Mr. Darcy's Dilemma and Delight

Jadie Brooks

ISBN: 1491253797
ISBN-13: 978-1491253793

DEDICATION

To my husband, Stan,
thank you for all your love and encouragement.

CONTENTS

JADIE BROOKS

ACKNOWLEDGMENTS

I want to thank my good friend and beta, Florence Solowianiuk. She has kept me going when I was ready to give up. Her questions and suggestions have been invaluable to my work.

I want to thank Betty Campbell Madden for her help in editing this story.

I am grateful to Molly Anne who took the lovely photograph used on the cover.

I would like to say how much I appreciate the online community for their support of this story.

Finally, I am glad for Miss Jane Austen's talented writing. Without her wonderful and enjoyable story *Pride and Prejudice* and its characters, this work would have not been written.

CHAPTER ONE

Fitzwilliam Darcy of Pemberley in Derbyshire inhaled deeply of the crisp autumn air as he stood in the paddock waiting for his horse to be brought to him. The day was perfect for his desired solitary ride. The morning sky shone bright, clear, and the air was cold. He had left the house eager for a good gallop away from the insipid, overly flattering attentions of Miss Caroline Bingley. Since he was a guest at Netherfield, the house her brother and Darcy's good friend Charles had leased, there were few places inside where he could avoid her.

The groom finally brought Darcy's horse, Paladin, to the mounting block. As soon as Darcy was in the saddle and out of the yard, the large bay obliged his master by galloping quickly over Netherfield's pastures. The two travelled with great pleasure over many acres of land before Paladin slowed and began to favour his left front foot. Darcy quickly pulled the animal to a stop and dismounted. After examining the horse's leg, he found that his mount had a loosened shoe. He knew he could not ride anymore without the risk of injury to the stallion.

Taking stock of his surroundings for the first time, Darcy realized he could see the spire of Longbourn church at not too great a distance. The road to Meryton lay between his location and the Longbourn estate. Grabbing up the reins, he guided his horse down the rise toward the road.

Darcy understood that most of his morning would be spent in the pursuit of a new shoe for his mount. He kicked at the grass and then upbraided himself for his irritation. Nothing could be gained in allowing free rein to the frustration caused by the inconvenience of having to find a blacksmith. Only aggravation and a bad mood would be the result. His father had never shown such a negative attitude, so he decided to follow his parent's example once again.

The late Mr. Darcy would also have been ashamed of his son's conduct during the past few weeks. He had allowed his distress about his young sister's near elopement to colour his dealings with the people of the small Hertfordshire

1

village. Lifting his eyes heavenward, he asked for patience and understanding of why this inconvenience should happen on such a fine day for riding. Drawing upon the sudden infusion of strength resulting from the prayer, Darcy moved on with resolve.

When he arrived at the fence that separated the field and the lane, he could find no gate through which to pass. To his left he spied a copse of oaks with a brook running through it. *Paladin could use the refreshment after such a ride, as could I,* he thought.

Guiding his horse toward the bubbling stream, Darcy thought he heard a woman cry out. He stopped and strained his ears to listen. Perceiving no other sound, he shook his head. *It must have been a magpie,* he told himself, remembering several swooping and diving across his path as he rode.

Darcy tethered Paladin within reach of grass and the stream before he stuffed his gloves into his coat pocket and crouched to scoop up a drink for himself. When he finally stood up again, he became conscious of the fact that he could not see the road from his position amongst the trees. Leaving his horse, he walked toward the place where he knew the lane to be. As he reached the edge of the grove, he viewed the road through a tall hedge of wild roses growing over the fence.

Pulling a face that expressed his annoyance at not being able to find a place from which to gain the road, Darcy made to turn back to his horse when he heard the sound of rapid foot steps on the lane. Curiosity got the better of him, and once more he peered through the gap in the hedge. He was astonished by what he saw.

George Wickham strode quickly up the lane toward the village of Meryton. He was buttoning his fall, which in most circumstances would not have seemed too unusual. Darcy knew of men who relieved themselves by the side of a road, however ungentlemanlike the action was. On the other hand, because of the bright, bloody scratches on Wickham's cheeks and the leering, smug expression upon his face as he straightened his uniform jacket, Darcy came to a completely different conclusion. He had seen that look on his former friend's face once before. In fact, it had been the final death blow to their friendship.

His own excellent father had sought to instil in both the boys that they were never to take advantage of the positions they held, Darcy as the master's son and Wickham as his godson and son of his trusted steward, in the Pemberley household. Not once did Darcy expect that those lectures had failed to reach the mark with George Wickham until he happened upon him hurrying down the back stairs, doing and looking much the same as he had at the present moment. Pushing past Darcy, he had grinned lecherously.

Darcy had chosen to use the back stairs since he had fallen from his horse while practicing steeple jumping. Remembering that the elder Mr. Darcy had visitors that afternoon and not wanting his father or his company to see him in such a state of dishevelment, he used the kitchen entrance to the house and the servants' stairs to go to his room to change.

All the while his newly acquired valet, Peters, had helped to make himself presentable, Darcy pondered the look and actions of his childhood friend. The expression on George Wickham's face caused him great concern, and the scratches on his cheeks spoke of a confrontation of some sort.

Once he was changed into fresh clothes, Darcy dismissed his valet and sought Pemberley's housekeeper, Mrs. Reynolds. She was not at her usual occupation for that time of day. When he inquired of a footman as to where she could be found, the servant told him that one of the maids had summoned her to tend to an emergency.

Darcy suddenly knew where to find Mrs. Reynolds. He would never forget the horror of what he found in one of the upstairs maid's tiny room, a bruised and terrified young girl of no more than fourteen. Mrs. Reynolds was giving her aid. The girl seemed to be mute and only whimpered and cowered when she saw Darcy standing in the doorway.

"Master Fitzwilliam, this is not a place for you," Mrs. Reynolds admonished. "Please leave. Tillie needs privacy."

Blushing as he bowed and turned away, Darcy ran down the stairs to find Wickham. When he found him, he trounced him heartily. While the young man lay moaning on the ground, Darcy managed to threaten him strongly enough that young Wickham never repeated that particular offense at Pemberley.

Wickham received no other punishment for the incident. The maid remained so traumatized that she did not reveal who had attacked her. Although she was not found to be with child, she requested a new position and was sent to work in the London house of the Earl of Matlock to protect her from further attacks.

Darcy explained to his father what he had witnessed on the stairs and what he suspected of Wickham, but after interviewing his godson, the elder Darcy believed his tale of innocence over his own son's observations. He cautioned Fitzwilliam against spreading falsehoods, and the two young men removed to Cambridge the next week with their former friendship destroyed completely.

Shaking himself from the memory, Darcy caught a glimpse of Wickham as he rounded a corner and out of sight. That was when an awful premonition flowed over him. Who was Wickham's latest victim? He had to help whoever it was. He owed her that much. Why had he not warned the villagers when he first found the cad in Meryton two days ago?

Making sure that his horse was securely tied, Darcy ran out of the grove and vaulted the fence. He sped in the direction from which Wickham had come. After running nearly a hundred yards, he heard a groan. Turning his glance in the direction of the sound, he spied a footpath leading away from the road. After travelling only twenty feet, he saw a young woman who lay on the grass curled into a ball, her knees tucked tightly against her chest.

As Darcy moved closer, his breath caught in his throat. There was no mistaking who the victim was. He had seen the cream-colored sprigged muslin and the green spencer too often within the past few weeks not to recognize the unfortunate young woman as none other than Miss Elizabeth Bennet.

Hurrying to her side, Darcy dropped to his knees. "Miss Bennet," he said gently. "May I be of assistance?"

When she did not answer, he touched her shoulder. Her panicked reaction alarmed him. She slapped at his hand and tried to move away from him.

"Miss Elizabeth, it is I, Fitzwilliam Darcy," he responded and removed his hand. "You are injured and need help. Please let me assist you to your family."

At the mention of her family, she stopped her feeble crawling and turned to him. "No, no, they cannot see me like this. I ... they will .... No, I must go away," she protested weakly, tears leaking from beneath her closed eyelids.

"But Miss Elizabeth, you are unwell," Darcy pleaded. "You must allow me to find your father or mother and to call a doctor."

"No!" she fairly screamed. "You do not understand. I am ruined, and if anyone learns of it, my sisters will be ruined as well." She began to sob uncontrollably. "I... wish he... had... killed me."

Raking his hands through his hair in frustration, Darcy tried to decide what to do. Miss Bennet was not to be reasoned with at the moment, but she did need care for her injuries. There had to be a way to get help without causing her any more trauma.

He ached with compassion for the young woman before him. His own sister had barely escaped a similar fate. Technically, she had not been ravished as Miss Bennet had been, but her trusting innocence had been lost, and her confidence had suffered a blow as well. Georgiana still refused to see all but a few of their closest friends and family, though her new companion, Mrs. Annesley, seemed to be helping her deal with her fears.

"Miss Elizabeth, is there any place where I can take you?" When she did not answer, Darcy asked another question. "There must be someone, your sister, perhaps? Miss Bennet would want to assist you. May I fetch her?"

"My sisters and mother went shopping in Meryton first thing this morning," she replied as her weeping quieted. "If I had only gone with them," she spoke with deep regret.

"Are you certain that I cannot bring your father?"

"He is also in the village. He had some estate business with my uncle Phillips. Papa took Mr. Collins along, so that I would be able to stay home." Slowly her voice lost all emotion. "I am alone as I should be."

"Come, Miss Elizabeth," he said as he offered his hand, having decided to humour her for the time being. "If you do not want to be discovered by your family, you will need to find shelter until we consider what can be done. Is there somewhere close by where you will not be seen?"

Elizabeth stared at his proffered hand. She could not understand why he would not leave her alone, but she could see the wisdom in his assertion. "The shepherd's cottage is only beyond that rise. Mr. Oscar left two days ago to visit his family in Kent. His only daughter gave birth to twin boys, and Papa gave him leave to visit them for a fortnight since he is not needed for the sheep at this time."

Finally, she accepted his hand and attempted to rise. It was then that the world began to spin wildly around her, but before she fell back to the ground, Darcy caught her in his arms. At first, she closed her eyes against the dizziness and marvelled that she could feel so safe in the care of a man so soon after an attack by another.

"Thank you, sir," she sighed and tried to lift her head, but the spinning began again. Her body ached, and she could feel the lump on the back of her head start to throb.

After a short walk, they viewed a small stone cottage. "Do you have a key?" Darcy asked.

"There is no lock." Her voice took on a sleepy quality which gave Darcy some concern.

Hurrying as quickly as he could without jostling Elizabeth, Darcy arrived at the cottage and opened the door. He had to bend his tall frame to enter. Once inside, he searched for a place for Miss Bennet. The only spot available was the shepherd's cot, which was where he laid her down as gently as possible and covered her with a surprisingly clean blanket.

For a moment, he stood mutely, surveying the small room. A gasp from Elizabeth brought him back to her side. She had turned her face away trying to find a comfortable spot to rest her head, and he detected a blot of red on the pillow. His concern increased as he saw that blood was seeping through her hair.

"Miss Bennet, your head is bleeding!" Reaching into his pocket, he dropped to his knees next to the bed and brought his handkerchief to rest on the bump.

"When he threw me to the ground, I struck my head on a rock," replied Elizabeth with a detached voice. "I was so stunned that I did not fight as I ought. I tried .... I think I scratched him."

He took her hands in his free one. "You need a doctor. If you will lie still, I will fetch one."

Jerking her hands from his grasp, Elizabeth tried to rise only to have dizziness overtake her once more. "Please, Mr. Darcy, no doctor," she pleaded, her breathing shallow, her face pale.

"Please do not excite yourself. Lie back. I will do as you wish, but if not a doctor, there must be someone I can summon."

Elizabeth pondered her choices. Although at the moment she wished for death, the stronger part of her knew she needed assistance. If she was to keep the attack quiet, she wanted an ally. Indeed, Mr. Darcy seemed to be one such person, but he could not nurse her.

As Elizabeth thought on the subject, she became so quiet that Darcy feared she had fainted. He had determined to go for help despite her objections when she said, "Sarah."

"Sarah?" he repeated in a baffled tone.

"Sarah is the maid we sisters share," she explained. "She will keep a secret. She has always been trustworthy. I frequently share things with her which I would share with no one else but Jane."

"I see," he said, relieved that she was both conscious and willing to receive assistance. "And where might I find this Sarah? Will I not have to apply to the house to find her?"

"No, she is in the rose garden, harvesting rose hips for jelly and our medicinals. Take the path outside to the barn. If you keep close to the hedge to the right of the barn, you may proceed undetected. Once you reach the break in the hedge, you will see the rose garden."

"I will be back as quickly as I can." He touched her shoulder lightly. "Please promise you will not move. I will not leave unless you promise."

Elizabeth lifted her gaze to his, and he saw a bit of her usual sparkle as she said, "Very well, sir, I promise I will not leave this cot. Indeed at the moment, I could not, even if I wished it."

Darcy was both worried and encouraged by her response. He stood and dusted off his trousers. Ducking through the doorway and closing the door behind him, he followed Elizabeth's directions and soon came upon a young maid snapping off rose hips and dropping them into a basket.

"Excuse me, but are you Sarah, Miss Elizabeth Bennet's maid?" Darcy inquired in much the same manner he might have asked about the weather.

The maid started at his question, but as she recognized the gentleman, Sarah curtsied and replied, "Aye, sir, I am. May I help you?"

"Miss Elizabeth tells me that you are discreet and can be trusted to keep a secret when need be. Is this true?"

The girl did not lower her gaze, but rather lifted her chin as she answered, "I would never betray Miss Elizabeth's trust, but I do not understand why you ask."

He lowered his voice to almost a whisper. "I must ask for complete secrecy. Your mistress was attacked and needs medical attention. However, she will not allow me to fetch a doctor. She has agreed that you might come and minister to her."

In her concern for Elizabeth, Sarah forgot her station and grabbed Darcy's arm. "Where is she? Take me to her!"

Darcy did not move but said in the same low tone, "You must bring water and clean cloths for bandages. Her head is bleeding. She is in the shepherd's cottage. I will go to her now. Are you able to come without detection?"

"Aye, sir, I am," Sarah held his eyes for a moment longer. "Go to Miss Elizabeth. I shan't be long."

As relieved as Darcy was to have someone else involved, he knew that Elizabeth needed a doctor's care. He began to ponder how it could be accomplished without her attack becoming public knowledge. He uttered a quick prayer for her healing as he reached the small building. Just before he entered the cottage again, an idea came to him that just might work, but he would need Miss Elizabeth's agreement and the maid's help.

It took a few seconds for his eyes to adjust to the dim interior of the cottage. Darcy moved quickly to the bed and looked down upon her unmoving form.

"Did you find Sarah, Mr. Darcy?" Elizabeth's voice startled him since he thought she was asleep.

"Yes, Miss Elizabeth, I did and she is bringing some water and clean cloths to clean your head wound."

"Thank you, sir," she replied wearily. "Since Sarah shall be here soon, you need not remain."

"Madam, I will not leave you," Darcy exclaimed as he pulled out a chair and sat down. "I have a plan whereby you will be able to receive a doctor's attention and no one, not even the doctor, will know the true cause of your injuries."

Elizabeth, who had been lying on her side facing the wall, attempted to turn over to look at him, but her pain was too great. She sobbed out in frustration. "What am I to do?"

"Lie still until Sarah gets here. I shall explain my plan then since her cooperation will be needed for it to work," Darcy said as he gently patted her shoulder.

"Very well," Elizabeth sighed. The pain in her head and body kept her mind occupied while they waited for her maid to arrive.

In a short time, Darcy heard footsteps on the front path and opened the door to admit the young Sarah. Since she was of a petite build and height, she did not find it necessary to lower her head to enter the cottage. Without preamble, she rushed to Elizabeth's side.

"Oh, Miss Elizabeth!" Sarah cried as she saw her blood-soaked hair. Depositing the jug and the cloths she had brought onto the table, she hunted for a bowl or a pot. Finally she found a clean, though chipped, bowl into which she dropped some of the rags and poured some of the water over them.

"Sir, would you please move the table and a chair closer to the bed?" the maid timidly asked of him.

Without speaking, he did so and stood back out of the way, but he watched as Sarah cleaned the wound, placed some kind of herbs against it, and bound one of the cloths around Elizabeth's head as a bandage. Once she finished her ministrations, Sarah looked to Darcy for further instructions.

With Sarah's help, Elizabeth had been able to turn to face away from the wall. The effort caused a new wave of dizziness, so she closed her eyes and waited for it to subside before she asked, "Mr. Darcy, you said that you had a plan."

"Yes, I do," he began, "but first I must ask what may seem a rather impolite question. Have you ever been known to have mishaps when you go for your walks?"

Elizabeth did not answer, but Sarah smiled. "I have heard that Miss Elizabeth does not always watch where she is going. Only last summer, she caught her foot in a snag of tree roots and suffered a mild sprain. Then there was the time, she raced ..."

"Sarah!" Elizabeth admonished. "You make me sound like a clumsy oaf or a hoyden."

"Never an oaf, Miss Elizabeth," Darcy interjected with a teasing smile. "However, since you have a bit of a -- shall we say -- history of mishaps, my planned explanation has a basis of truth."

Elizabeth was astounded by the smile and the tease, but she refused to focus on it. "And the explanation is?"

"You were running down one of the hills and slipped, hitting your head on a stone. I found you. Since I was concerned with the bleeding of your wound, I summoned Sarah to your aid before bringing you into your house." After pausing he said, "Once at the house, Sarah will ready you for bed. This way the doctor can be called. Since he will not see any other wounds or bruises, no one need know of them."

Elizabeth was quiet while she thought about Mr. Darcy's suggestion. Since she had no other plan to suggest and was certain that neither he nor Sarah would leave her alone, Lizzy finally assented.

Darcy gently lifted Elizabeth from the bed, making every effort not to cause her more pain. Sarah held the door open as he left the cottage. She swiftly took the lead back toward Longbourn House.

The butler, Mr. Hill, must have seen their approach because he had the door open before they had crossed the courtyard.

"What happened to Miss Elizabeth?" he called out in concern.

"She slipped and hit her head on a rock," Sarah answered as she reached Hill. "Mr. Darcy found her and asked for my help. Her head was bleeding, so I bound the wound before we came to the house." Her rapid recitation continued as she moved into the house ahead of Mr. Darcy and Elizabeth.

"Please, Mr. Darcy," Sarah said as she turned her attention to Darcy. "Her room is this way." Hurrying up the stairs, she led the way to Elizabeth's chambers with the butler following in the rear.

Since Darcy had lifted her into his arms, Elizabeth had felt safe and at peace, a very strange thing given the current situation. She closed her eyes and willed the peace to continue, but once Darcy entered her room and gently deposited her on her bed, all the turmoil of fear and pain returned. It took all of the little strength she had left not to cry out in protest.

"I need to borrow a horse so that I may fetch the doctor," Darcy explained as he turned to the butler, who stood in the doorway. "My own horse has a loose shoe."

"Of course, I shall see to it at once," Mr. Hill agreed and hastened to call for the horse.

"Miss Elizabeth, I shall leave you now," Mr. Darcy said earnestly, "I pray you will be well soon."

"Thank you, Mr. Darcy," was her fatigued reply.

Darcy motioned for Sarah to follow him to the hallway. Once they were nearly at the top of the stairs, he said, "I trust that you will keep watch over Miss Elizabeth. I shall return as soon as possible. Please make sure that you give me an account of her condition when I return."

"Aye, I will, sir." Sarah curtseyed and returned to Elizabeth.

CHAPTER TWO

Within minutes Darcy was on his way to Meryton. He felt some aggravation that the horse from Longbourn was little more than a nag, but it proved faster to ride her than to walk as he pressed the animal into a decent canter and arrived in the village in fairly good time.

Darcy dismounted and was about to inquire of a passer-by the whereabouts of the doctor when he heard his name.

"Mr. Darcy," Mr. Bennet called from the doorway of a shop on the other side of the street. He crossed the street and examined his own horse. "Have you taken to stealing horses, sir?" he teased.

Unaccustomed to teasing, Darcy reddened. "No, Mr. Bennet, my own horse nearly lost a shoe near Longbourn. I was for Meryton when I heard a cry and investigated. I found Miss Elizabeth Bennet had fallen and hit her head."

Mr. Bennet's teasing smile vanished in his concern for his favourite daughter as he grasped Darcy's arm and demanded, "My Lizzy is injured? Tell me what is being done for her."

"I brought her to the house and summoned a servant to attend to her before I came to fetch the doctor." He understood the man's worry as his own mind was racing in the same direction. "Please tell me where I can find him."

"Do not trouble yourself with that, Mr. Darcy," Mr. Bennet answered. "I will go to Mr. Jones straight away. Please go back to Longbourn and see to your horse. In fact, have one of my grooms bring it to the smithy. It is the least I can do for your helping my daughter."

"But, sir," Darcy protested. "How will you get back? Might you not need your own horse now?"

"I shall travel with the doctor." As an afterthought, he mumbled mostly to himself, "Mr. Collins can walk back on his own. He has gone to call upon the village vicar. I shall leave word for him while Mr. Jones calls for his carriage."

Darcy lost no time in making his way back to Longbourn. Concern for Elizabeth filled his breast as he nudged the horse along the road. When he finally reached his destination, he gave the footman Mr. Bennet's instructions and details as to the whereabouts of his horse before he moved to the house.

He was met by both Mr. and Mrs. Hill, who were obviously worried over the young miss. "Mr. Bennet and Mr. Jones will be along shortly," Darcy explained. "Is there any news of Miss Bennet?"

"No, sir, Mr. Darcy," Mrs. Hill murmured softly, "but I will go upstairs to stay with Miss Elizabeth and send Sarah down so that she may tell you what she knows."

The older woman ascended the stairs as quickly as she could and soon Sarah appeared.

"How does Miss Elizabeth fare?" he asked, anxiety in his tone.

"She is resting, though I can tell she is in pain," Sarah confided. As Darcy wanted to speak with more privacy, he turned to the butler. "I am thirsty. Is it possible that I could have some tea?"

"Of course, sir, I shall fetch some right away," Hill bowed and turned to go to the kitchen.

As soon as the man had left the foyer, Darcy lowered his voice. "I must ask you some very awkward and improper questions. Remember I only do so out of a desire to help Miss Elizabeth in every way possible." At Sarah's nod he continued, "As her maid, you must be aware of when she normally has her courses."

The girl blushed but again she nodded.

"Because of the attack and the fact that she will not allow us to tell her family, I must ask you to inform me whether or not, she ... whether they ... uh ...come," Darcy stammered, his own face tingeing red. After an embarrassed pause, he asked, "Are you able to read and write?"

"Yes, sir," Sarah whispered.

Darcy quickly pulled one of his gloves from the pocket in which he had stuffed them when he drank water from the stream. "Hide this in your pocket. Once you know one way or another, send this back to me with a note. Explain that you are returning the 'missing' glove if she does not have her courses, or that you 'found' it if she does. Do you understand?"

"Perfectly, sir," said Sarah as she bobbed a curtsey.

The butler again entered the foyer and was about to speak when Darcy said, "Thank you, Sarah. You may return to Miss Elizabeth. Please send my wishes for her speedy recovery."

Bobbing another curtsey, Sarah mounted the steps as rapidly as she could.

"Mr. Darcy," Hill said respectfully, "Tea is ready in the drawing room. May I show you in?" He opened one of the doors and waited for Darcy to enter.

"Thank you," Darcy said as he inclined his head and made his way to a chair next to the table on which an older woman stood arranging the tea and a few raisin cakes.

Turning back to Mr. Hill, he asked, "Would you bring me some writing materials? I find I have an urgent matter to which I must attend."

"Right away, sir," the butler replied as he exited the room.

As Darcy wrote a letter to his cousin Colonel Richard Fitzwilliam, Elizabeth fought hard not to remember the horrific event of earlier that morning, but every time she closed her eyes, she relived each moment: the surprise of seeing Lt. George Wickham, the uneasiness she felt at the strange expression on his face, the wish that she had not walked out alone with all her family gone from Longbourn, his obvious attempts to flatter her, her own vain efforts to return to the house, and finally and most ghastly, the attack itself.

She cried out with distress as a cloud of suffocating blackness threatened.

"Miss Elizabeth!" The soft voice and gentle touch of her maid dispelled the cloud. "You are safe. Do not thrash so. You will reopen the wound."

Tears rolled down her cheeks, but she quieted as Sarah put a glass of water to her lips and helped her to drink. "I do not know how I will ever sleep again. It is as if it is happening again as soon as I drift off."

"Miss," Sarah soothed. "It is not happening. It is only a memory and that will fade in time. If the doctor does not give some draught to help you rest, I know of something that will help you sleep without dreams for a few days."

The maid took Elizabeth's hand and squeezed it. "I am afraid that part of the healing will be in talking about it, in the remembering. Once you are ready, I will be here to listen if you wish it. Talking will help break the power of the deed."

Elizabeth stared into the younger woman's eyes. "How do you know this, Sarah?"

Holding Elizabeth's gaze, Sarah said, "My own mama told me about her sister, Sarah. I am named after her. My aunt was a beautiful young girl and a maid to a wealthy family. Mama told me that Aunt Sarah had been blessed that after the attack on her person, she was sent to work in another place. There she met an older woman who was a godly and compassionate person. The lady, a companion to the young daughter of the house, was able to minister to her deep emotional wounds. During the time my aunt was in the employ of that house, the older woman also taught her duties so well that eventually she became the young lady's personal maid. I am so happy that she was not brought down by the experience."

Sarah paused to pat Elizabeth's hand. "Did you never wonder why I speak so well as I do?"

"I admit that you seem more educated than most of the servants in Meryton," she replied honestly.

"When my aunt was allowed to visit our family, she gave me books and taught me elocution. She thought that I should be a good lady's maid some day. If my mama had not married again after my father died and then moved to Meryton with my step-papa, I think I could have been hired by some fancy lady in Town." She smiled ruefully. "However, I am much happier to be a part of this household."

"Sarah," Lizzy sighed softly. "I knew so little about you."

Sarah protested, "You did not need to know much. I am just a servant who speaks the King's English better than most."

"You are, now, more than a mere servant." It was Elizabeth's turn to squeeze Sarah's hand. "You are a trusted friend."

~*~

In his letter, Darcy sought the assistance Colonel Fitzwilliam in dealing with Wickham. Once again, the vile man could not be publically denounced as the villain he was in order to preserve the reputation of another innocent, young woman. He sighed and paused in his writing to drink his now lukewarm tea.

Knowing his cousin as he did, Darcy knew that the colonel had connections and ways of dealing with a man of Wickham's ilk. He hoped that the cur had not already fled his militia regiment. It would be vastly easier if he could be found immediately.

Darcy was at once glad he had made some preparations in case he had to deal once more with the scoundrel after the ordeal at Ramsgate involving his sister and Wickham. After the rogue left the seaside town, Darcy had bought up all of the man's debts with the local merchants, and even the debts of honour he had been able to uncover. He was not surprised at the extent of the man's obligations since he had paid off George Wickham's creditors in Lambton a few years before. The small village so close to Pemberley would have suffered greatly if he had not.

Happy to have the power in his possession to exact some punishment upon Wickham, Darcy wrote a quick note to his attorney instructing him to give the evidence to Colonel Fitzwilliam upon receipt of the letter. It had been impossible to make this move last spring after the failed elopement involving the cad and his sister because he knew that Wickham would have understood who wanted him punished and would have done everything in his power to expose Georgiana to scandal. By involving his cousin and the markers of debt from the two towns in this way, Darcy himself would be separated from the punishment. Hopefully, Wickham would think that his gambling and debts had finally caught up with him.

He reread over both missives, especially the one to his cousin in which he added some facts relating to another young woman who had fallen victim to Wickham. He wanted to be certain that he had written nothing in his explanations that would reveal who the young lady was or how he had come upon the information. Not for a kingdom would he betray the trust she placed in him, but Darcy wanted nothing more than to make sure that the villain would never harm another. Once satisfied with the contents, he sealed the letters, folded both into another piece of paper, addressed and sealed it, and slipped it into his pocket. Once he was able to return to Netherfield, he would send the missive by express on his way through Meryton.

The sound of a carriage brought him to his feet and into the foyer. Mr. Bennet and another gentleman whom he recognized as the local doctor, Mr. Jones, entered the house.

"Mr. Darcy," Mr. Bennet greeted him in earnest. "What news of Elizabeth?"

"She was resting as well as can be expected when I inquired upon my arrival. Perhaps it is best that Mr. Jones should see her immediately," Darcy suggested quickly.

"Yes, yes, of course." Mr. Bennet flushed. Turning to the doctor, he said, "Mr. Jones, Hill will show you to her room."

Turning to Darcy, Mr. Bennet invited him into his book room. Once inside he retrieved a bottle of brandy and poured himself a glassful after offering some to his guest, who declined.

"I know it is too early in the day for brandy, but I cannot seem to calm myself. The thought of my Lizzy's being hurt has always discomposed me." Mr. Bennet said half to himself.

"It is quite all right, Mr. Bennet," Darcy said reassuringly. "I do understand that you had a shock. I do wish I had been able to inform you in such a way as to minimize that shock."

After swallowing his drink, Mr. Bennet sat wearily in the chair behind his desk. Gesturing for Darcy to be seated, Mr. Bennet sighed, "Do not concern yourself about me, Mr. Darcy. There was no other way that you could have told me. Sometimes, I think that Providence gave me such a daughter so that I would be kept alert. I am too apt to hide out in this room and let my family do as they please, but my Elizabeth … well, just let me say that because of our deep affection and closeness of temperament, I am more alive and challenged.

Looking at the stern countenance of the young man sitting in front of him, Mr. Bennet asked, "Could you tell me what happened to Elizabeth?"

Darcy retold the story he had agreed upon with Elizabeth. He did not have much to add, although he did say that she was alert enough to recognize him and to speak to him coherently.

"I do wish she had gone with her mother and sisters, but she insisted she would not give up her walk for a mere bit of shopping," he answered, rubbing his face with both hands.

"Does she often go out for walks on her own?" Darcy could not help but ask.

Bennet sighed once more, "I am afraid that she has done so since as soon as she was out of leading strings. In that, I encouraged her independence. This part of Hertfordshire is a safe and peaceful place. And with such a devoted mother and so many sisters, might I say some very silly sisters, Lizzy needs time to herself. I suppose that I should insist that she take a maid or a footman with her, but I had thought she had grown out of her accident prone stage."

He paused for a long moment before he continued absently, "I am just thankful that she only fell and was not accosted by some villain. I do not know if I could live with myself if she had."

If took all of Darcy's self-control for him not to react to that statement from Elizabeth's father. It was plain why she sought to keep this news from Mr. Bennet. While Darcy was not convinced of the wisdom of this secrecy, he would not betray her trust in him. For a while the two men sat in silence, each in his own thoughts about the same young woman. Darcy began to fidget with worry as the doctor seemed to be taking a long time for his patient.

Her father's ponderings having followed a similar path of concern caused Mr. Bennet to suddenly stand. "I must see what is taking Mr. Jones such a long time." He left the room quickly with Mr. Darcy behind him.

Mr. Bennet had just reached the bottom of the stairs when a rabble of voices was heard from outside. The front door was flung open and a strident voice called out, "Hill, whose carriage is that? Is that not Mr. Jones's? What is happening? Has Mr. Bennet fallen ill?" Each question rose in volume and in hysterics.

"Mrs. Bennet!" Mr. Bennet bit off each syllable quietly but with firm command. "You will keep your voice down." When his appearance in obvious good health and his unyielding tone silenced his wife, he continued evenly, "Lizzy fell and injured her head. Mr. Darcy found her nearly unconscious, brought her home. Once she was given into the care of our servants, he went to Meryton where he found me. I came with Mr. Jones as soon as I could. The doctor is with her now."

Seeing his wife open her mouth in what would likely be a loud tirade about her second daughter and her lack of consideration of her mother's nerves, Mr. Bennet lifted his hand to silence her once more and then, with a quick move, took his wife's arm and manoeuvred her into the parlour. Gesturing for his daughters and Mr. Darcy to follow him, he made sure the door was closed behind them.

Mr. Bennet caught the eye of each of his family members before he spoke again. "Please consider that Lizzy will need peace and quiet if she is to heal quickly, so I will insist that if you must talk you keep your voice to just above a whisper." Receiving a general assent to his statement, Mr. Bennet relaxed and took a chair.

Though the conversation that ensued was not loud, it bordered on babble. Everyone seemed to have a question and wished to ask it at once. Again Mr. Bennet raised a hand and indicated that his wife should ask her questions first. "Maybe the rest of you will have your answers once your mother is finished."

Soon Darcy was recounting once again how he had come to find the injured Miss Elizabeth. He could not help but feel uncomfortable at being the centre of attention, so much so that he hid behind his habitual inscrutable façade. Only Mr. Bennet and Jane seemed to notice his unease and gave him the benefit of that notice. The rest of the family, to varying degrees, thought him cold.

After hearing Mr. Darcy's explanation, Mrs. Bennet decided that until such time they found out from Mr. Jones that Elizabeth was on her death bed, she would talk of more pleasant topics. She then asked after the health of the Bingleys and the Hursts.

Darcy opened his mouth to answer when doctor entered the room. He stood and went to the man. Mr. Bennet did the same and asked, "How is Elizabeth?"

"She is doing as well as can be expected," Mr. Jones answered. "I have given her a draught which will help her sleep, and I left some laudanum for pain. She will need bed rest and quiet for the next few days. I will come back this evening to see how she fares. If she does not have complications or an infection of the head wound, Miss Elizabeth should be fine by week's end."

"Thank heavens!" Mr. Bennet responded. "We will see to it that your instructions are carried out, Mr. Jones."

Mr. Bennet escorted the doctor to his carriage while Darcy went to stand at the window. He listened to the women behind him begin to talk about the items they had purchased while in Meryton, so that he was surprised when the soft-spoken Miss Bennet addressed to him.

"I must thank you for your help with my sister today, and thank God that you came upon her when you did," she said earnestly. "I shudder to think what might have befallen her if you had not been so close."

"It is my pleasure to have been of service to Miss Elizabeth." He knew his words were stiff and formal. He eased the formality when he said, "I am not used to receiving such thanks, Miss. Bennet. I am happy that I was able to assist her."

Jane nodded with understanding as she too hated to have much gratitude heaped upon her. "Just know that you have made a friend in me today, Mr. Darcy."

"Thank you, Miss Bennet." He bowed his head in acknowledgement.

Just then hoof beats could be heard at the front of the house. Darcy excused himself to discover if the groom had returned with his horse. It was indeed the case, so he took his leave, promising to return later to inquire after Miss Elizabeth's health.

CHAPTER THREE

Darcy was nearly to the end of the drive when he spotted a man in clerical garb turning from the Meryton road. Once they met on the lane, the cleric doffed his hat and bowed deeply. The man's greeting seemed rather overdone, but Darcy gave a slight nod in acknowledgement before he rode on into the village.

Arriving in Meryton, Darcy immediately dispatched the letter to his cousin by express. He pondered for a moment the wisdom of waiting for Fitzwilliam to join him to inform Colonel Forster of Wickham's character. Finally, he knew that if he did not do it immediately, his former childhood friend would likely hurt another if he did not flee the area. Turning his mount from the main street, he headed to where the militia's commander resided.

It did not take Darcy long to give his account of Wickham's deeds to the colonel, including the unpaid debts and unseemly behaviour toward young ladies. Of course, he did not reveal the names of the young ladies involved or how he came to have the information other than telling Forster a brief history of his own relationship with Wickham. Colonel Forster was truly upset at the news and promised Darcy he would see to it that Wickham was held under guard until Colonel Fitzwilliam or his representative came. Colonel Forster was incensed that a man of such unprincipled character should be in his regiment. He prided himself on having men of better than average moral fibre. Under his command, discipline was swift and harsh so as to keep his men in line and to make sure that the villages in which they were encamped did not regret his regiment's having been in their midst.

After promising to pay any of the man's debts that should come to light and exacting the colonel's promise not to reveal his involvement or that of his cousin, Darcy was satisfied that he had done all he could and finally made his way back to Netherfield. His thoughts drifted back to Longbourn and Miss Elizabeth. So many thoughts and feelings swirled around in his mind that he had a difficult time sorting through them. First of all, guilt raged at him. If only he had not been so proud, so arrogant as to think that he need not speak of his dealings with Wickham. When he recalled the sight of Elizabeth on the ground, so full of pain and terror, his heart throbbed with regret. He had saved his own sister from the same fate by a mere accident of circumstance. How could he have thought his silence wise? He hoped that God would forgive his conceited selfishness.

Other feelings fought for his recognition. He could not forget the tenderness he felt when she relaxed in his arms as he carried her. Her soft body fit so perfectly against him, causing emotions too foreign to name. Darcy shook his head when it seemed that his heart wanted to tell him that it was affection, even love, that had finally taken up residence there.

"Impossible!" Darcy cried out loud, startling his horse. After calming Paladin, he resumed his troubled ruminations. There was no way that he could be in love with Miss Elizabeth Bennet. Her position in life and her family's improper conduct would surely prevent an alliance between them. Immediately following that thought, his conscience berated him once more.

He shook his head. "Be honest with yourself, Darcy," he commanded barely above a whisper. "Wickham has put the true barrier between Elizabeth and myself. Unless ..." No, he would not think of "unless". He would help her as much as propriety allowed, no more. Urging his horse to pick up the pace, Darcy tried to push all thoughts of the lovely Miss Bennet out of his mind.

Once he arrived, he was greeted by Charles and Caroline Bingley before he even dismounted. "Darcy!" Bingley exclaimed. "We were concerned about you when you did not appear for breakfast. Fosset told us you left early for a ride. Are you well?"

Before Darcy could answer, Caroline began to complain. "Indeed, we were beside ourselves with worry. Charles would not send someone to look for you before now. He had just summoned a man to organize a search when you were spotted coming up the drive. It is vexing that you did not send us word," she chided as if she had the right to do so.

Bowing slightly as he moved up the stairs, Darcy apologized, "I am terribly sorry to have been the cause of concern, but I did not have the time to inform you that I was well. In fact, I did not think of it until I was on my way back here."

Before the butler could take Darcy's coat, Caroline asked incredulously, "What could have possibly happened to cause you to forget sending word to your hosts?"

The fulminating look Darcy gave Caroline made her close her mouth and redden. He turned to Charles and said, "I did go for a ride this morning, and after some time I found that my horse had a loose shoe. I was near the road from Longbourn to Meryton when I heard a woman cry out. I investigated and found that Miss Elizabeth Bennet had fallen and injured her head. I assisted her to

Longbourn and summoned her father and a doctor. Mr. Bennet insisted upon seeing to the re-shoeing of my horse. Once that was accomplished, I returned to Netherfield." Throughout the narrative his voice remained stern and formal and only more so after Caroline's gasp upon hearing Elizabeth's name.

Having already forgotten the reproving look he had given her just moments before, Caroline waited until Darcy ended his speech before she exclaimed, "Surely, Mr. Darcy, you did not fall for such an obvious ploy to capture your attention. I have always thought the Bennets to be a conniving lot."

Darcy seemed to grow taller as he turned and held her gaze for several seconds. "Miss Bingley," he addressed with a voice dripping with sarcasm, "I wonder if you could then explain how she could have known that I would be at that place at that time and that my horse would have a loosened shoe." He silenced her protest with a raised hand, pointing to the dark stain on his sleeve. "I wonder how this 'ploy', as you called it, could have included her bleeding profusely from the injury to the back of her head and how she could have 'connived' to bleed on my coat when I helped her to the house."

Turning his back to Caroline, he spoke to Charles, "May I ask for water to be sent to my rooms? I find I am in need of a bath."

"Of course, Darcy, and I will have Fosset see to having a tray sent there as well. You did not have breakfast."

"Thank you, Bingley." Darcy bowed and took the stairs to his chambers.

Once Darcy was out of sight, Caroline began a tirade against the Bennets in general and Elizabeth in particular. "I do not understand how Mr. Darcy can have been taken in by those scheming Bennets. I have known for a long time that Miss Eliza was trying her best to worm her way into Mr. Darcy's good favour, but this is--"

"Caroline!" Bingley interrupted brusquely, "you will not speak of any of the Bennets in this manner again. If you do, I will be forced to ask Louisa to hostess for me as I will send you to our relatives in Scarborough. I will also reduce your allowance."

"But, Charles, surely you can see ..." Caroline did not finish as she realized that her usually affable brother would not relent. Thinking that after his anger cooled she would be able to make him see reason, she nodded before heading up to find her sister to tell her of Eliza Bennet's latest plot to capture Mr. Darcy.

~*~

Just under three hours later, Darcy called for his horse. He could not be at ease until he knew how Miss Elizabeth fared. He told himself that there could be nothing improper with his going to Longbourn to ask after her.

19

As he exited the house, Charles called after him. "Darcy, are you heading for Longbourn?" Hastening down the steps, he asked, "If you are, may I join you? I am concerned about Miss Elizabeth as well."

Relieved not to be alone with his thoughts any longer, Darcy readily agreed, "I would be happy for the company, Bingley."

"Excellent!" Bingley beamed at his friend. "Just let me order my horse readied."

Charles had not had time to ask for details, as Darcy had spent the time since his return in his chambers. He was indeed worried about Miss Elizabeth's health, but the eldest Miss Bennet's emotional well-being concerned him the most. He knew that Jane was very close to her sister and any harm to Elizabeth would trouble her.

"How was Miss Elizabeth when you left Longbourn?" Charles finally asked as they entered the road to Meryton.

"The doctor had given her a sleeping draught and said that if her head wound did not get infected, he was certain that she would recover completely," Darcy explained in a tense tone.

"It is fortunate that you found her when you did," Charles said earnestly. "I am sure her family is grateful to you for your aid."

A dark look crossed Darcy's face. "I am sure that they would have been more grateful if I had prevented it in the first place," he muttered to himself.

"Darcy," said Charles in amazement. "Even you could not have prevented an accident."

"What?" Darcy shook himself from his darker thoughts. "You are right, Bingley; even I cannot prevent accidents."

For nearly all of the rest of their ride to Longbourn, the conversation was mostly one-sided, Charles trying with little success to engage his friend. All he received for his effort were short, almost curt replies.

"I just remembered the ball," Charles said, frowning. "I was going to have the cards sent out tomorrow, but I am sure I should postpone the affair until Miss Elizabeth is well enough to attend."

"Yes, Bingley." Darcy finally gave his full attention to what his friend was saying. "That would be most prudent. I am certain that the Bennet family would not wish to attend with Miss Elizabeth unwell."

The two gentlemen were greeted warmly upon their arrival at Longbourn. Mrs. Bennet's attitude toward Darcy had warmed a great deal although she was still more loquacious in her reception of Bingley.

After being introduced, Mr. Collins, having been apprised of Darcy's part in rescuing Miss Elizabeth and realizing his relationship to the parson's patroness, did not cease in expressing his gratitude and appreciation. He monopolized the gentleman's attention for many minutes before Mr. Bennet took pity on Darcy and invited him to his library for a glass of wine.

"Sir, I do apologize for my cousin's exuberance," said Mr. Bennet as he poured two glasses of burgundy liquid. "I wish I could say that this was an infrequent occurrence. However, Mr. Collins has the gift of abundant speech."

Handing the glass to Darcy, Bennet continued, "I must, however, express my own thanks once more for your kind assistance to my daughter. She and I are very close. I am aggrieved that she was injured, but the doctor assures me that your swift action and Sarah's herbs were indispensable."

"Please, sir," Darcy interrupted in discomfort. "I only did what was needed to be done."

"That may be, Mr. Darcy," Mr. Bennet answered gravely, "but I thank you all the same." He sighed deeply and forced a teasing smile to his lips. "I suppose you would like to know how she is doing."

"I would indeed."

"I looked in on her a quarter of an hour ago. Sarah told me that Lizzy has been sleeping peacefully since the doctor gave her the draught." He sighed again, "I think it will be a while yet before we know for certain that she is truly well."

"Uh... Mr. Bennet... sir," Darcy stammered in embarrassment. "Would you allow me to...I mean could I be so bold as to ask to be kept informed as to Miss Elizabeth's health?"

"Mr. Darcy, I would be pleased to do so, but..." Mr. Bennet smiled as he sipped his wine. "You are welcome to come here at any time to ask after her yourself."

"Thank you," Darcy breathed out the words, relieved, before he drank the remainder of his wine.

"Shall we rejoin the others?" Mr. Bennet asked as he put down his empty glass. "I promise to help keep my effusive cousin at bay."

CHAPTER FOUR

Darcy received a short note from Colonel Forster that evening. It seemed that his men found Wickham packing his things. Obviously planning to leave the area in a great hurry without informing his commander, he denied any intention of doing so. Wickham was placed under armed house arrest. This bit of news helped Darcy to rest easier that night.

Within a day of his sending the express to Colonel Fitzwilliam, Darcy received a reply from his cousin by special courier. He would send three of his most trusted men to retrieve Wickham from the custody of the militia's commander. Because of his father's, the earl's, many contacts in the shipping industry, Fitzwilliam planned to see that the blackguard was bound for the West Indies as soon as a vessel was available. Darcy wrote a quick note of appreciation and sent it back with the same messenger.

The next few days found Darcy and Bingley visiting Longbourn twice a day and once staying for family dinner. Mr. Collins continued his sycophantic notice of Darcy, but with the frequent intervention of Mr. Bennet and his two daughters, Jane and Mary, their cousin was kept busy enough to save their guests from too much unwanted attention.

In the meantime, Elizabeth was having a difficult time. Her wounds were healing well enough, but the aftermath of the attack left her emotions raw and in tatters. Lizzy was sure that, without Sarah's constant presence, she would have gone mad. Nightmares plagued her, and because she would not confide in Jane, her maid's knowledge of herbal remedies and her soothing attendance at night gave her the only rest she could achieve.

One day toward the end of the first week after the attack, Sarah felt she needed to let Mr. Darcy know of Elizabeth's troubled emotional state. She slipped down the stairs while her charge was asleep and quietly peeked through the door into the drawing room.

This particular afternoon found only Darcy, Bingley, Jane, and Mary in residence in the room. Mrs. Bennet was consulting the cook on the evening's menu while Mr. Bennet played backgammon with his cousin in the library. Mary sat reading a book, Jane and Bingley chatted quietly near the fire, and Darcy stood examining a painting nearest the door.

Sarah moved just inside the room and caught Darcy's eye. Without speaking she gestured for him to follow her. Checking to see that no one in the room took notice, he exited. With her finger to her lips, she walked down a hallway to a door leading to the back garden. After they left the house, she led the way to a bench hidden from the view of the house.

"I cannot leave Miss Elizabeth for long, but I wanted to tell you how she is doing," Sarah explained in a low tone. "As you must have been told, her head wound is healing nicely as are the bruises she received."

When she paused, Darcy inquired, "What is it?"

"I am deeply concerned for her emotional well-being. She has nightmares, deeply disturbing ones from the way she cries out and thrashes about. At first, the draughts and laudanum the doctor prescribed seemed to help, but she has begun to refuse them. She especially does not want to become dependent on the opiate," Sarah sighed, showing signs of fatigue herself. "I am going to try some of the herbs my mother told me about that might help with this sort of thing. I hope I can convince her to take them."

The maid twisted her hands, wondering if she should broach the subject of her aunt. "I think that I know of someone who could help Miss Elizabeth, but I do not know if she will talk to her."

Darcy did not think that another person should be privy to the secret, but he was interested in what the girl had in mind. "Who is it? How is it you believe she could help?"

"It is my aunt Sarah. She is a lady's maid, who is in Town with her mistress at the moment. Each year at this time she is allowed to come to visit us since we are the only family she has left." Sarah paused again while she prayed that her aunt would forgive her for what she was about to reveal.

"She was attacked as Miss Elizabeth was," the girl whispered so softly Darcy could barely hear her words. "She has found peace with what happened to her, and she might be able to counsel Miss Elizabeth."

"When will she be in Meryton to visit?"

"She is due in four days." A flush bloomed on her cheeks. "I would have to ask Aunt Sarah if she is willing to speak to Miss Elizabeth. I know that since my aunt is a mere abigail, I should not be suggesting this."

"At this moment, I think that rank should not be an issue." Darcy thought about his own attitude and wondered how many of his ideas of status had made him fail to see the correct ones.

"I will speak to her once she arrives," Sarah promised.

"Is there anything I can do?" A fierce storm of frustration rolled through him as there was little he could do since he was not allowed to see or speak to Miss Elizabeth whilst she was in her bedroom.

"Sir," Sarah crooned softly, patting his arm. "If you are a praying man, I would suggest doing so. In addition, the doctor said that she could come to the sitting room for a time tomorrow if she continues to improve. I will speak to Mr. Jones and suggest that only certain people be allowed to speak with her until she is feeling completely well. He has no liking for Mr. Bennet's cousin. Mr. Collins is forever trying to give him advice from Lady Catherine de Bourgh on the best treatment for a head wound. Apparently he wrote to her of Miss Elizabeth's fall. The lady has already sent two letters to him by express."

Rising to her feet, Sarah said quickly, "If you will excuse me, I must go to Miss Elizabeth now, but I will do all I can to see to it that you are able to visit with her in the morning." She told him what time the doctor would come so that he could arrive some time after.

"Thank you, Sarah. I appreciate your help."

After Sarah left, Darcy sat back down and pondered what he would say when he saw Elizabeth the next day. He had not been much help to his sister after the incident at Ramsgate. However, Georgiana had told him that when he let her talk about it without commenting on the right or wrong of her thoughts and feelings, she had been better able to deal with her disappointment at finding out Wickham's true motives. Would Elizabeth ever open up to him? Would it even be appropriate for her to do so? Perhaps speaking to this maid's aunt would be the greatest help. He sighed and lifted a wordless prayer for guidance. Finding no answers to his questions at the moment, Darcy returned to the house in time to receive another invitation to dine with the Bennets again.

~*~

The next morning Darcy slipped out of the house, having written a note to Charles as to his destination. He had implored the Lord in his prayers for wisdom in dealing with Elizabeth. Even now, in his thoughts, he referred to her without the "Miss." He told himself that he was merely feeling guilt and compassion. She needed a friend to help her through this most trying of times. He could never be more than that to her. He admonished himself to maintain propriety in his thoughts, so that he did not slip and call her by her Christian name in public.

Paladin sensed his master's unease and pranced nervously down the road. Before they entered the village, Darcy was able to calm the animal when he finally came back to himself. It would not do to have his horse bolt at a sudden noise and become a danger to someone.

His passage through Meryton was noticed by many of its occupants. He did not realize that speculation was growing as to the reason for his frequent trips to Longbourn. Mrs. Bennet kept her friends informed about his visits, and although she still saw no sign of his interest in any of her daughters, she was pleased that his visits seemed to encourage Mr. Bingley in paying calls to Jane.

Dismounting, Darcy saw that the doctor's carriage was still standing in front of the house. Hill opened the door and escorted him to the drawing room where Jane greeted him.

"Good morning, Mr. Darcy. I hope you are well," she said softly.

Darcy bowed and said, "Good morning to you, Miss Bennet. Thank you, I am well. How are you and your family today?"

Jane smiled serenely. "My mother and three younger sisters have gone to Meryton to shop. My father insisted that Mr. Collins escort them using our carriage."

"I wanted the house quiet for Lizzy's first trip downstairs after her accident as the doctor directed." Mr. Bennet spoke from behind them. "I am surprised to find you here at this time of the day, Mr. Darcy."

"I am sorry if I am intruding, sir," Darcy said as he faced the older man. "I must confess to having prior knowledge of the possibility of Miss Elizabeth's being able to venture from her room this morning. I hope you will not mind if I stay for a few moments to see for myself how she fares."

"Mr. Darcy, you are welcome to stay and visit," Bennet gestured for Darcy to have a seat. "May I offer you something to drink? I was just going to have coffee myself."

"Thank you. I would enjoy some coffee," Darcy smiled as he took a chair nearest the chaise that had been pulled closer to the fireplace.

"I take it black," he replied when Jane asked his preference as she poured for his father.

Darcy had just taken a few sips of the fragrant brew when he heard a shuffle in the doorway. He turned to see Elizabeth entering the room on the arm of the doctor. Darcy put down his cup, stood, and gave her a bow as he watched her being helped to the chaise.

Sarah followed closely behind and saw to it that Elizabeth was settled comfortably on pillows and covered with a soft wool blanket.

"I have asked Sarah to keep Miss Elizabeth's visit to a half hour as I have other appointments." After a quick good-bye, Mr. Jones exited the room.

"Miss Elizabeth." Darcy took her hand, bowed over it, and quickly released it before he sat back down. 'I hope you are faring better this morning."

"Thank you, Mr. Darcy. I am feeling better." Elizabeth did not look up. She was surprised at his presence so early in the day. However, there was something about his being there which soothed her tattered emotions. For the moment, the memory of the attack was overshadowed by the far more pleasant one of feeling safe in his arms. She felt warmth creep into her cheeks at the thought.

Seeing the colour rise in her sister's cheeks, Jane exclaimed in concern, "Are you too warm, dear Lizzy?"

"No, Jane," Elizabeth said and smiled reassuringly. "The walk down the stairs may have caused me to flush. I am perfectly comfortable with my arrangement. It is so good to be out of my room." Looking around the room, she noted the rest of her family's absence. "Where are Mama and my other sisters?"

"I gave them leave to buy a bit more frippery for the upcoming ball at Netherfield with Mr. Collins as their escort." Her father grinned at her. "It is a small price to pay for a bit of quiet for you."

"Thank you, Papa," she said gratefully. "I must admit that I wondered if I could endure Mama's enthusiasm in my present state."

"Well, well, my child," he chuckled. "Better your mama's exuberance than her nerves."

At that moment, Hill entered the room. "Sir, one of the tenants would like to speak with you. He says it is most urgent."

"Very well, show him into the library," he said as he moved to Elizabeth's side and leaned down to kiss the top of her head. "I shall return so that I may escort you back to your room."

Darcy wanted to apologize to Elizabeth about his failure to inform the people of the area of Wickham's evil character, but he could not figure out a way to do so with Jane in the room. He thought that he would have to wait and that he might actually be intruding at the moment. Determining to take his leave, he made to stand when Elizabeth spoke to her sister.

"Jane, dear, would there possibly be any apricot scones left? I find that my appetite is coming back, and I know I detected the aroma of them baking earlier this morning."

"Of course, Lizzy," Jane answered as she stood. "Could I bring you some tea to go with them?"

"Yes, please. I would enjoy that."

Elizabeth spoke as soon as her sister left. "I think you have something on your mind, Mr. Darcy."

"You are most perceptive, Miss Bennet," Darcy said after clearing his throat. He glanced up at Sarah, who was standing behind the chaise. "Sarah, would you mind giving us a bit of privacy? Might you take a chair across the room?"

Sarah curtseyed as she went to sit on a footstool on the far side of the room and gaze out the window.

In a near whisper, Darcy began, "Miss Bennet, I must apologize for a great failure on my part. If not for me, I am sure that you would have never been hurt."

"I do not understand you, sir." Her eyes filled with confusion. "Did you know of his plans?"

"No!" His voice was sharper than he intended, so he repeated more softly, "No, I merely mean that if I had been more forthright with my knowledge of him and his dealings with my family, he might have been prevented."

"The day I first met him, he told me that he was the son of your family's late steward," she said softly. "He tried to tell me of some mistreatment he had experienced at your hands. However, I could not believe him."

When she hesitated, he urged her to go on.

"I did not think that a gentleman with friends such as Mr. Bingley could keep such malevolence hidden from those around him." She dropped her gaze. "I admit I thought you a bit proud and disagreeable because, I confess, I heard your statement of my mere tolerable appearance, but you seemed to be very distracted at the time, so I thought that you might not have been quite yourself."

Darcy reddened with embarrassment that she had heard his insulting words. "I am mortified that you should have heard me. Please forgive me. I have only the excuse that I was still not over the emotional impact an incident of involving my sister, Georgiana, and Wickham."

Elizabeth covered her mouth with her hands. "Did he... was she...?" She could not finish her question.

"No, he had other plans for her." Darcy sighed while raking a hand through his hair. As quickly as he could, he explained Wickham's failed elopement attempt, his sister's companion's betrayal of trust, and Georgiana's heartbreak at finding the cad only wanted her dowry of thirty thousand pounds and revenge on Darcy.

"Oh, the poor girl!" Elizabeth cried as tears welled in her eyes.

"I knew of his other misdeeds. So you see, I could have, I should have said something." Darcy dropped his head into his hands. He was sure she would not want to see or speak to him again as he was certain it was what he deserved.

Silence reigned for several seconds while Elizabeth digested what he had just told her. It was obvious that he was weighed down with guilt for his perceived offense. She also understood his desire to protect his younger sister from the gossip that would have been birthed if he had made Wickham's part in the failed elopement known to the general populace. Was she not trying to protect herself and her family by a similar kind of secrecy?

Reaching out her hand, Elizabeth touched his arm. "Mr. Darcy, if you feel you are in need of my forgiveness, you have it, totally and completely. However, I would never fault you for trying to keep your sister safe from the vicious tongues of gossipmongers just as I am trying to do."

Darcy gazed into her eyes to search their depths for assurance of her sincerity. "But I might have prevented…"

"I do not know if what happened could have been prevented even if you had spoken what you knew. It might also have been prevented if I had not been so stubborn as to insist upon staying behind, if I had fought harder. I have been blaming myself for that for days." Tears began to fill her eyes.

"Please, Miss Bennet," Darcy took her hand and squeezed it. "You must not blame yourself." Pausing to take a deep breath and exhale, he managed a small smile. "It would seem that we are of a similar bent. We each like to think we have more power in our lives than we actually possess."

Smiling slightly through the tears, she agreed, "Indeed, we do, sir."

"I am sorry that I was so long, Lizzy," Jane said as she carried a full tray through the door. "Cook insisted that since Mr. Darcy was here this early, he must be in need of more than mere scones. As you see, she made up a fruit compote, added jam and clotted cream to the meal, and made up fresh coffee as well as tea for you, Lizzy."

Elizabeth quickly dashed the tears from her eyes while Darcy stood to block Jane from seeing her do so. He took the tray from Jane, bringing it to a table close to Lizzy's couch. *He is still trying to protect me.* Elizabeth thought.

"Thank her, for my part, Miss Bennet, as I am beginning to have quite an appetite." Darcy grinned as he finally noticed the heaping mound of foodstuffs on the tray.

As Darcy and Elizabeth sat eating in a companionable silence, Sarah watched her young mistress carefully for signs of weakness or pain. Her heart rejoiced when she saw no indication of either.

"Mr. Darcy," Elizabeth spoke at last. "Papa mentioned a ball at Netherfield. Has a date been set?"

"Mr. Bingley decided to postpone setting a date until you are well enough to attend. He wanted you and your family to be there." If he had not glanced at Miss Bennet when he heard her slight gasp at the mention of Bingley's name, he might not have seen the blush of pleasure or the look of longing that passed quickly over her face before it resumed its normal serene countenance. Jane Bennet did have feelings for his friend that were not evident to strangers. He congratulated himself that he had not made the grave error of trying to dissuade Charles from pursuing a closer association with her based upon a false assumption of her indifference.

"Please thank Mr. Bingley for me." Elizabeth looked up at her sister. "I would have been saddened to have missed the ball. I know my family all look forward to it."

"That is the precise reason I may come to regret my suggestion of another shopping trip." Mr. Bennet sighed dramatically as he re-entered the room and winked at Elizabeth. "Although I believe the quietude this morning is worth the cost."

Sarah looked at the clock and moved closer to Elizabeth. "Miss, it is time for you to return to your chambers."

Elizabeth looked up in surprise. "Oh, but I want to finish eating before I leave. I will not be long, Sarah, I promise." She lifted the last spoonful of compote to her mouth.

"Just a few more minutes," Sarah agreed since she was happy to see that Elizabeth seemed to be enjoying the repast and did not show overt signs of fatigue.

Darcy drained the last of his coffee and stood. "Thank you for the delicious refreshments, but I must go. I promised Mr. Bingley that I would inspect one of the barns with him to see what repairs must be done before winter is full upon us." Bowing to everyone, he took his leave.

On his way to Netherfield through Meryton, Darcy spied the Bennet ladies exiting one of the shops, a perspiring Mr. Collins following them with his arms full of packages. Fortunately, the loquacious cleric could not see much of the street because of the pile of parcels he carried, and most of the ladies were too busy chattering over their purchases to notice him. Only Miss Mary acknowledged him with a nod of her head.

CHAPTER FIVE

Once back at Netherfield, Darcy hoped that he had not kept Charles waiting. He quickly entered the house and asked the butler where his master could be found.

"Mr. Bingley is still at breakfast, sir," Fosset informed him.

A footman opened the door to the breakfast room. The whole party was at the table.

"Good morning, Darcy," Charles greeted him. "How did you find the Bennets this morning? Is Miss Elizabeth better today?"

Darcy noted that Miss Bingley and Mrs. Hurst exchanged a look that could only be described as one of derision. He would rather Charles had not mentioned his early morning visit to Longbourn, but he answered as he took a cup of coffee from the serving maid, "I did not have the pleasure of seeing all of the Bennets, but Mr. Bennet and Miss Bennet were well, and Miss Elizabeth was allowed out of her room for a short time. She does seem much improved."

"I am sure that we are all very happy to hear it," said Charles with his usual beaming smile. "I hope that means we will be able to set a date for the ball soon."

Darcy stood gazing out the window, wondering how long it would be before Miss Elizabeth would feel up to attending a ball. As much as he disliked that kind of event, the idea of dancing with her made his heart race unexpectedly. What was happening to him that he would look at a ball with anticipation and be so eager to be in the company of a certain young lady?

As he stood pondering this, Darcy did not notice that Miss Bingley had joined him at the window until she spoke to him. "Mr. Darcy, I wonder at your visiting the Bennets so often. I understand that Charles is currently enthralled with Miss Jane Bennet, but unless your admiration for a certain 'pair of fine eyes' has blossomed into something greater, I should think that you would be more circumspect lest the general populace and, in particular, her family get the idea you are courting Miss Eliza. I would not think it possible that you would stoop so low as that."

Darcy moved a few steps away from Caroline before he replied in a cold tone, "I wonder how that is any of your concern." He dismissed her by turning his back and asking Charles impatiently, "Will you be much longer, Bingley? I believe you said the matter with the barn was of some importance."

Since he was close enough to hear his sister's impertinent speech, Charles coloured and rose from the table, leaving a half full plate. "I am ready now, Darcy. Let us see to the matter straight away."

The two men had left the breakfast room and the house before Charles apologized, "Darcy, I am appalled at what Caroline just said to you. I promise that I will not permit it to continue. I shall speak to her about it as soon as our estate business is finished."

"It is not important, Bingley." Darcy tried to dissuade him. "I know how to act when something of this sort is said to me."

"Nonsense, Darcy!" was Bingley's adamant response. "Caroline has once again over stepped herself. If my home is to be comfortable for my friends, I cannot have her acting this way. It was bad enough when Miss Jane was ill and Miss Elizabeth stayed here to nurse her. No, I am resolved to act."

Darcy marvelled at how Charles had changed in the weeks they had resided at Netherfield. He had become admirably involved in Netherfield's estate business, and more than once now, he had stood up to his sister's diatribes. It was obvious that his affection for the eldest Bennet sister was not his normal fleeting kind of infatuation. All-in-all, it appeared that his affable friend was finally becoming a man in his own right.

This newly acquired maturity was evidenced during their visit to the barn. Charles asked questions about the roof structure and the roofing materials that might be used for the repairs. He listened to the steward and to Darcy before making a well-reasoned decision about the work to be done and did so with strong confidence.

On their way back to the house, Darcy slapped Bingley on the back. "You are well on your way to becoming a successful landowner, my friend."

"Thank you, Darcy." Charles grinned. "I have found I have a head for it. I do wish I had known this earlier. I could have had the estate my father wished for me a great deal sooner. I doubted my own ability and feared I would fail."

"I foresee that you will surpass all of your father's expectations."

Charles beamed at the compliment and agreed wholeheartedly without conceit.

Once back at the house, Darcy parted with Charles, and wanting to avoid the company of Bingley's sisters, he went to his chambers. A hearty blaze in the fireplace warmed the room. Pulling up a chair and stretching out his legs, he pondered his options. He knew full well that if Elizabeth was found to be with child, the scandal would touch her entire family. The very thing that she was trying to avoid by not reporting the attack would fall upon her anyway.

Only a quick marriage could solve that dilemma. Could he find a man to suit her? Was there someone to be found who would accept a child that was not his own? He was certain that money could make it happen, but somehow this choice sat suffocatingly upon his heart. His own growing attraction to the lovely, dark-haired girl screamed out against it as well.

He stood and paced the room as he argued with himself. Her family's connections and the conduct of some of them left much to be desired, but the lady herself was above reproach as was her elder sister. Elizabeth's liveliness and beauty would win over those of his family and friends who were important to him. Her loving compassion could very well help Georgiana once her own pain lessened.

After pondering for a while what impact his marrying someone of a lower social position would have on his sister's prospects, he decided that although there would be talk, no lasting harm would be done. Society would find other things to gossip and frown upon a long time before Georgiana's coming out. No, he would not use her social status or her family to keep him from the match. Indeed, if the unfortunate incident had not occurred, he was certain he would have still wanted to pursue her.

Stopping to stare out a window at the bright autumn colours, Darcy finally asked himself the question. *Then what is stopping you?* He sighed as the answer sounded clearly in his mind. *Wickham!* The thought of her defilement by Wickham and the possible result being a child was like a giant wall before him. Could he ever get over that obstacle? Would he be able to raise that cur's child as his own? What if the child was a boy? Did he wish for the son of George Wickham to inherit Pemberley?

Darcy rubbed his neck as a headache began to creep up the back of his skull. Frustration roared through him. Seeking relief from the tension and pain his ruminations had caused, he poured himself a brandy and tossed it back. Its heat burned his throat and stomach, but within a few moments he felt the soothing effects of the drink.

May God help me! Darcy thought as he resumed his seat by the fire and leaned his head back. The decision did not need to be made at this very moment, but he knew it could not be put off much longer. He would wait until the morrow to revisit the problem. Another day might bring enlightenment.

~*~

Darcy had not intended to return to Longbourn that afternoon, but Bingley entreated his friend to accompany him. Beside his desire to see Miss Jane Bennet again, Charles wanted to explain to his friend the outcome of his latest talk with Caroline.

Once they mounted their horses and guided them down the lane to the Meryton road, Charles said, "Again, I apologize on Caroline's behalf. She insists that she had only your welfare in mind when she spoke to you this morning. I have long known of her aspirations with regard to you. I have tried to tell her that you are not interested, but she has not listened."

Pausing to take a deep breath, he looked at the fields beyond the hedges. Seeming to change the subject, Charles said, "This is a lovely place. I am happy I took it. I enjoy the people of Meryton. I know that not all is up to your exacting standards, but Caroline sees no beauty in the countryside or appeal in the residents of the area."

"She has made her opinion of both perfectly clear," Darcy responded.

"Indeed, and she reiterated them when I spoke to her this morning after her unacceptable speech to you." Charles shook his head and sighed. "The short of it is that she will be joining our aunt and uncle in Scarborough or Bath as soon as it can be arranged. As they often occupy a house in Bath this time of year, I must first ascertain their whereabouts. I cannot send my sister to an empty house. I wish that I could tell you she will leave tomorrow morning, but it may be as long as a fortnight before she does. I do promise to rein her in as much as possible in the meantime. To ensure the quickest resolution to this situation, I have sent letters by express to both of my relatives' addresses."

"I appreciate your attempt, but I am not insisting that she leave," Darcy protested half-heartedly.

"I understand that." Charles nodded, his face grim. "However, I will not tolerate her haughty, self-important behaviour any longer. One would think by her actions that she had been born a titled lady. Our wealth came from trade, for heaven's sake."

"Who will keep house for you if she does not?" Darcy wondered how a ball could be planned and orchestrated without a hostess.

"I have already asked Louisa to do it." He smiled dourly. "Although her attitude is nearly as bad as Caroline's, she understands the boundaries I have set forth. Hurst nearly danced with joy when I informed him of my plans. Apparently, they have had many confrontations while Caroline stayed with them in London. He offered the use of his carriage, footmen, and a maid to accompany my sister to Scarborough once she reaches London and promised to see to it that his wife controls her actions and tongue."

Charles, finally able to shake off his sour mood as they neared Longbourn, sported a brighter than normal smile when he spotted Miss Bennet in the garden picking flowers.

"Mr. Bingley, Mr. Darcy, it is good to see you," Jane welcomed them with serenity.

"Miss Bennet, you are looking radiant this afternoon," Charles said as his gaze dropped to the ground. "I hope your family is well. May I ask after Miss Elizabeth?"

Jane's smile was indeed radiant as she answered, "They are all well, including Elizabeth. Her excursion to the parlour had no ill effects."

"Splendid!" Charles cried happily. "Is that not wonderful news, Darcy?"

"It is indeed." Darcy's heart lifted at the positive report.

"Will you not come in, gentlemen?"

After the men handed off their horses to a groom, the three made their way into the house. Mrs. Bennet greeted them just inside the foyer and quickly ushered them into the parlour where Mr. Collins and Mary sat discussing a difficult passage in one of Fordyce's Sermons. The cleric stood so quickly and bowed so low that he nearly toppled over.

"Mr. Darcy, Mr. Bingley, I am so happy to see you again." With great deference, Collins took Darcy's arm and tried to forcibly guide him to a settee where he indicated that Darcy should sit down while the clergyman prepared to monopolize the gentleman's conversation.

However, Darcy, being in no mood to pass his time listening to the man's verbose praise of Lady Catherine or her home at Rosings Park, wrested his arm from Collins's grip and moved to the opposite side of the room where Bingley stood talking to Jane and her mother.

Mrs. Bennet rhapsodized about the planned ball at Netherfield and all the lovely things she and her girls had purchased in Meryton. She frowned slightly when Darcy came up to them, but she soon forgot his presence in descriptions of ribbons and lace.

Darcy watched Charles and realized with an inward smile that his friend heard little of what Mrs. Bennet said, so lost was he in gazing into Jane Bennet's eyes. Though her countenance stayed tranquil as usual, the faint bloom on her cheeks and the fact that she continually twisted a handkerchief in her hands told him that she was not so calm as she seemed.

When Mrs. Bennet finally finished her discourse on accessories for the ball and turned to ring the bell for some tea, Darcy inquired of Jane, "Is Miss Elizabeth truly well after this morning?"

"Oh, yes!" Jane exclaimed, clasping her hands together in joy. "Mr. Jones said that if she fares as well tomorrow, she will be allowed to join the family for dinner the day after."

"Excellent news, indeed," he commented calmly though he inwardly praised God for His mercy. How he wished he could see her again! But too many visits would foster speculation. The words of Caroline Bingley ran through his mind.

"...I should think that you would be more circumspect lest the populace and, in particular, her family get the idea you are courting Miss Eliza."

As Darcy pondered the idea of courting Elizabeth Bennet, the longing he had been trying to quell for days burst forth. Her lovely face with its expressive, brown eyes drew him like none had ever done. He wanted to protect her even more than the day he found her on the ground, whimpering in pain. If she was found to be increasing, and he could overcome his misgivings as well as hers, they would, of necessity, need to be married quickly. It seemed logical that Mr. Bennet would likely be suspicious of his desiring so hasty a wedding if there was no earlier indication of Darcy's regard. Surely questions and possible accusations would arise. Elizabeth's reputation must not be tainted with even a hint of impropriety. At that moment, he resolved to act.

Excusing himself, he made his way to the library. After knocking and being bid to enter, he went in and closed the door.

"Good afternoon, Mr. Darcy," Mr. Bennet smiled up at him from behind his desk. "I am surprised to see you again so soon."

"Bingley asked me to accompany him," Darcy said, feeling the need to explain.

"So that gentleman is here as well?" The older man chuckled as he dropped his gaze to watch Darcy nervously twisting his signet ring. "Is there something about which you wish to speak to me, or were you merely trying to escape my cousin's exuberant deference?"

When he saw the light of genuine sympathy and the glint of humour in Bennet's eyes, his mouth curved into a smile. "A little of both, I would say. I do have something to discuss with you, but avoiding his overdone admiration of my aunt and Rosings Park is an added boon."

"Please sit down, sir." Mr. Bennet leaned forward in his chair with anticipation.

Darcy sat stiff and straight in the chair, finding that the words would not form themselves properly in his mind. He took a deep breath and held it for several seconds before he exhaled while trying to relax. "Mr. Bennet ..., that is to say, I wish to...," he stammered and paused to steel his resolve before going on. "I would like to ask your permission to court Miss Elizabeth." His relief at finally saying the words made him feel almost faint.

"You wish to court my Lizzy," Mr. Bennet repeated with a touch of incredulity. "I know that you have been visiting us frequently, but I had supposed that you only did so to encourage your friend. Are you telling me you fancy Elizabeth? That does not coincide with the reports I have heard of your previous opinions."

Darcy frowned and reddened, realizing that others besides Elizabeth and Charles knew of his insult. "Sir, I have already apologized to Miss Elizabeth for my ill-judged and completely inaccurate comment at the Meryton Assembly. Circumstances wholly unconnected to her or to the local society caused my foul mood. I beg your pardon as well since even that night I found myself fascinated by her beauty and lively spirit. Truly, sir, I do admire Miss Elizabeth greatly," he finished in a humble tone.

"Well, well," Mr. Bennet grinned. "It is an interesting turn of events. What does my daughter say to this courtship?"

"Your daughter is not aware of my intentions as yet, and I am not sure I want her to be so until I am sure this regard is more than a passing one."

"Are you often fickle in your regard for young ladies?" Bennet inquired.

"Sir, upon my honour, I have never felt this way about any other young woman. I merely thought to save her embarrassment if we courted publicly and either of us wanted to end it. But if you want to inform her of my application, I bow to you in the matter." Darcy's pride was taking a bruising, but the more he thought about it, the more he felt it likely needed a good flogging.

"I see no reason to withhold my consent," Bennet said thoughtfully. "And I think that we will keep the knowledge to ourselves at the moment, at least until Lizzy is completely well. I warn you that my daughter is stubborn. You will have your work cut out for you, trying to win her heart." His face took on stern lines. "Take care that you do not hurt her."

"I shall do my very best, sir," Darcy promised as he reached out his hand to Elizabeth's father.

As Mr. Bennet shook Darcy's hand, he thought, *you will do, sir, you will do, indeed.* "I believe that I will extend an invitation to dinner the day after tomorrow to both you and your jovial friend Bingley since Elizabeth is likely to join us. I promise to talk to Jane about arranging the seating so that you are close to Lizzy and far from my loquacious cousin."

"Thank you, sir," replied Darcy with enthusiasm. "I accept for us both. I know that we have no other plans." *I know that Charles and I would change them if we did,* he thought with inner candour.

When he walked back to the parlour, he saw that Collins was once again talking with Miss Mary while Bingley chatted amiably with Jane. Mrs. Bennet was no longer in the room. Catching Charles's eye, he suggested a walk in the gardens. Although he did not mean to invite the Bennet cousin, the cleric seemed to think the invitation included him, and so was more than eager to accompany them. Mary Bennet followed that gentleman as if she could not bear to be parted from him. Seeing the expression on Miss Mary's face, Darcy realized that she was infatuated with Collins. He filed the fact away in his mind as he pulled on his topcoat.

Mr. Collins moved to his side before Darcy knew what was happening. Mary walked on the clergyman's other side as they followed Jane and Bingley along a lovely garden path. Bright gold and orange mums spilled out from urns along the way, their colours complimenting the leaves on the trees and the brilliant foliage of the shrubs.

"This is a charming bit of garden, Miss Bennet," Darcy complimented.

"Thank you, sir," Jane replied from just ahead of him. "We feel that there should be a touch of colour during every season."

"Indeed, I am of the same opinion," Collins interjected. "Lady Catherine demands a great deal of her gardeners so as to maintain a beauty that befits her regal home." He began a monologue in which only Mary Bennet seemed interested.

It was not until Collins mentioned that his noble patroness had insisted that he choose a wife from his fair cousins that Darcy tuned his attention back once more. Lowering his voice a fraction, he confided, "I had thought to choose by seniority, but as I have been informed and see for myself, another has come before me. I decided to turn my attention to the next oldest of these lovely ladies." Looking smug at his own brilliance, he smiled satisfactorily as if waiting for the approbation of his companions.

Glancing quickly in Mary's direction, Darcy witnessed her pale face and her saddened demeanour. Immediately, he realized that he had a task to perform that would at the same time keep Elizabeth from having to entertain the parson's effusive proposal and possibly ensure the future felicity of her younger sister.

As swiftly as he was able, Darcy turned the subject back to Rosings and his aunt. He did not truly want to hear sycophantic rhapsodizing about Lady Catherine, but he did want to keep him from the subject of marriage and Elizabeth until he could figure out how to manoeuvre the cleric in another direction. Thus the conversation was not particularly to Darcy's liking, but there was an advantage to it. He could, again, ignore the man while formulating a plan. Finally the cleric's droning slowed enough for Darcy to inject a question of Mary.

"Miss Mary, I noticed a pianoforte in your parlour. Do I surmise correctly that you play?"

Mary blushed and smiled. "I do indeed, sir."

For a moment, Darcy could see her resemblance to Miss Elizabeth. "I hope someday to have the pleasure of hearing you."

Her face flushed an even deeper shade of pink that made her almost pretty. "I would be happy to do so when the opportunity arises."

"Oh, yes, Mr. Darcy, if I may say so, you are in for a rare treat," Collins gushed. "I have had the great joy of hearing my cousin Mary practice. I would dare say that playing would even give enjoyment to Lady Catherine."

Darcy was satisfied with this exchange. Now he felt he had the right course of action in mind. He excused himself for a moment to hurry to Charles's side. "Bingley, I have a great favour to ask of you."

"Anything, Darcy, I am at your service."

"I believe we should invite Mr. Collins to come shooting with us tomorrow."

Darcy's request bewildered Charles, but he quickly agreed, "If you wish it, certainly he may come."

Nodding, Darcy returned to the cleric's side. "My friend and I would like to invite you to join us for a bit of bird hunting."

"But, sir," Collins sputtered, "I have no firearm and have never shot one in my life."

"Do not trouble yourself about that, Mr. Collins." Darcy dismissed his objection with a flick of his hand. "We have plenty of guns and shall instruct you in the use of them."

Collins was extremely flattered by the invitation. He bowed and agreed wholeheartedly.

"Excellent," Darcy declared as he congratulated himself for his idea.

Again Darcy turned to Miss Mary and engaged her in conversation, taking the opportunity to find out her views on various subjects. The more interest that was paid to the young lady the more her visage shone. He did not wonder at her thirst for attention, being the middle and plainest of five daughters. He hoped he could redirect the clergyman's attentions and that in the redirection he could ensure her happiness, considering the qualities of the man.

After settling the time of the hunt, the men returned to Netherfield.

CHAPTER SIX

Mr. Collins arrived at Netherfield nearly half an hour earlier than he had been invited to come. However soon, the four men, including Mr. Hurst, made their way to the fields where the hunt would begin.

Mr. Hurst turned out to be a patient instructor in the use of firearms. He showed the cleric all things necessary for safety and accuracy. After several misses, Collins managed to bag a bird. The man beamed like a child at his achievement.

Darcy congratulated him on his success before taking him aside for a private conversation.

"Mr. Darcy, I must thank you for inviting me today." Collins spoke before Darcy could begin. "I must admit I was apprehensive about shooting, but I find I am quite fond of it. It is a pity that there is little opportunity at Hunsford for the sport."

"I might be able to see to it that you attend the gamekeeper at Rosings when he goes on one of his hunts," Darcy interjected, and before Collins could thank him, he said, "Don't thank me, as I have done nothing yet."

When Collins opened his mouth to argue, Darcy stopped him by lifting his hand. "Sir, I have something of a rather delicate nature to discuss with you. I hope you will forgive me if I speak of a personal matter involving yourself."

"Mr. Darcy, please do not trouble yourself. I have no qualms with hearing anything from you involving myself." He emphasized his acquiescence with a bow. "I have always been more than happy to listen to your excellent aunt, the Right Honourable Lady Catherine de Bourgh, whenever she condescends to offer me her advice, so I am ready and willing to hear what you have to say."

"Yesterday you mentioned your ambition to marry one of your cousins, and your decision is that the one would be Miss Elizabeth." Darcy looked down at the man and shook his head slightly. "Am I correct in my recollection of what you told me?"

"Yes, that is what I said." Collins's brow furrowed with worry at the stern look on Darcy's face. "I thought that it was only fair to choose the next in line."

Darcy rubbed his chin as if he were pondering the other man's statement. "I suppose it would be fair to the ladies, but what of fairness to yourself and your patroness?"

"I fail to understand you, sir," Collins gulped at even the thought of being unfair to Lady Catherine. "How could it be so?"

"I hope that what I am going to say will go no further, not even to my aunt," Darcy said gravely.

"Indeed, sir, my lips are sealed," he hastened to agree.

"Very well then," he said as he lowered his voice. "I wonder if you have noticed Miss Elizabeth's lively nature and her propensity to go for long walks alone." At Collins's nod he continued, embarrassed at repeating a falsehood, "It is said that her injuries were caused by her running about. My aunt would find this behaviour upsetting, do you not think?"

Collins thought about this for a moment before he protested, "But surely Cousin Elizabeth would settle down after we were married. Indeed as her husband, I would insist upon it."

"But, sir, I am not certain but that her nature is not already fixed at this point." Darcy paused to rub his chin again. "This is not my only concern, however."

"It is not?" Collins turned a bit green to think there could be more.

"Her taste in books and her ability at a musical instrument are mediocre at best. I have heard that she does not take the time to practice as her younger sister, Mary, does." He lifted a finger as if an idea just struck him. "In fact, I believe Miss Mary Bennet is far better qualified to be a clergyman's wife. She is admirably pious and constantly studies theological texts. I think I observed you and her discussing one such book just yesterday."

A pensive expression crossed Collins's face. "Miss Mary, you say? Yes, we did have an enlightening discussion yesterday afternoon. And as I told you, her playing is quite lovely." Then he said more to himself than Darcy, "She is not so handsome as Miss Elizabeth, but she does have a comely figure and a humble manner."

"I have one more comment, and then I will importune you no longer. I have every reason to believe that Miss Mary has a deep regard for you." Darcy paused to let that thought sink in. "I think that affection from one's wife is a thing to be greatly desired. You would not have to wonder if she accepted you for purely monetary reasons."

Collins stared at Darcy for several long moments. His thoughts were evident by the changing expressions on his face. When, at last, the looks of concern and worry gave way to ones of determination and satisfaction, the clergyman said, "I must thank you again for your interest in my well-being." He smiled broadly. "I believe I know how to act. Since in less than a sennight I must return to Hunsford, I think it would be most prudent to approach the lady as soon as may be."

"Indeed, Mr. Collins, I believe you are correct," Darcy said as he nodded solemnly. "And I think you will find Miss Mary amenable to your offer."

After listening to the cleric's abounding gratitude for another ten minutes, Darcy finally and not so subtly suggested that Collins should return to Longbourn and seize the moment. The idea was met with great eagerness, and it found Mr. Collins on his way back to the Bennets' home in a thrice.

~*~

The next morning Darcy took his breakfast in his room. He did not want to encounter Miss Bingley. Charles had not yet heard from his relatives in regard to his sister, so she still roamed the house as if trying to find a moment alone with Darcy. Having no desire to face an attempt by Caroline to catch him in a compromising position, he had taken to locking his doors at night, and he never entered a seemingly empty room without at least one footman to accompany him. Too often in his past, young women of the *ton* or their matchmaking mamas had tried to manoeuvre him into a position which would force him into marriage. He refused to fall into a trap now.

While he ate, read, and lounged in his chambers, Darcy could not fight the rising tide of emotions Elizabeth Bennet evoked in him. His thoughts constantly wandered to their last meeting. Even though still pale from her ordeal, her loveliness overwhelmed his senses. He was grateful that she found herself able to forgive him, even though he did not feel he deserved it. The fact that he was about to embark on a secret courtship, with only her father's knowledge, and approval seemed unreal and quite unsettled him.

Darcy stood abruptly and pulled the cord to summon his valet, Peters. He needed to ride off some of his disquiet. A good gallop on Paladin would set him to rights again. After ordering his horse to be brought to the house, his man helped him change into appropriate clothing.

"I will be back in time for luncheon," Darcy told his valet. "Is everything ready for tonight?"

"Yes, sir," Peters replied. "I will have your bath ready at three o'clock, if that suits you."

Darcy nodded and left his rooms.

~*~

Elizabeth sat at the window of her room with Sarah readying her things for the evening. Smiling, she spoke, "Is it necessary to do that so early?"

41

"It is, Miss Elizabeth," Sarah smiled and answered. "Since I must help all of your sisters in their preparations for this evening, I want to make sure that I am prepared to do my duty by you."

"I sometimes forget that your duties are so great," Elizabeth apologized.

"Oh, I did not mean to complain. I merely know how to make the best use of my time," she exclaimed before she added cheekily, "and since Miss Kitty and Miss Lydia will need much of my time, I must start my work early."

Elizabeth chuckled, "I see that I am in error and now am only surprised that you are still here."

The responding light laugh from Sarah gladdened Lizzy's heart. How she wished that she could ease the young maid's load. There was only one way that she could ever help her, and that would be for Elizabeth to marry a rich man. That way she would be able to keep a personal lady's maid.

Such fancy! She chided herself. There were few such men in her limited acquaintance and one obviously loved her dearest Jane. The other... she blushed at the image that flooded her mind of being carried in Mr. Darcy's arms. The pleasure of those few moments seemed to increase with each remembrance. Elizabeth was surprised at the turn of her feelings toward the gentleman. Admitting that his recent conduct had changed her opinion of him, she wondered if he could ever look upon her as more than a friend. Again she upbraided herself and moved to her desk to write an overdue letter to her aunt Gardiner.

After nearly an hour, there was a knock at her door.

"Come," she called as she folded and sealed her missive to her aunt.

When the door opened, she spied Sarah who curtseyed and said, "Mr. Jones has arrived to see if you are well enough to be allowed to join the family for dinner tonight."

Elizabeth handed the letter to Sarah and said, "See that this is posted as soon as may be, and bring the doctor here."

Bobbing another quick curtsey, Sarah did as she was told.

The examination did not take long and the result was favourable and even glowing. Mr. Jones told her that with frequent periods of rest and no undue exertions, she would be allowed to resume her normal activities in a few days time. He would come round to see her on the morrow to ascertain whether or not her excursion to dinner had had any adverse effects.

After faithfully promising to follow his instructions, she bade him farewell. Elizabeth was so elated at the idea of finally being free to move about as she wished that she could not help but give Sarah a quick hug. "I believe I have you to thank for my return to health," she lowered her voice, "even more so than Mr. Jones, though we shall not confess this to anyone else."

"No, Miss Elizabeth," Sarah replied as she blushed.

Elizabeth quickly made her way to Jane's room to share the good news. After a bit of private rejoicing, the two sisters proceeded to make the rest of the family aware of the doctor's favourable report.

Her father, though gratified at the encouraging account of his daughter's return to health, insisted that she rest after luncheon. Elizabeth obeyed with no complaints as she did want to be well for the evening.

~*~

The brisk ride restored much of Darcy's equilibrium. He bounded up the steps and into the entry just as Charles came down the staircase.

"Oh, Darcy," Charles exclaimed. "I am glad you are back. Come with me into the study. I have news."

Once he had closed the study doors behind them, Bingley spoke. "I received a letter from my aunt this morning. It was unexpected but not unwelcome. I suppose because of the fact that I sent an express and took the time and effort to make certain my correspondence was more legible than usual, she responded with the greatest haste. They were preparing to leave Bath the day my letter arrived, so they decided to meet Caroline in Northampton. Hurst's servants and carriage will only need to go that far. I began making arrangements as soon as I read my aunt's letter. Packing has commenced and a man has been dispatched to Town to see to Hurst's carriage."

"That is swift work, Bingley," Darcy declared with astonishment.

"I am determined to have Caroline out of this house as soon as possible. I know how you have been trying to avoid her, and I have noticed her loitering in rooms like a cat waiting to pounce on a mouse." Charles shook his head in disgust. "And I believe you are the intended mouse. I will not have it!"

Bingley strode to a cabinet and pulled out a bottle of brandy. "I need a drink. Care to join me, Darcy?"

Understanding that something else bothered his friend, Darcy accepted a glass even though he rarely drank so early in the day. After taking a sip of the excellent spirits, he asked, "If it is to be dealt with in such an expeditious manner, why are you still so overwrought?"

Taking his time the swirl the amber liquid around the snifter, Bingley merely sighed.

"Come now, Bingley, what has happened?"

"This morning after I told my sister what my aunt wrote to me, she tried to argue with me at first. I am certain that she thought she could get me to change my mind." He shook his head sadly. "I am afraid I have done so too many times in the past. However, this time I was not moved. That is when she began to rage against the Bennets, saying that they were mercenary and social climbing, merely out to trap wealthy gentlemen into matrimony."

Charles took a large gulp of his brandy and his face reddened as the liquid burned down his throat. After a few moments, he found his voice once more. "I tried very hard not to lose my composure, but her last words to me pushed me over the edge. She said that Jane Bennet did not care for me, that I should study her countenance, and that I would find that she shows me no real regard. She told me that if I offered for her, Jane would say yes so as to secure financial benefit for herself and her family." He slumped into a chair. "She also suggested that I ask you. She said she was certain that even if you might be infatuated with Eliza Bennet, you could see that her elder sister showed no sign of returning my affection."

Darcy moved to a chair closer to Bingley. "Charles, I admit that until recently I might have said that Miss Bennet showed no special regard for you."

"Until recently? What has changed?" Charles demanded eagerly.

"I watched more carefully and discovered that I was wrong." His anger toward Caroline Bingley rose, but he tamped it down, since it would not help his friend. "Miss Bennet is a private person, not unlike myself. She does not exhibit her feelings to many. I believe I caught glimpses of her true feelings for you, such as when you and I visited Longbourn a few days ago. I am quite certain that she does not seek your favour for any reason other than that deep regard. Please do not be discouraged by what your sister said. It seems to me that she is trying to lash out at you for sending her away."

A servant knocked on the door to announce that luncheon was served and put an end to their conversation.

"Let us eat." Charles stood, a smile brightening his face. "Thank you again, my friend. I am glad I talked about this with you."

~*~

The carriage ride to Longbourn found both of the gentlemen suffering from disquieted emotions, thus they travelled in silence. Charles was upset at himself for believing even for a little while that his angel was indifferent to him, and Darcy was uneasy because his feelings for Miss Elizabeth increased, it seemed, almost hourly.

Upon entering the drawing room, the two men found those gathered there in a joyous uproar. Collins and Mary stood beaming while Mrs. Bennet cried out in rapturous tones of her happiness. When she caught a glimpse of Darcy and Bingley, she called out, "Gentlemen, please come in and hear the wonderful news." Before they took a step, her delight gushed forth, "Mr. Collins and Mary are to be wed."

The gentlemen offered their congratulations and wishes of felicity while the two youngest Bennet sisters sniggered and giggled in turn. Mr. Bennet only smiled at the chaos before he offered Darcy and Bingley a glass of wine.

"You, sirs, must join me in a celebratory drink," Mr. Bennet declared as he directed his gaze toward the newly engaged couple. Lowering his voice, he spoke to Darcy. "I have been told that you were instrumental in guiding my cousin's choice. From what I hear, you were perceptive as to the favourable disposition of my middle daughter's feelings as well. Thank you for your assistance in this matter. I can see no better outcome than this for them both."

Darcy tried to protest, but Mr. Bennet would not hear it. He slapped the younger man's back before he changed the subject. "I think you will be happy to hear that Elizabeth is much improved and will be joining us for dinner. In fact, I was just going above stairs to assist her when you arrived."

Even though Darcy had been fairly certain Miss Elizabeth would be well enough to dine with the family that night, his heart leapt at the thought of seeing her once more. He felt heat warm his face and wondered at his precarious hold on his emotions of late.

Mr. Bennet had to bite his cheek to keep from smiling at Darcy's discomposure and obvious delight at the idea of seeing Elizabeth again. After a thoughtful moment, he sobered. If this gentleman was able to win Lizzy's heart, he, as her father, would be losing her to the man from Derbyshire. Sighing, he excused himself to go to Elizabeth's room.

Darcy followed Mr. Bennet as far as the drawing room door. He wanted to be able to offer Elizabeth his arm. It seemed like ages since he had spoken to her and had been able to witness her lovely, sparkling eyes as she teased. He looked around the room, found that one of the settees was unoccupied, and hoped that it would remain so. The desire to have a few moments to sit beside her made him wish that propriety did not prevent him from making a verbal claim on the seat.

Because Darcy was concentrating on his longing to be seated next to Elizabeth, he nearly missed her arrival. Quickly turning his attention toward her and bowing, he said, "How are you this evening, Miss Elizabeth?"

Smiling and curtseying, Elizabeth answered, "I am fine, thank you. I hope you are well."

"Yes, I am. I thank you." Darcy offered his arm. "Would you allow me to escort you to the settee?"

Elizabeth nodded and releasing her father's arm, placed her hand on Darcy's. The warmth of his glance made her heart race. She had not realized how a mere look could cause such a response in a person. Again the sense of well-being and safety filled her. It was as if nothing could harm her when she was with him.

Once she was seated, Elizabeth was surprised at the pleasure she felt when Mr. Darcy sat down next to her. Jane asked after her health from her position beside Bingley. After talking a few moments with her older sister, she spoke to Mary and Mr. Collins. "I wish to congratulate you both. I pray that you will have a long and happy life together."

Mary merely blushed and thanked her sister, while Mr. Collins spent five minutes extolling the magnitude of his delight at securing such a talented and virtuous bride. Finally, Mary was able to distract her fiancé so that Darcy was able to speak to Elizabeth. In a low voice, he asked, "I hope that you are truly recovering, Miss Elizabeth."

Elizabeth thought about the nightmares that still plagued her, though they were not so frequent. Her head no longer pained her, other than a slight soreness around the wound. As far as she and Sarah could tell, her other injuries were healing nicely. "I am greatly improved, Mr. Darcy. I hope to be allowed to resume my normal routine in a day or two."

Darcy's smile transformed his countenance, causing Elizabeth to catch her breath. "I am delighted to hear this news," he declared with obvious joy. "I have prayed daily for your swift recovery."

"Thank you, sir," Elizabeth said and blushed.

The pair sat in silence that was not at all uncomfortable. For Elizabeth, it afforded more of the pleasant feelings of safety and belonging. For Darcy, the emotions were far more unsettled but still enjoyable. The reality of being in her company always outstripped his imaginings of it.

Opening his mouth to ask how she kept herself occupied whilst convalescing, all such thoughts vanished as he tuned into what Lydia Bennet was telling her mother in a loud strident voice. "Yes, Mr. Wickham! I had gone to Meryton with Maria Lucas. We were just looking in a shop window when we heard a noise and turned to see Mr. Wickham being forced from his lodgings by three very large soldiers, not militiamen but regular soldiers, who escorted him to a carriage. Poor Wickham looked as if he had slept in his uniform and had not had time to shave in several days. I do wonder what is to become of him. It was almost as if he were being arrested."

As Lydia, Kitty, and their mother continued to exclaim aloud at the fate of Wickham, Darcy brought his attention back to Elizabeth who had turned white at the mention of the blackheart's name. He surreptitiously took one of her cold hands in his. "Do not be alarmed, Miss Elizabeth," he soothed as he caressed the back of her hand with his thumb. "This means that he is gone from the area. You will not have to see him again." He was elated to know that his cousin's men had arrived and taken the vile man away, but he was upset that her youngest sister's tale had distressed Elizabeth.

As her colour returned, Darcy became aware of the impropriety of holding Elizabeth's hand as he was doing. Giving her fingers a brief squeeze, he released them. "I do hope you will forgive me for taking such a liberty," he whispered.

Though she blushed, Elizabeth looked into his eyes and said with a faint smile, "What liberty is that, sir? I am not aware of your taking any."

Darcy's heart pounded. She did not take offense. What singular joy to know Elizabeth was not insulted by his actions! "Thank you, Miss Elizabeth. You are most kind to say so."

Elizabeth took it upon herself to change the subject. "How are the arrangements for the ball at Netherfield proceeding?"

"I dare say you will have to ask Bingley," Darcy answered with a smile. "He and Mrs. Hurst are often in conference about one or another matters pertaining to it."

"Mrs. Hurst? I thought that Miss Bingley would have charge of arrangements for the ball." Her voice rose with her surprise so that her question was heard by Bingley.

"Ah, yes, Miss Elizabeth." Charles coloured slightly before he said with obvious discomfiture, "Caroline is to travel to the north on the morrow to join our aunt and uncle on their way to Scarborough. There was a sudden need for her to do so. Louisa graciously consented to be my hostess in my younger sister's absence."

"I am sure Miss Bingley will be missed," Jane said in her usual gracious way. "Please tell her so when you see her."

Charles nodded without committing himself to any such thing. He thought that he would not be speaking with his sister for a long while, and after Caroline's tirade of this morning, she would not desire to hear Jane's message either.

Just then, dinner was announced and the guests and family proceeded into the dining parlour. Darcy, with Elizabeth on his arm, followed Jane's direction as to where he was to be seated. He was pleased to see that his place was to Elizabeth's right and Jane was to his right with Bingley next to her. Another observation showed that their chairs were at the opposite end of the table from Mrs. Bennet and Mr. Collins. Thus, the meal passed with relatively little discomfort.

Charles fielded many questions about when the ball would be held. Fortunately he had ascertained that Miss Elizabeth was on the mend, so he thus announced that the festivities would be in a sennight.

Mr. Collins bemoaned the fact that he was due back at Hunsford two days before the ball, but after a brief hushed conference with his future wife and mother-in-law, he decided that if he left the morning after the dance, he could reach Hunsford in time to prepare for Sunday services. "My noble patroness will surely understand if I wish to attend with my fiancée."

"I do not see how she can object, as she was the one to send you here to find yourself a wife." Mr. Bennet chimed in with a twinkle in his eye.

"I do believe you may be right, cousin," Collins replied, smiling happily at Mary. "Tonight before I retire I will be sure to write Lady Catherine to explain the reasons for my delay."

After dinner the separation of the sexes did not last long. Mr. Bennet saw that all three gentlemen were loath to linger long over their port. Mr. Darcy and Mr.

Bingley seemed especially eager to return to the ladies. Unable to watch them fidget any longer, he suggested they make their way to the drawing room.

Out of the safety of her own room, Elizabeth felt anxious now that Darcy was not with her. She upbraided herself for being foolish. How could the man's mere presence by her side make her more secure than when he was in the other room? Could it be that the mention of Wickham had given rise to this disquiet? Unable to answer her own question, Lizzy fidgeted in her chair next to Jane.

"What is wrong, Lizzy?" Jane asked quietly when she saw that Elizabeth's face had turned pale.

"I am well, dearest." Lizzy tried to reassure her, but when she saw that Jane was unconvinced, she added, "Although I could use a glass of water."

Jane quickly rose to go to the kitchen when the door opened and the gentlemen moved through it. She saw Lizzy's countenance brighten as Darcy moved toward her and took the seat Jane had just vacated. She signalled the maid who was coming into the parlour with a fresh pot of coffee. "Bring Miss Elizabeth a glass of water." She took the steaming carafe from the servant.

Bingley met Jane at the refreshment table. "May I be of assistance, Miss Bennet?"

Jane coloured when she saw Charles's huge grin. "Thank you, Mr. Bingley, but I believe I will be able to set the coffee pot down on the table by myself," she teased shyly. "May I pour you a cup?"

From his place next to Elizabeth, Darcy watched Bingley nod to Jane. "I wonder how long it will take my friend to propose to your sister," he pondered so softly that only Lizzy could hear.

Elizabeth laughed quietly. At Darcy's raised eyebrow, she explained, "If I tell you the source of my mirth, you will be shocked and even insulted by my impertinence." She paused to gaze at him with a challenge in her eyes.

"I am certain that would not be the case, Miss Elizabeth." His eyes danced as he tried not to smile.

"Very well, sir, be prepared," she warned, cheekily. "You sounded like my mother when you wondered about the timing of Mr. Bingley's proposal."

Darcy's barking laugh could have been mistaken for a cough. The room fell silent as everyone turned to look at him. He tried to hide his outburst by covering his mouth with his handkerchief and clearing his throat. Not daring to look at Elizabeth, he told her he would retrieve some coffee for them both.

As he made his way to the refreshment table, the servant entered the room with the water for Elizabeth. After thanking the girl, Lizzy grinned. Happy warmth filled her as she thought of how Mr. Darcy had been caught by surprise because of her jest. He did not seem to object to her joke at his own expense, which pleased her immensely. Taking a sip of the water, she gazed unseeing as she pondered the pleasurable emotions that gentleman was able to invoke in her.

With her mind thus engaged, Lizzy did not notice Darcy's return until he spoke. "I see that someone has brought you something to drink."

"Jane was worried about me and asked a servant to bring me water," Elizabeth told him, her cheeks warming.

"Did she have a reason for that worry?" he asked with concern in his voice.

"No, I was just a bit thirsty," she explained without looking up.

Darcy put a cup on the table next to her before resuming his own seat. "I am glad that I brought you the coffee then. Now you have a choice of liquid refreshment."

After sipping his coffee, Darcy leaned closer. "It is a good thing you warned me of your impertinence, Miss Elizabeth. Making me laugh as you did was impolitic, for I might be tempted to return the favour when you least expect it."

Elizabeth glanced up to see him smile and wink. Relaxing, she returned his smile. "I am certain that I do not fear your reprisal, sir. You obviously enjoyed my bit of humour; therefore I believe I look forward to your retribution."

Darcy's gaze turned serious. "I would not have you fear me."

"And I do not fear you, sir," Elizabeth explained. She wanted to tell him that fear did not enter into her feelings about him, but she knew she could not be so bold.

The rest of the evening passed too quickly for Darcy. However, once Elizabeth began to show signs of fatigue, he knew that he should take his leave.

"Miss Elizabeth, I think that my friend and I must be on our way back to Netherfield. I would not want you to become overly tired on your first real excursion back into society after your injury. I am pleased to have been invited to dinner." Darcy stood and bowed before asking that the carriage be brought round.

The time it took for the carriage to be summoned was spent in saying good night to the family. Bingley was obviously reluctant to leave, and Darcy no less so, but he knew that it was prudent that they depart.

Elizabeth rose and, with her sister, accompanied the gentlemen to the door. As Jane moved closer to Charles when he asked her a question, Darcy took Lizzy's hand and squeezed it gently.

"I am most gratified to see that you are doing so well. May God speed your complete recovery," he said as he gazed into her eyes.

The faint blush that came to her cheeks pleased him and disquieted her.
"Thank you, Mr. Darcy, I enjoyed your company and our conversation," she said and dropped her gaze. "Have a safe journey back to Netherfield."

"Miss Elizabeth." Darcy lowered his voice to nearly a whisper. "May I be so bold as to request the honour of dancing the first and the supper set with you at the ball?"

At this surprising application, Elizabeth lifted her eyes once more and smiled. "It would be my great pleasure, sir."

The delight of Darcy's asking her to reserve two dances buoyed her spirits so much that once in her bed, Elizabeth fell quickly into a restful and nightmare-free sleep.

CHAPTER SEVEN

Darcy made his way to the breakfast room in a happy frame of mind.

"Good morning, Darcy," Charles called out cheerfully. "Was not last night an enjoyable evening?"

"Indeed, it was, Charles," Darcy affirmed as he filled his plate at the sideboard. "I take it that your sister is on her way this morning."

"Yes, in fact, Louisa and Hurst decided to accompany her as far as London." Charles paused to take a big bite of toast piled high with strawberry jam. Once he had chewed and swallowed, he said, "I believe my brother thought it best that he see to Caroline's travel matters personally."

Darcy's relief at not having to work to avoid Miss Bingley any longer lightened his mood even more. He hoped that Elizabeth had not been too weary after her first full evening out of her room. Part of him wanted desperately to go to Longbourn to find out how she fared, but his more reasonable side told him he needed to be guarded in how many times he visited the Bennets. Rumours could ruin a young woman's reputation, and he began to think that his frequent visits to her home must certainly be a cause of speculation in Meryton just as there was because of Bingley's frequent attentions to Jane Bennet.

Determining to find another occupation that would distract him from thoughts of Miss Elizabeth Bennet, Darcy asked, "What say you to an inspection of the far pear orchards? I believe that your man said they are ready and that harvest was to commence today."

"Splendid idea, Darcy!" Charles grinned broadly. "I will ask Cook how many she might need for a pear tart…no, two tarts. We will bring them as a gift when we visit the Bennets tomorrow." His expression turned pensive. "That would be the proper amount of time to wait before another visit to Longbourn, would it not?"

Darcy chuckled. "I do believe that the offering of pear tarts would be sufficient to redeem yourself if it were not."

Charles laughed gaily as he spread jam on another piece of toast and gestured to the servant for more coffee. It was then that the butler brought the post in on a salver. Several were for Darcy, including one from Colonel Fitzwilliam.

As Charles opened his letters, Darcy broke the seal on his cousin's missive.

Darcy,

I am happy to tell you that my men were successful in their task. W. is in confinement on board a freighter bound for the West Indies. He will be assigned to a work crew on the ship and on the island. I have arranged that he will be indentured there with only food, lodging and ten pounds a year until he works off his debt. I doubt that he will live that long.

The ship sails in four days. My men will stay onboard until it departs. They tell me that he was extremely vocal in berating you and me, although they never told him who the perpetrator of his transportation was.

It does sound as though he has a guilty conscience, does it not? Thank you for allowing me to be involved with his punishment. I only wish you would have given me leave to do this after his failed elopement with our dear G.

I will keep you informed and tell you when he has left our shores for good.

I shall close by saying that I am not surprised that you choose not to tell me who you are aiding by asking for my help in disposing of that particular blight on society. I shall not press. Knowing and trusting you as I do, I am certain that there is a good reason for your secrecy. I have not told anyone of your involvement either. I would not want the evil Mr. W to have that information.

Your cousin,

Fitzwilliam

Darcy was relieved beyond words to know that the man who had been the bane of his existence for so long would finally be gone from his life. His smile broadened as he finished off his eggs.

~*~

The morning routine at Longbourn returned to normal as Elizabeth breakfasted with her family. Mr. Jones made an early visit and proclaimed that she could resume her usual activities as long as she continued to follow his previous instructions.

As Elizabeth walked into breakfast with Jane, she rejoiced that she was no longer confined to her room. Her dreamless and restful night's sleep had refreshed her as well. Taking her usual place at the table, she was greeted by her family, including a beaming Mr. Collins who sat across from her next to Mary.

"I am delighted that you are well enough to join us, Lizzy," Mr. Bennet said as he smiled broadly. "And in celebration, Cook has baked your favourite scones. Make sure that you eat heartily, or she may be offended."

"Thank you, Papa," she replied before taking a warm scone from the proffered dish. "I shall be sure to do justice to her fine baking."

The mood of the whole room was joyful and energized and soon filled with loud chatter. Mr. Bennet winked at his second daughter as he listened to his wife exclaim over the great attention Mr. Bingley had paid to Jane. Mrs. Bennet went on to ponder aloud how long it would be until the gentleman from Netherfield would offer for her. Lizzy watched her older sister turn pink and lower her gaze to her plate when she heard her mother speak so. Elizabeth smiled and fought back the chuckle that wanted to escape when she remembered the discussion on the same subject she had had with Mr. Darcy the previous evening.

The previous evening had been more than she had expected. Mr. Darcy's focused attentions had amazed and flattered her. His former aloofness and apparent disdain for others had vanished. His solicitous behaviour toward her since he found her after the attack, his apology for his rude and unflattering remarks, his polite response to her family's silliness, his skilful manoeuvring of Mr. Collins's attentions toward Mary, and his jovial reaction to her teasing combined to completely reverse her initial impression of him.

She sighed as she took another scone and accepted more tea from the servant. Lizzy tried to warn herself that thinking too favourably of that particular gentleman could end in heartache for her. Since her station in life was too far below his own, and that after the attack she was no longer a maiden, Elizabeth was certain that he would never consider her for his wife.

Suddenly Elizabeth had no appetite. She put the half-eaten scone on her plate and glanced around the table. No one seemed to notice that she was no longer eating. The conversation continued to be lively and cheerful. Not wanting to spoil the mood of her family, she nibbled at the food on her plate.

She startled when Jane spoke to her. "Lizzy, are you feeling well enough to join me for a walk in the garden. The weather is quite pleasant for this time of year, and I thought you might want to take advantage of it."

"I would like that, Jane," Elizabeth said as she tried to smile. The idea of going outside did not have the same appeal it usually did, but she told herself that she could always plead fatigue if the walk proved too uncomfortable for her.

Following breakfast, the two donned their pelisses and bonnets. It was then that Lizzy began to feel some unease. She reminded herself that she would not be venturing out alone. She would certainly be safe in Jane's company. Determined not to allow fear to keep her inside, Elizabeth opened the door and, taking Jane's hand, walked through the doorway.

The sun shone brightly in a cloudless sky. Elizabeth noticed that the autumn colours had deepened in the days she had been convalescing. The reds, yellows, and oranges of the trees and shrubs nearly overwhelmed the eyes. The autumn had always been her favourite season, but Elizabeth felt a sense of loss. Would her enjoyment of the fall always be tainted by the memory of the vicious attack? Her heart thumped in her chest at the painful question. Blinking back tears, she tried to keep her voice calm and even as she talked with Jane. It would not do for her sister to see her distress and begin to ask questions.

They walked through Longbourn's gardens with Jane carrying the bulk of the conversation. Elizabeth succeeded in keeping the discussion focused on Mr. Bingley and the ball at Netherfield.

Jane seemed content to speak of the young gentleman's easy manners and charming ways. "Mr. Bingley has been kind to us all by postponing the ball until you would be able to attend."

Upon reaching the gate that led to one of Elizabeth's favourite walks, Jane asked, "Lizzy, would you like to walk to the woods?"

Elizabeth tensed with fright. "No, I am afraid that I find myself quite fatigued. I believe that I should return to the house."

Although Lizzy tried to keep her voice even, Jane gave her a worried glance. "I am so sorry, dearest. I have forgotten not to overtax you. Let us go to the house immediately." She took Elizabeth's arm and guided her back toward their home.

"Do not fret, Jane," Elizabeth soothed. "I am fine. It is merely that I am not ready for a long walk just yet."

Still her sister fussed, and when they were finally inside, Jane insisted that Lizzy retire to her room to rest. Elizabeth did not argue. In fact she welcomed the time to ponder her emotions in private.

"Would you please ask Sarah to bring me some of her special herbal tea?" Lizzy asked when she sat on her bed.

"Of course," Jane hurried out of the room as soon as she made sure that Elizabeth was settled comfortably in bed.

When Sarah arrived with her special herbal blend of tea, she found Elizabeth lying with her forearm over her eyes. "Miss Elizabeth, is something wrong?" Sarah asked worriedly. She moved to the bedside and deposited the teapot and cup on the side table.

"No, there is nothing wrong with me, Sarah," Lizzy said as she threw back the coverlet and swung her legs over the edge of the bed so that she could sit up.

"Miss Jane was concerned when she found me. She said you tired quickly on your walk this morning."

"I am afraid I was not truthful with my sister," she confessed. "When Jane asked if I wished to walk into the woods, I could not tell her that I feared going so far from the house. And it was in the same direction where the...where my injuries..." She was not able to finish.

Sarah prepared the tea and sweetened it with a bit of honey just the way Elizabeth liked it. She handed her the cup and said, "Perhaps it is time for you to confide in Jane or at least talk to me about what happened."

Shaking her head, she snapped, "I cannot speak of it. I will not burden my sweetest sister with the knowledge. Do not ask me to do it."

"Forgive me, Miss Elizabeth. It is just that I see how holding this secret is hurting you. I want to help."

Elizabeth sighed and took the teacup from Sarah. "I know you want to help. Someday I will talk about it, but right now the very thought of reliving it frightens me."

"Very well, Miss Elizabeth," Sarah complied. "Just remember that I am ready to listen when you are ready to talk."

~*~

Although to both Darcy and Bingley that day and evening seemed to go on forever, it did pass. The following morning found the two gentlemen eager to visit Longbourn as soon as propriety allowed.

After eating breakfast and dealing with the day's correspondence, Bingley asked for a moment of his friend's time.

"What is it, Charles?" Darcy asked, looking up from the letter he was writing to his sister, Georgiana.

"I am going to propose to Miss Bennet today," he said in a rush, then paused to take a deep breath. With the exhale, Bingley requested a favour of Darcy. "I would like to have a private moment with Miss Jane. I believe that will be almost impossible inside Longbourn, so I am going to invite her, her sister Elizabeth, and you to walk out with me."

Darcy grinned inwardly, partly because of his friend's obvious discomfort and partly because of how opportune it would be to have the chance to walk alone with Miss Elizabeth. "Of course, Bingley, I would be delighted to help you achieve your goal of securing Miss Bennet's hand. I do not think there will be any hindrance to that end."

"Splendid!" Charles cried, as he rang for a footman. "I will have our horses ready within a half hour, if that will give you enough time to finish your letter."

"That should be sufficient." This time Darcy allowed the smile to form on his face. He had nearly finished the letter to his sister, but he added a few lines, hinting at the likely match between his friend and Miss Bennet. Before he signed the missive, he reread it. It was then he realized that he had given much of the space on the paper to descriptions of Elizabeth. Why was he not successful in avoiding thinking of her as merely Elizabeth?

Shaking his head, Darcy scanned the pages again. He had tried to convey her lively personality, her gentle but courageous nature, and her admirable loyalty to her family along with her appealing comeliness. Only Georgiana would receive his account without comment and, when she finally met Elizabeth, (he no longer told himself, if they would meet, but when) would quickly become her admirer. After signing, sanding, and sealing the letter, Darcy left it with the others to be posted, and, then, he made haste to change for the ride to Longbourn.

~*~

Elizabeth awoke with renewed vigour. Another night without nightmares greatly contributed to her positive outlook for the day. Something told her this day was going to be a wonderful one. Elizabeth quickly completed her morning ablutions as she waited her turn for Sarah's services. After choosing her favourite green day dress, she pinned up her hair.

At the knock, Lizzy bade the person to come in.

"Oh, Miss Elizabeth," Sarah exclaimed from the doorway. "You did not wait for me to help you."

"No, Sarah," Elizabeth smiled as she explained. "I was impatient to meet the day, but now that you are here, I will submit to your much more capable hands."

"Tsk, I will not be able to do any better than what you have done with your hair. There are only a few pins needed to secure it." After expertly finishing what Elizabeth had started, Sarah helped her into the frock she had chosen.

At breakfast, Elizabeth found that her appetite was renewed as well. She ate heartily and with great enjoyment. Not surprisingly, conversation at the table was of the Netherfield Ball. Her mother tried to wheedle Mr. Bennet into allowing her to take some of the girls to Town. She argued that Jane needed a new gown if she was to secure Mr. Bingley's affections, and Lydia, being a growing girl, could use one as well.

"Mrs. Bennet, it is my opinion that Jane could do nothing more to secure the affections of our neighbour at Netherfield. He is completely in her power now." He turned to smile at his becomingly blushing eldest daughter. "I believe it would be a cruelty to try to gild the lily."

"Oh, Mr. Bennet, how you try my nerves," cried out his wife. "I dare say that Charlotte Lucas will have a new gown, and she is not half so pretty as any of our girls."

"Mama!" Jane scolded. "That is unkind."

Just then Mr. Collins looked up from his heaping plate and frowned. He had not been paying attention to his future wife's mother, but if his cousin Jane did not approve of what she had said, it might behove him to inquire about it. However, before he could say anything, Elizabeth asked him if a date for the wedding had been set.

"No, Cousin Elizabeth," he answered while dabbing his mouth with his serviette. "We are going to walk to the church this morning to talk with your vicar, Mr. Scott, to set a date for our nuptials. My dear Mary and I would like to be married as soon as the banns can be read since being apart for long will grieve us both. However, my noble patroness, Lady Catherine, who will be attending, has provided me with several dates that would be acceptable to her. She has also suggested that we not be too hasty. She wants no hint of impropriety to be spoken against her clergyman. It would reflect upon her judgment in her choice to fill Hunsford's pulpit."

Elizabeth merely smiled and continued to eat.

As soon as breakfast was over, Mrs. Bennet accompanied Mr. Collins and Mary to the church. A few minutes after they quit the house, Kitty and Lydia decided to visit Maria Lucas. Thus ,with most of the family away from Longbourn and Mr. Bennet once more ensconced in his library, Jane and Elizabeth sat in the drawing room doing needlework and chatting as they rarely were able to do when the others were present.

"I wonder when Mr. Bingley will call again," Elizabeth said as she drew a needle through the linen in her hoop.

"Lizzy," Jane admonished. "I did not expect you to say such a thing."

"Come now, Jane." Elizabeth rested her work on her lap and stared at her sister. "I know that you were wondering the very same thing. If he does not come today, I will be very surprised. There is no doubt as to where his interests lie."

"Please Lizzy," her sister pleaded. "It is true such a thought had entered my mind, but it is unseemly to give voice to it."

"You sound like Mary and not my Jane. We are not in our rooms, so we are alone and may speak freely. I know you like him. Dare I say you love him? Why not confess it to me?"

Bright pink circles brightened Jane's cheeks. She did not look up from her embroidery but spoke in a hushed tone, "I do like him above any other man I have ever known. His manners are so pleasing and obliging. He has a handsome countenance. He is all my heart has ever wished for. I do not trust my own opinion as to his regard for me. His attentiveness extends to everyone. What if I am deceiving myself?"

Elizabeth hurried to Jane's side and wrapped her arms about her. "Jane, you are too modest. It is plain to everyone that Mr. Bingley loves you. Even Mr. Darcy mentioned his friend's regard for you."

"Mr. Darcy!" Jane cried. "He spoke of this to you?"

'Yes, he did," Lizzy answered, smiling at the memory of his laughing response to her teasing.

Jane's face turned even darker pink at this revelation. Finally she looked up and said, "I do not want to discuss Mr. Bingley any longer. Please honour my request."

"Forgive me, dearest." Elizabeth was immediately contrite. "I will drop the subject."

Jane had just whispered her thanks when Hill opened the drawing room door and announced, "Mr. Darcy and Mr. Bingley."

The two ladies rose quickly and curtseyed as the gentlemen bowed.

"I hope you ladies are well this fine morning." Mr. Bingley's cheerful voice filled the silence.

"We are, sir," Elizabeth answered, since it seemed that Jane could not find her tongue. "I hope you are as well." Her gaze fell on Darcy who stood close to the door.

"Both of us are very well," Bingley responded as he moved closer to Jane. He lifted the basket he had carried in. "My pear crop is excellent this year. I had my cook make two tarts for your family."

Jane took the basket and called for Hill to take them to the kitchen. "Thank you, sir, for your thoughtfulness."

While Charles blushed and accepted Jane's thanks, Elizabeth turned to their other guest and raised an eyebrow. "Mr. Darcy, will you not join us?"

"As a matter of fact, Bingley and I were wondering if you ladies would join us for a walk. That is, if you are feeling up to the task, Miss Elizabeth." His gaze locked on hers.

"I am not averse to having a ramble toward Meryton." Elizabeth thought she would be fine as long as they did not walk anywhere near the place of the attack.

After the ladies donned their spencers, cloaks, and bonnets, Bingley hastened to offer Jane his arm and guided her out the door. Darcy gestured for Elizabeth to leave the house ahead of him, but as soon as the door closed behind him, he reached her side and said, "I hope you are certain that a walk will not fatigue you."

"Thank you, Mr. Darcy, but I am positive that I will come to no harm." She looked around her with some anxiety, but when she glanced up and met his gaze, the fear eased.

Darcy observed Elizabeth's first tentative steps. She obviously felt uncomfortable, and he wondered what he could do to help her. He met her glance and watched as her worried look calmed.

Elizabeth tore her eyes from his, and she watched Mr. Bingley lean his head toward Jane and smile broadly. "I think this is the day," she said lightly.

"I do not understand your meaning, Miss Elizabeth," Darcy said, a trifle confused since he was not looking in the same direction she was. Thoughts of Bingley and his proposal intentions were, indeed, very far from Darcy's mind at that moment. His thoughts were more agreeably engaged as he gazed upon the beauty of his companion's dark eyes and creamy complexion. He was elated to see that she was much healthier even than two days earlier and that her fear had seemed to quiet after she looked into his eyes. He worked to squelch the pride he felt at the thought his presence might have been the reason for it.

Her laughter brought him back to the moment. "Surely, Mr. Darcy, you have not forgotten your contemplative question from the other evening about your friend."

Darcy fought a blush, but he followed her gaze to the couple ahead of them. "Of course, I remember. Now I see that you are very observant, Miss Elizabeth. My friend has informed me that he hopes to obtain your sister's agreement to be his wife."

Darcy thrilled to the utter joy that shone on Elizabeth's face. He fought the urge to touch the small curl that had escaped its confines and bounced against her right ear. When his hand reached up, he came to himself quickly enough to act as if he only intended to offer her his arm. "The road ahead is quite uneven. I would hate for you to misstep."

"Thank you, sir. It is kind of you to offer." Elizabeth rested her hand in the crook of his arm. Once more, she revelled in the feeling of peace that washed over her when in his presence. Any apprehension she had felt the day before with the very idea of walking out of the sight of her house had fled. Smiling up at him, she was struck breathless at his intense scrutiny.

For some distance neither of them spoke, as each enjoyed the pleasant day and equally pleasant companionship of the other. They proceeded slowly so that Jane and Bingley increased the distance between the couples until they disappeared from sight behind a tall hedge as the road curved to the right.

"I think we should give them a few moments of privacy," Darcy interjected into the silence. "I do not think that propriety will be injured by it."

"I believe you are right." Elizabeth smiled up at him as they stood alone in the lane. "I am so happy for my sister. Mr. Bingley is such a genial person... as is my dear Jane. I believe they shall have a felicitous marriage." She lowered her gaze to the ground as she sighed softly, knowing that this would not be her own lot in life.

"What sigh is this, Miss Elizabeth?" He tried to lift her chin so that she would look at him again. "Surely one day you will secure an equally happy match."

Jerking away, Elizabeth turned her back to him. "You of all people would ask such a question? Do you find pleasure in teasing me thusly since I can never hope to find that kind of joy? Who will have me after...?" Her voice trailed off to a mere whisper. She fought for composure. It certainly would not do to cry in the middle of a public road, even if they were currently alone. No, she could at least save herself the humiliation.

Straightening her shoulders, Elizabeth spoke, cutting off the protest that Darcy was about to make. "I believe we should join my sister and Mr. Bingley."

Her regal exit was spoiled by her stumbling upon a particularly deep rut in the road.

Darcy hastened to her side and helped her to regain her balance. He offered her his arm once more, and when she looked to refuse, he stated dispassionately, "I believe that you would not want to be injured again so soon, especially not at this time or place."

As Elizabeth took his arm, Darcy berated himself for upsetting the friendly balance they had achieved. How could he have forgotten what had happened and made such an insensitive statement? "Miss Bennet." His tone became formal and distant. "I beg you to allow me to apologize. I have no excuse, other than my thoughts were pleasantly occupied with your company and my friend's happiness. I did not... Please forgive me."

Without looking at his face, Elizabeth knew that Mr. Darcy was sincere in his confession of contrition despite the return of the formality of his tone. She, too, had nearly forgotten the attack in the joy of the moment. It said a great deal that a man like him would humble himself in this manner. How could she not forgive him?

As Elizabeth pondered this, she realized that she must apologize as well for believing that he would purposely hurt her in this way. She stopped and turned to him, still afraid to meet his eyes. "I am afraid that it is I who must apologize. I cannot believe that I accused you of such cruelty. I am utterly ashamed of my outburst."

"Elizabeth," Darcy murmured almost too quietly for her to hear before he spoke again more formally, "Miss Elizabeth, I believe that we should think on it no more. I took no offence at your words, and if you will believe that I meant none with mine, we shall continue as friends."

Finally glancing up at him, Elizabeth smiled and said, "Indeed, we shall."

As they rounded the bend, they spied Bingley and Jane standing in the middle of the road with hands clasped. Charles was the first to glance their way, and he fairly shouted in his delight, "Miss Elizabeth, Darcy, come and congratulate me. Miss Bennet has made me the happiest of men by consenting to be my wife."

Elizabeth and Darcy quickly joined the newly engaged pair. The sisters embraced as Jane smiled her most angelic of smiles.

Charles pumped Darcy's hand and thanked him for his encouragement. "I might not have proposed today without Darcy's steadying support."

"You are too modest, as usual, my friend," Darcy replied and then turned to face Jane. "Charles told me that he wished to propose this morning. I merely helped him to achieve the privacy he needed to do so."

"Thank you, sir," Jane said sweetly.

After a few moments more of cheerful talk, Charles indicated that he was eager to speak to Mr. Bennet as soon as possible.

Not surprisingly, Mr. Bennet approved the match wholeheartedly. Charles and Jane were of the mind to wait until the ball to make a formal announcement of their engagement. It turned out that Mr. Hurst had not only accompanied Caroline to meet her aunt and uncle Bradley; he had also been given the task of retrieving a certain item of jewellery that Bingley wished to give to Jane if she agreed to be his fiancée. Charles wanted to be able to present that particular item to Jane before the news was made known.

Mr. Bennet was more than happy to keep the news from his wife until the night of the ball. "I will be able to enjoy a little more peace until the announcement is made."

Soon after, whilst they all sat talking in the drawing room, Mrs. Bennet, Mr. Collins, and Mary arrived. Greetings were exchanged and refreshments ordered.

As Mrs. Bennet supervised the setting out of the tea things, she exclaimed happily, "Mr. Scott has agreed with a date a six-month from today. The banns will be published accordingly."

She turned to her husband. "I should like to take Mary into London to order her trousseau. Indeed, I think we must all have something made up for a wedding which Lady Catherine shall attend. It would not do to offend her sensibilities."

Elizabeth watched her father tease and torment his wife with protests and proclamations that he did not think such an excursion would be necessary. She knew that he merely toyed with her mother, but Mrs. Bennet did not seem to understand her husband enough to see what he was doing.

A blush of deep embarrassment crept up her face to think her father would not refrain from such teasing in front of others. Lizzy wanted to flee the room but was forced to endure further evidence of her parents' foolish and untoward behaviour. She tried to calm herself by sipping her tea slowly as she stood near a window while staring out at the garden.

"Do not upset yourself, Miss Elizabeth," Darcy whispered close to her ear.

Elizabeth had not noticed his moving from his friend's side as she had tried to block out her discomfort at what her parents were doing.

"I am embarrassed that you have witnessed this display." Elizabeth continued to sip her tea and look out the window, unwilling to meet what was certain to be a disapproving gaze.

"You are not responsible for your family's conduct." His tone was soft and reassuring. "And if you had ever had the opportunity to be in the company of my aunt Catherine and to experience her arrogance and officious interference in the business of others, you would be able to entertain with ease the harmless, if slightly inappropriate, actions of your parents."

Tears stung her eyes as Elizabeth realized that he was not offended or upset by the actions of her father and mother. It had never occurred to her that he would be so gracious and understanding of the foibles of those below his station in life. She might expect him to overlook such faults in those of the same rank but never the likes of her family. Ever since the attack, Mr. Darcy's conduct and attitude continued to show her that he was not the prideful or arrogant man she had supposed him to be upon first acquaintance. She was happy to have found out what kind of man he was and that he was becoming her friend.

Placing her empty cup on the small table beside her, she blinked rapidly to dispel her tears. "I do not know how to express my appreciation for your kind attitude."

"It is completely unnecessary," said Darcy as he finally caught her eye and smiled. "It does seem to me that your father should perhaps exert more control over himself and his wife. However, I have a sense that he has greater control than he shows."

"Truly, Mr. Darcy?" She was incredulous.

"Truly, Miss Bennet," he stated with a grin.

Elizabeth searched for a place to sit.

"Allow me, Miss Elizabeth," Darcy said as he guided her to a couple of chairs not far from where they had been standing. "I hope my observations have not distressed you."

Elizabeth gratefully sat down before she answered, "No, I am only discomposed." More softly, she said, "I had always supposed that you would not approve of my family."

"Perhaps in the beginning I was taken aback at their lively actions and vocal exchanges; however, I see much more love than malice in their dealings. Since I do not have to be concerned for my sister's lack of dowry, nor does she have to worry that she might be cast out of her home upon my death, I did not understand until lately the strain that those kinds of burdens could put on the emotions of a family with no heir. Forgive me if I have shown any disapproval of you or your family."

The relief that Darcy's words gave to Elizabeth was great. "Let us think on the subject no more."

Soon, Mrs. Bennet extended another dinner invitation to the gentlemen, which they readily accepted.

The evening's conversation flowed even more freely than it had previously. Although Jane and Charles had not publically announced their engagement, it seemed to Elizabeth that their very expressions of happiness would shout it to the world.

The engaged couples, one public and one secret, were nearly oblivious to their company. Mr. Collins was the consummate lover, asking after Mary's needs for more wine or another morsel of meat or potato or a bit of fruit. She blushed and fairly beamed under the attentions of her fiancé.

Charles Bingley was no less solicitous of Jane's wants and wishes although he was not as obvious about it. And when the group separated after the meal, he nearly followed the ladies, so loath was he to being parted from Jane.

Again, the men did not linger over their port but quickly rejoined the ladies for coffee. Cards were suggested as a diversion. Two foursomes sat down to play. Mrs. Bennet and Lydia played opposite Elizabeth and Darcy while Jane and Charles joined Mr. Collins and Kitty. Mary asked to be excused so that she could play the pianoforte for the company as she did not particularly like the game they were playing, and Mr. Bennet explained that he would enjoy observing the games better if he did not actually participate.

Lydia giggled more than the game warranted, and her mother talked more of hats than of hearts, but Elizabeth found that somehow sitting across from Mr. Darcy while knowing he was no longer looking on her family to find fault allowed her to relax and enjoy her rather eccentric family in a whole new way.

Darcy had to admit that the evening was one of the most unusual he had ever enjoyed. It was as if after understanding the true motives of many of the Bennets, he was able to look beyond much of the impropriety to view the obvious love that filled the house. Even the fawning Collins was more easily tolerated as Darcy observed the growing affection between the cleric and his fiancée.

Happily, Darcy noticed that Elizabeth no longer flinched every time her mother or one of her younger sisters spoke. She had relaxed and joked with Lydia about her risky card moves, to which Lydia merely laughed and told her it was part of her secret to winning.

All-in-all, the evening passed quickly and ended positively for everyone. The carriage was called for and good byes exchanged. As the gentlemen walked out of the house, it started to rain. For that reason, Jane and Elizabeth, who had walked out with them, had to hurry back in without a private farewell.

CHAPTER EIGHT

For the next two days, it rained continually. The weather kept the residents of Longbourn indoors and their neighbours away. By the second afternoon, Lydia and Kitty were at each other over minor things, such as who owned a certain length of pink ribbon or whose turn it was to page through the latest fashion publication that had arrived the day before by post.

Mrs. Bennet began to worry that the weather might even prevent them from attending the Netherfield Ball. Her husband teased her, asking if she had a premonition of a catastrophic flood. Elizabeth watched her mother as she complained of vexation and her nerves before retiring to her room.

Elizabeth and Jane worked steadily on their embroidery while Mary practiced on the pianoforte as Mr. Collins sat next to her turning the pages. Lizzy felt sorry for Jane, whose own fiancé could not be by her side because of the weather. She also could not help but feel a bit envious of her two sisters' having obviously found men who cared about them.

Sighing, she put down her handiwork. Elizabeth's spirit sank further under the weight of knowledge that she would, indeed, be the spinster aunt to her sisters' children. She had more than once joked with Jane about that possibility but had not actually been serious. However, there was now no chance for any other fate for her, and her heart and mind rebelled at the sentence to which her attacker had condemned her.

"I'm going to my room," Lizzy spoke softly to Jane. "I have a bit of a headache and shall lie down."

"Lizzy, do you require anything for your relief?" Jane's voice was heavy with concern.

"No, dearest, only a bit of rest and I shall be well again," Elizabeth reassured her.

Once inside her room, she threw herself on her bed and let herself weep. This time the grief seemed to reach deeper than anything she had felt before. At first, after the attack, the resulting deep-seated fear and physical pain had pulled at her, throwing her into nightmares. However, now that she understood the extent of her loss, anger and grief warred within her, and the result was a wrenching kind of agony from which she feared she would never fully recover. She knew no decent man would have her, and her father did not have enough money to bribe a greedy one into offering for her.

After several moments of weeping, Elizabeth dropped into a fitful slumber, but one, thankfully, without dreams. As she slept, Sarah came to look in on her, having been sent by Jane.

The young maid stood by Miss Elizabeth's bed. Her own heart clenched at the sight of the sleeping girl's swollen, red eyes. The poor miss had been crying again. Knowing this day to be the one during which her mistress should have begun her courses and thinking the weeping might have been the result, she quietly checked the small drawer where such supplies were kept. Nothing had been touched since Sarah had replenished them the month before.

Sarah bit her lip, trying to decide if she should send the glove to Mr. Darcy immediately or wait a few more days. Finally, she told herself it could wait until after the ball. Miss Elizabeth might just be late because of the recent trauma. If that were not the case and there was another reason, it would do no harm to let the family enjoy the festivities before they received the bad news. Besides, she thought that particular gentleman might have other ideas on how to help Miss Elizabeth. Having made the decision, Sarah laid a light quilt over Elizabeth and left the room.

Sarah truly wished that she could find a way for Miss Elizabeth to meet her aunt, for she had arrived and, with her, a surprise for the family. She brought her new husband, the valet of the lady's own husband. Her employer, Lady Ophelia Wilkins, had given her an extended time off from her work and the use of one of her carriages. It was one of the servant's carriages, but the loan gave them a lovely and less expensive trip from Town.

Sarah had told her aunt that she wanted to introduce her to Miss Elizabeth without giving her a reason other than that her young mistress was a very kind and generous person who had expressed a wish to meet the maid's family. The concept of a gentleman's daughter entertaining a servant was unheard of, so Sarah fretted that it would never happen, even if Miss Elizabeth consented. Sighing, the young maid left the room.

Elizabeth awoke to bright sunlight filtering through her curtains. The rain had stopped. Pushing herself up from her bed, she moaned from the stiffness caused by her awkward sleeping position. Her eyes felt scratchy and puffy, and she was quite thirsty. Moving to the table where the water-filled ewer stood, she poured a glass and drank it down quickly. After her drink, she pressed a wet cloth to her eyes, hoping to relieve the puffiness.

Somehow, the nap and the sunshine had tempered some of the grief. Elizabeth did not feel the despair so fully as before, though it still weighed on her heart. Shaking her head, she scolded herself out loud, "If I am to keep this secret, I must not give my family cause to wonder why I am so depressed, especially with the delightful prospect of attending a ball within days. I shall be cheerful. No one must suspect." With that self-admonition, she returned downstairs to join her family.

~*~

The next morning, as early as propriety allowed, Mr. Darcy and Mr. Bingley visited the Bennets and invited the Misses Bennet to walk out with them. Mary declined so as to stay with her fiancé who was working on his sermon. Kitty and Lydia agreed to walk as far as Lucas Lodge for they wanted to show Maria their favourite gowns from the newest periodical they had spent so much time perusing during the recent rainy weather. Both gentlemen were satisfied that the two eldest Bennet sisters would accompany them all the way to the village.

Before they left Netherfield that morning, Darcy suggested to Bingley that they invite the young ladies to have tea with them in Meryton. They had been fully prepared to treat the five sisters, but neither was upset that they would have the pleasure of Jane's and Elizabeth's sole company.

As the four walked down the lane toward the village, Charles and Jane again moved ahead so that they could have some private moments of conversation, which was entirely agreeable to Darcy as he wanted to talk with Elizabeth alone. He was concerned at her pale countenance, but what worried him most was the dull, lifeless look in her usually sparkling eyes.

"Please tell me why you are so sad today, Miss Elizabeth," Darcy asked gently after assuring himself that the other couple had gone far enough ahead for the conversation to be private.

Elizabeth sighed but did not answer. How she wanted to talk to someone about her feelings! But how could she tell Mr. Darcy what troubled her so? On the other hand, telling him that she was not sad would be a lie and an insult to the man who had been so kind to her.

Shaking her head, she simply said, "I cannot tell you."

"Are you ill? Do your injuries still cause you pain?" His tone became almost desperate. "You are so pale. I am worried," he finally confessed.

Elizabeth stopped in the middle of the road and turned away from him. "I am not ill or in physical pain." Her voice took on a choked quality. "It seems that daily

I more fully understand my predicament in life. It is difficult to accept, but I am certain that I will manage eventually." With the last statement she knew that she came perilously close to lying since she felt no such conviction.

Moving so that he was in front of her once more, Darcy lifted her chin so that he could look into her eyes. Once again, he could see the flatness of her gaze. She did not even fight him, but merely acceded to his examination without comment. Compassion and something deeper filled his heart, as he did the only thing he could think of to do. He pulled her into his arms and simply held her.

At first, Elizabeth stiffened in his embrace, thinking about the inappropriateness of his actions. They were standing in the middle of a public road where they could be noticed at any time. Soon, however, the compassion she had seen in his eyes and the warmth of his arms around her swept away her misgivings, and she relaxed against him. Tears pricked her eyes, but they did not fall. The gratitude she felt toward him welled up in her and soothed away much of the anguish she had been feeling. Here was a man she could trust and would never have to fear. It was as if she had spoken all of her concerns, and he had answered and properly dealt with them all.

Elizabeth savoured the feeling of well-being for several moments before she came back to her surroundings. She pulled away slowly since she did not want Mr. Darcy to think she was upset at his actions. Once his arms had dropped to his sides again, she caught his gaze and gave him a small smile. "Thank you, Mr. Darcy."

He searched her face before he spoke. "You are most welcome, and I am grateful you did not think me bold and improper."

"I would never believe that about you, sir," Elizabeth gave a faint smile and took his arm before he had time to offer it. "But I think we should make haste to catch up with Jane and Mr. Bingley."

As they quickened their pace, Darcy could not help but wonder if he should have suggested that Elizabeth speak with her maid's aunt. He was glad that his embrace had not upset her but felt at a loss when it came to helping her work through her grief. He prayed that he could find an appropriate time to recommend she share her ordeal with a person who, having gone through a similar experience, might be able to help her cope.

The small Meryton tea room could accommodate fewer than twenty patrons at one time, but the gentlemen had no trouble arranging for a table. The proprietor, happy to have such fine customers, seated them close to the tiny fireplace and quickly took their order.

Darcy was pleasantly surprised to find the place was clean and well maintained. The few other customers chatted quietly over steaming cups of tea. Per his instructions, the serving girl brought a tray of cakes and tarts so that they could make their choice. He was so pleased by the delicious array of baked goods that he asked the girl to leave two of each.

Both Jane and Elizabeth protested that it was too much, but the gentlemen insisted that their appetites were up to the challenge even if the ladies' were not.

For the next half hour, the four talked amiably. They shared bits of their childhood memories. Jane surprised her sister by relating several incidences where Elizabeth got the two in trouble. One that brought bright colour to her cheeks involved a frog and her mother's favourite hat.

"But I was certain Mama had taken the frog's lily pad to use on her hat," Elizabeth protested while trying to suppress her laughter.

"Poor Mama," Jane sighed with a teasing smile. "She was greatly upset to find the frog nestled in her favourite hat."

With a chuckle, Darcy said, "My own mother was the one who showed me how to catch frogs. She and I spent many a happy time hunting for tadpoles as well. We watched them grow. Every spring until she became too ill to do so, we were off to the pond." At this last statement, he sighed involuntarily.

Shaking himself from his melancholy, he asked, "Have you ladies had enough tea?" At their affirmation that they indeed had more than enough, he suggested that they return to Longbourn.

As they left the shop and the village, the group was the object of much observation that went unnoticed by all of the members of the small party, including the usually alert Mr. Darcy. However, his particular walking companion so held his attention that he did not perceive the interest of the hamlet's citizenry.

Again, Jane and Bingley outpaced Elizabeth and Darcy with no complaint on the second couple's part. Lizzy was comfortable enough with the propriety of the situation since she could see her sister and her fiancé up ahead while Darcy was glad of the opportunity to speak in private.

"Miss Elizabeth, I have something I would like to suggest to you," he began hesitantly, without looking at her. "Your maid, Sarah told me about her aunt and that she is currently in the neighbourhood, visiting Sarah's mother. I wonder if you might benefit by talking to her."

Stopping abruptly, Elizabeth stared at him in disbelief. "You think I should talk to a stranger about what happened to me? I am reluctant to speak of it to my closest sister. What makes you think I would feel free to do so with someone I do not already know and trust?"

Darcy retraced the few steps he had managed to take before he had realized she was no longer walking by his side. He ran a hand through his hair and sighed. "I do not know what will help. My only thoughts were that you might feel more at ease speaking to someone who has gone through a similar experience, someone who, according to your maid, has healed remarkably well, both physically and emotionally, from the attack upon her person."

He hung his head and said quietly, "I did not mean to discount you or your feelings in the matter. Please pardon my interference. I will not speak of it again." He straightened his shoulders and turned to go. "Let us walk on, shall we?" His heart was heavy with the burden of wanting to help but being unable to find a way to do so.

"Wait, Mr. Darcy," Elizabeth said after a moment. "I am so sorry. I know that you only want to help. I am afraid to speak of it. What if I lose control and weep in front of Sarah's aunt? What would she think of me?"

"Do you not think that she would understand completely what you are going through? It is very likely that she wept as well." By this time, Darcy had taken her hand and spoke in low earnest tones. "You trust Sarah with your secret. I expect that she would not have suggested anyone who might betray you."

Staring down at their joined, gloved hands, Elizabeth thought about what he had said. Finally, she looked up at him and asked, "How would one arrange such a meeting? It is not proper for a maid's relative to visit one of her employer's family members without at least a prior introduction."

"I believe I have the perfect solution. You and I shall go for a ride in my carriage. Of course, we will need a chaperone. You should suggest Sarah. We will then visit her mother's home. I am certain that there will be a private place for you to talk."

"I am grateful that you would think of this and volunteer to bring it about." She could not hold back the warm feeling of gratitude and squeezed his hand. "Thank you, Mr. Darcy, thank you."

"You are most welcome," he replied as he returned the gesture before he tucked her hand into the crook of his arm and started walking again toward Longbourn.

When they finally arrived, the gentlemen declined an invitation to dinner. Mr. Bingley was needed at Netherfield because he had been informed by Mrs. Hurst that many last minute details were in need of his approval. Mr. Darcy was loath to turn down the request, but he understood that his friend would need his company since Bingley hated this part of hosting a ball. Darcy knew that in this one point Caroline Bingley would have been the better choice for a hostess. She did possess a confidence in her abilities that her older sister did not.

As they took their leave, Mr. Darcy was able to have a few parting words with Elizabeth in the hallway.

"I will come tomorrow around ten. Would you please arrange with Sarah for us to visit, or do you think I should speak to your father about the carriage ride?" he asked softly.

"Yes, I think it would be wise for you to do so, and I believe that Papa is in his library." Elizabeth nodded toward the door. "I will go with you and explain that Sarah will be the chaperone."

It did not take long for Mr. Bennet to agree with the plan. In fact, he had begun to wonder when the young man was going to take an opportunity to court Lizzy without his friend Bingley and Jane present.

Darcy thanked Mr. Bennet, and both he and Elizabeth left the room.

"Bingley is probably wondering what is taking me so long," Darcy teased as they made it to the door.

"I doubt that he will even notice," she answered back in the same easy tone. She wondered at the fact that she could still joke with her emotions so unsettled, but she was happy for even a short moment of fun.

They found Bingley and Jane standing just outside the door doing what could only be called "billing and cooing." A footman, a grin on his face, stood in the lane holding the reins to their horses.

When Darcy asked if Bingley was ready to depart, Charles seemed surprised to see him. Elizabeth caught Darcy's eye and smiled knowingly.

Each gentleman bowed over his lady's hand, and Darcy added a quick. "I will see you at ten."

~*~

Elizabeth did not have a good night. Dreams of terror plagued her, so that when Sarah came to help her dress, she could barely manage to get up. It was only the knowledge that Mr. Darcy would be coming for her that motivated her to climb out of bed and allow Sarah to help her with the preparations.

"I am happy that I will be able to introduce you to my aunt. It is an honour for my family that you and Mr. Darcy would visit."

Once Elizabeth was dressed, Sarah bustled around the bedroom, tidying the place as Elizabeth sat unseeing, staring out of the window. All of the signs pointed to her young mistress having had nightmares again. The maid had hoped that she would be rid of them but supposed that it was too much to ask at this time.

"Would you like me to bring you a tray?" Sarah asked timidly, as Elizabeth did not move from her chair.

"What?" Elizabeth snapped back from her reverie. She shook her head to clear it. "No, I will go downstairs. I was just thinking about what I will say to your aunt. What happened to me is so shameful that I am afraid I shall not be able to speak of it."

"Miss Elizabeth, remember that she has also gone through something similar."

Elizabeth only sighed before getting to her feet. "Be ready to leave before ten. I do not want to keep Mr. Darcy waiting."

"Of course, miss," Sarah said as she curtseyed.

After managing to eat only a muffin and drink a cup of tea, Elizabeth went to the parlour to await Darcy's arrival. She could not settle upon an activity, so she finally merely sat with an open book in her hands. She barely noticed when her sisters and mother came into the room.

"I am so happy that the weather has turned out so fine and hope it will last through tomorrow evening," Mrs. Bennet announced to the room at large without expecting an answer.

Mr. Collins had just entered the room as Mrs. Bennet spoke and he responded, "I believe that we will see decent weather tomorrow. Have we not been praying for it?" He smiled down at Mary before taking a seat next to her at the pianoforte.

A lively conversation started between the two youngest Bennet sisters and their mother about how many of the officers would be attending the ball. Lydia bragged that her dance card was nearly filled already by the officers she knew. Kitty pouted at the announcement but soon remembered that she herself rarely sat out a dance at an assembly and was not likely to do so at the Netherfield ball.

Elizabeth hardly noticed Jane until her sister spoke quietly from the seat beside her. "Are you well, Lizzy?"

Sighing, Elizabeth answered, "I did not sleep well last night, but I am perfectly fine, if a little nervous about the ride I am to take with Mr. Darcy."

"Oh, Lizzy, you are not concerned about his behaviour, are you?"

"Oh, of course not," Elizabeth hastened to reply, smiling despite her anxiety. "I cannot say why I am nervous. I suppose that if I had slept better I would not be so nervous, but alas, I did not."

"Perhaps you should not go," Jane reasoned. "I am sure Mr. Darcy would understand."

"No, I shall go," Elizabeth almost wished that she could do as her sister suggested but she knew she needed to do this.

Sarah slipped into the room and curtseyed when she drew near to Elizabeth and Jane. "I will be in the entry. Mrs. Hill knows that I am going with you."

"Very good, Sarah," Elizabeth said softly.

Ten minutes later, Hill announced Mr. Darcy. After returning everyone's greetings, he turned to Elizabeth. "Are you ready, Miss Elizabeth?"

She nodded and took her leave of Jane and then moved to do the same from her mother.

"Oh, Lizzy, you will need a chaperone," her mother protested. "Take Jane with you."

"Mama, Papa arranged that Sarah would go as chaperone when he gave his permission for me to go for the drive," Elizabeth quickly explained before moving to the door where Darcy stood waiting.

"Well, I suppose it must be if your father has already arranged it," her mother conceded reluctantly.

However, after brief reflection, Mrs. Bennet realized that it seemed much more sophisticated and elegant that her daughter would go riding with a maid as a chaperone as those in the *ton* did. "Yes, yes, enjoy yourselves, and do not hurry your return. It is a fine day for a long drive," she happily urged them off with a wave of her hand.

The ride toward Meryton was quiet. Although Darcy tried to make conversation, Elizabeth answered in one or two words and was silent once more. Finally he decided that she must need the stillness and sat without speaking until they arrived at Sarah's parents' home.

The cottage was typical of Hertfordshire, small and squat, made of bits and chunks of flint and mortar, with a steeply pitched roof. The front garden would be lovely in the spring, Darcy thought as he surveyed the neat shrubs and bushes. A flat stone path led to the front door where Sarah's mother stood smiling in the doorway.

"Miss Elizabeth, I did not expect you," the woman moved quickly to her and curtseyed to both of them. "But you are most welcome."

"Mr. Darcy, this is Mrs. Brown," she began the introduction, "Mrs. Brown, this is Mr. Fitzwilliam Darcy of Pemberley in Derbyshire."

"It is an honour to meet you, sir," Mrs. Brown curtseyed again. "Please do come in."

They followed Mrs. Brown into the cottage. Inside, they found it small but very tidy. Another woman, younger than Mrs. Brown, curtseyed to them. She was introduced as Mrs. Henry Parker. They were told she and her husband were visiting with their employer's blessing after their recent marriage.

"It is such a pleasure to finally meet you, Miss Bennet." Her voice was cultured with none of the usual accent of those in service. "My niece has told me so much about you and your family. She is fortunate to work for your family."

Darcy felt Elizabeth stiffen beside him. He correctly surmised that she thought that Sarah had revealed what had happened to her and was upset.

"Is your husband away, Mrs. Parker?" Darcy entered the conversation.

"Mr. Parker went with my husband to his shop," Mrs. Brown answered for her sister.

After a short discussion about Mr. Brown's business, Sarah quietly asked her mother if she could speak to her privately in the kitchen.

"Of course, my dear, I was just going to suggest that we serve some of the shortbread I baked for the occasion of your aunt's visit. I am sure my sister will not mind sharing."

Mr. Darcy, who stood when the two left the room, indicated that he needed to see to something in the carriage and walked outside.

Mrs. Parker smiled as she watched the gentleman leave. "I believe your Mr. Darcy is not comfortable with strangers."

"He is indeed shy, but he is not my Mr. Darcy," Elizabeth said quickly.

Nodding knowingly, Mrs. Parker said, "I believe that our friends have left us alone for a reason, Miss Bennet."

Elizabeth was thankful that Mrs. Parker broached the subject. "Yes, Sarah told me that you might be able to help me."

Mrs. Parker only lifted a brow and waited for Elizabeth to go on.

After a long silence in which Elizabeth tried to think of a tactful way to start, she blurted out, "I was attacked."

"Do you want to speak of it?"

"No! Yes, I do not know," Elizabeth sighed as her eyes filled with tears. "I do not want to think about what he did to me. It was horrible and shameful, and now I am ruined."

Mrs. Parker moved to the chair closest to Elizabeth and patted her arm. "I felt that way after it happened to me. I suppose you already know that I was raped."

When she saw Elizabeth blush, she continued, "Sarah has my permission to speak of it if she feels it will help another. She is a very kind-hearted girl."

"I am glad that you are not upset that Sarah told me." Elizabeth reached into her reticule for a handkerchief and wiped her eyes. "She said that you found someone to help you and that you want to do the same for others."

"I only wish to give back some of the comfort I received." Mrs. Parker sat back in her chair and studied the younger woman before her.

"I do not wish to talk about or even remember what happened. I am afraid I will lose control of my emotions." Elizabeth swiped at her eyes once more.

"If you do not wish to tell me about the attack, I will not pressure you. Perhaps you can tell me how it has affected you. Are you having nightmares?"

"Yes, I do, and the ones last night were some of the worst." Elizabeth refused to remember the terror that plagued her the evening before. "But the worst is the fear during the day. I cannot leave the house without anxiety unless my sister Jane or Mr. Darcy is with me. And it is only with Mr. Darcy that I can go far from the sight of my home."

"Mr. Darcy knows what happened to you," Mrs. Parker stated.

"He found me just after the attack and helped me home. Mr. Darcy summoned Sarah, and since I would not allow them to speak of what happened, they came up with a tale that kept the attack secret from my family so that I could see a doctor. Mr. Darcy has been so kind and helpful to me." Elizabeth did not realize that she smiled as she spoke of Mr. Darcy.

"It is good that you have them both to help you."

"I do not know what would have happened to me without their help. I suffered a head injury as well during the attack." Elizabeth twisted the damp handkerchief in her hands.

"Are you well now?" Mrs. Parker asked.

"The doctor says that the head injury is healed, and I no longer have headaches."

"That is good," the older woman said. "I do wish that we had more time to talk about this. Since there is not much time, I will tell you something that helped me, besides talking through what happened to me did. You might write down your thoughts and memories of the attack, even the fears and the terror you felt."

"Oh, I could not do that!" Elizabeth interrupted. "What if someone found them?"

"I was going to suggest that as you write them, you visualize taking them out of your mind, and then once they are on paper, you crumple the paper and throw it into the fire as you again envision the power they had over you going up in smoke. Remember the act of destroying them each time the thoughts come back to haunt you, and mentally watch the paper burn. You may have to do this several times as more comes to your mind, or you need reminding."

Elizabeth was uncertain that it would work, but she said that she would think about it.

Mrs. Parker paused for a moment before she asked, "What has happened to the man who did this to you?"

"He has been taken away on other charges."

"So you do not have to worry about seeing him again?"

"Unless he escapes," Elizabeth whispered.

"The person who hurt me was never punished for it and is still in society," Mrs. Parker sighed. "There was little I could do to expose him considering our relative positions in society, so I do understand your fear of seeing your attacker again. Even though I was removed from the household, I feared I might see him in the future."

"How did you overcome your fears?"

"My friend, Mrs. Ellis who listened to me often as I shared with her, reminded me of what the Bible says about fear, 'Perfect love casts out all fear.' I pray daily that God's love will guide me from fear and fill me with His peace. More and more I am able to refuse the fear. It is not unlike an unwanted caller. I ask God to refuse its entry. I do not always succeed, but I am able to live my life as normally as possible."

Mrs. Parker paused a moment, wondering how to best say what she knew she must. "I must tell you that healing takes time, just as the injury to your head took time to heal. I imagine that you will still, on occasion, have headaches because of it. In like manner, you will need time and as the healing progresses, you will likely have recurrences of pain, fear, and the nightmares. Try not to be discouraged by that. It shall get better with prayer and continued effort on your part. Ideally, you would do well to speak to a close friend or relative about what happened. They will be close by so that they could help shield you when Mr. Darcy is not around."

Elizabeth hung her head because part of her had hoped that the woman might have an answer that would make everything better immediately. How could she talk to anyone else about the awful act against her person? She did not believe that she could be so strong or resilient as the woman before her. She had even gotten married, which Elizabeth was certain would never happen to her.

"May I ask you a rather personal question, Mrs. Parker?"

"I have nothing to hide, Miss Bennet," she smiled slightly, since she was certain what the young woman wanted to know.

"Does your husband know?"

"Yes, he does. I told him when he asked to court me." Her face glowed at the memory. "Henry did not reject me. I will never forget the compassionate tears in his eyes as I spoke of the attack. We were wed six months later.

"He is the valet to our master, Sir Harold Wilkins. Although it is not usual for such a valet and an abigail to marry, we obtained our employers' permission. Lord and Lady Wilkins also allowed us this extended holiday to visit our family since none of them were able to be at the wedding, and what with all of the Christmas entertaining they do, they will require our services for most of the month of December." Mrs. Parker sighed with obvious pleasure.

"You are most fortunate in your employers and your husband," Elizabeth said wistfully.

"I am, indeed, and I feel strongly that you will find someone who will wish to marry you despite what has befallen you."

Tears of deep longing welled up in Elizabeth's eyes, and she dashed them away quickly with her handkerchief. The idea of falling in love with a man who would overlook what had happened to her was very appealing.

Mrs. Parker seemed about to speak again when her sister and niece re-entered the room carrying a tray of biscuits, small mugs, and a pitcher of ale.

"I am afraid that we have used all the tea we had during our celebration of Sarah and Henry's marriage, but I can offer you some fairly good ale." Mrs. Brown poured ale into the mugs before realizing that Mr. Darcy was not in the room. "Little Sarah, please see if Mr. Darcy would like to come back."

The maid moved quickly out the door and found Mr. Darcy talking to his driver. She curtseyed and said, "Mr. Darcy, sir, my mother has refreshments ready in the parlour, if you will follow me."

Darcy nodded and walked after the girl into the house. There he found Mrs. Parker and Elizabeth sitting close to each other, nibbling on shortbread biscuits, and sipping from a mug.

Mrs. Brown stood and brought him a plate and a mug. Thanking her, Darcy sat and ate the food in silence. He was uncomfortable being the only man in the midst of four women, and two of them complete strangers, but he knew that Elizabeth needed him to exert himself to be civil.

"These are exceptionally good biscuits, Mrs. Brown." He took a swallow of the ale. It was decent quality and very likely the best they could afford. "Shortbread has been one of my favourite treats since childhood."

Darcy and Elizabeth took their leave soon after they finished the refreshments.

Mrs. Brown was delighted by the pair's visit and would have liked to share her pleasure with her friends, but her daughter had explained that they would not like being gossiped about, even in a positive light. She knew that her daughter was correct, so she would have to be content with telling her husband and new brother about the visit.

Once back in the carriage, Darcy asked, "Miss Elizabeth, would you like to drive farther into the countryside, or would you rather go back to Longbourn?"

"Oh, please, sir, if you don't mind, I would rather drive on for a while." If she could have, she would have gone for a long walk to ponder what had transpired with Mrs. Parker. She was happy with the knowledge that Mr. Darcy would allow her time to process her conversation with Sarah's aunt.

"As you wish," he said and leaned out the window to tell the driver what direction in which to go, and they travelled for quite some time in silence.

Elizabeth, being particularly grateful that Mr. Darcy did not try to make small talk or to question her about her talk with Mrs. Parker, reflected upon the peaceful countenance of the abigail. It was beyond her own imagination to think that she could obtain that kind of peace after what had happened to her, but on the other hand, she did feel more hope than she had expected to feel.

Being careful not to stare, Darcy glanced often in Elizabeth's direction, wanting to inquire about her conversation with Mrs. Parker, but knowing the timing was not right nor was it quite appropriate for him to do so. As had become his habit, he lifted a prayer for her as he gazed out the window without actually seeing what passed by.

After nearly a half hour, Elizabeth spoke softly, "Mr. Darcy, I believe I am ready to return to Longbourn."

"Of course," Darcy replied quickly and proceeded to relay his orders to the driver.

"I hope the drive has not fatigued you, Miss Elizabeth," he said when he noted the slump of her shoulders.

"No, sir, I have enjoyed the ride," she said and decided to explain her weariness. "I did not sleep well last night. I experienced several nightmares."

"I am very sorry to hear it. I hope that you will have better rest tonight."

"As do I, Mr. Darcy, as do I."

~*~

Once they arrived at Longbourn, they found that Bingley had found a bit of time to visit the Bennets after all, and Darcy was invited to join them. As he did not yet want to part from Elizabeth, he accepted and sat next to her on the settee.

Mrs. Bennet, being so pleased that these two eligible men were again in her home, allowed the young people to speak to each other without her usual verbose involvement. To her, it seemed that she did not need to give any encouragement at the moment. She would have her time to give her daughters more advice on how to promote themselves once the gentlemen departed.

After a quarter hour of conversation, Darcy and Bingley stood to leave. With little subtlety, Mrs. Bennet insisted that her two eldest daughters accompany the two gentlemen to see them out.

As they moved to the door, Darcy held back to have a final word with Elizabeth. "I will not see you again until the ball. This morning, I received a packet from my steward at Pemberley. I must read through the information, and from what the cover letter advised me, I will need more than this afternoon to sort through it and write my instructions in response."

With some of her former teasing manner, she replied, "I understand that estate matters can be time consuming. However, I hope that you will not be so taxed by the work as to prevent your fulfilling your commitment to dance with me."

"My tasks will be made lighter by the knowledge that I will have the pleasure of dancing with you, Miss Elizabeth," he answered so softly that only she could hear. He bowed over her hand and squeezed it gently before he left to enter his carriage.

Once the gentlemen went down the drive, Mrs. Bennet hurriedly ushered her two older girls back into the house like a hen with her chicks. Back inside, she insisted that Elizabeth tell her what had taken so long. Not being concerned about any impropriety happening during the lengthy drive, Mrs. Bennet merely wanted to hear about the excursion from her daughter, so that she would be able to give the best account to her neighbours. She rejoiced in the knowledge that the day before her own girls had been chosen for the honour of taking tea in the village's best tea room with the two most eligible gentlemen in the county. To top it off, today Elizabeth had been taken for a long carriage ride with Mr. Darcy. Caring little that her second daughter gave her few details other than that the drive was lovely, the matron knew that she had plenty to tell her friends, even if she had to make up the details for herself.

Her opinion of Mr. Darcy had begun an alteration within the last month. He no longer seemed so disagreeable nor so proud. It was almost inconceivable that he was interested in her least favourite daughter. However, she had seen with her own eyes that he singled her out for his attention. For a woman who was not known for her intellect, Mrs. Bennet was smart enough to understand what a fine match they would make. With that information in mind, she decided to assist her daughter in whatever way she could. She would make certain that Lizzy would look as well as possible for the ball.

Once more, Mrs. Bennet flew into raptures over the ball and bemoaned again the fact that the girls did not have new gowns. Then with a smug smile on her face, Fanny Bennet ordered Jane and Elizabeth to accompany her above stairs. Thus began a long day of looking through their gowns, discussing the additions or subtractions of ribbons or lace, and various alterations that could be made with the materials at hand. By the time of the ball, both girls were attired in gowns that could be mistaken for new and were quite flattering to both.

Typically, Elizabeth would have objected to such overzealous attention to herself and her wardrobe, but at this point in her life, the exuberance of her mother's focused interest helped to keep Lizzy's mind occupied during the day and exhausted her body sufficiently to keep the nightmares at bay at night.

CHAPTER NINE

The day of the ball found Mrs. Bennet in high spirits, especially since the usually fine, late autumn weather still held. The house fairly hummed with activity as the mistress ordered baths, naps, and extra fittings.

The niggling bite of fear Elizabeth felt as Sarah put the final touches on her toilette made her palms damp. Elizabeth worried about going into such a large company. The fact she would be with her family or Mr. Darcy for most of the evening kept the anxiety from becoming overwhelming. At first, she thought that she might ask Mr. Darcy's help in managing her trepidation. Her pride and her former self-reliance rebelled against the idea. Surely she could endure the ball without obliging herself to the man even more. Sighing, she faced the mirror again as prompted by her maid.

"I have just a few more pearls to place. You are a vision, Miss Elizabeth," Sarah said with awe in her voice. "I am sure there will be none prettier at the ball."

"You must not have seen Jane yet if you say so. We all know she is far more beautiful," Elizabeth disagreed amiably.

"Aye, Miss Jane is lovely," Sarah agreed. "But there are those who prefer the beauty of dark eyes and rich brown curls to the classic British, fair hair and blue eyes."

"Do not be silly, Sarah," she interrupted with impatience. "Even if I look well tonight, there is no reason for me to be so. I have no hope of a good match now. You know that is so." Despite the good fortune of Sarah's aunt, she was certain that the same was never to be hers.

Sarah said no more as she left to help the younger girls get ready, understanding that her young mistress knew not how Mr. Darcy watched her. It seemed that he was the perfect match for her favourite Bennet daughter. She had to be content to let things happen as they would.

~*~

The Bennet carriage took its place in the queue on the torch-lit Netherfield drive. The house glowed from the light of hundreds of candles. The staff of footmen was dressed in livery, more elegant than those typically seen in Hertfordshire.

Once the carriage door opened and the Bennets were assisted to the ground, they joined the many other guests who milled inside the entry, waiting to be announced.

Elizabeth held tightly to Jane's arm as the crowd seemed to press on every side. How could she be so fearful when nearly everyone attending was known to her? Even with this internal admonition, she did not release her grip on her sister. Slowly, the push of people moved on, and they were received by the hosts.

A glimpse of Mr. Darcy standing near Mr. Bingley soothed away much of her anxiety, and when he caught her eye, he smiled before making his way toward her.

"Miss Bennet, Miss Elizabeth," Darcy greeted them warmly. "If I may say so, you both look stunning."

After the two sisters curtseyed, Jane answered for them both, "Thank you, Mr. Darcy. It is kind of you to say so."

"It is no more than the truth," Bingley said as he joined the group. "You are very welcome, ladies." He also bowed, but his eyes were only for Jane as he quickly kissed her hand before releasing it. Mrs. Hurst caught his attention with a cough and a frown aimed in his direction. He nodded and said, "I would greatly like to stay with you ladies, but I fear I must perform my duties as host before I can have that pleasure. If you will excuse me until later?"

Mr. Darcy offered each sister an arm and escorted them into a less crowded section of the ballroom. "If the attendance so far is any indication, Bingley's ball will be a great success," he remarked as they observed the rapidly filling space.

"I believe you are correct, Mr. Darcy," Elizabeth began innocently, but added with a bit of her former liveliness, "It is likely that only grave illness or death would have kept Netherfield's four and twenty families from attending."

Darcy raised an eyebrow while a dimple played on his right cheek. "Indeed. A crush of people is always a good sign of a ball's triumph."

Charlotte Lucas soon joined them, greeting Mr. Darcy with a curtsey and Jane and Elizabeth with a kiss on the cheek. "Jane and Lizzy, you look lovely tonight, not that I am surprised," Charlotte exclaimed.

"As do you, Charlotte," Elizabeth said. "That is such a becoming shade of pink. I do not recall seeing the fabric in the mercantile in Meryton."

"Oh, Lizzy, you know my mother's habit," she said, her cheeks flaming. "Nothing would do but that she would send to London for material she spotted while she visited Town earlier this year."

Elizabeth felt rather than saw Mr. Darcy's withdrawal from such feminine topics of conversation. "Sir, do forgive us for digressing into subjects not interesting to a gentleman's mind."

"On the contrary, I am by no means offended since I have the honour of being in the company of three of the loveliest and well-dressed ladies at the ball."

"Such flattery, Mr. Darcy," Elizabeth protested, though she was pleased with his statement. "You have not seen all of the ladies who are attending."

"It is unnecessary that I do so in order to know the truth of the matter."

Any argument Elizabeth could have made was curtailed by the arrival of Mr. Bingley. "The dancing will commence shortly. I hope you ladies have come prepared to dance."

All three answered in the affirmative before Bingley turned to Jane. "Miss Bennet, would you give me the pleasure of your company while I make certain the orchestra is ready?" He offered his arm, which she accepted.

As the couple moved into the assembled crowd, Elizabeth was once again struck by the obvious affection displayed on Bingley's and Jane's faces. A pang of envy lanced through her, but she pushed the feeling away.

"Oh dear," Charlotte said suddenly. "I see that Maria is signalling me. Pardon me, but I must see what she is about."

Charlotte's going left an awkward silence in her wake. Since Mr. Darcy did not seem to have anything to say, Elizabeth said the first thing that came to mind, "Mr. Darcy, were you able to complete the pressing business of which you spoke to your satisfaction?"

"Yes, thank you for asking," he replied with a nod. "I was able to finish with enough time for a nap this afternoon."

"A nap?" She fought the urge to laugh at the image of Mr. Darcy needing an afternoon nap.

"Did not you and your sister rest this afternoon?" Darcy countered.

"Indeed, our mother insisted upon it."

"I wonder that you seem astounded that I should do so as well."

She coloured at what seemed to be a reproof. "I meant no offense. You do not seem the type to need extra rest."

A kind smile warmed his expression. "I know you did not. Pardon me if my manner of speaking suggested it. I am unused to the late hours required by such events as this. Because I usually rise early, I find that I must take the opportunity to rest, or I might fall asleep in the middle of a dance."

Elizabeth's trill of laughter pleased Darcy immensely. He had heard it far too little of late. The desire to find ways to give her cause for mirth grew in his breast. "Miss Elizabeth, I believe that the two gentlemen approaching us have in mind to ask you to dance. I hope you have entered my name on your card."

Looking up, Elizabeth noted Samuel Lucas and Frederick Long making their way toward her. "Do not worry, Mr. Darcy, I did not forget." She lifted the small card that was attached to her wrist by a ribbon. "Your name is ascribed in the proper places."

"I am glad to hear it."

Lucas and Long did indeed ask for a dance and were not surprised to find the first and the supper sets were spoken for. They asked and gained a place on her card.

Being in Mr. Darcy's company, Elizabeth was not experiencing the apprehension she had earlier anticipated. She was relieved and thought perhaps she would be able to enjoy the festivities without fear.

When the music began, Darcy took Elizabeth's hand to lead her to the dance floor. The light touch of her gloved hand sent a pleasurable tremor up his arm. He forced his mind to dwell upon the dance and not to ponder how delightful it would be to hold her hand ungloved.

For the next few minutes, they moved through the dance without speaking. Elizabeth was astonished at his graceful execution of the intricate steps and was silently thrilled to be his partner of choice. On Darcy's part, he only wanted to savour the pleasure of finally being able to watch her twirl, skip, and spin to the exceptional music.

Darcy finally realized that neither of them had spoken. "Miss Bennet, I believe we should have some conversation."

"Very well, Mr. Darcy," Elizabeth replied as she passed him in the dance. "Of what shall we speak?"

"I believe that I will cede the choice of subjects to you."

"I am not certain that is wise," she said as they separated to swing around the couple opposite them.

Once they were together again, Darcy said, smiling, "I thought that I was being polite."

"Indeed, you were, sir." Her eyes sparkled in the way that had caught his attention that first night in the assembly. "But you might find the topic I choose not to your liking."

"If it is one in which you are interested, I am sure that I shall enjoy it," he countered.

"Well said, sir, well said," she laughed lightly as they met again to move down the dance together. "I choose books."

"Books?" he queried. "That is a huge subject with many avenues to explore."

"I shall narrow it down," she tossed over her shoulder as they parted once more.

Darcy smiled, his heart light as he watched Elizabeth sashay around another dancer. He did so as well in his turn before rejoining her.

"How will you narrow it down, madam?" he teased.

"I will ask your favourite author."

The dance parted them once more.

Darcy was at a loss. He loved books but he could not say which one was his favourite. Once she laid her hand in his once more, he confessed, "I truly cannot say that I have a particular favourite. I enjoy Shakespeare but I dare say there are few who do not."

The final notes and steps of the dance prevented Elizabeth from replying. The dancers all clapped, after which Darcy offered his arm. They had travelled only a short distance before Samuel Lucas met them and began to talk about the weather and other polite subjects. He was obviously waiting until the next set began.

Darcy stepped back and observed the interchange between Elizabeth and her long-time friend. He learned that Lucas had recently graduated from university and returned home only two weeks previously. Guessing that Sir William's heir could not be more than three and twenty, Darcy wondered if he had come home looking for a wife. He ground his teeth against the surge of jealousy that gripped him, but upon further observation, he understood that Elizabeth was not returning the young man's interest. She was polite but with only that surface manner one uses with casual acquaintances and was slipping slowly away from Lucas. Chiding himself for his jealous mind, Darcy moved to stand beside Elizabeth and joined the conversation.

As soon as the orchestra played the chords to announce the next set, Lucas offered his arm, and with what seemed to be reluctance, Elizabeth placed her hand lightly on it.

Out of pure instinct, Darcy followed them as closely as he could without calling attention to himself. He placed himself against a wall from where he proceeded to watch the dance commence. Elizabeth seemed to falter until she spied him. Their gazes locked for several seconds before she visibly relaxed.

Darcy wondered at this reaction. *It is as if she is afraid unless she knows I am within view.* A rush of purely masculine satisfaction filled him. He wanted to be the man to whom Elizabeth looked for protection and reassurance. Though he understood that she was uneasy, he could not comprehend why, when the one who hurt her was no longer a risk to her. Determining in his mind that he would try to find a way to talk to her about this fear, he settled in to enjoy the vision she made as she danced.

To Elizabeth, the set seemed to go on forever. She only half listened to her childhood friend as he chatted on about his time at university, the friends he had made, the courses he had studied. Elizabeth could manage to tolerate it only because she was able to periodically glance at Mr. Darcy. His presence was a draught of water soothing her mind of the intense fear.

A few times during the dance when she lost sight of Darcy, Elizabeth caught sight of a red uniformed militia officer moving up the dance or along the outskirts of the ballroom. Twice, she nearly tripped when that flash of crimson caused a minute flashback of the attack. Fortunately, she righted herself in time so as not to call attention to her missteps.

When the set was finally over, Elizabeth did not wait for Samuel to escort her from the floor. She moved swiftly to where Darcy stood. "Please, sir," she pleaded, "Would you take me to my sister Jane?"

"Of course, it would be a pleasure." Darcy looked up to see Lucas a few paces behind Elizabeth. He leaned his head closer to her. "Do you wish for Mr. Lucas to join us?"

"Please, no," she whispered without looking back. "I want to see Jane, but do not leave me."

"I am at your service, Miss Bennet." He took her hand and slipped it through his arm. "I believe Miss Bennet is talking to Bingley in that alcove over there."

Elizabeth was relieved to see her sister and to feel Darcy's strong arm as he guided them through the milling crowd. She avoided looking at the people as they walked so as not to see a red coat. She took a deep breath. How could she be so fearful when dancing with an old friend? No one would harm her here. She wondered if she were going mad.

"Elizabeth, are you well?" Jane asked once Darcy and Elizabeth reached them.

"Why would I not be, dearest?" Elizabeth answered with a question.

"I thought you might be getting tired. It was not so long ago that you were injured."

"Do not worry," Elizabeth sighed. "Though I admit to feeling a tad bit weary, I believe if I can sit for a time that I will be fine."

"Here are some chairs, Miss Elizabeth." Bingley gestured a few feet to their right. "Why do not you and Miss Bennet rest in them, and Darcy and I will fetch some punch."

"No, there is no need." Elizabeth's voice betrayed her panic. "Sitting will do me just fine."

Since she already asked him not to leave, Darcy waited until the two ladies made their way to the chairs before suggesting to Bingley that he fetch punch on his own. Charles agreed and hurried off.

As soon as Elizabeth sat down with Jane on the chair beside her and with Darcy standing next to her on her other side, she began to calm. However, she began to wish that she had not come to the ball. Knowing that she would have to dance with men other than Mr. Darcy caused a shudder to roll over her.

"Are you chilled, Miss Elizabeth?" Darcy leaned down to inquire.

"No, sir," she replied quickly. "I am quite comfortable."

Soon Bingley arrived with two cups of punch. Both Jane and Elizabeth thanked him and drank the refreshment with enjoyment. Once they finished, Charles asked, "Miss Bennet, would you like to take a turn about the room." As an after thought, he added, "Miss Elizabeth, Darcy, would you like to accompany us?"

"Thank you, Mr. Bingley," Elizabeth answered a trifle breathlessly, "but I would prefer to sit here and rest before the next set."

Once Bingley and Jane took their leave, Darcy sat down next to Elizabeth. "If I may be so bold," he hesitated until she nodded. "You seemed distressed during your dance with Mr. Lucas. Did he say something to offend you?"

Twisting her hands in her lap, she replied sheepishly, "No, he did not."

"Miss Elizabeth, will you not tell me what it is that has you so nervous?"

"I am embarrassed to say," Elizabeth muttered.

"There is no reason for you to be embarrassed with me." He touched her arm. "I hope that by now we are friends." At her nod, he continued, "Friends share burdens, do they not?"

"Very well," she sighed, "If I am not in my own room, my home, or with family or close friends, I am overtaken by a great fear. Although Mr. Lucas is a friend from childhood, I have not seen him in several years. He seems more of a stranger than a friend."

Elizabeth stared down at her hands. "And I had forgotten I would see militia officers at the ball. You must have noticed that I almost tripped several times while dancing. At those times, I spied a red coat. If you had not been close by during the dance, I do not know what I might have done. I wanted to flee, so panicked was I."

"Etiquette requires you to dance the next set with Mr. Long," he stated flatly, more to himself than to her.

"Indeed, it does," she lamented. "If it would not require my family leaving, I would ask to go home immediately."

Darcy looked across the room and witnessed Mrs. Bennet chatting animatedly with one of her cronies while gesturing in their direction. He also noticed Long making his way toward them. "I will stay close by, so that you are able to see me, or I could join the set. Will that help to give you relief?'

"You would do that for me?" She looked up at him with gratitude in her eyes.

"I am at your service, madam," Darcy bowed his head in acknowledgement. "I must find a partner so I can be close by."

"It appears that Charlotte means to join us as well," Elizabeth informed him. "I am sure that she will dance with you."

In a few moments, both Long and Charlotte arrived. Elizabeth and Darcy stood and greeted them.

"Miss Elizabeth, I believe our dance is to begin shortly." Long offered his arm.

Manoeuvring his body so he could delay Elizabeth's leaving with Long, but in a way that would look as if he merely wanted to be close enough to speak to Charlotte, Darcy said, "Miss Lucas, if you are not engaged for this dance, I would be honoured if you would join me in it."

Charlotte blushed with pleasure at the invitation. "I am not engaged, sir and I would be delighted."

Stepping back, Darcy allowed Elizabeth to take Long's arm before he offered his to Charlotte. They walked toward the dance floor together just as the call to dance was made. Darcy made sure that he and his partner lined up next to Miss Bennet and hers. He fought the urge to simply go through the motions all the while listening to what Long was saying. Knowing that it was unfair and rude if he did so, he applied himself to polite small talk with Miss Lucas.

For Elizabeth, this set was easier than the one before it. Mr. Darcy's presence helped immensely to keep the fear and panic at bay. Even a glimpse of an officer barely affected her. Just knowing she could see him anytime she wished soothed her agitated emotions. Happily, no one else had asked for a place on her card. She prayed that no one else would.

By the time the set finished, Elizabeth felt more at ease than she had been all evening. Even though Mr. Long insisted upon escorting her back to where her mother sat gossiping with her neighbours, she was not upset because providentially, one of the women her mother was speaking to was Lady Lucas. For that reason, Darcy and Charlotte followed close behind.

The time before the next set was spent talking with the older ladies. Elizabeth's mother was particularly enthusiastic about the ball. Inwardly, Mrs. Bennet exalted that Mr. Darcy seemed so attentive to her Lizzy. It amazed her that he could be attracted to her impertinent, second daughter, but she had enough wisdom to believe what her own eyes told her and to keep her peace about her own amazement for the time being.

Lady Lucas smiled in pleasure at the honour Mr. Darcy had paid Charlotte by dancing with her. That gentleman had not danced with anyone besides Elizabeth Bennet. She did not expect that it meant he was interested in her spinster daughter, but it certainly gave her something to boast about for the next several days at least.

A few moments later, Mr. Bingley and Jane joined the group. The older ladies excitedly complemented their host on his home, the fine furnishings and decorations, and talented musicians. He accepted their gushing praise with grace and good humour.

Excusing herself to go to the refreshing room, Elizabeth asked Jane to accompany her. She did not know if she would be able to find Mr. Darcy when she returned so she glanced at him, her eyes pleading for him to understand her need. The slight nod he gave her pleased her as she linked arms with her sister and moved out of the room.

On their way back into the ballroom, Elizabeth talked cheerfully with Jane. As they moved through the doorway and into the throng, she scanned the room for Mr. Darcy, but she did not see him. He must not have understood her plea. As she swept her gaze over the crowd once more, she saw an officer pushing his way through the throng toward her.

Elizabeth froze as the dark-haired soldier came closer. In her panic, she was certain that the man was Lt. Wickham. Her mouth went dry and her hands turned to ice. As she tried to take a step back, her way was blocked. A buzzing sounded in her ears and lights shone so bright she could hardly see.

CHAPTER TEN

Just as consciousness seemed ready to slip from her grasp, she heard Darcy whisper in her ear and felt his hand at her waist, "I am here, Miss Elizabeth. I am sorry to have taken so long."

From a distance, Darcy had witnessed Elizabeth's terror as the officer approached her. Anger at the people who had caused his delay raced through him. He abruptly excused himself and hurried to her. Certain that she had been about to faint, he had spoken and touched her, careful to keep his gesture from the view of those around them.

The soldier stopped before them, bowed and said, "Miss Bennet, Miss Elizabeth, Mr. Darcy, I hope you are well tonight."

Darcy felt her tremble and wanted to whisk her from the room. Instead he hastily searched his memory for the man's name and said, "Good evening, Captain Carter."

Throat tight and dry, Elizabeth could do nothing but nod in acknowledgement.

"Miss Elizabeth, I would like to engage you for a dance this evening if I am not too late." The officer smiled charmingly.

Elizabeth's pale face prompted Darcy to act on her behalf.

"You are too late, Carter." Darcy spoke without a smile. "Miss Bennet's card is filled."

Surprise filled the officer's face. "It is my loss, more's the pity. I am sure your many partners will enjoy themselves." Carter bowed and quickly left.

Jane watched the entire interaction, from the fright in Elizabeth's eyes to the intervention of Mr. Darcy on her behalf. She was uncertain as to why Lizzy would look so frightened of Captain Carter and what she should do about it. She decided that the ball was no place in which to question her sister, so the conversation would have to wait.

Mr. Darcy disrupted Jane's train of thought. "Miss Bennet, would you help me find a place out of the crowd where Miss Elizabeth can sit down? I believe the crush has become too much for her."

"I think that the dining parlour may be the best choice. There will be servants preparing for the meal, but not many of the guests."

"Excellent suggestion!" Darcy held out his arms to both the ladies, and they moved to the dining room as quickly as it was possible without commanding undue attention.

Once they arrived and he had assisted Elizabeth to a chair in a corner, Darcy asked a passing serving girl to fetch a glass of sherry for her.

"How are you feeling, Miss Elizabeth?" Darcy took her hands, which he could feel were cold even clad in gloves, and tried to warm them.

Trying to force words past her throat proved impossible until the maid came back with the sherry. Elizabeth sipped the liquid slowly, holding the glass with two unsteady hands.

Jane could hold back no longer. "What is the matter, Lizzy? Why did Captain Carter frighten you so? Did he harm you?"

As the sherry warmed her, her voice was released. "No, dearest, Captain Carter has done nothing. I cannot explain why I reacted the way I did. Please forgive me for troubling you."

Darcy glanced at Jane. "Miss Bennet, might I ask you to find Bingley and bring him here to help assist Miss Elizabeth?"

Jane looked from Darcy to Elizabeth, certain that her sister would not want another person involved, and asked, "Lizzy, what do you want me to do?"

Elizabeth tensed at the thought of another having knowledge of her terror. She looked questioningly into Darcy's eyes, one eyebrow raised. He mouthed soundlessly, "Trust me." She knew that this was, indeed, one man in which she would always have confidence. Elizabeth nodded and replied quietly, "Please bring Mr. Bingley."

Watching Jane leave, Elizabeth fought the tears that threatened.

Turning to Darcy, she choked out, "Thank you, sir. I think I would have fainted if you had not come when you did."

"I am glad to be of assistance," he said, his tone solemn.

Seeing the compassion and the firm determination in his look, she dropped her gaze to her lap. She blinked rapidly to keep the tears from falling as she remembered the encounter with the officer. This fear, this panic! How could she overcome it? She would not think on it. Casting about in her mind for a subject that would distract her, she grasped the first that came to her. "Mr. Darcy, do not think me ungrateful, but Captain Carter will no doubt see the truth of the matter when I do not dance with anyone else but you."

"I believe I have a possible solution." He paused to draw a deep breath. After he exhaled, Darcy continued, "Which is why I asked your sister to fetch Bingley. With his assistance, I believe your dance card will be filled."

"Surely Mr. Bingley could not dance the remaining sets with me?" Elizabeth shook her head. Was it possible to ask her host for the use of a quiet room in which to rest until the ball was finished? No, that would not do since her extended absence would definitely cause speculation.

Darcy's swift answer showed he had given the matter some thought. "Since Bingley is not able to dance more than three with your sister, he will be allowed to do so only because all will know of their betrothal after supper. He will still be free to dance two with you. We will only need to find one other partner you can be comfortable standing up with, and I will claim the final set."

"Mr. Darcy," she replied in shock. "I cannot dance with you three times. People will think we have an understanding. No, that will not do."

Darcy wished to tell her that he wanted to proclaim to the world that there was an understanding between them. But as soon as he opened his mouth to speak Wickham's image floated through his mind. *Blast the man! Will I ever overcome such an impediment?*

"Very well, I will not insist, but since it is the final dance, you may choose to sit it out." He caught and held her gaze. "People are aware that you have been injured. No one would dare dispute your need for rest."

Fighting the disappointment that she and Darcy would never have an understanding, she concentrated on the matter at hand. She did see the wisdom in what he proposed. "Your plan is sound except for the other partner. I would be uncomfortable dancing with most of the gentlemen who would dance with me, especially the officers. Please do not insist that I dance with an officer."

"Of course not!" he exclaimed, tamping down the feeling of offense Elizabeth's statement caused. Darcy reminded himself that she was not herself and that she meant no insult. After a calming breath, he asked gently, "Is there no one else of your acquaintance with whom you would not feel afraid to dance?"

Elizabeth tried to think of someone. At first, her father came to mind, but he no longer cared to dance and would likely only tease her about wanting him to do so with her. He preferred to spend time in the card room or in a corner with other men who also no longer enjoyed the exercise. However, thinking of Mr. Bennet brought another to mind. "Mr. Collins," she said simply. "He is family and with his engagement to Mary, he is nearly a brother."

"I believe that is a good solution." He scanned what he could see of the crowd through the doorway. "I see Bingley and your sister are coming. Once they arrive, I shall speak to Charles before I seek out your cousin." He corrected himself, "No, I shall talk to Mr. Collins during the supper break as the supper set is due to begin any minute."

Bingley listened as Darcy explained that Elizabeth had not wanted to dance with a certain officer. "Understanding this, I impulsively told him that Miss Elizabeth's card was full. Because of my rather rash action, I must ask her friends to save her from the embarrassment that would come to her should this person find out she has no such partners."

Looking down at Elizabeth with a contrite expression on his face, he continued, "I have no doubt that others would have asked you to dance, but unless you object, I think it wise to find you a partner or two."

"I have no objection," she replied softly.

Charles agreed while apologizing that he had not asked sooner. He told her that he had fully intended to ask her. Knowing that his mind had been fully occupied by her sister, Elizabeth forgave him quickly and wholeheartedly.

The supper dance was called, and the two couples stood up together in the line. Elizabeth felt the most relaxed she had all evening. It might have been attributed to the sherry, but she knew without a doubt it was Mr. Darcy's presence most of all, along with Jane's, that gave her relief from the fear. Even the presence of officers did not stir up much anxiety. She only needed to glance in Darcy's direction to feel peaceful again.

Once the dance ended, Darcy moved quickly to her side and slipped her arm through his. "How are you faring, Miss Elizabeth?" he asked in a near whisper.

"I am well, thank you." Her sigh was one of contentment. "Although I admit to be in great need of a chair and a bit of food."

With a faint smile, Darcy said, "It is fortunate, then, that supper will be served. I believe that Bingley has reserved places for us at his table."

Elizabeth returned his smile as they were swept along with the rest of the guests into the dining room. She spied Jane standing next to Bingley and the Hursts. Darcy must have seen them too because he guided her around other guests until they arrived at the table.

"Please be seated," Bingley invited as he signalled for a server to bring out the wine he had ordered. Lowering his voice, he said, "As soon as the rest of the guests are in their places, I will make our announcement." He flashed Jane an adoring smile before he moved to intercept Mr. and Mrs. Bennet. It was only fitting that his angel's family be seated with his for this wonderful occasion.

Elizabeth greeted Louisa Hurst, complimenting her, "Mrs. Hurst, I dare say there has never been such a lovely ball held around Meryton."

"Thank you, Miss Elizabeth," Mrs. Hurst responded, pleased by the compliment.

Their conversation was interrupted by the arrival of Mr. and Mrs. Bennet as well as Mr. Collins and Mary, who had just joined her parents when Bingley came upon them to escort them to the table. Elizabeth's mother explained that her two youngest daughters wanted to dine with the Forsters, because they had become such close friends with the colonel's wife since the militia first encamped in Meryton.

Elizabeth sighed in relief that their hosts and Mr. Darcy would not have to suffer through exaltations about the militia and its officers. In fact, she was grateful for the reprieve herself, and decided she would rather listen to her mother's excited utterances or Mr. Collins's effusive praise of his patroness and Rosings Park than to have to hear about soldiers in red coats.

Soon the room filled with people chattering, laughing, and looking for places to sit. The servers who had set out the cold meats, cheeses, breads, and fruit brought out the wine and began to pour.

As the servants did their tasks efficiently, Bingley tapped a spoon on a glass. "Ladies and gentlemen, may I beg for your attention for a moment?" Quickly the assembled guests ceased their conversation to listen to their host.

"I wish to thank you all for coming tonight," he said, a brilliant smile gracing his face. "Since you are my neighbours and are fast becoming my friends, I would like to share my joy with you, as well as my home. The joy I speak of is this: Miss Jane Bennet has consented to become my wife."

The room erupted with happy babble, and most of it came from the host's own table. Mrs. Bennet nearly leaped over the table trying to reach Jane and Bingley. Her emotions seesawed between wanting to preen with ecstatic excitement over having another daughter engaged and the wish to scold her daughter and her own husband for keeping the news from her. The need to bask in the wonder of her good fortune won the battle. She told herself she could reproach her family in private.

After several toasts were offered, Bingley insisted that the guests return to their meals. He beamed at Jane before he reached into his pocket for the ring he had commissioned his brother, Hurst, to fetch from Town. He slipped the sapphire ring on her left hand.

Jane blushed as she examined the ring on her finger. She thanked him prettily before she allowed her family to see it. Soon, the room filled with the normal conversational tone of suppers such as these.

Filled with joy for her sister, Elizabeth again felt a twinge of envy, but she refused to dwell on it. There was nothing to be gained but bitterness, which could easily destroy the bond of sisterly affection between Jane and herself. If she allowed her heart to fill with resentment, her spinsterhood would be sour and lonely.

Darcy watched Elizabeth and thought he understood the battle within as it played over her face. He wanted above anything to bring the joy and sparkle back into her life. He ached to help her. A thought struck him with such force, he almost gasped aloud. *I love her. Truly, I have fallen in love with Miss Elizabeth Bennet.* His mind reeled while his heart sighed with pleasure at the acknowledgement. How was he to act upon this revelation? Was he strong enough to put aside his hatred of Wickham to help one more of his victims?

"Mr. Darcy?" Elizabeth's voice finally broke through his reverie.

"Excuse me, Miss Elizabeth," he apologized. "Would you please repeat that? I was not attending."

"It was not important." Her eyes were on her plate as she moved a few pieces of fruit around with her fork. "I merely asked if you would like some of the bread."

Darcy realized that he had not taken any of the food and took up the platter of bread and began to fill his plate from it and the other bounty around him.

After sampling a few bites, Darcy noticed that she had not eaten even one mouthful from her sparsely populated plate. He leaned closely and asked softly, "You are not hungry, Miss Elizabeth?"

It was her turn to colour. "I admit that I do not feel like eating. Perhaps the shock I experienced before has stolen my appetite."

He buttered a small slice of bread and handed it to her. "Eat this. It might rekindle your hunger." He smiled winningly. "Will you do it for me?"

Elizabeth took the food from him and nibbled on it. At first, her uneasy stomach seemed likely to rebel, but once she had finished the morsel, the queasiness she had been suffering vanished and hunger returned. "Thank you, sir. I do believe that you were correct. In fact, if I am not being too impolite in asking, would please serve me from that platter of cheeses?"

Darcy was only too happy to oblige Elizabeth, though her asking had not been perfectly according to the etiquette of the day. He served her cheese, cold slices of ham, and more bread and smiled as she ate with apparent appetite.

The conversation at the host's table continued to be pleasant and light. Frequently other guests approached the table to express their good wishes. Mrs. Bennet barely had the time to eat or drink because she would have a part in every interchange. For the most part, Mr. Bennet merely smiled at the happy couple and winked at his favourite daughter from across the table.

After another glass of the fine wine, Elizabeth relaxed enough so as not to panic when several of the officers offered their congratulations to Jane and Bingley. Only once did she feel anxiety, and that was when Darcy moved to speak with Mr. Collins about standing up with her. Embarrassment warred with her anxious feelings. How could she be allowing Mr. Darcy to arrange her dance partners? She felt that she had lost control, though she knew that, without his help, she surely would have humiliated herself and her family by fainting. However, she could not have danced with Captain Carter. No, she owed a great deal to Mr. Darcy and would not fight his assistance.

After partaking of the repast, the guests were entertained by several ladies who played the pianoforte or sang. Mrs. Hurst and Mary Bennet performed to the satisfaction of all. A few tried to prevail upon Elizabeth to sing or play, but she would not, claiming she was unprepared. Never in her life had she felt so reluctant to perform before her friends and neighbours. Anger toward her attacker roiled up within her. Following the anger, came the nearly ever-present anxiety. As in many times before, Elizabeth pushed down the fear and tried to think of something else.

Darcy spent much of the supper break observing Elizabeth. He read her face as her expressions changed with her thoughts. The look of fear and then anger that swept across her countenance gripped his heart. He might not think of proposing to her, but he certainly could help her through another bout of terror. However, he was unsure if he could assist her in dispelling the anger. Just a few moments before, he had caught a bit of conversation between Bingley and his intended and decided to act upon what he heard.

"Miss Elizabeth, would you like to take some air? I overheard your sister express a wish for some, but Bingley obviously cannot escort her alone. Shall we accompany them to the terrace before the dancing recommences?" He kept his voice level and as impersonal as he was able.

"I would like that above all things," she exclaimed quietly, "but do you think we have the time?"

"As the host, Bingley is able to postpone the dancing for a few additional minutes." Darcy stood and helped Elizabeth from her chair.

Together, they moved to where the engaged couple stood. "Bingley, would you and Miss Bennet care to accompany Miss Elizabeth and me for a bit of fresh air?"

"Excellent idea, Darcy!" Charles offered his arm to Jane, and they moved slowly from the room, through a short passage, and into another sitting room from which they could access the terrace more privately.

Both sisters inhaled and exhaled deeply as the group moved onto the tiled terrace. "It is lovely tonight, if a trifle cool," Jane expressed cheerfully.

"I will fetch you a shawl," Bingley quickly exclaimed as he dropped her arm in preparation to find her wrap himself. "I cannot have you catch a chill."

"No, please," she protested, retaking his arm, "just stay close and I will be fine for the few minutes we will be out here."

In the meantime, Elizabeth, being unaware of her actions, moved closer to Darcy. She sought both the safety and the warmth of his close proximity. He revelled in her movement. A surge of contentment welled within him. The knowledge that she continued to seek shelter in his presence made him smile broadly. How he wanted to be the first and only one she ever needed for such protection! No longer could he conceive of her belonging to another. The very thought pierced him to the soul. Unable to control himself, he covered her hands, which were clasped together on his arm with his larger and warmer one.

For a brief second, the gentle pressure of Mr. Darcy's hand upon hers caused her to lean against him even more than was entirely proper. Out in the night air with her beloved sister and her fiancé, Elizabeth forgot that the gentleman next to her was merely a compassionate friend. She almost believed that they could be something more.

Soon however, the reality of her situation reared its ugly head. She was fooling herself. Things had not changed. Her fate was sealed. She made to pull her hands away from Darcy, but he would not have it.

Pretending she had intended to move inside, Darcy whispered, "I do not want to go back to the supper room just yet. I will not have the pleasure of your company again until we sit out the last dance. Please indulge me for a few more minutes."

Nodding, she blinked tears of gratitude from her eyes. What a kind and wonderful man he was! Elizabeth sighed as she felt her earlier fury at Wickham attempt to rise in her again. It would not do; she would not allow that cad to ruin a lovely moment like this. No, she planned to cherish it as long as she could.

A sudden screech of laughter shattered the calm night. Someone had opened the doors from the supper room and come out onto that part of the terrace. Three officers were joined by three young girls, one of which was Lydia.

Elizabeth shrank back upon seeing them. "Please, let us return to the house," she begged in a ragged whisper.

"Bingley, I believe we should go back. Your guests will wonder what has become of their host." Darcy kept his voice low so as not to be heard by the others who stood talking and laughing such a short distance away. He guided Elizabeth back through the double doors to the supper room. Keeping her close to him, they moved into the ballroom where the orchestra sat tuning their instruments.

Standing next to the wall, they were joined by Charles and Jane and soon after, by Mr. Collins and Mary. Elizabeth was suddenly struck by how different this ball was from the assembly in Meryton. She stood comfortably talking not only with Mr. Darcy but also with her rather odd, male cousin. Both her sisters were radiating joy in the knowledge that they were loved. At the assembly, she had overheard Darcy's insult and would likely still be upset with him had she not been attacked and had he not come to her aid. Their vicar had often told his congregation that God sent blessings in the midst of trouble. She lifted a silent prayer of thanksgiving for that special gift of mercy that was Mr. Darcy.

As the dancing began again, Elizabeth smiled as Mr. Bingley guided her to the dance floor. Throughout the next sets, Mr. Darcy was near enough to her so that she did not experience panic. She did notice Captain Carter staring at her with curious eyes during the dances with Bingley and her cousin, but he did nothing more.

When the time came for the final set of the evening, Elizabeth was more than happy to sit down. Mr. Bingley escorted her to a settee while Darcy followed with Jane.

Jane searched her sister's face for signs of fatigue. "How are you faring, dearest?"

"I have decided to forego the last dance and sit here until it is time to leave." Elizabeth smiled up at Jane.

"Then I will stay with you." Concern filled Jane's voice. Turning to her fiancé, she asked, "You do not mind if I sit with Lizzy, do you, Charles?"

Though visibly disappointed, Bingley was about to agree when Darcy spoke. "Do not worry, Miss Bennet. I will attend Miss Elizabeth." He shook his head slightly when Jane tried to object. "As Bingley can tell you, I rarely dance as much as I have tonight. I will be most happy to stay here with your sister."

"Oh, yes," Bingley said as he agreed with his friend. "I do not ever remember Darcy dancing more than two dances before, three at the most. He dislikes the amusement so much in general." He winked quickly at Darcy.

"That is enough, my friend," Darcy cut Bingley off. "Take your lovely fiancée and enjoy your dance."

After giving Elizabeth one more examining look, Jane seemed satisfied. She laid her hand on Bingley's arm and moved to the dance floor with him.

"You do not have to stay with me, Mr. Darcy." Elizabeth told him although she hoped he would.

"There is nothing I would rather do, Miss Elizabeth." He did not look at her, but he smiled as he tracked the movements of the dancers. Darcy was content to be next to this lovely, if wounded, young woman. The idea that he loved her both thrilled and grieved him. It had never entered his mind that he would fall so completely for a country lass with no fortune and few connections. But here he sat, and the lack of money or the presence of embarrassing family members was not what stood in the way of his happiness. It was the vicious actions of another that had seemingly spoiled any chance he had for the delight of being her husband.

"I believe that we must have some conversation, even if we are not dancing," Elizabeth teased so as to keep the more sober thoughts at bay.

"I agree, Miss Elizabeth," he said as he turned his attention to her. "However, this time I will choose the topic." His dimples showed themselves as he smiled widely. "Tell me about your favourite poet."

Within the next half hour, the two discussed poetry, art, their favourite foods, and hobbies. Elizabeth was surprised to discover that Darcy sang and played the pianoforte, although he said that he did not play so well as her or his sister

Georgiana. He found that she did not particularly like fish but loved steak and ale pie. She did not often have the opportunity to eat it because her mother thought it too common to serve more than a few times a year.

Often, Darcy sensed that Elizabeth kept up the cheerful conversation for his sake. He respected her choice so much that he pushed aside his natural reserve to keep her entertained with stories about his finicky childhood eating habits and his secret fondness for hot chocolate. He made her laugh with a tale of going to the kitchen late one night to try to make himself a cup when he was about eight years old. The housekeeper found him covered with chocolate and sugar. After that night, Mrs. Reynolds would prepare him the hot drink at least once a week and never reported his nocturnal escapade to his parents.

Mr. Bennet came upon them a few minutes before the end of the dance. Her father felt gratitude toward Mr. Darcy. He had watched Elizabeth during the evening and everything he saw spoke of the gentlemen's regard for his daughter. *My little Lizzy will not be mine for much longer,* he silently mused.

"Lizzy, have you enjoyed yourself?" Mr. Bennet asked though he was certain of the answer. "I know how you love to dance. However, you did not dance this last set."

"Yes, Papa," she replied. "I found at the end of the preceding dance that I needed to rest, and Mr. Darcy has been pleasant company.

"Thank you, sir." Mr. Bennet searched the younger man's eyes as he said, "It was kind of you to sacrifice your time to entertain my daughter."

Darcy met his gaze without flinching. He understood Elizabeth's father was questioning him. *Are you still intent on courting my daughter? When will you speak to her about it?* With a slight nod, he said earnestly, "Sir, I can think of no one with whom I would rather have spent the last half hour. I thank you for allowing me the pleasure."

"Well said, sir," Mr. Bennet acknowledged Darcy's answer as the music ceased. "I see that it is time for me to call for our carriage. I will collect your mother and meet you at the door, Lizzy."

As her father moved away, Elizabeth stood and faced Darcy. "Again, I feel I must express my gratitude for your kindness to me this evening. Not only did you save me from humiliation, but you kept my mind from dwelling on unpleasant thoughts by your entertaining stories." She curtseyed formally.

Without thinking, Darcy took her hand in his before lifting it to his lips. All the while, his eyes never left hers. A surge of delight jolted through him. It was the first time that kissing a lady's gloved hand had given him such pleasure.

Finally, Elizabeth eased her hand and gaze away from him. What had just happened to her? Her heart raced, but this time it was certainly not from fear. She felt her cheeks warm, while the spot on her hand where his lips had pressed throbbed pleasantly. His eyes spoke of something she could not quite fathom. Surely he was not interested in her. He knew what she was, what had happened to her. It was not possible and yet...

"May I escort you to the door?" asked Darcy, his eyes no longer held the intensity of moments before, only their usual kind friendliness. He offered her his arm once more.

"Of course," Elizabeth agreed, and placed her hand on his arm. She followed his lead through the crowd, first to retrieve her outer garments and then to where her family awaited their carriage.

CHAPTER ELEVEN

The journey back to Longbourn was a noisy one. Mrs. Bennet could not seem to get the words out fast enough or with enough enthusiasm. She chided Jane for the secrecy concerning her engagement to Mr. Bingley, but it was without bite. Sighing over the grand house that would belong to Jane, her mother exulted that her oldest daughter would be able to host as many balls as she wished. On and on went the lady of Longbourn House, leaving little opportunity for Jane, or anyone else for that matter to speak.

Once they were inside the house and as her mother called to Mrs. Hill, so she could repeat the wondrous announcement of Jane's engagement, Elizabeth slipped upstairs to her room. She was glad to find Sarah awaiting her. Although she did not feel so tired as she thought she would at this hour, Lizzy knew that she would need assistance to remove her gown and such if she wanted to go to bed any time soon.

Sarah asked the usual questions about the ball and the dancing as she assisted the young miss out of her garments. The young maid felt concern for the tense, almost agitated look about Elizabeth. The night's entertainment seemed to have been enjoyable, but the servant wished she dared inquire as to what was bothering the young lady. Finally, after she removed the flowers, pins, and ribbons from Elizabeth's hair and prepared a cup of her special herb blend that would help with sleep, Sarah was dismissed to assist the other Bennet sisters, who were even now calling for her help.

After drinking half her tea, Elizabeth picked up her brush and stroked it through her hair without thinking about the task. Her mind whirled with the memories of the ball. Now that she was at home and in her room, the one thing that stood out from her experience at the ball was not the surge of panic at the sight of an officer or a red coat, nor the embarrassment of almost fainting in front of her neighbours and friends, nor the pleasant dancing and entertainment. The moment that her heart and mind wanted to revisit over and over was the very one in which Mr. Darcy had kissed her hand.

Even alone in her room, Elizabeth blushed at the memory of the warm pressure of his lips on the back of her gloved hand. She was well aware that it had not been altogether proper for Mr. Darcy to kiss her in such a way. She realized that the look he gave her as he did it probably was improper as well. However, the idea that his conduct was somehow indecent or ill-mannered did not seem correct. On the contrary, his actions had felt natural and wonderful. Elizabeth was about to scold herself once more for such fanciful notions when a knock sounded on her door. She called out, "Enter."

When Jane entered and closed the door behind her, she said quickly, "Oh, good, you are not asleep. May we talk or were you intending to go right to bed?"

Thinking she knew the topic Jane wanted to discuss, Elizabeth still could not dissemble. She was not sleepy; in fact, she felt a great nervous energy that she knew would keep her awake for some time. "I am too full of the ball to be able to rest just yet. What is it you would like to discuss, dearest?"

Jane stood behind her sister and took the brush from her hand. As she worked it through Elizabeth's hair, she caught her gaze in the mirror. "I want to understand why you were so frightened when Captain Carter came up to us. You say he has done nothing, but you have never reacted to anyone in that way before. You have been the brave one, the one to forge ahead or speak to strangers with little or no fear. Lizzy, what is wrong?"

As Jane spoke, Elizabeth dropped her gaze to her lap. Her eyes stung and her throat tightened. How could she tell her sister what happened to her? It would give her kind-hearted sister such pain. Yet if she did not explain, might Jane bring her behaviour to their father's attention in the hope of being of assistance to her?

Jane finished brushing her sister's hair and waited with great patience for her sister to speak. Finally Elizabeth stood, took her hand, and tugged her to the bed. Once they settled into their customary conversational positions against the headboard, she gripped her Jane's hand and said, "You must promise not to tell anyone what I am about to tell you."

"I promise you, but what is such a secret that I may not tell anyone?" Jane asked apprehensively.

Elizabeth took a deep breath and answered quickly, "I did not hit my head on a rock because I slipped on wet grass. A man attacked me and threw me to the ground. It was then my head hit on that stone."

"It was not Mr. Darcy." Jane stated the matter as emphatically as she tightened her grip on Elizabeth's hand.

"No, it was not."

"He was an officer." Her sister's logic was flawless.

Elizabeth nodded but said no more.

"You know who it was."

"I will not tell you who he was. He has been dealt with and is no longer in the area." Throughout the dialogue, Elizabeth's tone was flat.

Again, Jane squeezed the hand of her favourite sister and best friend. "Please tell me how it is that Mr. Darcy brought you to the house and was the one to summon help."

"Mr. Darcy heard my scream and saw the man leave. Soon afterward, he found me injured on the ground. I would not allow him to tell anyone what had happened. I just wanted to burrow into the ground and die."

"But, Lizzy, why would you not say something?"

"Jane, do you not understand that despite my innocence in the matter...I was...am ruined? And were the knowledge of this ruination made public, all of my sisters, including you, would be made to share in it. I would never allow what that awful man did to me to rob my family of its good name. I am certain that you and Mary would not be so happily engaged if I had been open as to the cause of my injuries."

By this time, slow, fat tears began to fall down both sisters' cheeks. Jane wrapped her arms around Elizabeth and rocked her for several minutes. Finally, she pulled back and found Lizzy a handkerchief and one for herself.

Elizabeth thanked Jane as she blew her nose and wiped her eyes. "Mr. Darcy and Sarah came up with the story I have told everyone. They were the only ones who knew the truth until now." She decided at that moment not to say anything of her talk with Mrs. Parker. It would only further injure Jane to know she spoke to a stranger before she confided in her beloved sister. "I beg you again to promise me you will not speak of this to anyone, not even Mr. Bingley. I could not live with the idea he knew of my disgrace."

"Lizzy!" Jane said sharply. "The disgrace belongs completely to the man who did this to you. I do not understand why the victim must bear the burden of guilt."

"It is the way things are. Maybe, one day, it might be different. I pray that it will be so." Elizabeth felt drained by the telling and the weeping, but for the first time since the attack, her burden seemed lighter. The deep bond of love she felt for her sister had forged another strong link. She sighed and tried to hide a sudden yawn.

"Dearest Lizzy," Jane's compassion filled her voice. "I will leave you so that you may sleep. I love you and will pray that God will give you true healing and freedom from this plaguing fear." She hugged Elizabeth once more before she left for her own room.

Pulling the covers up around her neck, Elizabeth pondered Jane's reaction to her tale and her own relief at the sharing. Perhaps the rest of what Mrs. Parker told her would help. As her eyes grew heavy and sleep overtook her, she hoped that her sister's prayer would be answered and soon.

~*~

As he knew he would, Darcy awoke much earlier than the rest of the house. Only wishing for a cup of coffee, he met a few blurry-eyed footmen while on his way to the breakfast room. A brown paper-wrapped package sat by his usual place at the table. He poured himself a cup and sat down.

The footman who stood ready by the buffet informed him, "It came by a groom from Longbourn about twenty minutes ago, sir. He told me it was urgent that you get it as soon as possible. I was going to bring it to you soon if you had not come down."

Darcy nodded as he picked up the parcel after he sat down. Once it was in his hands, he stared at the simple bow knot of twine that kept the paper wrapped around what he knew to be his glove and likely the note that would convey the message he had asked the maid to send. What would he do if Elizabeth was with child? He had not loved her at the time of the attack, but now she was so dear, he ached to be with her at that very moment.

The thought struck him. *Was she aware of her condition? Was that the reason for her emotional reactions of last evening?* He must read the note, so that he could decide what he would do about Miss Elizabeth Bennet. Already he was certain that if she were not increasing, he would continue to court her and eventually to propose. The possibility that she could be carrying Wickham's child made him hold back from untying the knot on the parcel.

Suddenly, Darcy wanted something much stronger than the coffee that was cooling in his cup, but calling himself a coward, he finally pulled the bow apart and folded back the paper. There in the palm of his expensive leather glove laid a folded bit of paper. Again, he fought the urge to postpone having the knowledge that was contained in the little note. Darcy lifted the paper from its resting place and slowly unfolded it. The hand was neat and unembellished. It read:

> *Mr. Darcy,*
> *I am returning your missing glove.*
> *Sarah Brown of Longbourn*

Darcy paled as he stared at the simple missive. He had no doubt that Elizabeth's maid was certain that her young mistress was pregnant. Suddenly, it seemed as if he could not hold his head up. Resting his chin in his hands, his eyes continued to peruse the paper in front of him. Its purport never changed, nor he did actually expect it to do so.

Finally, he stood, picked up his glove and the note, and strode to the study. Once inside, he poured himself a whiskey. The unprecedented action proved how distraught he was. Only the night before, he had realized he loved Elizabeth, and then today George Wickham's villainous deed had put a seemingly insurmountable barrier between them.

After tossing back the liquor, Darcy sat sprawled in a large wing-back chair. As the alcohol hit his empty stomach, it burned before it began to relax him. He thought of pouring another, but he did not want the numbness of being drunk. He stood quickly with the intention of pacing. However, the room spun, and he was forced to sit down again. It had been foolish to take that drink, and now he needed to wait until its effects dissipated.

Darcy understood that he had to approach the situation in a logical manner despite the strong emotions involved. He felt steadier when he acknowledged once more that he loved Elizabeth and wanted only the best for her. That she was with child, with Wickham's child, complicated the matter, but something needed to be done in a very short time if the scandal was to be averted. The shame would not only touch her, but it would hurt the family that she dearly loved. Remembering the fierceness with which she argued for secrecy regarding her attack for her family's sake told him that she might do something rash and possibly dangerous to herself if she thought her actions could protect the rest of the Bennets. No, he could not delay. He must find a solution, and do so with haste.

Raking his hands through his hair, Darcy stared across the room as if he would find the answer on that wall. Nothing could have surprised him more than what appeared before him. A vision of a babe being held in Elizabeth's arms arrested his frantic musings. The infant grinned toothlessly up at him. Her arms waved frantically. Her short, dark curls and sparkling eyes reminded him so much of Elizabeth's own as she, too, lifted her gaze to him and smiled.

The image shifted and this time a little girl of five or six turned from Elizabeth's side to look up at him. She squealed cheerfully, "Papa, I missed you," as she ran to him with arms raised. After he lifted her, she wrapped her little arms around his neck as she peppered his cheek with wet kisses. Finally with her small head on his shoulder, she whispered, "I love you so much, Papa."

The vision swirled and changed again. He thought he spied Elizabeth dressed as a bride inside a room in the chapel at Pemberley, but as he watched an older version of himself walked through the door toward her. She smiled when he reached her and said as she kissed his cheek, "I thought you would be late, Papa, and I would have to be wed without you."

His older self swallowed several times before he found his voice again. "I would never allow that, my sweetling. I had to see to your brothers. You know how they can get into mischief." Taking the young woman's hand, he tucked it into the crook of his arm. "Remember, your mother and I will always love you, and we are very proud of you." With that, he escorted her out of the room and toward the sanctuary.

Darcy blinked several times as his eyes stung with the longing that the scenes wrought in him. The vision or hallucination or whatever it was seemed to send the message that he should marry Elizabeth and claim the child as his own. A prideful part of him violently objected to the idea, but his heart smiled. To think that he might be able to show his love and to win hers caused elation to fill him. A life without her, without her wit and beauty, without her loyalty and compassion, was unimaginable and intolerable.

The surge of despair Darcy experienced when he thought of his life with no Elizabeth Bennet in it told him that his love for her was far stronger than his hatred of George Wickham. Never in a million years would he have guessed that he could contemplate raising a child that was not his own as if it were, but this vision had cleared his mind of thoughts that he might hate the child she was carrying. Marriage to Elizabeth was truly the only choice he had.

At that moment, he wondered how he might convince Elizabeth that it was the best and most prudent of options. Darcy sighed upon the realization that she might be harder to persuade than he himself had been. He would do it, since there was no other alternative.

Slowly getting to his feet, he made his way back into the breakfast room. Darcy wanted to eat something so as to counteract the effects of the whiskey. He had a great deal to accomplish and a very short time in which to do it. He hoped that Bingley would rise soon, so that he could entrust him with a message to Elizabeth. Ordering the footman to check to see if his host was awake yet, he mentally made a list of what he must attend to while in Town. There, he must meet with his solicitor to make up the marriage contracts, and to retrieve some special jewellery from the safe in his townhouse.

Darcy was just finishing his meal when he heard Bingley come into the room.

"Blast it, Darcy!" Charles slapped his back. "You need less sleep than anyone I know."

"I hope the footman did not wake you."

"No, no, I was awake," Bingley smiled dreamily. "I had such a wonderful dream about Jane, er, Miss Bennet. Unfortunately, when I woke and found it was a dream, I could not go back to sleep. I finally decided to get dressed and come to breakfast when Tillford knocked on my door."

As Charles accepted a cup of coffee, he turned to study his friend. "You wanted to speak to me?"

"Yes, I did," he said with determination. "I must go to Town on an important matter. I should not be longer than a day, two at the most. It is a matter of some urgency that requires my attention, and it cannot be delayed. I would like you to explain that to the Bennets when you see them next.

"Of course, I shall be happy to do so, but might you need my assistance?" queried Bingley.

"I thank you, Bingley," Darcy said with a faint smile on his lips. "But I am afraid that only I can accomplish the tasks that are before me. And they are not of a grievous nature. I merely wish I did not have to leave so suddenly, but it is for the best since it will hasten my return."

Darcy left the breakfast room and ordered his horse and one for his valet to be brought to the house. Since he would spend his nights in his house in Town, he did not need a bag packed. Within thirty minutes, he and his man were off to London.

The ride to Town was especially pleasant for Darcy with the delightful contemplation of marriage to Elizabeth. He refused to think of the complications that might arise when his family learned of his plans of marriage to a woman of lower social standing and no money. Cringing at the thought of introducing Mrs. Bennet and her younger daughters to Lord and Lady Matlock, he knew that none of that would change his mind. In fact, he was tempted to wait until he was married to say anything. The thought hovered in his mind for a short time until the reality of the scandal that might come from such action wiped it away.

He would arrange everything first and then invite his family when they could do little but attend or not. Darcy had no doubt that most of them would be won over by Elizabeth. Georgiana had always wished for a sister and would love her almost immediately. Indeed, all would be well.

Darcy planned and deliberated as he rode Paladin through the countryside and into the city. Once they reached Darcy House, he felt excitement coursing through him.

Mrs. Graves, his housekeeper, though surprised at his sudden and unexpected arrival, greeted him as if nothing was amiss. "Good day, Mr. Darcy, I hope that all is well. Miss Darcy did not tell me that she expected your return so soon. In fact, she and Mrs. Annesley have gone to visit Lord and Lady Matlock for a few days. Shall I send word to your sister?"

"Everything is well. I merely have unexpected business which requires my immediate attention. It is not necessary to call Georgiana home. I will be returning to Hertfordshire tomorrow or the next day, so I would not wish to spoil her plans," Darcy answered, almost relieved that his sister would not be there to ask questions that he might not wish to answer at present. She would be the first of his family to know after he was able to convince Elizabeth to marry him. He sent up a pleading prayer that she would not fight him on this matter.

"Very well, sir," the housekeeper said. "Shall I have hot water sent to your room before luncheon?"

"I will clean up shortly, but I have a note I want Barnes to take to my solicitor." He turned back when he reached his study door. "Just send the water and a cold meal on a tray to my room. I plan to leave to speak to Mr. Whitton as soon as I hear back from him."

At his desk, he reached for a pen and paper. Darcy wrote a short note requesting an appointment as soon as his attorney was free. Once he had dispatched the missive, he hastened to his chamber to clean the travel grime from his person. Peters had a fresh set of clothing set out for him and a basin of hot water on the stand.

When he had changed and was ready to leave once he heard from his attorney, the lunch tray arrived. The ride from Netherfield Park had whetted his appetite, so he ate with relish. As he drank the last of his tea, the answer from Mr. Whitton arrived.

The solicitor was free that very afternoon, which pleased Darcy very much. If all of his business went well, he would be able to return to Hertfordshire by the next day. He was eager to get back in order to see Elizabeth and to propose. A thrill of pleasure danced up his spine. The prospect of her being his wife and life companion grew in its appeal hourly.

His phaeton was called for, and Darcy made his way to the building that held Mr. Whitton's office. Once he arrived, he was quickly led back to the solicitor's private chamber.

"Mr. Darcy." The older gentleman bowed respectfully. "It was a pleasant surprise to receive your correspondence. Please be seated and tell me what I can do for you."

Darcy sat in a large comfortable leather chair while Mr. Whitton took the one beside it. His attorney never sat behind his desk when he did business. He once told Darcy he wished his clients to feel he was a trusted friend, and he would not have a piece of furniture come between friends.

"Sir, I am to be married soon, and I have come to arrange the marriage contract," Darcy blushed slightly since he had not even asked Elizabeth or her father for her hand. "I want to obtain a license as well."

Mr. Whitton extended his hand. "May I congratulate you, Mr. Darcy? And who is the lady?"

After taking a deep breath and exhaling slowly, Darcy confessed, "The lady's name is Miss Elizabeth Bennet of Longbourn in Hertfordshire, but I have not as yet made the offer."

"Are you not a bit premature in writing the contract and obtaining the license?" the other man inquired reasonably.

"I suppose it is unusual, but I wish to have everything arranged first. I believe timing is crucial. Will it be a problem for you?"

"No, sir, all I will need are the details of settlement. And I can arrange for the license as well if you are going to be married from Town."

"I believe that Miss Bennet will prefer to be married from Longbourn."

"Then I am afraid that I will not be able to help you obtain the license. You will need to purchase it from the local vicar," Mr. Whitton explained.

"Very well, I will do that once I have her father's permission. How soon may I expect the rest to be achieved?" Darcy leaned forward in his chair, eager for the process to be over.

"I suppose with the right incentives, it can be ready for you by tomorrow afternoon or early evening."

"You have my permission to pay whatever is needed to speed things along. I wish to be back in Hertfordshire by supper time tomorrow if at all possible." His tone was determined.

"Very well, sir," the attorney reached for a pad of paper and a pencil and began to ask pertinent questions.

About an hour later, Mr. Whitton put down his papers and stood as Darcy prepared to leave. "If you would please wait, I have something to give you."

Darcy's brow creased as he wondered what the man had for him. He watched as Mr. Whitton moved a panel behind his desk to reveal a safe. The older man swiftly unlocked it and reached in for a bundle of sealed papers. After sorting through the pile, he laid one aside before replacing the others and relocking the door.

Once the panel clicked into its original position, the attorney picked up the paper and turned around. "I hold here a letter your father asked me to give to you when you came to tell me you were going to marry. I do not know its contents, only that he gave it to me about the time you came home from Cambridge. I suggest that you read it at your leisure, as I do not think what it contains will require my legal advice."

Taking the offered missive, Darcy frowned down at the familiar Darcy seal and his own name written in his father's hand above it. Curiosity and the wish for privacy battled within him before he decided to wait until he reached his home to read it. He thanked Mr. Whitton, asked to be summoned when all was ready, and took his leave.

CHAPTER TWELVE

It was late when Elizabeth awoke. The sun played tag with the clouds, so that it appeared that it could not decide whether to shine or not. One particularly bright beam speared through her window as the sun broke through once more. She sat up quickly as she thought to take a walk before rain might come, when in the next moment, the idea brought fear to her heart.

Tears spilled down her cheeks as she felt again the pain of what had been taken from her. That man had done more than take her innocence and injure her body. He had wounded her spirit and stolen her freedom. Dashing away the tears, she rose and rang for Sarah. Elizabeth made the decision that she would walk even if it were only in the garden. As Jane had said the previous night, she had always been the brave one.

With determination building within her, she spoke out loud, "I will fight this fear. I will not allow this to keep me caged."

Sarah arrived so quickly that Elizabeth wondered if she had been waiting for the summons. She brought with her a tray with toast and tea on it. "Good morning, Miss Elizabeth. Did you rest well?"

"Good morning, Sarah," She answered. "I slept well. It is no wonder considering how late we came home. Is the rest of the family awake?"

"Miss Mary awoke early so as to see Mr. Collins off to Hunsford, and she is now resting in her room with a book. Mr. Bennet is breakfasting in his library." Sarah smiled as she related, "He told Hill that he wanted to avoid any rehearsal of the events of the ball once the rest of the family arose."

As the maid handed Elizabeth a cup of sweetened tea, she said, "I believe that Miss Jane is just now awake. I think I heard her moving about when I passed her door."

"Oh, you should take her something. I will be fine until you get back." Elizabeth sipped the sweet liquid and sighed as it soothed the slight queasiness in her stomach.

"Yes, miss," Sarah agreed as she set out clothes on the bed. "I will do that once you are dressed."

Elizabeth wanted to argue, but she knew that Jane took time to awaken fully, and would not expect Sarah to come right away if she were busy with one of her other sisters. She spread some jam on a piece of toast and bit in. There was something about the simple repast that tasted especially good this morning. Perhaps all the dancing had sharpened her appetite.

While she watched Miss Elizabeth eat, Sarah was glad she had chosen to bring the simple fare. She knew that women who were with child could experience sickness in the morning. From what her mother had told her, bland and uncomplicated food was what such ladies needed. It pleased her to see that her young mistress seemed to enjoy the meal.

Soon, Elizabeth finished her simple breakfast and allowed Sarah to assist her in dressing. As the girl worked, she asked about the ball, and Elizabeth told a few details, including the announcement of Jane's but held back from sharing the negative feelings she had experienced.

Once she was fully dressed, she would not let the maid help with her hair. "I am fully able to see to my hair. You are free to go to Jane."

As Sarah moved to the door, Elizabeth stopped her. Her maid's loyalty and persistent help prodded her to speak about the talk she and Jane had once they returned. "Please wait. I want to tell you something else. Last night once we were home, I told Jane what happened to me, about the attack."

"Oh, Miss Elizabeth, I am happy you finally did so." Sarah felt her own burden lighten. "May I ask how it went?"

"The only way it could have. She listened, asked a few questions, and then just held me as we cried. I am glad that I do not have to keep this from her any longer. You and your aunt were correct when you said that talking would help." Elizabeth sighed, "I just wish that the fear would be gone."

"It will be, I am sure," Sarah said with emphasis. "I have been praying against that fear and for your wholeness. God will not fail to answer. In fact, I am sure the answer has already begun."

"Thank you," Elizabeth said around the lump in her throat. "You may go now."

As Sarah went about her work that morning, she pondered as to whether she should tell Miss Elizabeth what she knew about the child. Mr. Darcy now knew and she was certain he would help in every way possible. Smiling, she thought about the tender way he had with Miss Elizabeth. Sarah would be very surprised if he did not love her. Perhaps he would ask her to marry him. Would not that be a wonderful end to such a horrible situation? Finally, Sarah decided that a few more days would not hurt, so she would wait to see what Mr. Darcy would do and how he would react before she informed Miss Elizabeth.

Elizabeth joined Jane in her room and invited her to take a turn about the garden before it rained. Her elder sister eagerly assented, and soon they donned their outer clothing and hastened into the yard.

They walked silently and slowly for several moments before Jane spoke, "You seem rested, Lizzy."

"I slept quite well after our conversation." Emotion caught in her throat, so that she could not say more.

"I am so glad that you trusted me with your burden." Jane's own voice was husky. "I cannot imagine the stress it caused you, having no one with whom to share it."

Clearing her throat and swallowing hard, Elizabeth explained, "I thank God that I was not totally alone. Mr. Darcy and Sarah helped me a great deal. I did want to spare you the pain, but it is so good to be able to be frank with you at last."

"Shall we go farther? You might feel better if you stretch your legs on one of your favourite hill trails," Jane suggested innocently.

"No!" Elizabeth sharp reply echoed across the grass. A well of panic built inside and threatened to overwhelm her.

Jane took her sister's hands in hers. Concern was etched across her face. "I am sorry for the suggestion, dearest. I knew you were avoiding your solitary walks, but I thought you could go with me."

Gripping her sister's hands in a desperate grasp, Elizabeth panted out, "I thought I...could, but it...feels as if...I cannot...breathe when...I think of...doing so."

With compassion filling her loving heart, Jane turned Lizzy back toward the house. "We will not go any farther than you wish."

At her viewing Longbourn, the fear ebbed. Elizabeth took several deep, calming breaths before she spoke. "I will not allow this fear to control me. If I am able to walk into the village in the company of Mr. Darcy, I should be able to walk out of sight of our home with you."

Steeling her resolve, Elizabeth linked her arm through Jane's and turned toward a trail that did not go near the place where she had been assaulted. Each step grew more difficult, but she forged on until they reached a bend that would take them completely out of sight of the house. Once they travelled about twenty more yards, her breathing became so shallow that she feared she would faint for lack of air. Perspiration snaked down her back as a chill wrapped its cold arms around her.

"Lizzy, we must turn back." Jane recognized the same symptoms of panic in her sister as occurred the night before when Captain Carter had approached them. "You have proved you could go beyond the garden. Shall we not try this again another time?"

Elizabeth allowed Jane to guide her back to the house. She did not notice her mother inquiring after their walk as Mrs. Hill helped her off with her pelisse, bonnet, and gloves. All she wanted was to be in her room. Once they had ascended the stairs and entered her room, Jane wrapped her shivering sister in a woollen shawl before she rang for Sarah.

When the maid arrived, Jane ordered a hot drink, explaining that Elizabeth had become chilled from their walk. She returned to her sister and began to chafe her hands in an attempt to warm them. Tears flowed down her cheeks as she apologized, "I should not have allowed you to walk that far. Please, Lizzy, forgive me."

Jane's plaintive cry returned Lizzy to her senses. Wrapping her arms around her sister, Elizabeth soothed, "Oh, Jane, it was not your fault. Do not fret. I needed to test my strength." She laughed mirthlessly. "It was not great, was it? However, I did not faint, and I walked farther than I thought possible a few days ago. I will call it a success, even if it is a small one."

~*~

Once Darcy reached his townhouse and informed the staff he was not at home to anyone, he locked himself in the study. Something told him that he would need privacy once he read the missive from his father.

He dropped into his favourite chair and stared at the letter for a few moments before breaking the seal. The strong, bold script that was unmistakably his father's made him wish he could discuss his present situation with him. He had been such a wise man and a compassionate one.

Pushing away these melancholy thoughts, Darcy unfolded the letter and began to read:

Pemberley
*12 June, 18_*
My Dear Son,

If you are reading this, two things have happened. The first is that I am no longer on this earth. I must say that since your dear mother's death, I have longed to be with her, and more so as the time has passed. I realize I am a selfish man to feel this way when I have two fine children who love me and depend upon me. However, as all of my doctors tell me I do not have long to live, I can indulge these thoughts with less guilt.

The notion of the event that will put this missive into your hands gives me great joy. You are to be married! To begin with, I will ask you to consider your reasons for marrying before I am free to wish you joy. Only the greatest love should cause you to enter into this blessed state.

I hope that your aunt Catherine has not pressured you into marrying your cousin, Anne. Quite often after Anne's birth, she would try to press your mother into agreeing to her plans to form an engagement between the two of you. My Anne, your mother, never once agreed with her. The only concession she made was that if you and your cousin should fall in love, she would have no objection.

For this reason, I will repeat myself by saying that if you are not in love with the lady, whoever she may be, find a way to extract yourself from the engagement. Any scandal that should arise from breaking an engagement will be of relatively short duration, but a marriage is for a lifetime. Do not subject her or yourself to that torture.

Darcy lifted his eyes from the page and gave a small chuckle. So his aunt had lied to him all these years. It explained why she never mentioned this supposed agreement between her and his mother until after his father's death. The relief from the small amount of guilt he had carried at the thought of disappointing the hopes and dreams of his dear mother almost counteracted the anger he felt toward his imperious relative. His resolve strengthened as he now knew his father would have supported him in his marriage to Elizabeth.

With a contented smile, he returned to his letter.

Before I am on to another matter I need to convey to you, I wish to express my pride in you. I do not believe that any father could boast of a better son. Fitzwilliam, you work so hard and succeed in ways that I had never foreseen. I do feel that you need to relax and enjoy yourself a bit more, but our home has not had an atmosphere conducive to levity since your mother died. I hope that you will forgive my selfishly indulging my grief. It is rather late for that now, but I ask just the same. As I made up my final will, I knew that you would need someone to help shoulder the burden of Georgiana's guardianship. Of course, I chose Richard because he is an honourable and capable man, but also I picked him because he is one of the few people who can consistently make you laugh. My thoughts were on your welfare as well as hers.

Now to the details I have delayed as long as I could. My postponement of sharing this story is no doubt the result again of my Darcy pride. I suppose I felt that if I did not repeat any of it, it would not be. I admit to trying to tell you a few times, but I never summoned the courage. It concerns my sister, Sophia. I do not think you are even aware that I had a sister, so I will begin by telling you a little about her.

Sophia was just shy of ten years my junior and my parents' joy. She was born while I was at Eton and, being a boy, her birth meant little to me until she was about five and I was preparing to enter Cambridge. I was home for the summer, and Sophia followed me everywhere she could. She begged to be allowed to go riding with me, and one day I decided I would grant her wish. Until that time I had not really known my pretty baby sister. I cannot say what happened during the hours we rode. Mostly she chattered and peppered me with questions about school and the world beyond Pemberley, since my mother never went to Town and my father made only rare trips on business.

By the time we returned to the house, I began to love her as a brother ought. I started to teach her to read and write, so that we could exchange letters. Sophia was a quick learner, and I received copious letters in her childish hand.

Our parents were happy that I had finally taken notice of my sister and began to share their plans for her education. As with most parents of our social circle, they wished that she would marry well, but they wanted her to find a man who would love her.

My father died three years after I left Cambridge which was a few months after Sophia's twelfth birthday. He had already taught me to manage Pemberley, so I was able to take over running the estate with few problems. However, once I was finished with mourning his loss, I went to London to find a wife. And there I was blessed to meet your mother.

Anne loved Sophia, but I think that my sister was jealous of your mother. She was fourteen by the time of our marriage. At times, I could not believe her bouts of temper and depression, but your grandmother and your mother said that she would grow out of it.

A year after our marriage, the old vicar of Kympton died, and I settled the living on a friend of mine from university. Being the second son of a baron, Croydon chose the church over the military. I had remembered him as a good, steady gentleman. I knew I could trust the flock to his care. As a way of showing my support, our family attended services there for some time.

Sophia began to seek out ways to assist the ministry there. We allowed it because she was so adamant that she needed to help the poor of our area. Once she told me of her shame at realizing that there were people who did not have enough to eat when she refused perfectly good food. We always sent a footman and a maid to accompany her.

When she turned sixteen, Croydon and Sophia came to me with a wish to marry. After I interviewed them both, I allowed that they could become engaged, but they must wait six months to marry. She was upset at first, but he soothed her and told her they must be patient. With their agreement to wait that long, the women of my family began to plan the wedding. It was during this time that we found that your mother was finally with child. We had feared she would never conceive, so we were overcome with joy.

About a month before the wedding, Croydon received word from his brother, who had become the baron the year before at his father's death, asking him to come home because his mother was ill. He never returned because within a fortnight the whole family had died from influenza. The estate and title went to a distant relative, and Sophia received nothing since they were not yet married.

Sophia grieved herself ill, or so we believed until we found out that they had anticipated their wedding vows and that she was with child. I went wild with anger and would have cast her out if your mother had not intervened. I can see now that my rage was actually self-directed, since I felt I could have prevented her ruin if I had allowed them to marry sooner.

For days, I tried to come up with a solution that would save the family name and her reputation. Finally, it was my steward, Paul Wickham, with whom I had shared our dilemma, who provided an answer. He knew of a family of some wealth in the north near the Scottish border who were childless. He and his wife would travel with my sister and stay with her until the babe was delivered. Sophia did not want to give up her child, but we finally convinced her that it was for the best.

The irony of the similarity to Elizabeth's situation was not lost on Darcy. Of course, it was not her fault that she was with child, but her family would suffer the same kind of shame his father had wanted to avoid. He scratched his head as he lifted the pages and read the rest.

From the letters I received from my sister and subsequent interviews with the Wickhams, Sophia was not well during her confinement. In fact, they were forced to hire a nurse who stayed with her for the last few weeks before the birth.

To our shock and grief, we received word that Sophia had delivered early and had died of birth fever soon after. The babe was sickly at first, but Mrs. Wickham stayed with him, seeing to his every need so that he finally grew strong enough to take to the couple they had arranged to adopt the baby. However, by that time, Mrs. Wickham's bond with the infant was so great that she pleaded with her husband to let her keep him. Mr. Wickham had also grown to care for the boy, so he petitioned me to be allowed to keep the baby and to bring him back as their own.

I granted their request both for their sakes, as well as mine. The baby was my nephew after all. And my guilt at sending Sophia away only to die so far from her home was my biggest reason for becoming his godfather. You know how his adoptive parents and I overlooked his behaviour. Yes, I understand that you thought I did not see his small acts of mischief as a child or his greater misconduct as a young man. Where he is concerned, I admit I am weak. I can only offer a sense of guilt that he would never be acknowledged as a member of the Darcy family as my flimsy excuse.

For all of this, I ask your forgiveness. By now you know my bequest to George of the living at Kympton. I am uncertain as to his ability to follow in the footsteps of his late father, but I am confident in your discernment when the time comes. I am sure you will give him a monetary settlement in lieu of the living, if need be.

You may wonder why I chose this time to have this letter put into your hands. I can only say that I wanted to have a hand in advising you about marriage, even if from the grave. I also felt the need to try to explain my actions regarding my godson. I suppose I should have written this in two separate letters, but I feared that should you know the truth immediately after my death, you would feel obligated to treat George differently because he is family. I know you have already paid off the debts he accumulated at Cambridge because of his connection to the family, and you did not want me to know of his folly. The Wickhams and I spoiled him. It was a disservice to him. I pray even now that he has turned out better than I feared he would.

Lastly, I must say to you that if you truly love the lady you are to marry, never allow a disagreement, society's whims, or anything else to come between you. Love her more than yourself, and you will be happy all your days.

Take care of your sister. I would not wish for her to know what I have shared with you, but I will leave that to your discretion.
God bless you, my son.
Your loving father,
George Andrew Darcy

Darcy laid the papers on his lap. Stunned by the contents of his father's letter, he sat and stared at nothing for a long time. Once his mind could begin to grasp what had been laid out before him, one fact stood out above all the rest. Like it or not, Wickham was his cousin, and because of that, the child that Elizabeth carried was already a Darcy by blood. It did not matter if she bore a boy or a girl.

Darcy lifted the papers and moved to the fireplace. After a quick rereading of the contents, he tossed the pages into the flames. This knowledge could not be allowed to find its way into the wrong hands. He would tell Elizabeth - he must tell her because nothing could be permitted to come between them. No one else could ever know about this. Watching the flames merrily consume the paper, he vowed to himself that he would always count the baby she carried as his own. He determined to never treat it with more or less regard than any other children they might have.

He bent to jab at the charred bits of paper in order to be sure they were all burned. Replacing the poker, Darcy rose and so did his confidence. He wished that he did not have to wait for the contracts. However, he did have something else to do before he returned to Elizabeth.

Moving to the shelves behind his desk, Darcy slid his hand down the vertical side of one of the shelves until he felt a slight indentation. With a quick push and pull, the section of the bookcase moved soundlessly out from the wall. Behind that part of the shelving was a hidden safe. Darcy took no time in working the combination and opening the door with a quiet click. In one of the many compartments, he found the jewellery casket he had wanted.

Darcy laid the ornate case on his desk and opened it. Inside, jewels and bright metals sparkled. He rearranged a few of the pieces while he looked for the ones he wanted, and after finding them, he removed a ring box and a smaller case covered in ruby satin. Placing the two packages on the desk before him, Darcy quickly returned the larger casket to the safe before locking it and restoring the bookshelf back to its proper place.

First, he took up the smaller box and pushed the button that popped open the lid. His beloved mother had worn this ring as had her mother before her. The circle of intricately designed filigree held a deep red garnet surrounded by tiny perfectly matched seed pearls. For a moment, he imagined it gracing Elizabeth's small hand. The thought thrilled him.

Setting down the ring box and turning to the satin covered case, he lifted the lid. Inside lay a three-strand pearl necklace with a pendant comprised of a teardrop shaped pearl surrounded by small garnets with matching earrings. Once, when Darcy had allowed his fancy to run away with him, he had pictured Elizabeth wearing this particular set on their wedding day. He remembered fingering the large drop when he was a child. His mother had always worn it to the balls held at Pemberley, and on one such evening, she had come to the nursery to say good night. He had begged to look at the pretty jewellery. His mother allowed him to climb onto a chair in order for him to be close enough to see it since she did not want to wrinkle her gown by lifting him. Recalling the weight and the cool smoothness of the piece, he smiled. Perhaps one of his children would one day ask for the same privilege.

Darcy replaced the lid and picked up both boxes. He would see that they were safely packed to take with him on the morrow. Ringing for Peters, he wished once again that he did not have to stay in Town another minute.

At the knock at the study door, he bade his man enter. "I must bring these with me. Make certain that whatever we carry them in seems innocuous."

"Yes, sir, I shall see to it." Peters bowed and took the jewellery from the room.

Now all he had to do was endure the time away from his beloved Elizabeth.

It was during this moment of longing for Elizabeth that a nagging voice in his head accused him of presumption. How could he devise all these plans for marriage and future children when he had not even asked for her hand? Would all of his plans be for naught? Perhaps despite Elizabeth's forgiveness of his disdainful and insulting remarks at the Meryton assembly, she would not have him. It was also conceivable that she would not want to keep the child because of who its father was.

A piercing pain stabbed his heart at the thought that Elizabeth might never be his or that the child for whom he had only recently come to care might be lost to him as well. He staggered to a chair and dropped heavily into it. After a few minutes of dark and agonizing thoughts, Darcy rubbed viciously at his stinging eyes and sat straighter. He would not give up until all hope was gone. Begging God's mercy in the matter once again, he moved back to his desk to see if there was anything amongst the correspondence there that needed his attention.

Within a half hour, he finished and left his office for his chambers. Whether he wished it or not, Darcy knew that his staff would have arranged a supper for him in the small dining parlour. He and Georgiana preferred the smaller room for family meals or when they were not entertaining many guests. So as not to upset the house staff's preparations, he dressed for dinner and ate the delicious fare in silence.

Darcy retired to his room shortly after dinner, prepared to read a book he had forgotten to bring with him to Hertfordshire, but the tome held no interest for him that night. His heart and mind were too full of Elizabeth and their child. He smiled sheepishly as he comprehended how fully he had accepted her babe as his own. How had it happened so quickly? It was a rather miraculous thing, and he would be forever grateful to the Lord for it, even if events did not proceed as he wished.

CHAPTER THIRTEEN

Mr. Bingley arrived at Longbourn early that afternoon. As he was shown into the parlour, Jane and her mother greeted him warmly. On the other hand, Elizabeth kept her eyes upon the door. She had expected Mr. Darcy to accompany his friend, as had been his wont and could not understand what was keeping him outside.

Seeing where Elizabeth's attention was focused, Mr. Bingley correctly surmised her questioning thoughts. "I am sorry, ladies. I have been remiss in my assigned duty. Mr. Darcy directed me to extend his apologies and to explain that urgent business has called him to Town. He told me that he would return tomorrow or the day after at the latest."

Mrs. Bennet frowned as she wondered if her second daughter had done something to cause Mr. Darcy to reconsider his interest in Elizabeth. "I hope that all is well with Miss Darcy," she exclaimed, louder than need be.

"Darcy told me that all is well, but the business was something that only he could handle," Bingley smiled confidently. "I suppose it is one of the many issues that will come up when one has such a thriving estate. And with winter so close at hand, I am sure that Pemberley has many such issues that need his attention."

With such reassurances, Mrs. Bennet turned quickly to discuss Bingley and Jane's upcoming wedding with no further thought of Mr. Darcy. Elizabeth, on the other hand, paled with concern. She tried not to think that she had somehow driven him away. Of course, he was not hers in the first place, but she had come to depend upon his presence and support. She strongly hoped it would be as Mr. Bingley said, and Mr. Darcy would return to the neighbourhood soon.

Elizabeth sat near the window and picked up her needlework. At the moment, her project consisted of several men's linen handkerchiefs. Her plan, after hemming them, was to embroider her father's and her uncle's initials upon them as Christmas gifts. The thought came to her that she should consider making some for her future brothers. Pleased to see that she had enough of the material for two or three more, she managed to finish blind hemming several before Mr. Bingley returned to Netherfield to dress and return for the evening meal with the Bennets

An hour after Mr. Bingley's departure, her mother rejoiced once again that her most beautiful daughter had been noticed by the handsome Mr. Bingley. She regaled Jane with all her desires for her eldest's nuptials. Insisting that the wedding and its following breakfast must be worthy of such a rich and agreeable young man, Mrs. Bennet talked on and on about lace and flowers, the fine wine and food that she planned to procure. Jane tried to interrupt her mother's narration with thoughts and opinions of her own, but Mrs. Bennet did not pay much heed to her eldest's ideas or wants.

After having listened to the rather one-sided discussion for as long as she could tolerate it, Elizabeth interjected, "Mama, I think that Jane should be the one to say how much lace or what her veil should look like. It is her wedding after all."

"Oh, I suppose you are right, if you put it that way," Mrs. Bennet reluctantly conceded with a wave of her hand. "But I am sure that I have had more experience with this sort of thing."

"I am certain that Jane will be pleased for your assistance, but I believe she should have some time to get used to the idea of marriage before she is forced to consider the details." Elizabeth winked at Jane who had joined her by the window.

"Yes, Mama, I would like a little more time before we begin our planning," Jane said calmly. "I thank you for your offer of assistance, but I believe it can wait."

Mrs. Bennet huffed and stomped from the room. She could be heard declaring to Hill in the foyer that she would visit Mrs. Lucas to discuss the many pleasures of last night's ball since her daughters were so disobliging.

"Thank you, Lizzy." Jane gave Elizabeth a brief embrace. "I did wonder if I would ever be able to extract myself from that conversation."

"Mama has no greater pleasure than planning our weddings," Elizabeth said with a sigh. "She must be beside herself at having two to plan."

"Why the sigh, dearest?" Jane inquired softly.

"It is nothing," Elizabeth tried to demur, but when she spied the look her sister gave her, she said, "I do not believe I will ever marry now. I almost wished that I could be the subject of our mother's wedding planning raptures."

"Oh, Lizzy," Jane scolded. "You will marry someday. Why would you not?"

"Jane," Elizabeth whispered, "you know I am damaged goods. No upright gentleman will have me. There is little hope of that." She set aside her basket of work and rose. "Please excuse me, but I find that I am in need of more rest."

With tears of compassion clinging to her lashes, Jane watched her sister leave. Surely Elizabeth was wrong. She had seen for herself the care and solicitude

Mr. Darcy had shown Lizzy the previous night. This was a man on the verge of falling in love, if he had not already taken the plunge. Shaking her head, Jane determined to be optimistic and moved to take up her own embroidery to work on in solitude while it lasted.

Elizabeth slowly plodded up the stairs, her despair draining her energy. As she reached her room, she remembered what Mrs. Parker had suggested. Could it be that the exercise would help ease her emotional pain? With a purpose now in mind, she moved to her little writing desk and extracted paper, pen, and ink. Since she always kept her pens in perfect repair, all she had to do was pull up her chair and begin to write.

At first, the words would not come. She had suppressed the memories for enough time that her mind seemed reluctant to allow them to resurface. However, she was finally able to start recording everything she recalled of the day. To begin with, Elizabeth penned her memories of the day that had been lovely and perfect for the solitary walks she loved. Because of all the pain and terror that had followed, she had forgotten how much she enjoyed herself at the beginning of her ramble that morning. She was surprised to feel herself smile at the recollection.

Pausing in her chronicling, Elizabeth had to take a deep breath. She knew that the next part would not be so pleasant to recall. She dipped her pen into the ink once more and forced herself to continue. It was then that the dam seemed to break, and memories of all sorts flooded through her and onto the paper. Wickham's false charm and flattery, her unease at being alone with the man, her desire to be away, the fear she felt at his sudden grip of her arm to stop her from leaving, the attack itself with its pain and horror, the pain in the back of her head from striking it on the rock, the humiliation that his mocking words had caused as he left her broken and bruised on the ground - they all were finally on pages of tear-stain, blotched paper on her desk.

Elizabeth had no sense of how much time had passed. Her cheeks were wet and her eyes felt swollen as she stared down at what she had written. After blowing her nose, splashing water onto her face, and drying it, she walked to the fireplace. Crumpling each of the pages, she tossed them one by one into the fire, and while watching them burn, she pictured the power the memories of that event had held over her heart and mind go up in smoke. Her heart raced, not in fear this time, but in hope.

Mrs. Parker had been right. The memories had not harmed her in the recalling. Her heart and mind felt free of the fester of the vile deed. She knew that she had not rid herself of what was done to her, but the heaviness was gone. As the last of the paper turned to ash, she straightened her desk by mending her pens, closing the ink pot, and sliding the remaining papers into place.

With her emotional burden far lighter, her body craved sleep. Elizabeth slipped off her shoes, crawled under the counterpane, and fell quickly into a two-hour, refreshing, and dreamless nap.

~*~

The next morning dawned to gloomily cloudy skies, but before the weather could depress his spirits, Darcy received word that his documents would be ready for him by one o'clock. He had no idea how his attorney was able to accomplish such a feat, but he did not question the outcome. After assuring himself that Peters would be ready, he ordered that an early luncheon be prepared, so that he could travel to Mr. Whitton's office by the appointed time.

Although impatience still caused him to pace the time away, his morale was high and his outlook optimistic. Darcy questioned his valet twice that morning to make sure that the jewellery was indeed packed and ready. He did not notice the perceptive looks his man gave him. If he had, he might have been embarrassed at how easily and how soon Peters had perceived the growing affection Darcy was experiencing for Miss Elizabeth Bennet.

The clock had just struck two when Darcy and his valet quit Darcy House. He patted the packet of legal papers in his coat pocket as they rode through the streets of London. Checking another pocket, he touched the bump the small ring box made there. He had finally taken it back from Peters' care. Somehow, marrying Elizabeth seemed to be more of a possibility with his mother's ring carefully stowed on his own person.

They arrived at Netherfield just before darkness fell. Bingley and the Hursts welcomed Darcy back. After he changed from his travelling clothes, he joined the family in the sitting room.

"I trust your business was dealt with successfully, Darcy?" Bingley asked while pouring them both a glass of wine.

"Yes, indeed, it was." Darcy could not help but smile. "I was able to conclude the matter expeditiously and to my complete satisfaction."

Darcy sipped the excellent wine for a few moments before his desire to discover how Elizabeth fared overcame his reticence to show interest in her. "Have you visited Longbourn since the ball?"

The Hursts' chuckles and Bingley's love-struck grin spoke volumes. "Indeed, I dined with them last evening."

"How did you find the family?"

"All were well, though Miss Elizabeth seemed a bit out of spirits," Bingley said absently. "Perhaps she has not fully recovered from her mishap."

Darcy wanted to hope that she missed him and, thus, she was out of sorts for that reason. However, the likelihood was that pregnancy was causing changes in her mood, especially if she was aware of her condition. He chafed at having to stay at Netherfield that evening. More than anything, Darcy wanted to rush to her and propose on the spot. So involved was he in his own musings, he nearly missed his friend's next words.

"I suppose it is a little soon to entertain after a ball. Regardless, I invited the Bennets to play cards and to partake of refreshments this evening. Mrs. Bennet was not sure that Mr. Bennet would be able to come, but she accepted on behalf of herself and her daughters." Seeing the small frown on Darcy's face, Bingley interjected, "Perhaps you would rather not be in company after such a quick journey. I could send word that tomorrow would be a better time."

"I have no objection." He paused to consider his words carefully before he continued, "However, you might send word of my return. They might not wish to share your company with me."

"Nonsense, Darcy." Charles wondered why he would say such a thing. "I told them of the very likelihood of your return today, and no one objected. Mrs. Bennet even remarked that she would be happy to see you again."

Inwardly, Darcy still had hopes for a positive reception by Elizabeth. By this time, they had reached a trust, a friendship of sorts. However, if she was aware of her condition, what might her state of mind be? Likely she would find an excuse to stay at Longbourn. He made up his mind that if she did not come to Netherfield, he would make his excuses and ride over to Longbourn and ask Mr. Bennet for permission to speak with her.

~*~

Elizabeth stood at the door, watching her mother and sisters enter their carriage. She had finally convinced Mrs. Bennet that she was not well enough to attend the card party. Her mother's comment that she would miss seeing Mr. Darcy puzzled her. Did her mother think that he had an interest in her, one such as Mr. Bingley had for Jane? She almost laughed, but the very impossibility of the thought brought tears to her eyes instead.

A shuddering sob escaped before she could quell it. Elizabeth hurried up to her room so that her father or the servants would not see her cry. Once she closed her door behind her, she sank onto the bed and wept as she recalled the events of the morning.

Her sleep had been a restless one, but Elizabeth awoke at her usual hour. When she noticed that the clouds were quite dark, she frowned. Rain meant that she would likely be unable to even try out her new resolve to walk a bit farther each day to conquer her irrational fear.

Sighing heavily, Elizabeth threw back the covers and sat up on the edge of the bed. It was then that a wave of nausea hit her. She barely made it to the chamber pot before she was sick. She was forced to sit on the floor with the pot between her knees while she continued to vomit. Finally, just as she felt the sickness abate, there was a knock on her door.

"Who is it?" she called out weakly.

"Sarah, miss," was the muffled answer.

"Come in." Elizabeth struggled to rise to her feet, but she was having difficulty.

As soon as Sarah entered, she understood the situation. "Oh, Miss Elizabeth, let me help you."

After assisting Elizabeth back to the bed, Sarah poured her a glass of water and brought it and the washbasin to where Elizabeth lay and helped her lift her head. "Rinse your mouth and spit it into the bowl," the maid instructed.

Once Elizabeth indicated that her mouth felt clean, Sarah encouraged her to slowly take sips from the glass while the maid went to the kitchen for some toast.

"Please promise you will stay abed," Sarah insisted. "I will not be long."

Elizabeth nodded her assent and Sarah left the room. Setting the glass on the nightstand, she rested her head back against the pillows while trying to understand why she was so ill. Had she eaten some spoilt food? It was possible that the rest of her family was experiencing the same malady this morning. Even now, she felt small twinges of nausea roll over her. She wanted to cry out in frustration. If she was indeed ill, she would need to forgo the card party at Netherfield. She would miss seeing Mr. Darcy. She had begun to wonder why that very thought brought her pain when Sarah knocked briefly and re-entered her room.

Sarah set a tray on the nightstand. "Please try to eat some of the toast." She offered a small plate which held triangles of toast spread thinly with honey.

With no real desire to eat, Elizabeth nibbled slowly on a piece of the toast. When she had finished the first, Sarah pressed her to eat another until soon the plate was empty, and her stomach had clearly settled. Sitting up higher in her bed, she drank from the cup Sarah offered.

Elizabeth was amazed at how much better she felt. "Thank you, Sarah," she said full of gratitude. "I do not understand why I was so ill."

Something in Sarah's expression caused her to ask, "What is it, Sarah? Do you know what is wrong with me?"

Sarah lowered her eyes to the floor and did not speak for several moments as if she was gathering her thoughts. When she finally lifted her gaze to Elizabeth's, compassion radiated from her eyes. She moved closer to the bed and sat beside Elizabeth without asking leave to do so and took one of her hands. "Nothing is actually wrong. But, Miss Elizabeth, I believe you will not be happy at what I must tell you."

Apprehension grabbed at Elizabeth's heart, making it race madly. "Please tell me, Sarah," she insisted.

"All of the signs suggest that you are with child," Sarah answered gravely.

"With child!" Elizabeth's screech filled the room as she pulled her hand free.

"Hush now, Miss Elizabeth!" Sarah commanded as she grasped her shoulders and shook her gently. "You would not want your family to learn of this."

Instantly Elizabeth froze, her hands flying to her mouth. Indeed, her family must never know. How could she bear to bring this scandal on her beloved family? It could ruin the happiness of Jane and Mary and any future chances of marriage for Kitty and Lydia.

"What am I to do?" she whispered in quiet desperation. "What am I to do?"

Sarah looked as if she had something to say but only wrapped her arms around her young mistress and crooned, "It will be well. You shall see. It will be well."

Elizabeth wanted to cling to the hope offered by Sarah's words, but she could not believe it. As tears began to flow, she buried her face against her maid's shoulder and sobbed. Several moments passed before she could take control of herself. Once she had, she wiped at her eyes and met Sarah's eyes. "I shall have to leave Longbourn. I will be forever estranged from my family. It is too much. How shall I bear it?"

"Miss Elizabeth!" Sarah scolded quietly. "There are other choices aside from exile. At this moment, you must bring yourself under better regulation, especially if you are to keep this from your family. Now you must wash your face, let me fix your hair, and help you dress."

When Sarah saw Elizabeth shake her head, she said sternly, "If you love your family, you will gather your wits and show none of your feelings about this. I am sure that Miss Jane will not be fooled, but you must not betray your secret, at least not until you have had time to think about your options. You still have the time to decide what you will do. So unless you want to continue in your grief and self-pity, you will get up and be about your day."

Elizabeth stared up at the young maid, astonished at her audacity, but as she allowed Sarah's words to filter into her grief-fogged mind, she saw the wisdom in what she had said. Elizabeth sat up slowly, feeling as if she had aged years in just minutes. "Please tell me what to do," she begged. "How shall I accomplish what you have told me?"

"Once you are dressed, I shall fetch you a bit of sherry." She paused before she explained, "You must relax a bit and the wine will help you. While I am gone, I suggest that you pray. The Lord knows your innocence in this matter, and I am sure that He will hear and answer you."

The matter-of-fact way Sarah spoke had a calming effect upon Elizabeth's heart and mind. Praying seemed the right thing to do since, at the moment, she needed a miracle to see her way out of her dilemma.

Between the sherry and the prayer, Elizabeth finally felt in control enough to join her family at the breakfast table. No one but Jane seemed to notice the change in Lizzy's demeanour, and she merely asked if she was well and accepted her sister's assurances that nothing was amiss.

Here was one result of the attack that nothing could erase. She could not do away with it with pen and paper. Again, despair tried to move into her heart as her newly won hope fought to remain. For the moment, all she was able to do was to ask the Lord to help her get through that day, especially since she had no desire to think of the future in the light of this new reality that was her life.

Elizabeth managed to make her way through the day without any open display of being upset, but when her mother began to fuss over what the girls were to wear at the Netherfield card party that night, Lizzy pleaded a headache.

"I suppose there is no real reason for you to go since Mr. Darcy has likely not returned," Mrs. Bennet muttered absently to herself.

Blushing bright pink, Elizabeth took to her room. She considered her mother's words as she sat at her window. Did her mother believe that Mr. Darcy wanted to court her? Is that what his attentions to her during the past month had wrought? Knowing her mother as she did, if Mrs. Bennet had gotten it into her head that Mr. Darcy was interested in her second daughter, she might have already begun to speculate on the subject to the neighbours.

First the babe, and now this conjecture about Mr. Darcy! How would she manage to live through it all? She did not know how long she stared unseeing out of the window, but a knock on the door brought her back.

"Come," she called.

Jane entered, carrying a tray with two cups of tea and a plate of biscuits. "I hope you do not mind my interrupting your reverie."

"Of course not, Jane," Elizabeth smiled genuinely.

"How is your headache, Lizzy dear?" Jane's look of concern made Elizabeth feel guilty for the small lie.

"I believe it is a little better."

Jane had set down the tray and offered Elizabeth a cup before she took the other chair and pulled it close to her sister's. "I do not suppose that you will be able to go with us to Netherfield tonight."

After sipping at the steaming tea, Elizabeth shook her head. "I do not think it would be wise. I will try to read if my head will allow and if not, I might impose on Papa to read to me for a short time. Then it will be off to bed early for me. I believe I just need more sleep."

Jane searched her sister's face while Elizabeth worked hard to keep any of her concerns from her expression. Her elder sister lifted the plate and offered Lizzy a treat.

"Thank you," Lizzy said and then teased, "I believe you shall spoil me, and I will come to live with you at Netherfield once you are married, so you can continue that occupation."

Jane laughed as Elizabeth had intended. "Oh, Lizzy, you could never be spoilt, and I would love for you to live with us once we are married. Of course, I would have to confer with Charles, but..."

"Oh no, Jane, I was only teasing. I would never dream of imposing upon your privacy at such a time." She smiled as genuinely as she could. "Besides, three miles is not too far. I plan to be back at traversing over hill and dale soon, no matter the weather. You shall eventually lose your shock at my having petticoats six inches deep in mud when I visit you."

"You will always be a welcome visitor in our home. I do not have to confer with Charles to tell you that." Jane leaned close and gave her a tight hug. "I love you, dearest sister."

"And I love you."

That evening Elizabeth took her dinner in her room, wanting to forestall any conjecture that she might be well enough to attend the card party after all. When it was time for her mother and sisters to depart, she made her way downstairs.

"Mama, will you please extend my apologies to Mr. Bingley and the Hursts for my absence. Explain that I am sure my headache will be of short duration, and that I will see them again soon."

Mrs. Bennet heaved a sigh. "If I must, but I have decided that you will miss seeing Mr. Darcy since you will not come. Now go to your room so that you will be well when he next visits Longbourn."

As her weeping ebbed, Elizabeth washed her face and blew her nose. In her mirror she saw her red, puffy eyes and blotchy face. She was happy that her family would not see her, for no one would believe that a headache would cause her face to look so wretched.

Elizabeth knew she must try to think of those other options Sarah mentioned that morning, but none came to mind except exile. The Bennets had little family beyond the Phillipses, the Gardiners, and Mr. Collins. She thought she remembered a maiden great-aunt in south-western England, but Elizabeth did not recall if she was still alive. How would she approach this relative if she was alive?

Would she be able to give up the babe she was carrying? At this moment, its existence did not seem real. On the other hand, how could she keep a baby whose father was such a man? It seemed impossible that she could do such a thing, especially since a woman with a child and without a husband would be cast as fallen and her family's reputation would be in ruins.

She sat still for over a half hour, pondering her situation and a painful, lonely future. Beyond tears, Elizabeth could not find the answer or the peace she longingly sought. The sound of a horse on the front lane barely broke her unhappy reverie. Since she knew that it could not be her family returning and likely only someone to see her father, she ignored it. Opening her book, she began to read.

CHAPTER FOURTEEN

The time for the Bennets' arrival had come, and Darcy stood watch at his chamber window. The night sky had cleared of clouds, and the moon bathed the front garden with its cool, silvery light. He could hear the rumble of a carriage coming up the lane and was able to witness the family's exiting of the equipage. When he saw that Elizabeth was not one of the ladies moving up the steps to the house, he quickly called for his man.

"Peters, have the stable saddle Paladin immediately, but do not have him brought to the house. I will come to the yard to fetch him," Darcy ordered brusquely, "and when you return, I shall have a note for you to take to Mr. Bingley. I have a rather important errand to accomplish."

Darcy quickly drafted a note, explaining that he would not be attending the card party after all. He apologized for not taking his leave in person, but as Bingley's guests had already arrived, he felt it most prudent to write out his intentions. Once he finished the missive, Darcy donned gloves and the same coat he had worn on his ride from Town, and while he waited for his valet's return, he checked the pocket to make sure the ring box was still there.

Not wanting his presence to be discovered by the Bennet ladies, he took the back stairs and went out the servants' door. Darcy blessed the moon for its light as he jogged to the stable yard where his horse stood ready for him.

Darcy rode cautiously along the road to Longbourn, all the while trying to puzzle out how he could insure a chance to speak to Elizabeth. Happy for his decision to ask Mr. Bennet for permission to court his daughter, he realized that he might use that fact to gain a private, if chaperoned, audience with her. As had become his habit, he lifted up a prayer for her well-being and wisdom in all his words and actions. Armed with a sense of purpose, he made good time reaching his destination.

Longbourn's butler welcomed him and ushered him into Mr. Bennet's library after a brief knock.

"Mr. Darcy, I did not expect to see you here tonight," Mr. Bennet said as he rose from his favourite chair. "I hope that nothing is wrong."

"No, all is well, and I do apologize for coming here uninvited, but I have a request of you and thought this a good time to find you alone."

"Ah, you know of Mrs. Bennet's and my daughters' presence at Netherfield." Mr. Bennet gestured to a chair and sat back down. "What can I do for you, sir?"

Now that the time had come to speak, Darcy lost the words. He took a deep breath to calm himself before he began, "You gave me leave to court Miss Elizabeth." At Bennet's nod, he continued, "I fully intend to continue the courtship, but I would like to speak to her alone. I ask that you grant me that unusual privilege."

Mr. Bennet's face creased into a frown. "I am not sure I should allow this."

"For your comfort's sake, I have no objection if you ask the maid Sarah to chaperone us." Darcy added, "I trust her discretion."

"It seems that you have thought this through." Mr. Bennet chuckled. "Very well, I will give you some time with my Lizzy. See to it that you do not abuse the privilege."

"Yes, sir," Darcy said solemnly as he nodded his head.

Mr. Bennet rose and escorted Darcy to the parlour. "Please make yourself comfortable while I summon Sarah and ask her to have Elizabeth come down."

Excusing himself, Mr. Bennet left the parlour to call the maid. Once Sarah arrived, he explained what he wished for her to do. She hastened to carry out her master's orders.

~*~

Elizabeth struggled for a time but finally was able to get so caught up in the plot of her book that a knock on the door ten minutes later startled her. "Come," she said absently as she began to read again.

Sarah opened the door and curtseyed. "Miss Elizabeth, your father wishes you to come to the parlour."

Elizabeth set her book on the table and moved to check her appearance in the mirror. She took a few moments to tuck stray curls back into place. The blotches had faded, and her eyes, though still a bit red, did not shout that she had been crying. Taking a deep, steadying breath, she left the room.

Her father met her at the bottom of the stairs. "Lizzy, I hope you are feeling better."

"Thank you, Papa, I am a little," she answered. "You wanted to see me?"

"Yes, come with me into the parlour." He took her arm and gently guided her through the door.

Elizabeth gasped in shock when she saw Mr. Darcy standing in the middle of the room. He bowed politely. She automatically curtseyed in response and waited for an explanation of his presence.

"Mr. Darcy would like a private word with you," Mr. Bennet told her as he nodded to the man not five feet away. Turning to glance toward the doorway behind him, he gestured for Sarah to enter the room. "I have given my permission with the stipulation that your maid shall attend you. Shall I order refreshments?"

Darcy would have rather gotten to the point immediately, but he knew tea might make for a more relaxing atmosphere. "I would enjoy a cup of tea, if it is not too much trouble."

Sarah went to fetch the tea while Mr. Bennet asked about Mr. Darcy's latest trip to London. Usually, Darcy would have given a cursory account, but he found that at the moment making small talk about the roads and weather to and from Town soothed his nerves.

Once Sarah arrived with a tray, Mr. Bennet took his leave. Elizabeth busied herself pouring out the tea, all the while wondering with great curiosity why the gentleman wanted to speak to her. Sarah moved to the corner farthest from the couple and took up the bit of mending she brought with her when she fetched the tea things. She could see that Miss Elizabeth was nervous and not a little uncomfortable, but Mr. Darcy seemed determined to have his say, though he did not seem to know how to start.

After the couple sipped tea in silence for a while, Darcy finally spoke. "You did not attend Bingley's card party."

"As you see," was her quick answer.

"Are you not well, Miss Elizabeth?"

"I admit to having a headache." Her back seemed to stiffen with each question.

Darcy searched her face for a moment. He was taken aback at her short, taciturn replies. He thought he perceived evidence of weeping about her eyes. "Is the headache caused by your previous injuries or something else?"

Just as Elizabeth was about to answer, Darcy caught her gaze with a kindly one of his own and lifted a brow. After a brief self-battle, she slumped against the chair back. "I am perfectly healed from that blow. This headache is of a more recent origin."

Glancing across the room at Sarah, Darcy levelled a questioning look at the maid. At her answering nod, he leaned forward in his chair and rested his arms on his knees. "I am your friend, Miss Elizabeth. I want you to always remember I want only the best for you. I hope I have shown that I can be trusted."

"You have been a true friend, and I do trust you," Elizabeth said as she held his gaze.

"Then I have a solution to what I am sure is the source of your headache," he offered softly.

At first, she did not understand what he meant. He was not even in Meryton when she had found out about her condition. How could he possibly know? It only took a quick glance in Sarah's direction, the maid's refusal to meet her eyes, and the resulting blush to her cheeks to tell her the man's source of this intelligence.

Elizabeth stood abruptly and made to leave the room, but Darcy caught her arm and guided her back to her chair.

"Please do not blame Sarah. I knew that this would be a possibility and wanted to be able to assist you as soon as it might ... should it become a reality." As he spoke, he moved his chair closer to hers.

Unable to meet his eyes, Elizabeth stared at her hands without speaking as embarrassment and shame rolled over her in waves.

Darcy placed his hand over hers and said, "I propose that we marry within a fortnight and retire to Pemberley as soon as we can. Our babe will be born on my estate. My staff is discrete. I will make sure that we have the best midwife and the best physician possible to aid you in the delivery." So settled was his heart and mind to the idea that this child would be his as well as hers, he did not even realize he had used the possessive form of we.

Stunned, Elizabeth looked up and pulled her hands from his. "Marry you? Our babe? Go to Pemberley?" she repeated with incredulity. "I do not grasp your meaning, sir."

"You told me from the first that you wanted to spare your family shame and ruin." He seemed to want his statement confirmed.

"That is true, but I do not see..."

He interrupted her. "I suppose you thought that you would have to leave Longbourn to disappear and never see your family again." The quick paling of her face told her he was correct.

"Another choice might be to find some trusted relative or friend who would allow you to stay with them until you give birth and give the baby to a worthy family for adoption." His heart squeezed in pain at the thought and the pain was echoed in her eyes. "I perceive that neither alternative is any more appealing to you than it is to me."

"But, sir, how is it your concern that you would consider this?" she pleaded. His offer and easy acceptance of her expected child made no sense to her. To hear him speak, one would think that he was the one who caused her to be in this situation.

"When I first was informed, I admit that I was not so sanguine about it as I am now." He picked up one of her hands and stroked the back of it with his thumb. He wanted to tell her that he loved her above all else, but the truth of his affections were too new for him to feel at ease expressing them. "I struggled for quite a while, but I am now convinced of the wisdom of our marrying as soon as possible. I am already in possession of settlement papers, and I will accompany your father to see Mr. Scott to purchase the license."

Again shock and astonishment showed on her face. "You have done all this for a child that is not your own?"

"I would like to share with you every part of my inner journey to my present outlook, but I fear that your excellent father will not give me that much time alone with you. I promise I will tell you as soon as I have another opportunity, but for now, I can promise you that I will never treat this child any differently from any other child we may have."

"I do not know how to respond." Elizabeth felt overwhelmed, but in a small place in her mind, joy wanted to spring forth at this very positive resolution to her horrible dilemma. The soft caressing circles that Mr. Darcy made on the back of her hand were nearly hypnotic.

"I had hoped that you would say 'yes'," he answered. "Then we could go to your father right now. I believe haste is imperative."

Elizabeth sat quietly as her thoughts raced. She could not organize them enough so as to decide what she must do. "I need more time to think about this. I never thought that anything like this would be an option for me. Surely you do not need my answer tonight. Please allow me time to consider this. I am sure that there are things I might want to ask you about this…proposal of yours."

The fact that she had not rejected him outright made it possible for him to accede to her wish. "I would rather not wait, but I know I have overwhelmed you with this sudden offer. I shall return for your answer in the morning the day after tomorrow. I promise to do my best to answer any questions you may have. I will come with Bingley, as I am sure he will have no objection to a visit at Longbourn." Retaining her hand, he stood. "Do not be concerned if it should rain. Bingley and I shall arrive by carriage if it does."

Elizabeth got shakily to her feet and tried unsuccessfully to remove her hand from his. "I am stunned, sir, by your kind offer, and I promise to give it all due consideration. Thank you for your patience, Mr. Darcy."

Holding her gaze, he lifted her hand to his lips. "I will pray that God gives you the right answer."

As his lips grazed the bare skin of her hand, Elizabeth trembled at the new sensation. The pleasant warmth enveloped her like an embrace. It seemed somehow impossible that such a simple gesture could affect her so much.

Darcy moved toward the door. The ingrained habit of courtesy forced Elizabeth to accompany him to the foyer to see him out.

Mr. Bennet peered out of his book room. "Ah, you are leaving us so soon, Mr. Darcy?"

"I fear I must," Darcy bowed as he answered. His mind was in turmoil. Would she accept his offer? He gathered and used every method he had ever learned to cover his roiling emotions. "I would not want to cause a recurrence of Miss Elizabeth's headache. Thank you, sir, for the time. If I may, I shall call again soon."

"Indeed, sir," Mr. Bennet replied with a smirk. "You are most welcome to call. Is he not, Lizzy?"

"Of course, Papa." Her father's knowing look and accompanying smile mortified her, and her face reddened. "Good night, Mr. Darcy. Have a safe journey back to Netherfield."

Doffing his hat, Darcy bowed once more and left the house.

Elizabeth turned to go but was stopped by her father's voice. "Do you have something to share with me, Lizzy?"

"I do not know what you mean, Papa," she replied, trying to sound nonchalant.

"Did he speak to you of anything of import?"

"I need a little time to think about what we discussed." It was the truth. Likely she would not sleep much this night.

Mr. Bennet searched his daughter's face before he smiled in the indulgent way he always did with Elizabeth. "Very well, Lizzy, but do not make the gentleman wait over long for your answer." After kissing her on the cheek, he went back into his library and closed the door.

Elizabeth made her way upstairs to her bedroom in a daze. Mr. Darcy had proposed to her! Was it truly possible he had done so, or was this some bizarre dream? She had not noticed that Sarah had followed her until the maid kept her from closing the door behind her.

"Miss Elizabeth," Sarah said softly as she stood in the doorway. "May I speak to you a moment?"

"Come in, but close the door." Elizabeth sat heavily on her bed. "What is on your mind?"

"Are you well? You seemed upset by what Mr. Darcy said."

"Did you overhear my conversation with Mr. Darcy?"

"I tried not to but I did hear a few words." Sarah stood rigidly in the centre of the room.

"Oh, Sarah, do sit down." Elizabeth motioned to the chair closest to her. "I am not displeased that you might have listened. I want to know what you heard so that I might be sure I understood Mr. Darcy correctly."

"I heard him mention marriage and the child. Did he make you an offer?" she asked breathlessly.

Elizabeth scowled and puffed out a breath. "It would appear that Mr. Darcy of Pemberley wants to marry me and raise the child as his own.' She rubbed her eyes and scowled again. "How is it that he would want to marry me and agree to say that the child is his?"

"Could it be that he loves you?" Sarah ventured softly. "He has treated you in a way which a person rarely sees a man do unless he is in love."

Laughing mirthlessly, Elizabeth shook her head. "Impossible. I am not his equal in social status, nor do I have a fortune. His family will not accept me, I am sure."

"Miss Elizabeth," Sarah put in gently, "you must think about everything he said. I did hear you tell him you would. I will leave you to it." She touched her mistress's shoulder lightly before she stood to leave. "I will bring you some of my special tea if you would like. After I bring it, I will help you dress for bed."

Elizabeth barely noticed the maid leave or when she came back. She woodenly submitted to Sarah's assistance with her clothing. Once she was wrapped in her warmest robe, she absently sipped Sarah's herbal concoction. Once she had finished, the young maid removed the tray, and with a "Do get some rest, Miss Elizabeth," she left Lizzy's room.

"Mr. Darcy proposed to me," Elizabeth said into the empty room. A flood of disbelief wanted to crash over her, but she knew it was so. The biggest question in her mind was "Why?" She puzzled over the question for quite some time before the futility of it became apparent to her. That would have to wait until she talked once again to Mr. Darcy.

Instead, she should be pondering the nature of her response, but how could she do it justice without having her first question answered? As Elizabeth put more thought into it, she discovered more questions came to her mind. How could he call the child she carried "our babe"? Had he considered the lowness of her connections and lack of dowry? What would his family think of their marriage? Would not the *ton* look down upon their union, especially with a child born so soon after the wedding? All of the queries required Mr. Darcy's presence, so they could not be answered now.

Elizabeth then asked herself a few questions. *Would I marry him if he loved me, and the baby did not exist? What are my feelings towards the man? Was it possible to endure the shadow that would be cast upon their characters because of an apparent anticipation of their wedding vows?* Here were things she could ponder and find at least some clarification of her own thoughts and feelings.

Knowing that she had trusted Mr. Darcy to keep such a horrendous secret and had found him to be worthy of her faith in him gave her the first clue to his value as a husband. His presence had always afforded her a great sense of peace and safety unlike that of any other person, even her beloved Jane. Had he not made sure that the vile man who attacked her was dealt with in a timely manner? The incident at the Netherfield ball had shown his discernment and care when he made sure that she would not be forced into dancing with a man who frightened her, even if that man was innocent of any wrongdoing. Never once had he upbraided her for the irrational fear that often gripped her. As she listed more of the positive attributes of the gentleman, Elizabeth became aware that not only had her feelings gone from her initial dislike to friendly regard, but it had moved into a deeper and more profound emotion, not unlike love.

She started at the place her thoughts had taken her. Did she love Mr. Darcy? Had she fallen into that state unaware? Elizabeth reviewed in her mind all of her interactions with him and found that there were many signs of her deepening regard that had escaped her notice at the time. Even without the panic that plagued her, she knew that her trust in his character and protection was not reasonable without a deep affection. Also, her responses to his touch bore no resemblance to what she experienced with other men. The two most memorable were his kiss to her hand and the touch of his thumb on the back of her hand that very evening.

Elizabeth wished that he could have explained himself instead of leaving her to wonder about his motives. Her speculations had only netted her one bit of information. She had very likely fallen in love with Mr. Darcy. The idea did not dismay her; in fact, it filled her with excitement and anticipation.

Having no doubt that her whole family would welcome the news of a betrothal between her and Mr. Darcy, Elizabeth wondered about his family and friends. They would likely object to a country upstart, and consider that she had finagled a proposal from such a wealthy and well-bred gentleman. She might find herself shunned by those close to him. If he loved her and had no objections to her status or connections, she decided that she could weather the deprivation of his family's company very well.

Just as Elizabeth rubbed at gritty, tired eyes, she heard her youngest sisters' laughter as they ascended the stairs, and her mother's high pitched exultation at the fine welcome they received, and how devoted Mr. Bingley continued to be toward Jane. She quickly blew out her candle, since she was in no mood to listen to Mrs. Bennet's retelling of the night's entertainment. There would be enough time for that on the morrow.

Weariness from the day's disclosures made itself known to her, so that Elizabeth slipped under the blankets and burrowed into her pillow. She had first thought that she would not sleep after hearing Mr. Darcy's offer, but as she closed her eyes, a contented peace flowed over her and she fell easily into a restful slumber.

CHAPTER FIFTEEN

Darcy slipped from his horse and handed the reins to the stable hand. Moving quickly in the shadows, he found the servants' entrance and entered. A young scullery maid made to scream when she saw him, but he held up his hand. "Do not be alarmed. I came this way to avoid disturbing Mr. Bingley and his guests."

Once the girl heard Darcy's voice, she calmed and dipped a curtsey. "Aye, sir."

Reaching into his pocket, Darcy found two coins and tossed them to her. "I hope you will not reveal my unorthodox entry into the house."

The maid shook her head vigorously and slipped the money into her apron pocket while not quite hiding a pleased smile.

Darcy stepped quickly to the back stairs and hastened up them. As he reached his room, he could hear the sound of voices filtering up from the game room, which was situated near the main staircase. Once inside his room, he threw off his jacket and waistcoat and poured a glass of brandy from the decanter that Peters always kept filled for his use before bed. He swirled the amber liquid around in the snifter. The glint of the light flashing off the wine reminded him of Elizabeth's eyes when they sparked with humour.

Sitting in the comfortable chair by the fire, Darcy sipped contemplatively at the brandy. It warmed as it slid down his throat. As the alcohol did its work, he relaxed, and he recalled the scene in the parlour at Longbourn. He took heart that she did not reject him outright, but she did not seem inclined to accept. Indeed, she seemed incredulous that he would ask for her hand.

When he had first seen her walk into the room and saw her pale cheeks and red rimmed eyes, Darcy had wanted no more than to take her into his arms and whisk her away to Pemberley. Only his deep sense of what was right and her father's presence had held him back from it.

He swallowed the last of his brandy and bowed his head. With great feeling and deep sincerity, Darcy poured out his heart in prayer, begging the merciful

Lord for favour in Elizabeth's eyes. "Please grant that she might come to love me. I pledge that I will love her all of the days Thou might see fit to give us together."

He swallowed hard against the painful lump in his throat and added with less fervour but the same sincerity, "Not my will, but Thine, be done."

A gentle touch of peace came upon him. Darcy knew that the prayer would be answered, but he did not know what the outcome would be.

As Darcy stared into the fire, he thought of the way Elizabeth's hand had felt in his and of her skin's velvety softness. Even now, the memory of its warmth seemed to flow into him as it had when he held it in his. He was surprised that she had allowed the liberty, but she had been likely overwhelmed by his proposal.

After a few minutes in this pleasant reverie, Darcy decided that he must put thoughts of her lovely attributes from his mind for the moment and consider her words about what his relatives' reaction would be to her family connections. During his battle with himself, he had not pondered how they would respond to his announcement.

Georgiana and Richard, he had no doubt, would support his decision wholeheartedly. He was certain that with time and exposure to Elizabeth's charms his aunt and uncle, Lord and Lady Matlock, would learn to value her, despite her low connections.

It was his other aunt, Lady Catherine de Bourgh, who would be unbending in her opposition to the match, since she had always harboured designs that he would marry her daughter, Anne. His cousin was of a sickly constitution and had never stood up to her mother in anything. He knew she did not seem to hold him in any particular regard, other than as a cousin, but she would have likely married him on her mother's demand. Given Anne's acquiescence to her mother's wishes, being wed to her would be like being wed to his aunt. The very thought of it made him cringe with abhorrence.

He had no doubt that those in his family who mattered to him would be the ones he could count upon to support him in his choice and to love Elizabeth as one of their own.

As to whether he would suffer any reproof or snubbing from the *ton* upon his marrying Elizabeth, Darcy nearly laughed at how little society's applause or criticism would affect him. If he had his way and she became his wife, nothing that people so wholly unconnected to himself could do would cause him even the smallest of bit distress. He would have such great reasons for happiness that he would never have cause to repine.

It occurred to him that it was a blessing that Georgiana was still too young to come out. When in a few years time, that event did happen, society would have found something else about which to titter and gossip. Therefore, his marriage to Elizabeth would have little negative impact upon his sister, and he was certain that Georgiana would greatly benefit from spending time with Elizabeth.

Darcy knew that he had a great deal to share with Elizabeth when he saw her again. There was one thing he needed to endure until then, and that was the whole of this night and the four and twenty hours after. He decided to make an early night of it after trying to read for a while.

~*~

Elizabeth awoke once more to a queasy stomach, but she stayed in bed, hoping that if she remained quiet and still, the nausea would pass. She had thought to leave a glass of water on the bed side stand the previous evening. Reaching for it, she raised her head a bit to sip at the water. The drink did nothing to improve her upset stomach, so she put her head back on the pillow.

She lay there trying to reason how she could see to another pressing need that required her to get up, but the solution did not come to her. Elizabeth had almost resigned herself to being sick once more when there was a knock and Sarah entered with a tray.

"Good morning, Miss Elizabeth," Sarah greeted her, as she moved the glass from the nightstand and set the tray. "I brought you some soda bread. I told Cook that it was a new favourite of yours, and that it would help you keep your headaches at bay if you had some first thing in the morning. I know that it was a falsehood, but I believe that it was for the best that I tell her thus. After all, it will soon become a favourite since it will help you in the mornings. Please eat some now, as your family is beginning to move about. Unless you wish to spend another day pleading a headache, you should have breakfast with the rest of the family."

"Thank you for your assistance, and I shall comply for that very reason." She picked up a piece of the bread and ate it slowly but determinedly. Once Elizabeth had finished the slice, she drank the tea Sarah had brought as well. Sitting up slowly, she was happy to find that once more the sickness had abated.

After Elizabeth used the chamber pot, she dressed with Sarah's help and was in the breakfast room in time to greet her father.

"You look well this morning, my little Lizzy." Her father smiled fondly at her when she kissed his cheek.

"Thank you, Papa, I do feel better," she replied as she took her place at the table. "How are you today?"

"I am well though I may have to use your excuse of a headache in order to escape to my library if your mother waxes too eloquently about last night's card party," teased Mr. Bennet.

"I did not use a headache as an excuse, Papa," she protested.

"I am quite aware that you were truly unwell, but a headache can be an elegant pretext to evade an unpleasant experience and much simpler than nerves."

Elizabeth laughed at her father's teasing, which had been her father's object. She opened her mouth to respond with a jest of her own when Mrs. Bennet and Jane entered the room.

"Oh, Lizzy, I am glad to see you here this morning," her mother rejoiced. "I want you to be well enough to receive callers today. I am sure that since Mr. Bingley mentioned he might ride over to Longbourn to see Jane, a certain other gentleman might decide to visit us as well."

"My dear Mrs. Bennet," Her husband quipped. "Why would Jane desire two gentlemen to call on her? I would have thought that now that she is engaged to Bingley, she would seek to discourage other suitors."

"Other suitors?" Mrs. Bennet objected in a high pitched voice. "What other suitors?" Finally she saw the amused grin on her husband's face. "Oh, Mr. Bennet, you do delight in vexing me! You know that I was not talking about other men visiting Jane at all. I meant that Mr. Darcy might very well call when Mr. Bingley does. Since it appears that Lizzy has caught his eye, I say we should do all we can to encourage him."

Mr. Bennet winked quickly at his second daughter before answering his wife, "My dear, I think you may have become greedy because of Jane's success with Mr. Bingley. And I have always had the impression that you disliked Mr. Darcy. I recall that you called him arrogant and disagreeable."

After opening and closing her mouth several times, Mrs. Bennet tried to explain herself. "I admit that I did not like him at first, but he did us such a great service by helping Lizzy after her fall. Also, he has been so attentive as to visit here nearly every day since she recovered." Her eyes brightened as she continued, "And the ball! Who could forget how he danced the first and supper sets with her? No, I will not be gainsaid. I am sure that he will be asking to court Lizzy soon. You just wait, Mr. Bennet. You will see."

Her husband nodded solemnly. "I will take your prediction and the reasoning behind it into consideration." He picked up his cup and drank his tea. *If she only knew,* he thought with glee, *if she only knew.*

To Elizabeth's satisfaction, the rest of the day passed in relative calm. Although her mother would on several occasions talk about how wonderful it would be if Mr. Darcy would seek to court her second daughter, Mrs. Bennet's effusions were more of a distraction than a distress.

Elizabeth worked on her needlework, read her book, and even walked with Jane a little farther down the lane before the fear took hold again. All-in-all, she spent little time thinking about Mr. Darcy or the baby, though neither was far from her mind.

It was not until mid-afternoon when Mr. Bingley called that Elizabeth fretted a bit. Part of her had hoped that Mr. Darcy would come despite his promise to wait until the next day. Bingley suggested a walk into Meryton, but Jane, being cognizant of her sister's fear of going so far from home, proposed that they walk in Longbourn's gardens instead. Her fiancé did not object, since he would be with his beloved in either case.

Elizabeth followed the couple at a discrete distance, thus allowing her sister and Bingley the ability to speak privately while maintaining propriety. Watching the obvious affection between the two, the brief touches, the bright smiles, and the rosy blushes, she felt something akin to envy. If Mr. Darcy were here, she, too, would have a strong arm to lean upon and someone with whom she could share the beauty of the day. Taking herself to task for the unbecoming emotion, she tried to steer her thoughts in a different direction, with only meagre success.

When they finally returned to the house, Elizabeth felt relief. She determined to keep herself busy enough to prevent her thoughts from straying often to the subject that they wanted to attend. Since she could not speak to Mr. Darcy until the morrow, it would not do to dwell upon questions that must wait until that time to be answered.

Mary was just rising from the pianoforte when they entered the parlour. This sight gave Elizabeth the idea to practice a piece that her aunt Gardiner had sent her recently. She went to the cabinet wherein the girls kept their sheet music and found the one she wanted. Moving to the instrument, Lizzy sat down, placed the paper on the stand, and began to play.

Soon she was lost in the lilting melody as her fingers moved across the keys. Elizabeth did not notice that the conversation in the room had quieted as she played. Once she finished the piece, she was completely surprised to hear the enthusiastic applause. Blushing, she nodded her acknowledgement.

"I say, Miss Elizabeth," Bingley exclaimed happily. "You played magnificently, though I am not surprised as I have heard you play before."

Both Jane and Mary complimented her performance, while Mrs. Bennet agreed that it was enjoyable before she turned the conversation to wedding clothes and décor. The same two sisters endured their mother's repetitive statements as to the proper number of dresses for a trousseau, and how they were to obtain enough flowers with which to festoon the church and Longbourn.

Kitty and Lydia entered the conversation when it was hinted that they might acquire more than one new gown, since there were to be two separate weddings. Lively chatter ensued about lace and ribbon.

Lizzy smiled as she watched Mr. Bingley's eyes glass over. She decided to rescue him, so she joined him in the corner of the room to where he had gone to escape the prattling of three Bennets and the attentive, though more quiet, Jane and Mary. He stood gazing at a particular pastoral watercolour that hung there.

"I believe that painting was done by my late, great-aunt Bennet," Elizabeth said quietly as she reached his position.

"It puts me in mind of a bit of woods near my aunt and uncle Bradley's home," he replied.

"That is where your sister has gone, is it not?" she asked politely.

"It is."

"I hope that Miss Bingley is well." She wondered at his unusually curt reply.

"I believe that she is."

"I apologize if I have asked amiss." Elizabeth could see that he was uncomfortable.

Bingley coloured and in a more pleasant tone said, "It is I who should apologize." He lowered his voice. "You see, my sister and I did not part on the best of terms. She insulted Mr. Darcy and said less than kind things about your family. I could not abide it any longer. So this is why I spoke so abruptly just now. I hope you will forgive me."

"Of course, I will forgive you," she whispered. "I am sorry to hear that you and your sister have had a falling out and that our family has had something to do with it."

"Please, Miss Elizabeth." He stopped her. "My sister has become a social snob of the first order. No one in Hertfordshire society was up to her standards. My aunt will help her to see the error of her way of thinking, or she will stay in Scarborough for a very long time."

Seeing that Bingley was becoming uncomfortable with the current topic, Elizabeth changed the subject by asking, "How was Mr. Darcy after his sudden trip to Town?"

Bingley beamed his unspoken thanks as he replied, "Darcy arrived last evening and seemed to have been able to conduct his business efficiently and successfully. He asked me to give his regards to your family and to you specifically. He will be joining me tomorrow morning when I call again."

Just then Jane approached and extended her mother's invitation to stay for supper.

"I am sorry, dearest, but I do not want to leave Darcy to dine alone since I rather neglected him because of the card party." When he saw Jane's consternation, he quickly said, "He was not upset, but he had wanted to rest after his ride from Town in any case."

After a few more minutes of pleasant conversation, Mr. Bingley took his leave. Elizabeth smiled to herself when she saw Jane's valiant effort to keep a placid demeanour before the family once her fiancé had gone. She moved to her sister's side and whispered, "I do believe he will be as forlorn without you as you are without him."

"Oh, Lizzy, please do not tease me so," Jane protested before she dropped her gaze. "I admit I wish he could have stayed longer, but I do not begrudge his duty to his friend."

"Of course, you do not, dearest Jane," Lizzy agreed. "You are too virtuous and unselfish to do so. You certainly are the angel that Mr. Bingley thinks you are."

Jane laughed softly while protesting that she was not angelic. "But I am so very happy, Lizzy. To be loved and to love in return is a wonderful thing. I pray that you will experience the same great blessing."

Elizabeth shook her head slightly at her sister's optimism. However, this time, she did not feel the same negative assurance that she would never marry. How she wished that she could share that Darcy had asked for her hand! She knew she could not until she knew what her own answer would be.

CHAPTER SIXTEEN

The day turned out to be the longest in Darcy's recent memory. During the morning, he wrote letters to his steward to catch up on all of his estate business possible. After lunch, he took a long ride on Paladin, forcing himself to stay to the other side of Netherfield Park. He did not want to be tempted to go to Longbourn since he was determined to give Elizabeth the time he promised, and since Bingley was to call there, he knew that his strength of will might weaken if his friend were to urge him once more to join him.

The Hursts retired to their rooms shortly after dinner, so that Darcy spent the rest of the evening playing billiards with Bingley. Since his mind was not on the game, Bingley beat him.

"I say, Darcy," Bingley teased. "I do not believe I have ever beaten you so soundly before. Are you well?"

"What?" Darcy started from his churning thoughts. "Oh, I beg your pardon, Bingley. I find it difficult to be attentive to the task tonight. Please excuse me, but I think I will retire for the night."

"Wait, Darcy, You cannot leave so early." Bingley poured two snifters of brandy. "At least stay for a while and have a drink with me." He offered one of the glasses to his friend.

"Very well," Darcy said as he took the drink. "But liquor will not make me better company, my friend."

"I merely wanted to share my recollections of my visit to Longbourn." Bingley leaned back and sipped his drink while closely watching his friend's reaction.

Darcy feigned a disinterested air as he inquired, "I hope the Bennets were in good health."

"Oh, yes, everyone seemed to be well indeed. My Jane was lovely, of course, and I must say that Miss Elizabeth looked to have gotten over her headache of last evening." Bingley thought he saw a quick look of interest on Darcy's face before he masked it. "Yes, we even had a few words of conversation while Jane had to attend her mother. Something about trousseaux, I believe."

"Was your conversation of a private nature?" Darcy tried to keep his heart from racing. He was not jealous of his friend, only a bit envious of his chance to talk to Elizabeth when he could not.

"Not particularly," replied Bingley easily. "I merely shared with her some of the reasons why Caroline is not residing here at present."

"I see."

"Miss Elizabeth was saddened to hear of our estrangement, but she did not ask any further questions. I believe that I must have shown my discomfort with the subject since she changed it by asking after you." This time he was certain that he spied a crack in Darcy's reserved façade. "I told her that you would be joining me to call upon Longbourn in the morning."

"I shall certainly enjoy seeing the Bennets again."

Darcy's flat response made Bingley laugh. "Darcy, I am not fooled. I must remind you that I am in love myself and easily see the symptoms in another, especially one as close as you are to me. Admit it, my friend, you are besotted," he demanded.

Without speaking, Darcy made his way to where the brandy decanter stood and refilled his glass. He lacked the patience to swirl the drink properly and thus downed the contents in two long swallows. The heat of the rapidly consumed alcohol nearly brought on a coughing fit. After clearing his throat a few times, he went back to his chair.

"Bingley, I do not feel comfortable with this line of discussion." Darcy paused and caught his friend's gaze. "Please be so kind as to drop the subject for the time being. I may be able to share something with you after tomorrow, but I am unwilling to do so now."

The earnest, pleading look in Darcy's eyes convinced Bingley that he would be wise not to press his friend any further. "Very well, Darcy, but I warn you that if you hurt my future sister, I may have to call you out."

"I can assure you that I have no intention of ever hurting Miss Elizabeth. You have my promise on that," Darcy pledged.

Soon after that conversation, Darcy excused himself to go to bed.

~*~

Elizabeth arose even earlier than was her wont. As she nibbled on the dry soda bread that she now kept in a tin next to her bed, she tried to keep her emotions under regulation. It proved to be a difficult task, since her heart raced at each thought of seeing Mr. Darcy that morning. Once her stomach was settled, she rang for Sarah and prepared to meet the day.

Only her father was present at the table because of the early hour. He smiled up at her. "You look better each day. It gladdens this old man's heart to see you well again."

"Thank you, Papa," she said as she kissed his forehead. "You are looking well yourself."

He chuckled. "I suppose that I am finally becoming immune to talk of lace, gowns, and trousseaux. I admit that I found I even had an opinion about some of the proposed dishes being served at Jane's wedding breakfast. Fortunately, I was able to keep that opinion to myself."

Elizabeth shared in her father's laughter, enjoying the rare time alone with him. She inquired about the new book he had been reading and, thus, began a discussion of current philosophers versus classic ones. Later, as the rest of the family drifted into breakfast, the conversation became more generally focused on weddings, so that Lizzy participated and listened less.

Jane, who had taken her usual place next to Elizabeth, asked, "Are you well this morning?"

"I am," she replied with a smile, "so much so that I hope that the weather will hold, for I would like to spend some time outside."

A half hour after the family finished breakfast, Bingley and Darcy arrived. Mrs. Bennet was ecstatic in her welcome, offering to have refreshments and tea served as soon as everyone sat down in the parlour.

"Madam, as much as we appreciate the kind offer," Bingley interrupted her exuberance, "Mr. Darcy and I would like to take advantage of the lovely weather to walk out with Miss Bennet and any of her sisters who would care to join us."

Mrs. Bennet's mind began to calculate how to manoeuvre the situation to the best matchmaking benefit. "I am sure that Jane and Lizzy will be happy to accompany you, but I have plans for my younger girls."

After admonishing her two eldest daughters to dress warmly, Mrs. Bennet fairly pushed the four young people out the door, and once it was closed behind them, she smiled in smug satisfaction.

After asking after the ladies' preference, the four walked toward Oakham Mount. As Bingley and Jane walked ahead, Darcy, with Elizabeth on his arm, kept his steps slow, so that soon the betrothed couple outdistanced them. They moved thusly in silence until the gentleman spoke. "Miss Elizabeth, I must say that yesterday was one of the longest days of my life. I do not say this to press you to pity me. On the contrary, I speak of it in the hopes you will understand that I was impatient to see you again. I do hope that I will be able to answer any questions you might have to your satisfaction, and afterwards, you will find it in your heart to be favourably inclined toward me." His eyes held only warmth and patience as he gazed into hers.

Elizabeth swallowed hard against the lump that wanted to form in her throat. His tender gaze helped her grasp the courage she needed to begin. "Thank you, sir. The first question I have is: why do you want to marry me?"

Darcy stopped and turned to face her, taking both of her hands in his. Before he spoke, he glanced up the road at his friend and his fiancée. Seeing they were completely preoccupied with each other, he said simply, "I have come to ardently admire and love you."

On the night Mr. Darcy proposed, Elizabeth had thought she could not be more surprised, but this straightforward declaration made her stare in stunned amazement. "You love me?" she asked in a hoarse whisper.

"I do love you, and I think I have loved you since I first met you, but it was not until the Netherfield ball I came to realize how deeply I felt it. I know I did not show any regard for you at the Meryton assembly, but I will spend the rest of my life making it up to you if you will allow me. Perhaps you shall even come to love me someday." Darcy had pulled her hands to his chest and he cradled them close.

Although her heart swelled with joy at his impassioned speech, Elizabeth found it hard to believe he had fully pondered the problems their union would bring. However, his declaration had one effect upon her -- it loosened her tongue, and out poured all of the issues she had wanted addressed. "How is it that you called the babe 'ours'? You know of my family's low connections and how silly some of them can be. Are you able to overlook that and call them yours? How will your family accept me? I am sure they expect you to marry better than a country gentleman's daughter. How will we escape the censure of the *ton* when this baby comes so soon after we are wed?"

The rapidity of Elizabeth's questions almost brought a grin to Darcy's face. Had he not already agonized over the exact same ones? He knew he must answer her, and without knowing where her affections lay. He released her hands before once more tucking one of them in his arm. "Is there a place close by where we could sit for a while? I would not want to catch up with your sister and Bingley before I have had a chance to fully explain my thoughts."

"There is a log not far from here, but I am afraid it is not on the road." She trusted the gentleman but was certain she did not want the scandal of being caught in a seemingly compromising situation.

"Very well, Miss Elizabeth, we will continue to walk if you are feeling up to it."

Darcy realized that she had not shown any signs of anxiety the whole of their walk and asked, "How is it that you seem to be less fearful today?"

"I have been venturing out on walks with Jane, although never so far as this." Her feeling of triumph over the plaguing fear showed on her face. "But I took the advice of Mrs. Parker." She proceeded to explain what the older woman had challenged her to do, from the writing of the attack to the burning of the paper it was written on. "I am not confident enough to believe that I will not experience the panic again, but for the moment, I would like nothing more than to continue our walk and our discussion."

"That is excellent news." Darcy smiled broadly at Elizabeth before his expression sobered. "I will endeavour to explain my reasons and my conclusions as it pertains to your very apt questions. I can only do so by relating two events to which I hope you will be able to give credence. I will begin by telling you what I experienced the day after the Netherfield ball and after I received a note from Sarah. I arranged with her to send me a note with one of my gloves I had given her the day of your attack. I asked her to tell me whether or not you had your courses in a coded message involving the return of my glove."

Rubbing his chin, Darcy tried to remain composed. "I admit that up until that time I had hoped against hope that you would not be found with child. Wickham's attack on your person and the possibility of your carrying his child seemed to add up to an insurmountable barrier between us. However, because of my failure to disclose that man's guilt and villainous ways and my newly discovered love for you, I felt compelled to aid you. Also, because I needed to make a decision, I closed myself into Bingley's study to weigh my options. Therein, I had what I suppose was a vision." He went on to describe the scenes he witnessed of himself and the child and how the experience had broken through the seeming impossible wall.

Tears stung Elizabeth's eyes as she listened to the narrative and watched his expression soften. "Your vision is a beautiful one, but I do not see that it is wise to make such a decision based on an apparition. And as I have told you before, you have no responsibility in the attack. It is not fair that that man's child should inherit anything from the Darcy legacy."

"Please, dearest, do not make yourself uneasy. There is more to tell." The endearment slipped easily from his lips as Darcy patted her hand before he went on, "As you know, I travelled to London that very day. I went to see Mr. Whitton, my family's attorney, so he could write the marriage contracts. I was surprised when he told me he had something for me. My excellent father had given him a letter with instructions to give it to me when I came to see the lawyer with the intention of marrying."

Again, he stopped walking and looked up and down the road. "What I am about to tell you is known by no one but myself. I have already burned the letter, so that its message will remain a secret."

Understanding his meaning, Elizabeth looked into his eyes and promised, "You may depend upon my discretion. I will never speak of it to anyone."

"I know that I can trust you." He breathed a soft sigh. Darcy then explained the whole of Wickham's Darcy connection. "So you see George is my natural cousin. There runs in his veins as much Darcy blood as there does in mine. Whether male or female, the child you carry is a Darcy, and I want to give the baby the Darcy name."

"It is sad that your father carried such a heavy burden," she said as the tears rolled down her cheeks. "How hard it must have been for him to lose a sister and to be unable to acknowledge her child as his nephew!" Reaching into her reticule, Elizabeth retrieved a handkerchief and dried her eyes.

Darcy's heart lifted at the compassion Elizabeth showed in her words about his father. He hoped that he had made progress in answering her questions. "The contents of the letter explained so many small things my father did for Wickham. If I had known, I might not have been quite so jealous of his attentions to a mere steward's son. I admit to experiencing jealousy often as a child and mostly due to a certain feeling of superiority over those beneath me in rank."

Sensing Elizabeth's withdrawal at his last words, Darcy hastened to add, "My father repeatedly taught me the responsibility that I would carry because of my wealth and status, but later as I grew into a man, I saw that while my wealth and status held a great deal of duty and accountability, it did not make me better than the butler or a poor country squire. My father often said, 'All is from the hand of God, and it is only by His mercy that it is not taken away.' and quoted from Scripture. 'To whom much is given, much is required.'"

He smiled wryly before he patted her hand again and continued, "You already know that I sometimes forget what my father taught me. When one is told through many and various means that one is greater than others, is quality, and is fawned over merely because of rank and wealth, it becomes easy to believe that lie.

"I shall not dissemble. There are those in my family who will have trouble accepting this marriage based only upon your social status, but the ones I hold dearest shall accept you, at first because I love you, and before long, they shall love you on your own merit."

He looked once more into her eyes so that she could see he meant what he said. "The only member of my family who will be truly upset with our marriage will be Lady Catherine who is my aunt on my mother's side. She has long campaigned for a marital alliance between my cousin Anne and myself. I have tried to dissuade her from the notion, but she will not listen."

Finally Elizabeth spoke up, "Will she not make it difficult for you in society if she spreads tales of a broken engagement? What is your cousin's opinion on all this? Is she not likely to be hurt by the reports as well?"

"First of all, I will say that I have never cared for society over much. I do what is needed when I am in Town so as not to bring shame on my family name. However, I would be completely satisfied if I never had to be in society again. Secondly, if my aunt tried to spread rumours about me, the rest of my family, being in possession of the knowledge of my wishes in regard to a marriage to Anne, would make things very difficult for her. She tends to be a despot at Rosings, but she has little real influence in Town. My cousin and I have discussed this at length, and she has no desire to marry me. More than once Lady Catherine has declared that Anne is addled in the head to refuse to marry me. Anne has begged me to convince my aunt that we do not suit, but I have been unsuccessful to date."

She wondered at a mother who would be so intent upon having her daughter married to a certain person that she would disregard the wishes of either party. Her own mother dearly wished for her girls to marry and might insist upon them accepting an offer to which they were not inclined, but Elizabeth doubted that Mrs. Bennet would ever think herself capable of forcing a young gentleman to marry contrary to his own wishes.

Elizabeth turned from him and began to walk again. Her mind was still in turmoil, although her heart grew more convinced that marrying Mr. Darcy was not only a solution to her predicament, but a very probable means of great love and happiness for her and her child.

She had never had a season in Town, nor had she ever been presented at court. Her life had been a happy one, for the most part. The lack of societal experiences had no bearing upon her. Could Mr. Darcy truly do without the same and not feel the lack?

Walking silently by her side, Darcy tried to gauge Elizabeth's reaction to all of his answers, but with little success. All that he could tell was that she was deep in thought, nearly forgetting his presence. He began to despair that she would ever accept him or love him as he did her. When he added her possible rejection and resulting loss of the unborn child he had already come to love as his own, tears sprang to his eyes. The thought tore through him like a jagged knife.

He must have gasped aloud at his painful thoughts because Elizabeth looked up at him at that moment. She saw the tears clinging to his lashes and the agony on his face. Her heart shuddered at the sight and her breath hitched. Touching his arm, she stopped walking. When she had caught his attention, Lizzy reached up to wipe a teardrop from his cheek.

"Why are you so sad?" she whispered as apprehension filled her. Did he finally discover in his heart of hearts that he would miss society's approval?

Taking her hand with his, Darcy said hoarsely, "You are too generous to trifle with me. It is apparent to me by the length of your ponderings that you have decided against my offer. And although the pain of losing you and the baby is greater than I can describe, I shall accept your decision. My love shall not change, but I will not speak of it again. Please tell me "No" quickly so that it will be done."

"I have another question, sir," Elizabeth said gravely. At his nod, she asked, "Have you truly thought through all of these things and decided that you still want to marry me?"

"Yes, yes, I have," he answered without pause, a glimmer of hope brightening his eyes.

"In that case, sir, I am afraid that you are labouring under some false assumptions." Elizabeth lowered her eyes to rest her gaze on their still joined hands. "You presumed that my lengthy quietude meant I would be rejecting your offer, and earlier when you told me you loved me, you implied that I was indifferent to you."

Darcy lifted her chin so that he could search her eyes for the truth. "What are you saying?"

"I am saying that I will marry you because I love you. The rest of what you told me helps me to understand you more fully, but what is of most importance is that you love me and the baby. All else, I believe, we can surmount together."

For a heartbeat, Darcy did not move, but soon he was overcome with pure joy. He laughed out loud before taking possession of both of her hands and kissing them repeatedly. "My dearest, loveliest Elizabeth, you have made me the happiest of men." Unable to contain his bliss, he crushed her to him. "Pardon me for this liberty, my love, but I cannot seem to help myself."

In a muffled voice, due to the fact that her face was buried against his coat, she said, "No pardon is necessary, since I find there is no place I would rather be than in your arms at the moment."

Darcy sighed contentedly while he enjoyed the feel of her so close to him, but soon his sense of propriety made him relinquish his hold on her.

It was then that he remembered the ring in his pocket. Darcy reached in and pulled out the box. "I have been carrying this since I retrieved it in Town. It belonged to my mother and to my father's mother before her. I hope that you will have the opportunity to pass it on to our eldest son's betrothed someday."

As Elizabeth looked on in astonishment, Darcy took off her glove and placed the ring on it before he kissed her hand. He stared down at her now beringed finger and then turned to smile into her eyes. "I will have to resign myself to waiting to see it again on your hand once we are back inside your home, for it is too cold for you to be without your gloves at the moment." He slipped the ring from her, and after placing it back in the box, he handed it to her.

Elizabeth could not believe that such a lovely ring would be hers. "I will wear it after we talk to my father." She tucked the box into her reticule.

Nodding, Darcy once more tucked her hand in the crook of his arm and began to lead them up the path from the road. This time, they spoke little and walked faster in order to catch up with Bingley and Jane. It was not until they reached the mount itself that they found the other couple sitting together on a large boulder and chatting quietly.

When Charles finally spied them, he stood and called out, "I was afraid that you had taken a wrong turn somewhere. Come join us. The view is excellent."

As Darcy and Elizabeth approached the other couple, Jane noticed something in their countenances that she had never seen before. As Charles offered his former place on the stone to her younger sister, she said, "Elizabeth, what is it? You are positively glowing."

Elizabeth glanced up at Darcy, who smiled and inclined his head as if to say he did not mind if she shared the news, if it were her wish. She leaned closer to her sister and whispered, "Jane, do you remember when you told me that I would someday marry, and I disagreed with you?"

When Jane owned that she did, Elizabeth said loudly enough for everyone to hear, "Mr. Darcy has asked me to marry him, and I have accepted him."

Jane hugged her, and Charles pumped Darcy's hand nearly hard enough to dislocate his shoulder.

"Wonderful news, Darcy! I wish you both great joy." Charles beamed as a thought came to him. "Since we are to be brothers, why do we not get married together?"

Both Darcy and Elizabeth tensed at the idea. Knowing that Bingley and Jane were to be married in the spring, Elizabeth was not certain that they would be able to attend the wedding, but it was impossible for them to share the date.

"We are honoured by your suggestion, but we are not going to wait until spring to be wed. Miss Elizabeth and I are going to be married by license in a fortnight, so that we might travel to Pemberley before the roads are impossible to navigate." Smiling down at Elizabeth with obvious affection, Darcy added, "I do not want to leave Hertfordshire without my wife by my side. It is selfish, I know, but I hope the Bennet family will forgive my impatience."

The four talked happily for quite sometime before Darcy suggested that they head back for Longbourn. He was eager to obtain Mr. Bennet's permission. Feeling fairly confident he would approve of the marriage, Darcy was less certain her father would agree to the timing of it.

Once they arrived at Longbourn, Darcy parted with the company to seek Elizabeth's father in his library. He entered the room at Mr. Bennet's call.

"Mr. Darcy, do sit down," Mr. Bennet said as he smiled. "I would offer you a brandy, but I believe it is too early in the day for that. Now, what may I do for you?"

"Sir, I have come to inform you that I have asked Miss Elizabeth to be my wife and she has agreed." His calm and formal tone hid the anxiety in his mind. "I would like your permission to marry her."

Leaning back so that his chair rested on only the two back legs, Mr. Bennet relaxed with his hands clasped over his stomach. He grinned mischievously. "You seemed to have gone from a secret courtship to an engagement rather quickly, Mr. Darcy."

"I suppose I have, but I greatly admire Miss Elizabeth and will make every effort to make her happy for the rest of my life. I have already had the marriage settlement drawn up and plan to purchase a license from Mr. Scott as soon as possible."

"This was the reason for your hasty trip to London?" Mr. Bennet asked, puzzled. "I do not understand the urgency. Even if you were to marry within a month, there will be plenty of time to publish the banns."

"We are to be wed within a fortnight," Darcy stated simply.

"What?" Mr. Bennet dropped his chair back on all four of its legs so hastily that the sound reverberated in the room like a pistol shot. "I do not understand your reasoning, young man. You would take Lizzy away from her family before Christmas?"

The abrupt noise startled Mr. Darcy. He took a deep breath to try to calm himself before he replied as reasonably as he could manage. "I am sorry, but we must return to Pemberley soon, since by mid December the winter snows will begin to make the roads quite impassable."

"Then, you shall wait until spring," declared Mr. Bennet, in rare raised voice. "Your friend, Bingley, has no problem waiting, so neither should you."

Elizabeth had not gone to the parlour with Jane and Bingley. She told her sister that she needed to retrieve something from her room. Once she exchanged her soiled handkerchief with a clean one, she quickly moved down the stairs and stood near the library door. It was not long before she could hear her father's voice, louder than was his wont. Realizing that Mr. Darcy might need her support, Elizabeth knocked on the door.

Upon hearing the knock, Elizabeth's father growled, "Come!"

Both gentlemen stood as Elizabeth came in quickly and shut the door behind her. "Papa, please lower your voice. Surely you do not want Mama to hear you and come to investigate." She walked to his side and led him back to his chair. "Please, will you both not be seated?"

Once they were back in their chairs, Elizabeth stood looking at her father and asked in a calm tone, "Why are you so angry, Papa? I thought you liked Mr. Darcy."

"Blast it, Lizzy, I do, or rather I did like him until he told me that he thinks you will be married within a fortnight." He slammed his fist upon the desk. "A fortnight! Did you agree to this?"

Moving around her father's desk to stand beside Darcy, Elizabeth placed her hand on his shoulder and looked at her father, her face set. "I did, Papa, and it is what will happen."

"I am your father, and I will say when, if, and to whom you will wed." Mr. Bennet's face reddened with anger as he watched his favourite daughter grip Darcy's hand as he raised it to hers on his shoulder.

"Papa, please listen to me," she soothed. "You know that I love and respect you, but it is important that we marry as soon as may be. If I did not wish to avoid a scandal, we would have eloped."

She looked at Darcy's disturbed facial expression as he rose to stand beside her, his hand on her back. "No, you did not ask me to elope. I merely wish my father to understand that we are serious about this.'

Returning her attention to her father, Elizabeth said, "Please, Papa, do not be angry at Mr. Darcy. He is doing what he feels is best for us."

Darcy watched as Mr. Bennet's glance moved from Elizabeth to him and back again. The older man's cheeks went from red to nearly white. He stood again and gripped the desk in front of him. "All this time I thought you were a gentleman and a kind of hero when you found Lizzy, brought her to the house after her fall, and made sure that a doctor was fetched for her. I was impressed by your solicitude, always asking after Lizzy's well-being as she recovered. I did not understand why you asked to court her in secret, but I allowed it since your explanation seemed sound. Instead, I find that you are a cad and a seducer."

"Oh, no, Papa!" Elizabeth exclaimed. "Mr. Darcy is the best of men. He has done no wrong. I promise you."

After searching his daughter's face for several moments, Mr. Bennet sighed with some relief before he asked, "Then you are not with child?"

When Elizabeth blanched and dropped her eyes to the floor, he raised his voice once more. "And you say he has done no wrong I do not think you understand what you are saying,"

"Papa, the babe is not Mr. Darcy's," she choked out, her throat closed in shame, and began to sob into her hands when she saw the look of disappointment and shock on her father's face.

"Why do you not marry the man you were... involved with?" Mr. Bennet then turned to speak in a stern voice to Darcy. "Why would you offer for such a woman?"

Darcy drew her into his arms as if to shelter her from her father's words, not caring about the impropriety of his action and explained sternly, "The person who is responsible is a vile human being whom no woman should be forced to marry. He attacked your daughter and forced himself upon her. He is now working off his many debts on a ship bound for foreign lands. And before you berate either of us for not telling you at the time, you must know that Elizabeth wanted to keep it a secret so as to keep the scandal from your door. She has always and only thought of her loved ones. Her first thought when she found she was increasing was to run away and disappear, to live the rest of her life without her family, dead to you all to save your family from ruin. And to answer your question as to why…it is simple, I love her with all my heart."

Mr. Bennet groped for his chair and slumped tiredly into it. He dropped his face into his hands, ashamed of his hasty judgments upon his Lizzy. He could hear her soft sobs and Darcy's quiet words as he tried to soothe her. After a deep inhalation of air, he sighed again and stood. Taking the few steps needed to bridge the distance between him and his daughter, he patted her back.

"Please forgive me, my Lizzy. I am a foolish old man." Lifting his mournful eyes to meet Darcy's, he said. "I beg you, sir, to accept my most humble apology. I offer no excuse for the many insults I hurled upon you. I would not blame you if you called me out."

"Sir, I do not claim to speak for Elizabeth, but I will accept your apology for her sake." His tone was solemn and cool.

Elizabeth lifted her face from Darcy's shoulder and turned to her father, her cheeks wet from weeping. She took the handkerchief he offered. "I f-forgive you, P-papa," she hiccupped. "I am s-sorry to have c-caused your distress. P-please do not repeat what we have t-told you. This baby will be raised as a D-Darcy, and we will not have any questions about its p-parentage."

"I promise I will never say a word," Mr. Bennet vowed. "Now, I fully understand your reason for wanting to have the nuptials as soon as possible. Your mother will be disappointed not to be able to plan for an elaborate wedding, but having the license will give her something to brag about to her cronies. Let me deal with her."

Mr. Darcy reluctantly released Elizabeth, and the three sat down so that they could discuss the details. He pulled out the contracts his lawyer had prepared according to his wishes and handed the papers to Mr. Bennet.

While her father read through the documents, Elizabeth reached out for Darcy's hand. She felt drained and embarrassed by all that had happened. She wanted above all else to be reassured that her beloved was not upset. As he took her hand in his, Darcy squeezed it and gave her a loving smile, which warmed the cold, fear-filled part of her heart. She could tell he wished to say something to comfort her, but he could not in the present company.

Her musings were interrupted by her father's declaration. "These are most generous settlements, Mr. Darcy. I am surprised and pleased at how well you have provided for Lizzy."

"A Darcy has always provided for his wife and family," Darcy replied with some pride. "I will do no less for mine."

"I would say that these settlements are far greater than mere provision. I commend you, sir, and I am even more ashamed of myself than before." Mr. Bennet sighed heavily. "It appears that my household will be greatly diminished in number before a twelve-month has passed."

Getting to his feet once more, Mr. Bennet held out his hand to Darcy. "I welcome you into our family, son."

"Thank you, sir," Darcy replied as he shook his future father-in-law's hand.

Elizabeth threw her arms around her father's neck and kissed his cheek. "Yes, thank you, Papa."

"Well, well," Bennet patted her shoulder and teased, "I think we will have to share the news, since you and I, sir, have been in this room too long for you to borrow one of my books. Let us get it over with so that I might return to my library as soon as possible."

It was no surprise that Mrs. Bennet was ecstatic at the news. At first, the blessing of having three daughters poised on the verge of matrimony was almost more than her nerves could handle. Mrs. Hill was summoned to bring her a restorative, but she soon overcame the strain and declared that the gentlemen must stay for luncheon to celebrate.

The meal was one of much conversation and rejoicing. At first, Mr. Darcy found it difficult to accept the constant attention heaped upon him by Mrs. Bennet, but once he glanced at Elizabeth down the table from him and saw her worried expression, he knew that he could and would withstand the excited chatter of his fiancée's mother, if only to put Elizabeth at ease.

His attention had been diverted toward Elizabeth long enough that he almost missed Mrs. Bennet's question. "Are you very certain that you must marry so soon, Mr. Darcy? I do so want to do you justice by having everything, including the wedding breakfast, be perfect."

"Madam, I am afraid that it must be so." He schooled his voice so that none of his impatience or frustration was apparent. "The weather in the north is often severe, and soon the roads will be impassable. You are aware of the many responsibilities pertaining to the running of an estate, and as you have trained your daughters so well in the running of a household, I will be extremely comforted to have her at Pemberley as its mistress. And now that I have been so fortunate as to win your daughter's hand, I, being a rather selfish man, do not want to wait so very long to have her as my wife. I hope that you will forgive me for taking her away so soon."

Smiling at Mrs. Bennet, he leaned toward her and said conspiratorially, "As to obtaining perfection for the wedding breakfast and such, I must tell you that after enjoying this and other fine meals at Longbourn, I can see no need for you to plan for any better. However, if you are concerned that there are items you wish to serve that are not readily available in Meryton, you only have to give me a list, and I shall see to it that they are procured from London at my expense."

"Oh, Mr. Darcy, you are too kind!" she cooed. "I will speak with my cook and begin planning this very afternoon. I am certain that there will not be many things needed from London, but I do appreciate the offer just the same."

Once the meal was over, the two gentlemen excused themselves, not wanting to overstay their welcome.

CHAPTER SEVENTEEN

The next few days passed in pandemonium. Elizabeth's mother made many lists, one for food, one for flowers, and another of items for Elizabeth's trousseau. She sent them off to Netherfield for Mr. Darcy's perusal and approval. Mrs. Bennet rejoiced when nothing she asked for was denied.

Once, during one of Darcy's morning calls, Mrs. Bennet bemoaned the fact there was not fabric to be had in Meryton that was good enough for Lizzy's wedding gown, nor a dressmaker skilled enough to make it if there were. He solved the dilemma by offering to take Elizabeth to Town in his carriage with her sister Jane and a maid. Once there, he would escort her along with her aunt Gardiner to Georgiana's modiste, assuring Mrs. Bennet that the woman, Madame Obier, would have the perfect fabric and would know all the latest fashions. She could also command enough seamstresses to finish the dress in a few days' time.

At first, Mrs. Bennet insisted that she must accompany her daughter to Town, but with the help of her husband, Mr. Darcy was able to convince her that it was crucial she stay at Longbourn to oversee the rest of the wedding preparations.

Flattered by her future son-in-law's compliments, she acquiesced.

Darcy knew that because of Elizabeth's fears, she would not be able to travel so far without him. He admitted to himself that he was not unhappy at the idea of having time away from the most trying members of the Bennet family and the added bonus of being with Elizabeth. His only distress about the situation was that her anxiety was what forced his accompaniment.

"Oh, Mr. Darcy," Mrs. Bennet gushed. "You are too kind to your future family. I daresay that this wedding will be remembered for its elegance and not for its haste. When Lady Lucas mentioned how soon you were to be wed, I assured her that you are very anxious to journey to Derbyshire before the weather turns foul, and that you are so much enamoured of my Lizzy that you simply will not wait until spring to become her husband." She sighed happily and proclaimed, "How romantic you are, my dear Mr. Darcy!"

157

Lydia, who had been sorting through some newly acquired ribbons at the table, had been listening and finally understood that her two older sisters were going to obtain new gowns in London. She asserted herself into the conversation. "Mama, it is not fair that Jane and Lizzy are to go to Town for new gowns. Kitty and I have to settle for new dresses from Mrs. Potter's shop in Meryton."

She glanced at Mr. Darcy, whom she still thought very proud, and said slyly, "I think that there would be a scandal if Lizzy and Jane wore new gowns from a modiste in Town while their younger sisters did not."

Mrs. Bennet sat in silence as she was torn between the obvious ploy by her daughter to gain another new gown and what even she could see would be imposing upon the more than generous largess of her future son-in-law.

Before her mother could reply, Elizabeth spoke, "Lydia, you were quite delighted with the new gown Mrs. Porter is making for you until you learned of our trip to Town. You will not trespass upon Mr. Darcy's kindness by being greedy."

Lydia pouted and flounced onto the settee in the far corner of the room, her arms crossed in obvious pique. When her mother did not argue with Elizabeth as she normally would, tears of anger and frustration gathered in her eyes. Just when she was about to cry in earnest, Mr. Darcy caught her gaze. A small smile of sympathy graced his face before he moved to sit in a chair beside her as Mrs. Bennet once more filled the room with her raptures on the subject of the wedding.

"Miss Lydia," he said quietly but with a bit of scolding. "It seems that you have forgotten whose wedding this is to be."

Sighing, Lydia swiped unladylike at her eyes with the back of her hand. "I know whose wedding it is, but I have ever wanted to have a dress from an elegant Town modiste, even a bonnet or lace from some fashionable shop would be wonderful."

Darcy studied the spoiled and selfish young girl and wondered how to respond. He had no problem with the idea of purchasing gowns for all the Bennet girls, but he did not want to set a precedent by giving in to Lydia's childish tantrums. Perhaps a bit of gentle correction would be the ticket.

"I understand you want this, but do you think it was polite to say so in the manner you did and in front of myself, the person who was offering the gift to your sisters?"

Lydia looked a little surprised at his calm and reasoning voice. He did not tease or berate like her father would, nor did he give in to her tale of deprivation like her mother. Pondering her actions was not her wont, but this man, who would be her brother, was giving her attention in a way she never before experienced. It caused her to consider what she had done. After a few moments of contemplation, she answered in a contrite tone rarely heard coming from her lips, "No, it was not. I apologize for speaking thusly. I hope you will forgive me."

Darcy nodded. "You are forgiven, Miss Lydia, but I wonder if you think you should apologize to your mother and sister as well for your outburst."

At first, the idea sparked anger in her again, but the patient look in Darcy's eyes extinguished it quickly. "I suppose you are right. It is hard to say I am sorry when sometimes I am not. Besides, it will make me appear foolish."

"No, Miss Lydia, admitting you are wrong may humble you, but you will not appear foolish. Your apology to me just now showed me that you understand what injury your actions can cause others. Your mother loves you very much. I think that she indulges you often because of that love, does she not? How do you think your sisters feel when their needs and wants are superseded by yours?"

"I suppose that they do not like it," she admitted, as she dropped her eyes to the floor.

In order to keep Mrs. Bennet from interrupting the conversation between Lydia and Darcy, Elizabeth kept her mother busy across the room with a discussion of whether they could find a place in Town from which to order flowers for the wedding, but all the while, she watched the interchange between her fiancé and her sister. She could tell that whatever he was saying was having an effect upon the young girl. Smiling, she turned back to answer a question as to her preference of roses or orange blossoms.

A few moments later, Lydia stood and walked to her mother and sister. "Mama, Lizzy, I want to apologize for my outburst. I was happy with the gown that Mrs. Porter is making for me before I heard of the trip to Town. I shall continue to be so."

The short and rather humble speech from Lydia astonished both Mrs. Bennet and Elizabeth, but they both accepted her apology. Soon, the mother and her youngest were clamouring on about how lovely the two older sisters would be, and that their beauty would reflect well on their younger siblings.

Elizabeth withdrew from them to make her way to where Darcy still sat. She sat in the place Lydia had just abandoned. "Whatever did you say to her?"

Darcy grinned. "I merely showed her that her actions were not acceptable."

"I believe, sir, that you said much more than that, but if you do not wish to share, I will not press." She laughed lightly before she said, "I must say that, whatever it was, it had a delightful outcome."

~*~

The next day, directly after breakfast, Darcy arrived in his carriage. As he entered the house, he was met by Mrs. Bennet, who exclaimed over the elegance of his equipage and that her girls would indeed travel in great comfort. He glanced at Elizabeth and could tell she was feeling nervous.

As Mrs. Bennet ordered the footman to see that the trunks were secured to the carriage, Darcy moved to stand by Elizabeth. "I hope that you did not have trouble getting ready for this hastily arranged trip."

She did not meet his eye as she said, "There was not much to pack since we will not be long in London."

Lowering his voice, he stated gently, "You are uneasy about leaving Longbourn."

Wringing her hands together, she admitted, "I am a little, but I know that were you not accompanying us, I would faint for fear."

"It is good, then, I am going with you." Glancing around quickly to see if anyone was looking their way, he urged her to the far corner of the entry. He then lifted her chin with his finger. "Please look at me, my love."

Once she raised her eyes to his, Darcy dropped his hand and asked, "Can you tell me what it is that makes you most afraid?"

Closing her eyes for a moment, Elizabeth thought about the anxiety that had plagued her of late. She thought it strange she had never asked herself that question. Was it fear of another attack? Or did she think suddenly that the whole world was no longer a safe place? Casting around in her mind, a simple answer came to her. She lifted her lashes and gazed into Darcy's eye for a second before she told him. "I feel helpless and powerless. Before the...," she paused to look quickly around her to insure herself that they still had privacy and then continued, "before it happened, I was so sure of myself and was positive I could handle anything that came my way, but now... I am no longer certain that I have the ability to do so."

Darcy took her hand in his. He thought that he would do anything in his power to give her back her confidence. An idea struck him. "I believe I know of something that will aid you in overcoming your feelings of helplessness. What say you to learning the art of fencing and how to shoot a gun?"

Elizabeth's wide eyes bespoke her astonishment at the suggestion, but her expression quickly changed to one of relief. "You would teach me these things?"

"I would and I shall," he promised. "But in the meantime, know that now you have me to defend and protect you. I will not allow anything to happen to you, dearest Elizabeth. Please remember that."

"Lizzy and Jane, are you ready?" Her mother's excited call interrupted their tête-à-tête.

"Yes, Mama," she answered, "I need only my cloak and reticule."

"I am ready as well," Jane said from where she had been waiting as she donned her pelisse.

Soon they all, including Sarah, entered the carriage, and after bidding the rest of the Bennets farewell, they left for Town.

At first, Elizabeth was plagued with an overall anxiety. She tried valiantly to hide her fear, but the other passengers were not fooled.

Darcy, who had defied convention to sit beside her, took her gloved hand from where she held it on her lap. "I beg pardon from you both at my continuing to take liberties, but I feel I must if I am to help Elizabeth to overcome her nerves."

The idea of her having nerves similar to her mother touched off a response that surprised everyone, including herself. Elizabeth began to laugh. The stunned looks on the others' faces only added to the ridiculousness of the moment and fuelled more laughter. It was Jane who first understood the source of Elizabeth's mirth and joined her in the mirth. Darcy and Sarah were not far behind, but only because the joyous sound of the sisters' laughter was so contagious.

Several minutes later, once their mirth had faded into an occasional chuckle, Darcy asked with a wide smile on his face, "Will you please enlighten me as to what I may have said that brought on this lively expression of merriment?"

Elizabeth could not help but grin. She felt completely at peace and knew the rest of the journey would cause little anxiety. "Sir, you mentioned that you wanted to help me to fight my nerves. I have always prided myself that I did not exhibit any of my mother's tendencies to nerves or the vapours. A rather amusing picture of myself calling for a restorative or retiring to my room ill with the effects of the same came to me. It was so ludicrous that I could not keep from laughing. I feel so much better, and appreciate that none of you thought I had lost my mind." She paused to look into his eyes, "I hope that I did not offend you by my lack of self-control."

"Indeed, I was not offended and instead am happy that I even inadvertently helped to relieve the situation." He patted her hand, which he still had in his possession.

The party began to talk about various things, only briefly touching on the wedding. Elizabeth and Jane exclaimed about the people, houses, and other points of interest they passed by. As they drew closer to London, Darcy described the area of Town in which he lived, as well as where the modiste's business was located.

Sarah listened with great interest to what they said, but she had trouble attending at times, for the privilege of riding in such a fine carriage had never been hers before. She tried to remember as many details as she could so that she could share them with her family when next she saw them.

For everyone, the trip to Town provided a lovely break from Mrs. Bennet's constant vacillating between elation and despair. Elizabeth's mother worried that the hasty marriage would cause gossip to arise and thus added more to her menu, decoration, and guest lists. The whole affair would be far more than Lizzy could have imagined, and certainly more than she wanted. Spending these few days with their aunt was a blessed reprieve from all the fuss and bother that was her mother. The bonus of being with Darcy without the constant attention her mother lavished on her fiancé thrilled her as well.

Since they had so little time in which to accomplish their task upon reaching London, Darcy ordered the carriage to stop at Darcy House before taking the ladies to Gracechurch Street. Miss Darcy was not at home. The butler told them that she had gone to visit a friend for the day. Darcy left a note for his sister, explaining his purpose in coming to Town so unexpectedly and that he would see her later in the day.

He had explained to Elizabeth that he needed to send his instructions to the *modiste* so that all would be in ready in the morning. He did not share that, in his message, he would tell Madame Obier to spare no expense on either gown in order that the dresses would be ready in two days. In addition to the wedding gowns, he ordered others for the winter months and any other garments to complete a suitable wardrobe for the new mistress of Pemberley. All but those for the wedding were to be shipped to his country estate as soon as they were finished. Since he knew that the *modiste* would understand what his future wife needed and would quickly discern her tastes, he had little doubt that his Lizzy would enjoy the surprise.

~*~

The Gardiners were pleased to see their nieces and to meet Mr. Darcy, and even though they would be making the trip to Longbourn themselves within a week, they graciously welcomed them and strove to make them most comfortable. Once the luggage had been sent to the sisters' usual guest room, Mrs. Gardiner served much welcomed refreshments.

Within a half hour, Darcy excused himself to return to his home. He was pleased to receive an invitation for himself and his sister to return the next evening for a meal. He accepted for himself and would inquire as to his sister's plans.

As Elizabeth walked him to his carriage, Darcy took her hand and kissed it. "I hope that you will manage while I ..." He interrupted his speech, realizing that it was a bit arrogant of him to think she would be in constant need of his presence while she was with her relatives.

"I believe I shall be fine as long as I stay indoors. Jane will be here with me." She lifted worried eyes to his. "However, I hope that you will be escorting us to the *modiste* tomorrow."

"It shall be my pleasure to do so," he assured her earnestly.

~*~

Mornings were still uncomfortable for Lizzy, and even more so since she was sharing a room with Jane. Sarah did everything she could to make sure that

Elizabeth's queasiness did not come to Jane's attention and thus alarm her. The Gardiners' guest chamber had its own dressing room and maid's bed, so Sarah was able to know when the sisters awoke in the morning and to bring tea and a little for them to eat before they went to breakfast. Elizabeth teasingly explained to Jane that Sarah had begun bringing her something after her injury, and since she liked the pampering, she had not discouraged the habit once she had recovered.

When Darcy arrived with his carriage to take them to the *modiste* the first morning, Mrs. Gardiner and her two nieces enjoyed the ride to the most fashionable of Parisian dressmakers. Elizabeth was astonished by Madame Obier's warm, enthusiastic greeting once Mr. Darcy introduced her as his fiancée.

"*Oui, bien sûr, Monsieur* Darcy, you sent the message to the shop. It arrives yesterday. I am so excited. There is a room ready just for you. This way, *s'il vous plait.*" Madame Obier gestured with a sweep of her hand toward the back of the shop. Her accent and her pattern of speech showed that she was indeed from France's capital.

They were shown into a plush room complete with tufted couches covered in maroon brocade. Chairs in similar lush fabrics were drawn up to a table covered with dozens of fashion sketches and fabric samples. Madame invited them to be seated on the sofas while she ordered refreshments to be brought. While they waited for the tea, the proprietress brought them the sketches. "The *Mademoiselles* will please look here to find what they like."

Mr. Darcy looked on with fond indulgence as Elizabeth and Jane began to look through the many pages, keeping a few from each pile. With helpful comments from their aunt, they narrowed down their selections. Mrs. Gardiner told them both to choose an extra because she wished to give them each one gown as a gift.

Once they had chosen their two favourites, Madame Obier exclaimed over their refined taste. "Now you will choose the *tissu.*" With that, she handed the ladies stacks of fabric samples.

Elizabeth found what she wanted quickly, while her sister had more difficulty. Lizzy had asked Darcy for his opinion, only to have him smile affectionately and tell her to choose any she desired.

"I will be happy with whatever you pick, since it will be merely gilding the lily anyway." He winked at her and then at the *modiste,* who proclaimed that he was indeed a wise man.

Jane finally had four different silks and two muslins in front of her, in a literal rainbow of pastels. She fretted at length over the lovely bits of material until, at Jane's urging, her sister and her aunt each chose one for her. At the look of delight in her elder sister's eyes, Elizabeth could tell that she was very pleased with the final choices.

The whole experience of shopping for a gown at a high style London *modiste* was nearly overwhelming to Elizabeth and Jane. Someone seemed to be ready to meet their every whim. When she mentioned in passing that she loved caramel, one of the shop girls was sent to a confectioners' for a box of the candy and returned within fifteen minutes.

While the ladies were measured in the privacy of another room (which seemed to take longer than it would to actually make the dress), Mr. Darcy conferred with the proprietress. "I would like to purchase bonnets for my fiancée's three younger sisters as a surprise. Would you be able to find them for me and have them sent to Darcy House?"

"*Bien sûr, Monsieur* Darcy," Madame Obier agreed. "All you must do is to tell *moi* what you want. I know someone who makes very wonderful *chapeaux*. What are they like who will wear *ces bonnets,* and for what occasion?"

"I believe they would like to wear them to the wedding." He scratched his head as he tried to recall what the younger Bennet girls had said during their many excited clamourings about their wedding clothes. He told the lady what he could remember and a little about their different personalities.

"*Très bon, Monsieur*, I understand and I shall find the right bonnets," she nodded her head and bowed several times.

A slow smile crossed her face before she suggested, "I, also, might suggest a gift for *Mademoiselle's maman.*"

"Oh, yes! Yes, of course," Darcy agreed, embarrassed that he had not thought of it. "What would you suggest?"

"I have a lovely shawl of *cachemire.* I think *les Anglais* call it cashmere," she explained as she moved to a cabinet and unlocked it. "It was to be for *un autre* customer, but she did not buy it."

Madame brought out a downy, grey bundle. After she unfolded it, she held it out for Darcy to inspect and touch. "*C'est perfection*, is it not?"

The delicate softness of the garment surprised Darcy. Suddenly, he did not want to gift his future mother-in-law with it. Something like this should belong to his Elizabeth. As he wrestled with himself, Madame Obier pulled out another bundle; this time it was a pale gold one.

Understanding the lady's clever conniving, he chuckled. "You are a shrewd business woman, Madame. Would you happen to have something like this in the same colour as Miss Jane Bennet's gown?

She smiled broadly and lifted the lid on a third box. Inside laid a pale blue shawl.

"Perfect! Please include them with the hats you procure."

As he considered what else Elizabeth might need for the winter in Derbyshire, he added, "Madame, I would like you to obtain a fur-lined cloak and matching hat and muff for Miss Elizabeth Bennet. As you are becoming familiar with her tastes, I will leave the choice to you, with one exception. I do not want any thing in orange."

"Of course, *Monsieur* Darcy," Madame Obier agreed. "*Rien d'orangé.* I know just the thing for the *mademoiselle.*"

Once the two sisters had finished with the measuring, Darcy took them all to a tea room for luncheon.

"Oh my, how do ladies of the *ton* manage?" Elizabeth exclaimed as she sipped a bracing cup of hot tea and nibbled on sandwiches. "I do imagine Mama and Lydia and likely Kitty would have loved doing it all, but I find I am exhausted." She blushed at her outburst, but Mr. Darcy only smiled tenderly at her.

"My dear Lizzy, you will have to become accustomed to this sort of thing, since it will be your mode of shopping," her aunt reminded her, "after you marry Mr. Darcy."

Darcy could see that Elizabeth was becoming more uncomfortable with the idea, so he said, "My sister would agree with your assessment of dress fittings and the like. Often, she will simply send a request for a pink or green dress or whatever colour she would like to meet a certain need she might have. Georgiana trusts Madame Obier to not pour on the lace or feathers as some are wont to do. She reluctantly goes into the shop occasionally to be re-measured, since she is not yet fully grown. Perhaps you might commiserate with one another tonight."

Her heart cheered by Darcy's light banter, Elizabeth entered into the conversation with greater enthusiasm as they finished their repast.

Darcy brought the three ladies back to Gracechurch Street before returning to Darcy House and his sister.

Upon entering the house, he encountered an agitated Georgiana, pacing the foyer. Concerned that some bad news had come while he was out, Darcy rushed to her and asked. "What is it, my sweet?"

"Oh, brother, you will say it is foolishness." She bit her lip and refused to look at him.

"Tell me so that I might decide if it is or not," he urged gently.

"I have been worrying since you told me last night that I would be meeting Miss Elizabeth and her family." She finally glanced up at him to see he was patiently awaiting her explanation. Sighing, she went on, "What if they do not approve of me? You know that I am so afraid of strangers that it takes me a great deal of effort even to be able to say 'hello.' How am I to manage a whole evening amongst them?"

Darcy pulled his sister into his arms and rubbed her back gently. "My dear sister, you shall find that my fiancée and her family are among the least intimidating people you will ever meet. My Elizabeth will charm you, mark my words. And the Gardiners, while not of our social circle, are genteel and gracious in their manner. I shall by no means be ashamed to call them family."

"Truly, Fitzwilliam?" she asked eagerly. "Do you think they will like me?"

"My dear Georgiana, they will be unable to help themselves."

~*~

In the Gardiners' front parlour, Elizabeth sat eagerly awaiting the Darcy's arrival. Although it had been only a few hours since she had last seen her fiancé, she could not help but feel the lack of his companionship. When her thoughts grew too anxious, Lizzy tried to imagine his hand holding hers, or even how she would feel after learning to use a gun or a foil. The image of her in fencing garb brought a happy smile to her lips.

"I do wonder what Miss Darcy will be like," Jane pondered aloud.

"From the things Miss Bingley and Mrs. Hurst said about her, she must be quite the lady. She plays the pianoforte very well and has many other accomplishments to her credit," Elizabeth answered as she, too, had been wondering the same thing. "I hope that we are not too common for her. Caroline Bingley, who claims to be Miss Darcy's intimate friend, never did like me, so I am a little concerned that I will not meet her standards."

"Oh, Lizzy," Jane admonished, "it is not kind to speak thusly of Miss Bingley. I admit that Charles's sister seemed a trifle lofty in her opinions, but I am sure that it was merely because she felt uncomfortable among strangers."

"My dear aunt, as you see, our sweet Jane is still the least critical of people." Elizabeth grinned and returned her glance to her sister. "Very well, dearest, I shall not speak ill of your future sister."

Elizabeth turned the conversation to Derbyshire, since her aunt Gardiner had spent part of her life near the small town of Lambton in that same county. Although she had often heard stories of the place, her curiosity was piqued by the fact that very soon it would be her home.

"As you know, Pemberley is only five miles from Lambton and owes much of its prosperity to that grand estate. I believe it is among the finest of estates in all of England and definitely the jewel of Derbyshire." Her aunt smiled fondly at the knowledge that it would be of this house her niece would be mistress.

"Thank you, Mrs. Gardiner." Darcy's voice startled the family. He and his sister had just arrived, and he had delayed the butler's announcement when he heard the topic of their conversation. He bowed before he apologized, "Please forgive my breech of manners. I prevented your man from speaking when I heard Pemberley mentioned. I am foolishly proud of my home and always enjoy hearing what others have to say about it."

"No apologies are necessary, sir," Mrs. Gardiner said after she curtseyed. She then turned to look at the tall, slender young woman who stood behind him. "And this must be your sister."

Darcy reddened with embarrassment. He had been struck by how lovely his Elizabeth looked and had forgotten that introductions had not been made. "Pardon me again, Mrs. Gardiner. This is indeed my sister, Miss Darcy. Georgiana, this is Mrs. Gardiner, Mr. Gardiner, Miss Bennet, and my fiancée, Miss Elizabeth Bennet."

Georgiana shyly acknowledged the introductions with a curtsey and a soft, "How do you do?"

After everyone was seated, Mrs. Gardiner ordered wine for her guests.

Elizabeth noted that Miss Darcy barely sipped at her drink and did not make a sound as the conversation flowed around the room. Moving from her place beside Jane, she took a chair close to the young woman. "Miss Darcy, I understand that you are an accomplished musician and enjoy playing the pianoforte."

Pink with embarrassment at being spoken to directly, she bravely lifted her head and said, "I do not claim to be accomplished, but I do enjoy playing very much."

"I have often heard of your proficiency on the instrument and hope to have the pleasure of hearing you play," Elizabeth continued the conversation.

"Oh, I am not sure that I would say I am proficient and certainly not enough to play in front of strangers," Georgiana protested.

Elizabeth, upon seeing the girl's discomfiture, endeavoured to change the subject. "Madame Obier told me that we must attend her once more tomorrow for a fitting. I did not understand that she would become such a fixture in my life when I agreed to this excursion to Town."

"Were you able to find a gown to your liking, Miss Elizabeth?" Georgiana asked timidly.

"Oh yes," Elizabeth exclaimed with enthusiasm, "I did, indeed, find one. However, I must say that I found it a difficult task in narrowing down my choices."

She leaned closer to the girl and spoke conspiratorially, "I hope I shall not shock you when I say that I was overwhelmed by the whole experience at the *modiste*. There were so many decisions and so many people intent upon meeting my every desire, when the only thing I truly wanted was not to be granted."

Darcy, who had been listening to his two favourite ladies' conversation with pleasure, frowned when he heard what Elizabeth said. He was happy that he had waited to see what it was that his beloved had desired but not received when he saw a subtle change in his sister's demeanour.

"Oh, Miss Elizabeth!" Miss Darcy glanced up and saw the slightly teasing but kind smile on the other lady's face and guessed, "Could you possibly mean you wished to be gone from the shop.

"I knew that you must be very clever, for it is indeed what I meant." She grinned broadly. "I hope that it shall be a long time before I have to endure the pleasure of shopping there again." She glanced quickly at Darcy in the hope that he had not been insulted by her little jest. Relieved by his indulgent smile, she sighed.

"Please do not think that I am ungrateful for the honour of being able to patronize such an establishment," Elizabeth said, as she turned her glance back to Georgiana. "I know that my mama will be overjoyed by the finery that I will wear to my wedding. I am sure that when I don my gown, I shall think it all worth the effort."

Georgiana's eyes lit in humour as she responded, "I have no doubt that my brother will think you very lovely."

"You are correct, my dear, but I do not need my fiancée to adorn herself in new finery to think she is the most beautiful woman of my acquaintance."

"Mr. Darcy, I do wish you had informed me of this before we spent so much time in Madame Obier's fine establishment," Elizabeth teased as she glanced in Darcy's direction.

"Indeed, I would have been perfectly content if you wore the same lovely gown you wore at the Netherfield ball," Darcy grinned and held her gaze. "However, I do not think that your mother would be so forbearing, do you?"

"Ah sir," Elizabeth sighed dramatically, "You have touched the heart of our reason for being in Town."

She turned back to Georgiana and explained, "My mother did not think that any offering in our local seamstress shop was good enough for my wedding. She is quite determined to make it an event that our small community shall likely never forget." Leaning in, she whispered conspiratorially, "I hope that your brother will not think that it is too much bother and expense and thus decide to call off the wedding."

Georgiana gave her brother a look of confusion. She had never expected her future sister to tease Fitzwilliam in such a manner. The look in his eyes told her that he was not at all angry at her lively banter. In fact, he seemed to take quite a bit of pleasure in the activity. "I should think that you might well ask for even more, since it is obvious my dear brother would deny you nothing."

The twinkle in his sister's eyes made Darcy's heart leap for joy. At one time, she had been a happy and playful child, but their father's death and Wickham's betrayal had cast a shadow over her usually ebullient but sensitive nature.

"I believe you are right, Georgiana," Darcy agreed as he winked at Elizabeth. "It is then fortuitous that I have a good income."

The whole party laughed and continued the task of getting to know one another. Georgiana and Elizabeth, along with Jane, found they had many similar tastes in music, art, and literature. Darcy's sister discovered that her future sister did not ride but enjoyed walking. She promised to help Lizzy find a horse so that she could explore the parts of Pemberley that could not be reached on foot.

Elizabeth did not disagree with Georgiana, but she knew that she would not be learning to ride for a considerable amount of time, both because of her condition and the fear that nagged her. She wondered to herself if she would even be able to walk alone at Pemberley.

Something of her feelings must have shown on her face because Darcy made his way across and sat in a chair close to her side. While Georgiana, in answer to a query from Jane, described the gardens at Pemberley, he leaned close and asked, "Are you well, my love?"

Shaking off the dark thoughts, Elizabeth smiled and answered, "Yes, I am well. I allowed a fearful thought to tax my mind for a moment, but no more. You are here, and your sister is a joy. Why should I be anything but well?"

The supper was an informal, family affair with the children present. At first, Darcy, who was taken aback by the younger Gardiners' presence, only spoke when he could not avoid it, but soon he understood that his hosts had a sound reason for it. He watched as Georgiana, charmed by the children, began to open up more, even to the point of agreeing to play for them before they retired to the nursery.

The two little girls were, in turn, quite taken by Georgiana. They asked her polite questions about her taste in music, fashion, and art. Darcy was astonished that children such as nine year-old Cassandra and eight year-old Bella spoke with greater poise and refinement than some ladies of the *ton*. It became obvious to him that the Gardiners were extraordinary people, who, despite their station in life, were worth knowing and not just because of their relationship to his Elizabeth.

So grateful was he for the Gardiners' wisdom that he started to speak to the two boys who sat opposite him at the table. Tom, the oldest at eleven, wanted to talk of horses and hunting, while Benjamin, age seven, wanted to hear about Darcy's soldier cousin after he heard him mentioned.

Elizabeth had been nervous that Darcy would not approve of her relatives' allowing their children to dine with them, but she thrilled to listen to her fiancé telling stories to her cousins. His patience in answering their childish and sometimes silly questions warmed her heart. By the time dinner was finished and everyone gathered in the drawing room to hear Georgiana play, Elizabeth could scarcely keep from hugging Darcy.

Darcy had joined her on a settee and was surprised when she took his hand in hers, squeezed it, and said, "Thank you!" before releasing it.

Quietly, he responded, "While I enjoyed the gesture, I do wonder what I may have done to deserve your gratitude."

Her smile dazzled him as Elizabeth lifted her eyes to meet his. "Do I need a reason to squeeze your hand?"

"I suppose not, but you thanked me. That is usually said in response to something a person has done."

"You were so kind to my young cousins," she whispered as Georgiana began to play. "I know that you were uncomfortable with the children dining with us, but you are such a gentle and kind man. Because of witnessing your interaction with them, I have such hope for the happiness of our future family."

Darcy held her hand closely in his, even though it was not completely proper. Finally understanding the necessity of relating to children more often than the strictures of society dictated, he began to see that theirs could be a different but extremely happy family.

After Georgiana's impromptu concert and after an extended round of farewells and goodnight kisses, the children were taken to the nursery by Mrs. Gardiner since it was actually past their bed time.

Georgiana insisted that Elizabeth perform. After demurring, she finally agreed to sing if Georgiana would accompany her on the pianoforte. Darcy thrilled to the sight of his two most beloved women getting along so well together. He looked forward to many enjoyable private concerts at Pemberley.

~*~

For Elizabeth, the following day was an exhausting one of trying on the gowns that had been begun and the various under things that Madame Obier insisted were needed for a proper trousseau, with subsequent fittings of all of the garments.

Darcy spent the time in a private sitting room reserved for gentlemen who waited for their ladies while they were involved in the various and sundry tasks by which a suitable wardrobe was completed. He enjoyed tea and cakes while reading a newspaper.

Elizabeth was more than grateful when the excursion was concluded for the day. Darcy took them back to the same tearoom as the day before for refreshments.

"Well, ladies, do you wish to return to the Gardiners' home, or would you like to do more shopping?" Darcy inquired.

When Georgiana and Jane exclaimed their desire to visit a notions shop they had passed on their way to the *modiste*, Elizabeth, being tired and greatly desiring a nap, reluctantly agreed to the plan. However, Darcy could tell that her agreement was not enthusiastic.

"Mrs. Gardiner, would you mind accompanying my sister and Miss Bennet to the shop?" he asked casually. "I have something that I would like to show Miss Elizabeth in a shop a few streets over. We will return in a half hour if you think that will be enough time for you."

Mrs. Gardiner agreed, but before she could state her preference about the time, Georgiana pronounced gaily, "Oh brother, we will need at least an hour, but are you certain that Miss Elizabeth will not miss going with us?"

"Do not worry about me, Miss Darcy," Elizabeth was quick to insist. "I would rather see what it is that your brother wishes for me to see."

"If it is settled, we shall return for you ladies in an hour."

Once the carriage arrived in front of the *modiste's*, Darcy offered the other ladies a ride to the accessory shop they wanted to visit, but they declined, stating that they wished to walk the short distance.

Darcy settled Elizabeth inside his coach, gave the driver instructions, pulled down the shades, and was seated himself next to her before he signalled he was ready to leave. For a moment, he watched her try to cover a yawn, and after seeing how fatigued she was, he confessed, "I'm afraid that I fabricated the story of having a shop I wished to show you."

Startled, Elizabeth looked up. "And what was your reason for doing so, Mr. Darcy?"

"I perceived that my fiancée is extremely fatigued, but she would not say so, since the others seemed quite anxious to visit a certain shop, and she did not wish to spoil their amusement." He moved closer to her and took her hand. "My love, you must not wear yourself out like this. You need your rest for the sake of both you and the babe."

Leaning her head against his shoulder, Elizabeth sighed. "I could not tell Jane or my aunt that I was too fatigued to enter another shop, or else they would have thought something wrong with me. I never tire before Jane. I did not want them to question me for fear I would confess all."

Darcy wrapped his arms around her and settled her head against his chest and said, "I believe that I was wise in my little charade. Rest against me for a while. We have an hour, and I have instructed my man to drive toward the nearest park. It will be quieter there, and with the shades drawn, no one will know exactly who is inside. He is to drive around for three quarters of an hour, then to my favourite bookstore. We will browse there for a few minutes if you feel able. You will be able to tell the others I took you to look at books."

"You are a brilliant man," was her drowsy comment, and within minutes she was fast asleep.

CHAPTER EIGHTEEN

Elizabeth benefited greatly from her rest and was in fine spirits when she, Jane, and their aunt and uncle joined the Darcys for dinner at Darcy House that evening. She was both excited and eager to see her future home, or rather one of them. It was a lovely old, red-brick townhouse in one of London's most fashionable districts, with a beautiful park across the street. The tidy front garden even now sported hardy mums amongst the shrubs and a few late blooming roses surrounding a bit of lawn on each side of the walk. There was a wrought iron picket fence with matching railings on each side of the wide stone steps leading to the front of the house.

Before they had even exited their carriage, the doors were flung open and both the Darcys met the party at the front gate. Georgiana greeted everyone with curtseys and smiles, while Darcy stood back and tried to keep from staring at his lovely Elizabeth.

Finally, after a nudge from his sister, Darcy said, "Welcome to Darcy House. Please excuse me for keeping you out in the cold. Do come in." He offered his arms to Elizabeth and Mrs. Gardiner. Mr. Gardiner followed with Jane and Georgiana on his arms.

The grandeur of the entry of the townhouse stunned Elizabeth breathless. The polished marble floor gleamed in the light from the chandelier that hung from the ceiling, which soared two stories above them. The centre of the floor sported what looked to be the face of a large compass. The staircase curved up to a balcony with three doors leading from it and a hallway at each end. She later learned that these three doors led to the family sitting room, the mistress's study, and the upper level of the library.

After the servants helped them off with their coats, Darcy asked if they would like a tour of the house before dining. Everyone approved this plan, so Georgiana and her brother guided their guests through the ground floor public rooms.

The first room was a formal drawing room. There were a number of groupings of furniture tastefully decorated in fine, deep-green brocade fabrics. Two tall windows, covered with lace curtains which hung underneath draperies of a paler shade of green matching upholstery, framed the massive fireplace of green-veined marble. A large painting of a sailing ship with a compass in the upper right-hand corner hung over the mantle.

Darcy and his sister accepted compliments on the beauty of the room before they guided their guests into the hall and on to the next room. Darcy smiled at the gasps he heard when he opened the double doors to reveal the library. The rich, dark wood shelves and panelling covered the walls two stories high, and a small staircase gave access to the second level. The collection of books was obviously the work of generations. Several comfortable chairs with oil lamps on small tables beside them were scattered around the room. It was apparent that this was a haven for the book lover. A variety of books sat on the tables as if the readers would come back at any time to resume reading where they had left off.

Elizabeth's curiosity was piqued by a glass-enclosed display case that stood in one corner, so she walked over to take a closer look. Inside it, she found a collection of antique compasses of all sizes and shapes.

"Mr. Darcy," Elizabeth said, catching his attention. "I can see now why there were compasses in other rooms of the house. Who in your family was responsible for the collection?"

"My great-grandfather, Alistair Darcy, was fascinated with them as a child," Darcy explained as he joined her at the case. "His father told him how ship captains used them to keep on course and gave him his first compass. It was that one." He pointed to a small brass instrument. "As he grew, he obtained more, some as gifts, and others he purchased for himself. He brought several back from his Grand Tour. When he took over Darcy House at his father's death, he commissioned the design in the front hall and the inlaid one in the ballroom, which you will see soon. He had this cabinet made, so he would have a place in which to keep them and to display them."

"Did he commission the painting in the drawing room?" Mr. Gardiner asked as he joined the pair.

"That was a gift from my great-grandmother, Patricia." He grinned and explained, "Her father, Admiral Lapcoff, had a similar painting. My great-grandfather saw the picture when he attended a ball at the admiral's home. That very night, he asked to buy it from the admiral, who refused to part with it for any price. It has been said that since Alistair Darcy had fallen in love with the picture, and the admiral would not sell, he determined to marry the daughter of the house with the hopes of inheriting it."

"He never did receive it, and he ended up loving the daughter far more than he did the painting," Georgiana interjected.

"Indeed, the Darcy men do seem to have a tendency to fall in love when they are occupied in a quite different endeavour." Darcy smiled adoringly down at Elizabeth. "And as I said, Patricia Darcy, nee Lapcoff, gave her husband the painting you saw in the drawing room. She had it done and presented it to him on their first anniversary."

From the library, they visited two small sitting rooms and Darcy's study before entering the ballroom. There were only a few candelabras lit, but the reflection from the large gilded mirrors on the walls brightened the room, casting a warm glow on the highly waxed sheen of the wood floors. The compass in this room was at least four times the size of the one in the entryway. Darcy was about to take them into one of the card rooms off the main ballroom when the butler came to announce that dinner was served.

They were led into the smaller of the two dining rooms. The mahogany table was dressed elegantly in ivory and gold, which glittered under the light of another large crystal chandelier, and if that were not enough illumination, several tall candelabras cast a warm glow over the fine settings.

Darcy could not help watching Elizabeth again to discover her reaction to this room. It was his favourite of the dining parlours, and he had begun to imagine her presiding over the table and welcoming guests as mistress of the house.

As if she sensed his scrutiny, Elizabeth caught his eye and smiled. "This has to be one of the most elegant, yet inviting, dining rooms I have ever seen." Her eyes twinkled as she asked mischievously, "Where is the compass in this room?"

Both Darcy and Georgiana laughed as they pointed to the table. "It is under the cloth," he explained. "My parents were not so fond of the devices as were my great-grandfather and grandfather, but they both loved the table and would not offend Grandfather's memory by replacing it, so the compromise was to keep the compass hidden under linen."

Soon, the party was seated, and after a prayer of thanks for the food and company was made, the meal began. Lizzy was surprised that though the food was well prepared, it was not ostentatious, but simple and delicious. She was even more surprised when one of the courses included steak and ale pie. When she lifted her eyes, she found Darcy watching her reaction. She could not help but smile broadly at his remembering her favourite dish. Her pleasure at his thoughtfulness almost brought tears to her eyes. Such a man was to be her husband! God had certainly been gracious to her.

Elizabeth almost wished that her mother could experience the fine food and lively conversation so that she might comprehend what fine manners truly were like. However, she knew that her mother would likely concern herself with nothing but an inventory of the room's contents and the estimated value of the same. She decided that she was completely satisfied that her first visit to Darcy House was attended only by her dear Jane and favourite aunt and uncle Gardiner.

The party broke up soon after the meal because Elizabeth, Jane, and Darcy were to leave for Hertfordshire early the next morning. Georgiana was loath to say goodbye, but she was reminded that her brother planned to come back with his carriage in a few days to escort her and their cousin Colonel Fitzwilliam back to Netherfield for the wedding. They would see each other again then.

~*~

The trip back to Hertfordshire and Longbourn passed uneventfully. The two sisters chatted first about how much their mother would like their new gowns and then moved on to more general topics. Once again, Darcy sat next to Elizabeth. By now, no one even thought about the impropriety of the act, since Lizzy was obviously much more comfortable with the arrangement.

Upon their arrival at Longbourn, Mrs. Bennet, who had been watching at the window for over an hour, stood waiting for them to exit the carriage. She greeted the girls perfunctorily before turning her biggest smile and most exuberant salutations to Mr. Darcy.

"How well you look, sir!" Mrs. Bennet gushed as she took his arm to guide him to the house. "I hope the trip from Town was pleasant. I have ordered some refreshments for you before you return to Netherfield."

Darcy did not want to insult his future mother-in-law, but he could not allow Elizabeth to be slighted in this manner. He refused to move forward and instead turned back to where Elizabeth stood with Jane. "Mrs. Bennet, as you can see, your daughters are a trifle fatigued by the journey, so I am certain that you will permit me to offer them my assistance into the house." He extracted himself from Mrs. Bennet's grip and offered an arm to each of the sisters.

Mrs. Bennet must have realized her error because she hurried ahead of the three to call for Hill to see that tea was served at once, while often glancing back to apologize for not considering her daughters' need for assistance. Once inside and after the outer garments were taken, Mrs. Hill told them she had warm water ready for the ladies in their rooms and for Mr. Darcy in a guest room.

"Oh, yes!" Mrs. Bennet cried. "I have been remiss again because of my excitement at your return. Girls, you may go to your rooms to refresh yourselves while Hill shows dear Mr. Darcy to the room prepared for his needs."

A quarter of an hour later, the group met again in the parlour for tea. Darcy made certain that he sat as close to Elizabeth as he could because he could tell that she was weary. Although he did not wish to be parted from her, he knew that he must leave as soon as he could politely do so in order that his intended could have some rest.

"Girls, girls!" Mrs. Bennet exclaimed more loudly than she should, "You must tell me about the shopping and your new clothes. I insist upon hearing all."

Jane took the lead in describing their trip to the *modiste*. Knowing her mother as she did, she tried to explain the process with enough detail that she would be satisfied, but without sounding gauche and insulting to Mr. Darcy's sensibilities. She succeeded as well as could be expected under the circumstances, if the reactions of her mother and the gentleman were any indication. If Jane had understood that her future brother paid little attention to the discussion because of his concern for Lizzy, she would have been less nervous about the conversation.

Elizabeth was so exhausted that she barely heard what her mother and sister were saying. Her fondest wish at that moment was to lie down and sleep. She sipped her tea slowly and nibbled on a biscuit but said nothing.

Observing that even after drinking a cup of tea, Elizabeth did not revive as he had hoped, Darcy rose and suggested that it was time for him to return to Netherfield. "I believe that the ladies are in need of a rest after our early departure from Town. I hope to have the privilege of seeing all of you again soon."

"Oh, Mr. Darcy, must you leave so soon?" Mrs. Bennet protested. "I am sure that Mr. Bennet and the other girls would like to make their greetings to you. They all had some business or another to attend to that could not wait, or so they told me."

"I am sorry that I have to forgo that pleasure for the time being, but I assure you that Mr. Bingley and I will return this evening for a call, if it is agreeable to you, Mrs. Bennet."

"Oh, yes, please do come," Mrs. Bennet said eagerly. "In fact, I invite you and Mr. Bingley to come for supper." She paused for a moment before adding, "Please extend the invitation to the Hursts as well."

"As soon as I speak to Bingley and the Hursts to ascertain if they are free this evening, I will send word to you." Darcy helped Elizabeth to rise from the settee and slipped her hand through his arm. "You will see me to the carriage, will you not, Miss Elizabeth?" He bowed and expressed his gratitude before he moved with Elizabeth to the door. "Thank you, madam, for your hospitality and your invitation."

Something in his manner of speaking and his look made Mrs. Bennet curb her impulse to follow the couple to the carriage. After all, it was imperative that she encourage the relationship in any way she could. She turned with a satisfied smile on her face and went to the kitchen to make sure that the cook had the meal well in hand.

"My love," Darcy whispered when they reached his carriage, "Promise me you will rest. You do not seem well, so pale and drawn."

"My dearest, Fitzwilliam," Elizabeth said as she smiled wearily up at him, "you do not need a promise from me, since rest is my immediate desire. I will even forgive your less than flattering description of my person."

Darcy opened his mouth to protest when he saw the sparkle in her eyes, despite her tiredness. His face softened as he said, "You know that I always find you the loveliest of women, even when you can barely stay on your feet." He lifted her hand to his lips and kissed it. "Until this evening, dearest Elizabeth, for I will be here even if Bingley has other plans. I find that I cannot endure the thought of not seeing you again today."

Elizabeth watched until Darcy's carriage drove out of sight before she re-entered the house. She was a little surprised to see Sarah waiting for her inside.

"Miss Elizabeth," Sarah said softly, "I will help you to your room." She took Elizabeth's elbow and helped her up the stairs. Once they entered Lizzy's room, the maid turned down the counterpane and helped her mistress to prepare for a nap.

Almost as soon as her head hit the pillow, Elizabeth was soundly asleep. Sarah covered her with a quilt and the counterpane before closing the curtains against the daylight. She left the room and quietly closed the door behind her.

~*~

Darcy could not help but worry about Elizabeth during the carriage ride back to Netherfield. She had looked so fatigued and wan when he left her. He had wanted nothing more than to put her back into the carriage and bring her to Netherfield with him. If she were under the same roof, he would be able to be certain of her care. *I will have to trust her sister and her maid to see to her needs in my absence,* he thought. *At least, I do not have to wait long before I will be able to watch over her as her husband.*

Once he arrived at Netherfield, Bingley greeted him warmly in the entry hall. "Welcome back, Darcy. I hope your journey went well and that you accomplished your purpose."

"The trip was without incident," Darcy said as he handed his great coat to the butler, "and I believe that the ladies were well satisfied, which is what we both wanted, is it not?"

"Indeed it was. Excellent news!" Charles exclaimed. "Would you like a drink?"

"If you would allow me to change from my travelling clothes first, I would be most happy to join you."

"Of course, my friend, of course." Bingley grinned. "I do not always think of these things, especially when I want to hear how my lovely Jane enjoyed her trip to Town."

Darcy turned as he reached the stairs. "I am afraid that I will have little to tell you apart from that she seemed to get on quite well with my sister, as did Elizabeth. I think you will have to wait to receive more in depth information until we dine at Longbourn tonight." He fought to keep from smiling as he added,

"Unless you have other plans for this evening. Your sister and her husband are invited as well."

"I have no other plans," was Bingley's earnest reply. "But I would change them if I did. It has been too long since I saw Jane. Louisa and Hurst are away for a few days. I am not sure where it is they went, but they plan to be back in time for your wedding."

Nodding in complete understanding, Darcy made his way to his chambers where his man was preparing a hot bath for him. "Peters, I do not know how you accomplished this so quickly since you arrived only a short time before I did."

"I have my ways, sir," was his only reply.

"However you did it, I appreciate it," Darcy said as his man helped him out of the travel-stained and wrinkled clothes. "I will be returning to Longbourn this evening. Make sure that my dark-green jacket and matching waistcoat are ready by six."

"Yes, sir, they will be ready."

Darcy slipped into the hot water and sighed. His carriage was one of the most comfortable money could buy, but his muscles needed the soothing heat to recover from the ride. Again, he hoped that Elizabeth would have time to rest before the evening.

Once he and Elizabeth were married, Darcy would insist that she nap every day. He would not allow anything to jeopardize her health or that of the child. The very thought of something happening to either of them made him shiver, despite the heat of his bath water.

Knowing that his friend was waiting for him, he did not stay long in the tub, but was dressed and back downstairs within thirty minutes. Darcy found Bingley in his study, absently minded swirling brandy in his snifter. He could tell that Charles was thinking about his fiancée, so he would not tease him for his lack of attention.

"I am sorry if I kept you waiting," Darcy said, as Charles did not hear him when he cleared his throat.

Charles startled so much that he nearly spilled his drink. "Oh, pardon me, old man, I was lost in thought."

"Thoughts of the lovely Miss Jane Bennet, no doubt," Darcy teased, unable to resist after all.

As Bingley poured Darcy a brandy, his face reddened, but he did not deny it. "I think you would do the same if you had been parted from Miss Elizabeth as I have been from my Jane."

"I dare say, you are correct," Darcy admitted as he took the snifter. "I am delighted that I did not have to test that theory."

"Please tell me that Jane is truly well," Charles insisted, a concerned look on his face.

"Of course, she is, my friend," Darcy soothed. "I would have summoned you to Longbourn if she were not."

Charles heaved a sigh and said, "Yes, I was certain you would, but I had to ask. When it comes to my angel, I am lost."

"I do understand, Bingley." Darcy rubbed his chest where his heart ached for his lovely Elizabeth. Since he did not want to sit and pine for her, he stood and suggested that they take their brandy into the billiard room. "Maybe the game will divert us until we are able to leave as soon as politeness will allow. And when the game does not do its job, we can take up a good book or even muck out one of the stalls, anything to keep you from mooning about."

Charles joined Darcy in a hearty laugh as he took up his cue to play.

CHAPTER NINETEEN

Elizabeth woke two hours later to the sound of her younger sisters' arguing as they passed her door. She could not help but smile at the familiar noise. *How will it be to live in such houses as Darcy House and Pemberley without the clatter that is Longbourn?* Stretching her arms languidly above her head, she decided that while she would miss her family, her new one would more than compensate for the deprivation.

Revived by the nap, Elizabeth checked the clock before ringing for Sarah to help her dress. She wanted to look her best for her beloved, so that he would know that not only did she rest well, but that she was back to herself again after the carriage ride from town.

Once she descended the stairs, she found her mother and Hill removing things from a large crate in the middle of the sitting room. Elizabeth had forgotten that her mother would have taken Mr. Darcy up on his generous offer to purchase items which could not be found in Meryton for the wedding and the following breakfast. She had meant to discourage her mother from doing so, but the shopping excursion had driven it from her mind. It now appeared that it was too late.

She hurried over to speak to Mrs. Bennet. "Mama, you must cease asking Mr. Darcy for things. I am embarrassed to find that you have been imposing upon his generosity in this manner. Please do not request any more from him."

Mrs. Bennet looked up from unpacking the crate. "Oh, Lizzy, do not be so silly. Your fiancé is a wealthy man, and I am sure that the things I asked for are mere trifles to him." She caught her daughter's stern and disapproving look and sighed, "Very well, but it is too late to order more anyway. I believe most of the rest will be coming tomorrow, with the flowers arriving a day before the wedding. I shall not insult Mr. Darcy by returning the things he has so kindly procured for us."

Elizabeth turned from her mother in frustration and strode to the window to look out at the cold, grey sky. If it were not so gloomy and threatening, Lizzy would ask Jane to go for a walk with her. It was not to be, however, so she took out the handkerchiefs she had been working on. She wanted to finish them all, so that she could wrap them and leave them with the rest of the gifts she had made for her family.

The idea of not spending the holidays with her beloved family, especially of being absent from her father and dear Jane, brought a lump to her throat. In fact, leaving her family at Longbourn was fast becoming a source of pain. Elizabeth scolded herself. By this time next year, she would be celebrating the season at her own home and with her own family. Indeed, this year she would be at Pemberley with her new husband and sister.

The very thought of Mr. Darcy soon becoming her own husband warmed her. How she did love him! Yes, she would miss her family, but she reminded herself once more that she would have so many wonderful reasons to be happy that any pain would dim quickly.

After finishing a few more of the handkerchiefs and noticing the time, Elizabeth folded up her work and went to her room to recheck her appearance. She took the time to wrap the handkerchiefs she had finished and left them in the drawer with the other gifts.

Elizabeth arrived in the parlour just in time to hear her mother telling Jane about the latest things for the wedding that had arrived from Town. She decided not to say anything in the hopes that by the time their guests arrived, her mother would be finished with the topic. Although her fiancé seemed to be able to withstand Mrs. Bennet's effusive gratitude, she did not want him to have to endure it.

Unable to keep herself from the window, Elizabeth stood in wait for the guests to appear. She was overjoyed when she finally saw the Darcy coach drive up the lane. Quickly, she moved to the entry and opened the door in greeting before the butler could do so.

Since she had been napping when Darcy's reply to her mother's invitation arrived, she had forgotten to ask if the whole of the Netherfield party would attend them at supper, Elizabeth was pleased to see only Darcy and Mr. Bingley alight from the carriage. It was then that Elizabeth felt Jane slip her hand through her arm. She smiled inwardly at the knowledge that she was not the only one happy to see their newly arrived guests.

Darcy smiled broadly as he spied Elizabeth in the doorway, waiting for him. "Miss Bennet, Miss Elizabeth, you both look lovely this evening," he called out as he hurried to them and bowed before reaching for his fiancée's hand. As his lips caressed it longer than was proper, he gazed into her eyes as if to relay his affection and regard.

Elizabeth did not notice that Mr. Bingley had taken Jane's hand in a fashion similar to Darcy's, since she could not tear her eyes away from the loving look in his. It was only her mother's voice that broke the spell.

"Oh, Mr. Darcy, Mr. Bingley," Mrs. Bennet effused, "It is wonderful that you have come. The girls are happy to see you, I am sure. Will not you come inside, since it is rather chilly out here?"

With her mother in the lead, Elizabeth and Jane entered the house, each on their respective beloved's arm. Her younger sisters were in the parlour, working at various tasks. Although they all rose in greeting, only Mary asked after their health and that of the Hursts. In turn, Mr. Darcy asked Mary how Mr. Collins was faring.

"He is well, thank you." Mary's cheeks coloured prettily as she spoke of her fiancé.

"I am glad to hear it," Darcy said, pleased that his impulse to turn Collins's attention toward Elizabeth's sister had brought such pleasant results. "He writes to you often, I take it."

"I am blessed that he is such a faithful correspondent. I rarely go more than three days without a letter from him."

"Oh, yes, and I doubt if he has to wait any longer than that for one of yours," Kitty chimed in with a giggle. "I wonder that you have enough for all of the postage."

"I have no objection to paying such an expense," said Mr. Bennet from the doorway. "It is far less than I have to put out to keep you and Lydia in ribbons."

Mary fairly beamed at her father's defence. "Thank you, Papa."

Mr. Bennet waved his hand to indicate that the two gentlemen return to their seats, since they had risen when he entered the room. "Mr. Darcy, I apologize that I was not here to welcome you all back from Town. In fact…," he paused to greet his daughters with a kiss on their foreheads, before he continued, "I have not even seen my two girls until this minute. Estate business can be very time consuming."

He shook the hands of his future sons-in-law before he took his usual chair near the fire. "Sir, I hope that the excursion to Town was not too taxing. I know that I would have found it beyond my ability to endure. If I allowed my wife to convince me to make such a trip, I fear that Mr. Collins would be in possession of Longbourn far sooner than expected." He winked at Elizabeth as his wife sputtered in protest.

"I am happy then that it fell to my lot to be the one to escort your daughters to Town," Darcy said in a smooth conversational tone. He had seen the wink and decided to join the teasing. "I would not like Elizabeth or the rest of your family to lose you in such a manner. It would not reflect well on me."

Mr. Bennet laughed heartily and said, "Well, Lizzy, I believe you will never be bored in this man's company."

This time Mrs. Bennet's protests were loud and profuse, beginning with "How could Lizzy be bored in such homes as will be hers?" and ending in, "Mr. Bennet, you do love to vex me."

The announcement of dinner cut off Mrs. Bennet's tirade, much to everyone's relief. Mr. Bennet offered his arm to his wife and led the way into the dining room.

One thing that could always be said about the mistress of Longbourn was that she could set a beautiful table and serve delicious meals. When she acted as hostess, she invariably outshone her neighbours. Although the table at Netherfield was adorned with finer silver and crystal and a greater variety of food, the people of the neighbourhood who had dined there remarked that something was missing that could always be found at the Bennet table.

This night, the seating was less formal than usual and far more agreeable to the gentlemen, as they were seated next to their betrotheds. The conversation flowed freely and pleasantly as the meal progressed. Mrs. Bennet had ascertained the favourite dishes of her future sons, going so far as making certain that each had the first servings of those dishes.

When the meal was complete and the ladies moved to the parlour, Mr. Bennet announced, "Let us retire to my library. I happen to know that its chairs are more comfortable, and I keep my best port there."

As the gentlemen settled in the library, Mr. Bennet tried to speak on a variety of subjects, but he found that Darcy and Bingley were rather distracted.

Finally, Mr. Bennet set down his port and said, "Gentlemen, I believe that I am poor company this evening. Why do you not join the ladies? I will be along later."

Elizabeth was surprised but pleased to see Darcy and Bingley enter the parlour so soon.

When her fiancé joined her on the settee, he confided quietly, "I believe that Bingley and I did not attend your father well. He told us to join you and that he would be along later."

"I fear that my father may only return to say his farewell to you," Elizabeth's voice was low as she confided. "He can take only so much talk of weddings, clothes, and lace. I must confess that even though it is our wedding being discussed, I have become weary of hearing of it.'

Darcy patted her arm before he said, "It is well, then, that our wedding is to be so soon." He paused and leaned in closer before he continued, "I must confess it seems it will not come soon enough for me."

Elizabeth's light laughter in response gave Darcy great pleasure. "Dearest, I hope that I will hear your delightful laugh often after we are married."

"You certainly will, as I do love to laugh."

"What are your plans for the morrow?" Darcy asked.

"I suppose that my mother will have many chores for me to do."

"I would like to propose a walk for the morning. I find that I cannot wait to see you until the dinner hour. I am grateful for your mother's invitation for us to dine again so soon, but it is still too great a time for me to wait. Poor Charles and I are dreary company when not in the presence of our ladies." The look on Darcy's face thrilled Elizabeth, as did his declaration.

"I accept, if we are properly chaperoned, of course."

~*~

After two days had passed, Darcy travelled to Town early in the day to fetch his sister Georgiana and cousin Colonel Fitzwilliam, both of whom would be staying as Bingley's guests. Darcy had promised that upon his return, the party would call in the afternoon around three o'clock, and it was fast approaching that time.

After smoothing her hair and dress, Elizabeth walked downstairs and to the front door. She opened it and peered out, hoping to catch a glimpse of the coach coming up the lane, but she was disappointed. How had he come to be so vital to her happiness? She wondered if he missed her as strongly as she did him.

As she moved to join her mother and two of her sisters in the sitting room, Elizabeth admitted to herself that she was a trifle anxious about meeting his cousin. He had assured her several times that the colonel would like her, but knowing the difference in social rank between his family and hers, she did worry. Elizabeth was also unsure of how the colonel and Georgiana would handle her mother and younger sister's silliness.

As Mrs. Bennet and Lydia chatted gaily over the guest list, Mary joined her on the settee. "You seem uneasy, Lizzy."

The look of warmth and compassion on Mary's face surprised and blessed her. Elizabeth patted her sister's hand. "I suppose I am a little nervous about meeting Mr. Darcy's cousin. What if he does not approve of me? His sister is a delightful young woman, and we became close very quickly, but it may be different with a man of Colonel Fitzwilliam's background."

"I cannot believe that he would not approve of you." Mary's intense gaze held her sister's as she explained, "You are the most lively and prettiest of us sisters. I had always been a bit jealous of your abilities to make others feel at ease, and now that I am to become a vicar's wife, I have been trying to emulate you so that I may be of use to my future husband in his parish."

"Oh Mary, that is such a lovely thing for you to say about me," Elizabeth cried softly as she impulsively embraced her sister. "I do believe that you will be a wonderful parson's wife, and the congregation will grow to love you very much.

"May God grant it be so," Mary replied humbly.

Elizabeth marvelled at the change in her sister's attitude. Since Mr. Collins proposed, Mary had become more thoughtful and less pedantic in her observations.

The sombre tomes of Fordyce's Sermons had been replaced by the more reflective readings of the Bible and the poetry of Milton. She was taking more interest in general household duties and was far less apt to moralize. All-in-all, Lizzy concluded that her younger sister was maturing and growing into a woman of substance. Still, she could not help but wonder if Mary would really be happy married to William Collins.

She was saved from further contemplation by the arrival of Mr. Darcy and his relatives. Hill showed the three into the sitting room. Elizabeth stood and curtseyed before she moved closer to them. She wanted to greet Georgiana with a sisterly embrace, but she was not sure how the colonel would take such informality.

Elizabeth turned her gaze to her fiancé and said, "I hope your journey went well"

"It was tolerable," Darcy said before he took her hand in his and kissed it. He did not relinquish it but tucked it into his own before he turned to his cousin.

"Richard and Georgiana, I would like to present Mrs. Bennet." He then smiled at his sister and said, "Georgie dear, you already have met Miss Bennet and Miss Elizabeth. Over there at the pianoforte is Miss Mary, and Miss Lydia is there by the table."

"Ladies, this is my cousin Colonel Fitzwilliam, and my sister, Georgiana Darcy."

"Colonel Fitzwilliam, Miss Darcy, welcome to Longbourn. It is an honour to meet you. Kitty, who is the fourth of my five daughters, is visiting her friend, Miss Lucas, and should be home soon." Mrs. Bennet moved forward to greet the newcomers. "Will you not sit down? Lydia, please tell your father that our guests have arrived."

After Mr. Bennet entered the room and further introductions were made, her mother ordered refreshments to be brought immediately.

"It is so good to see you again, Miss Georgiana," Elizabeth said as she took her place near her future sister. Darcy pulled a chair as close as he could and was content to merely gaze at his beloved.

"It is good to see you again as well," the younger woman replied with warmth.

"Did not Mrs. Annesley accompany you?" It dawned upon Elizabeth that Georgiana's companion was not with them.

"She did, but asked if she could accompany my maid to Netherfield," Georgiana explained. "Mrs. Annesley finds coach travel a bit tiring, I fear."

"I hope you are not too fatigued after your trip," Lizzy said as she enjoyed just being with Darcy and his sister.

"No, Miss Elizabeth, it was not tiring at all," Georgiana replied quickly.

"My cousin does not mention that we had to leave the carriage twice, so that the wheels could be extracted from the mud," Colonel Fitzwilliam remarked as he joined the conversation. "I do hope that your trip to Pemberley will be less eventful."

"I hope so too, and I have received word from Pemberley that the roads are faring better than those closer to Town," Mr. Darcy added calmly. "And the snows have held off so far."

When the tea and cakes were brought in, Mrs. Bennet poured and served the sweets to the guests. "Colonel Fitzwilliam, will you and Miss Darcy be staying at Netherfield until the wedding?"

"Yes, ma'am, it is our intention. After the wedding, I will then accompany Georgiana and her companion to London along with my parents. We all plan to travel to Pemberley a week or so after Darcy and his bride. My parents' home is but twenty miles from there, so it is not out of the way. Georgiana is eager to be at home for Christmastide."

Elizabeth leaned closer to Georgiana as the gentlemen answered her mother's questions about Christmas at Pemberley and spoke quietly, "Georgiana, I hope that my family will have the privilege of hearing you play soon. I have told them of your talent and proficiency on the pianoforte, and they are excited for you to perform."

"Oh, please, no, Elizabeth, you know that I am not always comfortable performing before strangers," Georgiana demurred.

"You know that I will not insist that you play, but you did so well at my aunt and uncle's home. My family here may be a bit more exuberant than the Gardiners, but they do appreciate talent. Also, I think you will find a kindred spirit in my sister Mary, although she does enjoy playing for an audience. She enjoys music and has recently taken to practicing some very lovely pieces that your brother obtained for her."

"I am not surprised, since my brother is the most generous of men," Georgiana praised Darcy.

"You shall receive no arguments from me. I agree with all my heart that he is a wonderful man. I am blessed to be marrying him." Elizabeth blushed when, as she was speaking, Darcy caught her eye and smiled a slow, warm smile.

"He is most taken with you. I believe he speaks of little else but your charms and accomplishments." Georgiana lowered her voice and leaned closer to place a hand on Elizabeth's. After a quick squeeze, she released it and added, "I know he loves you very much, and I am so happy for you both."

"I thank you, Georgiana," Lizzy said, her voice thick with emotion. The fact that Fitzwilliam would speak so freely of her and his feelings for her warmed her to the toes, and she was so full of joy that she felt like crying.

It was then that her mother's voice broke into their conversation. "I have sent out the wedding invitations to all of our family and friends. Do you wish me to send out any for you, Mr. Darcy?"

"That will not be necessary," he answered kindly. "I have seen to making certain my close friends and relatives are invited. The colonel's parents will be arriving the day before the wedding. I have not heard as yet from my aunt Lady Catherine. It may be that my cousin is not up to travelling. She is in poor health, you know." What he did not tell Mrs. Bennet was that he hoped that Lady Catherine did not deign to attend, since she would only bring contention and would likely scorn and insult his new family.

"I was hoping to meet my future son-in-law's patroness. I did invite Mr. Collins, and do hope that the great lady will allow him to attend."

The conversation moved on to talk of Pemberley, and after listening to Miss Darcy's and her cousin's descriptions, Mrs. Bennet once more marvelled at the grandeur that would be her second daughter's home. She mentally took note of all the details, so that she could relate them to all of her friends in Meryton. Lydia tried to turn the colonel's attention to herself, but though he was polite, he was determined not to show the obviously young and immature girl any special notice.

Soon, Kitty arrived, and she and Lydia moved to another corner of the room to gossip and giggle over the new additions to the Netherfield party. Elizabeth used her long-time acquired skills to keep the company entertained and diverted from her sisters' juvenile behaviour.

Already completely taken by Elizabeth, Georgiana again marvelled at her future sister's natural grace and vibrancy. She had no doubt as to why and how her brother would fall in love with such a woman. She could make anyone feel comfortable. Nothing seemed to faze her, although Georgiana saw that Mrs. Bennet and the youngest two could cause distress. Her brother's fiancée had the ability to rise above the foibles of her mother and adroitly turn most of the conversations back to safer topics. All-in-all, she looked forward to having her for a sister. She knew Elizabeth was one whom she could love and admire.

"I believe it is time for us to return to Netherfield," Darcy announced. "My sister has not had time to rest after our travel from Town, so if you will excuse us, we will take our leave until dinner tomorrow."

As Elizabeth and her mother arose to escort the visitors to their carriage, Darcy took her arm to keep her back. "Please, my dear, may I call upon you tomorrow morning. I have missed you so and would like to go out walking with you if the weather permits, and if not, we will spend the time indoors."

"I have missed you as well," Elizabeth sighed. "Please, do come. I have no fixed plans for the morning."

Darcy lifted her hand and kissed it slowly before turning it to place another kiss upon her pulse. "Until tomorrow, my love," he whispered huskily.

~*~

At Netherfield that evening, after they had partaken of a simple dinner and everyone had retired for the night, there was a knock at Darcy's door. When he opened it, he found his cousin waiting to come in.

"Richard, what may I do for you?" Darcy thought he knew what his cousin wanted, but he was not going to volunteer the information.

"You may ask me in and serve me a drink," the colonel said, as if the answer was obvious.

"Of course, do come in." Darcy led him to the sitting area beside the fireplace. He picked up the decanter of brandy and poured two snifters of the liquor.

Richard sprawled out in one of the deeply cushioned chairs. "This is a comfortable room. Bingley made a good choice to lease this estate." He took a snifter and held it in his palm, slowly swirling and warming the brandy.

Darcy decided to wait for his cousin to begin his questioning, if that was what he planned. At ease with the silence, he sipped the brandy and stared into the fire. He thought about how he wished that he could have spent more time with Elizabeth. However, with less than a week to go before the wedding, he tried to console himself that it would not be very long before they would not be separated again.

"You love Miss Elizabeth very much," the colonel stated simply.

"Yes, I do."

"I was greatly surprised to hear of your engagement." Richard watched as the candlelight sparkled on the surface of the brandy.

"I imagine nearly everyone who knows me is surprised," Darcy admitted calmly.

"Damn it, Darcy, what are you thinking, marrying a dowerless country chit?" The colonel's voice rose as he asked the question.

Darcy straightened in his chair, his face no longer relaxed or amused. "I will not stand for anyone insulting my fiancée. If you want to stay in this room or in this house, for that matter, you will refrain from any more derogatory remarks about her. Is that clear?"

Colonel Fitzwilliam did not often see his cousin in such a state. In fact, it was only during the incident with George Wickham that Darcy had ever lost his reserve and raised his voice in such a way.

"Darcy, I apologize," he sighed. "It is just so unlike you. You have always had such a head upon your shoulders when it came to women who wanted to lead you to the altar. I couldn't help but wonder..." The colonel stopped himself before he spoke what was on his mind, since he could see that his cousin was serious in his threat.

Leaning back against his chair once more, Darcy relaxed. He knew without a doubt that his cousin was concerned about him and did not know Elizabeth as he did. He decided to tell him something of their courtship, but nothing of her experience with Wickham. The more people who knew, the greater would be the possibility of exposure. He would protect his dearest love and their child from scandal if he possibly could.

"It is true she has little dowry, but she is of greater worth to me than any fortune would be." He smiled when he thought of what might have happened if she had continued to hold his unkind words spoken at the assembly ball against him, or if she had believed Wickham's lies. "She has never been impressed with my wealth or status. Besides, she is a gentleman's daughter, which means we are equals. At first, little about me endeared me to her. I even insulted her the day I met her at a local assembly. I was still in a rather foul mood over Georgiana's near elopement, and you know how I hate to dance with strangers. Bingley was trying to force me to dance. He said to me, 'I hate to see you standing about in this stupid manner.'" He joined with the colonel in laughter.

"The young pup is not afraid to speak his mind." Fitzwilliam chuckled once more.

"That night he certainly was not," Darcy went on, "and I did not really see her that night. The next time I had the pleasure of being in her company, it was under less than desirable conditions. Miss Bennet had taken ill while dining with Bingley's sisters. Elizabeth came the next day to nurse her sister, walking the entire three miles from her home to Netherfield. Soon, I began to understand what a lovely and compassionate woman she is."

"That is an admirable quality in a sister, but certainly not the basis for marriage," his cousin countered.

"I love Elizabeth more than I ever considered possible." Darcy's face softened as he thought of her. "And wonders of wonders, she returns my affection, which she told me when she finally agreed to be my wife."

"What do you mean, 'finally'?" Fitzwilliam asked.

"At first, she did not want to accept me." Darcy nodded at his cousin's incredulous look. "She felt that we would not suit, and that my status and hers were too different. Her own parents are not the most compatible. She wanted to marry only for the deepest love.

"Miss Bingley did not help with her constant references to her own intimacy of acquaintance with me and my family. She harped on what qualified a woman as accomplished. She had no idea that already I saw Elizabeth as being of a higher quality than any young ladies' academy graduate who wore only the highest of fashion could be." Darcy shook his head at the memory.

"I meant to ask you. Where is that particular young ladies' academy graduate?" the colonel inquired.

"She is off visiting an aunt of the Bingleys in Scarborough. I believe she will not be attending the wedding."

"Exiled, is she? For what offence?" Fitzwilliam did enjoy a bit of gossip, and since he had never cared for the brittle, social-climbing young woman, he wanted to hear what had brought about such a move.

"Bingley finally had enough of her rude comments to me and her constant insults concerning the Bennets, and about the two eldest sisters in particular." Darcy felt uncomfortable relating the events. "Please keep this to yourself. I know you love to gossip, but I would not have Bingley embarrassed by this becoming known."

Colonel Fitzwilliam knew how to apply discretion where it was needed, so he nodded his agreement. "I will not repeat any of what we speak here tonight."

"Thank you, Richard."

"So how did you end up engaged if she refused you?" Fitzwilliam would not be deterred.

"I did not say she refused me, I said that she did not accept me when I first asked her. She asked for time to think about my proposal, and after putting thought into it, she accepted me. She had already forgiven me my slight at the assembly and had discovered, upon examining her heart, she loved me too."

"All right, cousin, I see that you are convinced, but why must you be married so quickly? Why not be married in the spring? You could share your wedding with Bingley and the lovely Miss Bennet."

"I do not appreciate your questioning my motives," Darcy said fiercely. "But I will tell you this; I do not want to return to Pemberley for the winter without Elizabeth at my side, and she is in agreement with me. If you wish to know any more about my fiancée, I would advise you to ask Georgiana. She loves Elizabeth and will defend her right to become my wife and her sister with, for her, a rare passion."

"Very well, I will cease," the colonel said resignedly.

"Thank you."

"I do have a few questions about how it is that you came to write me about Wickham and your reason for having him tossed on a ship bound for the West Indies because of his debts. Why did you not just throw him into debtor's prison?" The colonel's own fury at his late uncle's godson had not abated since he tried to elope with Georgiana.

"As you know, I had bought all of his debt in Lambton and Ramsgate and some of his that I discovered in Town. I could not allow honest people to suffer, who in honour of my father's memory, had extended credit to Wickham," he said tonelessly. "It is likely that I planned someday to use his debts against him, but I could not do so in English courts. The possibility of Wickham blackening

Georgiana's name was too great. So I asked you to see to it that he was transported and put into servitude for what he owed."

"But why now and why here?"

"As usual, Wickham spread lies about my person and our dealings in Meryton, and one of the first persons he tried to impose his falsehoods upon was Elizabeth. She informed me herself that she had not believed a word he said." Darcy fought with his own sense of honour before he told his cousin only part of the truth of the matter. "Her younger sisters are fond of a man in a red uniform and were easily drawn to his easy manners and charming ways. Elizabeth was concerned that they and others might be drawn in by his charm. It was then that I shared with her the history between Wickham and myself and decided that I needed to act to protect my future family, as by that time, I had already understood my affection for her."

"I cannot say that I am unhappy with the outcome, for it seems that Wickham had not learned his lesson after my last encounter with him." The fierce, almost feral look in his cousin's eye startled Darcy.

"What happened the last time you saw him?"

"Let us just say that I enjoyed my attempt at rearranging his face, and may have broken a rib or two before I allowed him to leave his lodgings for other places. I told him that if I ever heard of him again, he would rue that day since I would not treat him so well then." The colonel stood and helped himself to more brandy.

"You said in your letter that he was packing to leave Meryton when Colonel Forster had him detained."

"Yes, and he was violent in his words toward the colonel and you, since he was sure that you were involved in his incarceration and deportation. It is fortunate that I dispatched three of my most trusted men, for Wickham talked at length about you. He tried to wheedle his way out of their custody with promises of rewards." Fitzwilliam's smile was sinister. "I believe he finally desisted after one of my men knocked out a few teeth."

Darcy smiled and felt no regret at the treatment his former playmate received at the hands of Fitzwilliam's men. It was only that he wished he could have been the one to administer it for Elizabeth's and Georgiana's sakes. "So the ship has been at sea for about three weeks now?"

"I believe so. As I told you, my men did not leave the ship until it set sail, and Wickham was bound the whole time. I left strict orders for the captain to see to it that he was kept in chains until they were out to sea." Fitzwilliam felt a warm satisfaction that they would never see the man again.

Darcy was content upon hearing this account and wanted to put the subject to rest. It was with that intention that he asked his cousin about his latest military assignment and what his opinion was as to the likelihood of his joining the forces on the continent.

Understanding that he had gotten as much information about his cousin's engagement as he could and realizing that he was no longer truly concerned at the rapidity of the marriage, Colonel Fitzwilliam began a longer discussion of his own current situation.

CHAPTER TWENTY

Upon their arrival at Longbourn the next evening, the party from Netherfield found that Mrs. Bennet had invited other guests to dinner. She introduced them to her nearest neighbours, the Lucases, and to her sister and husband, Mr. and Mrs. Phillips.

Since Darcy was already acquainted with them all, he easily slipped away to find Elizabeth, who was talking with two of her sisters. "I hope you are well after our walk this morning," he inquired as he smiled down at her.

"I am perfectly well, sir, as the company was more than tolerable," Her tone of voice contained the hint of impertinence that Darcy loved.

"I am glad to hear it." He smiled and turned to Mary and Jane. "And how are you ladies faring this evening?"

They both indicated that they were in excellent health, and Jane seemed about to add something more when they were joined by Bingley, the colonel, and Georgiana. For a time, small talk was in order until Mary invited Georgiana to view her newest piece of music at the pianoforte. Bingley not so subtly guided Jane to a settee in the corner.

"Your sister is a beautiful woman," Colonel Fitzwilliam commented as he watched the couple sit down and begin to talk eagerly to each other. "It is no wonder that Bingley is so besotted."

Elizabeth lifted a brow before she responded, "Jane is lovely, but I do believe my future brother understands her inner beauty is even greater than the outward."

"I meant no offense," he said, his tone defensive.

"Do not worry, Colonel. I am never offended by a compliment to one of my sisters." This time, Elizabeth smiled when she replied, "I am merely protective of Jane. If someone were to cause her pain, I would have a hard time forgiving the offender. She is full of grace and goodness and finds no fault in anyone she meets. It is very difficult for her to comprehend evil in others, since she is so good."

"A rare individual then, and a fortunate man, Bingley," he stated with a bit of envy.

"I dare say that he would agree with you," Darcy entered the conversation. He loved to watch his Elizabeth when her courage rose. She was loyal, which boded well for Georgiana and himself. "But as to the most fortunate, I claim that for myself."

Elizabeth blushed at the statement, so she decided to tease Darcy. "Colonel Fitzwilliam, your cousin has not always claimed to be so 'fortunate'."

"Ah, yes, Darcy confessed his social faux pas to me last evening," he said as he chuckled.

"Well, he has been forgiven for that, and I believe he finds me more than tolerable now." She smiled up into Darcy's face, and soon the two lost their awareness of any but each other.

Colonel Fitzwilliam decided that it would be best if he would leave the two relatively alone and find another conversation to join. He spied Bingley and his fiancée speaking to each other in a far corner of the room. He had no interest in disturbing them either. As he moved across the room, he saw three young girls happily chattering like a flock of finches. He did remember being introduced to them, so as he searched his memory for their names, one of them caught him glancing their way.

"Colonel Fitzwilliam, do join us and settle our query. We were just wondering if you are acquainted with Colonel Forster. He is the commander of the militia that is quartered in Meryton." The pretty, young girl tucked her hand in his arm and pulled him closer to the small group. "His wife is one of my best friends. We are so happy that the militia is in our area."

"Miss Lydia, is it not?" The colonel finally remembered her name.

"It is, and this is my sister Kitty and our close friend, Maria Lucas."

The colonel acknowledged each of the other girls with a bow. "I am happy to meet you again, ladies. I have not had the pleasure of making the acquaintance of Colonel Forster. However, my cousin did speak of meeting several of the officers, including the colonel."

Lydia lowered her head but looked up coyly through her lashes at Fitzwilliam. "I would like to know why you do not wear your uniform. I am sure that you look very handsome in it."

"I am sorry to disappoint you, Miss Lydia, but I am afraid that I do not look any better in uniform than I do in civilian clothes," he teased, his eyes twinkling.

"Oh, Colonel, you are too droll," Lydia laughed as she playfully slapped his sleeve. "You are fully aware that you are quite handsome, but I favour the scarlet of regimentals. It does add such distinction to a gentleman's appearance."

"I think you will find that the distinction you mention might be only on the surface," he replied as he thought of the likes of Wickham. "I know of some disgraceful officers who might look dashing in their regimentals, but who have no integrity at all. I would rather be known for my good character and conduct than for my good looks."

Lydia blinked up at the colonel, her hand still resting on his arm. No man had ever reacted to her flirting compliments in this manner. Could he have been trying to tell her something? "Are you saying that beauty is not to be desired, sir?"

"No, indeed, I am not, but I am saying that it should not be the weightiest measure. I know of a particular young man whose countenance would always be called handsome, but in his heart, he is as ugly as any African warthog. He can charm the ladies, but he always leaves them with heartbreak and sometimes in ruin." Fitzwilliam saw that he had the attention of all three young ladies by this time. "One should not trust that a man of fair appearance and manners is equally as fair in his dealings with others. One might find that a man of lesser beauty will be of the more sterling character."

He chuckled a little and continued, "I did not mean to lecture, but I am serious on this account. Pardon me, I will allow you lovely ladies to continue your conversation that I so rudely interrupted."

When he moved to go, Lydia prevented him. "You did not interrupt us, Colonel. We would love to hear about your history in the army. Have you seen much battle action? Do you think the French will invade England?"

Smiling, the colonel began a sanitized version of his military career, because something about the girl who still held tightly to his arm appealed to him, despite her age, naïveté, brashness, and too obvious fondness for a soldier's scarlet coat. For a quick moment, he pondered whether or not this young woman could change her ways, or if her personality was quite fixed.

"What can your cousin have to say to my sisters and Maria?" Elizabeth saw the three girls' attentive expressions and Colonel Fitzwilliam's serious demeanour as he spoke.

"I hope that he is not filling their heads with fanciful ideas." Darcy glanced at her. "Richard is not one of the soldiers who try for a conquest wherever they are, but he does like to weave rather farfetched stories of his exploits, and mine as well."

With an impish grin, Elizabeth said, "Maybe I should join them. I have not heard nearly enough stories of your misspent youth."

"I am afraid that you would be very disappointed." His own smile was relaxed. "I was a serious boy who rarely got into mischief unless I was following my cousin's lead."

"I shall believe your tale until I hear differently," she teased affectionately.

As the couple was enjoying a bit of conversation, they were joined by Samuel and Charlotte Lucas.

"Eliza, it is good to see you looking so well." Samuel bowed over her hand. "Mr. Darcy, I have not had the opportunity to congratulate you. I hope that you and Eliza will be very happy together."

"Thank you, Mr. Lucas," Darcy acknowledged him with a slight bow of the head. He had the feeling that Lucas was trying to goad him, but oddly, he felt no pang of jealousy. "Miss Lucas, it is a pleasure to see you again."

Charlotte studied her friend and found that her countenance showed her complete devotion to her fiancé. As pleased as she was, she could not help but be saddened by the fact that her best friend would be so far from Hertfordshire. She had just opened her mouth to ask about the wedding plans when her brother spoke.

"I admit that I was rather astonished to find not one, but three of our neighbours to be engaged, though I should not be surprised, since they are quite the prettiest in the county. I suppose I hoped that once I returned from University, I would court one of the fair Bennet ladies." He shrugged his shoulders as if it did not matter, but his eyes spoke of frustration.

"Mr. Lucas, I do not recall that you showed particular interest in any of my sisters, but there are still two of them who are unattached, if you are quite settled upon courting a Bennet." Elizabeth was clear in her way of addressing her neighbour and former childhood friend that she no longer wished him to address her by her nickname, and that she had never had an interest in a more intimate relationship with him.

"Yes, Miss Elizabeth, and lovely ones they are too." His reply and the slight nod of his head indicated that he had understood her meaning. "Perhaps I will reacquaint myself with Miss Kitty and Miss Lydia. If you will excuse me..." Again he bowed and left their company.

"Lizzy, Mr. Darcy, I hope that you are not upset by Samuel," Charlotte said, worried that her brother had offended her friend and her fiancé.

Darcy answered for them both, "Miss Lucas, I am not offended in the least, and I am sure that Elizabeth is not either."

"Oh, no, Charlotte," said Elizabeth grasped her friend's hand. "I suppose he was not as tactful so he could have been, but he did not upset me. I have always known how to handle him, have I not?"

Charlotte chuckled, relieved. "Indeed, you have."

"I am curious to hear examples of how my fiancée handled your brother, Miss Lucas," Darcy inquired as he grinned at Elizabeth.

Charlotte happily began a story which ended in Elizabeth's pushing Samuel into the duck pond on the Lucas property after Samuel tried to frighten her with a garden snake.

Soon, everyone was called to dinner. Again, Mrs. Bennet had laid a beautiful table and arranged the guests in such a way as to provide friendly and lively intercourse during the meal. Much to Darcy's pleasure, she had seated Elizabeth between his sister and himself, with his cousin across the table from them. He was not completely comfortable with the fact that the two youngest Bennets were on each side of the colonel, but he did notice that Fitzwilliam did not seem adverse to the arrangement.

After the delicious meal and the gentlemen had rejoined the ladies in the drawing room, Mrs. Bennet called upon the young ladies for music. Mary was prevailed upon to go first, and she entertained the assembled family and guests with one of the new pieces Darcy had obtained for her.

Once Mary had finished, she insisted that Elizabeth join her at the pianoforte and sing the song they had been practicing. While normally Lizzy would have been happy to perform for her friends and family, she felt a pang of anxiety and would have refused had Darcy not leaned to whisper in her ear, "Look at me, dearest, and remember that nothing will harm you here."

Taking his advice, Elizabeth joined Mary at the pianoforte, and she kept her eyes on him throughout her aria. Soon, the song and her fiancé's response to it cast out any anxious thoughts, and she was able to enjoy herself. As the music ended, she was almost surprised by the applause that swelled in response. After acknowledging her audience, Lizzy made her way back to Darcy's side.

As she passed Charlotte, her friend exclaimed, "Oh, Eliza, that was exquisite. You are getting better all the time."

"Thank you, Charlotte," Elizabeth replied, and she was blushing when she finally arrived at Darcy's side.

"I completely agree with your friend's assessment. Your voice and song were lovely," he said in earnest. "I hope to hear many a private concert once we are married."

"I hope to be able to astound you for years to come with my musical expertise, as I plan on following the advice Georgiana told me she often receives from your aunt Catherine," she teased. "The advice, as you have no doubt heard for yourself, is that one must practice most constantly in order to be truly proficient."

Darcy laughed, happy to see that Elizabeth was teasing him, and that the anxiety of earlier seemed to have subsided. He watched her as she listened to Maria Lucas's performance at the pianoforte. Her eyes closed in pleasure at a particular moment in the concert. What a wonder that she would soon be his! His sweet Beth! He blinked that his mind had conjured up the nickname. He had never imagined her as Beth before, but it seemed perfect. However, before he used it, Darcy sought her opinion on it.

"I have noticed that the Lucases often call you Eliza," he began. "Do you like that designation?"

"In truth, I do not, but I have been Eliza to Charlotte and the other Lucases so long that I dare not object." She paused to search for the right words. "I suppose that I did not mind it so much before Miss Bingley began to use it. It always seemed an insult upon her lips. I hope that you do not think less of me for saying so."

"Indeed, I do not," Darcy responded quickly. "It had always sounded the same to my ears as well when coming from Miss Bingley, which is why I do not care for it. I have thought of one that I wonder if you would object to my using, at least in private."

Elizabeth raised her brows in curiosity. "And what would that be?"

"Beth," he replied simply.

For several moments, she pondered the diminutive of her name, rehearsing the sound of it in her mind. Elizabeth looked into his eyes and smiled. "I think it is lovely, and since no one has ever called me thus, it will be special between us."

Darcy scanned the room quickly, and upon finding that everyone's attention was upon Maria and her performance, he lifted her hand to his lips for a kiss.

Once the music portion of the evening was concluded, Mrs. Bennet ordered coffee and cake to be brought in. Pleased with the pleasant conversations she noted taking place around the room, and that her unengaged daughters were receiving attention from the two unattached gentlemen present, she nearly swooned at the very thought that she could have all of her daughters married. Unable to contain the joy the idea brought her, she hastened to her sister's side.

"Oh, sister, what a successful evening this is!" she exclaimed as she squeezed Mrs. Phillips's arm.

Mrs. Phillips smiled at Lady Lucas to whom she had been speaking. "I was just telling Lady Lucas that it seems like romance is in the air at Longbourn."

Lady Lucas, who knew that her daughters were not so attractive as some of her neighbour's girls, could not help but feel the situation unfair. She knew Charlotte to be fairly on the shelf, but she could not believe that Lydia was any prettier than her own Maria, and she was more pleasant to be around than the Bennets' youngest. The only solace she had was that the colonel probably needed to marry for money, being a second son. Lydia had no more dowry than her own daughters, so the likelihood of a match was very poor, no matter what Mrs. Bennet's or Lydia's desires were.

"Colonel Fitzwilliam is a gentleman, to be sure," Lady Lucas answered noncommittally. "But he is not likely to be in the neighbourhood after the wedding."

A bit put out by her neighbour's negative opinions, Mrs. Bennet chose to ignore them. "I believe I noticed his special regard for my Lydia. I do have a sense of these sorts of things. I predicted that Mr. Bingley would offer for Jane, did I not?"

"You did, indeed, sister," Mrs. Phillips agreed. "Though I suppose you were surprised by Mr. Darcy's interest in Lizzy after his snubbing her at the first assembly ball he attended."

"I admit that it took me some time to comprehend his regard," Mrs. Bennet said, pensively. Then, she decided to change the subject, since even she could see that her good friend and neighbour was unhappy at the moment. "Lady Lucas, I suppose you are very happy to have Samuel home again. He seems quite the gentleman. You told me that he graduated with some honours, did you not?"

That was the perfect subject to elevate Lady Lucas's mood, and she began to relate her son's many accomplishments.

Across the room, midst the cluster of young women, Colonel Fitzwilliam laughed heartily. He knew that part of his appeal was his status and rank, but these girls were not like the young ladies of the *ton*. They did not put on the usual airs, and he found the lack of conceit refreshing. However, they did speak their minds with little thought to whether what they said was appropriate, especially Miss Lydia. He should have been put off by that fact, but he found the enthusiasm for life and the lack of artifice appealing. Of course, the youngest Bennet girl tried to flirt with him, but her efforts were not devious or cruel to the others. He came to the conclusion that she was merely very spoiled, but truly without malice.

Samuel Lucas stood on the edge of the merry group and observed the two remaining unattached Bennet girls. Lydia was far too vivacious for his tastes, but as he continued to watch, he saw that Miss Kitty was calmer and seemed to have more sense than her sister, though she tended to mimic her sister's ideas and actions. He decided that he was not averse to getting to know her better. And with Maria being her particular friend, he felt certain that he would have many opportunities to see Miss Kitty in the future.

Mary and Georgiana had been quietly discussing music and some of their favourite books. Mary had only recently begun to enjoy more variety in her reading choices by taking note of some of Elizabeth's preferences. The pair finished their dialogue on a new novel. Georgiana had obviously enjoyed the book. Mary, who was still overcoming her ingrained habit of moralizing, finally admitted that it had been exciting, if a bit beyond her idea of what was completely proper.

Having thusly exhausted that subject, they decided to join the other young people. It was at just the moment they arrived, arm-in-arm at the outer edge of the group, that Lydia posed a question to the colonel.

"I have been wondering if you remember Mr. George Wickham," she asked breezily. "He said that he grew up in Derbyshire, and since your cousins' estate is in that county, I thought that you might be acquainted with that gentleman."

Lydia did not notice that the colonel's face grew cold and stern at her question, but she was briefly aware that Miss Darcy's face had turned pale. When Fitzwilliam did not answer immediately, she continued to explain, "He joined Colonel Forster's regiment about two months ago and was very much liked by the people in Meryton, being so jovial and gentlemanly. Alas, he must have run into some trouble, for Maria and I saw him taken away by three brawny men who looked to be in the regulars, judging by their uniforms. I cannot understand what he could have done that was so wrong as to merit such treatment."

As Georgiana fought to stay upright at the mention of the man's name, Mary saw her distress. She put her arm around her new friend's waist and assisted her to a chair. Leaving her for a moment, she fetched a glass of lemonade from the refreshment table and brought it back to her new friend. "Here, drink this, Miss Darcy. It is suddenly quite warm in this room, and I am sure this will help."

The colonel seemed to grow in height as he stood staring down at Lydia. He looked at the young girl with a combination of disdain and pity. The chit was obviously not so perceptive as her older sister when it came to the charms of a vile man such as Wickham. Fighting within himself as to how to answer her, Fitzwilliam decided to be as gentle as possible.

"If you will remember, Miss Lydia," he began softly, "that earlier, I told you about the kind of men who seemed to be handsome and charming but were hideous inside. Well, Wickham is one of those men. I have known him since we were young. From an early age, he was shown to be cruel and a liar. More than once, I found him beating up on a younger boy, usually one of the servants' children. His clever tongue got him out of trouble more than it should have. He was also very cruel to animals. I will not trouble you with a description of the times I discovered those cruelties.

"Through my contacts in the army, I am privy to the circumstances of his latest crimes. All I will say is that he deserved the punishment which he was given. Finally, he was not able to talk his way out of the penalty for his vile deeds."

Lydia's mouth hung open. She could not argue with the colonel, for somewhere in her heart, she knew he was telling the truth, even though he was obviously leaving out details to spare the sensibilities of the ladies present. A feeling of shame washed over her for nearly the first time in her life and brought hot tears to her eyes. Colonel Fitzwilliam was right; she was too easily fooled by pretty looks and equally pretty words.

"I am sorry...p-pardon me," Lydia choked out before turning for the door and leaving the room as quickly as possible without causing a scene.

Fortunately, not many beside those within the group except for Darcy and Elizabeth observed Lydia leave. Concerned for both of their sisters, they stood and moved to join the colonel, who had excused himself from the group to follow Lydia.

"Let me see if I can help. It was something I said that upset her. She asked about Wickham and I exposed his character," the colonel explained, and quickly added when he saw the concerned looks on their faces, "In the most general of terms, of course."

Elizabeth nearly gasped, but concern for her sister overrode her own discomfort. "I will come with you. It would not be seemly for you to go to her alone," she said softly. She looked at Darcy and nodded her head toward Georgiana, who still seemed quite discomposed though not so badly as at first.

Understanding her, Darcy indicated that he would go to his sister. "Do not be long, dearest," he murmured as she left to follow the colonel.

A servant stationed in the hall told Elizabeth that Lydia had gone to the small sitting parlour. Upon opening the door, she saw her sister hunched over dejectedly, weeping into her hands. Elizabeth had seen Lydia cry or sob many times, but nearly always she had done so in a fit of pique or to garner sympathy. However, this time she seemed to be truly grieving.

"Hush, Lyddie dear, do not go on so. You will make yourself ill." Elizabeth used her childhood nickname as she sat next to Lydia and put her arms around her.

For several minutes, all that was heard in the room were the sounds of weeping and Elizabeth trying to soothe her. At first, Lydia would not be comforted, but finally, the sobs turned to sniffs and hiccups, then to deep sighs. Elizabeth drew back slightly and handed her sister a handkerchief.

"Tell me what is wrong," Elizabeth urged. "What has upset you?"

"I am such a foolish, foolish girl," Lydia said as she hid her face against Elizabeth's shoulder. "I believed a liar and thought you were wrong to marry the man who kept Mr. Wickham from what he claimed was his proper living. I did not know he was false in all he said."

Lydia looked up and caught her sister's gaze. She looked so much younger with her face blotchy and her eyes still wet with tears. "I thought that I could have been in love with him, and that he might have loved me if he had not been taken away. He said such lovely things to me, and that you were jealous of me. I think that I would have even eloped with him if he had asked." She hiccupped again and fairly wailed, "Oh, Lizzy, how wrong I was to believe him!"

Colonel Fitzwilliam pulled up a chair and sat down close by, but he kept his counsel while Lydia poured out her story. Once she finished speaking, he spoke in a gentle tone. "Miss Lydia, do not fret so. As I told you, he is a deceiver who has had much practice. He has tried to seduce many young women, and even succeeded in some cases. He is not someone to weep over."

Lydia turned her eyes to the floor. She swiped at her eyes a few times before she murmured, "I do not weep over him. I weep because I am ashamed of myself. I believed him, especially when he told me that Lizzy was jealous of me. It made me feel good, even superior."

She raised her gaze to her sister. "I have been jealous of you for a long time, Lizzy. You are so pretty and smart, and Papa and Jane love you above the rest of us. I wish you loved me too," Lydia added wistfully.

"Oh, my dear Lyddie, I do love you, as do Papa and Jane," Elizabeth wrapped her arms around her again. This time, there were tears in her eyes too. "Forgive me for not showing you so that you understood it."

Lydia held tightly to her sister for a moment before she smiled through her tears and exclaimed, "Truly, Lizzy?"

"Truly, Lyddie, I do."

"I do forgive you, but I think I am the one who needs your forgiveness." Lydia pulled back and gripped her sister's hands. "Lizzy, will you help me become more like you and Jane? I know you will be gone soon, but we could write to each other, and mayhap someday Mr. Darcy will allow me to visit."

"I gladly forgive you and would love to help you, but I believe that you are going to be fine. Remember that Jane and Mary will be here for longer than I, and I think that even Kitty could help, if you listen to her." Elizabeth paused to find the right words. "You have been spoiled, it is true, but that was because we all loved you so much. You were the sweetest and the happiest baby I had ever seen. No one wanted to squelch that in you, so we catered to you too much. I realize now that it was wrong, and now you do too. You have it in you to change. And remember, I will pray for you as well. God will help you if you allow Him."

Lydia smiled for the first time and leaned in to kiss Elizabeth's cheek before she turned to the colonel. "I need to apologize to you for my impertinence. And I think that something I said upset Miss Darcy. Will you explain to her that I did not mean to offend her?"

"Miss Lydia, I accept your apology and will speak to my cousin. I am not able to explain what it was that you said to upset her, but I know that you did not intend to do so. Georgiana is shy and may seem standoffish, but she does not hold a grudge and will eventually feel comfortable enough to speak freely about herself, especially if you are able to tell her what you told us about your experience with Wickham. Just give her time."

Fitzwilliam wanted to comfort Lydia in a more tangible way, but he could not. He took pleasure in the fact that one of the questions he had asked himself about this pretty young girl had been answered in such a roundabout way. It did, indeed, look as if she was capable of changing her ways. A person would just need to wait and see how successful she would be.

In the meantime, Darcy hastened to his sister's side. "Georgie, dearest, are you well?"

She looked up at him, her pale face showing her distress. However, her eyes were more peaceful than he would have expected. "I will be well, brother. Miss Mary has been most kind, and since few have noticed my reaction, I believe I shall recover from the shock soon." She cast a grateful glance at Mary as she spoke.

Darcy watched as Mary lightly stroked Georgiana's hand. The smile of acceptance and concern on Elizabeth's sister's face convinced him that he could speak more freely than he normally would have. "Forgive me for not preparing you for the likelihood that you would hear that he had been in the area. I thought that since he had been gone for over a month, there would be little chance it would be spoken of. I am so sorry for my error in judgment."

"There is no need for you to apologize," Georgiana patted his hand with her free one. "It was just such a great shock. I am so glad that Miss Mary was with me. She kept me from falling to the floor in a faint and brought me a cool drink to help settle me."

"Miss Mary, I do not think I can ever thank you enough for your aid to my sister." At this very moment, all he could think of was how grateful to God he was for most of the Bennet sisters, even though Darcy had to force down the anger he felt toward the youngest. He was hopeful that Elizabeth had been able to convince Lydia to curb her tongue concerning Wickham, or he would have to take measures to stop her.

"Sir, you owe me nothing. I only did what I could to assist Miss Georgiana," Mary humbly asserted. "Elizabeth's obvious affection for your sister and my own growing fondness for her gave me no other choice."

"You have my gratitude, nonetheless." He smiled at Mary before turning back to his sister. "Would you like for us to leave now? I am sure that we could manage it without insulting our hosts."

"Thank you, brother, but no. I would prefer to stay so that no one will think that anything untoward has occurred. I believe that Mary and I will adjourn to the pianoforte and see if we can play a duet, if you think that the Bennets would not mind."

Darcy marvelled at his little sister's bravery. "I am sure that if you apply to Mrs. Bennet, she will be happy to oblige you, since you did not have a chance before to play."

As he watched Mary and Georgiana walk to where Mrs. Bennet held court with her cronies, Darcy experienced great pride. His sister was truly maturing into a gracious and elegant young lady. He saw his future mother-in-law's eager assent to the girls' question and heard her announcement of the additional musical number.

Samuel Lucas, Maria, and Kitty stood huddled in a tight group. Lucas had not heard all the discussion between the colonel and Lydia, but his sister and her friend had told them enough to reinforce his opinion that the youngest Bennet girl was not for him. Her impertinence and cheek would never do in his home. He lifted his eyes to Kitty Bennet and saw genuine concern for everyone involved. He watched her twist her hands together as she glanced from Miss Darcy to the door and back again. It also seemed that she understood that her sister was in the wrong, and yet still wanted to comfort her. He was pleased that she did not interrupt Mr. Darcy as he talked with his sister. Yes, Catherine Bennet was indeed worth getting to know better.

As the music began to swell, Darcy wondered when Elizabeth and the others would return. He hoped that it would be soon, for he desperately needed his beloved Beth at this moment. Just when he had begun to ponder going to search for them, the three re-entered the room. A subdued Lydia was flanked by Elizabeth and his cousin.

He hastened to them and asked, "Is all well?"

Elizabeth nodded at Lydia's questioning look, encouraging her youngest sister to speak. Her voice was thick from crying, but quietly earnest. "I am much better than I have any right to be after my imprudent conversation, and my unspeakable foolishness in believing that man's tales about you and my sister. I must ask your forgiveness, Mr. Darcy, and I will seek the same from your sister once she and Mary are finished playing." When he did not speak, she sighed in resignation, "I will not importune you any longer, since I know that I do not deserve your pardon."

She moved to leave, but Darcy reached out his hand to stop her. "Miss Lydia, please stay. Please give me the opportunity to answer you." He took a deep breath and with the exhale, tried to release all of the bitter feelings he harboured toward her. The foolish young girl was his lovely Beth's sister. If he had not dealt with Wickham when he did, she might have been ruined or even worse, forced to marry the blackguard. "I forgive you, since it is obvious that you are repentant, and I do know how easily young women fall victim to his flattery and fine manners. I hope that you will be wiser in bestowing your esteem in the future."

"Oh yes, Mr. Darcy! Thank you, sir! Lizzy has promised to help me learn to be more of a lady. I am young, but I believe that I have learned a great lesson this night." She gave her sister a quick, grateful smile. "I think that the music is close to the end, so if you will excuse me, I will make my apologies to Miss Darcy."

"Miss Lydia, will you permit me to escort you?" Colonel Fitzwilliam asked gently. "I believe the presence of her old cousin will help to steady Georgiana"

"Of course, Colonel, if you think it will help Miss Darcy," Lydia readily agreed.

"Then shall we?" He offered the young woman his arm and they proceeded to where the pianoforte stood in the other corner of the room and waited for the duet to end.

"Oh my love, how can I express my gratitude for your forgiveness of my foolish, little sister?" Elizabeth clung to his arm as she beamed up at him.

At his beloved's reaction to his answer to her sister, any lingering resentment toward Lydia seemed to vanish. "How could I not forgive her, since I did not deal with his presence in Meryton in a timely fashion?" He returned her loving smile with one of his own.

His expression sobered when he asked, his voice deep with concern, "How do you fare after being forced to speak of the villain?"

Her face registered surprise. She had not really thought of Wickham's actions toward herself while she dealt with Lydia. There had been no anxiety for her own well-being, only for her baby sister. "I must admit that I had not given it a thought. I merely wanted to help my obviously distressed sister, so that I could rejoin you and assist you in comforting poor Georgiana. I am very happy to say that I am well and in decent composure."

"Wonderful!" He placed his hand over hers on his arm and squeezed. "Shall we join our sisters, or should we wait?"

"From what I am able to discern, Georgiana does not seem to be upset at the moment. I suggest that we tarry to see if we are needed. I believe that they will be better able to deal with what has happened without our intervention."

"I will accept your opinion, as I see that Lydia is more distressed than Georgie looks to be at the moment." He could not help but smile as his own shy sister seemed to be trying to comfort Lydia. "They do appear to be coming to an understanding. I did not know that either of them had this kind of strength in them."

Elizabeth gave a soft laugh. "They are our sisters. How could they not have the potential? This night has not ended as I thought, but all-in-all, I find I am quite pleased, especially if the change in Lydia is a permanent one."

"I believe the Lucases are preparing to leave. Let us join our sisters, Miss Maria, and my cousin." Darcy guided her back across the room.

They arrived in time to hear Georgiana warmly say, "Miss Lydia, you must not trouble yourself any longer. I think the sooner we forget that person, the better off we will all be. Someday I might even be prevailed upon to tell you how he fooled me as well."

"Oh, Miss Darcy, you are too kind. I shall endeavour to live up to your graciousness." Lydia was beside herself with relief. She smiled broadly at Elizabeth and embraced her quickly.

"Lizzy, I am so glad that the Darcys are to be part of our family." She grinned at Mary and added shyly, "God has truly blessed us."

The atmosphere within the group was now one of relief and camaraderie. Smiles graced all of the faces, and as the conversation went on to less serious things, the girls laughed together happily.

Darcy watched his cousin as he entered into the teasing banter. The colonel stood close by Lydia's side, and although she smiled up at him a few times, she did not appear to be trying to garner his attention as before, but merely wanted to include him in the conversation.

Leaning close to Elizabeth's ear, Darcy whispered, "I think that the crisis has passed and our sisters can truly be friends."

Elizabeth smiled her agreement as her mother called her over to where she stood by the door. "I think we are wanted to say our farewells to the Lucases as well as to my aunt and uncle, who also seem to be leaving."

She turned to Maria and said, "Maria, dear, your mother is waving to you."

"Oh," she sighed. "My family is ready to leave." Maria bid a good evening to everyone by name and walked with Elizabeth and Darcy to the door.

"My dear Mrs. Bennet, your dinner was lovely as usual. I have not been able to master that sort of pastry with which the lamb was covered. I hope that you will someday allow your cook to teach me the technique," Lady Lucas gushed. "And our musical entertainment tonight was perfection. Please, Mr. Darcy, would you express my pleasure to Miss Darcy for her splendid performance? I am sure that we rarely hear anything so fine in Meryton."

"I would be happy to do so, but I felt that all of the young ladies did an excellent job, your own daughter included. This neighbourhood has much talent indeed," Darcy did not want any of the girls to feel slighted.

Maria beamed her thanks. She could not help but feel pleased at the compliment, although she thought that Miss Darcy had been quite the best performer of the evening.

Soon after the Lucases and the Phillips left, the Netherfield party slowly took their leave. Many compliments to the cook and the hostess were given along with praise for the performers.

Colonel Fitzwilliam quietly expressed his admiration at Lydia's contrite seeking of forgiveness from all parties involved. Because of the attraction he felt for the youngest Bennet daughter, he was pleased that in his position as Darcy's cousin and co-guardian to Georgiana, there would be plenty of time to observe whether or not Lydia was truly repentant. He wondered if he would one day truly envy his cousin his freedom to choose a wife without thought of fortune or rank. Shaking himself mentally, he bade good evening to the rest of the Bennets and boarded the carriage.

The farewells among the four younger girls were heartfelt and slightly melancholy. Finally, Lydia suggested that Georgiana join them in the morning, for she planned to redo an old hat and desired her new friend's advice. "Mary is very welcome to join us. I would be happy to help her with one of her bonnets as well if she would like." It was agreed that Georgiana would come to Longbourn at ten, much to the satisfaction of all.

Darcy pulled Elizabeth into the dark corner of the entry once the rest had gone outside. "I want to tell you again how proud I am of you and your sister. Our child will have a wonderful mother and many lively and affectionate aunts, will she not?"

Everything within Elizabeth seemed to melt at his words. She wanted little more than to kiss him at that moment, but since they had chosen to wait so that they would have their first kiss as man and wife, she lifted his hand to her lips and gently laid her lips on his knuckles. "I love you, Fitzwilliam, more than I can say."

His eyes crinkled as he smiled. "I love you, too, my sweet Beth. I am so happy that soon we will not have to say good night at the door of your parents' home." He turned the hand with which she still held his so that he could kiss her palm. "Until tomorrow," he said before he slipped her arm through his and guided her outside where he bowed and climbed into his waiting carriage.

~*~

Georgiana was quiet on the carriage ride to Netherfield, only speaking a few words. Once they arrived and had shed their outer garments, Darcy took her aside.

"I thought that you might still be upset by the events of this evening." Darcy took her hand and led her into a small parlour and shut the door.

Georgiana sighed as she sat on a settee. "No, I am well. It is just..." She stopped and struggled to find the words.

Waiting with strained patience, Darcy searched her face for any signs of what was bothering his sister. When she did not continue, he finally asked, "Just what?"

"I wonder if the Bennets truly want me to visit them tomorrow." She hurried on when he frowned, "I am a relative stranger, and I believe that they were only being kind by their invitation."

"Would you like to hear my opinion?" He was relieved she was troubled merely by her shyness, and not by the events of the night.

At her eager nod, Darcy said, "Miss Lydia and Miss Kitty are not the kind of girls to say one thing and mean another, like some people of our acquaintance. I believe that Miss Lydia, in particular, is eager to make a better impression on you. She is fond of decorating bonnets, and she can see that you have good taste. Will you not give her a chance?"

Georgiana smiled and said, "When you put it like that, how could I not? She was most kind to include me in the conversation before we had to leave. I have not had much experience with young ladies my own age since I left school. Miss

Lydia and Miss Kitty are more open and lively than any of my fellow students. Perhaps I shall benefit from their company."

"Perhaps you shall, my dear," Darcy agreed, though with a bit of trepidation. He would accompany his sister to Longbourn so that he could insure that Georgiana was not upset again. "You need to prepare for bed, so that you will be completely rested for your foray into the realm of millinery."

Georgiana laughed with genuine delight and arose. After bidding Darcy good night, she left to go to her bed chamber.

CHAPTER TWENTY-ONE

Lydia was up early for her and joined Mr. Bennet and Elizabeth for breakfast. "Good morning, Papa, Lizzy. I hope you both slept well."

Mr. Bennet merely stared as his youngest daughter kissed her sister's cheek and then his own. Lizzy smiled and said, "I did, thank you. How are you this morning, Liddie?"

"I am excited and a bit nervous. I have never entertained such a cultured young lady, and after last night, I fear I might say something that will offend her." She sat in her regular chair and waited for her sister to pour her a cup of tea. "Thank you, Lizzy."

"I am certain that you will do well enough. I will stay in the room at least at first, if that will make you feel more comfortable." Elizabeth passed a plate of ham to Lydia.

She took a couple slices before she reached for the boiled eggs in a bowl next to her plate. "Oh, Lizzy, that would be wonderful. Are you certain that Mr. Darcy will not mind staying in the same room with us girls?"

"I am sure he will be fine with the idea." Elizabeth saw that their father was still gaping at Lydia with a puzzled look on his face.

"Would it be asking too much for me to be informed as to what happened last evening to make you so nervous?" Her father focused his full attention on Lydia, and his tone held none of its usual disdain or mockery.

For a few moments, Lydia concentrated on pulling the shell from her egg. Fortifying herself with a deep breath, she raised her eyes and said softly, "I asked Colonel Fitzwilliam if he were acquainted with Mr. Wickham. I was sure that I could find out more about how Mr. Darcy had mistreated him. Instead, I was told of his habitual lying and his loose moral character. I did not realize that he had hurt Miss Darcy in some way."

Lydia's eyes filled with tears, but she did not appear to notice. Clearing her throat, she continued, "After I heard of his wicked dealings from the colonel, I apologized to everyone, including the Darcys and the colonel. I must say that they are very gracious people. They forgave me without reservations. I have asked Lizzy to help me to reform my behaviour. I am wholly ashamed of my flibbertigibbet ways."

Mr. Bennet listened in wide-eyed disbelief as Lydia spoke. The contrite look on her face did more to convince him than her words. "I admit to being very surprised to hear this. You have never expressed such contrition before."

"Oh, Papa, will you forgive me for how I have behaved? I truly wish to stop being the spoiled brat of the family, although I feel certain that I will fail often since my habits are of long duration." Two large tears rolled down her cheeks as she eagerly awaited her father's answer.

Affection and something akin to shame displaced the incredulity on his face. For a moment he seemed unable to speak, but finally he whispered, "I do forgive you, my little Lyddie. How can I not when I desperately need yours? I have allowed my girls to grow up at the mercy of their own devices and their mother's, doing little but showing my displeasure by mocking and teasing. Maybe if I had been more of a man and stood up for what was right by all of you ..." He sighed deeply without going on.

Both of the girls hastened to their father. Lydia threw her arms around his neck as she once had done when she was a very little girl. "Oh, Papa, I forgive you and I love you. I have not told you in such a long time. Will you be patient with me as I endeavour to change my ways?"

"I believe that we all will need a great deal of that particular commodity in the next weeks and months, but I shall try if you will." He patted both Lydia and Elizabeth on the hand before shooing them back to their breakfast.

Lydia cheerfully began to describe what she had in mind for the morning once Miss Darcy arrived. She asked Elizabeth if she had any lace or ribbon that she could spare to use for trimming bonnets. Her request had none of the usual wheedling tone, and she seemed quite ready to accept a negative answer if it were given. That very change of tone and attitude made Elizabeth want to grant her appeal. "I believe I have some of each that are just waiting to be used." She could not but smile at the pleased and eager thanks her sister gave her.

A few minutes later, the other three girls joined the table. "Mama has ordered a tray to be brought to her room. She told me she is not well disposed this morning," Jane explained as she helped herself to the food that was passed to her.

"Does Mama know that Miss Darcy is to visit us this morning?" Kitty asked.

"I do not believe so," Lydia said and could not help but sigh. "I suppose the right thing to do is to inform her, is it not?" She looked to her father first and then to Elizabeth.

"I believe that we must fulfil your mother's wish to be undisturbed this morning." Mr. Bennet winked before he said teasingly, "Unless you girls fail to keep quiet enough to allow her to rest."

"We shall certainly do our best, Papa," Lydia said with a grin and soon afterward excused herself to organize her things.

Later Elizabeth found Lydia and Kitty stifling giggles as they placed bits of ribbon, lace, and feathers in piles by colour. "You may choose what you wish from this box," she offered as the two smiled in welcome.

"Oh Lizzy, this is too much. Surely you do not mean that we can pick anything we want," Lydia protested as she opened the box to reveal bunches of pretty trim.

"I suppose I do not mean that you should use all of it, but since I know how well you are able to decorate a hat, you likely will not want to pile all of these things on one hat," Elizabeth teased with a wink.

Both girls clapped their hands over their mouths to keep from squealing with laughter. Kitty was still a bit in awe of the fact that her older sister and her constant playmate, Lydia, seemed to have formed a bond such as never had been before. She felt a trifle off kilter and almost jealous of the new intimacy, but she forced that unkind emotion away. Lizzy was a kind and loyal sister, and now she seemed to want to be in their company. Lydia had almost stopped her bossiness and even had deferred to Kitty's opinion several times already this morning. All-in-all, the changes were for the better.

On the strike of ten, the Darcys arrived along with Bingley and the colonel. Elizabeth hurried to usher everyone into the sitting room, explaining that her mother was not feeling well and was resting in her chambers.

Only after receiving assurances that Mrs. Bennet was only fatigued and not ill did the company relax. The two betrothed couples settled themselves in separate corners of the room apart from the table where the four young girls, including Mary who, though she had no bonnet to re-trim, wanted to share in the camaraderie, sat discussing how best to do the redecorating.

The colonel stood near Georgiana's chair, actually enjoying the way the girls related to each other. He noticed that Lydia did her best to include his cousin by asking her to describe the hats she had seen in Town and seeking her opinion as to the choice of colours to match the feathers and lace she had applied to her bonnet. He still saw the liveliness of her character, but it seemed to be tempered by a self-control he had not seen in his previous contact with her. One thing that was glaringly absent was the flirtation of the evening before. Occasionally, she would catch him watching her and she would smile, but the glance was brief and no different from her acknowledgment of a similar glance from one of her sisters. All-in-all, Colonel Fitzwilliam began to believe that the young woman truly wished to change her ways.

After about an hour and a half, the ladies declared that the bonnets were looking splendid. Jane decided to call for a light luncheon of sandwiches and cakes to be served. Everyone was happy with the prospect and waited in the sitting room with a great deal of general conversation.

The trays of food had just arrived when Mrs. Bennet made her appearance. She stood in the doorway, feeling rather put out that her daughters were not seeing to the details for the wedding as she had expected them to do.

Her husband placed his hand gently on her shoulder and whispered in her ear, "The young people have had a great deal of enjoyment from the break in the routine of wedding preparations. If a few hours missing from a task will leave it unfinished, I say leave it unfinished. Our Lizzy will be leaving us soon. Let us join our family and our guests and enjoy the time we have before our family is minus one."

Stepping forward, he offered his arm. "Shall we, my dearest wife?"

Something about the tone of his voice brought a blush to Mrs. Bennet's face and a quickening of her heart. She gazed up into his eyes, took his arm, and smiled. "Let's shall."

~*~

With only three days left before the wedding, Elizabeth and her sisters were making up small keepsakes to be given to the guests. The bundles contained small sachets of lavender, pieces of hard candy, and a few coins. These gifts were not usual at weddings in Hertfordshire, but her mother had gotten the idea and would not be gainsaid.

They were nearly finished tying the ribbons to close the parcels when Darcy and Bingley were shown into the sitting room. The colonel and Georgiana had stayed at Netherfield so as to allow the two gentlemen time with their ladies. The men greeted everyone before joining their fiancées. Mrs. Bennet, who was especially proud of her idea, spent some time explaining how she had come up with the plan.

Both of the men showed proper attention to what she had to say, though it was quite obvious that they had little interest in this trifling detail. Just as Elizabeth was about to suggest that her mother serve refreshments, a commotion was heard from the hall.

"Mr. Collins, ma'am," Mrs. Hill announced.

"My dear Mr. Collins," Mrs. Bennet exclaimed in greeting. "We were not expecting you until tomorrow, but, of course, you are very welcome. Mary is looking very well, as you can see."

Bowing to everyone, Mr. Collins's stern expression only softened when he looked upon his fiancée. He cleared his throat before he spoke hesitantly, "I am afraid that I have grave news from Rosings to impart."

Glancing at Darcy, he coloured. "Do not fear for Lady Catherine, She is well though not in the best of spirits. Please forgive me, but I am afraid what I have to say will cause distress to all and to you, sir, most particularly."

"What is it, Mr. Collins?" Darcy asked with a hint of impatience.

Collins took a deep breath before he began, "When I received Mrs. Bennet's kind invitation to your upcoming nuptials. I was deeply honoured and wished to share my familial felicity with my patroness. I went to Rosings with that intent in mind. However, it became apparent after my arrival that Lady Catherine did not share my opinion on the matter. She had just received an invitation from Mr. Darcy, and she asked me if I had prior knowledge of the attachment between her nephew and my cousin. I owned that I did not. What happened next was quite unsettling."

Elizabeth could see that her cousin was quite upset and that the telling discomposed him. She glanced at Mary and saw her pale, worried look.

Collins took a handkerchief out of his pocket, wiped his brow, and then he continued, "After some rather unflattering comments about my Bennet relations and Cousin Elizabeth in particular, Lady Catherine told me that I had a choice to make. She insisted that I either come here immediately to persuade my cousin to give up her nephew, or if I failed to convince..." He trailed off as he glanced first at Elizabeth and then at Mary. "She ordered me to break off my engagement and sever all ties to this family until I inherit the Longbourn estate."

At his words, Mary burst into tears, and Elizabeth rushed to her side and wrapped her arms about her.

Darcy moved to where Collins stood and glared down at him. "You will not convince either of us, so you might as well leave now and tell my aunt that I do not want to see her again. I begin to wish I had never encouraged your attentions to Miss Mary. Now if you are quite finished, you may leave."

For a moment, Mr. Collins stood still, red-faced and silent. He did not know what to do first. His beloved sat sobbing in her sister's embrace, and Mr. Darcy stood poised to expel him from the house. Finally, he found his tongue. "Oh, sir, you do mistake me. I did not come here to try to dissuade you from marrying Cousin Elizabeth, nor do I have any intention of breaking off my engagement to my beloved Mary."

Mary's weeping ceased, and she raised her head while she searched his face for the truth. The joy on her face when she saw his sincerity was something to behold.

Collins moved quickly to where Mary sat with Elizabeth, dropped to his knees, and took her hands. "My dearest Mary, I would never do something so despicable, especially not on the whim of another. I do have to tell you something that may distress you. When I refused to do as Lady Catherine demanded, she withdrew the Hunsford living from me and gave me a day to pack my things and leave the house. We will have to wait to be married since I think it will be difficult for me to find another position without good references, which she informed me she surely will not give. I must say that I have been greatly disillusioned by that lady's lack of Christian charity toward her own family and ours. I fear I will have to join a friend of mine who runs a mission in east London. The work will not pay enough for the support of a married couple, so we will have to wait to be wed until I have re-established my good name. It pains me greatly to say this."

Tears began to track down Mary's cheeks once again while Mrs. Bennet, who had been silent while Mr. Collins told his tale, began to wail and call for her salts.

Mrs. Hill quickly brought and administered them. When that did not seem to calm her, Elizabeth suggested that her mother might go to her chamber to rest. With the help of Hill and Sarah, the mistress of the house was assisted above stairs.

Quiet thus restored, Darcy asked to speak with Mr. Collins in a corner of the room. "I do not understand how it is possible for my aunt to take away the living once it is granted to you. You have not committed any crime or even an indiscretion that would warrant your refusal as a vicar. I have given the livings which are in my possession to give. I have no power to withdraw them without due cause."

Mr. Collins's face reddened with embarrassment. He shuffled uncomfortably for a few moments while he gathered his thoughts.

Collins began, "I know that I am not a clever man. My own father told me enough times that my behaviour bordered on stupidity and cowardice, and therefore, I must make my way in life by learning how to flatter and ingratiate myself to those above me in status. Since I was a coward, the life of a soldier was not for me. He decided that I would study for the church."

Clearing his throat, he went on, "When my name came to Lady Catherine's notice just after my ordination and the retirement of the old rector, she invited me to an interview for the position. I had never been in a house so lavishly furnished or on grounds so well maintained. The lady herself was so imposing that I nearly fled in fear."

He paused to take a deep breath before he continued, "She told me that as a young man so new and untried at parish duties, I could not or, rather, should not expect the largess that she was ready to bestow upon me. She outlined the provisions, described the parsonage, and explained how much I would be able to earn if I accepted her offer of the living. She told me that with her connections and help I might one day aspire to a bishopric.

"Indeed, I was shocked at what she described and was ready to agree immediately when she told me that she had one stipulation. I would have to sign an agreement to the effect that if I displeased her in a significant way, she had the power to replace me immediately. Apparently, the former vicar did not allow her to command him so well as she would have liked.

"She did not say this in so many words, but I understood her meaning. Also, Lady Catherine hinted that if I did not accept, she had enough influence in society to see to it I would have a great deal of trouble finding another position higher than a curate. For all the above reasons, I signed the document and began my service at Hunsford."

Collins sighed and wiped his brow again with his handkerchief. Without looking up from the floor, he said, "So you see that my father was correct; I am stupid and a coward. I bowed and acquiesced to most of her whims. I wrote most of my sermons under her guidance. I doubt if I would have ever stood up to her if I did not love my fiancée so much as I do. I do not wish to lose her. And I knew of your great esteem for my cousin Elizabeth. I could not even consider trying to dissuade you from marrying her."

Darcy stared at the clergyman in astonishment before a begrudging respect for the man began to form. "You have proven your father wrong and shown yourself to be a man of both understanding and courage. I must say that I am duly impressed that you would stand up to my formidable relation in defence of your family and future bride. I want to apologize for my aunt's unseemly behaviour, and for the fact that in taking the living away from you, she necessitated the postponement of your wedding. Because of your stand, I promise to work to find you a living that does not require the kind of servile deference Lady Catherine demands. Also I shall speak to my uncle Lord Matlock to see about the legality of the contract you signed."

Something about Darcy's statement caused Collins to stand taller. Instead of his usual self-deprecating response to a compliment, he simply bowed and said, "Thank you for your kind words, sir. I would appreciate any assistance you could give me, Mr. Darcy."

Turning to Jane, who was the eldest of the Bennets in the room, he said, "If my family will allow me to stay until the wedding, I would like to have my things brought in. I have a hired wagon waiting for me in front of the house. Since Lady Catherine gave me such little time to find a better conveyance, I hired one of the farmers' wagons."

"Of course, Mr. Collins," Jane agreed quickly. "You may use your former room. I will ask Papa where to put any of your other belongings while you see to your trunks."

Mr. Bennet was quickly informed of the events Collins related and began to wonder if he had underestimated the clergyman. It could be that this particular son-in-law would not act so pompous and self-important as he had first thought he would. Perhaps the love of his middle daughter had wrought a great change in him.

Once the better news was related to Mrs. Bennet in her bed chamber, she flung back her covers and cold cloths and rejoined everyone with many exclamations of joy and gratitude to her future sons-in-law. In no uncertain terms, she declared herself to be blessed above all women that three of her daughters had found such fine, upstanding gentlemen to marry. Her elation was so great that Mary's weddings would not need to be postponed, that she insisted upon a special dinner celebration and that everyone would stay for it.

By evening's end, even Mr. Collins had tired of her effusions and retired early, and Darcy and Bingley departed after bidding quick and private farewells to their respective brides-to-be.

"Do you think you will be able to help Mr. Collins find a suitable living?" Elizabeth whispered as she walked with him to his horse.

"I believe so. There are some attached to Pemberley and others to Matlock." Darcy did not desire to spend their few moments of privacy speaking of the parson and his problems, but he knew that Elizabeth was concerned for her sister so he continued, "Our family has many other contacts as well, so that by the time we are finished, few people will believe what my aunt might say about Collins or your family. She has done a great deal to alienate herself from people in Town. At this point, her influence in society is mainly a figment of her own imagination. I am certain that we will be able to minimize any damage done by what she might say."

"Thank you for telling me this, Fitzwilliam," Elizabeth squeezed his hand. "It eases my mind to know it."

"I am glad I could help you, dearest." Darcy bowed over her hand and kissed it. "Good night and sleep well."

CHAPTER TWENTY-TWO

The next morning was likely the most hectic Elizabeth had ever experienced. Her mother made all of her girls rise early in order to make certain everything was ready. Fortunately for Lizzy, her habit of late was to be up before the rest. Sarah brought her the usual soda bread and special tea, so that she did not keep her family waiting.

Breakfast seemed to take on the atmosphere of a party. All five of the girls, being in high spirits and more in tune with each other than they had ever been, could not seem to stop giggling and chattering. Even her father was more than usually chipper and kept his normal sarcastic remarks to a minimum.

However, once Lydia, Kitty, and Mary followed their mother to the sitting room for some last minute instructions, Mr. Bennet could not keep his peace. He looked at his oldest girls and said, "I marvel at the changes in my daughters. The youngest three, whom I have always known to be silly and ignorant, have become quite calm and interested in books and discussions of something besides fashion and gossip in the past few days. That is, until this morning, when all five of you have become giggly and have displayed unusual sisterly communion. Have you all been drinking some tainted water? I find myself quite discomposed by these alterations in my daughters."

Jane and Elizabeth glanced at each other and could not keep from laughing until a genuine scowl on Mr. Bennet's face caused them to cease.

"Oh, Papa, do not frown so," Lizzy gently admonished. "My sisters and I have merely taken the time to understand each other, and we find that we truly enjoy one another's gifts and personalities. I am sorry if our laughter distresses you this morning. I suppose we are so silly today because we all, in our own ways, are nervous about the changes to take place, and we wish to seize the little time left until the wedding to take pleasure in one another's company."

Jane had reached for Elizabeth's hand when she spoke of the changes. "Yes, Papa, we are going to miss our Lizzy. I think that maybe the younger girls will feel the separation even more since, until now, they have not taken the opportunities I have had to know her. I know that you too will miss your favourite daughter."

When her father started to shake his head, Jane only smiled. "Do not bother to deny it, dear Papa. Everyone knows it, and I have never resented the fact, for she is my favourite as well, but I wonder if you would try to know your younger daughters better while they are still at home. Mary will soon be wed, and both Kitty and Lydia will likely find husbands sooner than we think. Be happy that your children have finally found friends in one another."

Tears filled Mr. Bennet's eyes, and he nodded. "I will certainly try, although I do hope you will allow me a little time to grieve the loss of my Lizzy."

Elizabeth jumped up and hugged and kissed her father. "Papa, I am not dying, I am merely getting married. And I will come for Jane's wedding and, hopefully, for Mary's as well. I will not forget my beloved family."

"See that you do not, Lizzy." He kissed her cheek and with a shooing motion, said, "Go on now; I am sure that your mother has many things she thinks need to be done before tomorrow. I shall take myself to my library."

Even though many of the tasks their mother gave them to do had already been done at least once, the girls cheerfully worked side by side, talking and laughing over memories of their childhood. It was into this jovial atmosphere that Mr. Darcy and Georgiana were announced.

Lydia and Kitty cried out in delight and raced to meet their newest friend. They pulled her to the table to see what they had been working on. Elizabeth stood in a far more sedate manner and curtseyed. The dignified way that she walked to her fiancé belied the excited pleasure seeing him afforded her.

"I did not expect to see you today," Lizzy pretended to scold him.

"I do beg your pardon if my presence is unwelcome." He tried to sound hurt and offended, but he could not manage it when she grinned at him. Chuckling, he admitted, "I have something to give to you, your mother, and your sisters."

At that moment, Mrs. Bennet entered the room and welcomed her very soon-to-be son. "To what do we owe this pleasure, Mr. Darcy? I had not thought to see you until the morrow."

"Georgiana and I have some things to give you. Please excuse me for a moment while I summon the footmen who have charge over the items."

Soon, Darcy re-entered the room, followed by two liveried footmen carrying boxes. They deposited them upon the table Mrs. Bennet indicated to them.

The girls gathered around in anticipation.

Darcy lifted a square, grey-print box and handed it to Mrs. Bennet. "This is for you, madam, with my best wishes."

Lizzy's mother tried hard to hide her excitement as she lifted the lid and pushed back the tissue that covered the dove-grey shawl. As she fingered the soft folds, her eyes filled with tears. "Oh, my dear Mr. Darcy, how exquisite it is!"

Picking up the shawl, she wrapped it around her shoulders and sighed. "It is like wearing a cloud, so soft but yet it is so warm. I am sure that I have never owned anything so wonderful. Oh, thank you so much!" Moving quickly to his side, Mrs. Bennet rose on her toes and kissed his cheek before she searched her pockets for a handkerchief.

Next he handed a box to Jane, who slowly lifted the lid. As she raised the pale-blue shawl to her cheek, she beamed and said, "It is lovely, Mr. Darcy. I thank you."

Counselling the younger girls to wait to open their gifts at the same time, Darcy gave each a hat box. Though it was quite obvious that they were to receive new hats, they waited with unabated expectancy until he gave them leave to open their gifts.

At first, silence reigned as they each examined their bonnets. Finally, the three began to talk at once, expressing their thanks and pleasure in a babble of sound. When their mother was called upon to inspect the lovely confections, which obviously had come from an exclusive millinery shop, the volume rose to another level.

Jane and Elizabeth were concerned that the Darcys might be uncomfortable at the outburst of the others. However, as they watched, they saw that both brother and sister were enjoying the enthusiasm over the gifts.

Smiling, Darcy met Elizabeth's eyes, held her gaze, picked up the last box, and moved to put it in her hands. "I hope you like this," he whispered in her ear.

Shivering from the warmth of his breath on her ear, Elizabeth opened the box to find the golden shawl otherwise identical to the others. Darcy took it from its bed of tissue and laid it across her shoulders. She ran her hands up and down the downy fabric, the feel of which was like no other she had ever known, almost as soft as fur. "Oh, my dearest, I love it. Thank you." She spoke softly as she laid a hand on his sleeve.

"You are more than welcome." He grinned in satisfaction.

Mrs. Bennet asked the Darcys to stay for some refreshments, but they declined, explaining that they too had many things to accomplish before the wedding. After another round of happy thanks, they took their leave.

Elizabeth took her gift to her room, marvelling at her fiancé's generous nature. She could hear Kitty and Mary merrily exclaiming over the bonnets Darcy had given them. Just as she closed the drawer in which she had placed her shawl, there was a knock on her door.

"Come," Elizabeth called as she straightened and faced the door.

Lydia entered the room with her bonnet in her hands. The look on her face was one of a strange combination of pleasure and disquiet.

"What is it, Lydia?" she asked, hoping that her youngest sister was not going to express some disparaging remark about the gift.

"Oh, Lizzy, I do not deserve this beautiful present," Lydia sighed as she laid the bonnet on the bed. "Mr. Darcy should not have bought this for me. I was such a terror when I pouted about you and Jane getting new gowns from Town. I think I should have him take it back or give it to someone more deserving than I."

"Do you not like the hat?" Elizabeth could not think of any other reason for Lydia to refuse the gift.

"Oh, I truly love it!" she proclaimed in protest. "It is quite the loveliest I have ever seen." Sighing once more, she gazed longingly at the pretty confection of lace and feathers. "I should be grateful for what I have. I am trying to learn from my mistakes, and I believe that I should not accept it."

Lifting the bonnet, Elizabeth set it on her dresser before she sat on the edge of the bed and reached out for Lydia's hand. "Come sit by me, Lyddie."

Lydia did as she was bid, while still looking at the hat.

"Lydia, look at me a moment," Elizabeth ordered. Once she had her sister's attention, she began, "I do not think that you should refuse the gift from Mr. Darcy and his sister. He would not have given it to you if he did not think you should have it. Besides, all of us are given gifts which we do not merit. In fact, is not the very nature of a gift that it is that which we do not earn? I am convinced that both Mr. Darcy and Miss Darcy would be hurt if you did give it back."

After giving her sister a hug and a kiss on the cheek, Elizabeth stood and handed the bonnet back to Lydia. "Let us take your hat to your room, and then we must find out if Mama has something for us to do."

Lydia's eyes filled with tears as she held the hat in her hands. She sniffed once and then with a great smile on her face, led her sister out of her room.

Mrs. Bennet did indeed have more repetitive things for her daughters to do, but the sisters did not complain, for they understood that the family would be changed forever on the morrow. They talked and laughed, enjoying themselves throughout the day and into the evening as they worked and dined.

After supper that evening, Mrs. Bennet asked Lizzy if she had finished her packing.

"Of course, Mama," answered Elizabeth with an indulgent smile. "I have not forgotten a thing. The only things left besides my present clothing and my nightclothes are my wedding clothes."

"Let us make certain, Lizzy," her mother insisted and grasped her hand. "Come, my dear, I want everything to be perfect for you and your Mr. Darcy."

She escorted Elizabeth to her chambers and said, "Please wait for me. I have something to give you."

Elizabeth sat on the edge of her bed, wondering what her mother could want to give her. She did not have long to ponder because her mother quickly entered the room with a box in her arms.

With ceremony, Mrs. Bennet laid the item on Elizabeth's lap. As she lifted the lid, she saw that it was a pale-green nightdress of silk and lace and with it a robe of the same fine material.

"Mama, this is lovely!" Elizabeth looked at her mother. "I did not expect anything like this. You and Papa are already doing as much as possible."

"I know that we have not been as close as perhaps we should have been, but I will not have you go without something beautiful on your wedding night. And before you ask, I did not use any of Mr. Darcy's funds for this. I asked your aunt Gardiner to retrieve this for me from a shop we both know about in Town. I sent an order as soon as I knew you were to be married."

Elizabeth hugged her mother and thanked her.

Pulling back and smoothing nonexistent wrinkles from her dress in embarrassment, her mother insisted, "Enough of that, Lizzy; I just did my duty by you and that brings to mind the other matter I would like to discuss." Mrs. Bennet paused, looked down at her hands, and cleared her throat. "Tomorrow night, you will become a wife in truth and deed. Many mothers would tell their daughters to lie still and let their husbands do what they do so that it will be done quickly. They would say that it is the woman's duty to do so in order to produce an heir."

Feeling her cheeks flame with embarrassment, Elizabeth did not know how to stop her mother's flow of words, and until this moment, she had not considered the wedding night. The idea of it struck her as frightening, even if the man was her beloved Fitzwilliam. Her experience with Wickham made the thought of intimacy distressing and even alarming. She was about to interrupt her mother when her next words caught her attention.

"Your Mr. Darcy obviously loves you very much, and I know you love him as well. When two people love each other, the conventional wisdom of the wife being a disinterested participant should not apply. I am certain that he will be gentle and will help you enjoy the process. There is a bit of pain at first, but it is of such short duration that it hardly signifies. My late mother told me that the marriage bed was a gift from God, not a duty or a curse. I found that it was so as well."

Finally, Elizabeth did interrupt, "But, Mama, I have heard you talk with Lady Lucas and Mrs. Long of the bother and of the duty, and you did not sound positive about it."

"Yes, I know," Mrs. Bennet sighed. "I did not, and I suppose it was dishonest of me, but I could not say otherwise without embarrassment. I did not think that I would be thought a proper gentleman's wife if I bragged how about I enjoyed my husband's attentions in that regard. Do you think that we have five daughters merely for the sake of trying for an heir?"

Elizabeth's mind refused to think deeply upon that question, but she did decide to ask another. "How is it then, that we have no more siblings?"

Her mother blushed and refused to meet her daughter's eye, but answered, "After Lydia's birth and the resulting infection I suffered, I was told by the doctor that I would not be able to conceive again." Her face turned an even brighter shade of red before she continued, "And he has been proven correct."

Understanding her mother's meaning, Elizabeth said nothing more.

"Do you have more questions, Lizzy?" Mrs. Bennet noted her daughter's flushed face and the negative shake of her head. "Very well, then, I have only one more thing to say. Since God has blessed the marriage bed, it is not something to fear, so trust the love that Mr. Darcy has for you, and you will experience that blessing as well.

Mrs. Bennet bestowed a rare kiss upon Elizabeth's cheek before she bade her good night and left the room. Lizzy sat in stunned silence for a long time, trying to take in what she had just heard from her mother. Often, she had thought it odd that her parents managed to live with as much harmony as they did, what with the vast differences in their personalities and tastes. Granted, her mother still was a pretty woman and her father a handsome man. Could it be that she knew so little about married life that she did not understand that the affection her parents held for each other managed to keep them happy in such a seemingly unbalanced union?

Taking a deep breath, Elizabeth stood and walked to her window. She could see nothing outside, but she knew that in the morning she would take the lane below and meet her beloved at the Longbourn church. Would she be able to trust him with all of her being? She had experienced an attack that had taken her innocence and filled her with fear of the very act, but she knew in her heart that she would never suffer anything of the sort at the hands of Fitzwilliam Darcy.

Even as the paralyzing fear rose in her breast, she forced herself to visualize the burning pages she had written turn to smoke and ash before her. As she calmed, she thought of her beloved's kiss on her hands and the few embraces they had shared, all of which were lovely and delightful. She would not be afraid of her married life because she knew that Darcy would be there with her.

Without ringing for Sarah to help her undress, she quickly readied herself for bed and slipped under the covers after she brushed out her hair and plaited it. Her final thought before sleep overtook her was one of joyful anticipation.

CHAPTER TWENTY-THREE

The day of the wedding did not see the sun. Grey clouds hung low in the sky, threatening, but never quite delivering, rain. In contrast to the gloomy weather, Elizabeth awoke with a light and happy heart that even the extra strong bout of nausea did not dim. Once her stomach settled, she hurried through her toilette and felt impatient that Sarah seemed so slow while she helped Elizabeth to dress.

"What is the matter, Sarah?" Elizabeth finally asked in irritation, but when she caught the maid's eye in the mirror, she saw what looked like tears. She softened her tone. "You are crying. Are you unwell?"

"Oh, Miss Elizabeth, I am sorry," Sarah sniffed. "It is just that I will miss you when you are gone."

"Oh, Sarah, it is I who should apologize. I believe that I have forgotten to tell you a very important bit of news." Lizzy smiled warmly.

"What news, Miss?" Sarah gave Lizzy her full attention.

"I asked Papa and Mr. Darcy and they both agreed that you will come with me to Pemberley and be my abigail."

"I am to go with you?" Sarah squeaked out.

"I hope you are pleased," Elizabeth said a trifle worried. "I am so sorry that I neglected to tell you. If you need more time to say good bye to your family, I am certain that you may have it."

"I am sure that when I explain to my mother she will not be upset. I do not have much to pack." She was quick to assure her mistress that everything would be fine.

"If that is so," Lizzy teased, "might we complete my dressing? I do have a groom awaiting me at the church. He is likely to be there at this very moment, as he likes to be early."

Sarah giggled and quickly went back to tending to the business of readying the bride for her wedding. Once Elizabeth was completely dressed, coiffed, and veiled, she studied her likeness in the mirror. The dress was a simple column of light gold silk that simmered as she moved. Its only adornment was a bit of gold trimmed lace at the neckline and hem. Her plain veil was trimmed with the same lace as her gown. She wore the pearl and garnet necklace and earrings Darcy had pressed into her hand just before he left after his quick visit the previous day. The large pearl at her neck took on a reflected gold glow from her gown.

Elizabeth was extremely happy about the gift. However, most of her joy came from knowing that she was about to become the wife of a wonderfully loving man, and to think he had overcome a seemingly insurmountable impediment. He appeared to be genuine in his excitement about the baby. How was it possible that God had given her such a man to love? As her eyes began to sting, she swallowed hard, refusing to allow herself to cry. She then turned to pick up her new shawl and pulled it about her. Draped about her shoulders, the golden cashmere added an extra touch of softness to her apparel.

A knock at the door told her it was time to leave for the church. Sarah opened the door to Mr. Bennet, who, upon catching sight of his daughter, stood in stunned awe. Finally, he found his voice, though it was thick with emotion, and he said, "You are truly a vision of loveliness, Lizzy. Your Mr. Darcy will be greatly pleased."

"Thank you, Papa." she smiled and kissed his cheek. "I suppose Mama and my sisters have already gone to the church."

"Indeed, they left a quarter hour ago." He offered her his arm. "The carriage is awaiting us, my dear."

After the short ride to the church, a footman opened the door and handed them out. Elizabeth suddenly felt a chill of apprehension slide down her spine. Gripping her father's arm much tighter than necessary, she allowed him to guide her into the vestibule.

The small foyer to the sanctuary was decorated in an array of tastefully arranged flowers and ribbons, which included a pair of tall potted gardenias that flanked the door into the sanctuary. The fragrance swirled around her as she passed by.

An usher opened the doors, and her father led her slowly through them. At first, seeing all of the people on either side of her caused Elizabeth to be gripped with the familiar panic. Her fingers dug into her father's arm. He patted her hand and continued to move toward her husband-to-be. Flashes of the crimson of militia uniforms in the crowd made her feel faint until she turned her eyes to the front and saw Darcy standing tall and strong and waiting for her, only her. Each step closer to him brought greater relief from anxiety. She relaxed and smiled at her beloved.

Darcy sensed Elizabeth's anxiety as soon as she entered the sanctuary. It took all of his strength not to race to her and bring her to the altar himself, but he would not embarrass her or her family. He watched as she scanned the room, and her face grew more pale. He prayed that she would look up at him. When she finally did, his relief was great as he saw her calm and smile.

In general, Darcy was not one to smile broadly in public, but he could not hold in the joy he felt as he saw her love radiating toward him. She was to be his forever. His heart seemed to jump with the happiness at the thought. When she arrived at his side and her father placed her hand in his, he allowed the contentment of the moment to wash over him.

Just as the vicar opened his mouth to begin, there was a loud commotion in the back of the church. Darcy did not turn until the parson asked, "Madam, what is the meaning of this?"

Darcy and Elizabeth turned in surprise to see Lady Catherine striding purposefully up the aisle toward them.

"I object to this marriage!" Lady Catherine declared in a loud, strident voice.

"On what grounds, madam?" Mr. Scott was obviously upset at the interruption.

"This man is already engaged to my daughter. I insist that this ceremony cease." Darcy's aunt had already latched onto his arm and tried to pull him away.

Darcy wrenched his arm from her grasp and turned to see that Elizabeth had lost all of her colour and was swaying on her feet. He put his arm around her to steady her before turning his attention to the clergyman. "Vicar, may we please use the anteroom for a more private discussion?" He lowered his voice to a whisper. "Elizabeth needs to sit down."

Mr. Scott nodded and gestured to a door to the right of where they stood. He then spoke to the congregation. "Ladies and gentlemen, please be patient for a few moments. I will investigate this matter immediately."

He led the way, with Darcy supporting Elizabeth, Mr. Bennet, and lastly Lady Catherine following, with that lady vocal in her displeasure at the further inconvenience to her person.

Once they were inside and the door was closed, the Reverend Mr. Scott offered a chair to Elizabeth before he did the same for the formidable Lady Catherine. Her displeasure at taking second place to a country miss was evident on her face, and she opened her mouth to voice that displeasure when the clergyman held up his hand. "Madam, I do not know who you are, but I would like to know why you feel you have the right to disrupt this solemn and holy sacrament."

Lady Catherine was stunned into silence, as she was not accustomed to being addressed in such a manner.

"This is my aunt Lady Catherine de Bourgh," Darcy said by way of introduction.

He then turned to Mr. Bennet and the vicar. "Mr. Bennet, Mr. Scott, I would like to make it perfectly clear that I am not now, nor have I ever been engaged to my cousin, Miss de Bourgh. My aunt has long held the idea that we were meant for each other, even to the point of insisting that my own dear departed mother agreed to the scheme. My father assured me that she had only agreed we would marry if my cousin and I did fall in love. I wish to go forward with the ceremony, unless Miss Elizabeth has been so distressed by the outrageous conduct of my aunt that she wishes to beg off."

He turned to search Elizabeth's face. She was still pale but she did not look so forlorn as before. Darcy took her hand and stood rigidly next to her.

"This is preposterous! I will be heard!" Lady Catherine stood and bellowed in a manner more like a fish wife than the wife of a baronet and daughter of an earl.

Elizabeth arose from her chair, her courage and her ire building. When Mr. Bennet stood to her other side, communicating with his facial expression and his stance that he supported the couple, the shock of Lady Catherine's interruption gave way. In its place flowed a soothing sense of peace.

As the vicar, it was Mr. Scott's duty to investigate allegations such as Lady Catherine had made, but although he was neither a tall man nor full of figure, he had a commanding presence that did not rely upon raging and threats. He moved closer to the lady and spoke in a soft but firm tone. "If you wish to remain on the premises, you will lower your voice. Now what documentation do you have to show me that would prove your allegation?"

"I do not need to show you proof. My word is good enough for the likes of you." She stared into his eyes and saw that the parson was not convinced. She sputtered, "From their infancy, my sister and I planned their union. They are descended on the maternal side from the same noble line and on his father's from a respectable, honourable, and ancient family. Their fortunes on both sides are splendid. They are destined for each other, and now this upstart without family, connections, or fortune is trying to insinuate her way between them. It is not to be borne!"

"Madam, I see no impediment to this marriage taking place. The wishes of distant family members do not hold sway. If Mr. Bennet, who is a gentleman and your nephew's equal in that, does not withhold his permission, we will return to the sanctuary and resume the service." Mr. Scott's demeanour was calm and reserved as he turned to the door.

Mr. Bennet spoke clearly and firmly, "I wish for this marriage ceremony to go forward, as I believe my daughter and her fiancé do as well.

"I will not have it. I have family and connections that will ruin you all. I will have my way. In fact, I insist upon it!" Lady Catherine screamed.

She turned on Elizabeth. "It is all your fault. You and your arts and allurements have made him lose sight of his duty to his family. I will not allow you to ruin all my plans." With her hands outstretched and claw like, Lady Catherine moved as if to attack Elizabeth, but Darcy and Mr. Bennet sprang forward to grasp the lady's arms and push her back into the chair.

The action of her father and Darcy were so swift that Elizabeth barely had time to feel alarm. She was grateful, however, that they were there to guard her.

The door to the little room opened quickly, and Lord Matlock entered and closed it. He immediately went to his sister, who was struggling to rise from the chair. "Catherine, you will cease this outrageous noise!" he ordered. "You are making a laughingstock of our family. You have no right to disrupt this wedding, and if you say or do one more thing, I will see to it that you are sent away indefinitely. I have several places in mind in the north that would accommodate you. They are more comfortable than Bedlam, but they will serve quite the same purpose.

"As you are aware, I still have power of attorney, and am trustee over your and Anne's affairs. Your husband did not trust you with his estate and only allowed you to remain at Rosings until Anne reached the age of thirty or when she married, and only afterwards if Anne deems it. I have been at fault for not curbing your imperious and outlandish ideas of this marriage between Darcy and your poor daughter."

The earl turned to Darcy, Elizabeth, and her father. "I apologize for this unfortunate disruption, and I will see to it that Lady Catherine does not disturb you any longer. Is there a way by which I could take her from this room without going back through the sanctuary?"

Mr. Scott pointed to a small panel on the end wall. "That is a rather small, private entrance. It is not often used, but I am sure it will do for your purpose."

"I will not be removed!" Lady Catherine cried out.

The earl grasped her shoulders and brought her so close that their noses nearly touched. "Catherine, listen to me if you say one more word, I will have you gagged and taken back through the sanctuary. In that way, everyone will witness your humiliation. You have a choice, but either way, I will have two of my footmen keep guard over you while I return for the ceremony. I will deal with you as soon as it is over."

For a long moment, Lady Catherine seem to ponder her options before she pulled herself from his grip and, with what dignity she could muster, walked to the panel and waited for someone to open it. Lord Matlock nodded to Mr. Scott, and the vicar opened the small door. She was quickly assisted outside by her brother, and the panel was closed once more.

The four remaining stood in silence for several seconds before Darcy turned and spoke to Elizabeth. "Do you still wish to marry me after you have experienced my aunt's actions in person?"

When she lifted her eyes to meet his, Elizabeth witnessed a look of fear and anxiety that she had never seen on his face before. Gently, she touched his cheek and smiled. "I believe you once warned me about that lady. Nothing that she said changed my mind. I would think you might be embarrassed to return to the church now after her disruption."

"I would endure any trial necessary to have you as my wife," he declared as his expression relaxed in relief. "Mr. Scott, do you wish to speak to those gathered before we go back."

"That is an excellent idea, Mr. Darcy," Mr. Scott agreed. "I will only need a moment."

The vicar slipped through the door, but left it ajar so that those inside could also hear what he had to say. "May I please have your attention," Mr. Scott said into the din of muffled conversation. Almost immediately there was silence, as everyone leaned forward to catch what the parson wanted to tell them.

"I have heard the objections of the lady who interrupted the ceremony and have found no grounds or impediment to the marriage of Mr. Fitzwilliam Darcy and Miss Elizabeth Bennet. Thank you for your patience in this matter. We will resume the ceremony. As he pushed the door completely open, the vicar spied Lord Matlock slipping quietly back into the church and into the pew next to his wife.

Arm-in-arm, Darcy and Elizabeth followed the parson back to the altar with Mr. Bennet just behind them. As they took their places in front of the vicar, Darcy took Elizabeth's hand in his before the vicar began again. After that, neither of them was quite aware of the proceedings, even though they responded correctly and at the right places.

All that Darcy could think was that Elizabeth soon would be his forever. His aunt's audacity had not shaken his lovely Beth, and he rejoiced that she loved him enough to overlook the insult his relative had given her and her family. He felt a bit of guilt that his initial thoughts of the Bennet family had nearly mirrored those of Lady Catherine. What would have happened if he had actually expressed those thoughts to her when he proposed? The very idea made him want to blush with shame that he ever could have felt himself above his lovely Elizabeth and her family.

Once the ceremony was complete and the marriage registry signed, Darcy and Elizabeth took their first walk as husband and wife. A cold wind whipped at them as they hurried to the carriage that waited to take them the short distance to Longbourn for the wedding breakfast.

"I hope that you are warm enough, my darling Mrs. Darcy," he said as he quickly wrapped the heavy carriage rug around her.

"I am perfectly fine, husband." She smiled adoringly at him before she snuggled as close to him as possible.

Her action gave Darcy all the encouragement he needed to pull her into his arms. For several seconds, he merely gazed into her eyes, revelling in the love he saw there. Finally as he watched her eyes drift to his mouth, he lowered his lips to hers.

The first touch of his mouth on hers was a revelation of sorts. Elizabeth had known that she would enjoy his kiss, but she had not understood the wondrous feelings she would experience. Her eyes closed as she surrendered to the sensations.

When he pulled away, Elizabeth nearly whimpered in protest until she realized that the carriage had halted. "We are at Longbourn."

Darcy chuckled at the sound of disappointment in her voice, which echoed his own. "Yes, my dear, I believe that we are. Shall we go in?"

"I suppose that we cannot merely drive on to London," she teased.

"After the gossip that will inevitably arise as a result of the actions of my aunt, I do not think it wise to circumvent attending the wedding breakfast." Darcy kissed her quickly and moved to the door just as a footman opened it.

Once out of the carriage, Darcy assisted his new wife to the ground and saw the Bennet equipage coming up the drive.

"I suggest that we go inside. We shall be warmer there, and I am certain that your mother would like us to greet the guests as they enter the house."

Mrs. Bennet did indeed wish that the newlyweds stand and receive all of the guests. Elizabeth thought that by the way her mother acted, one would think that she had been the sole reason the couple was now married.

Darcy kept a close watch on Elizabeth for signs of fatigue, but throughout their time in the reception line, she seemed to be well and enjoying herself. Once all the guests had arrived, his new mother-in-law escorted them to the main table set up in Longbourn's largest room, since the dining parlour would not accommodate so many.

With Darcy and Elizabeth finally seated at the head table, Mr. Bennet stood from his seat at his daughter's right and addressed the crowd. "Thank you all for coming to join us in celebrating the marriage of Elizabeth and Mr. Darcy. I must say that it was a unique service, which we all will not soon forget." He paused while polite laughter filled the room and looked at his wife, who was frowning and gesturing for him to get on with it. "As my lovely wife no doubt wishes me to get to the point, I would like to offer a prayer before we enjoy the food."

After those gathered bowed their heads, Mr. Bennet began, "Holy and loving God, we come to ask Thy blessing on this couple, who have just entered into the holy state of matrimony this morning. Please grant them health, long life, and happiness. May they look to Thee in their daily lives and raise their children to know Thy grace and love.

"We thank Thee for the bounty of which we are about to partake. May we always be grateful for Thy mercies and blessings! In Christ's name, we pray, amen."

Elizabeth and Darcy were then directed to the long sideboard that fairly groaned under the abundant array of food upon it. Neither was particularly hungry, but they took a sufficient amount, so that Mrs. Bennet would be satisfied that they had enough. Once they were seated again, the other guests were invited to serve themselves.

Due to their rank, Lord Matlock and his wife were the next to fill their plates and to join the head table. Not long after, Mr. and Mrs. Bennet, Mr. Bingley, Jane, Mr. Collins, and Mary sat down as well and began to eat.

Lord Matlock took a deep swallow of wine before he spoke, "Mrs. Darcy, Mr. and Mrs. Bennet, on behalf of the rest of my family and myself, I want to apologize for the rude and outrageous conduct of my sister. Please extend my apologies to all of your family on my behalf. I had no idea that she planned to interrupt the service when she asked Lady Matlock and me to escort her to the wedding. My wife and I had hoped that she had come to her senses.

"She will no longer be a problem for your family, I promise. She will not be given the same freedoms as before." Looking from Darcy to Elizabeth and then to Mr. Bennet, the earl added, "You can be sure that what I told her in the anteroom will be accomplished as soon as possible, Anne will be looked after so that she will not be inconvenienced by her mother's absence."

Finally, Lord Matlock turned his attention to Mr. Collins. "Sir, I also believe that you have received injuries at the hand of my sister. I would like to make amends by letting you know that you shall retain the living at Hunsford with an increase in compensation. My sister had no right to make you sign that infamous contract. Please know that I will completely understand if you choose to leave a curate in charge of the parish. I do have another parish that is due to become vacant in the spring which I could offer to you, but I know that the parishioners at Hunsford are in great need of a shepherd."

Collins stared in disbelief as Mary stifled a gasp at what the earl said.

"Lord Matlock, I am honoured that you would bestow this kindness upon me, and I accept with gratitude," Collins replied in a breathless voice that lacked its usual fawning tone. "You have made both Miss Mary and me very happy."

After those at the table expressed in their own individual ways their acceptance of the earl's apologies, the mood lightened even more. Mrs. Bennet was particularly satisfied with the outcome, since her second daughter's wedding had not been cancelled, and now it was certain that Mary would also be wed.

Darcy reached for Elizabeth's free hand and squeezed it lightly. She glanced at him with a loving but questioning look.

"I just wanted to make sure that you are truly here and that this is not all a wonderful, if slightly odd, dream," he leaned in to whisper in her ear.

With a chuckle, Elizabeth whispered back, "No, my dear husband, this is no dream, merely the reality into which you have willingly stepped."

Their intimate conversation was interrupted by Lady Matlock's call. "Mrs. Bennet, this is one of the loveliest wedding breakfasts I have ever attended. How clever the decorations are! And the food--I declare I have not eaten better in the entire *ton*. You and I shall have to join forces to host a ball to introduce your daughter as Darcy's wife. I am sure that it shall be the talk of Town."

Mrs. Bennet was struck nearly speechless because of the compliments. It took her several seconds to find her voice, and much to Elizabeth's and Darcy's surprise, she did not screech but instead answered in a very rational, for her, tone, "I would be delighted to do so. However, I have two more weddings to plan within the next five months. I am not certain that I would be able to find the time to assist you with a ball."

"Oh, my dear, Mrs. Bennet, two more of your daughters married! What a lovely thought! Since our oldest, Oliver, was married in February of this year, I have hoped to see my Richard married as well, but no girl has caught his eye. I quite despair that he shall ever find a wife. How fortunate you are! I have always wished for a daughter, but I have had to be content to spoil our dear Georgiana." Lady Matlock continued to gush about the good fortune of her hostess for several more minutes, and both Lord Matlock and Mr. Bennet cast looks of sympathy at each other.

"Husband," Elizabeth whispered, "You did not tell me that your aunt would get along so well with my mother."

"Indeed, I did not expect it myself," he assured her softly. "She is not usually this amiable with strangers." He paused to look around him to be sure that no one was listening to him before he said, "I wonder if there is something in the wine."

The tinkle of Elizabeth's delighted laughter thrilled Darcy as his own deeper tones joined hers.

"My cousin and his new bride seem to be very happy," Colonel Fitzwilliam commented at the sound of the newlyweds' merriment. He was seated at another table close by with the two youngest Bennet sisters, Georgiana, the Lucas family, and the Gardiners.

"Oh, yes, they certainly do," Lydia sighed. "I am happy for them, though I do wish that Pemberley was not so very far away. I shall miss Lizzy very much, and I am beginning to think I will miss my new brother as well."

"Oh, Miss Lydia, I feel guilty that I will be privileged to live in the same house with them both," Georgiana exclaimed in dismay.

"Please, Miss Darcy, do not be troubled on my behalf." Lydia smiled sweetly at her new friend. "I have had Lizzy all my life. I must begin to share her with her new family." Lowering her voice as if to tell a secret, she said in a stage whisper, "I believe that I will be allowed to come to visit later next year. I heard my new brother - how wonderful that sounds - say that my family should come in the summer or early fall."

"I had hoped that you could come sooner, but I suppose that with the two weddings in the spring and early summer, there will not be time for that." Georgiana was delighted with her new sisters. "Miss Kitty, I hope you plan to visit as well."

"Oh, of course," Kitty blushed as she had not been attending to the conversation as she ought because of Samuel Lucas's presence at her right side. He had been charming her with witty stories of his university days and his plans for improving his father's crops with a new kind of grain that was more resistant to mould in the rainy English weather. His ideas kept her interested because he explained them so well. "I would very much like to accompany my parents to Pemberley," Kitty added, not wanting to sound unenthusiastic about the idea.

"Georgiana, you must allow your brother and new sister some time to become accustomed to married life before you insist they invite a horde of people to Pemberley," the colonel admonished gently.

"I do understand that, cousin." Georgiana waved her hand as if to push aside his words. "Besides," she lowered her voice and said to Lydia, "We all will be invited to Hertfordshire for the weddings, so I will see you then."

Lydia grinned broadly and sighed contentedly, "Things have turned out so well even after Lady Catherine's unexpected disturbance."

Turning to Colonel Fitzwilliam, she asked timidly, "Is it wrong of me to wonder what went on behind the door of the anteroom?"

He smiled and shook his head. "I doubt there was a person in the church who did not wonder that very thing. Of course, we did hear a great deal of what my aunt said."

"Indeed, one could not help but hear it," Georgiana replied, and everyone at the table laughed.

Meanwhile in the midst of all the jovial conversation at the head table, Mr. Collins sat completely silent, in awe of the honour and blessing he had been given by receiving back his living.

Finally, Mary touched his arm and quietly asked, "Mr. Collins, are you well?"

"I am most definitely well, my dearest Mary," he replied with a wide smile. "How could I be anything else when God has shown such favour to us? I have been thinking that we need not wait the six months that Lady Catherine had previously required."

"Do you truly think we could be married sooner?" Mary asked in breathless eagerness.

"It is possible now, but we must ask your parents to see if they would consent to our changing the date." He took her hand in his and kissed it quickly. "I shall approach your father later today, once the Darcys have gone."

The next hour passed with much lively conversation and general good humour. Finally, however, Darcy decided that they must depart for London so as to reach Town before dark. The farewells were long and brought forth tears and laughter all around.

After Elizabeth kissed her family one last time, Darcy handed her into the coach before he climbed in and sat down opposite his wife. The second, smaller, servants' carriage stood behind them waiting to depart. At Darcy's signal, the drivers flicked the reins and they were off to London and the beginning of their new life together.

CHAPTER TWENTY-FOUR

Elizabeth waved to her family until the carriage reached the turn onto the Meryton road. She leaned back against the squabs and sniffed, trying to hide the tears that filled her eyes. Darcy had been watching her, and thus he realized that she was fighting to keep from weeping.

He quickly moved to sit beside her and wrapped his arms around her. "Do not feel you must hide your sadness from me, dearest. I do understand that you will miss them all." His voice was tender and soothing.

"Oh, my dear husband," Lizzy cried, giving full vent to her tears. She did not quite understand why she felt so sad at this moment. More than anything, she had wished to marry Fitzwilliam and to be with him forever. She loved him with all of her being, so she wondered why she had the desire to cry. When the torrent of tears was finally over, she reached into her reticule for a handkerchief.

"I do not know what came over me. I promise that despite recent evidence to the contrary, I am not a weeper." Elizabeth looked into his eyes. "Please do not think that I regret marrying you. I would not change that for worlds."

Darcy dipped his head and placed a light kiss on her mouth before he straightened and stroked her cheek. "I thought no such thing. I know that you love your family. Of course, you would feel the loss of their company. Your feelings for your family give me great hopes for our life together. Our family will be a close and loving one because you are such a loving person." He pulled her close for another kiss and a hug.

"Thank you, dearest Fitzwilliam," she said, and she laid her head on his shoulder and sighed contently.

"Are you warm enough?" he asked as he reached for the lap rug that had fallen from her.

"If you will stay right here with me and share the cover," she teased when he busied himself tucking the woollen blanket over her. She reached up to remove her bonnet and set it on the other seat.

In response, Darcy moved even closer, and after seeing to it that the rug was tucked around them securely, he pulled her back into his arms with her head against his chest. A surge of contentment flowed over him. *This is my wife, snuggled in my arms. Beth is my own wife, carrying a Darcy, the first of another generation of Darcys.* This time tears, ones of joy, stung his eyes, but he did not mind. He kissed her hair before leaning his cheek against the top of her head as he felt her body relax. The rocking of the carriage soon lulled them both into sleep.

The cessation of movement awoke Darcy, and he felt Elizabeth stir in his arms.

"Are we in London already?" Her voice was slurred with sleep.

"No, I believe that we have stopped to change horses." Darcy moved to the window in time to see one of his footmen readying to open the door. "We have time to refresh ourselves. Would you like something hot to drink? They have several choices here."

Elizabeth reached for her bonnet and secured it on her head as she replied, "That would be delightful."

After giving the signal for the footman to open the carriage door, Darcy alighted from the vehicle. As soon as he helped Elizabeth to the ground, Sarah was at her side.

"I was told by Peters there is a comfortable room in which you can refresh yourself, Mrs. Darcy. Shall I accompany you?"

As Elizabeth looked around her, she saw that the inn was clean and busy. People hastened about their business, paying little heed to the new arrivals. However, she began to feel anxious at being in such a crowd, and she groped for her husband's arm.

"I am sorry, dearest," he whispered, realizing what she was battling, "Of course, I shall walk with you into the inn and return for you as soon as I can. Sarah will go with you and stay until I come back."

Once inside the inn, Elizabeth calmed somewhat. After refreshing herself and upon returning to the main room, she was glad to see Darcy waiting for her at a small table close by. He had before him two steaming mugs.

"The coffee is quite good here, and I had them add plenty of cream and sugar just the way you like it," Darcy said once she sat down. Sarah stood off to the side, and when he noticed the maid there, he asked the innkeeper to show Sarah where the servants were having their drinks.

"This is good coffee," she told him as she sipped from the mug. "How much longer before the carriage will be ready?"

"It shall be ready as soon as we finish," he answered. "Are you hungry?"

Elizabeth shook her head and then drank more coffee. She did not meet his eyes, being both upset and embarrassed that the anxiety still plagued her.

"What is it, dearest?" His soft voice was filled with concern.

"I do so wish that I could overcome this fear. I am sorry that you must attend me in this way."

"My love," he whispered so quietly that she looked up to be certain that he had spoken, "it is my joy to attend you, joy that is only dimmed at your discomfort. We shall work together, and I believe that you shall conquer your fears."

Soon, they were back on their way. Darcy sat beside her once more with his arm around her. Now that Elizabeth had rested and had had the coffee, she began to ponder her position as wife to a man such as Darcy. She did not know what would be required of her. Although her mother had given her the skills to run a household, she was certain that she would be out of her element when she tried to manage those of Darcy House and Pemberley.

Her insecurities played through her mind as her husband talked of what they would encounter on their trip to Pemberley the next day. She heard little, since she fought to maintain her composure. Added to the mixture of fears and doubts of her own ability was the memory of her mother's discussion of the night before. Suddenly, she felt as if she was smothering under the weight of her concerns, and she began to breathe rapidly and push out of Darcy's arms.

"What is wrong, dearest?" Darcy asked with worry clouding his features as she moved to the other side of the coach.

Her only response was to turn away as she continued to fight for air. Darcy realized that she must be feeling great panic. Though he did not understand the cause, he moved to the other side and took her hands.

"Elizabeth," he said gently, "you must slow your breathing."

When she fought to pull her hands away, he raised his voice and ordered in a firmer tone, "Look at me!"

This time she complied, but he saw wild panic in her eyes. Darcy forced down his own anxiety as he spoke with authority. "Take a deep breath and hold it. That is right. Now let it out slowly. Again in, hold it, and out slowly."

After a few more deep breaths, Elizabeth calmed. Her face, pale from the ordeal, flushed pink as she struggled not to cry.

"What happened to frighten you so, sweetest wife?" Darcy pulled her into a hug before releasing her to search her face.

"I am such a foolish girl," she confessed. "First, I began to think of how I knew so little about being the mistress of large estates such as yours. I began to fret that I would disappoint you with my ignorance." She paused to dash away a tear that escaped. "I am thoroughly embarrassed to speak of what else came to my mind when I catalogued my inadequacies."

"Dearest Beth, you are more than capable to learn the requirements of managing our homes. Our housekeepers are both kind and patient and will likely be honoured to give you what little training you will need." Darcy lifted her hand to his lips and softly kissed each knuckle. "But please tell me what else has distressed you so."

She sat in stillness, her eyes cast down as her face reddened. Darcy finally understood and prayed silently for wisdom, as he knew he would need it. He had thought to delay this particular discussion until they had reached Darcy House, but it was not to be. He must reassure her so that she would be at peace.

"Did your mother speak to you of..." he trailed off, his own cheeks colouring at the subject.

"Yes," was her quick whispered reply, partly relieved that he had not made her tell him but had guessed the topic, but also concerned that she might not manage well in that area either.

"Please do not be troubled." He did not know how to tell her what he wanted to say. Darcy took a deep breath before he said, "I have been thinking about our marriage bed. I shall be completely honest. I look forward to... That is to say that you are a beautiful..." He raked a hand through his hair and began again, "I believe that given your condition and the reason for it that we shall not...uh...consummate our marriage until after the baby's birth, and, then, only when you feel you are ready and willing. I promise you now that you shall never suffer me to impose upon you without your consent. I love you too much to cause you any distress."

Elizabeth finally looked up and held his gaze as if she wanted to see the truth in his eyes. "You would wait for me?" she asked in an awed but tremulous voice.

"I have already waited my whole life for you. I would wait a great deal longer so that you would be comfortable." Darcy did not flinch from her scrutiny.

Gratitude and love overflowed within her, so that Elizabeth lifted her hands and held his face while she leaned in to kiss him. This kiss was the first she had initiated and, therefore, was all the more thrilling to her new husband, but because of his promise, Darcy enjoyed the caress without making further demands upon her.

When Elizabeth pulled back, she smiled and sighed, "I love you, Fitzwilliam Darcy of Pemberley."

"And I love you, Elizabeth Bennet Darcy, formerly of Longbourn." Once more he tucked the robes around them and settled her against him. This time he asked her various questions of her childhood and her tastes in music, etc. Although he would have rather spent the time in more intimate conversation, he knew that she needed the time to regain her composure. Thus he would give her that opportunity.

They reached Town with enough daylight left so that they could see the bustle of activity that was London at that time of year. Elizabeth was able to recognize the street in which Darcy House stood as the coach turned into it. She put on and straightened her bonnet before leaning down in order to catch a glimpse of one of her new homes through the carriage window. When the lovely building came into view, she glanced over at her husband and smiled. "I can hardly credit that this is to be my home. Are you certain that I am not in the midst of a lovely, though fanciful, dream?"

Darcy laughed in delight over Elizabeth's renewed wonder at the house. He was eager to discover what her reaction would be to the ancestral home in Pemberley. Darcy House was a newer acquisition, having only been in the family for four generations. "You are completely awake, and this is, indeed, your home, our home."

Once the coach stopped, he quickly helped his wife to the ground and into the house. He felt her stiffen at the sight of the household staff standing in two lines to receive their new mistress, but he soon saw that she had garnered the courage to meet each of them, her natural grace finally rising to win the approbation of all assembled.

Mrs. Graves explained that she had ordered hot water kept in readiness for their arrival. She ordered servants to prepare baths for the master and mistress before saying, "Mrs. Darcy, I will show you to your room."

"I shall assist my wife, Mrs. Graves," Darcy answered pleasantly. "Please prepare to have our supper sent to the master sitting room when I ring for it in about an hour."

Mrs. Graves bobbed a curtsey and left to give the order to the kitchen staff.

Darcy left Elizabeth in Sarah's care and went to his own chambers to wash the travel dust from his person. Peters had laid out a change of clothes and waited to help his master dress. Once his bath was over and he was dressed, Darcy waited for Elizabeth to finish, knowing it would take her longer than himself. He thought to read, but realized that he had left the book he had been reading behind at Netherfield, so he decided he would go quickly to the library for something with which to occupy himself for the next half hour.

As Darcy silently opened his chamber door, he hesitated upon hearing the words 'master and mistress'. Normally, he would not have eavesdropped, but the maid's voice he heard was not a familiar one. Gossip was discouraged in his houses, so he wished to find out who the servant was so that he could have Mrs. Graves put a stop to it.

"Polly, you should not say so," the second maid protested.

"Oh Mattie, no one will 'ear," the one called Polly said, dismissing the other's concern. I ain't never seen 'im afore, but the master is right fine to look at, no denyin'. I just bin thinkin' the reason the wedding 'appened so fast like was cause she be in the family way."

At the other maid's gasp, she chuckled and said, "Can't say I blames the mistress since 'e's so 'andsome and all."

"But, Polly, you mustn't repeat this. Mrs. Graves would dismiss you for sayin' such things about the new missus."

"Well, I 'ave already wagered with Crans, the chamber maid at the Cunninghams next door, that we won't be seein' no blood on the sheets come mornin'." Polly lowered her voice to almost a whisper. "I done asked for the 'onour of cleanin' the mistress chambers tomorra. I'll shows ye the proof then. If I be wrong, I'll do yer chores along with mine for a day."

Footsteps could be heard down the hall as the two maids moved away from the door. Darcy was stunned by the audacity of this maid Polly, but he was also aware of how such rumours could take on a life of their own when spread by servants from house to house. It was one of the reasons that he had always insisted that his housekeepers discourage any gossip. He wondered what he could do to prevent this particular maid from spreading this bit of scandal without letting anyone know that he had overheard what the maids said.

He had to protect Elizabeth from this. With God's help, he and Sarah had kept any hint of the attack from coming to public knowledge, and he knew that once they were at Pemberley, the staff would never reveal any suspicions even if they did have them, but without the proof of which the maid spoke, his wife could bear the brunt of foul gossip. After spending several minutes trying to come up with a plan, Darcy finally decided to turn his mind to other matters in the hope that the solution would come to him later.

Dismissing the idea of retrieving a book from the library, Darcy moved into the shared sitting room to await his bride, and he was not there long before she joined him. She had changed into a lovely blue silk gown, trimmed in ivory lace. She still wore the necklace he had given her. Her hair was swept back from her face with two ivory combs and twisted in a simple bun at her neck. He fought within himself not to pull her into his arms and kiss her with all the passion that he felt at seeing her beauty.

"My dearest, loveliest Elizabeth," he breathed out as he stared at her in wonder.

"Do you like the gown, dear husband?" she asked, her cheeks rosy at the way he looked at her.

"Indeed, it is lovely, but you, my darling Beth, are the most beautiful woman I have ever beheld." He paused and raked a hand through his hair as he tried to calm his ardour. "I thought that when I saw you this morning, that you could not be lovelier, but I can see that I was wrong."

"I think that you, sir, are blinded by your affection for me." By this time, she had reached him, and she lifted her hand to touch his cheek. "However, since I think that you are by far the most handsome man I have ever known, I believe that this bodes well for our union, do you not?"

Darcy took her hand in his and brought it to his lips. After he had kissed it, he said, "I do. It bodes very well indeed." He slowly and gently pulled her into his arms and kissed her, all the while keeping tight rein on his responses.

"I believe it is time for me to ring for our supper." He moved from her to the bell pull.

Elizabeth smiled at him in gratitude. She knew that he was working to keep his promise to her, and she loved him all the more for it. The feelings his kisses and embraces produced within her were the most wondrous she had ever felt, but until she was more comfortable with them, she would seek to enjoy them in an unhurried fashion.

The rest of the evening passed in a pleasing manner. Elizabeth could not have said exactly of what they spoke or what they ate or drank. She only knew that they had spent several hours happily together, snug in their common sitting room away from the world. Darcy read aloud to her, and he promised to continue reading to her while they travelled to Pemberley.

When it finally became clear to Darcy that his new wife was tiring, he rang for Sarah to help Elizabeth get ready for bed. While they waited for the maid to come, Darcy said, "I would like to wish you good night once you are ready, so please knock on the door between our bed chambers."

"Of course," Elizabeth answered nervously.

About thirty minutes later, there was a soft knock on the adjoining door. Darcy, still fully dressed, walked to it and entered his wife's chamber. He found Elizabeth sitting in a chair near the fire in a light green robe over a matching night dress. She did not look comfortable, though she was striving to appear at ease. Her hair lay in a long plait over her shoulder half way to her waist. The picture she made was one of innocence and purity.

Darcy swallowed hard as he gazed upon his lovely wife, seeing her obvious nervousness. He moved to her, knelt in front of her, and took her hands in his. "Beth, my darling I am humbled that you are my wife. I will thank God every day for His gift." He kissed each of her hands before he stood and pulled her to her feet. "You must sleep. We shall leave early, and it will be a long day." He lifted her into his arms, and once they arrived at her bed, he laid her down on the smooth sheets, as Sarah had already turned down the covers. After tucking her in, he leaned down to kiss her.

"I love you, my sweet Beth. Sleep well." He made to leave, but Elizabeth prevented him by catching his hand.

"Dearest Fitzwilliam, I love you too," she said, barely above a whisper. She then tugged on his hand while lifting her head. "Kiss me again," she whispered breathlessly.

He obliged her with a much longer kiss than the previous one, but he broke the contact as he felt his control slipping. "Sleep, my lovely wife. I will see you on the morrow."

"Sleep well, my beloved husband." Elizabeth relaxed back into the pillows and sighed.

When Darcy looked back upon reaching the door, he spied a faint smile on her lips. An answering one brightened his face as he moved back into his bed chamber. As he started to close the door, he decided that he wanted to be able to hear Elizabeth if she should need him, so he left it open a few inches.

Darcy was extremely glad he had left the door ajar when after a couple hours, he heard Elizabeth whimper and cry out in her sleep. He leapt from his bed and hurried through to her room. He found her thrashing violently at some unseen assailant, shaking her head from side to side, and calling out for help.

Hurrying to her side, Darcy strove to wake her by touching her shoulder but she recoiled from him. *She must think I am Wickham,* he thought grimly. Deciding that she would be more fearful if she woke in the dark, he quickly lit several candles before returning to her side.

His heart nearly seized at the tears that rolled down her cheeks as she continued to be locked in the nightmare. Darcy grasped her hand and began to talk to her. "Elizabeth, my love, wake up now. You are dreaming. It is only a dream. Please wake up for me, my darling Beth."

Just as he had begun to despair that she would not awaken, her eyes popped open and searched wildly around the room. When she finally saw Darcy, Elizabeth gasped in joy and pulled his hand to her cheek. "Oh Fitzwilliam, I thought that you had left me with… The dream was worse than the attack because you walked away. You did not help me." Her voice trailed off as she wept against his hand.

Darcy sat on the bed and pulled her close. "Sweet Beth, I am here. I will always be. I love you." He rubbed her back and planted kisses on her hair as he soothed her. "It was only a dream, only a dream."

After letting out a shuddering sigh, Elizabeth repeated, "It was only a dream."

"Let me find you a handkerchief," Darcy said as he carefully laid her back against the pillows. He was not well versed in the layout of a lady's dresser, but he looked in what he thought was a logical place for such things and found one. After handing it to Elizabeth, he poured her a glass of water and brought it to her.

After that she seemed to have regained her equilibrium, and she smiled up at him. "Thank you, dearest. I am sorry to have wakened you. I did not expect this tonight."

"There is no need to apologize." He pulled the covers up around her and kissed her forehead. "You must get back to sleep, my dear."

Darcy had just turned to go back to his room when Elizabeth cried out, "Fitzwilliam, would you please stay? I do not believe I would be able to sleep without you in the room."

"Let me fetch my robe and I will sit by the bed until you fall asleep."

"No, you need to rest as well. Could you not..." Even in the dim candlelight, he could see the blush that spread across her face. Struggling against the embarrassment, she continued, "Might I ask you to... I believe there is more than enough room in the bed for ..."

When it did not seem that she could finish her sentences, Darcy realized what she wanted. "Are you certain it is what you wish?"

Closing her eyes, Elizabeth nodded in the affirmative and whispered, "Yes."

Darcy blew out the candles and walked to the other side of the bed. After a brief inner struggle, he lifted only the top two covers, leaving one that could be a barrier between them. Slipping in, he lay very still on his back, not wanting to cause Elizabeth the least bit of fear.

"Thank you, Fitzwilliam," Elizabeth breathed out softly before she turned on her side toward him.

Soon, Darcy heard her breathing slow, so he knew she had fallen asleep. He turned on his side to face her and smiled. He wanted his wife in every way possible, but his contentment at her request for him to stay was enough for him at the moment. After gently caressing her cheek, he closed his eyes and drifted into sleep himself.

CHAPTER TWENTY-FIVE

Darcy became aware of a warm weight upon his shoulder and the light fragrance of roses filling his nostrils. As he opened his eyes slowly, he saw his wife's brown hair as she snuggled into his shoulder with her small hand on his chest. The weak winter sun barely lightened the room enough for him to know it was morning. They would need to arise soon, so that they could make their way toward Pemberley in good time.

Instead of waking his wife, Darcy decided to indulge himself, so he buried his face in her hair. Tendrils of its shiny brown curls had escaped the braid and formed into a kind of coronet. At this moment, he desired nothing more than to stay abed with his lovely wife, but after enjoying the innocent pleasure of being so near her for a short time, he kissed her hair and then her forehead, hoping to wake her gently.

She did not respond. He had just lifted his hand to touch her when she lifted her face to his and asked, "Must we wake so early? I am comfortable here."

"I am as well, but we have a long three days of travelling ahead of us," Darcy explained before placing a quick kiss on her mouth, "So I must get dressed, as must you."

Elizabeth sighed as she turned over to reach for the tin that held her soda bread. "If I must arise, I must fortify myself first," she told him as she took out a piece. "If you will ring for Sarah, I can finish this before she gets here with my tea."

Darcy crawled out of bed and pulled the bell cord. "How long before you will be ready to go down to breakfast?"

"I should be ready in half an hour, unless you object to me dressing myself and my hair plainly today. I do not wish to have my lovely new things soiled by travel." She hoped that he would have no objections.

"That is a fine idea," Darcy smiled his satisfaction at her practicality. "I had planned to do the same during our trip. If you do not object, I will rejoin you and escort you to the dining parlour."

"I would be delighted, Fitzwilliam," Elizabeth said as she beamed up at him from her position on the bed. "Would you mind waiting until Sarah arrives? I do not want to be alone."

"I believe that I will fetch my robe first, but I would be happy to wait until she comes." He quickly moved through the door, grabbed up the robe from the end of the bed and rejoined Elizabeth as he donned it. He noticed Peters arriving as he took up the robe, and he gave his valet a brief nod but did not speak as he left his chamber for hers.

About ten minutes later, Sarah arrived with a small tray on which sat a cup, saucer, and a tea pot. She curtseyed quickly when she spied Darcy sitting in the chair next to the bed, and then she served her mistress her special blend of tea.

"Mr. Darcy, sir, I did not bring you anything," Sarah said in embarrassment. "Would you like me to fetch you some tea?"

"No, Sarah, I do not desire anything at the moment." He stood and kissed Elizabeth's hand. "I will see you soon, my dear."

Peters was already waiting to shave Darcy when he re-entered his bed chamber. Sitting down, he leaned against the back of the chair and revelled in the knowledge that he would spend the next three days almost exclusively in his lovely wife's company.

Darcy was ready in fifteen minutes, but he knew that he should not return so soon, so he sat at his writing desk and took out some paper. However, he merely sat staring at the adjoining door. He wanted to go to her, but he waited another five minutes before he went to the door and knocked. When there was no answer, he opened the door to find the room empty.

At first, he was surprised and wondered if she had misunderstood him and had gone downstairs without him, but then he heard muffled voices and realized that Elizabeth was still in her dressing room with her maid.

He smiled as he looked around the room until his gaze fell upon the bed on which he had spent part of the night with his wife. The bedclothes were tossed aside to reveal crumpled, but pure white sheets. Suddenly he remembered that that the maid, Polly, would soon be coming to clean the room, and she would find those unstained sheets.

Shoving his hands in his pockets in frustration at his inability to find a solution that would keep Elizabeth from becoming the gossip of the house and beyond, he felt the solid metal of his pen knife. Darcy brought it out and stared at it for a moment before listening to make sure that neither Elizabeth nor Sarah seemed to be coming back into the room.

Darcy quickly opened the knife and hastened to the bed. He slipped the blade along the side of his left index finger, making a small cut. Leaning over the bed, he allowed the blood to drop onto the middle of the sheets. When he thought that he had soiled them enough, he wrapped his finger in his handkerchief, hid the spot from the view of his wife and maid by tenting a bit of the blanket over it, and quickly left the room.

His man did not look up from the chore he was doing, which allowed Darcy to move to his writing desk once more. Sitting down, he acted as if he were mending a pen with his knife.

"Ouch!" Darcy murmured as if he had just cut himself. "Peters, I just sliced my finger while mending my pen. Bring me a bandage." He exhibited his finger that was wrapped in the handkerchief.

"Of course, sir," Peters assented, though privately he wondered at his master injuring himself. *Perhaps his mind was preoccupied with his pretty new wife.* He shook his head slightly at the foolishness before he located the clean strips of linen he always kept for emergencies. After washing and drying the wound, the valet tied the bandage securely. "Make sure that you keep this dry and clean. I think that if you do, it will heal well and quickly."

With his finger bandaged, Darcy went back to Elizabeth's chamber and found her waiting for his arrival. He gave her a quick kiss good morning and said, "You look rested, my love."

"I feel rested," she answered while smiling her unspoken gratitude. "I am ready for our trip to Pemberley."

As Darcy offered his arm to escort her to the door, he rested his left hand on hers.

"What happened to your finger?" Elizabeth exclaimed.

"It is nothing." Darcy kept his voice nonchalant. "I was mending a pen and the knife slipped. Peters tells me it is hardly worth bandaging."

Elizabeth scanned his face, and he smiled. Thus reassured, she smiled back.

As the couple moved into the hallway and down the corridor, Darcy tried to think of a way to discover one particular maid's reaction to seeing the sheets, but he could not come up with one. Although he wanted the new servant to receive at least a warning, he knew that he could not be the one to give it. Also, if he mentioned his concerns to his housekeeper, it would expose what he heard and possibly what he did to thwart the maid's purpose. Deciding to ponder it later, he walked his wife to the breakfast room.

Elizabeth had a healthy appetite this morning and ate the deliciously prepared food with relish. "Fitzwilliam, your chef is very talented. I could eat entirely too many of these pastries. I would like to give him my compliments once I am finished," Elizabeth enthused before taking another bite of the fruit-filled confection.

"I am sure that he would be pleased to receive your accolades," Darcy answered with a smile. "He has certainly outdone himself this morning. I do believe that you impressed him on your earlier visit to Town."

"I am as delighted to dine on his lovely cooking now as I was then. If we stay here too long, I fear that I would gain weight." She grinned and sipped her tea.

They were just finishing the meal when Mrs. Graves entered the room.

"Mr. Darcy, sir, I would like to speak with you on an urgent matter." She twisted her hands in agitation as she looked from her master to her mistress.

Elizabeth understood before her husband did that the housekeeper wanted to speak to him in private. "I shall go to the kitchen to speak to the chef about obtaining some of the pastries to take with us on our journey." She stood and exited the room.

"What is it, Mrs. Graves?" Darcy asked with a bit of impatience.

"Pardon me, sir but something has come up, and I need your advice. I know that I am supposed to handle matters that pertain to the household staff or speak to the mistress, but this is a delicate subject." She glanced at the door by which Mrs. Darcy had left the room. "You see, Peters came to me after overhearing a couple of maids arguing in the mistress's chambers. One of them, Polly by name, is new here. She has worked here for under a month."

Mrs. Graves took a deep breath and exhaled before she continued, "She was saying that she had only been joking when she said that the mistress's sheets would not be spoiled and had agreed to do Mattie's work for her if they were not. Peters came to me in a hurry, and I found them still at it."

Her face was red with embarrassment. "I arrived just in time to hear Mattie taunt Polly, 'I warned you not to gossip. What will you say to Crans next door? It better be the truth, or I will speak to Mrs. Graves,' she said." The housekeeper wrung her hands. "Oh, Mr. Darcy, Polly talked to one of the neighbour's maids about her vile conjecture about the mistress."

"I must say that if she had not spoken to the neighbour's maid, I would know how to act, but I would not like to arouse speculation by dismissing her at this point. What is your opinion, sir?"

Darcy was glad that the maid had been found out. He pondered for a few moments what the wisest course of action would be. Finally he said, "I believe that Mattie should discreetly inform this Crans person of what they found. Give her instructions to say that gossip is forbidden at Darcy House, but because of the circumstances, you told her to explain that what Polly had said was false. I would have liked for Mattie to inform you of Polly's gossipy ways, but unless she had been involved in the spreading of the rumours, she is not to blame.

"As for Polly, I wish that she will be kept to work below stairs. I do not ever want her to be working in or around the family rooms. And she is not to have her next two half days off. Mattie will enjoy that bit of extra time to herself while Polly does Mattie's chores as well as her own. Watch her carefully, and let the staff know that they are to report any further gossip from her. Inform her that this is her last chance," Darcy said it in such a way that told the housekeeper that he was holding back his anger.

"Very good, sir," Mrs. Graves answered and curtseyed, "I will see to it right away."

Just as the housekeeper left the breakfast room, Elizabeth re-entered. "Chef Marcus had already prepared a basket for our journey, but he added a few more of the pastries just for me." She noticed his expression was more serious than when she had left and came to stand beside Darcy.

"I hope that the business Mrs. Graves had to speak with you about was not too dire."

"Not dire, just a matter of some delicacy," he replied with a smile as he took her hand in his. "Usually, Mrs. Graves would consult you in household matters, but I believe she was correct in seeking my advice this time. I hope that you are not upset that she did not."

"Of course not," she said as she smiled. "I am not quite in the practice of dealing with household matters as yet, so I am not upset at all. I suspect that I will need a great deal of experience to know how to be the proper mistress of such large houses."

"I have all the confidence in the world that you will do fine, and Mrs. Reynolds and even Georgiana will assist you during the transition." He kissed the hand he held before saying, "I believe that we should make haste to depart if we are to keep to our schedule today."

CHAPTER TWENTY-SIX

The trip to Pemberley went as smoothly as could be expected during the early part of December. Since Darcy had sent ahead to the coaching inns in which he planned that they would stay, they were clean and with ample accommodations for the party.

Because the inns were not large enough to have adjoining bedchambers for them, Darcy and Elizabeth shared a bed once more. She was happy that she did not have to beg her husband to stay with her, and he was delighted as well.

Elizabeth had never travelled to Derbyshire, which gave Darcy the pleasure of indicating all of the landmarks and explaining their interesting histories. He read more from the book he had begun the day before, much to his wife's entertainment. They revelled in the opportunity to share in private conversations. Before the end of their journey, they had come to a fuller understanding of each other's likes and dislikes and delighted in the fact that so many were of such similarity. Just after noon on the third day of travel, Darcy began to fidget in his seat.

"What is it, Fitzwilliam?" Elizabeth asked with a twinkle in her eye. "I am certain that my young cousins squirm less during a long ride."

Darcy looked startled for a moment; then he smiled. "I feel like a child who is eager for a treat."

He took her hand in his and kissed it. "My lovely Beth, we are very close to the village of Lambton, which is only five miles from Pemberley. I am excited to show you your new home as well."

"Oh my," Elizabeth gasped in mock horror. "I am afraid that you shall now be subjected to my own fidgets. Since I had no idea we were so close, I will now become quite impatient to see our home."

Darcy laughed out loud at her teasing, took her in his arms, and kissed her soundly. A few moments later, he leaned back against the squabs and relaxed with her head on his chest. "I am now quite content to enjoy the rest of our journey," he sighed.

"I am happy to know that I am a cure for the fidgets," he could hear the smile in her voice.

"Indeed, wife, I believe it shall be discovered that you are a cure for many things that have ailed me."

Not long after this interlude, Elizabeth noticed that the carriage must have entered a village because of the sound of cobblestones under the wheels.

Darcy straightened and leaned to open the carriage curtains. "This is Lambton. Pemberley is near," he said, without attempting to hide the excitement in his voice.

Pointing to the village green and an wide, old tree, he said, "I used to run everyday to that tree in the chestnut season. He grinned as Elizabeth peered out the window.

"What a lovely village! The green is beautiful." She, then, saw that most of the villagers stopped what they were doing to stare at their carriage as it passed them by.

"I think that the people are very curious about our little caravan. Do you suppose that they know about our marriage?" asked Elizabeth, who had forgotten her fears in the excitement of seeing the village but, now, leaned back out of sight in a sudden fit of anxiety.

"I am certain of it," Darcy smiled as he had not yet become aware of her changed demeanour. "I did not prohibit Mrs. Reynolds from telling of our marriage when I informed her. It was not something I wished to hide. My servants are not gossips…," he paused to think the word, *usually*, before he continued, "But I do not believe the news could be contained, and the people of Lambton are no doubt very interested in seeing the new Mrs. Darcy."

It was then that Darcy turned to see Elizabeth's pale countenance. "Oh, my love!" he cried out and pulled her to him. "I am so sorry. I should have known that this would discomfort you. I will pull the curtains shut immediately."

When he made the move to do so, Elizabeth shook her head. "No, please do not. I shall be fine. I just require a bit of time to overcome it. Hold me tightly, and I shall do so even sooner."

After only a few minutes as the carriage moved out of Lambton and into the countryside, Elizabeth relaxed her hold on her husband and lifted her head. "I am certain that I will eventually become comfortable with the prospect of visiting the village and the others in this area. However, for the moment, I must prepare myself to meet Pemberley. Elizabeth took a small mirror out of her reticule and surveyed her hair. Finding relatively little to repair, she retrieved her bonnet from the seat across from her and secured it in place.

"I must say that there is a benefit to married life I had not expected," Darcy said with a pleased smile on his face.

"And what may I ask is that unexpected benefit?" she asked with an answering grin.

"The benefit is of watching my wife transform herself into a proper lady after I have had the pleasure of seeing her in her less formal state."

"I must say that you do not look the very proper gentleman I first met at the Meryton Assembly, either. Moreover, I can say that I am eternally grateful that you do not show me that particular person often."

"I hope that you will not meet with that gentleman again, for he almost was the means of my losing the chance to win your good opinion." Darcy's tone turned more serious.

Elizabeth chuckled as she leaned in to kiss his cheek. "Please do not worry yourself, as I am confident that I now know how to handle him."

The couple sat together in silence for a while until the carriage slowed to a stop. The footman opened the door and let down the step. Darcy hastened out of the coach and assisted Elizabeth to the ground.

She was surprised to see that they were not in front of a house, but at the side of the road near a bend. "What do we here, Mr. Darcy?"

Smiling at her puzzled look, he said, "Mrs. Darcy, I have something to show you. I would ask you to trust me enough to keep your eyes closed until I tell you to open them."

"Of course, I trust you," she told him as she took his arm and closed her eyes. Elizabeth relied on his guidance by clinging tightly to his arm as the terrain they walked upon was not smooth.

After they had walked on for a few moments, Darcy stopped and turned her a quarter turn. He watched her face as he said, "You may open your eyes now, my sweet Beth. Behold Pemberley."

When Elizabeth opened her eyes, she could hardly believe what she saw. They stood on high ground overlooking a perfect view of a small valley. A mirror-like, lake-sized pond reflected the image of a beautifully grand home of golden stone, three stories high, on a gentle rise beyond. There was none of the artifice so often seen in the stately homes of the wealthy. Nature had not been contradicted, but instead had been embraced with a grace rarely achieved.

"Oh, I did not imagine such a wonderful place!" she cried out in awe. "It seems to have grown as an exquisite flower from the countryside. How can this be Pemberley?"

"I am so happy that you approve," he said in a tenor that was almost a sigh. "I had hoped that you would love it as much as I, but I admit to being a trifle nervous that you would not."

"Oh, my dearest, how could I not approve or love it?" She snuggled close to him while squeezing his arm. "If the inside is as wonderful as this prospect, I do believe I will never want to leave. May we hurry home? I have a great desire to see the whole place in closer proximity."

Laughing at her eagerness, Darcy led her back to the carriage and helped her into it. His heart swelled at her praise, and his joy in his choice of a wife seemed to grow beyond his wildest expectations.

It was Elizabeth's turn to suffer true fidgets as they travelled the last half mile to Pemberley, but finally they reached the house and the carriage stopped. Once the footman let down the steps and Darcy had exited the coach, she was ready to jump down. However, she succeeded in reining in her eagerness so as to allow her husband to assist her to the ground.

Before them stood an archway into an open paved courtyard. A small fountain graced the centre, and though it was not running because of the winter season, it was beautiful in its simple, cylindrical design. Twin staircases flanked the landing onto which double doors opened.

As they reached the doors, Elizabeth felt an unexpected sense of belonging. This huge and lovely building was to be her home for the rest of their life together, and it seemed to be beckoning her to come in and experience its welcoming warmth. When she glanced toward her husband, she saw Darcy smiling down at her, taking in her reactions to the house.

"Oh, my dear husband," she whispered in excited awe, "Let us go in. I cannot wait to see our home."

So it was that the whole of the Pemberley staff beheld their usually rather sober master with a huge, satisfied smile on his face as Mr. Darcy and his bride walked through the front door.

Because of her position and seniority, Mrs. Reynolds was the first to offer a proper curtsey and say, "Welcome home, Mr. Darcy."

"Thank you, Mrs. Reynolds," Darcy smiled at the diminutive woman whom he had known since he was four years old. "I would like to present my wife, Elizabeth Darcy."

Turning to Elizabeth, he began the introductions of his staff with his housekeeper. "This is Mrs. Reynolds."

It did not take Elizabeth long to realize that the household at Pemberley was a great deal larger than that of Darcy House in Town. However, that realization did not intimidate her so much as she would have expected. Each of the servants seemed extremely eager to make her acquaintance. Whether it was because of that eagerness, or the feeling of welcome she had experienced as she drew near the house, she felt none of the anxiety she had at Darcy House.

Soon, however, the weariness of the journey and the excitement of being in her new home made their effects known to her. Elizabeth had begun to lean more heavily upon her husband's arm by the time the introductions had been concluded.

Darcy, ever aware of her needs, understood, and after dismissing the rest of the staff, asked the housekeeper to have a tray sent to their sitting room as soon as possible. He escorted Elizabeth above stairs, to the right, and down a long corridor to their suite of rooms.

Inside their private sitting room, Elizabeth stood transfixed. Although it was decorated in an older style, its elegance fit the house perfectly. A rich, deep blue covered the walls, which were framed with gleaming white woodwork. Lovely matching blue brocade curtains framed the large sparkling windows, and the light coming through them brightened the room even though the sky was not sunny.

The furnishings were also not of the current mode, but they looked invitingly comfortable. Elizabeth walked around the room, picking up small *objets d'art,* running her hand over the lush velvet of the sofas and chairs and the smooth polished surfaces of the tables, and gazing up at the beautiful paintings of pastoral scenes that hung on the walls. She would have continued thusly much longer if there had not been a knock on the outer door.

At Darcy's call to enter, the butler, Davis, entered with a large tray. He was followed by Mrs. Reynolds, Sarah, and a younger girl.

"I did not think such a large group was needed to bring us a tray," Darcy teased as he moved to Elizabeth's side.

"Oh, Mr. Darcy," Mrs. Reynolds chided with a smile and with the same tone as he. "I only came to see that everything is to your liking and thought that I would familiarize Mrs. Darcy's maid with the equipment in the bathing chamber, since Mrs. Darcy will likely be wanting a bath after the meal. And Tina is-"

"There is no need to explain further," Darcy interrupted with a laugh. "Go right ahead with your work."

Taking Elizabeth's elbow, Darcy guided her to the loaded table where Davis had just laid out the contents of the tray: freshly sliced bread, pots of butter, honey, and preserves, a bowl of fruit, and a pot of tea. The sight of the lovely spread caused Elizabeth's mouth to water, making her realize how hungry she was.

The food was as delicious as it looked, and by the time they had finished, Elizabeth wanted to see more of her new home.

"When may we tour the house?" Elizabeth asked as she placed her empty tea cup on its saucer.

"I believe that Sarah has drawn your bath," Darcy replied. "If you are not too fatigued when you are finished, we can begin to see the rest of the house, but since it is so large, for your sake, I think we should not try to accomplish it all in one day."

"Very well," sighed Elizabeth, "I do need to freshen up, but I do so want to see more of our beautiful home."

Darcy showed Elizabeth to the door that led into her bed chambers. The walls were a warm and sunny yellow, as were the draperies and the bedcovering. Obviously feminine in taste, it was not frilly or overdone in lace, which pleased Elizabeth immensely.

"Oh, Mr. Darcy," she cried as she clasped her hands together in delight. "I do believe that I stepped into a dream. Is this truly to be mine?"

Chuckling, Darcy answered, "Yes, Mrs. Darcy, this is yours. I am happy that you like it, for here too, there was not time to remodel. Besides, I would not do so without seeking your opinion."

"I do not see a thing I would change. It is a lovely, lovely room."

Just as Elizabeth finished speaking, Sarah entered the room through a door to the side. After curtseying, she apologized, "Pardon me, Mrs. Darcy, but your bath is ready."

"Of course," Elizabeth said in a formal manner that was contradicted by the smile on her face. "If you will excuse me, sir,"

Darcy gave her a deep and ceremonial bow in return, but his expression gave away his happiness. "I will be about my own bath and will meet you in our sitting room when you are ready."

There was another revelation in store for Elizabeth when she entered the bathing chamber. Inside, she found a gleaming copper tub, and over against the wall above it was a large tank made of the same copper. Pipes ran from the tank to the tub.

"Is it not an amazing device, Mrs. Darcy?" Sarah asked as she helped Elizabeth remove her clothes. "I am told that there is a great cistern on the roof that feeds tanks leading to several of the bed chambers. The tanks are heated by oil burners underneath, and both the heated water and unheated are fed by gravity into the tubs. Such convenience I have never seen before."

As Elizabeth slipped into the water, she agreed as the perfectly balanced temperature of the bath soothed her travel weary muscles. "It is amazing indeed."

A little less than an hour later, Elizabeth rejoined Darcy to begin her tour of Pemberley. She did feel a trifle tired, but she would not forego seeing at least a few rooms before she would give in to rest.

"You may choose where we shall begin," Darcy said after he pulled her into his arms and kissed her.

Elizabeth sighed and laid her head on his chest. "I think I would like to see the library and then the music room. After hearing Miss Bingley's praise of both when my family dined at Netherfield, I wish to see if her praises were warranted."

She heard his laugh rumble through his chest and lifted her eyes to meet Darcy's smile.

"Then, Mrs. Darcy, let us to the library."

Elizabeth thought that she had been prepared by seeing the Darcy House library, but she quickly found that she was not. The room was much larger than its equivalent in Town and included an expanse of north facing windows, so that even in the late afternoon of a winter's day, it was much brighter than the usual library. It was a full two stories high, with more than the mere balconies of the townhouse's version. The second level boasted a chamber that, though indeed not of the size and breadth of the lower one, was even larger than her father's book room at Longbourn.

She asked to explore the second level, and upon reaching it by a circular staircase, Elizabeth completed a circuit of the balcony before moving into the inviting reading chamber. A large bay window which looked out over the north side of the gardens sported a comfortable built-in seat, strewn with lovely pillows. Darcy showed her a door hidden behind one of the bookshelves that led into the hallway. After surveying the furnishings of the room, Elizabeth wanted to see more of the main section below, so the two proceeded back down the stairs.

"I do not believe that I have ever seen so many books in one place in my life outside of one of the great lending libraries in London that Uncle Gardiner took me to once when I was in Town. Just to look, of course, since I was not able to afford the subscription price to borrow from such a prestigious place," Elizabeth exclaimed as she turned in a circle, trying to take in everything at once.

When Elizabeth stopped, she saw Darcy standing a little ways from her, smiling at her expressive face. "I suppose that you are inured to all of this splendour."

"Indeed, I am not," he denied as he moved to take her hand. "Oh, I suppose that I do not catch my breath when I enter the room as I witnessed you doing, but I am quite aware that the legacy my family has handed down over the generations is very special. I endeavour never to take it for granted, I assure you."

"I did not intend to insult you, my dear," she said with contrition. "I believe that my own reaction quite surprised and embarrassed me."

Darcy lifted her chin and asked, "Why embarrassed, my sweet Beth?"

"Should I not be more sedate and complacent in my reactions? Is it not bad form to be so unguarded in one's admiration of things? I would hate to become like my cousin Mr. Collins and begin to ask the cost of the glazing or the mantle piece, or like Miss Bingley and start to praise your excellent taste." She tried to sound teasing, but her heightened colour showed that she truly was embarrassed.

"Oh, my dearest, loveliest Elizabeth," Darcy pulled her into a close embrace. "I would never think that of you. In fact, I am finding that I relish your innocent pleasure as you explore our home." He paused to grin down at her and wink. "I could easily show you the records of all the expenditures if you are indeed interested in the costs, and as to praise, I will accept every bit that you wish to give, since I know that you have never sought to flatter me or ingratiate yourself."

He was rewarded by her hearty laugh and a quick kiss. Elizabeth pulled away from him, though she grasped his hand. "What I would truly like to know is how you keep track of all of these wonderful volumes. I would not begin to know how to find a book I might wish to read. As much as I love to explore amidst such abundance, I fear I would be lost."

"The books are catalogued here." Darcy gestured to a desk upon which stood several bound volumes. "Before any book is shelved, it is recorded with the date, cost, etc. I believe that one of my great-grandmothers of about two hundred years ago was the one to begin the current method of classification and recording. She even left detailed instructions as to the proper way to proceed, although I seriously doubt that anyone has needed to look at them for direction." At her questioning look, he explained, "Each of the Darcys who have been in charge of the catalogue has received complete instruction."

Elizabeth carefully opened what looked to be the newest of the volumes in the catalogue. After leafing through it for a few moments, she found the newest entries. "You are the current librarian," she stated with a smile.

He nodded his head and said simply, "I am."

"I hope that you will teach me the ways of the Pemberley library, for I believe my biggest indulgence will be in finding and buying new books for our home."

"I would be delighted to tutor you in all things bibliothecal."

"I look forward to it," she said as she put the volume back into its place.

For a few moments, Elizabeth ambled about the room before she turned and asked, "Do you have a favourite book amongst all of these?"

"I believe I do," Darcy admitted as he walked to a lower bank of shelves that housed some very large books. He reached down and pulled out a volume that measured three feet by two feet and was over four inches thick. Bringing it to a table that stood between two of the windows, he beckoned Elizabeth to join him.

"My great-grandfather Darcy had an unmarried sister who loved to do watercolours and also loved Pemberley. My great-aunt lived to the age of eight and seventy and painted nearly until the time of her death. As her favourite subject was the Pemberley estate, she left behind a great many renditions of the inside, the gardens, and the park.

"Later, it was my grandfather who wanted to preserve the visual history of the time, so that after his aunt's death, he had the pictures bound in this book. It was my joy when my father would show me the way Pemberley looked during his great aunt's lifetime. I think my first memory of the library includes this volume." Darcy's eyes softened at the memory.

Elizabeth looked carefully at the pictures as Darcy turned the pages. "I should like to spend an afternoon going through the book. However, I am very eager to see the music room before the light fades completely."

"Pardon me, I quite lost myself in the memories," Darcy said as he was brought back to the present.

"Do not worry yourself, my love," she whispered as she reached up to kiss his cheek. "Shall we go to see what treasures await in the other room?"

"Indeed," Darcy agreed as he returned her kiss. After putting the volume back into its place, he tucked her hand into his and guided her out of the library and down the hall to the music room.

The music room was two doors down from the library. Darcy opened a set of double doors before he ushered her inside. The room was papered in gold and white stripes above white-panelled wainscoting. All of the furniture was upholstered in gold and white brocade and was placed in pleasant groupings conducive to both listening and conversation. The instruments, a pianoforte and a harp, stood in a place of honour.

Elizabeth was drawn to the pianoforte, and she caressed the gleaning wood before she sat down and played a few chords. "It is a beautiful instrument. I have never seen such a one."

"It is a Christmas present for my sister, but I hope you will play it as well. I do enjoy hearing you play," Darcy explained.

"I fear I do not play well enough to do it justice," she sighed.

"My sweet Beth, I have rarely heard anything that gave me more pleasure than when you played in Meryton."

"I begin to wonder about your taste, dearest. I know that I play ill and need to practice more." Elizabeth rose from the pianoforte and smiled at her husband. Again, she moved her hand over its surface. "However, I believe that I would have greater motivation to do so with this beautiful instrument as an inducement."

Her reward was hearing her husband's deep chuckle.

Without glancing at Darcy, Elizabeth began to explore more of the lovely room. "I believe that this would be a comfortable place in which to play and to enjoy others' playing."

It was at that moment she spied an instrument case in the corner behind the pianoforte. "Does Georgiana also play the violoncello?"

She glanced at her husband in time to see his blush.

"It is yours, is it not?" she asked with genuine pleasure lighting her face. "Oh, how I love the instrument! Will you not play for me?"

"I am not in good practice," he protested as she came to him and pulled on his hand.

"Please, my love," she pleaded and caressed his face.

The pleasure of her touch made it impossible for him to deny her. "I will, but you must accompany me. We shall play a Christmas carol. I believe that I will avoid embarrassing myself if we do, since my cousin Viscount Matley has informed me that I will be required to play at Christmas."

"There will be music, then? How delightful!" Elizabeth smiled hugely as she sat at the pianoforte and found only a single set of sheet music. "Is there more sheet music than what is here?"

Darcy went to a cabinet close to his violoncello and brought out a stack. "Oliver asked me to practice this." He handed her a copy of *Hark the Herald Angels Sing.*

Elizabeth watched with great interest as Darcy extracted his instrument from its case, tightened the strings, retrieved and rosined the bow. She gave him the pitch from the pianoforte to which he toned the cello. She smiled brightly when he looked up and caught her gaze.

"Shall we begin?" he asked.

Several times, Elizabeth almost lost her place as she watched Darcy playing. His long, slender fingers worked over the neck of the violoncello with expert ease as his other hand drew the bow across the strings. She had never accompanied a stringed instrument before. The pianoforte and the cello seemed made for each other.

When the impromptu concert concluded, they heard applause from the doorway. The couple looked up to see Mrs. Reynolds and Davis standing there smiling, along with two maids and a footman.

"Please pardon our interruption, Mr. and Mrs. Darcy," Mrs. Reynolds said. "But we could not help ourselves. The music was so wonderful, so like when your mother and father would play together."

"Thank you, Mrs. Reynolds," Elizabeth said as she realized that her husband was not going to respond.

The housekeeper bobbed and asked, "Is there anything I might have brought to you?"

"No, thank you," answered Elizabeth, "We do not need anything at the moment."

The group of servants moved away and went about their chores as Elizabeth turned to Darcy, who still sat with his bow in his hand, a slight frown on his face.

"I hope that you are not dismayed that they stopped to listen," she said timidly.

"What?" Darcy seemed to come out of his daze. His face reddened, but he spoke, "Pardon me, my love. I was lost in a recollection of my childhood."

"I hope that it was a good memory."

He did not speak while he put away his instrument, and Elizabeth began to worry that something was wrong. She was about to speak again when Darcy settled the encased cello back into its spot and came to sit beside her.

"I remembered a Christmas when my parents played this very carol together. The violoncello was his, and he played far better than I. The servants' applause brought it to my mind." He sighed and continued, "My parents liked to allow the staff to listen to one of their informal concerts during the holidays. In fact, I believe that was the last time they played together. My mother went into her confinement a few months later and Georgiana was born. Since she never regained her strength from the birth, she could no longer play. Christmases were less festive after that, although Mother always made certain that my father played for us so that we could have music."

Elizabeth leaned her head on Darcy's shoulder and squeezed his arm. The pair sat in that way for several moments before she fought to stifle a yawn.

"My dear, I believe it is time for you to rest. We will have a light supper once you awaken." He rose to his feet and helped her to hers. "Come, let us to our chambers."

After a nap and a delightful supper of some of the best cold ham and cheeses Elizabeth had ever tasted, husband and wife spent the rest of the evening talking and reading in their sitting room once Darcy told her that the rest of Pemberley would still be waiting for her exploration on the morrow.

It was still early when Darcy noticed that his wife was becoming fatigued. He called for her abigail after informing Elizabeth that he thought she should retire.

"Are you tiring of my company already, sir?" He detected a hint of annoyance in her tone as she moved toward the door to her bed chamber.

"No, indeed, I am not," he answered patiently, "For as soon as you are ready for the night, I had hoped to join you once more. That is unless you do not wish it." His voice trailed off as she continued through the door.

Darcy sat down and sighed heavily. He rested his head on his hand while trying to decide how to apologize when he felt a hand on his shoulder. He looked up to see Elizabeth, her eyes glazed with unshed tears.

"Please forgive me, Fitzwilliam," she whispered contritely. "I am so sorry I was so cross. You are right. I am very tired. I just did not know how to ask for your company in my bed again tonight. I wanted to be with you longer."

Darcy turned in his chair, pulled Elizabeth onto his lap, kissed her with barely restrained fervour. Just when he felt his control slipping, he pulled away. "My beloved Beth, I am so happy that you do not wish to be separated from me, since I feel the same."

He set her back on her feet and led her to her chamber door. "Let us ready ourselves for bed. Just knock on the adjoining door once you are ready."

Rather breathless from their kiss, Elizabeth smiled up at him and entered her chamber once more and found Sarah laying out her night dress. With the maid's help, it did not take her long to change and to have her hair plaited.

After dismissing Sarah with a thank you, Elizabeth moved timidly to the closed door that led to the master's chamber. She knocked and was surprised to hear him bid her enter.

Elizabeth had not yet seen her husband's bedroom. It was decorated in a deeply masculine shade of burgundy with accents of forest green and tan. The effect was warm and fit Darcy well as he stood near the fireplace, having just added fuel to the blaze. He wore a robe of navy trimmed with a gold braid.

Her heart leapt at the look of utter adoration in his eyes as he moved to take her hand and draw her in farther into the chamber. "I hope that you do not mind if we sleep here tonight," he asked tentatively before he rushed on, "I have dreamed often of you here."

When she blushed but did not reply, Darcy stammered, "If you would rather, I mean, we can sleep in your bed, um, pardon me, my dear." He stopped speaking as words failed him in his embarrassment.

With his eyes lowered to the floor, Darcy did not see the smile on his wife's face. It was not until he felt her hands on his face that he raised his gaze.

"I have no objection to sleeping here, Fitzwilliam," she said as she lifted to her tiptoes to kiss him.

The thrill of having her initiate another kiss overwhelmed him as he wrapped her tightly in his arms. After covering her face with kisses, Darcy finally controlled himself enough to move them both toward his bed. The counterpane and blankets were turned back invitingly.

Elizabeth stepped out of his arms, but instead of climbing into the bed, she moved back to the adjoining door. Just before she opened it, she turned to catch his eye. "I must not leave the candles burning. I will also need my tin of bread for the morning."

Having spoken thusly, she slipped quickly into her chamber only to return within a moment holding a single candle and the bread tin. She set both on the bedside table before removing her robe and slippers and moving under the covers.

Unable to help himself, Darcy pulled his wife into his arms, resting her head on his shoulder. "I love you, dearest, loveliest Elizabeth," he whispered into her hair.

"And I love you, my dearest Fitzwilliam," she told him with a contented sigh.

It was not long before Darcy felt his wife relax and her breathing slow to a rate that told him she was asleep. Despite the fact that they had not yet united physically, he marvelled at how close he felt to his new wife. After lifting up a silent prayer of thanksgiving and petition for the well-being of his wife and child, he too surrendered to slumber.

CHAPTER TWENTY-SEVEN

Darcy and Elizabeth spent the next several days almost constantly in each other's company. They toured every room in the house and walked all of the paths near Pemberley that they could when the weather permitted. Although the temperatures were cold, it had not yet snowed in earnest.

This morning, only a few days before their Christmas guests were due to arrive, the winter sunshine seemed to beckon them outdoors once more. After they had walked in silence for a few moments, Darcy asked Elizabeth which way she wanted to proceed, since they had come to a spot where the paths veered in several directions. When she did not answer, he looked down to see that her attention was on a small stand of holly bushes which sported bright red berries.

"Elizabeth?" Darcy said as he brought them both to a stop. "Are you well?"

The concern in his voice broke her reverie. "I am sorry, Fitzwilliam," she apologized as her face reddened. "I was thinking of Christmas."

"I hope your thoughts were not of an unpleasant nature."

"Indeed, they were not," she said, smiling up at him. Tugging on his arm, Elizabeth indicated her desire to continue walking. "I had realized, however, that I have very little by way of gifts for everyone."

"Do not trouble yourself, dear," Darcy said as he returned her smile. "There will be gifts enough. I have arranged for the purchase of gifts for all my family, as I have always done."

Unexpected irritation rose in Elizabeth. Without thinking, she gave voice to it. "You have arranged? Do I have no say in the gifts? Do you not trust my taste?"

If Elizabeth had been looking at her husband, she would have seen the shock and bewilderment upon his face. However, her pique was still heated, and his lack of response did nothing to cool it. She pulled her hand from his arm and turned back toward the house.

"Elizabeth!" Darcy exclaimed as he grabbed her arm to prevent her from leaving. 'I do not understand why you are so upset with me."

"You do not understand that I would like the courtesy of having my questions answered? Instead, you say nothing." Again she had pulled her arm from his grasp and stood with her hands on her hips.

Darcy could not explain even to himself the thrill of pleasure he experienced at the sight of his wife standing before him in such an irritated state, but he wisely suppressed the smile that threatened to play across his face. Instead, he stood as calmly as he could and said, "You feel that my purchasing presents for my family officious?"

"No, yes, no," she sputtered and stomped her foot. "I would have liked to be a part of the acquisition of those gifts."

"Most of the gifts were purchased before we were even engaged," he explained. "I have found that if I do not buy some items every few months, I experience quite a state of agitation to obtain gifts in the weeks preceding Christmas, since I am often not in Town the month before the holiday."

Darcy took a few steps toward her as he saw that Elizabeth's ire was calming. "I have purchased a few gifts since we met." Once he reached her, he offered her his hand. "Forgive me if it seemed that I did not trust your taste."

Ignoring his hand, Elizabeth burst into tears and flung herself into his arms. The anger she had experienced just moments ago dissolved as shame took its place.

With soft murmurs of comfort and acceptance, Darcy patted her back. Finally, he felt her push away.

"I am so sorry, Fitzwilliam," she sniffed. Elizabeth pulled off one of her gloves and searched the pocket of her spencer for a hankie. After she found one and put it to use, she dared to look up, afraid that she had offended Darcy.

"I am not upset," Darcy said softly as he helped her on with her gloves. "I admit to being surprised that you did not simply ask me about gifts for the family."

This time, Elizabeth did not speak immediately, but she slipped her hand into the crook of her husband's arm as they began to walk again. The fact that he did not repeat himself or insist that she explain her outburst shamed her even more.

After a few more minutes, she spoke. "Again, I apologize for my unkind aspersions upon your character. I fear that I cannot explain why I did not think about the gifts until now, let alone fail to ask you about them." Her voice caught on a sob before she continued, "I fear the only excuse I might have is my emotions are not under good regulation. I fear that our baby is wrecking havoc on my moods. I have no other explanation."

"I forgive you, dearest," Darcy sighed as he kissed the top of her head.

A thought came to him. "Would you like to know what we are giving to my family?"

Elizabeth laughed softly. "No, I do not need to know just as I am sure that you do not have a desire to know what gifts I left at Longbourn for my family."

"I would not mind knowing what you gave them. It would ease my mind that the ones I had delivered there are not duplicates."

A tinge of irritation sparked in her mind at the statement, but this time she did not allow it free rein. "You sent gifts to my family." It was a statement, not a question.

"I had already purchased the rifle that Charles had desired but could not find, as well as token gifts for the Hursts. I wanted your family all to know that I value them as well, so I ordered kid gloves and lace sent to your sisters and a muff to your mother. For your father, I bought a volume by Wordsworth after he mentioned he wished to obtain it, but had not yet found the time to do so."

Elizabeth's eyes stung at her husband's thoughtfulness.

"Those are all perfect, thoughtful gifts," she responded as she leaned against him. "I could not have thought of better ones."

Something in the tone of Elizabeth's voice made Darcy think that she was not completely satisfied. When she hesitated to say anything further, he said encouragingly, "However..."

Looking up, Elizabeth smiled a little. "However, I would like to be included in the decisions about what gifts to buy."

"I believe that I can agree to that with one exception." He grinned down at her before he continued, "I will not seek your advice when finding gifts for you, my love."

The musical lilt of her responding laughter lifted his spirit. He worried about his wife's moods, and until they could speak to others about her pregnancy, he had no one from whom to seek advice except her maid, Sarah, who was not really old enough to know much about such things. Darcy pulled his wife's arm tighter against his side as they continued on their ramble about the gardens.

When they reached the house once more, Darcy was required to deal with estate business with his steward since he wished to have everything seen to before his family arrived. He excused himself from Elizabeth, leaving her to her own devices until dinner.

Elizabeth returned to her room to refresh herself before she went to the library. Her curiosity about the pictorial history of Pemberley that Darcy's grandfather had had put together from his aunt's watercolours drove her to explore the book.

However, once she entered the book room, Elizabeth spent over an hour meandering around the vast chamber, reading the titles, caressing the bindings, discovering many volumes unknown to her. Upon finding a first edition of *Gulliver's Travels,* Elizabeth sat down in one of the comfortable chairs and began to page through the volume. The book had been a favourite of hers as a child. She smiled as she reread some of her best loved portions of the story.

Eventually, Elizabeth returned to her original purpose in coming to the library. She found the large bound folio, but she struggled for several minutes to lift it to the table by the window. Shaking her head, she walked to the door and searched the corridor for a footman or servant to help her.

After walking a short distance and turning a corner, she found a footman. "You are Gilbert, are you not?" she queried.

"Yes, ma'am," he bowed deeply. "May I be of assistance?"

"Indeed," Elizabeth said. "Come with me."

She hurried back to the library with the young footman following. Once inside she moved to the place where the folio was kept. Elizabeth pointed to the volume that she had only budged an inch or so from its place. "I cannot seem to lift this book on my own."

With Gilbert's help, Elizabeth was able to retrieve the book and set it on the table so that she could look through it. "Thank you. That will be all."

Elizabeth barely noticed the footman leave as she reverently turned back the cover and slowly began her perusal of the beautiful art work within. It was there that Darcy found her, lost in visions of Pemberley past.

"I was told I would find you in here," Darcy said gently as he moved to her side. "You did not retrieve this by yourself."

"No, a footman did it for me," she said with a rueful smile. "I had no idea that it was so heavy. Pemberley is a weighty subject, indeed."

He laughed before he said, "Mrs. Reynolds has prepared a bit of luncheon for us if you are able to tear yourself away." Darcy could see that she was not racing through the volume, but studying each picture with serious attention.

"Might I leave the book as it is, or does it need to be put back in its place each time?" She asked as she slipped the attached ribbon bookmark onto the open page.

"If you plan to return to it today or tomorrow, I believe that merely closing it will do."

"Very good," she exclaimed happily. "I do not want to be rushed in my examination of all of the renditions. Today, I discovered what our chambers looked like in your father's great-aunt's day." Elizabeth assisted her husband in closing the book. "I must admit that I am very happy with what your mother had done to the rooms. They have so much more light and openness to them now."

"I am glad that you are pleased with them," Darcy answered as he offered her his arm. "Shall we go to the dining parlour? I am feeling hungry."

Elizabeth slipped her hand into the crook of his arm. "As am I."

They ate in what she came to think of as the family dining parlour. It was small and more intimate. Darcy had informed her that his parents had liked to dine there when they had no company, and often, he had been allowed to have breakfast or dinner with them there.

While they were conversing over a particularly delicious dessert, a footman brought in the post.

Elizabeth asked, "Did not the post come this morning?"

"Yes," said Darcy absently as he sorted through the letters. "One of my men usually rides to town in the early morning to collect the post, but this came by my special courier. I dispatched several business letters a few days ago, and these are the awaited responses." He set the pile of mail aside and picked up his spoon to finish his dessert.

"I have written a few letters to my family, but I suppose it is too soon to expect any in return," she sighed, suddenly missing her family. "I suppose that they are very busy with Christmas coming, and, of course, Jane will no doubt be working on the plans for her wedding and spending time with Mr. Bingley." She put her spoon down, no longer hungry.

Darcy looked up to see the pained expression on her face. "The post is rather slow in reaching Pemberley at times, which is why I use a courier if I feel the need for haste. I could send him to Longbourn with any letters you might wish to write and have him wait for any to you if you would like."

"Oh Fitzwilliam!" she cried in delight. "I would like it very much. I will go to my study straight away."

"Haste is not necessary since I must read my business letters and discuss them with my steward before I can write my instructions. I have an appointment with him after breakfast tomorrow. I hope you are able to postpone writing to your family until later today, since I have something else planned for this afternoon."

~*~

Elizabeth did not write letters or return to the library at all that day. Once they finished their midday meal, her husband took her to Lambton. He told her that she might find gifts there, even some more for her family that they could have delivered by Epiphany, or if the presents were small enough, they could be sent with the courier. The village was larger and more prosperous than Meryton, with many more shops in which to browse.

On the carriage ride to Lambton, Elizabeth had pondered what she might buy and made a mental list. Upon alighting from the carriage, the Darcys walked up one side of the village's high street and down the other while she examined the window displays.

Finally, Elizabeth indicated which of the shops she first wished to enter. It was a draper. In its window was displayed a beautiful length of pale pink silk run through with silver threads. It would be perfect for a dress for Georgiana.

The proprietress, Mrs. Higgins, greeted the couple warmly. Her smile was welcoming. "Mr. Darcy, it is good to see you again."

Darcy bowed and said, "Mrs. Higgins, I would like to present my wife, Mrs. Darcy. She is looking to purchase last minute gifts."

"I am honoured to make your acquaintance, Mrs. Darcy. Do you have anything particular in mind?"

Elizabeth smiled and returned the greeting with poise and grace. "Indeed, Mrs. Higgins, I am interested in that length of silk in the window. I have not seen the equal to it since I was in Town."

"Oh, that is a lovely piece, is it not?" Mrs. Higgins removed the bolt from the window and laid it out on the cutting table. "One of my clients asked me to order it from London for her granddaughter's coming out, but when she brought her in to see the fabric and pick out a pattern so my girls could make it up, she found out that her granddaughter hates pink. There was no reasoning with the girl, so the lady ordered a light green silk instead. She did not want the pink and told me to sell it or send it back."

"How dreadful for you!" Elizabeth understood the financial hardship it must have been for Mrs. Higgins.

"I have been hoping that someone would buy it." Mrs. Higgins sighed. "The lady is too good a customer for me to raise a fuss, or she might have taken her business elsewhere."

Elizabeth glanced at Darcy who grinned and shrugged. "I will take it," she said decisively. "Please wrap it up, and I will send a footman by to pick it up."

Turning to his wife, Darcy asked, "Is there anything more you wish to see here?"

"I would very much like to look around." She turned to an exhibit of ribbons and lace. "You have some lovely lace. It is very finely crafted."

"You have a good eye, Mrs. Darcy. This is the handiwork of a woman who lives just outside the village. She just brought this particular lace in yesterday, hoping that someone might fancy it before Christmas."

"Is there enough here to trim a dress?" Elizabeth fingered the tiny tatted stitches that depicted flowers and vines.

"Yes, I believe there is," Mrs. Higgins said eagerly. "I will measure it if you would like."

Shaking her head, Elizabeth said, "There is no need. I will take it as well."

Turning to Darcy, she spoke softly, "Would you please wait outside for a moment? I need privacy."

He smiled indulgently. "Of course, my dear, I will be outside."

When the tiny bell over the door tinkled and signalled the door's opening and closing, Elizabeth spoke to Mrs. Higgins in a near whisper, "Do you have any plain men's linen handkerchiefs? I would like to embroider some as gifts."

Mrs. Higgins gleefully brought out her complete selection, including those for ladies.

Elizabeth was pleased that for a small shop in a small village, Mrs. Higgins's establishment featured such items of quality. She picked out four handkerchiefs of the finest linen for the men. Just as she thought she was finished, she spied the ladies' hankies. One style in particular caught her fancy, a plain white one with a bit of lace work in one corner. Although the lace work was not as lovely as the tatted lace she had just purchased, the effect was quite pretty.

Quickly going through her memory, she counted up all of the female staff at Pemberley and ordered that number plus several more in case she had forgotten someone. She also ordered two dozen men's handkerchiefs of the lesser but still good quality, so that she could give one to each of the male servants in the house.

When she left the shop, Elizabeth was smiling happily, as was Mrs. Higgins.

Darcy offered his arm to his wife and asked, "Where are we to go now, Beth?"

"To the bookstore," she answered with a sparkle in her eye, "Unless my last purchase has worried you."

"I can safely say that I am not worried that you will spend too much." He grinned down at her. "I am certain that after your purchases, we will have enough to feed ourselves through the winter."

Her delighted laughter thrilled Darcy. He rejoiced that she liked to tease him and could enjoy his own feeble attempts at humour. His chuckles joined hers as they made their way along the storefronts until they reached the Lambton Book and Map Shoppe.

Just inside the door, both Elizabeth and Darcy inhaled deeply and sighed.

"I love the smell of books. I will always think of my father when I do," Elizabeth explained shyly.

Laying his hand over hers as it lay upon his arm, Darcy squeezed it and said, "As do I."

"Mr. Darcy!" A loud, reverberating voice sounded from the back of the store. "Have you finally brought your bride in to meet me?"

Elizabeth was surprised but pleased to see her usually reserved husband receive and reciprocate a bear hug from the man who rushed into the front of the store. Laughter filled the shop as the two men saw her astonished look.

"My dear, this ancient codger is Fred James." Darcy took her hand and pulled her over to meet the older, rather dusty looking fellow whose eyes still twinkled with humour. "Fred, you old goat, this is my wife. Mrs. Elizabeth Darcy."

Swallowing her surprise at her husband's informal appellation, she curtseyed and said, "I am pleased to meet you, sir."

"I suppose you are astonished to see your staid and stiff young man being rather rude to an old distinguished gentleman such as myself." He took her gloved hand and kissed it lightly. "Darcy here has been coming into my store since he was a young child. He loved to come with his father. I would give him a lemon drop, a picture book, and send him to sit and read over there." He pointed to a small, worn children's chair in the front corner close to the window.

"One day when he was about eight or nine, he came into my store alone." Fred smiled as he watched the blush stain Darcy's cheeks. "He came up to me and asked for two lemon drops. I asked him why he thought that he should have two, he told me that since I was so old and would likely not live long enough to eat them all myself, he wanted to help me."

Elizabeth covered her mouth to keep from laughing out loud. "Did he truly say that?"

"Indeed, he did," Fred assured her. ""I was only about five years older than his father, but I suppose that I looked like I was on my death bed to an eight-year-old. Eventually, his father found the two of us sitting on the floor behind the counter eating lemon drops."

"I was punished once we returned to Pemberley. My father was not pleased that I had left the footman he had put in charge of me. He did not allow me to return to this shop for two months." Darcy sighed dramatically. "I sorely missed those lemon drops."

"I believe that eventually my books became the draw to my shop, not the lemon drops," Fred said. He leaned behind the counter and pulled out a battered looking bowl heaped with yellow candies. "I still keep them here. Have one, Mrs. Darcy."

Elizabeth took one of the hard candies and popped it into her mouth. The tart-sweet burst of lemon made her mouth water pleasantly. As she enjoyed the treat, she watched Darcy grin boyishly at the shop's owner before the older man offered him the bowl.

As they silently sucked on the candy, they browsed the shop for a few minutes. Elizabeth was happy to find books for her father and her sister Mary. She brought the books to the counter.

A thought occurred to Elizabeth as the last of the candy dissolved in her mouth. "Mr. James, do you find these lemon drops in Lambton or do you order them from somewhere else?"

Fred James smiled and answered as he efficiently wrapped the books, "My sister and brother-in-law own the confectioner's and tea shop three doors down. They have several flavours of drops for sale, but my favourite has always been lemon."

Turning to her husband, Elizabeth said excitedly, "Do you think that we might purchase some for the children of the tenants? I believe they would be very happy to receive a special treat at Boxing Day. You know better than I do how many there are. Would you go to the confectioner and order what you think would be sufficient? I would like to find some music for Georgiana as I see that Mr. James has a good selection of that as well.

"Of course, my dear," Darcy agreed eager to do whatever she asked of him. "I will be back as soon as I can."

"Why do you not order us some tea? I find that I am very thirsty," she explained.

"I would be happy to do so." He bowed to his wife and Mr. James. "If you will excuse me, Fred, I must be off to do my wife's bidding."

"I knew that once you fell, my boy, you would fall hard. I am happy for you both." Fred smirked as he returned the bow.

Once Darcy left the shop, Elizabeth spoke softly, "I know that your shop is an unusual one for a small town. From what I have seen here, you carry a wide selection of books for a variety of tastes. I wonder if you know of any books that my husband might like that he does not have already."

'As a matter of fact, I thought when you both came in the shop that he would inquire about a book he asked me to find for him. He lost the second volume of a collection of six while he travelled to Kent two years ago and asked me to procure a replacement. He told me that he thought that he left it in a posting inn, but it had not been recovered. I have been making inquiries and had only just found and purchased one for him."

"Wonderful!" Elizabeth exclaimed. "Please wrap it up for me and put a small 'E' in one corner, so that I will know which one it is. Now I must look through your music."

Nodding his approval, Fred replied, "Before I do as you instructed, allow me to show you the newest music pages, as Miss Darcy is a regular in my shop. She has not been in for several months, so she will likely not have seen the newer pieces."

Once he showed her where to look, he quickly wrapped the book and set it with the others.

Elizabeth smiled as she left the book shop. She felt as if she had made great progress on this shopping day. Confident that she could find the rest of what she wanted to purchase, she moved to stand by the door to wait for her husband to come back for her. She marvelled at the fact that she had not felt panic even once during the entire outing. It seemed the longer she stayed at Pemberley, the calmer she became. It was one more reason to thank God for her marriage.

CHAPTER TWENTY-EIGHT

Back at Pemberley, Elizabeth instructed the footman to take all of her purchases to her study. She had not used the mistress's study often, as she preferred to be with her husband in his study or the library, but the room would afford her the privacy she needed to sort through everything.

Bundles of ribbons, pairs of lace fingerless gloves, and other miscellaneous items had been added to the fabric, lace, books, and sheet music Elizabeth purchased. Happy that many items were already wrapped, she made quick work of adding a tag with the recipient's name on it. Later she would seek out Mrs. Reynolds for her advice on how to present the gifts to the staff.

When she finished organizing her packages, she rang for a footman and Mrs. Reynolds. Elizabeth gave instructions for her personal gifts to be taken to her dressing room once the footman arrived.

As he was leaving, Mrs. Reynolds stood at the door. "How may I be of assistance, Mrs. Darcy?"

Elizabeth pointed to a stack of packages on her desk. "I have purchased small gifts for the house staff. I am not certain as to the proper way to distribute them."

"The late Mrs. Darcy would assemble everyone in the staff dining hall just before noon on Christmas Eve. She would give the gifts to each person from the lowest to the highest. She would stay for a glass of punch from the bowl on the servant's table. The house staff is given a time in which to eat their yuletide meal. I always make certain that they do not partake too freely of the bowl. One would not want to have inebriated servants on such a day."

"What about the gardeners and stablemen?" Elizabeth asked in a panic. She had not thought to buy gifts for them.

"Oh, the master sees to them and makes sure that they have a feast as well. He orders it delivered from the inn at the same time as the house staff's meal. They are always happy to see the holidays. No other estate master is so generous," Mrs.

Reynolds boasted, "and now the mistress is proving to be as generous as the master."

"Thank you, Mrs. Reynolds," Elizabeth said as she blushed. "I am certain that without your assistance in the last few years, my husband would not have such a sterling reputation."

Returning the topic back to the gifts, Elizabeth asked, "Would you mind assisting me in preparing the gifts? I will have Sarah to help me, but I have a few other things to see to before our guests arrive and would be grateful for the extra hands."

"I would be honoured to help, mistress." The housekeeper curtseyed and smiled happily. "When would you like me to attend you?"

"In about an hour in my private chambers," she told Mrs. Reynolds. "My husband insists that I rest after our shopping excursion, and I see the wisdom in his plan. I will have Sarah find you once I am ready."

Elizabeth rested almost the entire next hour and even slept for part of it. However, when she woke, she hastened from her bed as the excitement of the season surged through her. After ringing for Sarah, she was ready in a short time and bade her maid to fetch the housekeeper.

The threesome sat at a round table under a large window, cutting ribbon, folding a shilling into the handkerchiefs, and tying the bundles with lengths of ribbons. In a much shorter span of time than Elizabeth had imagined, a large woven basket was filled with the gifts and ready for distribution when the time came.

"Let us hide this in my wardrobe," Elizabeth suggested. "I want this to be a surprise."

After picking a few bits of ribbon from her gown, Elizabeth sighed in satisfaction. "Let us have some tea. I believe that we deserve a reward for our hard work."

"But, mistress, with due respect, would it not be unseemly for me to take tea with you?" Sarah knew that though not usual, a housekeeper having tea with the lady of the house was acceptable, but she had never heard of a maid, having tea with her mistress in the company of another.

"Sarah," Elizabeth said in a stern, but mocking, tone. "Am I not the mistress of Pemberley?" Upon receiving a nod from the girl, she went on, "I have such a position in life and in my own household that I may dictate what is seemly, rather than be dictated by it." With her nose in the air and a faux imperious look on her face, she was foiled in her attempt at haughtiness by a laugh that came from behind her.

"Sarah, my wife is correct," Darcy said as he continued to chuckle. "Mrs. Darcy is capable of choosing when to relax society's strictures. I believe that especially in her own chambers, she is the first and final authority on manners."

He walked farther into the room and kissed his wife's hand. "I will not disturb you any longer, my dear." He bowed to the three and left the room.

The next half hour passed in pleasant conversation. Elizabeth asked questions about the tenants of Pemberley, as she had not yet had a chance to meet any of them. She discovered that many of the families who worked the fields and woods of Pemberley had been there for generations. Some of the offspring of the tenants had gone on to other professions, but rarely did the entire family leave, so well-loved were the estate and its owners.

Sarah shared her experiences in being welcomed into the Pemberley staff. Already, she had developed friendships with several of the other maids. She had worried that her presence as a newcomer would have been resented, but she had been relieved that it had not been the case.

Elizabeth was pleased that she had decided to take a little time out of her day to visit with these two women. Wanting to be the best mistress that it was in her power to be, she understood that the people who worked in her new home were a contented lot and that contentment would be of great help in her accomplishment of her goal.

That evening after dinner, Elizabeth and Darcy sat in their small sitting room. He read a book while she worked as quickly as possible to monogram the men's handkerchiefs she had purchased in Lambton. Since she decided to do a single, simple letter on each, she was able to finish her work before it was time for bed.

As she worked, Darcy asked, "I hope that you are not too fatigued by our shopping today."

She placed her work in her lap and smiled brilliantly. "Oh, no, I think I was energized by it. I will admit that your suggestion that I rest once we arrived at home was a good one, but I did not need more than the hour's rest to completely recover." Elizabeth lifted an eyebrow to indicate that she knew he had not suggested she rest but had actually ordered it. She tried not to become upset at his hovering, and most of the time, such as that afternoon, she was able to do so.

~*~

After a refreshing night's sleep and a delicious breakfast, Elizabeth was finally able to return to her perusal of the Pemberley pictorial. As she turned the pages and viewed the many rooms her husband's relative had painted, she felt as if she were being guided through another time.

The gallery was shown to be much the same as it was at the present except for the portraits that had not yet been painted. The large nursery was obviously of a bygone era with the older furnishings and out-dated children's clothing. Elizabeth wondered if she should look over the current one with an eye to redecorating it, but she decided that she should wait, since she did not want any speculation to arise from her interest.

Nearly an hour later, Elizabeth came upon a section that displayed several rooms decorated for Christmas. One in particular grabbed her attention. It was of the grand front staircase. Garlands of holly tied with ribbon were draped gracefully down the banister. The effect was beautiful and welcoming.

Elizabeth quickly stood, and after slipping the ribbon back in to save her place, she closed the book. She left the library to seek out the housekeeper with questions about decorating Pemberley for the holidays. She found Mrs. Reynolds in her small office.

"Good morning, Mrs. Darcy," Mrs. Reynolds greeted her with a smile. "Is there something I might do for you?"

"Good morning, Mrs. Reynolds," Elizabeth returned the greeting. "I would like to know how the house will be decorated for Christmas. Do you have plans for it?"

"Mr. Darcy told me to talk to you about that very subject. He did not know if you would have ideas of your own, or if you would wish to continue with the traditions of the former mistress. I forgot to speak of it to you yesterday. I apologize for not doing so then. I must say that our decorations have not been elaborate for many years now. The family spent most of the holidays with Lord and Lady Matlock since the late Mrs. Darcy passed."

After seeing the watercolours in the library, Elizabeth knew what she would like to do, but she asked about the former traditions before she decided if she would go ahead with her plans. There was no harm in combining old ideas with new ones.

Mrs. Reynolds proceeded to explain how and where the decorations were arranged. She spoke of evergreen boughs festooning the mantles and side tables, large vases of red roses from the orangery, and the Yule log. "Mrs. Darcy also used to love holly, and she would personally drape garlands of it on the main staircase banister. I used to make mistletoe swags to hang in various rooms," she said in a wistful tone. "When he was little, the current master loved to catch his mama under the mistletoe. He would exclaim joyfully that he would kiss his mama, but he would insist that his father come to lift him up so that he could bestow his kiss properly. After he kissed her, Master Fitzwilliam would declare that since his father and his mama were now both under the mistletoe, they must kiss each other as well. He would be so pleased to see his parents act as if they had been caught out. When they finally kissed, he would clap his hands and laugh the sweetest little laugh."

The housekeeper reached into her pocket for a handkerchief and dabbed at her eyes. "Pemberley was such a happy place back then." She looked at Elizabeth and smiled. "I believe that it will be that way again. You have made the master so happy."

"I thank you, Mrs. Reynolds. I am blessed to be wed to a man that I find easy to please." Elizabeth got to her feet and said, "You have been most informative. I will leave you to your duties."

"Please let me know if you have any more questions, or if you might need assistance with anything, Mrs. Darcy."

Elizabeth paused to think for a moment before she answered, "Actually, I would like to gather some holly today. Could you show me where I could find the tools, gloves, and outerwear I will need? I noticed that it looks as if it will snow, and I would like to bring it in before the bushes are covered."

Elizabeth turned to leave, but she stopped when another thought came to her mind. "Would you happen to have wide red ribbon? If there is enough, I could tie bows of it on the holly garland."

Mrs. Reynolds beamed and said, "We do have a great deal of it. It may not be as new as it once was, but we have kept the ribbon that the late Mrs. Darcy used in a chest made of cedar. I do not believe that the insects have taken any notice of it. I will see to locating it as soon as I summon John to show you where the clipping tools are."

Walking to where Elizabeth stood, Mrs. Reynolds motioned for her mistress to go ahead of her. "I will find my old woollen coat for you and the leather gardening gloves I use when I pick roses. They should keep you warm and safe from the holly spines."

She stopped and eyed the dress Elizabeth was wearing. "Might I suggest that you wear a dress that you do not care about, in case it should happen to become torn a bit or soiled?"

"That is a splendid idea!" Elizabeth smoothed the material of the blue morning gown she was wearing. She did not wish to ruin such a beautiful new frock. "I have just the thing. I brought a few of my old gowns because I thought I might want to wear one when I took a long walk around Pemberley, but this is a much more practical reason." With those words, she excused herself to go change.

~*~

Darcy rubbed his neck as he raised his head. He had been going over the ledgers and business correspondence, first with his steward, and then alone for several hours. His stomach grumbled, which caused him to smile.

I am surprised that Beth has not summoned me to join her to eat, he thought to himself. *It is certainly time that she has something.* Pushing back from his desk, he stood and straightened the desk, putting away the ledgers and letters, and setting the sealed missives out to be posted.

Slipping back into his jacket, he rolled his shoulders to remove the last of the stiffness. As he moved toward the door and passed by a window, something caught his eye. Darcy stared down and across to one of the back gardens and saw a petite figure in a long, hooded brown coat reach up to cut a large sprig of holly that was loaded with bright red berries.

Seeing that it had begun to snow, Darcy frowned as the figure dropped the clipping into a large basket before rising on tiptoes and reaching high up on the bush for another sprig. This time the hood of the drab coat fell back off the head of the wearer to reveal her identity. *Elizabeth! What is she doing out in this weather?*

He watched as she cut off the branch and laid it in the basket before she laughingly replaced the hood over her hair. "She will catch her death!" he exclaimed as he ran from the room and down the stairs. Not waiting to don his own greatcoat, Darcy raced along the snow-dusted path to where he knew Elizabeth was.

When he was about twenty yards from his wife, Darcy called out, "What do you think you are doing out here?"

Elizabeth turned to him with a welcoming smile which faded as she took in his coatless condition and his scowling visage. "Just what it looks like I am doing. John and I have been cutting holly so that I may festoon the main staircase." She pointed to the gardener, who was cutting branches from another bush not fifteen feet away and who had another nearly full basket of holly at his feet.

"If John is doing such a good job, why are you out here doing the same in this weather? You will catch a cold," Darcy could not keep his voice from betraying how upset he was.

Hooking her cutting tool over the side of the basket, Elizabeth took a few steps toward her husband and lowered her voice. "I enjoy cutting holly, as did your mother, according to Mrs. Reynolds. And I am perfectly warm, since I had the wisdom to venture out-of-doors in the proper attire, unlike yourself. I believe it would be sensible for you to go back into the house to find a coat or a cloak before you find yourself unwell for the holidays." She turned and walked back to the basket without waiting for his response.

"You will return to the house at once," Darcy ordered as he moved to grip her arm.

Elizabeth stared at her husband, anger building in her, but as she looked up, she spied the gardener staring at them with curiosity in his glance.

After pulling her arm from Darcy's grasp and straightening her shoulders, Elizabeth addressed the gardener, "John, I believe that we have enough holly. Would you please bring your basket into the stillroom? I will be there in a moment to show you where I want it to be placed to dry."

"Yes, ma'am, I will do it straight away." He bowed and lifted his basket.

With a cold demeanour, Elizabeth turned back to her husband. "Would you please be so kind as to carry this basket into the house? I am certain that you will not allow me to do it."

Darcy did not answer, but he did lift the basket from the ground. Suddenly, he truly felt the cold as the snow that had accumulated atop his head slid down his neck. By the time he had the unwieldy container in his grasp and had turned, he found that Elizabeth was already far ahead of him walking toward the back of the house.

The back door was opened for her by one of the maids. Elizabeth did not turn to see if Darcy followed her inside. Her hurt feelings and her anger left her wanting to sting him in some way. *Let him stand in the cold holding the basket. It would serve him right for being so imperious. Me catch my death? Was I the one who came outside without the proper covering?* Stomping her boots both to rid them of clinging mud and snow and to vent her frustration, Elizabeth struggled out of the old coat. Finally, the maid helped her with it.

"Thank you, Molly May," Elizabeth said. "Is John in the stillroom?"

"Yes, ma'am," Molly May answered and curtseyed.

"Please have some tea made for Mr. Darcy and myself. I will have mine in my bed chamber. I believe that my husband will take his in his room."

Elizabeth swept out of the small entry hall toward the stillroom. Once inside, she gave quick instructions to the gardener to lay out all of the holly on the long tables which were already lined with old sheets. "Once Mr. Darcy brings in the other basket, you can do the same with it."

Just as she had finished her sentence, Darcy walked in and set his load next to the other basket. He looked quite cold and his hair and cravat were soaked. "Thank you for your assistance, sir. I ordered Molly May to make you some tea. We would not want you to become chilled, now would we?" She turned on her heels and left the room.

Darcy stood for several moments staring at the empty doorway. Behind him, he could hear the rustle of holly branches as John arranged them on the table. Finally, the dampness of his clothing began to make him truly uncomfortable. He did not start shivering but was very close to it, so he decided that he could use a hot bath.

Striding out of the stillroom and up the back stairs, Darcy entered his bedchambers through the servant's entrance. Once inside, he rang for his man while he stripped off his wet clothing. He donned his heaviest robe and went to the fireplace to add fuel to the fire. There he stood when Peters joined him.

"I want to bathe right away."

"Yes, sir. I have started to draw you a bath as Mrs. Darcy instructed me," Peters said without any sign that it was unusual for the mistress to request the master's bath and at that time of day. He left his master sitting close to the fire and frowning into it.

A few minutes later, there was a soft knock at the door of the sitting room, Darcy thought for a moment it was Elizabeth come to apologize, but when he asked who was there, he found that it was merely a maid with hot tea. He bade her enter, and as soon as she deposited the tea tray on a table, she left.

"Elizabeth thought of all of this, even in her pique at me," he murmured as he poured himself a cup.

There were also some scones and butter on the tray, and upon seeing them, his stomach rumbled once more. By the time Peters returned to tell him his bath was ready, he had drunk a cup of tea, eaten two scones, and was pouring another cup.

"I will finish the tea while I bathe," Darcy told his man as he stood and walked to the bath chamber. As he eased into the hot water, he hissed in pleasure. Peters placed a small table next to the tub, so that his master could have a place for his cup.

As the chill left his body, so did a great deal of the annoyance he had experienced upon seeing his wife labouring in the snow. A memory of himself as a child helping his mother fill the same type of basket with holly entered his mind.

"Mama, why do you not order the gardener to do all of this?" he recalled asking his mother as he watched one of the under-gardeners cutting holly from another bush.

"I love to cut holly to decorate the stairs," she explained. "Do you not like the way it looks running down the banisters?"

"Oh yes, Mama, I like it very much," the child responded. "But it is cold, and I thought that Papa would not like you to become chilled."

Laughing, his mother looked into his eyes. "Your Papa does worry a great deal about me, but he knows that I will do this if it is within my strength to do so. You must remember that there are times that even a papa should not argue with his wife, especially at Christmas time. Besides, I am warmly dressed for this weather as are you." His mother planted a cold kiss on his cheek and went back to her work.

Darcy raised his hand to his face as, for a moment, he could almost feel the chilly caress on his cheek even after such a long time. His mother had only a few more years of cutting holly before her health and strength declined and kept her indoors and mostly in her bed.

He knew that his wife was much stronger than his mother, but he could not help but worry about her in her condition. How he wished that they could speak to a physician about this! However, it was too soon to do so without causing whispers about her virtue.

Darcy sighed as he thought of his actions of the morning. It had been foolish for him to race out of the house with no outer clothing. The more he thought about it, the more embarrassed he became. However, the ridiculousness of his actions and speech during the whole affair suddenly overwhelmed him, and he started to laugh.

Peters peered through the doorway of the dressing room where he had been waiting until Darcy would need him. He saw that his master was still in the tub and seemed to be overcome with mirth.

After Darcy's laughter subsided, Peters moved into the room and said, "Would you like more hot water, sir?"

"No, I am ready to get dressed."

Peters helped Darcy into a robe as he rose from the tub. It did not take long for the valet to assist his master into dry clothing. He tied a simple knot in Darcy's cravat, per his usual daytime habit at Pemberley.

Once he was fully dressed, Darcy dismissed his man. He wanted to find Elizabeth to apologize, hoping that she would understand that he was concerned for her well-being and that of the babe. Leaving the dressing room, he crossed his bed chamber to open the adjoining door to his wife's room. However, Darcy hesitated once he reached it. Would she want to speak to him? He wondered if he should wait until later to talk to her. Shaking his head, he realized that he was merely stalling, so he knocked. There was no answer, so he knocked again only louder this time. Still no response came from the other room. Darcy thought that she might not be in her chambers. He decided to see for himself if she was there. If Elizabeth was not in her room, he would find her, for now his heart cried out to see her.

Opening the door, he looked for his wife and found her curled upon the bed under the down filled counterpane. A tray holding a tea pot and a half eaten scone sat on the table next to the bed. Obviously, Elizabeth had fallen asleep after her outing earlier.

He smoothed back a curl that had come loose and fallen across her forehead. Love filled him as he gazed down on her. She looked peaceful with a slight smile on her lips. How could he have scolded her so? She had only been trying to make Christmas brighter and lovelier for everyone by cutting the holly.

Pulling a chair closer to the bed, Darcy sat down to wait for Elizabeth to awaken. He wanted nothing more than to be with her at this moment. Sighing contentedly, he leaned back against the chair; his long legs stretched out before him. Darcy looked about the room, taking in the small details he had not noticed before.

Elizabeth had already put her individual touch upon the space, a small silver ink well upon her writing desk, a collection of shells placed attractively on a shelf alongside a neat row of her books, a silver backed brush with a matching hand mirror and perfume bottle that sat next to a dainty, lacquered tray on her dressing table. He thrilled at the lovely evidence of her residence in the mistress's chamber. Elizabeth had moved in and settled herself, just as he had wished her to do. He was not sure why seeing it made his heart so light, but Darcy knew that they would reconcile and that their bond would be all the stronger for the experience.

Smiling broadly, Darcy looked at the bedside table and spied a book he had seen his wife reading recently. Since he did not know how much longer Elizabeth would sleep, he took up the book and began to read.

It was in this occupation that Elizabeth found him an hour later when she awoke from her nap. "Does the Pemberley library not have books enough to keep you from reading mine?" she asked sleepily.

"Elizabeth!" Darcy sat up in the chair and put down the book. Taking her hand in his, he kissed it. "I trust you rested well."

"Well enough," she replied while pulling her hand away. Elizabeth rolled to the other side of the bed and got up. Walking to the window, she stared out at the blanket of snow.

"I am glad that I brought in the holly when I did," she murmured quietly to herself.

"You were wise to do it when you did," Darcy said from just behind her. Putting his hands on her shoulders he turned her to face him. "Would you please accept my apology for my ridiculous outburst this morning? When I finally understood how foolish I looked and sounded, I had a great laugh at my own expense. I am sorry that I acted the way I did. I admit that I was worried for your sake and that of our babe, but I did not think. I reacted in haste. Please forgive me."

At first, Elizabeth stiffened at his touch and refused to look him in the eyes, but as his words and humble tone reached her ears, she glanced up to see his beseeching expression. Her resentment melted at the sight. Leaning into his embrace, she whispered, "I forgive you. I am sorry that I reacted with anger."

"I understand your anger, though I am surprised that you did not laugh at my folly." The sound of his voice seemed to rumble in her ear as it rested on his chest.

"I suppose that if the babe were not in residence, I might have smirked at your absurdity, but he changes my moods at the oddest moments."

"She...," he corrected before he kissed the top of her head.

"You are very sure of yourself, sir," Elizabeth said as she pulled back to smile up at him.

"I am," he answered with a grin. "Now, I believe that we should see if the holly is dry, for it will take a great deal of time to decorate the banister. My family is set to arrive the day after tomorrow."

Darcy rang for her maid, who restored order to Elizabeth's garments. The pair soon walked down the back stairs to the stillroom.

As they descended the stairs, Elizabeth asked, "Will your family be able to make it to Pemberley safely in this snow?"

"Often the first snow does not stay long, but in the event that it does or there is more, my uncle will know what to do. Matlock is only a two-hour ride away, and if the snow is deep enough, they will come by sleigh. I remember that three years ago, Georgiana and I rode to Matlock in ours."

As they reached the door to the stillroom, Darcy said, "I think you would enjoy an open sleigh ride in the snow, and I promise to wear the proper clothing whenever I venture outside this winter."

"It is a wonderful idea!" Elizabeth squeezed his hand before entering the room. "Shall we get to work, sir? That is if you are still wishing to be of service to me?"

"I am ever your faithful servant, madam," Darcy smiled and bowed to her.

CHAPTER TWENTY-NINE

Many hours later, holly festooned the banister. It turned out that Darcy remembered the way his mother had tied the sprigs to the railing so that it was usable when climbing the stairs but still had a very lovely drape.

Elizabeth enjoyed working along side her husband and hearing him speak of his parents in such loving terms. She was treated to stories of his childhood Christmases. It warmed her heart that many of his favourite recollections of the season involved taking baskets for the tenants on the estate, especially the little gifts of candy and wooden toys given to the children. She was happy to hear this, since many masters, including her father, distributed gifts to his tenants as well, but rarely remembered the children.

Once Elizabeth had tied the last bow at the bottom of the staircase, Darcy tugged on her hand and pulled her to the front door for a better view of their handiwork. "I do believe that we have done an excellent job," Darcy declared with his arm around her shoulders. "Georgiana will be thrilled and will likely want a part in the work next year."

"That will be lovely," Elizabeth sighed and leaned her head on his shoulder. "And when our children are older, they can also be a part of it if they wish to do so."

"Our children, I like that thought." He lifted her chin with his free hand and lowered his mouth to kiss her.

"Fitzwilliam, we are not in private," she scolded as she blushed, but she did not move away from him.

"The staff is discreet and will not think ill of our showing a little affection in public." He grinned down at her rosy cheeks. "I can recall coming upon my parents while they were kissing or holding hands. I felt..." he paused to search for the right word before he said, "secure when I saw them thusly engaged."

Elizabeth sighed again. "My parents were not affectionate with each other, and rarely with us, once we were past our early childhood. I want our children to know that we love each other and them." She caught his eye and smiled mischievously. "So I suppose I will be able to put up with your public displays, Mr. Darcy."

"Indeed," Darcy agreed before he crushed her to him and kissed her again.

~*~

The party from Matlock arrived late in the morning two days later. As Darcy had predicted, the snow of earlier in the week had melted, so that their guests arrived in a large coach and six.

Darcy and Elizabeth stood in the courtyard archway. Once the footman opened the door to the carriage, Colonel Fitzwilliam jumped down and assisted first his father and then his mother from the vehicle. He then stepped aside as a tall, thin man unfolded from the coach and turned back to help a pretty young woman down.

Elizabeth was curious as to the identity of the couple, for couple they surely were, if the smiles of affection were any indication. She was about to move forward in welcome when Colonel Fitzwilliam moved back to the carriage to help another two young women from the coach, one of whom was her new sister.

Georgiana smiled hugely and rushed to her brother. "Oh, Fitzwilliam, it is so good to see you," she cried as she hugged him. She then turned to Elizabeth and embraced her. "Elizabeth, you look lovely. I can see that you both are well."

Smiling good naturedly at his sister, he offered his arm to Elizabeth. "Let us greet our guests, and I will introduce you to the ones you have not met as yet."

"Uncle and Aunt, welcome to Pemberley! You will remember my wife," Darcy could not help but smile fondly at Elizabeth."

"Of course, we do," Lord Matlock exclaimed as he kissed her hand.

Lady Matlock kissed Elizabeth's cheek and said, "You look as if my nephew has been treating you well, my dear."

"Indeed, he has, your Ladyship," she blushed prettily. Darcy's aunt was so warm and open, quite the contrast to the stark, cold demeanour of his aunt Catherine.

"My dear, let me present you to my older son and his wife." Lady Matlock turned to the couple who stood close by. "I would like to introduce you to the Viscount and Viscountess Matley. Oliver and Rebecca, this is the new Mrs. Darcy."

"I am happy to meet you both," Elizabeth said as she curtseyed. "Welcome to Christmas at Pemberley." She marvelled at the differences in their relative heights. The viscount was well over six foot, taller than either his brother or his cousin, who were the tallest men of her previous acquaintance. Lady Rebecca was even shorter than Elizabeth herself. The disparity in their stature did not seem to affect them at all.

"My dear," Darcy's voice brought her back to the task at hand. "I would like you to meet my cousin, Miss Anne de Bourgh. Anne, this is my wife, Mrs. Elizabeth Darcy."

The two women curtseyed to each other before Elizabeth announced, "It is rather cold out here for more socializing, and I am sure that our guests would like to go to their rooms to refresh themselves."

The idea was heartily agreed to by everyone, and the group entered the house, where servants were gathered to help everyone with the outer garments and to assist them to their rooms.

"Once you are refreshed and settled, please feel free to join us in the parlour for tea." Elizabeth extended the invitation before she went to speak to Mrs. Reynolds to make certain that there would be a room prepared for Miss de Bourgh. The housekeeper assured her mistress that extra rooms were always prepared for unexpected guests at Christmas.

Darcy joined her as she dismissed Mrs. Reynolds and surveyed the grand parlour. "Do not worry, my love. Between you and Mrs. Reynolds, not a single detail has been overlooked." He wrapped his arms around her and pulled her close for a brief hug.

"I am sure you are right, but I am, nevertheless, very nervous." She took a deep breath and exhaled slowly. "In fact, it is the first time since arriving at Pemberley that I have felt uneasy. From the first time I laid eyes on the house, I felt safe and at peace."

"Pemberley has that effect on people. I know that I am most at ease when I am in residence here."

Elizabeth caressed his cheek before she moved to a table and shifted a doily a fraction of an inch. She lifted her eyes to see Darcy smiling at her. "Oh, very well, I know I am fidgety. Come sit with me, and tell me a little about your cousins. I did not know that Miss de Bourgh would be joining us."

"I suppose that it is because my aunt Lady Catherine is not in residence at Rosings. My uncle told me after our wedding that he fully intended to fulfil his promise to his sister. She is likely spending the holiday on one of my uncle's small estates near Scotland," Darcy explained.

"I admit to feeling sorry that Lady Catherine is going to be alone for Christmas," Elizabeth sighed.

"But, my dearest, she would have made everyone miserable if she had stayed here," he protested.

Elizabeth sighed once more but said resignedly, "I know, but this is such a sad time to be alone."

"I would suggest that you and I pray for her change of heart toward our marriage. I know that my uncle wishes for her to be reconciled to the family. We know that God is able to melt hard hearts."

A joyful smile brightened her face. "I believe that is an excellent suggestion, Mr. Darcy. You are a wise man."

Again, Darcy pulled Elizabeth into his arms. "I admit to being wise at least once in my life, Mrs. Darcy," he said before kissing her. "I married you, did I not?" he asked when he came up for air.

Pushing out of his embrace, she scolded him with a grin that belied her words, "Mr. Darcy, I do not think you are being wise or proper at the moment. We have guests who might come upon us at any moment."

"Cousin, you should heed your wife's admonition." The colonel laughed at the surprised and embarrassed look on both their faces. "Although I am sure that you have an excuse, being newlyweds and all. My brother and his wife, too, seem to forget proper decorum at times when they believe themselves to be alone."

Darcy stood and offered his hand to his cousin. As he shook the colonel's hand, he caught his eye and said, "I begin to anticipate the time that you will marry, Richard. Oliver and I will enjoy exacting our revenge on you."

"But you do realize that I do not have a hope of finding love and domestic felicity as you and my brother have done. I must look for a wife among the likes of Miss Bingley." Colonel Fitzwilliam dramatically placed his hand over his heart and sighed.

"Colonel Fitzwilliam, you speak of my future brother's sister," Elizabeth admonished teasingly. "It is most impolitic."

Darcy watched his wife as she teased his cousin, who grinned and shot back a rejoinder. There might have been a time when he would have felt jealousy at their interaction, but he was secure in the conviction that his wife loved him and that she would never betray him. He also knew that Richard was an honourable man who would not play loose with another man's wife.

"Tell me, Richard," Darcy interrupted their banter. "How did my uncle manage Lady Catherine? Is she truly established in the north?"

"I will allow my father to give you the details as I was not a party to the move, but she is, indeed, in the north, quite near the Scottish border in one of the small estates Father uses as a hunting lodge. From what I understand, it was not a pleasant journey." His smile held no mirth. "I do not know if we will ever see her again. She was most seriously displeased and determined not to change her opinion about your marriage."

Before Darcy or Elizabeth could respond, Lord and Lady Matlock entered the room, followed by Viscount Matley, his wife, Miss Darcy, and Miss de Bourgh.

"I say, Darcy," Lord Matlock boomed merrily, "Pemberley fairly shines with Christmas cheer."

"Indeed, Nephew," Lady Matlock said excitedly. "The front stairway looks as lovely as it did when your dear mother was well enough to see to the decorations."

"I must give all the credit to my dear wife," Darcy said as he smiled down at Elizabeth at his side. "She would have holly on the banister."

"My husband fails to explain that he worked with me on the task."

"What wonders you have wrought, my dear Mrs. Darcy!" the viscount exclaimed. "One would not have thought he could be so domestic."

A gentle, teasing laughter filled the room as Darcy grinned at his elder cousin with no embarrassment on his face. Once the room was quiet again, he said, "Matley, I recommend the exercise. It is quite satisfying."

Once again laughter echoed through the room as servants entered with trays of tea and cakes. The guests enjoyed the refreshments as they became more acquainted with the new Mrs. Darcy. The talk became more general in topic as they discussed the trip from Matlock to Pemberley and the likelihood that it would snow before they returned home.

That evening as the guests were readying themselves for dinner, Elizabeth sat on the chaise in their private sitting room with her feet up, her head resting against the back, and her eyes closed. Darcy had just entered the room and he was admiring his wife from the doorway of his chambers.

"I hope you are not too fatigued, dearest."

Without lifting her head or opening her eyes, she answered, "I admit that I am enjoying the respite, but I will be fine by dinner time."

"My family is impressed with Pemberley," Darcy said as he pulled a chair next to the chaise. His voice was warm and deep with appreciation. "It is alive once more, thanks to you."

"Fitzwilliam, you give me too much credit," she protested. This time she met his gaze. "I think that they are pleased to see you happy." She lowered her head to hide her smirk. "Although I do think that I might take a little credit for that."

"Imp!" Darcy chuckled. "I will leave you to rest now and go down to play billiards. Richard is bound to want a rematch, since I trounced him last time we played. I will beat him again to show him it was not an accident."

However, before he could stand, Elizabeth pulled him over for a kiss which warmed her completely. It was with reluctance that she moved away from Darcy. "I will see you at dinner." She lay back on the couch and closing her eyes, she smiled.

As Elizabeth relaxed, she thought of Christmas and the gifts she had acquired for her husband. They seemed insignificant and paltry compared to the great love she wished to express. Even a few moments ago, she had wished for him to remain with her. Her whole being had wished for the kiss to lead them where she was more and more willing to go, and where she knew he wanted to go as well.

Pondering the thought gave birth to a greater yearning to be Fitzwilliam Darcy's wife completely.

At first, her pondering turned to the act itself. Since her attack, Elizabeth had tried to reject thoughts of such intimacies. Her fear was that if she shared in that way with her husband, the spectre of Wickham's brutal assault would come between them. However, now as she reflected upon her husband and his loving ways with her and the times of affections they had shared thus far, she did not know of one time in which she even remembered that evil man. The more she considered, the more she came to the conclusion that her dear Fitzwilliam would do everything in his power to spare her any distress or discomfort. With her beloved's help, she knew that vile deed would not be allowed to rule this part of her life.

Would it harm the babe? Would it be more prudent to wait until after the birth to consummate their union? How she desperately wished to confer with her aunt Gardiner! Surely, she would know such things. Elizabeth cast about in her mind for someone at Pemberley who could advise her, and that was when she came upon the idea of speaking with the housekeeper. Mrs. Reynolds was discreet, and with grown children of her own, she would know the answer to her questions.

Elizabeth frowned when she realized that she would have to be careful with the wording of her questions so as to not reveal how far along in her pregnancy she was. The fact that they had been married just under three weeks did not preclude her being with child. An idea came to her and she smiled softly.

Pulling the throw more tightly about her, Elizabeth relaxed and fell into a restful sleep.

The evening's meal and conversation sparkled with laughter and teasing. The three male cousins were often joined by the two female ones in trying to outdo the others in reciting stories of one or the other's childhood misdeeds or mischief. Elizabeth spent much of the time storing up the tales, as it gave her a truer understanding of her husband and new family. Darcy had been a typically rambunctious boy, but he was never mean-spirited and took the consequences of his actions with good grace.

She was surprised to hear that until Miss de Bourgh contracted a serious bout of scarlet fever at the age of ten, Darcy's cousin had been an active child, following after her male relatives and entering into their high jinks with enthusiasm whenever they were together. After the illness, Lady Catherine curbed nearly all outdoor activity for her daughter. This was the reason, according to Lady Matlock, Anne never recovered her full strength and vigour.

Once the meal ended, the ladies retired to the parlour and left the men to their cigars and port. Elizabeth enjoyed a pleasant half hour with her new female relatives before the men rejoined them.

"Darcy, it is time that we practice our music," Viscount Matley declared. "Georgiana, Rebecca, and Richard, come with us. I want this to be the best Christmas performance ever."

The two male cousins protested, half-heartedly on Richard's part, since he liked to tease his brother, and more strongly on Darcy's part because he did not want to leave Elizabeth alone with his aunt, uncle, and cousin.

Glancing up, Elizabeth caught Darcy's eye, and with a nearly imperceptible gesture and a smile, she indicated that she would be fine.

Darcy was still reluctant to go, but as he watched his wife turn her attention to Anne and his aunt, he left, following the rest to the music room.

"I look forward to this year's concert with great anticipation," Lady Matlock exclaimed. "Last year, only Oliver and Georgiana took part." She sighed quietly before she seemed to shake off the melancholy. "Our family has been blessed with musical talent, and now with the addition of Rebecca, we are in for a treat."

"And I am so happy to be a part of the audience this year, Aunt." Anne smiled. "That will have to be my contribution since I never learnt."

"Mrs. Darcy," the countess inquired, "Do you play or sing?"

"I do, but very ill," Elizabeth answered. "I do not take the time to practice as I ought."

"I am sure that you are just being modest, Mrs. Darcy," Anne interjected.

Elizabeth shook her head. "I assure you that I have little of the talent that Georgiana has."

Turning to the countess, she asked, "Does your Ladyship play and sing?"

"I am afraid that I have no talent at all. I can barely carry a tune well enough to sing in church. I could be called one of those able only to make a joyful noise unto the Lord." Lady Matlock laughed lightly. "And please call me Aunt Maud. This is a family gathering, and we should address each other as such."

"Thank you, Aunt Maud," replied Elizabeth. The feeling of welcome she was experiencing from Darcy's relatives completely washed away the dismay and hurt that Lady Catherine had inflicted. She continued, "I would be most happy if you both would call me Elizabeth. I am happy to be a part of this family."

Both of the other ladies assented, and Lady Maud was about to ask another question when Lord Matlock joined them. "My dear," he spoke, "I hope that you ladies will excuse me, but I find I must be for bed early tonight."

Lady Matlock stood and took her husband's arm. "I believe I will retire early myself. Thank you, Elizabeth, for the lovely meal and conversation. Please extend our thanks to your husband as well, and our apologies to the rest for not taking our leave personally. We will see you at breakfast."

Once Lord and Lady Matlock left the room, Elizabeth and Anne were seated once more. Anne said, "I am glad to have you to myself."

Elizabeth arched a querying brow. "It is an unexpected opportunity."

Anne chuckled lightly. "I asked Aunt and Uncle if they could leave us alone this evening, since I knew that the rest of my cousins would be practicing. I wanted to get to know the woman who took Darcy away from me."

Elizabeth's heart sunk and her cheeks paled. Was she to be interrogated or upbraided like she had been by Lady Catherine? Fitzwilliam had told her that Anne de Bourgh had not wanted to marry him, but had he been mistaken? Anxiety caused her breath to become laboured as she tried to think of something to say while she stared at her hands in her lap.

Anne placed her hand on Elizabeth's as she said in a contrite voice, "I apologize, Elizabeth. That was a poor jest. My cousin and I have always cared for each other, but we were never in love. I might have agreed to marry him if he had wanted. I have never been courageous enough to stand up to my mother. However, Fitzwilliam told me that he would only marry for the deepest love."

This time Elizabeth's cheeks burned with embarrassment. She cleared her throat a couple times before she answered, "It is I who should apologize. I am not usually so slow to comprehend a joke. Fitzwilliam told me about your mother's supposed arrangement. I had hoped that he had not been mistaken about your feelings in the matter."

"I assure you, Elizabeth, that I felt no pain, only happiness for my dear cousin at his marriage." It was Anne's turn to look down at her hands as she tried to formulate what to say next. "I also want to apologize for my mother's outrageous behaviour at your wedding. I am so ashamed that she would cause such an embarrassing spectacle."

"Oh, please," exclaimed Elizabeth quickly. "There is no need for you to apologize. I have already forgiven your mother, and certainly I do not hold her actions against you. I must say that I feel bad that you are to be alone at your home now that your mother has been moved to the north."

"I do not fully understand what this will mean for me. My aunt and uncle came to Rosings right after your wedding when they brought my mother with them so that her things could be packed. Mama was so very abusive in her speech regarding you and Darcy, so much so that Uncle Vincent summoned a physician to sedate her. Apparently, he had also sent an express to his housekeeper at Briar Mist, which is the name of the house where my mother is now residing, and had the place readied for her.

"Two days later, the nurse companion arrived. Mrs. Martin is an Amazon of a woman with a gentle but steely attitude. She has worked with difficult people in the past and came highly recommended. Uncle Vincent sent several men along for the journey, and two have stayed behind to insure her safety and compliance."

By the time Anne had finished her story, tears stained her cheeks, but she seemed unaware of them. "I am sure that I will miss her when I go back home to Rosings, but I feel guilt at how little her absence troubles me at the moment. In fact, after so many dull Christmases with only my mother and my companion, Mrs. Jenkinson, as company, I am thrilled to be here with the rest of my family."

Elizabeth drew out her handkerchief and offered it to her new cousin. "And to think, I often wished for a quieter holiday at Longbourn when I had the blessing of lively sisters and both parents."

"Thank you, Elizabeth," Anne said as she dried her eyes. "I feel better now that I have spoken of it. I know that things will be quite different for me, but I am optimistic that I will enjoy my new life as mistress of Rosings."

"May I ask you how you pass the time at Rosings?"

Elizabeth watched a blush tint Anne's cheeks. "Since according to my mother I am sickly, I am rarely allowed to walk about the grounds of Rosings. I do read a great deal, though our library is not extensive or varied. Lady Catherine has an aversion to many of the modern writers and poets. If it were not for the housekeeper, I would have memorized the whole of the library at Rosings by now."

"What did your housekeeper do to help?" Elizabeth could not refrain from inquiring.

"I gave her money to purchase books for me. She has a set of rooms that are quite out of my mother's way in that part of the house. Mrs. Justice has a lovely little library which she allows me to peruse at my leisure. She trades in books that we do not wish to keep. My cousins have gifted me with new volumes and kept the knowledge from my mother as well." Anne grinned with a hint of the same mischief Elizabeth had seen on Colonel Fitzwilliam's face.

"Surely reading is not all that you do," Elizabeth said with a grin.

"Indeed, it is not," Anne replied. "My mother allowed me to tour Rosings with my phaeton and pony as long as the weather was good. She did not know that I did most of the driving. She thought that it was one of the grooms or Mrs. Jenkinson who did so, and we made certain that she was never privy to the truth of the matter. I would have been forbidden to ride out, and my companion would have been dismissed. I also enjoy handiwork, such as embroidery and crochet, but mine is not out of the common way."

Anne looked down as she twisted nervously at the handkerchief in her hands, seeming to be having an inner debate as to whether she should share with her new cousin.

Finally, Anne lifted her head and caught Elizabeth's curious gaze. "I also spend a great deal of my time … writing."

"You must have many correspondents," Elizabeth commented.

Anne laughed lightly. "You mistake my meaning, Elizabeth. I write stories, novels, you could say. I have not shared this with any of my family, so please do not say anything about it," she pleaded in embarrassment.

"Of course, I will not speak of it to any of the Fitzwilliams, but I do not keep secrets from my husband. I hope you will understand that?"

Anne reddened for a moment before she nodded her agreement. "I understand."

"Why is it that you do not tell the rest of your family of your hobby?" Elizabeth inquired softly.

"I have never wanted my mother to know. She would undoubtedly tell me that I am wasting my time. I have only allowed Mrs. Jenkinson to read a few of my shorter stories. She said that she enjoyed them, but I am not certain whether she is flattering me or telling me her true opinion."

"What kind of stories do you write?" Elizabeth's curiosity increased.

"Romantic ones, but not any of the usual gothic type, I assure you," she confessed. "I know that I have not experienced romance, but I have such ideas that will not be repressed. I write of ordinary people and places and of extraordinary love that overcomes great obstacles. Sometimes I hear a comment or a brief account from one of the tenants at Rosings while I am out on one of my rides. I ponder on it, and soon a story forms in my mind."

Elizabeth smiled at the enthusiasm in Anne's voice and on her face. "Would you permit me to read one of your stories sometime? I admit to being very interested in your work. Your excitement about the subject is contagious."

"Oh, I do not know if I could." The woman's face flushed pink. "I am afraid that you will tell me it is horrid or that you will lie and tell me it is good when it is not, but either way the joy of writing will be lost to me."

"I must assure you that I would only be truthful, but I will not press you to allow me read one of your stories." Elizabeth placed a hand on the other woman's arm. "I will not think less of you if you do not share, or if you do and I do not like the story. We are family now. I have always loved my family, even when I did not completely approve of their actions."

"Thank you, Elizabeth," Anne whispered. "I will think about your request."

"It is enough for me," Elizabeth said before she changed the subject. "Your companion did not accompany you?"

"Mrs. Jenkinson is visiting her sister and family. She has not spent Christmas with her family since she became my companion ten years ago." Anne sighed before she continued, "I realized when Aunt Maud told me that we would travel to Matlock and then on to Pemberley, that poor Mrs. Jenkinson must miss being with family as much as I did, so I gave her a month off. I will be with my family and have no need to keep her near me during this time."

"How thoughtful of you!" Elizabeth proclaimed. "I am sure that she is enjoying herself."

"She wept with gratitude when I told her," Anne choked out before she cleared her throat. "She was overjoyed at the prospect, even though she tried to talk me out of it when she found out how far I would be travelling."

Soon the conversation turned to discussion of Elizabeth's family and that is what they were talking of when finally the musicians joined them.

"I see my parents are keeping to their usual schedule," the colonel commented as he entered the room, followed closely by Darcy, who made his way quickly to Elizabeth's side.

"Yes, both Aunt and Uncle expressed a desire to retire early," Elizabeth answered with a grin as she watched the surprised but pleased look on her husband's face at her use of the familiar appellations for his relatives. "They asked us to give you their apologies for not waiting to take their leave of all of you."

"Elizabeth and I had a lovely time getting to know each another," Anne added happily.

"Elizabeth, is it?" Viscount Matley laughed. "I hope that privilege will extend to the rest of us."

"Indeed, sir," Elizabeth's fine eyes sparkled as she answered. "I would be happy if you all would use my Christian name."

"I believe that I speak for all of us when I say that we would be honoured to agree and hope you will do so with us as well," Matley said as he sat next to his wife near the fireplace.

The rest of those gathered agreed, and a lively conversation began, continuing until the viscount and his wife excused themselves for the night. They were soon followed by the others.

Once Darcy and Elizabeth were in bed, he said, "I will be at the groomsmen's dining hall at the noon hour. I should not be longer than a half hour. You will be engaged with the house staff at that same time, will you not?"

"That was my intention, but I have thought that perhaps I could distribute the gifts prior to their meal, so that the staff could enjoy the full hour. Would you approve such a departure from the established custom?"

Darcy smiled at her thoughtfulness and kindness to the Pemberley servants. "I have no objections. In fact, I believe that I will do the same. I am certain that we will hear no objections from the staff. First thing in the morning, I will inform the head groom. He will spread the word."

"And I will speak to Mrs. Reynolds." Elizabeth lifted her head and kissed her husband's cheek. "Thank you, my love, for listening to my suggestions. You make me feel that my ideas have merit."

"Even though I acted to the contrary earlier in the week, I am happy to see you take the initiative in household matters. I have been thinking about enlisting your involvement in other estate management areas. I do not mean that you will be burdened with the everyday running of Pemberley, but there are new innovations in farming and the like that I would like to discuss with you. You have shown me that you have a keen mind, and I would be unwise if I did not avail myself of your insights. Of course, I do not insist upon it."

"Oh, Fitzwilliam," she crooned happily, "I would love to know more about our home and its running. I will prayerfully consider any matter you wish to discuss with me."

Elizabeth cuddled close to her husband and sighed. More than ever, she wanted to express her love. This seemed to be a sign that she should proceed with her talk with Mrs. Reynolds. She sighed once more and let sleep claim her.

CHAPTER THIRTY

Snow that had begun sometime in the night greeted the household as they awoke the day before Christmas. Breakfast was a lively affair as the family gathered in the more intimate small breakfast parlour. The chef had prepared several special treats, which were welcomed with enthusiasm.

"I declare that I have not tasted anything to compare with this pastry," Lord Matlock announced as he savoured the flaky apple-filled triangle on his plate.

"Chef tells me that our Pemberley orchards and creamery produce apples and butter that are unsurpassed," Darcy told him proudly.

"I was afraid you might say that, for while I might be able to tempt your chef away from Pemberley, I would be unable to move the orchards or the creamery. I wonder how it is that there is such a difference between Matlock and Pemberley," the earl sighed.

"I have to say that I am happy that you have only a few occasions to sample such rich foods. I do not believe it would be healthy for you to do so regularly, my dear husband," answered Lady Matlock.

Laughter flowed around the table, and soon conversation turned to what was in store for the next two days. Elizabeth informed the guests that the servants' dinner would make it necessary for their midday meal to be at a later hour than usual. With that in mind, she gaily admonished the guests to eat heartily of the breakfast offerings.

Once she finished her breakfast, Elizabeth excused herself to meet with Mrs. Reynolds. Her heart seemed to speed up as she thought of what she would ask the housekeeper. She wondered if it might be a mistake to talk about the subject, but she did not wish to wait any longer. There was no doubt that Fitzwilliam trusted his housekeeper, so she decided she could as well.

After knocking at Mrs. Reynolds door and hearing a muffled, "Enter," Elizabeth moved quickly into the room and closed the door behind her.

"Good morning, Mrs. Darcy," the housekeeper said as she stood and curtseyed. "What may I do for you?"

Elizabeth motioned for the older woman to sit as she did the same. "I have a suggestion for the servants' dinner or rather, for the distribution of the gifts."

Mrs. Reynolds nodded and Elizabeth continued, "I would like to change the timing of the servants' festivities today."

At the housekeeper's frown, Elizabeth smiled and said, "I do not mean to curtail them, only to add some time before the meal. I felt that if I hand out the gifts during the hour, it would not give much time for everyone to enjoy themselves. What I propose is to have as many of the staff as possible gather in one of the rooms closest to the servants' dining hall. I shall distribute my gifts to all assembled and dismiss them to the meal afterwards. If there are any others whose tasks preclude them from the earlier gathering, I shall await them inside the dining hall. I hope this will not cause an undue disruption in your schedule."

"Oh, Mrs. Darcy, I am sure it shall not!" Mrs. Reynolds exclaimed. "The servants and I try hard to finish our duties, so that the family is not inconvenienced by our holiday celebration. I shall make your wishes known as soon as you are finished here. Thank you so much for your concern for the staff."

"It is my pleasure," Elizabeth shyly acknowledged before she took a deep breath and said, "I have another, more personal, subject to discuss with you. This is not something that I thought to discuss with my mother, and she did not broach it with me."

Mrs. Reynolds held her peace while the young mistress struggled to find the words to say what she wanted to say.

After another deep breath, Elizabeth explained, "I have missed my courses this month. I know it is quite early to think that I might be with child, but as I am never late, I think I may be."

The bright smile on the housekeeper's face warmed Elizabeth's heart. She took courage from it and continued, "Since I am not experienced with these sorts of matters, I..." She twisted her hands together as her face reddened. "That is, I want to know... if ... when... must we refrain from..." Elizabeth could not go on in her acute embarrassment.

Mrs. Reynolds's face softened in sympathy. "Are you asking if you must keep from marital congress if you are with child?"

Elizabeth nodded, feeling gratitude that she did not have to say more.

"No, indeed, you do not have to refrain. If there is a babe, it is quite small and safe where it is growing." Mrs. Reynolds smiled. "Often, couples will enjoy that aspect of their marriage well into the last month. Most midwives that I know will tell you the same. It is only when a pregnancy is difficult, or when there is some complication that abstinence is called for. So, my dear Mrs. Darcy, do not worry yourself about this. You will not truly know if you are with child until the quickening. You will feel a fluttering where the child grows within. That is the best sign we have, although sickness in the morning can be another early sign. If you experience any stomach upset, please tell me, and I will see what can be done to ease your discomfort."

Mrs. Reynolds then stood and held out her hand. "I want to tell you that I hope to soon be able to congratulate you.

Shaking the older woman's hand, Elizabeth smiled and said, "Thank you for your kind advice. I am glad that I came to you."

"You are most welcome, and remember that I am always available anytime you wish to talk, Mrs. Darcy." Mrs. Reynolds curtseyed.

Elizabeth returned the gesture and turned toward the door. "I appreciate knowing that, and now I will allow you to get back to your work."

As she left the housekeeper's room, Elizabeth thought about how she would inform her husband of her intentions. She was certain that she would not be able to speak the words, and without giving him at least an idea of what she wanted, she thought he would be confused and even reluctant unless he understood. Finally, she decided to write him a letter that she would give to him after they returned from the Christmas Eve service in Pemberley's chapel.

Fitzwilliam had explained to her that it was a tradition that if the family was at home for Christmas, they would worship the Christ Child at midnight in Pemberley's own little chapel. As the Bennets had the same custom, Elizabeth enjoyed the continuity. God willing, throughout the following years, they would celebrate the blessed holiday with their children and extended family.

Hurrying to her own study, Elizabeth locked herself inside to pen her Christmas letter to her husband. The missive was surprisingly easy to write once she began. The words of love and determination flowed freely onto the page. After rereading what she had written, she sanded, folded, and sealed the paper. Slipping the letter into her dresser drawer, she smiled in expectation. If all went as she hoped, she would soon experience her true wedding night.

As she stood to leave the room, Elizabeth was struck with a feeling of unease like a ghost of the fear that came after the attack. It slipped around her heart and squeezed. The pain and horror of the attack seemed ready to reassert themselves. Her palms began to sweat and her breath came in quick pants.

Elizabeth reached back for the arm of the chair and lowered herself back into it. In part of her mind, she knew that she needed to use the tools she had learned to fight the memories. When she whispered, "God help me," it became slowly easier to focus her thoughts on the mental image of the burning paper. With her mind's eye, she watched the smoke rise up the chimney. She began to feel calmer.

"The man is not here," Elizabeth told herself aloud. "My husband is not that man. He is kindness itself and will never willingly hurt me. I can trust Fitzwilliam's love and care for me. It will be well." As she spoke the words, the fear ebbed away, and anticipation and excitement took its place once more. Taking a couple deep, reviving breaths, she stood to return downstairs.

Elizabeth joined the others in the blue parlour. She wished she could have stayed in her chambers, but she knew that would have given rise to too many questions. Moving across the room, she sat next to her husband, who was talking to his cousin, the viscount, about one of the musical pieces scheduled for the evening. When Darcy almost absentmindedly took her hand and lifted to his lips, she relaxed and smiled. *I am where I belong,* she told herself.

For an hour or so, they passed the time congregated; playing cards, reading, or in pleasant conversation. Finally, Colonel Fitzwilliam stood at the end of the game he had been playing with his brother, his brother's wife, and his father and walked to the window.

After peering out onto the snow-covered landscape, Richard announced, "I think we should don warm clothing and enjoy the snow. It is no longer coming down, and knowing Derbyshire weather as I do, I think it is the best chance we will have to enjoy the white stuff. By tomorrow it could turn very cold, or the present snow could be melted into a slushy mess. What say you, Darcy, Matley? Should we escort the ladies out into the wintery garden?"

Elizabeth glanced up to see Darcy frown. She thought he was caught between agreeing to the outing and keeping her inside the warmth of Pemberley. Deciding that he needed a little encouragement, she excused herself from her conversation with Georgiana and Anne to move across the room to her husband.

Resting a hand on his arm, Elizabeth spoke in a low tone, "I will dress warmly as will everyone else. You will be with me the whole time to prevent me from falling, or whatever else your fertile mind is envisioning might happen to me. I will make certain that there will be warm refreshments ready for us upon our return." She smiled winningly at him. "Might I remind you that I can't stay outside long because I must be ready for the servants' celebration? Please, Fitzwilliam."

Darcy's heart refused to obey his more cautious mind so he answered, "Very well, but no snowball fights." He winked at his wife before he lifted his voice and said, "Richard, my wife has convinced me that an outing is a good idea. I suggest that we change into clothing more appropriate for the cold. Anyone who desires to make the trek in the snow, please meet by the back terrace doors in half an hour."

Before going to her chambers, Elizabeth arranged for tea, coffee, hot chocolate, and biscuits to be readied for them upon their return to the house. She arrived at her room to find that Darcy had already summoned Sarah to help her. The maid had laid out her warmest clothing, including thick woollen stockings and petticoats. Soon, she and her husband made their way to the back of the house to meet with most of the rest of the party, all warmly attired and ready to brave the wintry cold. Only the earl and countess decided to remain indoors.

As the group moved through the large glass double doors, Elizabeth smiled. She had always loved a snow-covered garden, though in Hertfordshire rarely had she experienced one in which there was so much of it. On those times when the snow fell and stayed for more than a few hours, she and her sisters would build snowmen and have snowball fights. Since Darcy had forbidden the latter, she decided to propose the former.

"May we go out onto the lawn and make a snowman?" asked she with obvious eagerness.

Before Darcy could object, both of his male cousins expressed their agreement with the scheme, and each led the lady on his arm out into the white expanse. He looked down at his wife and over to his cousin Anne, whose hand was laid on his other arm.

"Are you certain that you are well enough to stay out in this cold?" Darcy directed this question to his cousin, but he truly wished to have his wife answer it as well.

"Oh, Fitzwilliam, I am not so fragile that I cannot spend half an hour in the cold." Anne glanced around him to meet Elizabeth's eyes. "I have not had this pleasure in far too many years."

She let go of Darcy's arm and reached for Elizabeth's hand. "Let us find a place to begin. Rebecca, Georgiana, Oliver, and Richard have a head start on us."

The two women trudged through the deep snow to an open space and began to pack the snow into a ball before they rolled it into a much larger base for their creation.

Darcy smiled a trifle begrudgingly. He still felt protective of his wife, but as he observed her pleasure in the act of playing in the snow, he could not suspend her enjoyment. He decided to help Elizabeth and his cousin so that they might finish and go back into the house that much sooner.

The trio talked happily, reminiscing about their childhood adventures in the snow for about twenty minutes, and was just adjusting the sticks they were using as arms when Anne was hit in the back with a snowball that exploded in a fine mist of icy fluff.

"Richard Andrew Fitzwilliam," Anne shouted as she turned around to see her cousin grinning proudly back at her. She quickly moved behind the snowman and ducked down to grab a ball of snow. "I will pay you back for that." She followed up her threat by throwing the packed orb at him. However, the icy missile hit Oliver instead.

Soon a hail of snowballs whizzed back and forth between the cousins, with Elizabeth and Darcy trying to stay out of the fray. They were unsuccessful, however, since Darcy's cousins joined forces to attack him, and as a consequence, Elizabeth was hit. She screeched and laughed when some of the icy powder ended up down her neck as one of the snowballs hit her shoulder. Unable to resist the temptation to join in any longer, she made her own ammunition and threw it back.

At first, Darcy did not realize that his bride had joined the battle. After sending several packed snowballs at the others, he looked to see if Elizabeth was out of the line of fire when he saw her lobbing a ball at Richard. Her aim was accurate, and she landed one full in his chest. Darcy tried to be put out at her seeming disregard for his request, when he understood that he had actually been quite unreasonable in the first place. She was healthy, and if her expression was any indication, his wife was thoroughly enjoying herself.

Darcy pulled out his pocket watch to look at the time after the battle had raged a while longer. Realizing that it was nearing the time for both of them to see to the distribution of gifts to the servants, he called out, "I do not want to end this bit of childish delight, but it is time for my wife and me to be about our duties as master and mistress of Pemberley. You are more than welcome to continue if you wish. There will be hot refreshments inside when you are finished waging your frozen war."

By that time, Elizabeth had arrived at his side, grinning in delight. "I hope you are not displeased that I joined in. I have not had the pleasure in so many years that I could not help it."

Sighing in an overly dramatic way, Darcy replied, "I suppose I will forgive you this time." He could not keep a smile from curling his lips. He put one of her gloved hands into the crook of his arms and guided her back into the house.

Once they were inside and helped out of their snow covered outer garments, Darcy wrapped his arm around her waist. "I hope you did not catch a chill, my love."

Leaning into him, Elizabeth replied, "I did not have a chance to get cold, but I think I will have a cup of hot chocolate in my room while I change into dry clothes."

She moved into the parlour that held the waiting hot drinks. Elizabeth asked that hot chocolate be brought to her chambers and one to the master's when he gave a nod to her questioning glance. After she made certain that her guests would have hot drinks and fortunately there was plenty of hot water for a bath if they should so desire, she hurried up the stairs to her room.

Inside, Elizabeth again found Sarah laying out clothes for her. Her maid had hung her under things before the fire, so that she was instantly warmed as she slipped into the garments. Once she had donned her dress, cap, and shoes, Elizabeth sipped from the hot chocolate another servant had brought to the room.

"I have something for you, Sarah," Elizabeth announced as she moved to her dresser and pulled out a drawer. She unwound the bit of cloth with which she had covered the gift and presented the prettily wrapped bundle to her maid.

"I did not want to embarrass you or cause hard feelings toward you from the others. However, I could not resist giving you something as a token of my appreciation for your care and friendship. Please open it."

Sarah blushed as she laid the gift on the table and pulled the ribbon from around the package. She neatly folded the ribbon and tucked it into her pocket before pulling off the wrapping. Gasping at the sight of the pale green shawl and matching gloves, she lifted her grateful gaze to her mistress.

"Oh, mistress," she whispered as she fingered the softness of the wool. "I have never seen the like. Thank you so much! They are lovely."

"You are welcome," Elizabeth said with a smile. "I must go to Mrs. Reynolds now before I see the rest of the staff. I want to see you enjoy yourself at the luncheon."

Elizabeth pulled another package out of the same drawer and left the room. She found Mrs. Reynolds seeing to the last minute details of both the servants' luncheon and the meal that would be served to the family and guests after the staff's celebration.

"Mrs. Reynolds, do you have a minute?" Elizabeth asked courteously.

"Oh, of course, Mrs. Darcy, how may I help you?" the housekeeper replied with a curtsey.

"Let us go to your office." Elizabeth gestured in that direction before walking from the room with the older woman following her.

Once inside the housekeeper's office, Elizabeth handed her the wrapped package. "I wanted to give this to you privately. You are such a treasure, doing your job with such diligence and skill and I believe, with a great deal of love. Mr. Darcy and I would like to give you a small token of our appreciation and esteem."

After unwrapping the gift, Mrs. Reynolds opened an ornately decorated box to find a silver and mother-of-pearl ink well, a stack of fine paper, several delicately crafted metal dip pens, sealing wax, a seal with the letter R on it, and a bottle of fine blotting sand, each in its own cloth-lined compartment.

The housekeeper stood staring at the gift for several moments before she laid it carefully on her desk. "Mrs. Darcy, this is too much. Mr. Darcy is always so generous during the year. I cannot... I do not..." She wiped at her eyes and sniffed, "Thank you, and please give my most heartfelt gratitude to Mr. Darcy as well."

"You are welcome," Elizabeth said as she gripped Mrs. Reynolds hand and squeezed. "Now, I believe I must retrieve the gifts for the rest of the staff."

"Please let me send someone to help you. I know how heavy the baskets are."

They had just moved from the office when Elizabeth spied Sarah in the hallway. "I think that Sarah and I can manage," she told her, gesturing for her abigail to join her.

In very little time, Sarah and Elizabeth arrived in the designated room to see that the servants were entering into that parlour from various doors. From their bright and eager faces, she had no doubt that their happiness was equal to the season.

The chatter hushed as Elizabeth and Sarah moved farther into the room. They placed the baskets on a table put there for just that purpose. She glanced about the room, meeting the smiles with one of her own.

Mrs. Reynolds finally nodded to indicate that all were present. Elizabeth smiled even more broadly as she said, "Happy Christmas, everyone. Mr. Darcy and I would like to thank you all for your faithful service. I have not been mistress here for very long, but I know without a doubt that we are blessed to have some of the best people in the country working for us. Your loyalty and dedication to your duties are only some of the reasons that Pemberley is so celebrated in Derbyshire. I thank you again, and would like to give each of you a gift to celebrate the birth of our Lord."

The distribution of the gifts took longer than planned, for many of the staff wished to say something to their new mistress. Once it was accomplished, Elizabeth joined the servants in their dining hall for a cup of punch. They toasted her and Darcy with many words and hearty cheers. Their warm well-wishes for their future life brought tears to Elizabeth's eyes and a great affection to her heart for them all.

Once the exuberant ovation had quieted, Elizabeth, noticing that they would not have as much time as planned to dine, said, "I will take my leave, but please do not worry about quitting your luncheon quickly. We will not suffer for waiting another half hour. Again, happy Christmas to you all."

Elizabeth left the room to a chorus of "Happy Christmas to you, Mrs. Darcy!" She smiled as she made her way to the large gold drawing room where she thought she might find her guests.

As Elizabeth entered the room, the gentlemen stood, and Darcy walked to her and whispered, "I can tell by the expression on your face, it went well for you."

"Indeed, it did," she answered back quietly. "However, our meal will be a bit later than planned. Everyone seemed to want to wish me a happy Christmas or to thank us both for our gifts. We have a wonderful staff."

"Aye, we do," he agreed.

Darcy raised his voice to address the whole room. "Our midday repast will be later than planned, although I do not think we will faint from hunger." His glance landed on the table still half-filled with food and drink.

Everyone laughed and resumed their former conversations as Darcy guided Elizabeth to a sofa near the massive fireplace. He brought her a glass of sherry from the loaded table and sat comfortably next to her, smiling both inwardly and outwardly at his wife's rapport with the servants and staff.

CHAPTER THIRTY-ONE

The rest of the day passed pleasantly as the family talked, played cards, read, and generally enjoyed a relaxing time until everyone filed into the music room for the anticipated Christmas concert.

The small audience sat cosily on comfortable settees as the musicians tuned their instruments one final time. The viscount nodded to the others, and they began to play -- Georgiana at the harp, Lady Rebecca on the recorder, Darcy at the cello, Lord Matley at the pianoforte, and Colonel Fitzwilliam sang a solo.

As the melodies of the season turned the lovely music room into an enchanted place of worship, Elizabeth closed her eyes and savoured the beauty of the sound. She was transported back to childhood memories of Christmases past. Tears stung her eyes as she felt the longing for her own dear family, but soon the magic of the songs turned those sad tears into ones of joy as she thought of the dear new family of which she was now a part.

Near the end of the concert with Georgiana at the pianoforte, Matley insisted that the four members of the audience join in the singing. Darcy joined his wife on the settee during this time, his clear baritone weaving with Elizabeth's light soprano to enrich the carol and knit the bond of their two hearts even tighter.

Elizabeth was surprised when she heard more voices join in on the singing. Glancing behind her, she realized that many of the servants stood crowded in the large double doorway. She smiled at them before she rejoined the song.

"It is one of our traditions for as many of the house staff as possible to listen to the family Christmas concert and to join in with the singing," Darcy whispered in her ear.

Smiling broadly, Elizabeth squeezed his hand as she revelled in yet another of the family traditions, which, though new to her, were now as dear as if she had observed them her whole life. Their babe would be a fortunate child to grow up in such a loving environment.

After a few more songs, the family retired to one of the parlours where two tables sat, one loaded down with Christmas fare and the other filled with gifts. As with her own family, the Darcy household exchanged gifts on Christmas Eve, and from Elizabeth's vantage point, there seemed to be a great many of them to be had.

Darcy led his wife to stand in front of the room's massive fireplace. "Elizabeth and I want to wish you all a very blessed Christmas. We are so very happy that you could join us for our first holiday together. Personally, I want to thank you, my dear family, for making my beloved feel so welcome." He paused, deciding not to mention Lady Catherine's attitude toward his wife.

He continued, "As was the habit of my father and his father before him, I would like to read the Christmas story and pray before we partake of the supper and gifts. Please be seated."

Helping Elizabeth to a comfortable chair, Darcy took the one next to her. He lifted the large family Bible into his hands and turned to the place marked by a long ribbon. Darcy smiled softly as he read from the book of Luke, chapter two, "'And it came to pass in those days, that there went out a decree from Caesar Augustus, that all the world should be taxed. (And this taxing was first made when Cyrenius was governor of Syria.) And all went to be taxed, every one into his own city.

"'And Joseph also went up from Galilee, out of the city of Nazareth, into Judaea, unto the city of David, which is called Bethlehem; (because he was of the house and lineage of David:) to be taxed with Mary his espoused wife, being great with child.

"'And so it was, that, while they were there, the days were accomplished that she should be delivered. And she brought forth her firstborn son, and wrapped him in swaddling clothes, and laid him in a manger; because there was no room for them in the inn.

"'And there were in the same country shepherds abiding in the field, keeping watch over their flock by night. And, lo, the angel of the Lord came upon them, and the glory of the Lord shone round about them: and they were sore afraid.

"'And the angel said unto them, Fear not: for, behold, I bring you good tidings of great joy, which shall be to all people. For unto you is born this day in the city of David a Saviour, which is Christ the Lord. And this shall be a sign unto you; ye shall find the babe wrapped in swaddling clothes, lying in a manger.

"'And suddenly there was with the angel a multitude of the heavenly host praising God, and saying, Glory to God in the highest, and on earth peace, good will toward men.

"'And it came to pass, as the angels were gone away from them into heaven, the shepherds said one to another, Let us now go even unto Bethlehem, and see this thing which is come to pass, which the Lord hath made known unto us.

"'And they came with haste, and found Mary, and Joseph, and the babe lying in a manger. And when they had seen it, they made known abroad the saying which was told them concerning this child. And all they that heard it wondered at those things which were told them by the shepherds.

"'But Mary kept all these things and pondered them in her heart.

"'And the shepherds returned, glorifying and praising God for all the things that they had heard and seen, as it was told unto them.'"[1]

A reverent hush lay softly on the group as they pondered the story they had just heard. The silence was finally broken when Darcy cleared his throat and began to pray, "Our loving and gracious heavenly Father, we are grateful to Thee for the gift of Thy Son Jesus. May we always remember the end of His perfect life when we celebrate His birth. Christ came to die for us in order to have fellowship with us. Thy mercy shown to us in such abundance should be more than enough reason for us to praise Thee every day of our lives.

"Thank Thee for the bounty of good things of which we are about to partake. We are not worthy of Thy great blessings to us, but we ask Thy assistance in our feeble endeavours to be so. In the wonderful name of our Saviour, Jesus Christ. Amen!"

As echoes of "amen" sounded in the room, Elizabeth reached over to squeeze her husband's hand. She expressed her own silent praise for the home in which she now lived and for the man whose love for her made it possible.

She stood and motioned to the food-laden table. "Please come and enjoy the delicious fare that Chef has prepared for us."

The meal was enjoyed by everyone, and they all expressed their pleasure many times throughout the supper. When they had finished and were comfortably settled into chairs and settees around the fireplace, Darcy stood and announced, "I judge by the heap of gifts on the table that we should begin the exchange in order to be ready for church at midnight."

The group answered his statement with delighted laughter, since they all knew they had plenty of time to open their gifts.

"Uncle," Darcy said as he turned to Lord Matlock, "I believe it is your task to play Father Christmas and distribute the gifts."

The answering laugh from Lord Matlock reminded Elizabeth of her childhood image of how Father Christmas would sound. The rich and booming quality of his expression of mirth warmed her heart as she waited for the gifts to be dispensed.

Many cries of thanks and gratitude filled the air as the gifts were unwrapped. Georgiana was especially happy with the pink silk and lace. She declared that she wished to have it made into a gown for the first ball Elizabeth and Darcy would give at Pemberley as husband and wife.

Elizabeth was overwhelmed by the generosity of her new family. Never had she expected to receive such thoughtful, lovely, and useful gifts. As she opened each one, she understood in a new way how blessed she was. They all had seemed to put a good deal of thought into each item. One of her favourites was a bound journal from Anne de Bourgh with a note inside that she should keep a record of her new life as a married woman. Lizzy truly liked that idea. Darcy gave Elizabeth several pieces of jewellery he had had made for her. He whispered to her that he had ordered them made when he travelled to London to have the marriage contract drawn up. She was particularly fond of a brooch made of garnets and pearls and hair combs adorned with the same gems, both of which matched the necklace she wore on her wedding day.

"It seems that our family approves of the presents you found for them," Darcy said softly for her ears only.

"I am happy they like them," she replied. "I am amazed at how they were able to find so many items I would have chosen for myself, if given the chance."

"I have more gifts for you," Darcy promised in the same low tone. "However, they are of a more personal nature, which means that you will have to wait until we come back from services tonight."

Elizabeth smiled up at her husband and said, "You took the words out of my mouth, Mr. Darcy."

Darcy chuckled and lifted her hands to his lips. "I am intrigued, Mrs. Darcy."

It was then that Darcy's attention was called to a different quarter when his uncle again thanked him for the gift of a travel chess set of carved ivory and onyx. Conversation flowed around the room as each person shared their happiness with the day.

Soon the time came for them to make their way to the chapel. Darcy had ordered two sleighs to be readied to take them the short quarter mile to services. The gentlemen helped the ladies into the vehicles, where they were tucked under rugs and their feet warmed by heated bricks. As they departed, footmen trotted ahead, holding lanterns aloft to light the way.

Elizabeth was delighted with the chance to experience a midnight ride, even if it was a short one. The bright night sky was illumined with countless stars, making her wonder if the first Christmas might have had such lovely stars. She almost expected to hear the heralding angels.

During the short trip, Darcy could not keep his eyes off his wife. Her joy at her experience thrilled his heart. How he loved her and thanked the Lord that she was his! He certainly yearned to be her husband in all ways, but at that moment, he was content to watch her.

The service was short but poignant, filled with all of the joyfulness that the celebration of the birth of a Saviour can bring. The small chapel was filled to overflowing with many of the household staff standing in the back and at the sides of the sanctuary. Songs of praise seemed to lift those congregated into heavenly realms.

Once the vicar had prayed and pronounced the benediction, Darcy, with Elizabeth on his arm, led his family from the chapel. They stood outside, waiting for the sleighs to return while exchanging holiday greetings with the few neighbours who travelled to Pemberley Chapel for the service. It seemed that the neighbours had been eager to meet the new mistress and had been willing to brave the cold to do it.

Elizabeth was extremely happy when their sleigh pulled up. As much as she enjoyed meeting the neighbours, she wanted to return to the house. The letter she had written seemed to cry out to be put into the hands of its intended recipient.

Her eagerness must have been evident to her husband because as he handed her into the sleigh, Darcy whispered, "Do not worry, my love. I will make sure that we make it to our rooms as soon as possible."

Darcy's words were prophetic, as it was not many minutes after returning to the house that each family member wished the other, "Happy Christmas and a good night," before all retired to their own bed chambers.

Following the last guest up the staircase, Darcy put his arm around Elizabeth's waist and whispered, "I am happy that I was correct in my estimation of how quickly we would be able to be alone in our rooms."

Elizabeth only smiled up at him by way of an answer. Her heart seemed to have taken up residence in her throat as she thought of the letter lying in her writing desk. Would Fitzwilliam think her forward or improper because of what she asked in the missive? Maybe she should wait to give it to him. Would the fear come back to her again unexpectedly? How would she manage if it did? Her thoughts whirled about in such a way that she did not immediately notice that they had entered their sitting room until Darcy's anxious voice called out her name.

"I beg your pardon, my love," she croaked out as her face turned crimson. "I was completely lost in my thoughts. Did you say something to me?"

"There is no need for pardon, dearest," Darcy insisted as he pulled her into his arms. He wondered what could be causing his wife to seem so uneasy. "I was only worried that you did not speak when I asked if you wanted some wine before I brought you the last of the gifts."

Looking up at his face, concern still evident on it, Elizabeth caressed his cheek and smiled as the anxiety left her body. Here was the man who loved her enough to love and raise a baby that was not his own and who had proven that even when he was upset with her, he would not turn against her. She knew that tonight would be perfect, no matter what his response to her request would be.

After kissing him quickly, she said, "I think I would like a small glass of the plum wine your aunt and uncle gave us."

"An excellent idea!" Darcy smiled and found one of the bottles from the Matlocks' estate he had sent to their rooms earlier. He knew that the wine was of a fine quality and that it would help ease what seemed to be his wife's flustered nerves. He poured out two glasses and took one to his Beth. "Here you are, my love. I think you will approve."

After taking a sip, Elizabeth smiled up at him. "It is delicious. I will have to tell Aunt and Uncle how much I like it."

Darcy took her hand and led her to a table on which sat a large box tied with a giant red bow. Elizabeth had not noticed it when they entered the room. He pulled out a chair and indicated for her to sit. "I have been excited to give this to you. I wish to fulfil a promise I made to you."

Pulling at the ends of the ribbon, Elizabeth removed it from the box before she lifted the lid. Inside, she found a fencing mask, a foil, and padded fencing vest along with a white jacket and breeches. When she came to the last item, she frowned. "I am expected to wear these?"

"I saw no other way that I could teach you to fence than to have you wear the proper clothing. A gown would hamper your movements and keep you from defending yourself." Darcy saw the look of trepidation on his wife and promised, "I know that we can trust Sarah not to say anything, especially if you explain the reason you are learning to fence, and I shall order all of the servants away from the ballroom when we practice."

She still did not look completely convinced, but Elizabeth nodded her acceptance. Thinking that this was the only gift Darcy was going to give her, she stood to go to her desk for the letter when he reached behind the box with the fencing gear and handed her another much smaller one of ornately carved and inlaid woods and mother of pearl. For its size, the gift had weight to it, so she placed it on the table in front of her before she undid the latch to open it. Before her lay a beautifully crafted pistol, undersized in comparison to any she had seen before. On the grip was a silver and gold replica of the Darcy crest, surrounded by tiny garnet cabochons.

"Oh, Fitzwilliam, it is so very lovely!" Lizzy exclaimed enthusiastically. "It is almost too beautiful to be truly a weapon."

"I assure you that it is indeed a weapon." He reached over to lift it from its velvet-lined bed. "It has a unique firing system. A friend of mine from Cambridge has been working on this weapon, which fires more than one shot before need of reloading and is easier to reload than conventional guns. This is one of only a few prototypes. I have one as well, although it is a bit larger. I have spent some time practicing with my own piece, so that I will be able to teach you how to use yours."

"Thank you, Fitzwilliam," Elizabeth threw her arms around Darcy's neck. "The fact that you thought to find such things for me to help me overcome my fears overwhelms me with love and gratitude."

Elizabeth kissed him soundly and pulled out of his arms to hasten to her desk. After retrieving the letter, she handed it to him before she lost her courage and said, "Please read this and know that I mean every word from the bottom of my heart."

With curiosity, Darcy unfolded the missive and began to read.

> *Happy Christmas to you, my dearest Fitzwilliam,*
>
> *I am compelled to write this letter because I do not believe I could speak the words out loud. Firstly, please know I have considered long what I want to relate and am firm in my resolve that it is what I wish.*
>
> *Secondly, I have to tell you once more of my great love for you. Although I did not always have the same regard for you as I do now, I am happy to say that loving you and being loved by you makes me the happiest of women. You have shown me more than kindness since you found me that day. I never expected that you would want to marry me or that you would love the babe as you do, but it seems that each day you find a new way to show your love, even when I am not always so pleased by its expression.*
>
> *As I have pondered the love that I feel for you, I realized that we are missing one thing to make our marriage complete. I know that you told me that we would wait until after the baby's birth to consummate our marriage, but I do not wish to wait.*
>
> *My darling husband, I want us to become one in every way it is possible for us to be. I blush to even write the words, but please, Fitzwilliam, make me yours.*
>
> > *Your grateful and loving wife,*
> > *Elizabeth*

Darcy reread the letter before lifting his eyes to hers. He searched her face for confirmation of what she had written and saw her faint embarrassment and a bit of apprehension but no hesitation. His heart began to race at the thought of loving her as he had desired to from the first night of their marriage.

After taking several deep calming breaths, he asked, "But what of the babe? Will it not come to harm if we...?" He could not finish the sentence for his own discomfiture.

Elizabeth leaned forward in her chair to take his hands in hers. "Mrs. Reynolds assured me that no harm would come to the baby. It is still so tiny and is quite safely sheltered within my body."

Darcy's face paled in shock. "You told Mrs. Reynolds about the baby?"

"No, my love, I only told her that I have not had my courses this month. I asked her if marital relations would injure a baby if there was one. She was very helpful and told me that often a husband and wife safely engage in such until close to the birth unless the doctor instructs otherwise."

Elizabeth's smile grew as she remembered the scene of the day before. "She also told me that I could only be certain I was with child once I felt the quickening, but that stomach upset was another early sign."

As Elizabeth spoke, Darcy visibly relaxed. He had no worries that his housekeeper would spread any gossip, but he also did not want her to think less of them.

"My dearest, do you truly want this?" he questioned hoarsely. Darcy determined to seek only to know her true desires and not his own on the matter. He could not help but wonder if Wickham's attack would make her nervous of the intimacy. He would wait any amount of time needed to help her be at ease with the marriage bed.

Elizabeth stood, and since she was still holding his hands, she tugged until he stood as well. She wrapped her arms around his waist, looked up at him, and said, "I admit to being somewhat fearful. I do not think someone in my position could be completely without trepidation, but truly, I want it more than I can say."

A broad smile brightened Darcy's face as he lifted her into his arms. "I believe it is time for us to go to bed."

"Shall I ring for Sarah to help me undress?" she asked with an answering grin on her face as all thoughts of Wickham's actions were banished by the loving expression upon her husband's face.

"No, I believe I will be quite able to assist you tonight." And with that he carried her through the door to his chamber.

---

[1] *The Holy Bible -- The Authorized King James Version*

CHAPTER THIRTY-TWO

The sound of the chamber maid seeing to the fire awakened Elizabeth. The bed curtains sheltered her and her husband from the outside world, and the thought caused her to smile. She lay comfortably on her side with Darcy spooned against her back. Never had she expected the feeling of belonging that now filled her entire being.

The night before had been beyond her imagining, and Elizabeth finally understood what her mother had told her before the nuptials. More than the exquisite pleasure they had experienced was the complete sense that she and her beloved had indeed become united. They were now two halves of one whole in the great, God-ordained mystery of marriage. When an overwhelming urge to see her beloved husband's face came upon her, Elizabeth turned in his arms, only to find him smiling at her.

"Good morning, my love," he whispered softly before he kissed her.

Once the kiss was over, Elizabeth returned in a low voice, "Good morning, my dearest husband."

Darcy turned to move back the bed curtains. Upon finding that the maid had finished her chore, he took Elizabeth back into his arms and inquired, "How are you faring this morning?"

A broad smile covered her face and her eyes danced with joy. "I do not think I have ever fared better. I did not know that I could feel this way. I believe that I can say without a single doubt that this is the best Christmas Day of my entire life."

Darcy's deep chuckle and smile made the day seem even better.

"Happy Christmas, Beth, my beloved wife." He kissed her on the nose.

After she returned his greeting, Elizabeth sighed exaggeratedly. "I suppose we will be required to greet our guests sometime this morning."

"Yes, my dear," he said with a laugh. "I am afraid that we must spend time with them. It would be inhospitable not to do so."

"If we must," Elizabeth said after another dramatic exhalation. "Would you please ring for Sarah so that she will bring my tea?"

Before Darcy could do as she asked, Elizabeth placed a hand on his arm. "I love you, Fitzwilliam."

A look of deep adoration suffused his face as he leaned in to kiss her once more before he said, "I love you, dearest, loveliest Elizabeth."

~*~

Breakfast was delayed because the party had gone to bed so late. Indeed, it was not late by Town standards, but it definitely was according to country manners. As each of the guests arrived in the breakfast parlour and filled a plate from the sideboard, cheerful greetings of "Happy Christmas" were exchanged.

Elizabeth was surprised to find a small pouch near her place at the table after she had filled her plate and sat down. She looked up at her husband and saw that he was grinning. "What is this, sir?" she asked.

"Mayhap it is another gift from Father Christmas," Darcy answered mysteriously. "I would suggest that you open it to find out."

After lifting the pouch from the table, Elizabeth realized that it was one of the courier packets she had seen upon her husband's desk. Her speculation was correct, for when she lifted the flap, she found several letters. Since the top one was in the familiar hand of her father, she had to suppress the desire to squeal in delight.

A few letters from her family had come the first week after their arrival at Pemberley, but she had not received a missive for almost a fortnight. She had been assured that the post was not always reliable during the winter months. The snows or heavy rains could cause many delays.

"When did they come?"

"I sent a courier along with your most recent correspondence to your family and the gifts we purchased for them when we were last in Lambton." Darcy explained as he relished his wife's happiness at receiving the correspondence. "I told him to wait for any letters they might want to send back. A heavy snow storm in southern Derbyshire slowed him down enough that he only arrived late last night. I did not know of his return until a few minutes before arriving to breakfast."

"Thank you, my dear, for thinking to do this." She patted the stack of letters and began to eat heartily. Wishing to extend the pleasure of anticipation, she did not hurry her meal.

Just the knowledge of the missives was a comfort. Throughout the holiday preparation and celebration, Elizabeth had missed her family at Longbourn. Of course, her husband and his family had done much to keep her from overwhelming feelings of homesickness, but she could not help but long to hear how they were doing. Fitzwilliam had obviously understood her well enough to know how much the letters would mean to her.

Once she had finished her breakfast, Elizabeth excused herself, went to her study, and sat in a comfortable chair. Randomly pulling one from the pile of letters, she began to read the one from Lydia.

Dear Lizzy,

We were all very surprised to see the rider from Pemberley with letters and parcels. None of us expected to receive more gifts from you and your husband besides the ones that we already received.

I am certain that your husband must be one of the most generous of men. Oh, Lizzy, I hope that I will be able to find such a man when I am older. I have truly worked on improving myself since you have been gone. At times, I do fall back into my old silly ways. I admit that at times I am drawn to flirt with officers, but I really try to emulate you and Jane. Hopefully, I have not been too much of an embarrassment to my family. I find I miss you dreadfully now that you are gone. Jane is helpful, but you seem able to help me understand things so much better.

The Christmas Assembly was so much fun. I confess that I danced as much as ever, but I tried to remember to keep my tongue under good regulation as you advised. I do think I must have succeeded, for people were quite astonished that I did not giggle or run about as in the past. I tried very hard to imitate Jane's serenity, which was difficult. She is such an angel.

I even sat with Mary at supper. Do you know that she smiles more often since becoming engaged to Mr. Collins? I still lack understanding of what she sees in him, but I know she is happy.

I did laugh, in private of course, after my mother took me aside at one time during the night to see if I was feverish. Poor Mama, I do not think that she knows what to do with me these days.

Please extend my thanks to Mr. Darcy and my affectionate greetings to Miss Darcy. I look forward to seeing you all again for Jane's wedding.

Your affectionate sister, Lydia

Elizabeth looked up from the letter and smiled widely. It warmed her heart to see how Lydia was working on improving herself.

Next was a missive from her mother.

My dear Mrs. Darcy,

Elizabeth could not help but laugh at her mother's formality and endeavour at pretention. She returned to the page before her.

I do hope that this missive finds you and your illustrious husband in good health and enjoying your holiday with his family. I am certain that you will enjoy a bountiful Christmas, as Mr. Darcy has already proven his generosity with his outpouring of gifts to us. Please do give your dear husband our thanks for the presents he has so graciously bestowed upon us. Knowing his good taste from his previous gifts, I do not have to open them to be sure that they are of excellent quality and value.

We continue in health and good spirits at Longbourn. Mr. Bennet continues to vex me by not allowing us to go to London after Boxing Day. I am sure that Mr. Bingley and Mr. Collins would be much happier with their respective brides if they were to appear in new gowns from Town on their wedding day.

Jane and Mary, along with their fiancés, have agreed that it would be more economical to be married in a double ceremony, so I am pleased to tell you that they will be married the first Saturday in April.

I must admit that I am relieved to have a longer period in which to plan this time. No one in attendance at your wedding has ever spoken negatively about the arrangements for your nuptials, but I am sure that I could have managed a grander affair if you had given me more time. Ah well, you were married by a license, and few could afford to do so.

The Gardiners will arrive later today. I am afraid my nerves will be greatly tried by the sound of all the children, but I will bear it without complaint, as always.

Your father tells me that I must close since Mr. Darcy's man wants to leave post haste.

    Sincerely yours,

    Mother

PS: I do hope that you have been attentive to your husband's needs. I am certain that he is very desirous of an heir.

Again, she laughed at her mother's typical style. Elizabeth could almost hear her mother's voice as she read what she had written.

In her letter, Kitty also told her of the Christmas assembly and how Lydia had changed, but most of her communiqué was on the subject of Mr. Lucas. At the dance in Meryton, Samuel had asked if he would be allowed to seek Mr. Bennet's permission to court her. Two pages were barely enough to hold all of Kitty's raptures on the subject.

The letter from the middle Bennet sister was the next and rather surprising in its tone. Mary did not moralize or preach, but rather she wrote simply and directly of her thoughts on the preparations for the holiday and the wedding. The biggest surprise was her confession of a wish that she, too, could be married quickly as Elizabeth had. Mary and even Mr. Collins were apparently becoming taxed by her mother's raptures and excessive plans.

Elizabeth could tell by what Mary wrote about her betrothed that her affection for him was growing even deeper. This fact made Lizzy happy. She knew that her soon-to-be brother could be trying, but from what she was reading, he had begun to work on being less sycophantic. He had even managed to take a logical stand during a debate with her father, who did not hesitate to show his admiration for the well thought out argument.

Her father's letter was the second to the last she pulled from the bundle. Elizabeth opened it in eager anticipation.

> *My little Lizzy,*
>
> *Your old father misses you quite dreadfully. It is evidenced by the fact that you are receiving this letter. We are all well, but there have been many changes in our family life, not the least of which is your absence.*
>
> *I do miss you, my Lizzy, but I am faring better than I had expected, though it seems I have you and your new family to thank for it. Lydia, it seems, has taken your advice to heart and has taken great strides toward reining in her old silly ways in exchange for much more prudent pursuits. Soon after you left, she asked me to teach her to play chess, since you enjoyed it so much. Imagine my surprise to find that she has an aptitude for the game. Of course, she is not yet very adept at it, but I believe that she will someday be nearly as good as you are.*
>
> *This is not, however, the most astonishing of her actions. One afternoon we had plans for her to read with me from one of your favourite books of poetry. I had been struggling for some time with the estate accounts. I could not balance them and was very frustrated when she knocked on the library door. I admit that I barked at her because of my aggravation.*
>
> *Lydia did not take offence as I had expected, but instead, she asked me what was bothering me. I was so shocked by this unusual reaction that I explained my dilemma. She asked if she could look at the ledger and I allowed her to see it. Within minutes, my youngest, and heretofore the one I had thought the silliest of my daughters, pointed to the double posting of a bill from the butcher and told me what the correct sum for the particular week should be. I was so pleased at finally being finished with the accounts that I offered to allow her to buy some new ribbons. I was certainly surprised that she politely declined my offer, saying that she had already spent her pocket allowance and would wait for new ribbons until it was time for her next allotment.*

I must say that my eyes were opened. I realized to my great shame that I had never taken any time to know and understand my three youngest daughters. After you were born, and I found a like-minded soul in you, I allowed my wife to take over the education and shaping of their minds. I determined on that day that I would break out of my complacency and tend to my girls before I lost the opportunity.

Mary and Kitty are not so eager to spend time with their old father as Lydia is, but I found that as I persevere, they are warming to the idea. Mary is blooming as she basks in the love of Mr. Collins. She seems to be open to reading a broader range of books than she has ever done before. I have enjoyed several debates with her on the merits of certain tomes. Her bent is still toward a more spiritual outlook, but it has been tempered and has softened, no longer so judgmental as it had previously been.

Mr. Collins, too, has surprised me with his tender regard and actions toward my middle daughter. I have received two letters from him since you left, and although they were still quite wordy, they were not full of the obsequious compliments and false humility that characterized his former missives to me. He is due to arrive this afternoon to spend the holidays. Since your aunt and uncle Gardiner are also coming, he is to stay at Netherfield as Mr. Bingley's guest. All-in-all, I believe that I will be able to tolerate all of my sons-in-law, present and future.

Kitty spends a great deal of time at Lucas Lodge when her young man is not visiting at Longbourn. I am certain that she wrote that the young Lucas scion has asked to court her and received my permission. I believe that it is a good thing that you have married, my dear, because if it were not for the reduction in costs that your leaving has afforded us, I would not have the funds for the extra food that is needed to feed him. There is, however, a benefit to his coming. I have learned a great deal about the newer farming techniques and have decided to make use of them in the spring.

I suppose that I should close, so that the young man who is at this moment enjoying Cook's fine fare can complete his task of delivering the letters we have all written to you.

I look forward to reading your letter and to seeing you in April. Greet my son-in-law and his family for me.

I remain your affectionate father,

Thomas Bennet

Lizzy was pleased that her father had decided to get to know his younger daughters better. It seemed that many changes were taking place at her old home.

Eagerly, Elizabeth opened the final letter, the one from Jane.

Dearest Sister,

I scarcely know how to begin, as so many things have happened since you left Longbourn. Everyone is well, but the most astounding alterations have overtaken the family.

Lydia seems to be the one most transformed. She rarely mentions an officer or red coat. Although she is still lively and enjoys laughing as much as ever, my sister makes better choices as to the time and place in which she gives rein to her amusement. She has spent a great deal of time with my father in his library and comes to my room to talk about how she can be more of a lady. She even walks out in the mornings, though I do not think she goes so far as you once did.

My mother has been worried that Lydia is not acting as she would normally. After the Christmas Assembly, she called on the apothecary to buy a tonic for her youngest daughter. It took Father, Lydia, and myself to convince Mama that Lydia was merely maturing. Finally, when Lydia told her that she was trying to be more like Miss Darcy, Mama seemed to comprehend and has not bothered Lydia about it since.

Charles and I almost wish that we could have been married when you and Mr. Darcy did. We are tiring of the constant wedding planning. We have made one adjustment that will, I am sure, restore peace sooner to the halls of Longbourn. We are to share our wedding day with Mary and Mr. Collins.

Mary had approached me to ask if we would consider it. She had seen the turmoil caused by my mother over Charles' and my nuptials and did not want to be the sole target of the same machinations. After my betrothed and I discussed it, we decided to agree. Although Mama did complain a little about the change, we were able to convince her of the likelihood that she could save money and have still more guests and decorations with a combined ceremony. I smile when I hear her talk of the plans as if they were her own idea.

I hope that you, my new brother, and his sister are doing well and will enjoy a wonderful holiday. I have not read your latest letter as yet because we are to hurry our writing so that Mr. Darcy's man can leave to ride back to Pemberley.

I long to see you again, dearest Lizzy. My wedding day cannot be soon enough for me for more than one reason.
Your loving sister and friend,
Jane

Elizabeth sighed from pure happiness. The reading of the letters had dissolved the feeling of homesickness she had been experiencing during the past couple of days. It was as if she had had an intimate talk with her entire family. Quickly, she stowed the letters in her desk and hurried to find her husband to thank him again.

CHAPTER THIRTY-THREE

That morning after church service, it was obvious that the whole group was in a festive and jovial mood, which paved the way for the rest of the day. Throughout the day, much laughter and happy conversation rang out. First, the colonel suggested a walk in the snow and promised no repeat of the previous snow fight. Everyone, including the earl and countess, took a turn about the cleared paths through the gardens.

Once they had all returned from their bracing ramble and enjoyed some warming tea, Viscount Matley said that he would like to practice some music and suggested that any of the others who would like to do so should join him, so that they could have another concert that evening. The viscountess, Richard, and Georgiana joined him, leaving the remainder of the party to pleasant conversation.

The rest of the day passed in familial harmony and enjoyment with good food and drink a seemingly constant part of the merriment. Music and games of charades and cards added to the festivities. By the end of the day, each person vouchsafed that it had been one among the most agreeable holidays they had ever spent.

~*~

As previously planned, Boxing Day at Pemberley was to include the whole of the party. Two sleighs were ordered, and the boxes to be given to the tenants were divided between the two conveyances.

Smiling, Elizabeth watched as the footmen loaded the sleighs with eagerness and enthusiasm. In keeping with another Pemberley tradition, both the household staff and otherwise, were given most of Boxing Day as their own holiday from work. Since she had worked out a schedule with Mrs. Reynolds beforehand, Elizabeth knew that the family meals would have been prepared in advance so that only a couple servants would be required to serve them. If a need would arise that the mistress and housekeeper had not planned for in advance, Mrs. Reynolds would see to it herself if at all possible.

Darcy and Elizabeth, along with Anne and the colonel, rode in one of the conveyances while the Matlocks, the Matleys, and Georgiana took the other. Those of the tenants to whom the Darcys brought food were completely charmed by the new mistress and delighted by the jovial attitude of the robust colonel and the somewhat shy Miss de Bourgh. The lemon drops and other candies that Elizabeth distributed did not fail to win the hearts of the children wherever they stopped.

The tenants that the Matlock's party visited were perhaps not so relaxed as those visited by the Darcys, but the honour of being brought food by an earl and a viscount made up for any lack of ease. For many a year to come, the people of Pemberley would speak of the mistress's first Christmas on the estate as the finest and most generous they had ever before experienced. From that day forward, old and young alike sang the praises of Mrs. Darcy and told of the obvious love the couple shared.

After four more days, and with the snow having melted enough for the journey, the Matlock party left for their estate. The routine of the household became more sedate, though not indolent. Elizabeth and Georgiana, under the capable guidance of Mrs. Reynolds, learned more of the household management of Pemberley.

Elizabeth had insisted that her new sister gain more knowledge of running a household along with herself, as Georgiana would someday be the mistress of her own home. Lizzy felt that her new sister needed to know more than simply how to preside as hostess as she had done for her brother before his marriage.

Although there were many differences between Pemberley and Longbourn, many of the principles she had learned from her mother stood her in good stead as mistress of her new home. More than once, Mrs. Reynolds marvelled at Mrs. Darcy's knowledge and ease in the execution of her duties. It was obvious to the housekeeper that this was not merely a country gentlewoman. She was proud to work for such a well-trained and competent mistress. She thought to herself, *I will be able to do my work, happy with the knowledge that such a lady is mistress.*

The rest of Elizabeth's time was varied and fulfilling. The company of her beloved and his sister kept her happily engaged. Long conversations with Georgiana helped her understand the young girl. Although Georgiana seemed timid, Lizzy soon found that her new sister merely tended to observe before becoming involved in discussions. She did enter into discourse more freely as she felt more at ease with her company. In that respect, she was very much like her brother.

Darcy began to teach Lizzy how to fence and to use her new gun. At first, they spent more of their time on the fencing lessons due to inclement weather, but often on a snowy but sunny day, the couple could be found at target practice. Nothing had prepared Elizabeth for the pride she felt in finally hitting the target. She also learned the care and cleaning of her weapon.

Fencing was good exercise, but she did not enjoy it so much as she did firing her small gun, and soon, her growing middle became a hindrance to the activity. Elizabeth realized that, in any case, she would not likely defend herself with a foil. The expertise she was gaining using her pistol worked to assuage the fears caused by the attack. Acquiring the skills needed to use the tiny weapon helped her feel a great deal calmer and in control, despite the fact that she knew she would likely never have to use it. She continually thanked God for His gift of her husband. He was helping her once again in regaining more of her former equilibrium.

~*~

As the days turned into weeks and months, hints of spring began to make their presence known. By early March, the final snow of winter had disappeared. Snowbells and crocus pushed their way through the soil to be greeted by birdsong and budding trees.

One brightly sunlit morning, Elizabeth prevailed upon Darcy to join her in a tour of the grounds. For days, she had desired to tour the park about which she had heard so much. So it was that after the ground had dried sufficiently and Darcy had finished all the arrangements for the early spring planting, he agreed to show his bride the lovely environs of Pemberley.

Arm in arm, the couple first walked down to the small lake in front of the house and around its perimeter. From there, they moved onto a path that led to a stream and through a lovely grove of tall oaks. The ground next to the path was covered with violets and tiny daisies.

"Oh, Fitzwilliam, I love violets," Elizabeth exclaimed happily. "I would like to pick some."

"Of course," Darcy agreed as he watched the delight play across his wife's lovely face. Her countenance fairly glowed with health. She had stopped feeling queasy in the mornings and had a good appetite. Her figure, though as lithe as ever, had changed. Soon they would have to announce that she was expecting because he was certain that some of the staff had already observed her body's alteration.

As he opened his mouth to raise the subject, Darcy heard Elizabeth's surprised cry of "Oh!" and saw her straighten from picking the flowers, her free hand over her stomach.

He rushed to her side in panic. "What is it, Elizabeth?" He scanned her face for signs of illness but found only a brilliant smile. "Are you well? Is there something wrong with the babe?"

"Oh no, we are both well indeed," she replied giddily. "I felt the quickening. It was like tiny flutterings right here." She showed him by placing his hand where she had felt the movement.

"I cannot feel anything," Darcy exclaimed in disappointment. He pushed his hand a little harder against her.

"I can barely feel it myself. It is so light." Lifting her hand to his face, she said, "Do not be discouraged. I am certain you will have many opportunities to experience the baby's movements."

"When do you suppose that we should make others aware of your condition?"

"Soon," said she as she smiled at him. "I think that some of the staff already suspect. We have been married for over three months now. I believe that we should begin at Easter. We are to travel to Matlock for the holiday, are we not? And if we send the news ahead of us by post to the rest of the family, the excitement may be somewhat less intense by the time we reach Longbourn."

"An excellent idea, my love, but I would like for us to tell Georgiana first before we go to Matlock. Would you object if we told her at dinner the day before we leave?" Darcy looked eager for her agreement.

"Oh, Fitzwilliam!" she cried. "I would love for her to be the first to know about the baby."

"Until that time, we will continue to keep the news to ourselves."

~*~

Georgiana was completely thrilled by the news, as was all of the family at Matlock. His aunt spent a great deal of time with Elizabeth, planning how she would come mid-summer to help decorate the nursery. They spent time working out a list of baby clothing that would be needed.

Elizabeth admitted to Darcy upon their retiring for the night that she was overwhelmed by the sheer volume of things a tiny baby seemed to need.

"I hope that my aunt does not take too much upon herself," he commented. "I am sure your mother might want to be involved in the planning."

She sighed, "I am certain that she will, but I hope to discourage her from coming for the birth. I truly wish that she not suspect that the baby is early. Mama does not always practice discretion in what she says, as you well know."

"I will talk to your father. He will understand that you wish to be recovered from the birth before your mother comes." He pondered the situation for a few moments before he said, "I think that we will invite your family here in late

September. You should be well by then. Your mother will have ample opportunity to fuss over you and the baby at that time."

"That is a brilliant solution," Elizabeth cried enthusiastically and added with a grin, "And if we just happen to be planning a ball at Michaelmas, she will be more than happy to agree to the plan,"

"Only for you, my love, would I assent to give a ball," he agreed with reluctance, "if you think that you will be up to the task."

"With my mother and our sisters to assist me, I am certain I shall."

"Then it is settled; we shall give a ball."

~*~

That night Elizabeth had a nightmare. This dream was not the usual one in which she relived the attack. This one began with the delivery of the baby. Everything went fairly well until the midwife handed her the infant and said, "How could you have thought to fool us, Mrs. Darcy. How could you bring another man's child into the Darcy family? It is obvious that this baby is not your husband's."

Before she could speak, the room filled with family, friends, and servants, all chanting over and over, "Not your husband's, not your husband's." Elizabeth tried to find Darcy in the crowd, but the faces were indistinguishable blurs.

The baby began a thin, sad wail. Elizabeth began to rock the infant in an effort to soothe it, but as it continued to cry, she joined it. Her voice thick with tears, she called out, "Fitzwilliam, where are you? I need your help. Our baby will not stop crying. I do not know what to do."

The vague outline of a tall, dark man began to emerge from the misty crowd. Elizabeth's heart temporarily leaped with joy. "Fitzwilliam, you are finally here. Come see our baby."

Her joy quickly turned to terror when the man's face came into focus. It was George Wickham, smiling broadly down upon her. "Your husband will not help you this time. I came for what is mine. You did not really believe that Darcy would let you keep my bastard. Besides, you do not truly wish to be reminded of me everyday, do you?" He snatched the baby from her arms and ran back into the mist.

Momentarily, she felt relief that she would no longer have to face the misty crowd's scorn about the baby. However, at the idea of losing the child, she was overcome with grief. Elizabeth tried to get out of the bed to go after him, but the midwife held her down. "It is better this way. The babe would not be welcome here."

Crying out in anguish, Elizabeth fought to sit up.

Darcy awoke to his wife's weeping and thrashing about in her sleep. Recognizing the signs of a nightmare, he pulled her into his arms and whispered softly, "Elizabeth, my love, it is just a dream. Wake up for me, dearest. Hush now, hush."

Slowly, his words had the desired effect. Elizabeth ceased her struggling and relaxed. Opening her eyes, she rasped out, "It was a horrible dream," and began to weep against his shoulder.

"Do you think it would help to tell me about it?" Darcy asked steadily, though he felt anything but steady himself.

For what seemed like ages to Darcy, Elizabeth merely continued to weep into his shoulder. Just as he had decided to call for Sarah's assistance, his wife ceased her crying, moved out of his arms, and reached for her handkerchief.

Darcy waited until after she had wiped her eyes before he pulled her back into his embrace. "Shall I call for Sarah? What can I do to help?" As he asked the questions, he rubbed soothing circles along her back.

After a few small sniffling, false starts, Elizabeth began to describe her dream. Fear, regret, and even guilt coloured her voice when she reached the part where Wickham took the baby. "I cannot believe I felt relieved for even a moment. I have come to love this little one. How could I even think of such a thing?"

Darcy quickly sent up a prayer for wisdom. He did not know how to comfort his wife. Having no experience to fall back on, he decided to speak from his heart. "I know not what to tell you. Dreams are such mysterious workings of our minds. You must know that when you give birth, I will be close by. Although I might wish at times that we were not in the position of having a child that is not of my body, know that I do look forward to greeting her upon her arrival. I shall never allow anyone, especially Wickham, to come between me and the babe."

Reaching down, Darcy lifted her chin with his finger. Once she met his gaze, he said, "I love you more than I can say. My heart aches for what you have suffered, but I have been so proud of your strength and resilience. We shall trust that God will help us through whatever comes our way."

Elizabeth listened to Darcy, and once she looked into his eyes, she saw the love reflected there, Understanding dawned upon her that although he could not guarantee she would not have nightmares again or have problems because of her ordeal, he would walk beside her. They would overcome it.

"I love you, Fitzwilliam Darcy, with all of my heart. Thank you for loving me and for the patience you have shown to me. I am so blessed." Elizabeth lifted her head and kissed him with all of the emotion flowing within her. Soon, the nightmare was forgotten in the passion of the moment. It was quite some time before the couple returned to sleep, and this time their slumber was uninterrupted and restorative.

~*~

The Easter service at the Matlock parish church was lovely and inspiring. Elizabeth was introduced to many of the congregation she had not met at the large dinner party that Lord and Lady Matlock had hosted in their honour that week.

After breaking her fast the next morning, Elizabeth went for a solitary walk around the grounds. Darcy was seeing to the last minute plans for their travel to Hertfordshire on the morrow. Matlock House was grand, majestic, and, no doubt, a masterpiece of architecture, but she already missed their lovely home at Pemberley.

As she walked, Elizabeth daydreamed of how it would be once the baby was born. She and Fitzwilliam would truly be a family with the birth of the little one. Smiling broadly, she thought that her husband would likely be a doting papa if his behaviour toward her was any indication. She would have to keep diligent watch so as to keep the child from being spoiled by him.

Elizabeth decided to return to the house as she wanted to check on the packing of their things for their leave taking. The excitement of seeing her family again quickened her step. As she rounded a curved hedge that lined the path and took the fork in the path that led back to Matlock House, she noticed a figure striding toward her dressed in scarlet.

A fog of fear, the one which had been her companion when she was still at Longbourn and during the earlier days of her marriage, clouded her vision and halted her step. Elizabeth reached for her reticule before she realized what she was doing. However, she had not thought to carry her pistol that morning. The terror of the attack had lessened so much in the past few months that she had left the gun in its original case in her trunk while at Matlock.

Just as she thought that she would faint from fear, Elizabeth lifted up a prayer and remembered the words of her maid's aunt Sarah. She brought to mind the vision of the smoke rising from the fire she had made using the pages upon which she had written of the attack. Those images dispelled the fog in which she was held captive just in time to comprehend that the uniformed officer who was now even closer to her was none other than Colonel Fitzwilliam. Besides, her mind logically told her, Wickham would no longer wear the red coat of a militiaman. He was likely nearing the West Indies, if not already there.

"Richard," Elizabeth greeted him with a shaky voice. "I am surprised to see you in your uniform."

"Ah, yes," he answered with a quick bow and a grin. "After you left for your walk, two express letters for Father and a dispatch for me from my major general arrived. One of the letters for Father was from the steward at Rosings asking for his assistance with a problem there, while the other was from Aunt Catherine's companion. It seems my aunt is in poor health and wishes for my father to attend her.

"Both are urgent enough for personal attention. However, as my father cannot be in two places at once, he has asked that being as familiar as I am with Rosings I go to Kent to see to the need there while he travels to Briar Mist to visit my aunt.

He paused in his speech to offer his arm as they began to walk back to the house. As they moved down the path, he continued, "My own dispatch, though not so pressing, asked that I tend to some matter for the major general in Kent after my leave. I thought that I would conclude the business and see to the concern at Rosings. I will then go straight to Hertfordshire. I do not want to miss Bingley's wedding. I came to find you so that I could bid you farewell, for I am off as soon as we return to the house. Father will leave first thing in the morning."

"I do hope that Lady Catherine will recover and that the matter at Rosings is not too serious," she said, expressing her genuine concern.

"I am fairly certain that I will be able to resolve the situation at Rosings quickly," he assured her. "However, I am concerned about my aunt. Father is worried as well, but we can only do so much. I believe that he plans to ask his own personal physician to accompany him. If anyone can help Aunt Catherine, Mr. Connelly can."

Soon, the colonel bid his family farewell, and he rode off to the south.

The rest of the family tried to hope for the best. Anne de Bourgh was the most worried. No matter the past, Lady Catherine was her mother, and concern for her prompted Anne to ask to be allowed to accompany her uncle to the north. After some discussion, she was convinced that the trip could be made more quickly without her, and since the viscount and his wife were leaving for their estate, Lady Matlock wanted her companionship.

CHAPTER THIRTY-FOUR

The travellers, including the earl and the Darcys, breakfasted early and were off before seven o'clock. The route Darcy planned for them to take was different from their usual one, as they would not travel through Town on their way to Hertfordshire.

Elizabeth soon was lost in the grandeur of the ever changing scenery. As their carriage travelled south through the luscious spring greenery and lovely bursts of colour from the flowering trees, shrubs, and fields, she became more excited about the journey and their destination.

As Elizabeth had expected, Darcy endeavoured to make the trip as pleasant and comfortable as possible. Each place they stopped, whether for a change of horses, for meals, or for the night, proved his care for her well-being and that of his sister. He had made the arrangements ahead of time so that the finest of food and drink were available. Only one other time had she travelled in such luxury and that was on their wedding trip, which was also carefully arranged by Darcy.

It rained on the second day of their travel, but, happily, it was not enough to bog down the wheels or to slow down the trip in any appreciable way. So it was that late the afternoon of their third day, they arrived at their destination.

"Welcome to Netherfield," Charles Bingley greeted them as soon as they climbed down from the carriage. "I hope your journey went well."

"Thank you, Bingley," Darcy answered. "It did."

"Let us go in," Bingley waved his hand toward the door. "I am sure that you all would like to refresh yourselves."

Darcy offered his arm to his wife as Bingley did the same for Georgiana. Elizabeth leaned heavily on her husband. The last part of the journey had not been on good road, and she was greatly fatigued.

"I believe that is a good idea," Darcy spoke as he felt the difference in Elizabeth's hold on his arm. "Elizabeth is tired and could use the rest."

"Of course," Charles exclaimed and nodded to the housekeeper. "Mrs. Nichols will show you to your rooms."

Darcy rejoined Bingley after changing from his travelling clothes. Elizabeth and Georgiana had both decided to rest before coming back downstairs.

"Congratulations, Darcy," Charles proclaimed as he poured them both a glass of brandy. "Jane told me of your news. I think it is wonderful."

"Thank you, Bingley," Darcy answered as he took the snifter from his friend. "We are delighted."

"I hope that Mrs. Darcy is well."

"She is tired, as must be expected after such travel," Darcy explained. "However, she has been feeling quite well."

"I am glad to hear it." Charles took a good swallow of the brandy before he changed the subject. "I hope that your plans for the spring at Pemberley are going well. I remember how much time you spent on outlining the plantings the one spring I spent with you there."

"I was able to get everything into place before I left." Darcy sipped at his drink. "How are you doing with getting Netherfield ready for the season?"

Charles coloured and coughed nervously. "I was hoping to speak to you about it, Darcy. I find I am not so prepared for the task as I had hoped. Would you be so kind as to meet with the steward and myself sometime tomorrow or the next day?"

"I believe that I can find some free time to do so," Darcy said while trying to keep from smiling at his friend's discomfort. "Although I would have thought that you would ask your future father-in-law for help."

"I had thought to do so as well, but it seems that every time I go to Longbourn, I am either pleasantly distracted by my betrothed, or Mrs. Bennet will not hear of my discussing business when there is a wedding to plan," Charles told him sheepishly.

"I suppose it is a good thing, then, that we are not staying at Longbourn, or we would not find the time either," Darcy teased.

"Too true, my friend, too true," Bingley chuckled.

There followed a lengthy discussion of the Darcys' trip and the happenings in and around Netherfield until Elizabeth joined them an hour later. Both men stood at her entry into the sitting room.

"Mrs. Darcy, I hope that you rested well," Bingley greeted her with a bow.

"I thank you; I did," she answered with a small grin. "I have a favour to ask of you as my future brother."

"Anything," Bingley agreed quickly.

"I would have you address me as Elizabeth or Lizzy," she said with a lift of an eyebrow. "I think it would be proper to do so, since we will be family soon enough."

Charles laughed delightedly and agreed, "I am happy to do so, Elizabeth, and I must insist that you call me Charles."

After Bingley ordered tea and refreshments, he asked after Georgiana.

"She was quite fatigued and wished for a bath once she rested," answered Elizabeth. "I think she will be down in half an hour or so."

Once the tea tray arrived, Bingley asked Elizabeth to pour. With tea and biscuits in hand, they had settled in for comfortable conversation when they heard rapid foot steps in the hall. The butler entered the room quickly before handing a letter to Bingley. "Pardon my interruption, sir, but this just came by express for you."

Bingley stared at the direction on the missive and frowned. "It's from my sister Caroline. I wonder what she could want."

Keeping her voice low, Elizabeth said, "I believe that we should allow Charles some privacy to read his letter. Since Georgiana has not joined us, we could see how she is faring."

Nodding his agreement, Darcy stood and helped Elizabeth to her feet. "Bingley, you will want to read your letter. If you will excuse us, we shall take our leave to see how Georgiana is doing. The trip from Pemberley was rather taxing for us all."

Charles stood. "Of course, Darcy," he said. "I hope that Miss Darcy is well."

"I am certain that she is merely in need of a good rest and shall be fine." Darcy left the room with Elizabeth on his arm.

~*~

"Caroline is engaged!" Charles announced as they settled into the carriage drive to Longbourn for supper that evening, his voice conveying his astonishment.

"That is surprising news," Elizabeth asserted. "Will she be attending your wedding?"

"No, she will not," Charles replied. "I did invite her along with my aunt and uncle, but I told her in no uncertain terms that she should be on her best behaviour or she should not attend. Her letter explains that with her wedding to plan, she could not dream of travelling so far."

"Who is her intended?" Darcy asked. "Is he someone with whom you are acquainted?"

"No, I have never met the man," Bingley explained. "Sir James Montague, a baronet who was visiting his sister in Scarborough. They met at a private ball given by mutual friends of the sister and my relatives. Apparently he is a widower with two grown sons.

"Caroline told me Sir James has a house in Town and in Bath along with his estate in Shropshire. She went on for a full page about his style and grace, his grand carriage, and his fine mode of dress. According to her, Sir James could give Beau Brummell lessons in fashion. She sounds exceedingly satisfied, almost triumphant."

"If I may be so bold as to ask," Elizabeth waited for Bingley to nod before she continued, "do they plan to marry soon?"

"They plan to be married in mid-May in Town. I gather that there are many parties and balls to attend before the season is over. They will take a belated wedding trip to Scotland and Ireland to visit a few of Sir James' properties there."

"Will they have enough time to be certain of their regard and compatibility?" Elizabeth asked.

"I would not be surprised if my sister did not concern herself with either of those considerations," Charles sighed. "She will have the prestige and status she has always sought after."

Georgiana sat quietly and listened carefully to the conversation. She was not surprised at the news. Mr. Bingley's sister had gone after Darcy with such force and diligence that Georgiana had feared for her brother. As for her own opinion of Caroline Bingley, she had felt uncomfortable with that woman's fawning and insincere attentions. Smiling with happy contentment, she glanced at her brother and his wife as they sat next to each other. *I could not have wished for a better brother or sister.*

"My aunt and uncle will arrive at Netherfield for the wedding on the morrow." Charles glanced around the coach's interior. "We shall be a small but merry party, since the only other guests scheduled to arrive are your cousin Colonel Fitzwilliam and the Hursts."

"I hope we will have time to get to know your aunt and uncle," Elizabeth said, "We shall be very often at Longbourn during the daytime. My mother has written that she is greatly looking forward to our assistance."

Georgiana said with a smile, "I am looking forward to renewing my acquaintance with your family. I so enjoyed spending time with your sisters on my last visit."

"My family, especially my sisters, have written to tell me of their excitement at seeing you again. I believe that Kitty and Lydia have several surprises in store for you," Elizabeth said teasingly. "I only hope that you will not be too overwhelmed by their enthusiasm."

"Oh, no, Lizzy," Georgiana protested. "Your younger sisters are lively, 'tis true, but once I spent time with them, I found that I enjoyed their animated spirits and creativity."

Soon, the carriage pulled to a halt in front of Longbourn. When the footman opened the door, a happy chorus of voices could be heard welcoming them. They alighted from the coach as quickly as possible. The Darcy ladies were greeted with hugs and kisses by the Bennet ladies.

Darcy smiled indulgently until he too was given a kiss on the cheek and a quick embrace by his mother-in-law. He was more accustomed to such expressions of affection than he had been prior to his marriage, but he nevertheless could not keep the blush from his cheeks.

When the volume of each voice rose as each of the Bennets tried to communicate something of importance to the new arrivals, Mr. Bennet's voice boomed above the din, "Pardon me, ladies. I believe that there is sufficient time to convey all of the news without injuring our ears. Come. Let us go into the house."

Darcy offered Elizabeth his arm and turned to do the same for Georgiana, only to find that Lydia and Kitty had each taken one of her arms and were escorting her into the house while chattering excitedly. He took a step toward the house when he felt a hand take his free arm.

"My dear, Mr. Darcy," Mrs. Bennet smiled brilliantly up at him. "I was so thrilled to hear that my Lizzy was expecting a child. What wonderful news! I am so happy for you."

"I thank you, Mrs. Bennet," Darcy said graciously. "We are pleased as well."

"I believe that she is almost as pretty as Jane now. Her condition is becoming to her."

Darcy bit back an angry retort and merely said flatly, "I know of no other I consider more beautiful than Elizabeth."

"Oh, of course." Mrs. Bennet stumbled over her words, realizing that she may have upset her son-in-law. "Lizzy is a lovely girl."

Once inside the house, the party was ushered into the parlour to await the call to dinner. Many questions about the trip from Derbyshire and the condition of the roads were fielded by Darcy and Elizabeth, while Lydia and Kitty kept Georgiana occupied as they tried to tell her of all the preparations for the wedding.

"Oh, Miss Darcy!" Lydia exclaimed. "You must come to my room to see the gown I designed for the wedding. We have time before dinner, I am sure."

As Lydia stood and took Georgiana's hand to help her to her feet, she glanced across the room at Elizabeth and saw her frown. Her enthusiasm faded somewhat. *Am I acting like my old self?* she wondered.

Turning back to Georgiana, she said in a much quieter tone than before, "We can wait until after dinner, if you would like."

Not having seen Elizabeth's look, Georgiana insisted eagerly, "I admit to being curious to see the gown."

Lydia smiled and moved toward the door to the hall when she heard Elizabeth's voice. "Lydia, may I see your dress as well?"

Relief and joy bloomed on Lydia's face. "Of course, Lizzy, I would be delighted to show you both. But we must hurry. I would not want us to be late for dinner."

Once the three entered Lydia's room, the youngest Bennet girl hurried to her closet to remove the gown, which was enveloped by a covering made from an old, patched sheet. With Lizzy's help, the cover was removed to reveal a beautiful gown of pale green with a front fall of lace gathered under the bosom and ending at the hemline. Gold beading trimmed the neckline and the tiny cap sleeves.

"Oh, Lydia," cried Georgiana. "It is lovely, quite as lovely as any fashion plate I have seen. Did you truly design it?"

Lydia blushed with pleasure at the compliment. "I did," was her quiet affirmation. "I could not have achieved it without the lovely lace that Lizzy and Mr. Darcy sent me at Christmastide. They were so generous in the gifts they gave me."

Smiling, she turned to Lizzy, who had not spoken. "I must thank you again for the generous Christmas and birthday gifts. I did not expect such wonderful ones."

Her eyes were bright with unshed tears when she wrapped Elizabeth in a tight embrace. Lydia softly whispered into her ear, "I love you."

Returning her hug, Elizabeth returned quietly, "And I love you." More loudly, she said, "You have made wonderful use of the lace. I am sure I would not have ever thought to do such a thing with it. You have always had an eye for design, so I suppose I should not be too surprised."

With a wink, she added, "I hope that you will not outshine your sisters at the wedding."

"Oh, Lizzy!" Lydia laughed and said, "You have not seen their dresses. They are so beautiful. They both asked for my opinion as to fit, styles, and colours. I was so pleased to be asked. I dare say that no one will even notice me once they walk down the aisle with Papa."

"We shall see, Lydia; we shall see," Elizabeth said as she retrieved the gown's covering. "I believe it is time to put your dress away, for I am certain that dinner will be announced at any moment."

As they returned downstairs after securing Lydia's gown once more in the closet, Elizabeth felt a hand on her arm as Georgiana moved through the door to the front parlour.

"Lizzy," Lydia whispered hesitantly, "Are you upset with me for asking Georgiana to see my gown? I know I was a bit exuberant. I am sorry if I embarrassed you or Mr. Darcy."

Elizabeth turned to face her sister. As she laid a hand against Lydia's cheek, she said quietly, "I was neither embarrassed nor upset. I admit that I thought that you might be slipping back into your old ways, but I quickly understood that although you are trying to change your behaviour, no one should expect you to change who you are. As I told you before, you have always been a happy person, eager to interact with others. Since you and Georgiana have become friends, it is completely understandable that you would want to show your gown to her."

She leaned forward and kissed Lydia's cheek. "I am proud of you, Lydia, very proud indeed."

Lydia could not contain a squeal of joy as she hugged Elizabeth tightly. "Thank you, Lizzy; it means so much to me, since I have worked so hard to change. It has been difficult and at times I do fall back into my old habits." She straightened herself and grinned. "Let us go back to the parlour before Mama comes to find us. She has been so excited to have you and my new brother to dinner."

Arm-in-arm and smiling, the two sisters returned to the parlour.

~*~

The dinner was a lively and enjoyable one. Mrs. Bennet had outdone herself with three courses and a fine dessert. After the meal, she led the ladies to the parlour. She served everyone tea before seating herself next to Elizabeth.

"Lizzy, you do look well. I was so pleased to hear your news, though the way you are showing, I wonder if you might have twins." She squeezed her daughter's hand before she whispered conspiratorially, "You found out that your mother was right about marital duties, did you not?"

Elizabeth blushed deeply and stammered, "Please, Mama, it is not a proper subject for the parlour."

Heaving an aggrieved sigh, Mrs. Bennet agreed as she glanced about her, "I suppose you are right. There are unmarried girls in the room."

"Have you seen a doctor or a midwife?" She changed the subject.

"Yes, Mama," Elizabeth said and smiled. "Fitzwilliam could not be easy until I was seen by both. Each gave me instructions and told me that I was in excellent health."

"I hope that I will be able to convince your father to make the trip to Pemberley for the birth. I am sure that you will want me by your side."

Elizabeth paused to think how to deal with this not unexpected statement by her mother. "Mama, I had hoped that you would instead come in the early autumn to help me with a ball I wish to give around Michaelmas. I was certain that you would want to be there when Lord and Lady Matlock arrive. Lady Matlock told me that she hoped to see you, and if you come for the baby's birth, I know that Papa will want to go home within a fortnight or so after. You know how much he hates to be away from Longbourn."

Mrs. Bennet opened her mouth to object, but she seemed to weigh the options. Finally she spoke, "I believe you are quite right, my dear. With a doctor and a midwife, you shall not require my presence for the birthing, but you shall certainly need my assistance for the planning of the ball. Oh, Lizzy! What a wonderful thing! A ball with an earl and countess and perhaps even a duke in attendance! Even the one at Netherfield was not nearly so grand."

Listening to her mother's effusions with half an ear, Elizabeth watched her sisters chatting gaily about the wedding. Both Jane's and Mary's faces were overspread with dreamily contented smiles. Lizzy thanked the Lord that they had found men to love who both were honourable and respectable.

During a pause in which her mother took a breath, Elizabeth asked, "Mary, when is Mr. Collins due to arrive?"

"He should be here in two days' time. I believe that he was to find a curate to fill the pulpit for a month. We are to go to Essex on our wedding trip. The Earl of Matlock has offered us the use of one of his favourite fishing cottages. It is located on the river Wick near Wickford. We will stay there for a fortnight before returning to Hunsford." Mary was obviously very pleased with the prospect of the trip.

"That sounds lovely, Mary," Elizabeth said, "and very kind of Lord Matlock."

"Indeed, it was very kind," Mary answered. "Mr. Collins tells me that his Lordship is trying to make up for Lady Catherine's interference in our family's dealings."

Soon after this exchange, the men returned to the parlour. Mrs. Bennet swiftly moved to where Charles joined Jane at the other side of the room. Darcy took the opportunity to take the place she vacated to sit next to his wife.

"How are you doing, my love?" he asked softly.

"I am well, though a bit tired," Elizabeth smiled at Darcy, her eyes twinkling. "I would not object if you were to suggest after a quarter hour or so that we leave for Netherfield in order that I can rest."

Darcy nodded his assent while smiling back at her.

Moving a chair closer to the couple, Mr. Bennet beamed at his daughter. "I see that your husband takes prodigious care of you, Lizzy. You are the picture of health."

"Oh, yes, Papa, Fitzwilliam is diligent in his care." She winked at her husband before saying, "He can be almost annoying in his attentiveness to my well-being."

"Ah ha, is that the way of it?" Mr. Bennet chuckled merrily. "You have found the one flaw in Lizzy's character. She does not like to be told what to do."

"I think that she and I have come to an agreement on that score," Darcy replied as he took her hand and squeezed it gently.

"Yes, Papa," she said as she returned her husband's gesture, "I am learning to listen to suggestions, especially those regarding my health and that of the baby."

"I am happy to hear it." Mr. Bennet grinned cheerfully before he lowered his voice and said, "Darcy here tells me that you are to give a ball after the baby is born. It is a clever way to keep your mother at Longbourn when you give birth. I will gladly attend if I have your promise that I may spend most of my time at Pemberley in its famed library."

"I doubt that we could keep you from it, Papa."

A short time later, Darcy announced that it was time to return to Netherfield, as Elizabeth needed the rest. The farewells were nearly as enthusiastic as the greetings had been and nearly twice as long, but they finally managed to leave and were at Netherfield ere long.

The party from Pemberley made their way to their chambers as soon as they could, for the long journey and the excitement of the evening's gathering could not help but cause them fatigue, however pleasant the company at Longbourn had been. Elizabeth fell asleep nearly as soon as she lay down, with Darcy following soon after, spooning comfortably against his slumbering wife.

CHAPTER THIRTY-FIVE

Midmorning the next day, the Bradleys, Bingley's aunt and uncle, along with the Hursts, arrived to stay until the wedding. Once the new guests had refreshed themselves, they joined Charles and the Darcys in the front parlour for some tea and cakes. Introductions and polite inquiries as to the health of all involved were exchanged as the refreshments were served.

Mrs. Bradley complimented Bingley on the charm and beauty of the house and grounds. "You have found a comfortable home for yourself, Charles."

"Thank you, Aunt," he answered, pleased.

"When will we have the opportunity to meet your fiancée?" his uncle asked in a booming voice.

"The Bennets are to dine with us tonight. You will meet my Jane and the rest of her family at that time, as well as the Lucases. We shall be quite a merry party."

Elizabeth glanced around the parlour as she sipped her tea, only to spy Louisa Hurst speaking animatedly to her Uncle Bradley. Mr. Hurst was not hovering over a decanter of wine as had been his previous habit. He seemed to be fully involved in the conversation with his wife and her relative. She could not help but wonder how these new people would react to her family and friends. Knowing that her own mother and, to a lesser degree Lady Lucas, could try the heart of a saint, she hoped that the presence of the new arrivals might temper her mother's enthusiasm.

As Elizabeth listened to the conversation flowing around her, she was struck with the realization that she had never been so at ease in the company of the Hursts before. Always in the past, Louisa had seemed to join with Miss Bingley when Caroline vied for Darcy's full attention and seemed to take great pleasure in tossing barbs in Lizzy's direction. However, Charles' older sister sat in apparent enjoyment as she took part in the conversation, instead of playing with her bracelets out of boredom.

The contemplations had barely crossed her mind when the very object of her thoughts rose to draw near to where Elizabeth sat. Indicating a chair next to Elizabeth's, Louisa Hurst asked if she might join her.

"Of course, please do sit down, Mrs. Hurst," Elizabeth said as she gestured to the seat. "How was your trip to Hertfordshire?"

"It was a pleasant journey." Mrs. Hurst smiled and said, "Indeed, it is difficult to imagine a pleasanter one, given the company. My aunt and uncle are delightful companions. The roads were in good repair as well, so that I enjoyed myself immensely. The only thing that marred my enjoyment was Caroline's refusal to attend, although I understand she has a grand wedding to plan."

A soft, teasing smile crossed Louisa's face. "But perhaps the trip would not have been quite so pleasant if she had come."

Elizabeth bit back a chuckle. "I understand that Miss Bingley's fiancé is a baronet."

"He is," Louisa assented, "He is an older gentleman, but from what Aunt and Uncle Bradley tell me, he is kind and seems quite taken with Caroline."

Louisa lowered her voice and whispered, "I should not say this but I was greatly surprised when I heard that Sir James is thirty years Caroline's senior though it does seem an advantageous match for my sister. I am certain that she will enjoy being addressed as Lady Montague."

After glancing around her, Mrs. Hurst said in the same low tone, "I know that I have been improper in my speaking thusly about my sister, but I have one more remark to make about her absence. My husband is very pleased that Caroline has found a match. She embarrassed him a great deal which was the reason, though not a very good one, that he seemed lost in a bottle so much of the time. In such a stupor, Mr. Hurst could ignore her remarks and socially superior affectations. Once again, he is the man I married. I can only hope that she will wed the man and enjoy her own home."

Elizabeth felt compassion for the woman and patted her hand. "We shall speak of it no more, but I must say that I am glad for your entire family because of Miss Bingley's good fortune."

"Thank you, Mrs. Darcy," Louisa said as she smiled.

"Please convey my wishes for her health and happiness," Elizabeth said with resolve to think no more of the woman who once fancied Darcy so much.

"Of course, I shall do so." Mrs. Hurst nodded her head.

~*~

That evening the party was indeed a merry one. Lady Lucas and Mrs. Bennet were less boisterous than usual, but they were still animated. With Jane's assistance, Bingley had organized the seating into a comfortable arrangement.

Mrs. Bennet and her neighbour were seated near each other but away from the Hursts and their party, with Darcy, Elizabeth, Jane, Bingley, and the others of the Lucas and Bennet families as buffers between them.

Darcy watched as Mr. Bennet and Mr. Bradley talked of sport and horses. Mr. Hurst contributed to the conversation from across the table. Mrs. Hurst sat next to Mary and surprised everyone by asking about the future Mrs. Collins' plans for her new home. It seemed that the entire party enjoyed the meal and the exchanges with their neighbours at the table.

~*~

After the gentlemen returned to the company of the ladies, Darcy, standing close to his wife as she chatted with her sister Jane, noticed that as his mother-in-law became more comfortable with the newcomers, she began to speak more loudly and with less tact. He also noticed Louisa Hurst wince at one inappropriate remark Mrs. Bennet made to Mrs. Bradley.

Darcy had just decided that it might well be a good time to speak to Mrs. Bennet when he saw Mr. Bennet move to her side. After giving a slight bow to Lady Lucas and Mrs. Bradley, his father-in-law took his wife aside, speaking quietly, yet earnestly, to her. At first, she seemed to argue with him, but soon she nodded quickly. When he saw an empty settee near Mr. and Mrs. Bradley, he guided his wife to the seat, sat down with her, and patted her hand.

Happy to see that Mr. Bennet was at last taking his wife in hand to control her more unbefitting outbursts, Darcy smiled and looked to see if his Beth had witnessed the interplay between her parents. The expression of relief upon her face told him that she had indeed seen it.

Charles asked who among the ladies would favour them with some music. When no one volunteered, he asked Mary if she would play for them. She agreed to play, but asked Georgiana to sing along with her playing. It took a bit of persuasion until finally she consented.

The duet was so well received that the whole company insisted that they perform another, which they did. Following their second piece, Elizabeth was cajoled into playing for the group. Darcy watched with great pleasure as she played one of his favourite tunes. From his position, he was able to enjoy not only her superb performance, but also her loving glances at him. At the end of the song, his applause was the loudest and longest.

"You amaze me, my love," Darcy whispered when she returned to him. "Your playing tonight surpasses any I have heard."

She blushed prettily before she answered him in a low voice, "You must not have listened to my sister."

Darcy offered her his arm and only smiled as he escorted her to a seat.

Charles asked his sister to play for them. Louisa surprised the whole room when she only agreed to do so if her husband would join her for a duet as she played. They performed beautifully together with the rich baritone of Hurst blending well with the bright soprano of his wife.

As the applause faded, the butler quietly moved to where Bingley sat and said softly to his master, "Mr. William Collins and Colonel Richard Fitzwilliam are in the entry. They did not wish to disturb the company by being announced."

"Very well, Fosset," said Bingley in reply. "Tell them I will be with them in a moment."

Charles rose from his seat and moved to where Darcy sat. After a quick, low conversation, the two slipped nearly unnoticed from the room. Elizabeth was the only one to observe the men leaving. It was only the pleased look on her husband's face that kept her in her seat. With such an expression upon her beloved's countenance, there could be no need for alarm.

"Colonel Fitzwilliam, Mr. Collins," Bingley proclaimed as he met them in the hall and shook hands with each in turn, "I am pleased to see you, though we did not expect either of you for another day or so."

"Bingley, I am sorry to interrupt your entertainment. We meant only to stop in to inform you of our arrival. We stopped first at Longbourn, but we were told that the family was at Netherfield. Hence, we shall go to the inn and return tomorrow."

"Nonsense, Colonel, we are only surprised to see you and Mr. Collins so soon," Charles argued. "I was told that Mr. Collins was not expected until sometime tomorrow afternoon and that you would likely not come for another day or two. However, your rooms are already prepared for you."

"I was able to complete my business at Rosings more quickly than I expected, thanks to Collins here. In fact, it was he who first observed the problem, made Rosings' steward aware of it, and encouraged him to write to my father. With his help, we made short work of the difficulty. I decided to show my appreciation by offering to convey him to Hertfordshire in one of the many carriages at Rosings."

After the colonel's explanation, Darcy nodded his approval. "I have always thought that my aunt had far more carriages than she could ever use," he confessed light-heartedly.

It was then that Darcy glanced at Mr. Collins. In appearance, the man looked very much the same as he always had, but something in his demeanour and bearing bespoke of a change. He no longer bowed and smirked in the obsequious way that had been his habit. The clergyman merely nodded and acknowledged the colonel's tale without speaking or interjecting any of his usual compliments. There was still an air of deference about him, but it no longer seemed so overdone as in the past.

"Come, let us go into the drawing room," Bingley gestured down the hall. "There are those with whom you already claim an acquaintance and others whom I shall be happy to introduce to you both."

"Of course," the colonel agreed happily.

As they walked toward the drawing room, Bingley offered to send for some refreshments for the new arrivals. "You must be hungry and thirsty after your journey."

"I will have something to drink now," Fitzwilliam answered. "However, since I will need to retire shortly, I ask that the food be sent to my room. After I greet everyone, I shall go upstairs."

Mr. Collins nodded his agreement with the colonel's statement and arrived at the entrance to the drawing room.

Just inside the door, the colonel scanned the room before he said, "Ah, I see you correctly stated that there are some in the room with whom I am not yet acquainted."

Bingley first led the men to where Louisa stood with their uncle, aunt, and Hurst. Once the introductions had been made, they moved around the room greeting the rest of the company.

When they had first come into the room, the chatter had dimmed, but soon everyone returned to their own conversations as they realized that they would have their turn to speak to the gentlemen.

After greeting Mr. and Mrs. Bennet and the Lucases, Mr. Collins made his way to Mary's side. She blushed prettily when he kissed her hand.

"Miss Mary, you look lovely tonight," Collins complimented her with feeling.

"Thank you, Mr. Collins," she replied softly. "I am happy that you were able to come earlier than expected."

"As am I, dearest," was his fervent reply. "Colonel Fitzwilliam was kind enough to offer to share one of the carriages from Rosings. I had been able to see to all of my affairs at Hunsford. I am certain that all shall be in readiness for us upon our arrival in a month."

Georgiana, who had lost her patience, rushed forward to greet the colonel. "Cousin Richard, we did not expect to see you for a few more days."

The colonel kissed his young cousin's cheek before he explained the situation.

Lydia Bennet, however, remained with her sister Kitty and Samuel Lucas and watched the colonel as he moved around the room speaking jovially to all. Formerly, she would have pushed her way into their company, demanding her share in the conversation, but now she understood how inappropriate her conduct had been. She knew neither of her two eldest sisters would have ever been so forward or impolite. No matter how tempting the prospect of speaking with Colonel Fitzwilliam was, she would be patient and wait, hoping that he would want to seek her acquaintance once more.

The time finally came when the colonel and Georgiana joined the two Bennet sisters and the Lucas scion. "Miss Catherine, Miss Lydia, Lucas," Fitzwilliam bowed in greeting. "It is delightful to see you all again. I hope you are all well."

After curtseying, Lydia spoke, "As you see, we are well. I hope you had a pleasant journey to Hertfordshire."

"A very pleasant one," he answered with a grin. "Your cousin turns out to be an interesting conversationalist, even if the subject most on his lips is your sister Mary."

"Indeed?" Kitty and Lydia said at once, incredulity evident in their voices.

"Indeed," he answered. "Mr. Collins has improved a great deal since we first met. He told me that he had been taught from a young age to value rank and wealth as virtues above all else and that the possessors of such virtues were to be held in awe and reverence. However, his experience with Lady Catherine and her subsequent fall in his estimation gave cause for him to reflect upon his long held beliefs. As the weeks and months went by, both at Hunsford and here in Hertfordshire, your cousin realized that as a clergyman, he had failed his Lord and his parishioners by his constant attentions to only one of the flock under his care. He resolved to spend time in private devotion and more public ministrations in imitation of his Lord."

"I can just hear him speaking thus," Kitty cried out with a giggle.

"I have given you a fairly accurate recital of what Mr. Collins said to me, but that does not in anyway detract from what I perceived as an honest and sincere change in him." Colonel Fitzwilliam felt a bit of offence on behalf of the clergyman, as he had had a good deal of interaction with the man. He decided to ignore Kitty Bennet's remark.

He watched in pleased surprise as the youngest Bennet daughter seemed by her disapproving expression about to scold her older sister. Fitzwilliam decided to forestall the confrontation and said, "Miss Lydia, I was promised liquid refreshment by Mr. Bingley. Are there tea and coffee set out somewhere in the room?"

"Yes, of course, Colonel Fitzwilliam. Allow me to show you the way," Lydia agreed quickly.

The colonel, after excusing himself from the other two, offered Lydia his arm. They walked in silence until they reached the small table upon which were laid out the tea and coffee things, as well as cakes and biscuits.

Lydia offered to pour for the colonel, to which he agreed. She decided that she would like a cup of tea as well, and after each had a full cup, Fitzwilliam found a place for them to sit on a settee against the wall.

"You are not inclined to poke fun at your cousin?" the colonel inquired lightly.

Lydia blushed a bright pink when she thought of how in former times, she would have laughed heartily with Kitty. Indeed, she would have been the first to burst forth into snorts and giggles. She had been surprised at the idea that Mr. Collins could be good company until she thought of his recent kind words and gestures toward her family. He seemed devoted to their middle sister, and she to him.

"I admit that I used to mock his manner of speaking and his odd kind of walking, but I can see that he has worked to change the habits that were the most unappealing." She took a sip of tea before she went on, "As I have been endeavouring to modify my own behaviour since you were last in Hertfordshire, I am hopeful that you might have observed that I have been at least moderately successful."

"Indeed, Miss Lydia," he said seriously. "I noticed that you have matured in your actions and words. I saw the genesis of it after that discussion of a certain reprobate soldier. I must say that I am pleased to see the fruits of that beginning. It is not always easy to overcome long-held habits of behaviour."

"Oh, Colonel Fitzwilliam!" Lydia exclaimed, "I am pleased that you are able to see the difference. I have found it a great deal of work to change. I am so blessed to have sisters who do assist me in my new path. I have failed miserably at times, but I am determined to succeed." She paused and smiled. "My father has been teaching me to play chess and has given me some of Lizzy's favourite books to read. I have also begun to help him with the household accounts. Who could have known that I would love chess and numbers so well? Reading is still not my favourite of pastimes, but I have benefitted from the time I have spent doing it."

"I admit that I do not find reading so satisfying as my cousin does, but I have been known to crack a book and enjoy the activity." The colonel grinned as he spoke. "May I ask what your favourite pastime is? Might it be chess?"

She laughed quietly as she shook her head. "No, though I like to play chess, I would rather design gowns or, best of all, play my harp."

"Your harp?" the colonel asked in a surprised tone. "I did not know that you played an instrument."

"My mother insisted when we were younger that we all learn to play the pianoforte," Lydia answered. "Only Mary and Lizzy continued. I did not have the interest, and Mama was never very strict with her younger daughters. I had always loved the harp. I can recall the times that I was present when Agatha Long would play. I could think of nothing more lovely or heavenly than the melodies she performed for us."

She sighed with the remembrance before she continued, "Papa would not purchase one for me. He thought that it was too great an expense when he was sure that I would soon tire of the necessary practice. He was probably correct, since I was a flighty girl then."

"If that is so, how did you convince him to change his mind now?" Fitzwilliam inquired.

"Oh, my father did not change his mind," Lydia said, smiling happily. "My sister Elizabeth and Mr. Darcy gave me the harp among other presents for my sixteenth birthday in early February. They even hired a master to teach me. Once my father saw my diligence in practicing during the first few weeks, he informed my brother that he would see to the music master himself."

"Will I have the privilege of hearing you play?" Colonel Fitzwilliam tried to keep the eagerness from his voice. The harp had always held a particular interest for him. His first infatuation as a callow youth of twenty had been for the beautiful Lady Julia Ashton, whom he had seen perform on that instrument at a musicale hosted by her parents. She had been six years his senior and the wife of an earl. Those two facts were all that it had taken to cool his ardour for the woman, but he had loved to listen to that particular stringed instrument ever since.

"I do not feel that I am quite ready for an audience. I can only play scales and a few very simple songs with any success," Lydia protested with many blushes.

"But surely you have played for your family," he argued.

"Of course, my parents and my three sisters at home have heard me practicing," she admitted. She set her cup aside, clasped her hands in her lap, and stared down at them. Lydia wondered if she should tell him that Lizzy and Georgiana were coming for a visit the next morning and had extracted an agreement from her to play for them. She had felt obligated to agree since the harp was a gift from the Darcys.

"I am certain that Mrs. Darcy will want to observe your progress for herself." It seemed as if the colonel had read her thoughts. He continued, "And that being the case, I do not see the harm in my sitting in on the recital. I am family, after all."

After a few more protests on her part, Lydia finally agreed to allow him to hear her if the two Darcy ladies did not object to his escorting them to Longbourn the next day.

Certain of his ability to wheedle his way into the visiting party the next morning, he thanked her for the kind invitation and began another subject while forgetting that he had arrived tired, hungry, and with road dust on his clothing. Colonel Fitzwilliam wanted only to continue in the company of this vivacious, yet newly reserved, young woman. In the back of his mind, he understood he was treading upon a dangerous path. Her age and lack of fortune made a match with her a very unlikely and imprudent alliance, but for the time being he ignored that more sensible part of himself in favour of enjoying the company of the lovely Miss Lydia Bennet.

Elizabeth watched her family around her. How things had changed in the months since Mr. Bingley had first let Netherfield. There were so many alterations that she could scarcely take them in. Her mother spoke with whomever would listen, but her father kept his wife from being either too loud or too embarrassing. The biggest surprise was that her mother seemed much happier and calmer under her husband's watchful eye.

"Your youngest sister seems to have matured a great deal since we last were in Hertfordshire," Darcy commented as he arrived with a cup of tea for her.

After Elizabeth thanked him and took a sip of the beverage, she answered, "She has, but she is not the only one who has altered since that time. I was just pondering all of the changes and how remarkable they are."

They talked for several more minutes as they continued to observe the rest of the party, until Darcy noticed Elizabeth trying to hide a yawn. "I think it is time that we retire. You are fatigued."

Sighing softly, she agreed, "I believe that you are correct, even though I do not like to admit to being weary. Let us take our leave."

CHAPTER THIRTY-SIX

At breakfast the next morning, Elizabeth and Darcy were surprised when Colonel Fitzwilliam arrived even before the rest of the party. He tended to enjoy a ride before breakfast and usually did not arrive at the table until later.

Darcy was about to inquire about his cousin's change in his routine when Georgiana entered the breakfast parlour.

"Good morning, everyone," she greeted them cheerfully. "I am surprised to see you here so early, cousin." Her tone reminded both men of Elizabeth's usual teasing manner.

"That I am, dear Georgie," Richard agreed quickly. "I wanted to be able to wheedle my way into your morning visit to Longbourn. I have heard a rumour of a private harp recital, and since you are perfectly aware of my delight in hearing that particular instrument, I wish to join you."

"I have no objection if Elizabeth does not," Georgiana replied with a smile.

"Lydia might object as she has only just begun her lessons," Elizabeth answered.

"Ah, my dear cousins," the colonel grinned in triumph. "I had the rumour from a very reliable source. It was Miss Lydia herself who gave her permission for my attendance this morning. Therefore, I shall be ready whenever you are and only wait upon your convenience."

Once it was settled to everyone's satisfaction, the party finished their breakfast and left for Longbourn just before ten o'clock. The group included Darcy as well, once he found that Mrs. Bennet would be in Meryton with three of her daughters, bent on finding some last minute items for the upcoming wedding. They spent the short drive plying Richard with questions about his impromptu trip to Rosings. They were both pleased and surprised that the problem that had caused the steward to call for assistance from the family had been solved relatively easily with the help of Mr. Collins.

Their arrival at the door of Longbourn was a much more subdued affair than usual. Without Mrs. Bennet's enthusiastic greetings, the foursome were quietly shown into the smaller parlour that housed the pianoforte, and now the harp, and served as the music room.

Lydia rose when the party entered, and after all courtesies were exchanged, she invited them to be seated. She sat in the chair near her harp and nervously smoothed her skirt before she pulled the instrument into position.

"I do apologize in advance for the simple tunes I will play and for any mistakes I am sure to make." Lydia took a few deep breaths and began to play. At first she felt anxious, but slowly her love for the instrument and her natural aptitude eased the tension in her body. The result was that the simple melodies seemed to take flight and flowed around the audience, leaving them charmed.

Lydia was taken by surprise upon completing the second song when her small audience began to applaud enthusiastically. She could not help but blush when her sister cried, "Oh, Lydia, that was wonderful! You played so well."

The colonel and Mr. and Miss Darcy seconded Elizabeth's praise before the two Darcy ladies rushed to embrace Lydia. They chattered happily about the music and their pleasure at having been allowed to hear her.

They were brought out of their conversation by Darcy, who had moved to where they stood. "My dear Miss Lydia," he began, "I must say that upon hearing your performance, I wish that we had gifted you with the harp at Christmas. I look forward to the next time we will have the pleasure of one of your recitals."

Darcy watched as the youngest of his new sisters swallowed several times before she curtseyed and answered him. "Thank you, Mr. Darcy. It is very kind of you to say so. I must tell you once more of my gratitude for the gift. The instrument is lovely and a joy to play. I promise I shall not neglect to practice in order to measure up to your expectations."

"No one who has had the honour of listening to you play would think you neglectful in that area, Miss Lydia," Colonel Fitzwilliam said and Darcy nodded his agreement.

After a few more moments of conversation, Elizabeth looked at the mantel clock. The hour was fast approaching when her mother would return, and since she did not wish to spoil the pleasant mood of the visit by Mrs. Bennet's taxing treatment of her husband, she said, "It is nearing time for us to return to Netherfield, and I wish to greet my father. Please excuse me while I do so."

"I shall join you, my dear," Darcy said and moved to his wife's side. He offered her his arm, and they left for Mr. Bennet's library.

After a brief but pleasant visit with Mr. Bennet, the Darcy party left for Netherfield. The conversation on the short trip comprised mostly of a discussion of Lydia's performance and the obvious talent she had displayed that morning.

That evening and the next few days before the wedding passed in a blur for Elizabeth. There were neighbourhood soirees, luncheons, dinners, and card parties. It would seem that all of the four and twenty families of the area had conspired together to fill each day with activity. She grew more tired as the days went on, but she did not wish to spoil Jane's time to shine. Also, she wanted to spend as much time as possible with her sister before her wedding.

It was for this reason that Elizabeth attended luncheon at Longbourn the day before the wedding, when all she had wanted to do was to crawl back into bed as she went to her room to change for travelling to the Bennets'. Shaking her head, she told herself that she might be able to nap before they dined at the Lucases' home that evening.

Darcy worried when he spied his wife as he entered her chamber after he had changed. "Are you well, Elizabeth?" he asked.

Elizabeth smiled bravely as she answered, "Only a little tired, Fitzwilliam. I will be fine." She did not tell him of the headache that was slowly making itself known to her, so intent was she to fulfil her promise to herself to spend as much time with Jane as she could.

Not entirely confident that his wife was as well as she proclaimed, Darcy nevertheless offered his arm to escort her downstairs. He noted that Elizabeth leaned more heavily than usual, but he thought that if she were indeed tired, it was not surprising that she did so.

Several carriages took the entire Netherfield party to Longbourn. The rocking and jostling of the coach did little to alleviate the headache Elizabeth suffered. By the time they reached her parents' home, she was feeling lightheaded as well.

Elizabeth thought that she might ask Jane to use her bed for a few minutes in the hope that time in a reclining position might help her to feel more like herself. However, it was not to be, for just as Darcy helped her from the carriage, her head spun wildly. As she lost consciousness, Darcy was able to catch her before she hit the ground.

Mrs. Bennet began to screech, while most of the rest looked on in panic. Mr. Bennet stepped forward and directed Darcy to carry Elizabeth into the front parlour and to a large sofa. He refused to allow anyone but Jane into the room while calling for a servant to fetch the apothecary.

Jane brought forward a vial of smelling salts, and Darcy thanked her as he held it under Elizabeth's nose. After a few seconds, she turned her head away as she swatted at Darcy's hand. "Why am I here?" Elizabeth asked weakly. She lifted a hand to rub her temple in an effort to soothe the pain throbbing there.

"You fainted," Darcy said, almost scolding. He was kneeling beside her, rubbing her icy fingers. "You frightened us."

Before he could say more, Jane pulled a chair close and spoke, "Papa has sent for the apothecary. How are you feeling, Lizzy?"

Elizabeth dropped her gaze so that neither her husband nor her sister could see her eyes.

"Elizabeth, please tell us the truth," Darcy's voice was filled with concern. "Fainting is not a good sign. There might even be something wrong with the babe."

Swallowing back tears of contrition, Elizabeth whispered, "Forgive me, Fitzwilliam. I did not tell you of my fatigue and the headache I awoke with this morning. I did not want to curtail my time with Jane. I see now that I was unwise."

"Do not fret, my love," Darcy kissed her hand while trying to quell his unease. "I am certain that Mr. Jones will put you to rights, and if he permits it, we will make our way back to Netherfield, so that you may rest for tomorrow." He was not entirely sure of his assertion, but he wanted to appear positive before his wife.

"Yes, Lizzy," Jane exclaimed. "I am sure Mr. Darcy is correct. I shall come with you to nurse you as you have done more than once for me. That is, if my brother will allow it."

"I have no objections," Darcy smiled at his sister-in-law. "I believe that Elizabeth would be very happy if you did."

"But, Jane, Mama will be upset if you were to leave," Elizabeth protested even though she would very much like to have her sister with her for a last private time together.

"Do not worry, Lizzy. I will speak to Papa while Mr. Jones is with you. He will be able to manoeuvre things. Since the rest will stay for the meal, my mother will have enough guests to satisfy her, I am sure." Jane smiled serenely and winked. "After all, she will have the son of an earl at her table. Mama shall be in her element."

Thus it was accomplished that after Mr. Jones examined Elizabeth and declared her merely in need of one of his draughts, rest, and quiet for the remainder of the day, Jane accompanied her sister and Mr. Darcy back to Netherfield while the rest of the party stayed for the planned luncheon at Longbourn.

The scheme had not come off without a great deal of fussing and lamentations on the part of Mrs. Bennet, until Mrs. Gardiner teamed up with Mr. Bennet to reason that it would be more important that Elizabeth be present at the nuptials of her two sisters than at the luncheon or the party at the Lucases that evening, which Jane would attend as planned. She was also reminded that she must consider her future grandchild's health as well.

Mrs. Bennet finally ceased to complain about the inconvenience or the absence of her two daughters and her son-in-law. She began to think that it was quite her own idea as she repeatedly explained the reasons to the others as they arrived for the meal. As Lady Lucas was one of the select few who had been invited to the private meal, Elizabeth's mother was able to personally inform her of the change of plans for that evening.

By the time the Darcys and Jane made it back to Netherfield, the draught Mr. Jones had given to Elizabeth had begun to work to alleviate her headache. Despite her protests, Darcy carried her to her chamber and summoned her maid to help her to bed.

A few minutes later, Jane entered the room with a tray of hot chamomile tea and buttered toast. "I have brought you a bit of refreshment."

"Thank you, dearest Jane," Elizabeth said as she slipped under the covers. Sarah adjusted the pillows so that her mistress could sit up to drink her tea. After stirring some honey into the cup, Jane handed it to Elizabeth.

"Sarah, please tell Mr. Darcy that I am in bed and having a cup of chamomile tea before I try to rest." Elizabeth sipped at the warm brew and smiled at her sister before she sighed, "I feel a trifle foolish for not simply staying abed this morning. I could have injured the baby and been kept from your wedding."

"All will be well, Lizzy," Jane said as she patted her sister's arm. "I can tell that your head is better, and I believe that you will be well after a good nap. I will stay with you until I must leave to dress for the Lucases' soiree."

"I am sorry that you feel you must stay with me."

"Nonsense, Lizzy," said Jane, shaking her head. "There is no place I would rather be on this day. Tomorrow I depart my maiden life to join my life with Charles's. I am content to be spending this time with you, even if you will be sleeping for part of it. I have missed our chats and our companionable silences." Jane took the empty cup and plate from Elizabeth, set it on the tray, and helped Elizabeth recline on the bed as Darcy walked through the door.

"How are you, my dear?" Darcy asked with anxiety.

"I am feeling much better," she said as she reached out to take his offered hand. "The draught has all but chased the headache away, and the tea and toast have also helped. I believe I shall rest quite well now."

Kissing his wife's forehead, Darcy told her he would stay in the room while she slept. He then ordered a light collation to be brought to the room for Jane and himself.

Elizabeth awoke after two hours, feeling much better. She smilingly asserted that she would be well enough to attend the evening soiree, but neither her husband nor her sister would allow it. However, they did agree after some wheedling on Lizzy's part to her reclining upon the chaise near the fireplace so that she and Jane could talk more comfortably. The visit passed by quickly until it was time for Jane to return to Longbourn. The others had returned to Netherfield hours before and were resting or readying themselves for the Lucas party as well.

A soft knock sounded at the chamber door. When Darcy opened it, he found Bingley.

"How is Mrs. Darcy?" he asked quietly.

"Elizabeth is much better," Darcy announced happily. "Do come in to say hello."

Charles made his way to where Elizabeth sat and bowed to her and Jane. "You are looking well indeed. I am so glad to see it. Louisa and the rest asked me to give you their regards. Is there anything that I can send for on your behalf before I return Jane to Longbourn?" he asked eagerly.

"Thank you for your inquiry. I am feeling quite a bit recovered. Give my thanks to the others for me. I have no needs at the moment, and as you see, my husband is quite at my beck and call in the event that I should have need of anything." Elizabeth smiled up at her very soon-to-be brother.

"Excellent!" he exclaimed before turning to Jane. "My dear, I believe we must go now, so that your mother is not distressed that you will not have time to make yourself ready for the evening's entertainment."

After giving Elizabeth a hug and bidding adieu to both the Darcys, Jane left the room with Charles.

A while later there was another knock upon the chamber door. Thinking it was one of the maids, Darcy called out, "Enter."

Both Elizabeth and Darcy were surprised to see Lydia smiling brightly at them. Before either one of them could speak, she explained, "I was worried about you, Lizzy, even though Jane said that you were doing much better after a nap. I convinced Mama that I should come back with Mr. Bingley to find out if Jane, in her optimism, had the truth of it." She paused to lower her gaze to the floor and went on, "Besides, I was jealous that Jane was able to spend more private time with you."

"Lydia," Elizabeth said with a grin. "Do come and sit by me." She held her hand out as she lowered her feet to the floor and sat upright.

As Lydia sat down beside her older sister, she glanced at Darcy and saw him frowning. "Oh, Mr. Darcy, please forgive me," she cried nervously. "I did not ask if I could indeed stay. I shall only stay a moment, and then I will walk back to Longbourn."

"Of course, you will do no such thing, Lydia," Elizabeth protested as she looked to her husband.

"No, indeed, Miss Lydia," Darcy said as he softened his expression. "I am merely surprised that you are here so close to the start of the soiree at the Lucases. Shall you have time to get ready?"

"Oh, I do not plan to attend," Lydia answered quietly. "I have convinced my parents that you are in need of company, so that you will not feel forlorn at missing the entertainment tonight."

"It is not necessary that you sit with me," Elizabeth told her. "Mr. Darcy will be here."

"Oh, Lizzy," Lydia exclaimed. "You will be leaving for Pemberley on the morrow." She sighed forlornly. "The house will seem so quiet with only Kitty and myself left at home and with her so involved with Samuel Lucas. A party at the Lucases' does not appeal to me nearly so much as spending time with you."

"I do not have any objections to visiting with you for a few hours." Elizabeth squeezed her youngest sister's hand. "I suppose that my husband can find something to entertain himself lest we bore him with our female conversation."

"I will find myself a book and read in the library for a while as you visit," said Darcy with a grin as he stood and exited the room.

For a few hours, the sisters chatted about a sundry of topics until Lydia heard the chime of the clock. Her face fell into a sad mien as she said, "I suppose it is time for me to return home."

Elizabeth rang for a servant. When she arrived, Lizzy asked that a carriage be ordered to take her sister home along with a maid to accompany her.

After some time, Darcy entered the room to inform them that the carriage and maid were ready to take Lydia back to Longbourn.

Lydia took her sister's hand, "I must say that although I am glad that Jane will be at Netherfield, but I wish that Pemberley was not such a great distance from Hertfordshire."

"Dear Lyddie, you will come to see us in the autumn," Elizabeth soothed. "There is to be a ball."

"I know," Lydia said as she tried to sound more cheerful. "And as much as I look forward to a ball, it is not so much a cause for rejoicing as it once was. Maybe once I have proven that I am truly improving, you will invite me alone to Pemberley."

Elizabeth grasped Lydia's hand. "Oh, Mr. Darcy and I do not need any more proof of your improvement." She glanced at her husband to see his nod at what he understood she wanted. "We may just insist that you stay on with us once Papa and Mama return to Longbourn. The babe shall want for another aunt to spoil him or her. Would you like that?"

Lydia, in great delight, threw her arms around Elizabeth while proclaiming, "It would please me above all things to do so. I shall go distracted with the thought." Trembling with the excitement the idea of an extended stay with her sister brought about in her, she took a deep breath to calm herself. She dropped her arms from around her sister's shoulders and continued, "I shall wait to think about it until you have obtained Papa's consent. He might not wish for me to be away from Longbourn. I am, however, grateful that you would suggest it."

"I shall certainly ask Papa, but I am positive that he will agree," Elizabeth said as she kissed Lydia's cheek. "I will speak to him on the morrow at the wedding breakfast."

The women stood and embraced once more before Lydia left to get her outer garments.

Darcy went to his wife and kissed her before saying, "I shall not stay long, but I shall send Sarah to you. You need to retire early so that you will be well for the wedding and the journey tomorrow."

Elizabeth patted his cheek. "I am sure that you are correct. I shall, however, await your return before I get into bed." When Darcy opened his mouth to protest, she stopped him by saying, "Sarah may assist me in my preparations, and I am certain that I will be quite ready to retire by the time you are back."

"Very well, my sweet Beth," he replied and kissed her again.

CHAPTER THIRTY-SEVEN

The next day, nothing happened to mar Mrs. Bennet's triumph of marrying off two more of her daughters. The weather was neither too hot nor too cold. The sky wore its finest blue, with only a few of the purest white clouds for accessories. Even the birds seemed to sing just for the couples.

Mr. Bennet and his two youngest daughters were ready in a timely fashion. Although Jane and Mary thought they might suffer under the scrutiny of their mother, their aunt was able to distract and steer her toward the less disruptive task of overseeing the final preparations for the wedding breakfast. However, all of the servants were so diligent in their assigned duties that the mistress of Longbourn could find no fault in them. Her sojourn to the kitchen gave her only enough time to see to her own toilette, so she was thus prevented from further plaguing her daughters.

The guests filed into the Longbourn chapel until there was only room left for the Bennet party, who were the last to arrive. Mrs. Bennet and Mrs. Gardiner were escorted to the front of the church by Mr. Gardiner.

The two grooms stood handsomely dressed in dark gray morning coats, silver brocade waistcoats, and cream coloured breeches. The joyous anticipation of seeing their respective brides shone brightly on each man's face. Although Mr. Bingley's smile was by far the broader, Mr. Collins's was all the more striking by its complete and unfeigned genuineness.

The quiet murmur of the congregation hushed completely as the doors at the rear were opened to admit the two brides, each holding an arm of their father. Again, Jane was by far the lovelier of the two, but the light of love brought a beauty of countenance to Mary's face that caused more than one person to wonder why they had always thought her to be plain.

As Mr. Bennet first gave Jane's hand to Bingley and, in turn, Mary's to Mr. Collins, he felt a twinge once again in his heart. His daughters were quite rapidly leaving the nest, and although he was quite certain each had made a good match, he could not help but think of the day they had each come into the world. Despite what most of his acquaintance might surmise, he did not regret having so many daughters, only that he had not an heir to inherit Longbourn and provide for his wife and any unmarried daughters when he passed away, although it would appear that he might not have to concern himself about leaving any spinsters behind at his death.

The ceremony was as lovely as usual, especially when one observed the shy glances between each couple. Once the vicar introduced the newlywed Mr. and Mrs. Bingley and Mr. and Mrs. Collins, Mrs. Bennet could be heard to say, "Thank you, Lord," in a voice thick with happy tears.

Bingley led his bride out of the church with the Collinses close behind. Lydia and Kitty were among the young girls who held aloft a flower-bedecked arch and tossed petals at the couples as they walked underneath. Two open carriages awaited the newlyweds to convey them the short distance back to Longbourn for the breakfast.

Mr. Bennet offered his arm to his wife, so that they could lead the rest back to the house. He was surprised at how quiet she was as they walked. "Is something amiss, my dear," he asked as he looked down at her.

"Oh, no, Mr. Bennet," she cried as she smiled brilliantly up at him. "Nothing is wrong. I am just so happy that I feel about to burst from it. What did I do to deserve such joy?"

"My dear Mrs. Bennet," he patted her arm. "For a start, you gave birth to all these lovely young women with whom the Lord decided to bless us."

"Oh, to think, I have three daughters now so well settled," she sighed and squeezed his husband's arm. "How wonderful it is!"

Once everyone had entered the house, the festivity advanced famously, with the guests enjoying the company, the food, and drink. At first, Mrs. Bennet began to fuss over perceived but unreal problems, but Elizabeth and Mrs. Gardiner were able to convince her to enjoy her company and the thrill of a perfect wedding and breakfast after plying her with a few glasses of the fine wine Darcy had provided. The couples mingled with the guests, smiling and accepting the good wishes that flowed from the many friends in attendance, after they had partaken of at least a small portion of the delicious meal Mrs. Bennet had had prepared.

Darcy saw to it that Elizabeth ate well before she also moved about the house, talking to her friends. He kept watch on her to make certain that there was no repeat of the incident of the day before. As far as he could tell, his wife was feeling refreshed and eager to share in the conversations of those around her, with no evidence of fatigue.

Finally, the time came for the two couples to leave for their respective wedding trips. The Collinses set out for the earl's cottage in Essex. The Bingleys would travel first to London for a week's stay in the Darcys' townhouse and then on to Ipswich for a fortnight.

Having left instructions with Longbourn's groom to bring the Darcy carriage round once the newlyweds carriages were summoned, he guided his wife to bid her farewells to all of her family. He tried not to worry as she wept with each goodbye. *It is merely an emotional time for her. She will be fine,* he endeavoured to convince himself.

Finally, he was able to hand his wife into their carriage for the trip north. Before he entered their conveyance, Darcy checked once more with his cousin Richard to see that all was ready for Georgiana to travel with him back to London to stay for a few weeks at the Matlock town home. His aunt had invited all three of the Darcys to visit, but Darcy had wished to have a little time alone with his wife.

Once the earl returned from visiting his sister, the Matlocks were to travel back to their country home and would bring Georgiana to Pemberley on their way. His aunt had written of planning a great deal of shopping and some concert attendance while their niece was with them. Darcy smiled when he remembered the excitement that shone on Georgiana's face at the idea of going to a concert in Town.

Elizabeth leaned back against the seat and sighed. She reached into her reticule for a handkerchief and wiped her eyes.

"Are you well, dearest?" Darcy asked in evident concern.

She sniffed and gave him a smile. "Of course, I am well, only a bit sad at the changes in my family. However, I shall be fine. You know that I am not fit for melancholy."

Wanting to help elevate her mood, Darcy inquired into Elizabeth's thoughts on how the wedding and following festivities had gone. He smiled as she animatedly chatted about the loveliness of her sisters' gowns and the fine food and decorations at the wedding breakfast. Soon, she was sharing more about her revised relationships with her family and talked about Lydia's acceptance of her invitation for an extended stay.

"So your father has given her his permission?" he asked.

She grinned sheepishly at him. "I am afraid that I made certain that he would agree." Her eyes twinkled as she continued, "I agreed to give him not only full access to the library at Pemberley but also agree to the availability of your best port as well."

Darcy barked out a laugh. "It is good that my supply of books and port is ample enough."

"Indeed," Elizabeth agreed as she leaned her head on Darcy's shoulder. "Thank you for being so understanding. It will give me much pleasure to have my family at Pemberley and especially to have extra time with Lydia."

Soon, they arrived in Meryton and passed through the village, nodding to acquaintances as they did so. Their carriage was joined by the servants' equipage on the road outside of town, near the entrance of the lane to Netherfield. They were not to take the London road at the crossroads a few miles ahead of them. With the Bingleys staying at Darcy House in Town, they had chosen to take the more northerly route back to Derbyshire.

That first day of travel was uneventful until about an hour before the final stop for the night, when it began to rain heavily. The carriages were quite weather tight, but everyone was very happy to enter the inn and find hot tea and coffee ready for them, as well as a hearty meal of steak and ale pie.

"My dear, I fear you will find yourself with a spoiled and fat wife if you continue on this course," Elizabeth commented between bites of the savoury dish.

"Never," he proclaimed with a smile. "You know I have tried these past months to no avail." Her laughter warmed him more than the excellent food and drink.

~*~

The rain continued to fall as they got into the carriage for the second day's journey. The roads were muddy, for the most part, but relatively passable until the final leg of the journey. They had to stop several times so that the footmen and drivers could remove mud from the wheels or push one of the carriages out of a deep rut. They were but a few miles from their destination and passing through a village when someone flagged them to a stop.

"What is it, Holmes?" Darcy asked a footman through the window he had opened.

"Sir, the man says that the bridge ahead be out. He says we should go to the Fox and Hound. They have rooms there for the night." The footman bowed and motioned for the stranger to come forward.

"What is this I hear about the bridge being out?" Darcy demanded in a firm tone of the man who came to stand next to Holmes.

A stout young man of about eighteen wearing a long coat of oil cloth touched the rim of his dripping broad hat and nodded. "Aye, it be out since this noon. The rains have swollen the water something fierce. It be days 'til it can be repaired. Sir, we have a fine inn, and there still be rooms for ye there. The other road north still be passable. If ye be following me, I will show ye." The man's uneducated pattern of speech reminded him of many Darcy had encountered during his previous stays in post inns.

Darcy nodded to both the men and leaned back to close the window. "This will cause a delay, but it cannot be helped," he sighed.

"We can be thankful that there is an available inn, although I hope that it is clean," Elizabeth said.

"We always travel with a change of bedding for just such an occasion." Darcy frowned at the rain as it splashed against the windows. "I am more concerned that the roads will be passable on the morrow. If not, we will need to extend our stay here."

"Let us not borrow trouble." Elizabeth squeezed his hand as she said, "At the moment, I wish only for a good cup of tea and a decent meal."

Once they made it to the inn and entered through the large darkly panelled door into the crowded and noisy pub, the innkeeper, a Mr. Sawyer, bowed low and gestured to a small private dining room.

"Sir, we be honoured that ye be here," he bowed once more and said, "My wife and one of our maids be seeing to the preparing of our best chambers. As ye can see, we have tea, coffee and ale ready for ye. Your meal be forthcomin' as soon as ye desire."

"We would like to refresh ourselves before we do anything else." Darcy informed the brawny man.

"Of course, sir," he hastily agreed as he turned to the servants at the back of the room. "Show these fine people to where they can refresh themselves and be quick about it."

After a quick visit to the refreshing rooms, the Darcys returned to the dining parlour and found Peters and Sarah overseeing the setting out of the things for the meal.

Elizabeth accepted a cup of strong, sweetened tea after she sat at the table. She looked about the room, which was panelled in the same wood as the rest of the establishment. It was almost black with age and smoke. Happy to notice that it was as clean as the previous inn in which they had dined, she nodded when the serving maid offered her a platter of venison and roasted potatoes.

Remarking upon the tastiness of the meal, Darcy dismissed the young girl. Before she left, the maid whispered to Sarah that there was a dried apple tart on the sideboard if the gentry wished to partake of a dessert.

All-in-all, the stay at the Fox and Hound turned out to be a pleasant one. While they breakfasted that morning, the innkeeper asked if he could speak to Darcy in private after he had eaten. Darcy met with Mr. Sawyer in a small back room that served as the innkeeper's office.

"Thank ye, sir, for coming," the man said nervously. "I don' mean to be afrightenin' ye, but there be places on the north road which ain't safe for gentlefolk such as yerselves. We have been having highway men robbin' folks lately between here and Greystop where ye will be rejoining the road ye were wantin' to travel on before the bridge went out. I have four of my most trusted friends who would be more than happy to escort you. They be good shots and strong in the bargain. Miller would be going back to his home in Greystop, where he be the innkeeper, so he wouldn't be chargin' ye much to go with ye. They all be ready as soon as ye are, sir."

Although unhappy with this latest development, Darcy knew that if the man was correct, they did need more protection than his two drivers and four footmen. He agreed to the escort after inquiring how much the four men would want in return. Their price was not too dear, so after making arrangements for the time of departure, he returned to the dining room and explained the new situation to Elizabeth.

"I am nervous about this, but I want to go home as soon as we can." Darcy paced the small room and raked his fingers through his hair.

Elizabeth lifted her reticule and said, "I have my 'toy'."

Darcy reluctantly smiled. "You have your 'toy', and all of the men have theirs. Any highwaymen will be surprised at how well armed we all are, but I do not wish for you to be in such a situation."

"Nor do I, but it is better that we are forewarned," she said as she came to his side and stopped his movement. She lifted onto her toes and kissed his cheek. "I will go and see if there is anything needed for the trip. Mrs. Sawyer has already ordered a food basket for us and hot bricks for our feet."

Darcy lifted her hand to his lips for a quick kiss. "Thank you, Beth, for calming me."

"I am at your service, sir," she teased, her eyes sparkling with delight.

As the day progressed, the rain lessened and had stopped completely once they arrived in Greystop. The detour had added an extra day to the journey, but with better weather, tomorrow's trip would not be so difficult or uncomfortable as the previous day's unless the rain returned, which did not seem likely.

Mr. Miller ushered his guests into the Lion's Head Inn, calling to his wife and daughter to come serve the gentleman and his lady. Darcy entered with Elizabeth on his arm and looked around the establishment. It was even cleaner than the Fox and Hound. Inside the public room there were several customers who surveyed the new arrivals with curiosity before returning to their drinks or food.

"Mr. Darcy, this is my wife, Tilly," Miller said as he smiled proudly. "She is my business partner as well as my wife. I would not have half the profits I do if she did not do what she does around here."

Darcy was surprised and pleased to see the man's pride in his wife and his acknowledgement of her contribution to the inn's success. The man sounded more educated than Mr. Peters or others of the innkeepers he had met. It crossed his mind that the man reminded him of Mr. Gardiner in his manner and his attitude toward his wife. Darcy bowed and introduced Elizabeth. He asked to be shown to their chambers so that they could refresh themselves and that a meal be ready for them in half an hour.

While Elizabeth listened to her husband discuss the details of their stay, she rubbed her hand unconsciously over her rounding stomach before she pushed a fist into her lower back. As her body changed to accommodate her growing child, she found that the usual stiffness and aches of riding in a carriage for long periods were intensified.

Mr. Miller quickly agreed and asked that his wife show the Darcys to their rooms. "My daughter usually attends to these matters, but she must be busy elsewhere."

Mrs. Miller looked worried as she hastily replied, "She is not well today."

Turning back to the Darcys, Mrs. Miller said, "Sir, if you please follow me."

Mrs. Miller showed them to the inn's best rooms. The furnishings were simple but comfortable. A pitcher of hot water sat ready for them with fresh clean towels laid out next to it. "Please ring for me when you are ready. I shall come to take you to the dining room." She paused before she added, "Mrs. Darcy, while you eat, I could order hot water for a bath for your comfort. In your condition, it can relieve aches and pains."

When Elizabeth raised a questioning brow, the innkeeper's wife answered, "I noticed you rubbing your belly and your back. No matter how well sprung a coach is, it can be jarring to one such as yourself."

"Thank you, Mrs. Miller. I would appreciate a hot bath very much."

Once they had finished refreshing themselves, the Darcys were shown into the private dining room. Hot food was laid out for them on the table. The couple moved farther into the room before they dismissed the inn's servant. Elizabeth went to the sideboard where the drinks were set. She prepared tea for them both. As she did this, her reticule which hung from her right wrist, threatened to upset the cups. Stopping mid-task, she switched the purse to her left arm.

Sarah stood quietly just inside the room to the side of the door, awaiting either orders or dismissal. Her mistress liked to prepare tea for herself and her husband when she could during their travels. A slight smile crossed her lips as she thought of her lot in life. The Darcys were good and kind masters whom she would serve to her best ability as long as she was able.

As she was thus pondering, the door slowly opened. Expecting a servant, Sarah barely glanced that way. For this reason, she was shocked when she finally noticed a scruffy man, dressed in dirty, shabby garments. She stood in incredulous confusion for a second, wondering how this derelict could have the audacity to enter a private room. As Sarah watched the man move toward the Darcys, she saw that he had a pistol in one hand. She also realized that he had not taken notice of her presence in the room. Deciding to take advantage of that fact and to go for help, Sarah reached out to catch the door before it closed completely. Just as she slipped out of the room, she heard Mr. Darcy cry out, "Wickham, what are you doing here?" before she shut the door quietly.

CHAPTER THIRTY-EIGHT

Elizabeth had just set the tea cups on the table in front of Darcy when he jumped up and nearly knocked over the chair. At his cry, she looked toward the door and gasped. Grabbing her husband's left arm, she moved slightly behind him. Part of her wanted to panic, but she would not allow it. She needed her wits about her if she and Fitzwilliam were to survive this ordeal.

"Well, now, Darcy, is that any way to greet an old friend?" Wickham smiled toothily and said, "Miss Elizabeth, it is a pleasure to meet you again. I enjoyed our last encounter so very much. Happily, I was in a position to observe your entry into this fine establishment and heard the proprietor speak your name. Thus I decided to renew my acquaintance with you both. I noticed your delicate condition as I watched you, Miss Elizabeth. I knew I had to come to see you both. It is interesting that you are such a fertile kind of woman."

"How is it that you are here and not in the West Indies?" Darcy asked, ignoring Wickham's disgusting comments.

Wickham chuckled derisively. "So you know about that, do you? I thought you might have had something to do with my hasty departure from Hertfordshire, and I imagine your cousin the colonel was your errand boy as usual. I merely jumped ship just before we entered the channel. Once we had set out for sea, they untied me, never thinking that I would jump ship so far from land. I am sure the intrepid sailors did not miss me until I had reached the shore. You must recall my talent for swimming long distances. It came in very handy this time for certain. Likely you would have received word months from now of my being lost at sea. "

He took a couple steps closer so that he reached the table. Raising his gun so that the couple could see it, he reached forward, took one of the cups, and sipped from it, all the while keeping them in his sights. "Very good, Miss Elizabeth. I have always liked my tea the same as Darcy here. You must be very helpful to that gentleman. I admit that I am surprised that you would agree to be his mistress, but I suppose you had few choices, given your obvious condition."

"You will not speak to my wife in such an insulting manner." Darcy leaned forward and glared at the other man. His heart pounded frantically as he lifted up a desperate prayer for help.

"Oh, ho, you married her?" He bowed slightly toward Elizabeth. "Made him think the child was his, did you?" When Darcy made to lunge at him, Wickham waved the pistol at him, which forced the couple to take a few steps back.

"Did she neglect to tell you that the brat is mine? Did she tell you how delightful our encounter was? I considered returning and partaking of that enjoyment once more before I left the area, but I was rudely removed before I had the chance."

"The babe is as much a Darcy as I am. I have no doubt of that." Darcy stood tall and looked straight into the other man's eyes. "And before you say something else insulting about my wife, I know what you did. I came upon her after your attack. I even saw you leave. You are a villain of the worst sort, and I wish that I had allowed Richard to have his way in dealing with you. The world would be a better place without the likes of you."

Wickham narrowed his eyes as he watched Darcy's stance. He could tell that here was a man bent on protecting his wife at all cost.

"You will not escape punishment this time, Wickham," Darcy bit out in agitation.

"Oh, I believe I will, my old friend," Wickham argued. He tried his usual cocky smile, but it lacked some of its usual confidence.

He pointed the pistol at Darcy's heart and said, "Mrs. Darcy, I want you to come over here. You will be my protection and companion. I am sure that you would not want your husband dead. First, Darcy, put your money clip into her reticule. You always did carry far more than you needed."

"No, I will not come with you!" she cried out and held tightly to Darcy's arm.

"I would prefer you come willingly rather than kicking and screaming after I kill him, but I will have you as a hostage either way. It does not matter to me which you choose." Wickham shrugged his shoulders as he lifted the pistol and pulled back the hammer. "I have little time left in this hamlet. Soon my recent activities will come to light, and I wish to be far afield by that time."

"Please," Elizabeth paled and called out, "no, I will do as you say. Do not shoot, and I will come quietly with you."

Wickham eased the hammer back and lowered the gun slightly as he watched the silent interplay between husband and wife. He understood that Darcy would rather die than have his wife taken from him. The thought made him smile more broadly. Indeed, he would have his revenge.

Looking into Darcy's eyes, she held out a hand palm up for the money clip. He reached into his pocket and pulled out the money he had there. Elizabeth opened her reticule and slipped it inside. While her hand was in her bag, she let go of the money and took hold of the small pistol but did not bring it out, merely holding the whole thing close to her side. She took a few steps until she was around the end of the table.

This movement split Wickham's attention, but since he believed Darcy to be the bigger risk to him, he kept his eyes on him and commanded in a loud voice, "Bring the money to me, woman. I want to get out of here."

Elizabeth moved closer without a sound, and once she was close enough to the cad, she let the reticule drop to the floor while quickly bringing the pistol barrel to his temple. "Put the gun on the table and take a slow step back."

"You would not kill me," Wickham said shakily as if to convince himself.

"Oh, I will pull the trigger with pleasure if you do not do as I say." Elizabeth's voice was cold and flat with no hint of fear. "You will be dead before you can do anything else." To emphasize her point, she cocked the pistol.

It was the tone of her voice and the click of the hammer that convinced Wickham to acquiesce, and as soon as Wickham put his pistol down, Darcy came around the table and grabbed the other man's arms, trying to twist them behind him. In one last effort to escape his punishment, Wickham began to struggle to free himself and get his hands on his gun once more. This attempt was foiled as Elizabeth grabbed up the pistol from the table and moved away from the struggling men.

Finally able to get a stronger grip on Wickham's arms, Darcy called out breathlessly, "Keep your gun aimed at this poor excuse of a human being so that I can tie him up until we can find the constable."

"That will not be necessary, sir," a voice behind them announced.

Elizabeth and Darcy turned to see Mr. Miller and two burly men in the doorway. Miller held a large flintlock. Wickham struggled again to free himself from Darcy's grasp, but although Darcy had been surprised by the newly arrived men, he had not loosened his hold.

"Mr. Darcy, among my other duties, I serve as the constable of our town," Miller said. "We have a nice, secure lockup here. This person," he spat out the word with disgust, "will be held there until the magistrate can question him. First thing tomorrow morning, I will summon the magistrate, Sir Clark Duncan. He is in residence this month and at his leisure to administer justice."

The two men took hold of Wickham forcibly and tied his hands behind him. They marched him out of the door while he shouted curses at Darcy and the other men. Just outside the door, those in the room heard a crunching sound, a grunt of pain, and no more noises from the prisoner.

"Sir, I am so sorry that you were subjected to this blackguard at my inn. Your maid here," Miller pointed to Sarah, who had just entered, and continued, "finally located me and told me what was happening in this room. I had just found out that my own daughter had been harmed by that rotten scoundrel. She was reluctant to tell anyone because he told her no one would believe her, and that she would be called a whore." The man was clearly angry and upset.

"It would seem that he has been involved in the highway robberies round these parts, as well as taking liberties with other of the young ladies in this and other villages close by. He has been using my inn as a headquarters of sorts. We have arrested someone we believe to be one of his accomplices. The stupid bloke tried to exchange a bit of stolen lady's jewellery for drinks at the town's other public house. This one is likely to hang for the robberies, especially since he seemed to enjoy beating his male victims in front of the ladies to show off his power over them.

Darcy put out his hand to the innkeeper. "Mr. Miller, you have done us a great service. I cannot begin to thank you. That man's name is George Wickham, and he is an escaped prisoner. He was to work out his many debts on a ship and later on in the West Indies when he jumped overboard into the channel and swam to shore. I will testify to this with the magistrate as well.

Elizabeth placed her hand on Miller's arm and said, "Is there anything that I can do to help your daughter? Trauma such as she has suffered is hard to overcome."

"It is very kind of you to ask, ma'am, but I do not know what can be done in this case." He sighed in despair and said, "If she is with child, I suppose she will have to be sent away, and if she is not, it will still be hard for her to find a husband. I know that we are not quality folks, but the better of us do have standards. I would hate to see my girl married to a ruffian, just because that..." He paused to search for the right word and continued without finding one, "chose to attack my Jenny."

Darcy studied the man before him, a person in obvious pain over what had happened to his daughter. Pondering a solution, he spoke in a kind tone, "Mr. Miller, I am grieved indeed for your misfortune and that of Miss Jenny. I am grateful to you and your friends, since I am not certain what might have transpired if you and your men had not come as soon as you did. For that reason, I would like to offer assistance to your daughter. I own a large estate in Derbyshire, near the village of Lambton. I have many people working for me. I believe that I would be able to find a decent man who is in need of a wife. I shall provide a dowry that will aid in securing such a man. I vow that I shall investigate all the men whom I will suggest, so that your daughter shall have the best possible chance at felicity in marriage."

The older man stood in silent astonishment for several moments, blinking back tears before he hoarsely uttered, "It is too much, sir. You do not owe me such generosity. I only did what was right in my duty as a man and an officer of the law. That should be my only reward."

Darcy took a step closer to Miller and lowering his voice, said, "I shall insist upon it, sir. I knew what he was, and though I tried to have him punished for his debts and other acts of villainy, I know now I should have called for a harsher punishment, knowing him as I do. If you will allow us to stay long enough to ascertain what is to happen to Wickham, I shall begin my enquiries as soon as I reach my home. I will not be gainsaid in this matter."

Mr. Miller locked eyes with Darcy, who did not flinch at the examination. Finally the innkeeper held out his hand and proclaimed, "You are welcome to stay at Lion's Head as long as you wish and as my guest at no charge."

Darcy shook the man's hand but protested that he would pay for the accommodations.

"Pardon me, sir, but I shall be as firm in my resolve as you are in yours," Miller replied with a bow of the head. "And I shall leave you so that I may have the hot food and tea replenished and brought to you." With a crisp nod to both of the Darcys, he left the room.

Darcy turned to Elizabeth and saw that she was sitting in a chair next to Sarah, gripping her hands. They were both trembling with tears running down their faces.

"My dear, are you well? What can I get for your present relief?" He quickly reached his wife and knelt before her.

Elizabeth swallowed several times before she found her voice. She continued to grip one of her maid's hands while slipping the other into Darcy's. "I am merely shaken from the ordeal, but I am well. I am so grateful to Sarah for her quick thinking. We must reward her for her help."

"Oh, no, Mistress," Sarah sniffed. "I want no reward. I could not have done other than to go for aid when I saw that man with a gun. If I had been a man, I would likely have defended you myself, but I was not brave enough to try or smart enough to know how to do it. I am so happy that you and the master are safe." She reached into her pocket for a handkerchief and wiped her eyes.

"I too wish to express my gratitude for your swift service to us both." Darcy offered his hands to help both the women to stand. "I want you to find some food and to rest for the night. We will not need your assistance tonight. And if you see Peters, please tell him he need not attend me either. Mrs. Darcy and I will discuss how you shall be rewarded for your swift action."

Sarah bobbed a curtsey and exited the room.

Darcy pulled Elizabeth into his arms and held her as tightly against him as her growing shape would allow. "My brave, darling Beth, are you truly well?"

"I am indeed," she said against his chest. "I am completely well and free of the fear that his first attack caused me. I am so glad that you gave me that gun and taught me to use it."

He kissed the top of her head. "As am I, dearest; as am I."

CHAPTER THIRTY-NINE

Following an intense dream in which she relived the day of her attack, Elizabeth awakened the next morning with some of her former fears beginning to plague her once more. She determined to ask Darcy if she could go to the prison to see for herself that Wickham was there. Once the servants had left them in privacy to eat their breakfast, she did just that.

"Why would you want to see him again, dearest?" Darcy worried about what his wife was thinking.

"I had a horrid nightmare about the attack. I believe I need to see once and for all that he is securely locked up," she answered, while gazing steadily into his eyes. "In my mind, I know that he has lost his power to make me afraid or to harm me again, but I have not completely convinced my heart of that fact. I believe that seeing him behind a barred door shall be the persuasion my heart needs."

"If you are certain it is what you wish, I shall inquire of Mr. Miller," Darcy said as he touched her arm.

Elizabeth lifted her face to him and smiled with gratitude.

Half an hour later, Miller guided them up the high street to the middle of the square in which stood the small round building that served as the village's gaol. A man stood at post on each side of the building's one entrance. Heavy iron bars made up most of the door, with a huge beam lying across it to hold it closed. The padlock that locked the beam in place was massive and obviously well maintained since there was not even the hint of rust or dirt to be seen upon it. When the guards spied Miller and the Darcys, they stood straighter.

"The prisoners be safe in the lockup, sir," one of the men said quickly as if to reassure the constable of the fact.

"I am certain they are, Black," Miller answered with a nod. "These fine people would like to have a look at one of them."

"O' course, sir," Black replied, "but neither ain't so pretty right now. They had a bit of an accident, they did. They be a bit messed up."

365

Miller held back his grin. He understood that his men had taken out their anger on Wickham and, to a lesser degree, the other man the night before, but he knew that they had not fatally injured either prisoner.

"Black, make sure the prisoners are back from the door," Miller ordered.

The guards both laughed, but Black did look through the bars to be sure before he said, "They ain't moved from the floor but to moan since they got here last night."

"Come ahead, sir," Miller said quietly to Darcy.

Darcy put his hand over his wife's where it lay on his arm. His look asked if she still wanted to view the man. When she nodded quickly, he guided her to the small building.

Moving tentatively to the bars, Elizabeth glanced in and saw the two prisoners on the floor. Although there was no light inside, the sun at the moment was streaming into the place, and it fell upon Wickham's face. An involuntary gasp escaped her as she glimpsed the swollen and bruised face of the man. One eye was so puffy that it was obvious that he would not be able to open it. There was a smear of dried blood across one cheek which bespoke of a broken nose and split upper lip.

Elizabeth was surprised at her reaction to the sight before her. She felt little pity or even sympathy for the fallen man before her, but even more shocking was the lack of triumph in her heart. It was as if in seeing the broken man before her, she was able to release the hatred, but not wish him to be free from his just punishment. As she turned back to Darcy, she sent up a silent prayer for his soul and asked to return to the inn.

On their way back to their rooms, Darcy inquired, "Are you well, dearest?"

"I am indeed," she answered softly. "He will likely be hanged, will he not?"

"Yes," he said simply.

"God have mercy on his soul," Elizabeth pronounced without emotion. "I shall ask God for His help in forgiving the scoundrel, for I have no compassion at the moment. However, as I have seen in the last months, forgiveness is freeing. God will avenge, with the help of the law."

"You are an amazing woman, my love," Darcy said with wonder apparent in his voice. "I am not certain I will ever forgive him. I feel great hatred for the man."

"Ah, yes, as I do, or did for a long time," she sighed. "I am certain I shall struggle for an equally long time with this issue, but as I viewed him lying on that dirty floor, I knew that he was defeated and that even what he meant as injury, God has used to our good. I could wish that I had never experienced what I have, but I would not want to be anywhere other than where I am right now. I am your wife, beloved by you, and awaiting the birth of our first child. He will be as wanted as any of our children."

"Indeed she shall," Darcy said, smiling down at her.

~*~

The Darcys stayed in Greystop for two more days while the magistrate questioned them in private. Sir Clark was respectful of the women involved and said that with all of the testimony he had obtained from witnesses and their signed statements, he was certain that they would not be required to be at the trial. It might be necessary for Mr. Darcy to be present, as he was aware of the details of Wickham's previous offenses and his debts and had heard the man's account of his escape from the ship. The magistrate promised to contact Darcy when he knew what was required of him.

As they awaited the packing of the carriage, the couple breakfasted one last time in the private parlour. Jenny served them efficiently and without a word as she had been taught. When Darcy left to see that everything was in readiness for their departure, Elizabeth spoke to the girl, stopping her from leaving the room. "Are you well?"

The girl bobbed a quick curtsey. "Aye, ma'am, I am very well, thank you."

"Mr. Darcy and I are concerned about you. Please be sure to inform your parents of any problems you may have. We wish to help you."

Jenny blushed deeply as she responded in a near whisper, "My papa told me of your kind offer. Please believe that I... we do not expect you to do anything."

"Yes, we do understand that, but we are more than willing to do as we have promised. It will be an honour to help such a deserving family. You should not have to suffer because of another's evil deed."

"Thank you, ma'am," Jenny answered as she bobbed another curtsey and left quickly when she was dismissed.

~*~

The rest of the trip to Pemberley was uneventful and fairly swift. Their arrival at the house was met by both the housekeeper and the butler. The staff had been informed by express of their delay. Speculation as to its cause had circulated throughout the servants' quarters. The main concern was that something had happened to the mistress or the expected babe, but relief fairly radiated from the two once they spied their master and mistress alight from the carriage in obvious good health.

"Welcome home, Mr. and Mrs. Darcy," Mrs. Reynolds declared.

"Thank you, it is good to be home," Darcy answered for them both. "We will be needing to freshen up. Please see that we have a tray of tea and food in our sitting room in a quarter hour."

Elizabeth smiled happily at the two as she passed them upon entering the house. She felt some fatigue, but the very fact that she was finally home cheered her in both body and spirit. The tea tray had arrived once both of the Darcys had washed and changed.

After pouring tea for them both, Elizabeth sat in her favourite chair near the fire. "It is so lovely to be home once more, Fitzwilliam." She sipped her drink and nibbled on some of the small sandwiches from the tray.

"I agree wholeheartedly," he replied as he settled into his chair with a plate of food. "Will you want to rest this afternoon?"

"Oh, no, I only wish to finish our refreshments before taking a walk around the garden. There are so many new flowers and plants to see. It is amazing how things can change in a month's time."

"Very well, my love, as long as you do not tax yourself," Darcy said and, with a twinkle in his eye, continued, "Should you like me to attend you?"

"Very much," she grinned as she answered. "I am certain that I shall need a strong arm to lean on and a listening ear for all of my raptures on the beauty of the gardens. Do you think that you will be able to manage such a task?"

"I do believe I shall be able to handle it."

~*~

For the rest of the week and into the next, the Darcys stayed close to home, only venturing into the village once for church. The day after they arrived home, Fitzwilliam had insisted that the doctor be summoned to examine Elizabeth for any adverse results of the encounter with Wickham. The physician found her to be in excellent health, and the pregnancy was progressing according to schedule, with the baby arriving in early September.

Elizabeth and Darcy had not shared the circumstances of her pregnancy with the doctor, nor did they think it necessary. Knowing that the child was actually due early in August, they would not lie about it to anyone, but they would just wait until the baby was born and see what people might say.

Georgiana arrived after a fortnight with Colonel Fitzwilliam and his family. Since his father, the earl, had sent word that he would not be returning for some time, he had asked his son to escort his mother and Georgiana back to their respective country homes. The countess and her son did not stay long after they refreshed themselves and ate a light meal. They wanted to make it to the Matlock estate before dark.

The Darcy family enjoyed a happy reunion. The younger woman had several gifts for the baby, including a richly crafted christening gown purchased by Lady Matlock. Rattles, stuffed animals, and a doll were among the toys she brought.

"Georgiana," Elizabeth exclaimed as she unwrapped the packages. "You must have bought out half the shops. These are wonderful. I am sure the baby will be the best dressed and most spoiled niece or nephew that ever lived."

Giggling, her sister-in-law said, "I fully intended to be the doting aunt, spoiling the children dreadfully."

Darcy entered the parlour to hear the ladies' laughter. "What is this? Why was I not informed of a party?" He tried to sound stern, but his smile belied his words.

"Oh, Fitzwilliam," Georgiana cried, "I could not wait until you were back from your duties to show Elizabeth what I brought for the baby. Come look at this cunning little rattle. It has a pony painted on it that looks just like my Dotty."

After Darcy had duly admired the baby things, he asked to speak to Elizabeth alone in his study. Georgiana waved them off with promises to move everything to the nursery, which was being updated with fresh paint, wallpaper, and furnishings.

Closing the study door behind them, Darcy guided Elizabeth to the settee and sat down with her.

"Is something wrong, my love?" Elizabeth was worried by the blank expression on his face, since it was his usual habit to hide negative emotions behind an unreadable look.

A small smile crossed his face as he shook his head. "I cannot hide anything from you, can I?" He sighed softly before he went on, "Richard brought a letter from my uncle. He is well, but he states that Aunt Catherine is not. He had been afraid that she called for him so as to convince him to allow her to return to Rosings. Instead he found that she had had a fit of apoplexy and is mostly bedridden. However, though her speech is slow and slurred, she is still able to make her opinions known.

"Uncle Vincent is glad that he brought his personal physician along, since there is none close by Briar Mist. Mrs. Martin had done a very good job in caring for Lady Catherine. The doctor said that there is a chance that with proper exercises she could recover some of the use of her right side, which is almost completely paralyzed, but there is also a good chance that she will have another attack."

"Does Uncle Vincent plan to bring her back to Matlock or Rosings?" Elizabeth asked him. Although she was not fond of the older woman, she did feel sympathy for the Fitzwilliam family and for Anne de Bourgh.

"The doctor does not think it prudent to move her at this time. He has sent for more nurses to help in her care. My uncle has already asked that Anne travel to see her mother and will await her arrival." Darcy rubbed his chin as he thought about the rest of the letter.

"There is more, is there not?" Elizabeth laid a hand on his.

"Yes, there is," he sighed out resignedly. "Mrs. Martin told him what happened the day Lady Catherine fell ill. In the days leading up to that fateful one, my aunt had written many letters to friends and other more distant relatives. My uncle decided that he did not trust her, thinking that she might try to sully your name in the eyes of anyone who might listen. With that in mind, he ordered that all of her outgoing letters be sent to him. He would examine them, send any acceptable ones on their way, and destroy the unacceptable.

"This worked well until the day when my aunt found the packet that was to be sent to my uncle and opened it. She screamed and ranted at the servants and Mrs. Martin about their betrayal and incompetence. Nothing that Mrs. Martin could say would calm her. The nurse went to call for the two footmen to help her to restrain Lady Catherine, so that she could administer a sedative powder, when my aunt collapsed."

"Will you be travelling to see her as well?" Elizabeth asked with trepidation.

"No, Uncle Vincent asked that I not come." He shook his head sadly. "As I said before, my aunt's speech is slow, but she now blames us both for her illness. She has even gone so far as to claim that you somehow poisoned her."

Elizabeth gasped at this news. Her mind could not comprehend such delusion. "She said that? She thinks I would poison her? What if someone believed her?"

"Dearest, my uncle will not allow her to see anyone who might believe her," he soothed as he wrapped an arm around her shoulders. "The doctor will inform the new nurses that Aunt Catherine is delusional. His people are well experienced in dealing with the mentally deficient, and they will not have any reason to give credence to her mad tales. And the doctor hopes that seeing Anne again will calm her, since my aunt calls for her often and fears for her safety as well."

"I am relieved to hear your reassurances and that you shall not have to travel north to see her." She leaned her head on Darcy's chest and relaxed.

"I have no plans to leave you any time soon," Darcy said and kissed the top of her head. "You are my most important priority."

Elizabeth smiled and lifted her face to his and kissed him. "You are mine as well.

CHAPTER FORTY

In the middle of June, the Darcys were at breakfast when the daily post was brought to them. Two letters arrived addressed to Fitzwilliam. The first was from the magistrate, Sir Clark of Greystop. Since Darcy and Elizabeth had not shared the details of their encounter with Wickham, he decided to discuss the contents of the letter from the magistrate with Elizabeth in private.

The other missive was from Lord Matlock stating that he had returned to his estate along with his niece, Anne. He told them that Lady Catherine remained the same in body and mind. Seeing her daughter had helped for a few weeks until Lady Catherine asked after Darcy and was told that he was unable to visit, as his wife could not travel in her delicate condition. The tirade that followed caused fear that she would have another fit of apoplexy, but she did not. She had to be sedated for several days until it was decided that when she was stable, the earl and Miss de Bourgh would return to their homes. Nothing was being accomplished by their remaining.

"I am sad that the lady is so confused and upset. I had hoped that once she understood how happy we are...," Elizabeth said as she caressed her rounded belly. She was having difficulty sitting close enough to the table these days. Leaning forward, she reached for her tea cup and sipped from it.

"I have never been as close to Aunt Catherine as I am to Aunt Maud. Aunt Catherine was always a cold and demanding woman. My father instilled in me a great sense of familial obligation, and we visited her often, especially when my uncle and my mother were alive. Once my own father passed, I could not manage more than my yearly stay at Rosings because of, among other reasons, her insistence that Anne and I were to wed. She was so stubborn and almost fanatical in that insistence, but I admit even I am surprised that she carried the idea so far as to interrupt our wedding and then to try to lie about both of us to her friends and acquaintances." Darcy absentmindedly spread jam on a piece of toast that he really did not want. "It is good that my uncle thought to censor her mail, or there would be a great scandal about the family. He shall have to spend a goodly amount of money to keep knowledge of her condition from becoming known in the *ton*."

"Will he be able to achieve it?" she asked quietly. Looking around the room, she realized that Darcy had quietly sent the servants from the room before he began the discussion.

"I believe he will," Darcy stated as he dropped the toast on his plate without eating it. "He has the resources to make it happen, and Briar Mist is a long way from London."

Georgiana had listened to the conversation until she finally commented, "I cannot help but be glad that she will no longer torment you, brother. You would always be in such a state after an Easter visit to Rosings, though I had no idea how difficult it was for you until now. I am happy to finally be able to become more acquainted with Cousin Anne. I like her very much."

"As do I," Elizabeth told her with a smile. "I am happy that she will be able to return home." She turned to her husband with a question, "Do you think that she will be able to come to our ball?"

"I believe she will if you invite her personally," Darcy answered her with a smile and a wink.

"I shall write and invite her as soon as we are finished here."

Once breakfast was over and Georgiana had left for her morning music practice, Darcy asked Elizabeth to join him in his study. He wished to relay the news contained in the missive from Sir Clark.

Darcy led Elizabeth to their favourite settee and helped her to sit down before joining her. He lifted an official looking document. "This is from the magistrate, Sir Clark. He has looked into the matter of Wickham and is sending him to Derby to await trial in the assize court there. It will be another six months before the circuit judge arrives to preside over the proceedings. Wickham will be in the prison there for the time being."

Elizabeth felt her stomach clench with fear. Her voice was small and breathy when she asked, "Would he be able to escape?"

"Oh, dearest, please do not be afraid." he gripped her hands firmly in his and reassured her in a confident tone, "I had already left word with Mr. Miller that to prevent just such an event, he was to hire two men to serve as additional guards to escort him to Derby and stay as such for whatever time is needed. They will not let him escape. I am completely certain of it."

There was something in her husband's tone that doused the panic that had tried to build once more. She would trust in her husband's abilities and would not allow herself to slip back into the old terror. "Thank you for doing this for me, my love."

"No gratitude is needed," he said calmly. "I am just doing what I need to do to keep you safe."

~*~

As her time of delivery in early August drew near, Elizabeth began to fuss about the nursery, calling for changes to be done even though the room had already been completely redecorated a few months before. Once she finished directing a servant as to the moving of furniture, she began to unpack and refold all of the baby items while making an inventory of everything. When she was asked what she thought might be missing, she could not give an answer other than that she felt compelled to be certain that everything was in readiness for their child.

One afternoon Darcy found her seated in the rocking chair next to the cradle, singing a soft lullaby and caressing her swollen belly.

"Beth, you look so beautiful," he said as he entered the room once she finished her song.

"Oh, Fitzwilliam, I feel so huge and awkward," she complained as she struggled to get to her feet.

Darcy helped her rise and kissed her lightly on the lips. He looked down at the mound under her dress that held their child and saw the material move as the baby kicked. "I believe she is anxious to greet the world."

Following his gaze, she chuckled. "My singing seemed to calm him, but now he heard your voice and is happy to know you are here."

"I shall be pleased when she arrives, so that you will stop calling her a he," Darcy teased as he lifted her chin and looked into her eyes. "Are you well, my love?"

Breathing out a sigh, Elizabeth could not help but smile at the oft repeated question. "I am well, just impatient and worried. I want to hold the baby now, and from our calculations, I should have been delivered over a week ago. What if something is wrong?"

"I admit to being impatient as well, but from everything I have read, babies come when they come. She is still active, which is a good sign." He tried to encourage her, but he was beginning to become concerned about it as well.

"But what if something is wrong?" She leaned forward awkwardly, trying to put her head on his chest.

Darcy turned her to the side so that she could rest against him without her belly between them. He put his arms around her. "Do not worry, my love. Everything is fine. What do you say to the idea that if the baby is not born within the next week, we shall call for the doctor and tell him you are feeling anxious about the babe?"

"I believe I am able to wait another week." She sighed again. "However, the midwife is coming to examine me about that time, and the doctor is scheduled to arrive for his stay in a fortnight. I am certain that babies come early or late, even without our particular circumstances. I do not wish to stir up any gossip, if we can help it, by stating that I am worried that the baby has not come."

"As you wish, dearest." Darcy kissed her forehead and urged her toward the door. "Now it is time for dinner. I want to make sure that my two girls are fed."

"And I would not want my two boys to go hungry," she cheekily retorted.

~*~

The Darcys received surprise visitors mid morning during the second week of August. Jane and Charles Bingley were announced and brought into the small family parlour where Elizabeth and Darcy were enjoying a quiet time of reading.

"Jane!" Elizabeth exclaimed as she struggled to her feet.

Darcy hastened to assist her, and once she stood, Elizabeth embraced her sister as much as she could. She laughed when her belly bumped into Jane's, but suddenly she stepped back and thought she noticed that her sister sported a slight bulge.

"Dearest Jane, are you with child?" Elizabeth asked in an excited whisper.

A bright blush spread across Jane's face as she nodded. "I have suspected for some time, but I have just felt the quickening. I decided that I would not tell you until we arrived at Pemberley. We planned this trip so as to surprise you. I so wanted to be here for your lying in. I hope that you do not mind that we did not ask for an invitation."

Elizabeth quickly glanced at Darcy to gauge his reaction, and when he smiled broadly, she knew that he was happy for their company. "Of course, we do not mind. I am so happy to have you here." She took her sister's hand and led her to the sofa. "And to think I shall be an aunt soon as well. What wonderful news!"

Darcy turned to Bingley and asked, "Do you wish to refresh yourselves? I am certain that Mrs. Reynolds has already seen to preparing chambers for you both. I shall ring for her and have her show you to them."

"I am sure that we both would appreciate that as it has been a long trip." Charles beamed his thanks to his friend.

About a half hour later, the Bingleys and the Darcy were back in the sitting room awaiting the refreshments that Elizabeth had ordered. At a knock at the door, Darcy bid the servant enter. The butler followed with a bottle of wine and glasses on a tray.

"We must have a toast." Darcy proclaimed. "Charles, I am so glad to hear your news and pleased that you came at this time."

Once the wine was poured and distributed, Darcy raised his glass. "To your health, Jane, and the health of my niece or nephew. May God grant you many children with their parents' goodness and optimism."

Both Bingleys blushed and thanked Darcy. After the toast, Elizabeth poured the tea and offered the small cakes and fruit.

Once she finished serving, she moved to sit next to her sister. Holding Jane's hand tightly in hers, Elizabeth asked, "Do my parents and sisters know of your news?"

Again Jane's colour rose in her cheeks. "No, we decided not to inform them until after they arrived here for the ball. We, rather I, thought that my mother would be in such a state that she would somehow prevent our coming alone. I knew you did not wish Mama to be here for the birth, so we did not say anything except that we were going to travel a bit and would see them at Pemberley."

Distress evident on her countenance, Jane confessed, "I am ashamed to have dissembled by not telling my mother or father, but I so wanted to be with you without the uproar that Mama can provoke. I hope that you do not think less of me for it."

"Indeed, I do not," Elizabeth responded, and it was echoed by the two men.

"Mrs. Bingley," Darcy began and then continued with, "Jane, I am happy that you came, for Elizabeth has needed a female family member with her. I am certain that I have not always been so understanding or so helpful as you shall be."

When Elizabeth opened her mouth to protest, Darcy stopped her with a smile and said, "I have tried to the best of my ability, but I believe that you will be of great comfort to Lizzy."

"I shall endeavour to do my best, sir," Jane said as she bowed her head and smiled.

After the excitement of the Bingleys' news died down, there were questions about the trip and the health of their families in Meryton and Hunsford. Charles told them of his sisters. Hursts had gone to visit the Bradleys in Scarborough. Lady Caroline Montague was somewhere in Scotland with her new husband.

Bingley then asked if the ladies would excuse him and Darcy as he had a matter of business to discuss with his brother-in-law. Both Jane and Elizabeth were eager for some privacy, so they smilingly insisted that they would be fine by themselves.

"Where is Georgiana this morning?" Jane inquired as the men left for Darcy's study.

"She has gone to visit a neighbour who has recently returned from an extended trip visiting family in Wales. They have been friends since childhood but have not seen each other in a few years. I think it shall be good for her to have a friend her own age so near." Elizabeth offered her sister more tea and cakes.

Jane accepted the tea and sipped it for a few moments as Elizabeth told her of how she had decorated the nursery. "I shall show you after we have finished our tea.

"I am so happy that you came, dearest Jane. I was becoming quite a fidget lately. It is such a pleasant surprise. How did you know I would want you here with me for the birth?"

"I admit that the foremost reason we are here is your lying in. However, it is not the only reason. Charles is discussing the second reason with your husband as we speak." Jane's normally serene smile brightened with her excitement.

"Do tell me." Elizabeth demanded.

Sipping her tea, Jane seemed to be enjoying drawing out the moment, but when she saw the frustration on her sister's countenance, she relented.

"We want to purchase an estate near Pemberley."

Elizabeth nearly squealed as she exclaimed, "You are going to live in Derbyshire? What about Netherfield?"

"Indeed, it is our fondest wish to be closer to our best and closest friends," Jane declared decidedly. "As to Netherfield, there has been a purchase offer and the people wish to take possession by Christmas. We could have offered to purchase it ourselves, but it was not long after our wedding that we realized that Netherfield was much too close to Longbourn. Mama finds it necessary to visit nearly every day, and has taken to giving both Charles and me advice about the running of the place. Once I found her countermanding my orders to the housekeeper about the meal I planned for a small dinner party the next day.

"I must admit that I nearly lost my temper when she said that we should not have lamb. As you are aware, my mother is not fond of it and tried to say that beef should be served in its place. I had ordered roast leg of lamb because it is one of Charles' favourite dishes, especially the way Cook prepares it. I believe I spoke rather harshly to Mama, asking her to come to me if she had a question about something in my household. She was not pleased when I told her that lamb would be served at the dinner and that if she did not like it, she did not have to attend." Jane finished her tale with cheeks, reddened with embarrassment and some shame.

"Oh, Jane, my dear brave sister," Elizabeth proclaimed happily. "You did just the right thing. I am sure that my mother soon got over her pique and boasted to all her friends how well you see to your husband's tastes. She likely told them she taught you to act thusly."

Jane giggled as she did when they were girls together at Longbourn and agreed, "I did hear her tell Mrs. Long that I served the lamb especially for my husband, even though her own mother did not care for it. It did, indeed, sound like a boast rather than a complaint."

Soon, the two sisters were lost in their conversation as they tried to catch up on all and sundry. It was thusly that their husbands found them.

"I can see that we were not missed," Darcy said teasingly from the doorway.

"Indeed, I do not think they even noticed our absence." Bingley sighed dramatically, but could not hide the smile on his face. "I wonder if they will be upset at our interruption." He moved into the room toward where the ladies were sitting.

Elizabeth and Jane laughed and stood.

"We have been inconsolable in your absence," answered Elizabeth as she gestured for the men to be seated.

In answer to the hopeful and questioning look on his wife's face, Charles announced, "Darcy is aware of two estates that are available for sale at this time. We shall investigate them both. If they prove to be good investments, we shall all go to view them."

"Wonderful!" the two women exclaimed at the same time and began to pepper Darcy with questions about the estates, the primary one being how close to Pemberley the two houses were.

CHAPTER FORTY-ONE

The first several days after the Bingleys' arrival were spent in pleasant conversations and diversions. Elizabeth had not known that a visit from her sister would calm her so much. She knew without a doubt that her husband loved her and would care for her to the best of his ability, but having a beloved female relative with her at this very momentous time helped her feel less vulnerable and fearful. Each morning she thanked the Lord for the blessing of Jane.

When the midwife arrived to examine her, Jane asked to be in the room, and Elizabeth was happy to oblige her. Mrs. Norris did not object, so they left for the mistress's chambers. Elizabeth did not question her until she finished her examination.

Mrs. Norris smiled as she stood from her task. "You be doing fine, ma'am. The baby might be a tad early. Signs are there."

When the midwife saw the surprise on Elizabeth's face, she tried to reassure her. "I seen many a babe decide to coming a bit early, and there ain't usually a problem 'cept the child is small and likely to need coaxing to eat. That won't be no trouble. I know a good wet nurse. She is experienced with early babes."

"I wish to feed the baby myself for at least the first few months," Elizabeth said firmly.

"That bein' the case, ma'am," Mrs. Norris answered with a delighted smile. "I kin teach you how to manage it."

The midwife did not know if she should speak her mind, but decided that if a lady like Mrs. Darcy would shun the habit of most of the gentry of using a wet nurse, she could chance it. "I think it be a good thing you want to do. You will recover faster and the foremilk be good for the babe."

She lowered her voice and whispered, "And you likely won't be falling with child so quick like if you be nursing the babe."

Both Elizabeth and Jane blushed a bit at hearing the information.

Elizabeth had previously planned to ask Mrs. Norris about what would happen if the babe was late, but the midwife's reassurances that everything was going well made her decide against it. She rang for a maid to see Mrs. Norris to the kitchen for refreshments before she left for her home.

~*~

It was two days after Mrs. Norris's visit that the pains began. At first she thought they were merely muscle spasms in her side and back. She and Jane had walked the gardens extensively the day before, and for this reason, Elizabeth did not even mention them to anyone. However a strong, sharp pain and severe contraction of her belly caused her to understand that the baby was coming.

After the pain had passed, Elizabeth awkwardly stood from her place on the sofa next to Jane. The four adults had been spending a comfortable time before dinner when the pain had hit her. She rang to summon Mrs. Reynolds before she cleared her voice and stated calmly, "Mr. Darcy, I believe that you should send someone for the midwife and the doctor."

A stunned silence hung over the room before Darcy and Jane understood at the same moment what Lizzy was saying. Jane gasped and Darcy came quickly to her side.

"It is time?" he asked hoarsely.

"I believe so, my love." She grasped his hand and smiled a bit weakly.

"I will send a footman immediately." He squeezed her hand before releasing it and making his way to the door. He paused before he opened it. "Is there something I can do for you before I go?"

"No, I have already rung for Mrs. Reynolds, and she knows what is needed, even better than I do," she quietly assured him.

Jane came to stand beside her as soon as Darcy left and motioned for her own husband to follow their brother from the room. "Oh, Lizzy, I am so excited for you."

"I admit that I am excited and a bit afraid," Elizabeth said as her voice quavered.

"You will be well, Mrs. Darcy," came the calm and steady tone of Mrs. Reynolds.

The housekeeper asked her pertinent questions about the timing and intensity of the pains and told the two women that there would be plenty of time. She did suggest that they retire to the prepared birthing room, and she would bring them some tea.

The doctor and the midwife arrived, and the time of waiting began. Darcy was almost beside himself with worry and concern for his beloved wife and the baby who was trying to enter the world. Bingley tried to cheer him with little success. Finally, what got him through the trial of waiting was a fervent prayer for both his wife and their babe.

Through the evening and into the night, Jane brought them updates on Elizabeth's progress. She told the men that both the doctor and the midwife were pleased with how things were coming along. They predicted that the child would be delivered before midnight. So it was that at eleven sixteen in the evening on the seventeenth of August, 1813, that the baby was born. Jane found Darcy pacing the parlour while Bingley dozed in a chair by the fire.

Darcy stopped when he heard Jane's footstep. "Tell me!" He demanded briskly.

His sister-in-law smiled and touched his arm gently. "Your family awaits you in Elizabeth's chambers."

Without a word, Darcy hastened from the room and bounded up the staircase, two steps at a time. He arrived outside Elizabeth's room rather breathless, so he stopped and waited for his breathing and his heartbeat to slow to a more normal rhythm. Knocking softly but without waiting for admittance, he entered the room. The sight that awaited him was the most awe-inspiring he had beheld since his wedding day.

Elizabeth lay back against a mountain of pillows, staring down at a tiny red-faced infant, who was busily feeding at its mother's breast. His wife caressed short, dark curls that adorned the baby's head. The smile on her face rivalled any painting of the Madonna he had ever seen. His eyes stung as he moved quietly toward the bed.

"Come see our baby, dearest," Elizabeth spoke softly, without taking her eyes from the baby.

Darcy pulled a chair close to the bed and took a closer look at the little miracle in his wife's arms. He could not speak for the lump in his throat, but he reached out to touch one of the hands that lay open against the swaddling. As he touched the tiny palm, impossibly tiny fingers wrapped around his index finger. At that moment, he knew that he would love this child for the rest of his life.

He lifted his glance to Elizabeth and saw her watching him with a smile and tears in her eyes.

"You are showing an odd lack of curiosity about whether we have a son or a daughter," she teased as she caressed his weary face. "It must be your fatigue."

"No, my dearest Beth," he replied as he captured her caressing hand in his. "I know that we have a daughter." He turned his attention back to the little one who was holding his finger and his heart in her tiny grasp.

"I asked Jane not to tell you," Elizabeth protested with a pout.

"Indeed, she did not tell me," he said before he kissed her hand. "You forget that I have seen her before. In the vision I had, she was a bit older, but there is no mistake. This is our Sophia."

"Sophia?" She chuckled softly at his emphatic pronouncement. "I did not know that we had decided upon a name."

"No, I suppose that we had not, but the moment I saw her, I knew that she was Sophia." Darcy looked into Elizabeth's eyes. "I hope that you do not object to the name."

"Of course not, I think it is a lovely name, but I thought we might name her after your mother."

"If we did that, your mother might be offended," he said thoughtfully.

"Not if we call her Sophia Frances Anne Darcy."

Darcy pondered the name for several seconds before he leaned over the bed, lifted the tiny hand which still held his finger, and kissed it. "Welcome to the family, Sophia Frances Anne Darcy," he said, with joy evident in his voice.

It was at that moment that the baby girl pulled away from her mother's breast, opened her eyes, and stared up at Darcy. She gazed unblinking for a long moment before she yawned and fell into a sound sleep.

This time, Darcy did not try to blink away the tears of joy and love that filled his eyes. He bowed his head and began to pray, "Dear heavenly Father, we thank Thee for Thy mercy on Elizabeth and Sophia. Please return my wife to health quickly and keep them both in Thy care daily. Help us to become good parents for this little one, and may we always look to Thee for our guidance and strength, in the name of Christ, amen."

"Amen," Elizabeth whispered. She then stifled a yawn.

"Oh my love, you are exhausted," Darcy said as he let go of her hand and gently pulled his finger from the baby's grip. "I must leave you and allow you to rest."

Reaching for his hand, Elizabeth protested, "Do not leave us. There is room on the bed for you. I know that you must be tired as well."

His smile brightened the room. He quickly pulled off his boots and outer clothing before he helped Elizabeth into a more comfortable position for sleep, then slipped into bed next to his family. Darcy placed his head on the pillow close to his wife and put one of his hands under the baby's head. The last thing he thought before he fell into slumber was that he was the happiest and most blessed of men.

~*~

The whole of Pemberley rejoiced at the birth of another generation of Darcys. The mistress of the house was pampered in her confinement to her chambers. Despite the custom of most of the upper class in British society, Darcy refused to stay away from his wife and daughter for more than it was necessary for him to tend to estate business and visit with his sister and guests.

After a week of being confined to bed, Elizabeth began to rebel at the forced confinement. She abhorred the idleness and the boredom, so she conspired to get out of bed whenever she was left alone in her chambers.

When first Darcy caught her at the window seat, staring out at the changing landscape, he threatened to have someone keep watch on her at all times. However, when he saw her reaction to the statement, he realized that it would be cruel to force such a lively woman to keep to her bed for the customary month. He consulted with the midwife as to Elizabeth's state of health and was told that she was doing very well indeed.

According to Mrs. Norris, she did not agree with the social strictures put on gently bred ladies. It was her experience with the tenants' wives that the ones who recovered the quickest were the ones who renewed their daily activities the soonest so long as they did not overtax their strength. In the midwife's opinion, Mrs. Darcy should be allowed to eat at least one meal with her family if she desired it and to walk a short time in the garden each day.

Elizabeth rejoiced at her release from what she had begun to think of as a prison. She took great pleasure in walking on Darcy's arm through the fall flowers and colours. Understanding her need for frequent rests, she did not object when her husband escorted her back to her chambers afterward. More likely than not, Sophia was awaiting her, ready for another meal.

Near the end of that first month after Sophia's birth Elizabeth was churched and the baby was christened. The Bingleys were appointed as the godparents, and there was a quiet celebration back at Pemberley. The Darcys revelled in the quiet before the arrival of the Bennets and the Matlocks. As much as they loved their family, they knew that soon the quietude they enjoyed would be absent for several weeks at least.

The day that the Bennets finally arrived at Pemberley was a rare warm one. Elizabeth had invited Charlotte and Samuel Lucas to visit as well, since she was such a good friend to the former and likely soon to be sister to the latter. The Darcys and the Bingleys were waiting in the blue parlour when the guests were announced. There were many embraces and declarations of congratulations as everyone talked at once. The Collinses had been invited but parish duties prevented their coming. Mary sent word that they would attempt to make the journey in the spring after Eastertide.

Mrs. Bennet demanded that Elizabeth sit down and tell her how she fared. It did not take long for Lizzy's mother to be convinced that her daughter's health was good, so she thus declared that she would see her granddaughter.

"Mama, it is Sophia's nap time," Elizabeth answered firmly. "I believe it is best that she have her rest, and while we await the summons from her nurse, you shall all partake of tea and the refreshments that Chef has prepared especially for you."

That statement more than anything calmed Mrs. Bennet's excitement. To think that the Pemberley cook, likely a French chef at that, would make something especially for her. And why should he not? Was she not the mother of the present Mrs. Darcy? She smiled and patted her daughter's hand while she waited to be served.

About a half hour later, a maid came quietly to Elizabeth's side and whispered, "Miss Sophia is awake, ma'am." She curtseyed when she was dismissed and left the room.

Elizabeth stood and addressed her family, "Please excuse me. I must see to my daughter. I shall bring her down once her needs are met."

Turning to her mother, she asked, "Would you like to accompany me, Mama?"

Slightly confused as to why Elizabeth would be seeing to her daughter instead of having a nursemaid bring her to be introduced to the rest of the family, Mrs. Bennet nonetheless rose to follow her from the room.

"Lizzy, do you not employ a nurse for the baby?" she asked as she hurried to keep up with Elizabeth's quick pace.

Without turning back, Elizabeth replied, "We have several nursery maids."

"Then why is it that you must go to the baby?"

"It is time for her midmorning repast," Elizabeth replied as if it were obvious.

Mrs. Bennet said nothing until they reached the door to the nursery. "I cannot believe that you are seeing to that task yourself. What are you thinking? I am sure that it is not done in your sphere of society. What will the Matlocks think?"

"It is a natural thing, and as my midwife informed me, good for both of us. There is a wet nurse for the times when my obligations require me to be unable to come to Sophia in good time, but I do love these times with her and shall not give them fully over to another."

Elizabeth opened the door in time to hear an impatient cry from her daughter. She laughed softly as she settled into the rocking chair and signalled for the maid to hand her the baby. Sophia's cries calmed as Elizabeth pulled her close and opened her dress.

Once the child was eagerly nursing, Elizabeth looked up at her mother. "Please do sit down, Mama." Speaking to the maid, she said, "Amy, bring that chair over here for my mother; then you may leave. Have a bit of tea in the kitchen. I shall ring for you when I need you."

Mrs. Bennet sat quietly observing her daughter as her granddaughter nursed. There was something of bliss and contentment in the picture. As the mother of five children and the wife of a country gentleman with little money for nurses or governesses, she had always hoped that her girls would have husbands who could afford the luxuries she had not been able to experience. However, as she remembered how she had cherished the times of solitude and communion when she nursed the first four, she realized one of the reasons she had indulged Lydia was because she had been unable to have that time to bond with her youngest, due to illness at her birth.

Tears filled Mrs. Bennet's eyes and spilled down her cheeks, but the lady was unaware until Elizabeth handed her a handkerchief and asked gently, "What is it, Mama? Are you well?"

After wiping her eyes and blowing her nose, Mrs. Bennet nodded and sniffed. "I am perfectly well, thank you." A tender look came to her face as she reached out to touch the baby's soft hair. "It will take me some time to become accustomed to being a grandmother."

Dabbing at her eyes once more, Mrs. Bennet said, "She looks so much like you did, Lizzy. I remember holding you thusly and thinking that although I should have given your father a son, I could not repine, for you were so beautiful. It was not until I had Mary that I began to suffer with my nerves.

"Oh, Lizzy, the thought of not having a son was so frightening. It meant that when we might lose your father, we would be left without a home. I am sorry that I did not practice frugality as I should have to help your father put aside monies for our future. God has been good to have found such wonderful husbands for you three girls. I am heartily ashamed of myself for my worry and for my spendthrift ways, and for the fact that I did not always show my love for you as I should have."

"Do not concern yourself with that. There is nothing to be done for it now." Elizabeth lifted the baby to her shoulder and began to pat and rub her back. "I love you, Mama. And now that we have Sophia, I am certain that I understand you much more now than I ever have."

Sophia's rather noisy burp made both women laugh. After Elizabeth put her to the other breast, she said, "Do you approve of her name?"

"I admit that I am very pleased with it." Mrs. Bennet hesitated before she went on, "I am happy that she will not have to be called Fanny. I never really liked my Christian name nor the shortened version of it, but you and Mr. Darcy honoured me greatly by giving it as a middle name to this dear child."

The rest of their private time was spent in discussing Elizabeth's experience with the birthing. Mrs. Bennet was grateful that the baby's birth had been relatively easy. When her mother talked of her experience, Lizzy was surprised that she did not complain or elaborate with details.

Once the baby was fed and her nappies were changed, Elizabeth laid the infant into her grandmother's waiting arms. Mrs. Bennet cooed, tickled and kissed the baby until Lizzy suggested it was time to introduce Sophia to the rest of the family.

Again, her mother surprised her by handing Sophia back to Elizabeth, saying that it was more fitting that she should be the one to present her daughter to the rest of the family. Once they arrived in the drawing room, they found the others in quiet conversation groups.

Mr. Bennet was talking to his son-in-law when Darcy abruptly stood and walked to where his wife stood. "I was beginning to worry. You do not usually take so long."

"I beg your pardon for taking so much time." Elizabeth smiled up at him. "But our daughter wanted to become acquainted with her grandmama. Now she would like to meet her grandpapa."

Elizabeth made her way to where her father was sitting, her mother and husband following closely. Mr. Bennet smiled broadly up at her as she arrived at his side. Bending over slightly, she laid the baby in his arms. "Papa, please meet Sophia."

"Oh, Mr. Bennet, is she not the most beautiful baby?" her mother cooed as she moved to the other side of her husband's chair. "She looks so much like Lizzy did."

"She is indeed a beautiful babe," Mr. Bennet admitted, but he added, "But I am not surprised. Her mama and aunts were pretty as well. Were they not, my dear?"

Mrs. Bennet's countenance softened and she smiled at her husband. "That they were, dear, that they were."

Soon, Charlotte and the two youngest Bennet daughters came to see the baby. After exclaiming over her, each one demanded to be allowed to hold her niece. Sophia was passed from one doting relative to another until the excitement of the process caused the tiny Miss Darcy to fall fast asleep.

CHAPTER FORTY-TWO

Two days later, the Matlocks arrived with Viscount and Viscountess Matley, the colonel, and Anne de Bourgh. The plans and preparations for the ball began in earnest almost immediately. Lady Matlock and Mrs. Bennet spent hours in conference with Mrs. Reynolds. The older ladies told Elizabeth that she would be excused from most of the planning, so that she might continue to improve and completely regain her strength before the time of the ball.

For the next fortnight, Elizabeth marvelled at how calm her mother remained. Although a few times she came upon her mother in what could have been called a fit of nerves, all that was needed to soothe her was for Lady Matlock to speak to her in her dignified and serene way or for her father to take her hand and whisper something known only to them. It seemed that the honourable lady and Mr. Bennet understood how to quiet Mrs. Bennet.

Thusly, the Darcys enjoyed a lovely time with their family and friends. Fitzwilliam and the other men spent time in sport, both hunting and fishing. The ladies who were not in on the planning sessions walked, chatted, played music, and, in general, had a wonderful time together.

The Gardiners arrived three days before the ball. They had not been able to come earlier due to Mr. Gardiner's business obligations. They brought gifts for the baby, which the Gardiner children were eager to bestow upon their newest cousin. It must be said that the younger ones were rather disappointed that Sophia was so little and would not be able to join them in play for some time. However, Eleanor, who was the eldest at the ripe old age of nine, found great delight in the pretty little girl. She spent as much time as she was allowed holding the baby and watching either the nurse or Elizabeth as they cared for her.

It was just before supper the day after the Gardiners arrived that an express came for Darcy. The butler told a footman to find the master and give the missive to him. Darcy was in their private sitting room, waiting for Elizabeth to finish with

Sophia before they went down to the dining room. At the footman's knock, he bade him enter. Taking the letter, he dismissed the servant.

"Who was at the door, my love," Elizabeth asked as she entered the room.

"A footman brought an express," Darcy answered distractedly as he examined the outside of the note. "It was posted from Derby."

Elizabeth's heart clenched with fear. "Could he have escaped?"

Moving quickly to her side, Darcy pulled her into his arms. "I doubt that very much. Come to the settee with me, and I will open the letter to find out the news."

He guided her to the sofa, and they sat down, Elizabeth nestled close to his side as he broke the seal, unfolded the paper and read.

> *Derby, Derbyshire*
> *19 September, 1813*
> *Dear Sir,*
>
> *As one of the parties injured by one George Wickham, I am required by the court to inform you that two days ago, George Wickham died of an infectious lung fever. He is one of several inmates who succumbed to the disease.*
>
> *This closes the case. No other action on your part will be necessary. He was buried in the county's pauper's field.*
>
> *If you have any questions regarding this matter, please feel free to contact this office.*
> *With respect,*
> *Allen Dent, Esq.*
> *Assize Court Clerk*

The two sat in silence for several moments, trying to fully comprehend the import of the short missive. Finally, Darcy refolded the letter and put it in his coat pocket. He wrapped his arms around his wife and whispered, "It is over."

"It is over," Elizabeth echoed. As she sat in her husband's arms, she marvelled that she felt nothing but relief that the man could not harm her or her loved ones again. "Thank the Lord," she finally sighed and held tightly to Darcy.

~*~

On the morning of the ball, the household staff bustled around with last minute duties to perform. Elizabeth slipped into the room before she went to break her fast. Everything in the grand room gleamed and sparkled even without the candles being lit. Footmen were busy pouring water into the large flower-filled urns which stood in the corners and next to pillars at the sides of the room. The chamber that was to serve as the supper parlour was filled with beautifully dressed and decorated tables. A card room on the other side of the ballroom held every necessity for the enjoyment of those persons who, like her father, preferred cards to dancing.

Taste and elegance abounded in all of the rooms. Elizabeth relaxed and began to feel great anticipation of the evening's festivities. She was slowly closing the door to the ballroom when she heard her name being called from the staircase. Turning, she spied her mother and youngest sister coming her way.

"Mama, Lydia, good morning," Elizabeth said warmly.

"Good morning, Lizzy," the two women answered in unison.

Mrs. Bennet kissed her daughter's cheek and teased, "I see that you could not wait until this evening to see the ballroom."

Lydia grinned at the faint blush on her elder sister's face. "Do not worry, Lizzy. I peeked yesterday and hoped to see the progress this morning myself."

She slipped her arm into Elizabeth's to guide her back to the ballroom door when Mrs. Bennet spoke, "Let us go to breakfast first. The servants shall have more accomplished by the time we are finished."

Smiling at Lydia, Elizabeth turned and linked her other arm with her mother's, and they made their way to the large breakfast room to join those gathered there. Darcy, Lord and Lady Matlock, Viscount and Viscountess Matley, the Bingleys, Mr. Bennet, and Anne were already partaking of the delicious fare. The rest of the party soon joined them to eat and enter into the lively conversation, the primary subject of which was, of course, the ball.

As she bit into a slice of buttered toast, Elizabeth watched her father and mother. Mr. Bennet, who had stood with the other men when the ladies entered the room, moved to intercept his wife and escort her to a seat next to his own. He ordered a cup of tea for her before he moved to the sideboard to fill a plate for her. To say that Elizabeth was astonished by her father's solicitude would be an understatement. The other surprising thing she witnessed was the lack of the usual fluttering or silly outcries from her mother. Instead, Mrs. Bennet blushed prettily and waited quite patiently for her husband to bring her a plate of food. Before she could question her parents' actions, even in her mind, she was asked about Sophia and was distracted from the thought.

Throughout the day, Elizabeth kept expecting her mother to erupt in a fit of nerves, but as the time of the ball drew near, she understood that it would not be the case.

The whole party retired to their quarters after an early dinner to prepare for the evening. Inside her dressing room, Elizabeth sat quietly in her dressing gown as Sarah coifed her hair. As she could no longer enjoy merely ribbons and jewelled pins to adorn her plaits and curls, she had to choose a turban or feathered cap, which was more appropriate for a married woman. Her abigail busily pinned atop her curls the tiny silk hat festooned with small feathers that had been dyed green and white to match her gown.

As Elizabeth watched the transformation, she smiled at the image in her mirror. She found it difficult at times to comprehend that she was truly a wife and mother, for she still often thought of herself as the girl who loved to tramp about the countryside and even climb a tree on occasion. However, when she held her infant daughter or was held in her husband's arms as they fell asleep at night, the idea was not so difficult to believe.

"Sarah," Elizabeth said as the maid finished with her task. "You are a marvel. I look every bit the lady of the manor. I did not think it was possible to banish the hoyden that was Lizzy Bennet."

Sarah grinned and patted her mistress's shoulder. "Oh, she is still in there."

"She is indeed," came a deep voice from the dressing room door.

Darcy moved into the room and walked around Elizabeth as if to inspect Sarah's handiwork. "You are lovely, my dear. I am very happy that you are my wife. If you were not, I am afraid I would make a fool of myself fighting off my rivals."

Elizabeth merely chuckled and said, "You have become quite a flatterer, husband. And I might well have my head turned if you continue."

She stood and took his arm. "You, however, must go back to your own dressing room. Sarah has still more to accomplish before I will be presentable for the ball, and you are not dressed either. You may call for me at the appropriate hour."

Arriving at the door, Elizabeth gently pushed him through it, and smiling, she closed it firmly. She then turned back to speak to her abigail. "Sarah, I have something I want to speak to you about." Elizabeth moved from the dressing room into her bed chamber. Glancing back at her maid, she motioned toward two chairs that stood side by side next to the window and said, "Come let us sit."

Once they were seated, Elizabeth said, "Before you finish with me, I want to thank you for your service to me and my family."

Sarah blushed and opened her mouth to reply, but Elizabeth went on, "I have never once regretted the faith I placed in you. You have aided me in so many ways that I do not believe I could ever thank you enough. Having said thus, I wish for you to know that Mr. Darcy and I have not forgotten your swift action in regard to Mr. Wickham. We have also not forgotten our promise to reward you for going for help."

Again Sarah made to speak, but Elizabeth silenced her with a raised hand. "We have decided that you are to have a holiday. You will travel back to Hertfordshire with my family and have a month to visit your family. This shall be in addition to your regular holidays."

Smiling broadly at the maid's stunned countenance, Elizabeth continued, "If you wish to stay longer - you do have your regular fortnight of holiday still coming to you - you may do that as well."

Tears of joy ran down Sarah's cheeks. For a long moment, she tried to speak. It was not until Elizabeth handed finally her a handkerchief and Sarah had wiped her eyes and blown her nose that she found her voice and exclaimed, "Oh, thank you, Mrs. Darcy! But you must know it is too much. I only did what I needed to do. I could not see harm come to you or the master."

"That may be, but we are intent upon this." Elizabeth patted Sarah's arm. "You shall go, and you shall have a wonderful time with your family."

Rising to her feet, Elizabeth motioned to the open dressing room. "However, now you must work, for I must be ready for the ball."

It was about an hour later that a knock came from the adjoining door. Sarah had just fastened the last of the tiny buttons on the gown, and Elizabeth was once again standing before a mirror scrutinizing the full effect of the deep emerald green confection she wore. She did not turn to greet her husband as he joined her.

"Do you think I will do?" Elizabeth didn't expect an answer since she could see in the glass that Darcy was smiling his approval as he gazed upon her.

"I believe that there is something amiss," he said calmly.

Elizabeth turned quickly in surprise and opened her mouth to ask what was wrong with her appearance when her husband handed her a box. She opened it to find a lovely emerald and diamond necklace and bracelet.

"Oh, Fitzwilliam," she gasped in astonishment. "They are exquisite."

"They are nothing to your beauty," he whispered as he lifted the necklace and placed it around her neck. Once he had fastened it, he performed the same office with the bracelet over her gloved wrist.

Taking her hands he pulled back slightly to examine the affect. "Perfection," he proclaimed emphatically. "I do love that shade of green, especially on you, my love."

"It was your love of the colour that made my decision when I saw the silk in the shop." She paused to look closely at her husband's similarly coloured attire and chuckled. "I see that you were informed as to the exact shade I would wear. Your waistcoat matches perfectly."

"I wished that no one tonight would have any doubt as to whose wife you are. I knew that you would be so beautiful that I would indeed be in need of some sort of sign to that effect." He moved closer and, one by one, he kissed her hands.

"Thank you, husband," said she as she smiled brightly. "I believe that we should make our way to the ballroom. It would not do for us to be late for our first ball as husband and wife."

Grinning, Darcy offered her his arm and guided her out of her chambers.

~*~

After greeting each of their guests in the receiving line, the Darcys moved into the ballroom. The earlier sparkling effect that Elizabeth had witnessed was bathed in the golden glow of the hundreds of candles hanging in the several large chandeliers. The jewels the ladies wore added to the crystal shine. Lizzy felt that she was in a fairyland.

Elizabeth knew that she and her husband would soon open the dancing, but she felt compelled to find her mother and Lady Matlock to thank them for the beauty before her.

"My dear," she said as she squeezed Darcy's arm. "Do you see your aunt and my mother? I must express my gratitude for the splendid arrangements."

After a brief survey of the room, Darcy guided her to where Lord and Lady Matlock stood chatting amiably with her parents and the Gardiners.

Elizabeth made her curtseys in turn to all before she exclaimed with enthusiasm. ""Lady Matlock, Mama, everything is exquisite. I do not think I have ever seen anything lovelier. Thank you so much for taking on this task."

"It was a pleasure, you can be sure." Lady Matlock answered quietly. "We wanted your first ball as Mrs. Darcy to be the very best. Besides, your mother is a joy with whom to work. Her ideas were quite innovative, and she is so very amenable to suggestions. We got on quite well, did we not, Mrs. Bennet."

"Indeed, we did, your Ladyship," Mrs. Bennet agreed, her face beaming with happiness and pride.

Mrs. Bennet might have said more, but the orchestra signalled the commencement of the dancing. As Elizabeth took Darcy's offered arm, she was astonished to see her father offer his arm to her mother. Mrs. Bennet blushed as prettily as a maiden at her first ball. Darcy led Lizzy to the head of the line, and soon most of the guests had joined them.

Georgiana had been allowed to attend, but she was permitted to dance only with her relatives. Colonel Fitzwilliam partnered with her for the first set. Nerves seemed to be practicing the steps of the set in her stomach as the musicians struck up the first chords of the song. However, soon she was enjoying herself as her cousin chatted with her in his amenable and entertaining way.

As the music stopped and the colonel escorted her back to where her aunt and her cousin Anne stood, Georgiana was becomingly flushed and smiling happily.

"I can see by your countenance that you are enjoying your first dance, my dear," Lady Matlock commented with a smile.

"Oh, yes, Aunt," the young woman agreed as she looked up at her cousin, Richard. "Thank you, Cousin, for the set. I did not know I would like it so much."

Just then Lydia Bennet came up to the group, and after greeting everyone, she drew Georgiana slightly apart from the rest. "Miss Darcy, I did not get a chance to tell you before how lovely your gown is tonight."

"Thank you, Miss Lydia," she said quietly. "You look lovely as well. Is this one of your creations?"

"No," Lydia sighed ruefully. "My mother would do nothing else but buy it from a London *modiste*. It is pretty enough, but I did have a design in mind. I suppose I shall have to wait a while to have the design made up."

"Have you drawn it?" Georgiana asked eagerly. "If so, I would like to see it."

"I shall draw it for you, for I left the original at Longbourn."

Georgiana lowered her eyes and whispered, "Do you think you might design one for me. You have such a talent. I could tell you what I would like if it would assist you."

"I would love to do so!" Lydia said excitedly. "We shall have such a grand time."

"I would like to have a grand time now," Colonel Fitzwilliam interrupted the girls' private chat and offered his arm to Lydia. "Miss Lydia, I believe that this is our set."

As they walked to their position in the line of dancers, Colonel Fitzwilliam commented as casually as he could, "Miss Lydia, would you permit me to tell you how lovely you look tonight?"

He noticed the pleasing colour that moved over her cheeks as she said, nearly in a whisper, "I would, and I thank you for the compliment."

The silk of her pale lavender gown rustled as she moved to her side of the line to face him. Lydia hoped that the colonel could not hear her heart as it thudded in excitement over the prospect of dancing with such a gentlemen. She had stood up for the first set with a nice enough fellow, a Mr. Evans from one of the neighbouring estates to Pemberley. He had been pleasant and knew the right words to say, but he had not been the colonel. Even as they spoke of similar subjects to those she had already covered with Mr. Evans, none seemed as mundane as they had before. Oh, how was she to get over this infatuation?

Having spent hours in pondering the appeal of the man before her, Lydia had concluded that it was not that he was a soldier, although that was what had first drawn her. She knew impartially that he was not handsome like his cousin Darcy or like her new brother Bingley. However, the more she got to know the man, the handsomer he seemed.

She had come to the conclusion that it was how Colonel Fitzwilliam had treated her after her disastrous outburst in favour of that vile Lieutenant Wickham that had first caused her to understand the colonel's worth as a gentleman. Even so many months later, Lydia could not think on it without wanting to berate her stupidity and naiveté. *I hope I will never be so fooled by such a scoundrel again.*

"Miss Lydia." Fitzwilliam worried as he saw a frown cross the young woman's face. "Have I offended you with my silly speeches?"

A blush once more suffused her face, but a bright smile replaced the frown as she denied the thought. "Of course not, Colonel, I am afraid an unpleasant thought came unbidden to my mind. I promise to work diligently to keep any more from intruding."

A movement of the dance parted them for a moment or two before they were once more near enough to speak to each other.

"I am happy to hear it," Fitzwilliam grinned as he replied. "I would hate to be the cause of a frown on such a lovely face as yours."

Lydia laughed appreciatively. "You do have a golden tongue, Colonel Fitzwilliam."

"I speak only the truth, Miss Lydia," he said in obvious sincerity.

"Then I must thank you once more for the compliment."

He nodded before they moved apart to sashay around the neighbouring dancers. The colonel had trouble keeping his mind fully on the steps of the dance as he thought about Miss Lydia Bennet. Having noticed the handsome young man she partnered with for the first set, he could not help the spike of jealousy that stabbed at him. There was no reason for him to have such feelings. Because of his lack of fortune, he was not able to follow his heart.

Lydia Bennet showed a great many signs of improvement from the days of their first acquaintance. She acted much as her older sister, Elizabeth, with liveliness and good humour, and she lacked the childish pique and silly disregard for others' feelings that he had first observed. No, he knew that she had endeavoured to improve herself, and he inwardly applauded that effort.

Shaking himself, Colonel Fitzwilliam smiled ruefully at the direction of his thoughts. As he took Lydia's hand to make their way down the dance, he wondered if there would ever be a chance for the two of them. Inwardly, he sighed and decided to enjoy the present and let the future work itself out.

On one side of the ballroom, Elizabeth stood with Charlotte Lucas, watching her guests, thinking how different things were from when she first met her husband, who was now dancing with a beaming Georgiana.

"I am surprised that you are not dancing, Lizzy," Charlotte commented with a smile.

"I find that I tire more easily than in the past," she replied with an answering grin. "No doubt it is due to my daughter's birth. Also, I find that I am not so eager to join in if my husband is busy. You see, I am a thoroughly besotted wife."

Their shared laughter was interrupted by the arrival of a gentleman. The tall, pleasant looking man bowed and greeted Elizabeth, "Good evening, Mrs. Darcy. I apologize for my tardiness. I was detained on a visit to Mrs. Phelps."

"I hope that she is well," Elizabeth said with concern.

"She is in good health, but her spirits still suffer the loss of her husband." The man sighed and shook his head. "It has not been three months since he passed, and the loss of a marriage partner of forty years is not easily grieved in such a short time."

It was then that the gentleman noticed Charlotte's presence. "Pardon me," he said as he bowed to her. "I was very rude to interrupt your conversation."

"Oh, I am sorry," Elizabeth exclaimed, "Please allow me to introduce you to my very good friend, Charlotte Lucas. Charlotte, this is Reverend Mr. Philip Gregory. He is the vicar of the village of Kympton, not three miles south of Pemberley."

"I am pleased to meet you, Miss Lucas. Your home is in Hertfordshire, I presume?" he inquired politely.

"It is, sir," Charlotte answered as she curtseyed. "Mrs. Darcy's former home, Longbourn, and my home, Lucas Lodge, share a border. Mrs. Darcy and I are long time friends."

"How are you enjoying Pemberley?"

"Very much indeed," Charlotte replied with a smile. "The house and grounds are lovely, but it is the company of my friends that I am enjoying the most."

Charlotte was intrigued by the man before her. He looked to be in his early forties with deep smile lines on his face. His sandy hair was in need of a trim and it kept falling over one eye. With interest, he gazed with eyes of golden hazel into hers. Never had she encountered a person with whom she felt so comfortable so quickly.

For a few quiet, yet not uncomfortable seconds, the two looked at each other before Elizabeth spoke. "Mr. Gregory and his family have been at Kympton for four years now. His three children are delightful little scamps."

Charlotte's heart sank as she heard her friend's words. "Is your wife not here with you tonight?"

Mr. Gregory's face sobered when he replied simply, "She died three years ago of childbirth fever after our youngest was born."

"Oh, I am so sorry," Charlotte said anxiously. "I did not know."

"It is quite all right, Miss Lucas. You could not have known." He summoned a smile that seemed bittersweet. "Rose left me with three lovely children. The baby survived. I named her Patience Rose, after her mother."

"Little Patty Rose, as her brothers call her, is one of the sweetest natured children I have ever known." Elizabeth re-entered the conversation. "Only Jane was as sweet."

Charlotte was about to ask a question about the vicar's sons when Darcy and Georgiana joined their little group. The three had not noticed that the set had ended.

After greetings were exchanged and the Darcys chatted about the set, Mr. Gregory spoke in a lowered voice, "Are you engaged for the next set, Miss Lucas?"

"No, I am not." Charlotte smiled and blushed.

"Then I would like to ask you to be my partner for it."

"I would be delighted," she consented with alacrity.

As the newly acquainted pair chatted while waiting for the next set to begin, Darcy asked, "Mrs. Darcy, has anyone asked you for the next set?"

"No, sir," she answered cheekily, "I am free, if you wish to ask me."

"I was hoping that we could take a turn about the room." He grinned down at her. "We can have a better conversation that way. However, if you wish to dance, I am ever your servant."

Elizabeth's delighted laugh turned more than a few heads in their direction. "I would by no means suspend any pleasure of yours, and I do feel more inclined to conversation than dancing at the moment. I have enough of the sets spoken for already, including the supper and last sets with you. Let us stroll and chat, shall we?"

As they walked around the perimeter of the ballroom, the couple smiled and greeted the guests who were not on the dance floor. They stopped for a while when they came to the earl and countess and Anne de Bourgh with them.

"Aunt Maud, I must thank you for your wonderful arrangements for the ball," Darcy said as he took the lady's hand and kissed it.

"Oh, Fitzwilliam, you must know that I enjoyed doing it very much." She smiled broadly before adding, "Your mother-in-law is a joy, and we hardly disagreed on anything."

"Anne, how are you tonight?" Elizabeth inquired. "I hope you have been able to dance."

"Thank you, Elizabeth," she answered with a smile. "I am enjoying myself greatly and have danced the first two sets before deciding to rest for this one."

After seeing that her aunt and uncle were in conversation with Darcy, Anne lowered her voice and said, "I have something to tell you. I am all excitement to share it with you. Perhaps we might speak privately during supper."

"I had planned to go to the nursery for a few minutes after supper. I would be pleased if you accompanied me."

Anne's smile and nod were answer enough, but she also squeezed Elizabeth's hand and said, "I look forward to it."

Soon, it was time for the supper dance, and the couples lined up for it. Elizabeth noticed that Charlotte Lucas was partnered once more with Mr. Gregory.

"It seems that our vicar is quite taken with Charlotte," observed Elizabeth quietly as Darcy passed her in the dance. "I would be pleased if something serious came of it."

"Indeed, Miss Lucas would make an excellent parson's wife," Darcy said as he came close to his wife once again. "I wonder how she would take to his children."

After a few seconds of separation, Elizabeth replied, "I do not see how she could help but fall in love with them, especially little Patty Rose."

"I suppose we shall have to wait to see what happens."

Darcy changed the subject as they walked down the dance. "I am a trifle concerned, however, with my cousin's obvious preference for your youngest sister. She is even younger than Georgiana and has little fortune."

Elizabeth frowned as they came to the end of the line and took their places across from each other. She glanced at her sister as she was escorted down the dance by the colonel. The pair chatted animatedly and smiled broadly as they spoke. The couple's mutual regard was evident. What her husband had said was true enough.

Taking her husband's hand, she passed to the other side of the line of dancers. "I do not think that age is so much a factor as is the lack of money. I believe that I should talk to Lydia. I would hate for her to be hurt," she whispered softly.

"I shall speak with Richard as well to find out what he is about," Darcy promised.

After the dance and eating a bit of supper, Elizabeth and Anne quickly made their way above stairs to the nursery. Sophia lay sleeping soundly in her cradle, with the nursery maid working on some mending in a corner near by. When the servant made to stand, her mistress waved her back down.

The two ladies peered into the cradle. Smiling, Elizabeth kissed her fingers and touched her daughter's head. Nodding toward the door, she led Anne out into the hall.

Once the door was closed again, Elizabeth asked, "Shall we go to my sitting room for a few minutes? It will afford us some privacy."

"That is a good idea, Elizabeth," agreed Anne happily.

Once they were inside the sitting room and seated next to each other on a settee close to the fire, Elizabeth turned to Anne with a look of curiosity. "What is it that you have to tell me?"

"I am to be published!" she exclaimed hurriedly. "Once I summoned the courage to let you and then Darcy read my work, and after you both said such kind things about it, I thought to submit it to a publisher. Two days before we set out for Pemberley, I received a reply and an advance of royalties."

"Oh, Elizabeth." Anne grabbed Elizabeth's hands tightly. "I can scarcely believe it."

Returning the pressure to her new cousin's hands, Elizabeth let out a tiny squeal. "Oh Anne, how perfectly wonderful! To think I shall be related to a published author." Unable to restrain herself any longer, Elizabeth threw her arms around the other lady and hugged her tightly.

Anne returned the embrace before pulling back. "I did not say anything earlier since only you, Cousin Darcy, and Mrs. Jenkinson even know of my writing. I plan to tell the rest of the family in a day or two, as I am not quite ready to endure the effusions I shall experience once they all know. It will be published under the pen name Jenny Lewis."

They talked for several more minutes before they realized that they would be missed if they did not return soon. In fact, on the stairs the two met Darcy, who had come to find them.

"Is Sophia well?" His brow creased in concern.

"She is well and was sleeping quite soundly when we left the nursery some minutes ago," Elizabeth reassured him gently and patted his arm. "We took longer because Anne had some important news to impart to me."

Turning with a questioning glance at Anne and upon receiving a smiling nod, Elizabeth said quietly but with animation, "Anne is to be published. She received word just a few days ago. Is that not exciting news?"

"Indeed it is," he agreed wholeheartedly. "Congratulations, Anne. I enjoyed your story once you finally allowed me to read it. Your work is very good. I am certain that you will be a success."

Soon after, Darcy escorted the two ladies back to the ballroom. The rest of the ball passed pleasantly for all.

Mrs. Bennet and the countess happily received praise for the wonderful decorations, the fine music, and the delicious food that was served. Mr. Bennet stood beside his wife, her arm resting on his throughout most of the evening. Unlike his usual habit, he did not hide in the card room or find some older men with whom to talk. He seemed to enjoy his wife's company and the dances they shared.

Feeling the inevitable fatigue after such an evening's entertainment, Elizabeth nonetheless sat with Darcy on a settee in front of the fire in their sitting room, sipping a glass of wine. "I do not think I have ever enjoyed a ball so much as this one." She sighed contentedly as she relaxed against his side.

"Nor I, my love," Darcy replied and kissed her temple. "I had no rivals for your affections with whom to contend. Most of our family was there, and I know they enjoyed themselves."

"I talked to Lydia," she said softly. "She does not have any expectations of the colonel. She promised that she would not do anything to encourage speculation or embarrass the family. I still believe that she harbours feelings for him, but she does understand that the circumstances are such that they cannot wed."

"And I spoke with Richard," Darcy sighed. "I could tell that he is very much enamoured with your sister. However, he is very much aware that his situation in life makes it difficult, if not impossible, for them to marry. He told me that he hopes his finances will not always be such, but he holds little hope that Lydia will remain single by the time that he is more financially secure."

"It seems rather hopeless, but I shall pray for their happiness, no matter the outcome." Elizabeth put down her glass and cuddled in closer to her husband. "After all, my love, you and I might never have been married if circumstances had been different."

Darcy pulled his wife upon his lap and kissed her ardently. He pulled back slightly and breathlessly said, "I believe that we were destined for each other, my loveliest Elizabeth. Our story would have turned out with us together, no matter the beginning."

EPILOGUE

Twenty years later-

Fitzwilliam Darcy stood gazing out of the main drawing room window on a beautiful summer day in June. Everywhere he looked, he saw flowers and brilliant greenery. His lovely wife, Elizabeth, had spent hours planning the design and overseeing the planting of the front gardens for this day. He sighed and then felt a warm hand take his.

"Fitzwilliam," she said, her voice rich with sympathy, "They will not live far from Pemberley. We shall be able to see them daily, if we wish it."

He looked down into the fine brown eyes that had captured him all those years ago. "I know, my sweet Beth, but I feel like Sophia was a babe just a short time ago. How is it that she is to marry the day after tomorrow?"

"How is it that we have grown old?" she asked saucily and reached up on her toes to kiss his cheek.

"You, my love, have not changed." Darcy wrapped his arm around her and pulled her close. "However, I have become a melancholy, old fool, but you are still the same lovely, impertinent woman I married these twenty years ago."

Their conversation was interrupted by a knock at the door. At a bid to enter, a servant came in and announced, "A carriage has been seen approaching the house. You asked to be notified, sir."

"Thank you, Fulton," Darcy said and offered his arm to his wife. "Shall we welcome our first guests?"

As they walked along the corridor toward the great entrance, Darcy's mind slipped into remembrances of the past twenty years. So many things vied for his attention. Finally, the thoughts of his oldest child won out.

Despite the circumstances of her conception, his precious Sophia had ever been his delight. He and Elizabeth had decided very early on that they would never mention that event to any one, especially not to Sophia. Even as the memory of the fateful day tried to impose on his conscious thought, he quickly pushed it away with remembrances of his little girl's birth and early childhood. Only one other female, his wife, held his heart in a tighter grip. Of course, he had tried very hard to keep from showing special favour for his first daughter, but in his heart of hearts, he knew that he had not always succeeded. She had grown into a beauty with charm and wit much like her mother, but with much of the Darcy reserve, as one or the other of his relatives would often remark.

She was to marry a good man of modest fortune and some property who, by all appearances, loved her as she loved him. Michael Grantley was the much younger half-brother of Georgiana's husband, Stephen Grantley. The Grantleys had been neighbours to the Darcys for several generations. Georgiana's husband was several years younger than Darcy, but George and Anne Darcy had been good friends with his parents. Stephen's mother had died while he was still at Eton. His father had remarried a much younger woman when his son was sixteen. Two years later, Michael Grantley was born.

After having only a younger sister while growing up, Stephen doted on his baby brother and had taught him many things that only a big brother can teach. Although Michael's mother was a kind woman who cared for the needs of her step-children, she did not like Derbyshire, especially during the winter. She preferred to spend her time in London or in Bath visiting her sister, which she did with far more frequency once Michael went to Eton.

Georgiana had begged to postpone her coming out until after she turned nineteen, and as Darcy and Elizabeth were in no hurry to push her into society sooner than she was comfortable, they agreed. Stephen and Georgiana met at the Michaelmas Ball the year following her coming out.

The two young people were drawn to each other almost upon their introduction. Stephen asked permission to call while he danced the supper dance with her, and she agreed. It was only a few weeks later that they talked of their future lives together, but when Grantley approached Darcy for permission to marry Georgiana, he was surprised to be told that they would have to wait. Concerned that they were too precipitous in forming an engagement, Darcy insisted that they court for a year. He said that he would give them his blessing if after that time, they were still inclined to marry. For the young couple, the following nearly twelvemonth was the longest of their lives, but at the next Michaelmas Ball, Darcy allowed them to announce their betrothal, and they married two months later.

The couple had only two children, a girl, four, and a son, two. Like her own mother, Georgiana had struggled to bear a child. She did not conceive for many years, and then she suffered several miscarriages before their daughter, Elizabeth Belle, was born. Their son, Daniel, followed two years later.

The Grantleys' father died two years after Stephen married Georgiana. When a year of mourning was over, the senior Mrs. Grantley moved to Bath to stay with her sister. Since Michael was in school and Bath was so far away, he spent his holidays with his older brother at Grantley Hall. Five years after his father's death, his mother remarried and moved to London with her new husband.

Instead of having to seek an occupation as was often the case with younger sons, Michael Grantley inherited an estate from his maternal grandfather. According to his grandfather's will, he had to spend the time after graduating from the university until he turned five and twenty, learning to run the estate. Since Grantley's father had been aware of his younger son's inheritance, he had trained him well in estate management from an early age. The house smaller than Grantley Hall, being only about the size of Netherfield Park, but it was only fifteen miles from Grantley Hall and Pemberley.

Since Michael grew up so close to Pemberley, it would not come as a surprise that he and Sophia knew each other from an early age. However, he did not really notice her as other than a nuisance who wanted to follow him around when their families visited each other, until she turned seventeen and attended the Pemberley Michaelmas Ball that year.

Since Sophia was not out, she was not allowed to dance with anyone except a family member. While she enjoyed watching the dancers and mentally went through the steps, Sophia did not see Michael hurrying through the crowd. He had been trying to avoid a certain young lady and her mother. He collided with Sophia near the doors to the terrace.

Often, Michael would say that he fell in love with Sophia at the same time that he actually fell onto the floor with her. With great embarrassment, he had apologized to her as he assisted her to her feet. That was when he had realized who she was and how lovely she had become.

Soon, Sophia's chagrin had turned to amusement as Michael nearly fell over himself, trying to atone for his clumsiness by offering to fetch refreshments, a servant, or even a physician. Finally, she was able to convince the large crowd that had formed around the couple as they struggled to their feet that she was well and needed only to sit for a while.

Michael did not leave her side the rest of the evening, and soon they began to talk and reminisce, finding they had much in common. Sophia enjoyed the easy friendship that developed, while his heart was lost to her.

His estate kept him busy for the next year, during which time he rarely left his home. Michael wanted to learn as much as possible, so he only visited his brother and wife at Christmas and Easter. All the while, his greatest motivation was to make a good home for his future wife, whom he hoped would be Sophia Darcy.

Eighteen months later, he had come into his inheritance and decided it was time to win the heart of his lady. He travelled to London, and during Sophia's first season, Michael danced with her for the first time. They laughed over their collision at the fateful ball. Soon, they caught up with each other's lives, and Sophia began to fall in love with him as well. It was only a matter of time before he formally asked to court her and was given permission. The courtship lasted six months before Michael proposed and was accepted.

Just before Darcy and Elizabeth reached the front door, it was being opened by a footman as two lanky teenaged boys eagerly rushed outside. Darcy smiled at his sons' excited chatter. He led Elizabeth through the open doors and turned at the tap of footsteps behind them. Their twelve-year-old daughter, Amelia Anne, on the arm of eight-year-old Edward, her youngest brother but one, had just descended the stairs., Sophia walked behind the pair, holding the hands of the two smallest Darcy children. Tobias (or Toby to the family), who was six, and Grace, nearly four, chatted happily with their big sister. He swallowed a lump that formed in his throat as the children came closer and smiled again, this time at his eldest daughter.

Sophia, now the same age her mother had been at her own marriage to Darcy, returned her father's smile. Sophia's likeness to her mother was uncanny, though she was a few inches taller. The only recognizable Darcy feature was her dark-blue eyes. She had told him many times when she was growing up that she was glad to have his eyes, because she thought her papa had the best eyes in the world.

"Oh, good," Elizabeth declared, "I had hoped that you heard of the arrival. I think it is your grandparents."

She smiled down at the little ones, who had obviously just awakened from their naps. "Are you excited to see Grandmama and Grandpapa?"

"Oh, yes, Mama," the pair cried in unison, bouncing on their toes.

"Will they bring us gifts, do you think?" Toby asked breathlessly.

"We shall just have to wait and see, shall we not?" was her only answer as they continued out of doors.

Darcy was again lost in thought. How could he have been so blessed with such a family? His two eldest sons, who at the moment laughed together at some private joke, were handsome and intelligent young men. He was proud of the gentlemen they were becoming. He could recall the births of all of his children, but the arrival of the "heir and a spare" caused great rejoicing amongst the people of Pemberley. He was told by his valet that many a toast was made to the health of the newest generation of Darcy males. He had been most happy that each of his sons had been delivered safely and that his beloved Beth had not suffered any harm in the process.

Once the family, including the seven Darcy children, was assembled just beyond the outer archway, they waited for the arrivals, some more patiently than others. The two older boys, eighteen-year-old Bennet, and sixteen-year-old Charles (Charlie to his family and friends) had moved to stand on either side of their father. Edward wanted very much to stand with his mama, but he decided that he must be a man and join his brothers and father. Toby and Grace stood close to Elizabeth, wide eyed and obviously excited.

Sophia reached for her mother's hand and whispered nervously, "Will they approve of Michael? Grandpapa always said that there would be no one good enough for his little Sophia."

"Oh, sweetheart, do not fret," Elizabeth soothed as she squeezed her daughter's hand. "Grandpapa said the same thing about me. And as you know, he is very fond of your papa."

"It is the Bennet carriage, Mama," Edward called from his position next to his father and two older brothers and bounced on his toes, while the two younger children had to be restrained from running up the lane to meet the coach.

Darcy held back a chuckle as he watched his two older sons try to stand tall and dignified while it was obvious that they fairly hummed with suppressed excitement. The youngest of the three stopped bouncing and straightened himself to his whole height while he copied his brothers' stances. The two older hid their smiles as they talked of seeing the rest of their family soon.

Glancing up, Darcy caught Elizabeth's smile as she reassured Sophia about her grandfather's opinion of her fiancé. Darcy could remember the time, nine months to the day from the first Pemberley ball at Michaelmas, when he had had to reassure and comfort his father-in-law at the birth of the heir to Longbourn.

Thomas Bennet II arrived quite easily for a child born to a woman two years shy of forty. A healthy and robust baby, he charmed all of his family. It was fortunate that most of his sisters did not live close, for they all doted on him and his brother, Robert Bennet, who had joined the family eighteen months later. The doctor who had told Mrs. Bennet after Lydia's birth that she could not bear another child had been completely amazed. His amazement was even greater when she was delivered of the second son.

The Darcy pair of brothers and the Bennet pair acted more like siblings than nephews and uncles. Many a summer in their childhood was spent at Pemberley, Longbourn, or Westfield Hall, the Bingley estate, along with the Bingley cousins.

"I am so happy that they are come," Amelia Anne said. "They could not be here Christmastide because of Grandmama's illness. Are you certain she is well enough to travel? The girl pushed an errant blonde curl behind her ear and smoothed imagined wrinkles from her lovely pink frock.

"You know that your grandfather wrote that your grandmother is well and back to her old self. There is nothing to worry about, my dear."

A minute or two after she finished speaking, the Bennet carriage pulled to a stop in front of those assembled. A footman opened the door and assisted Mr. Bennet and a young man to the ground. The two were joined by a boy of seventeen who jumped down from the top of the coach. Mr. Bennet had just assisted his wife to the ground when near pandemonium broke out. Kisses and embraces, hand shakes and back slaps were exchanged before Darcy raised his voice above the din.

"Let us all return inside. I am sure that as soon as you have all been shown to your rooms and refreshed yourselves, there will be food and tea laid out for you in the drawing room."

"I, for one, am starving," Thomas, the older of the two Bennet boys declared.

Laughter rang out as Mr. Bennet slapped the boy's back. "You are always hungry, son. It is good that your brother Darcy helped me increase the yield on the estate, for I would not have been able to feed you all these years on my former income."

"Thomas," Elizabeth said in a laughing voice, "I had Cook prepare many of your favourite foods, and he made plenty of them."

Thomas Bennet II smiled down at his sister. There was no doubt that they were related since they shared the same dark hair and sparkling brown eyes. Although he was over twenty years her junior, they had always been close.

Soon, Mr. Bennet picked up Grace, while Toby tugged him by the other hand toward the house. Elizabeth could hear her little son ask his grandfather in a loud whisper if he had brought presents.

"I am an old man," her father answered. "How am I to remember what might be packed in all those trunks we brought with us? We shall have to wait until your grandmother has them unpacked."

The children giggled at their grandfather's teasing and began to speak over each other in an effort to tell him what they were learning from their nanny.

As they made their way into the house, Thomas hurriedly took his sister's arm while her oldest son took the other. The two boys were very close, but there had always been something like a sibling rivalry for Elizabeth's attention. Thomas insisted that since he was her brother and born before Bennet, he should get more of her time when they were together. His nephew disagreed, citing the fact that he was her son. As little boys, it had been fairly easy to keep the rivalry from becoming too heated. She would hold both boys on her lap, read to them, and tell them stories of her childhood and of Darcy's. It became a little difficult when they were too big to occupy her lap, but soon they raced each other for the privilege of sitting next to her during the family hour.

Once the two boys attended Eton and now Cambridge, first Thomas, and the next year Bennet, their friendly competition turned to academics and sports, in which they both excelled. At their present age, they enjoyed teasing each other by competing for the privilege of escorting Elizabeth, as now, but in all other matters they were the best of friends.

After the guests refreshed themselves and then sat down to partake of the food and hot tea, they divided into groups. The boys, except for Toby and Edward, ate in one corner, laughing and talking about Bennet's new horse. Edward took a seat close to the window that overlooked the distant drive as he eagerly awaited the arrival of more of the family. The girls cuddled together next to their grandfather with the youngest Darcy boy seated upon Mr. Bennet's lap as he asked Sophia about her beau. Standing nearby, Darcy smiled as his father-in-law teased his oldest daughter.

Turning his attention toward his wife, Darcy watched Elizabeth join her mother on a settee after she finished pouring out the tea for the rest. He listened with interest as his mother-in-law spoke.

"Lizzy, you look well," Mrs. Bennet stated as she sipped her tea.

"Thank you, Mama," she answered with a smile of genuine affection. "As do you. I am glad that you are recovered from your illness this winter. Papa's letters made it sound serious."

"I think your father was too concerned," Mrs. Bennet replied as she looked toward her husband, affection clear on her face.

"He does not want to lose you, I am sure."

Elizabeth then changed the subject with a question about her brothers and how they were faring in school. Her mother's answer was full of pride as she related how well they had done in their studies that year. Mrs. Bennet's countenance brightened as she spoke of her youngest children,

"You do not look like a grandmother," Elizabeth observed quietly.

"How you do go on," her mother scolded playfully as she blushed. "I sometimes feel old, but I try to stay young for your brothers."

"They have grown much since I last saw them. I am proud to have such brothers."

"Your own are growing into fine young people as well." Mrs. Bennet sighed, "And to think our Sophia is getting married."

"I am certain I shall weep at the ceremony," Elizabeth confessed.

Her mother nodded as she took Lizzy's hand and squeezed it. "I know I did at yours."

"Did you indeed?" Elizabeth asked in astonishment.

"Yes," Mrs. Bennet admitted with a smile. "I cried at all of my girls' nuptials, but I believe I shed the most tears at your wedding. You were my first to leave, and you wed such a kind and generous man. I was so very happy for you, my dear."

Darcy did marvel at times at how much Mrs. Bennet had changed through the years. She was not always so calm as she was now, but more often than not, she was composed and far more rational than she had been when he first met her. Late motherhood seemed to have slowed the aging process for her as well. The Bennets' renewed love had wrought a wondrous thing in both of them.

The whole room quieted when Edward cried out from his position at the window, "I see more carriages. I think it is the Fitzwilliams and the Collinses."

Darcy stopped him, as Edward prepared to run out to meet them. "We shall wait for them in here."

The boy was disappointed, but too well behaved to show it. Instead, he took up his post near the door to await his relatives' arrival. He did not have to wait long, for five minutes later, the butler showed the newest guests into the drawing room.

Mr. and Mrs. Collins came into the room first followed closely by their two daughters, Anne and Mary Jane. The pair looked to be twins, but were fifteen and thirteen respectively. Although not the prettiest of the Bennet granddaughters, they were clever and witty. Amelia Anne rushed to greet them before pulling them to where their grandfather stood awaiting them.

Again, there was a round of hugs and kisses that was interrupted soon by the arrival of retired Colonel and Mrs. Fitzwilliam, each holding one of their two-year-old twin boys. Four more children came into the room behind them. The oldest, a pretty girl of thirteen named Sylvia, walked sedately, while the younger three boys were being herded by a harried nursemaid. The boys, stair-steps in relation to each other, ranged in ages of nine, eight, and five. They rushed past the nurse, with the two older joining Edward and the youngest finding Toby by their grandfather.

"Lydia!" her mother cried as she rushed to throw her arms around her. "It has been so long."

Darcy observed his cousin and wife as they were greeted by the rest of the family. He shook his head slightly as he remembered the youngest Bennet daughter. It was still amazing to him that his sister-in-law could have changed, admittedly with some struggles, from a spoiled, self-indulgent girl to a confident and competent woman and wife.

Richard and Lydia Fitzwilliam had married almost fifteen years ago when she turned one and twenty. Fitzwilliam had not taken that long to admit, at least to himself, that he was in love with the youngest Bennet daughter. For two years, it was his financial situation along with the war with Napoleon which kept them apart. When he finally came back to England once the little emperor surrendered at Waterloo, Richard was called to aid his cousin Anne when she inherited Rosings upon her mother's death.

Anne's novels had become extremely popular, and she had no inclination toward estate management. Soon, she realized that her cousin was more than up to the task of running the estate. After much discussion, the colonel retired from the army to manage and become the steward-tenant of Rosings, sharing the income with Miss de Bourgh. This allowed her to continue her writing and to travel as she wished.

After managing Rosings for nearly a year, Fitzwilliam travelled to Pemberley to visit the Darcys and to see their children. Lydia was visiting her sister and working on a design for Georgiana's wedding gown. He found the youngest Miss Bennet to be lovelier than ever before, and the changes he had first witnessed over the previous three years were firmly set as a part of her personality. The time they spent in each other's company convinced them both that their original attraction had stood the test of time.

Fitzwilliam travelled to Hertfordshire to ask Mr. Bennet for permission to court Lydia with the intention of marrying and was granted the privilege with the proviso that they wait to wed until she turned one and twenty. The courtship, which was carried on mostly at a distance, was not an easy one for either of them, but very soon after her birthday, they were wed and took up residence at Rosings.

During the time of the courtship between Fitzwilliam and Lydia, and unbeknownst to all but her attorney and physician, Anne de Bourgh's health began to decline. She willed Rosings to her cousin Richard. A year after the Fitzwilliams' marriage, she breathed her last, surrounded by her family and friends, who greatly mourned her loss. The royalties from her writings were to be used to continue the operation of a girls' school in the village of Hunsford, which she had founded soon after her first book was sold.

After returning her mother's embrace, Lydia Fitzwilliam pulled back and greeted her sister before looking around the crowded room. "It is good that Pemberley is so large, Lizzy. Else, we would not all fit."

"It is fortunate indeed," Elizabeth laughingly agreed. "Especially since not everyone is here as yet."

Later that day in the largest of the formal sitting rooms, the adults and young people age thirteen and older awaited the call to dinner. The bride-to-be and her fiancé begged that these younger ones be allowed to attend. Since the gathering would be made up almost entirely of family, the Darcys agreed to the less formal arrangements.

Jane and Charles Bingley, along with Samuel and Kitty Lucas, had arrived with their families in tow. The Bingleys' estate was only fifteen miles away, and the Lucas family had been invited to stay with them while they attended the wedding.

The Bingleys' two sons stood talking to their cousins and younger uncles. The boys were nearly the same ages as Bennet and Charlie Darcy. William Bingley was the oldest at nineteen and attended Cambridge with Thomas. The previous fall, Bennet had joined his cousin and uncle at Cambridge, and the three were currently on summer holiday. At the end of the school break, Robert Bennet and Charlie would travel with their cousins to university for the first time for the Michaelmas half. Off to the side but still in the thick of things, Samuel Lucas II lounged in a chair. At fifteen, he was the only one of the boys who had one more year at Eton before he would join the rest at Cambridge.

Across the room, the bevy of pretty girl cousins and friends giggled, talked excitedly, and sometimes louder than was truly acceptable. A parent or two would look up when the volume reached an uncomfortable level. It only took a raised eyebrow or a quick shake of the head, and they would quiet for a time.

Millie Bingley, a fair-haired beauty at fifteen, sat between Anne Collins and Kate Lucas on a settee. In chairs pulled close to complete a circle, Sylvia Fitzwilliam and Mary Jane Collins flanked Sophia, who was being peppered with questions about her wedding clothes, flowers, veil, and her betrothed. They collectively decided if Sophia did not answer with enough detail, they would prevail upon her sister Amelia Anne to elaborate later. This interrogation continued until the butler announced the final guests' arrival.

"Reverend and Mrs. Phillip Gregory, Mr. and Mrs. Stephen Grantley, and Mr. Michael Grantley," Fulton intoned formally, effectively silencing the room.

Darcy and Elizabeth, who were joined by Sophia, greeted the newest guests with bows and curtseys before introducing them to Mr. and Mrs. Bennet.

"Mr. and Mrs. Bennet, you remember Reverend Gregory and his wife, Charlotte, and my sister, Georgiana, but I do not know if you have had the opportunity to meet my sister's husband, Stephen Grantley." Darcy finished with a nod to Sophia.

"Grandpapa and Grandmama, I would like you to meet Michael Grantley, my fiancé. He is the younger brother of my Uncle Grantley." Her cheeks bloomed with a pretty blush, as her intended beamed at her before shaking Mr. Bennet's hand. He also bowed gallantly over Mrs. Bennet's hand.

"It is a pleasure to meet you both," Michael said politely.

"Oh, you are a handsome one, and with such elegant manners as well," Mrs. Bennet smiled coyly up at him.

Mr. Bennet shook the young man's hand before commenting, "You had better be more than a pretty face and nice manners. My granddaughter deserves the best."

Bowing his head in acknowledgement, Michael Grantley replied, "Indeed, Sophia deserves all of that. I shall spend the rest of my days trying to make her happy."

"Grandpapa." Sophia's voice took on a touch of scolding. "You promised that you would not tease my fiancé."

"I will behave, my dear." Mr. Bennet chuckled. He turned and said, "I would like to become acquainted with you, once Sophia introduces you to those you have not yet met."

"I would be honoured, sir," Michael said with deference.

Slipping her arm through her fiancé's, Sophia guided him toward the others. Darcy watched as his daughter and her fiancé traversed the room, speaking to everyone. The younger of the children present seemed especially pleased to have such attention from the happily engaged couple. He smiled despite the lump in his throat. His little girl would be leaving too soon.

A gentle pressure from his wife's hand on his arm brought his attention back to the conversation at hand. Stephen and Georgiana had just joined the group, which included Jane and Charles Bingley.

"How are you tonight, Georgiana?" Jane asked.

"I am well," she answered. "And how are you and yours?"

"Exceedingly well, thank you." Jane raised an eyebrow before she enquired, "Did you leave your children at home?"

"Oh heavens, no," she exclaimed. "Lizzy Belle would not let me leave without her. She has been looking forward to the children's ball, as she has been calling it for weeks now. Daniel's nurse and I escorted them both to the nursery. I think there is no other name to call what I found there. I believe the only thing missing from a real ball was the lack of musicians. I was told that Mrs. Parks will be playing the harp for their dancing."

Georgiana turned to her brother and said, "It is a good thing that the Pemberley nursery is so large; otherwise there would not be room for dancing and for the games that are set up. Oh, and the food table looks delightfully good."

Just then, dinner was announced. Darcy offered his arm to Sophia and Michael escorted Elizabeth into the formal dining parlour. The rest of the guests followed them. After everyone found their seats, the master of the house asked Mr. Gregory to bless the meal.

Once the prayer was over, Charlotte sat next to her husband and across from Jane and Charles. She surveyed the table before she said, "Jane, I meant to ask if the Dowager Lady Montague will be joining us."

"No, Caroline is still in Town," Jane explained. "Since Sir James passed, she has kept to Town except in July and August. She has always preferred it to the country. From what she writes, the dower house is too draughty and cramped for the winter season."

Overhearing Jane's speech, Darcy understood that his sister-in-law was casting a positive light on the life of the dowager. After her marriage to Sir James,

Caroline had not taken to her step-sons, and the feeling was mutual. While Montague was alive, an unsteady peace reigned. Her stepsons had always disdained their father's second wife for her connection to trade, so much so that after Sir James death nearly all ties were severed. Because his will gave her a townhouse in London, use of the dower house, and an allowance for the upkeep of both, the new baronet could not exclude her completely from his estate. However, the income that had been settled upon Caroline by the marriage contract did not give her enough to live as she had when her husband was alive.

For the years of her marriage, Caroline had treated her own relatives with disdain and could have put Lady Catherine de Bourgh to shame as far as haughtiness went. Her behaviour toward the Bingleys and Hursts had been so lacking in cordiality that they rarely communicated with her or she with them.

"I believe Elizabeth told me that Mr. and Mrs. Gardiner and family would be staying with you," Charlotte inquired.

"Yes, they will arrive tomorrow. However since all but their second son, Benjamin, who is in the Navy, will be here, there is the need for their extended family to be spread between the Grantley estate and ours. Mr. Gardiner and his eldest son have recently expended their wholesale business, which the reason they could not come earlier," Jane answered.

A bit farther down the table, Mrs. Bennet enjoyed the company of her youngest daughter and her husband. "Colonel, I hope that everything is well at Rosings."

"Yes, ma'am, it is very well," he replied, smiling inwardly at his mother-in-law's continued use of his military rank. He did not mind, but he had not been Colonel Fitzwilliam for many years and did not miss that time in his life.

"I see that the earl and countess are not in attendance," Mrs. Bennet probed.

"My brother and his wife will attend the wedding," he replied. "Since my father's death two years ago, my mother is not comfortable being from home overnight. And since Matlock House is near enough to Pemberley, they will arrive the morning of the wedding, returning home soon following the breakfast. Matlock's children will stay for a few days to visit with their brood of cousins and friends."

"I am sorry to hear about your mother," she sighed. "I have missed our times together. I am not a diligent correspondent. I shall apologize for my lack, and if she will forgive me, I shall be more faithful in the future."

"I believe she will enjoy being in your company again, Mother Bennet," he commented cheerfully.

Conversation flowed freely and enjoyably around the table. The young people contributed to the liveliness of the chatter, feeling fully the privilege of being part of the group.

Just before the meal was over, Sophia, who sat next to her father in the place of honour, spoke to her mother seated on the opposite side of the table, "Mama, I promised Amelia Anne and the younger girls that I would bring Michael to the 'ball' before it was their bedtime. Might we be excused once dinner is finished?"

Elizabeth smiled indulgently at her oldest child. "Of course, you may, my dear. I would not like to deprive the attendees of the guest of honour. The young people are to return to their rooms once dinner is over, so it will be a good time for you to go. Just do not allow Edward and Amelia Anne to keep you. The family is looking forward to your performing for us tonight."

Once the last covers were removed, Darcy stood with the young couple and said, "I will accompany you. I want to see this marvellous 'ball' I have heard so much about. I shall be able to make certain that our guests of honour do not fail to reappear."

The threesome made their way to the nursery, along with several of the younger members of the dinner party who had been dismissed for bed. Inside the room, they found a happy pandemonium. Some were twirling in the middle of the room to the music of the harp. To one side of the room, others were playing skittles, while still others sat at small tables watching the activities with sleepy-eyed enthusiasm. The various nurses held vigil over the skittles tournament, tapped their toes as their charges danced in front of them, or watched the drowsy ones, ready to take them to the bed chambers that already held several of the youngest children.

As soon as some of her cousins and siblings took note of Sophia's presence, they ran to her side, tugging on her arms or hugging her, while trying to tell her of all of the wonders of their ball. Once the music stopped, even more of the children surrounded the couple and Darcy. After many minutes listening to talk about the lovely dancing, the enjoyable games, and the scrumptious food, Sophia kissed and hugged all who would allow it before saying good night to them all.

~*~

The house was a veritable hive of activity the next day. The men folk, young and old, spent the morning after breakfast in gentlemanly pursuits, such as riding or fishing. The ladies took their time, making sure that all was ready for the next day.

At midday, the Darcys hosted a picnic which held a two-fold advantage -- it kept the children out-of-doors while allowing the staff some time for last minute preparations for the wedding breakfast.

Darcy and Elizabeth watched as Mrs. Fulton, the former Sarah Brown, orchestrated the setting out of the food while the younger children raced about the grounds and the older ones found places in the shade to converse.

"Mrs. Fulton, you have done yourself proud," Elizabeth remarked to her former abigail. Sarah had taken over as housekeeper ten years ago after a full year of working under Mrs. Reynolds, who had wanted to retire and spend time with her daughter and grandchildren. Sarah had fallen in love with the under butler, Stanley Fulton, shortly after they met, but since a lady's maid was not allowed to court, she did not allow her feelings to show. However, she began to train to take over as housekeeper after her mistress found her crying forlornly.

It turned out that Fulton had asked to court her, but she had declined him because of her loyalty to Mrs. Darcy. Elizabeth would not hear of her turning her back on happiness for the sake of continuing as her abigail. As Elizabeth had been about to inquire among the staff as to who might have an interest in learning the tasks of the housekeeper, she immediately fell upon the idea of Sarah being the perfect one. Sarah and Stanley Fulton were married a few months before she took over for Mrs. Reynolds.

"I learned from the best, Mrs. Darcy," Sarah said with a smile. "Speaking of Mrs. Reynolds, I heard from her just yesterday. She sends her best wishes to the family on this happy occasion and especially to Miss Darcy. She is grieved that her health does not allow for a trip to Pemberley for the wedding. She told me that she was to send a gift and a letter explaining everything to you."

"Yes," Elizabeth answered with a sad tone, "I was saddened to hear that she cannot attend. Although given her age and the distance, it is not surprising."

Once the food was ready and the meal announced, the group gathered around the heavily laden tables to enjoy the feast. After the meal the family enjoyed a few games before the younger of the children were finally taken to the nursery for much needed naps, while everyone else divided into groups and played cricket, fished, walked, or sat in the shade to talk or read.

Finally, Elizabeth reminded the betrothed couple that they were needed for the rehearsal at Pemberley Chapel. The event garnered mixed reactions. Most of the girls begged to be allowed to watch, while most of the boys wished to stay where they were. However, Thomas, Bennet, and William offered to escort the girls to the chapel. Being in the company of their girl cousins had recently become a pleasant and desirable activity rather than the annoyance it had been in their earlier years.

At the chapel, the betrothed couple met with the rector, who gave them instructions as to what was expected of them during the service. Laughter, teasing, and a bit of frustration peppered the practice, but when it was finally over, everyone smiled in anticipation of the actual event on the morrow.

Elizabeth insisted that the evening be an early one, since the wedding was scheduled for eight in the morning, so it was an excited group that retired after a simple supper.

~*~

Rising earlier than was his wont, Darcy stared out the window of their shared sitting room, feeling keenly the imminent departure of his daughter. His heart squeezed in sorrow, while his head told him that she was not lost to him, only venturing into another phase of her life. So involved in his thoughts and feelings was he that he did not know that Elizabeth had joined him until Darcy felt her warm arms wrap around his waist.

"You are brooding again, my love," she stated softly, leaning against him as he pulled her closer.

He sighed, "You are correct. I am indeed brooding, and I thought to get it over with before you rose. I promise that I am happy that she has found someone to love her as she deserves." Kissing the top of her head, Darcy said resolutely, "I shall smile and show Sophia that I do not regret her choice."

"Our girl understands her papa and mama will miss her, and she is likely going through a great deal of trepidation as well." Elizabeth looked steadily into her husband's eyes. "I remember well how nervous I was. I knew you were the best of men, but it was hard to think I would have to leave the only home I had ever known to be a wife, mother, and mistress of a large estate. We shall all get through this too and be happier for the experience."

Darcy laid his lips on hers for what he intended to be a light kiss, but it turned into one of passion and need. Lifting his head slightly, he scanned her face to find the familiar look of desire mirrored there. Taking her hand, he whispered huskily, "It is much too early. Let us return to bed."

~*~

Hours later, Darcy walked toward the Pemberley chapel. Family and a few guests from the neighbourhood were milling around the courtyard, smiling and chatting with great joy. As he passed the carriage that was to convey the newly married couple back to Pemberley, he saw all of his sons except Toby, along with a few cousins, tying things to the back.

Darcy smiled to himself, but he saw that their clothing was in danger of becoming soiled. He knew that his daughter and his wife would be unhappy if the boys were not presentable, so he spoke to them. "Boys, I believe that will do. Please hurry back to the house and clean up. Your mothers will be seriously displeased if you show yourselves the way you are."

The younger of the boys tried to wipe away the dirt that clung to their clothes, but the older ones merely grinned and nodded before each one of them grabbed the hand of a younger one and raced back toward the house.

"Do not tarry; the wedding is to begin shortly," Darcy called after them.

When he heard an answering "Yes, Father" or "Yes, Uncle," Darcy smiled once more and resumed his walk to the chapel. Even more guests stood inside the foyer. He thought that it was a good thing that the Pemberley chapel was larger than most, but there would still be many standing. The windows would be open so that those of the staff who wished to do so could hear the proceedings. Scanning around, Darcy spied his wife leaving a room off to the side. She beckoned to him.

"Sophia is inside waiting for you, my love," Elizabeth said a low voice.

Taking out his pocket watch, Darcy checked the time. "If our sons are not back in ten minutes, please send someone for them. They got a bit soiled while decorating the carriage."

Elizabeth laughed happily. "I shall do so if needed, but I do not believe it will be necessary. Go to our girl now." She gave his arm a slight shove.

Smiling, Darcy said, "Very well," before he left his wife to open the door.

Inside, he found Sophia staring out a small window on the other end of the room. The pale ivory gown she wore flowed to the floor from a gathered waist. The sleeves, with layers of lace and puffed just below the shoulders, left the lovely white skin of Sophia's neck exposed. The same lace circled the bottom of the skirt in several tiers. On her head, she wore a coronet of white roses with a thin gauze veil attached that trailed down to the middle of her back. Around her neck lay a string of perfectly matched pearls which had belonged to Michael's mother.

Sophia turned at the click of the door. She smiled when Darcy reached her and said before she kissed his cheek, "I thought you would be late, Papa, and I would have to be wed without you."

He felt his throat tighten and his eyes sting as chills ran over him. The final of the visions about Sophia had come true. Darcy coughed twice before he found his voice. "I would never allow that, my sweetling. I had to see to your brothers. You know how they can get into mischief." Taking her hand, he said, "Remember, your mother and I will always love you, and we are very proud of you."

Just then, there was a knock at the door. At his call to enter, it opened and Elizabeth came in. "The boys are inside now," she said and caught her daughter's eye. "Are you ready, my dear?"

"Oh, yes, Mama," Sophia exclaimed with enthusiasm.

"Very well, I shall take my place." Elizabeth glanced at the misty-eyed smile on her husband's face. "I will see you both inside."

Once his wife left the room, Darcy offered his daughter his arm. With her hand on his arm and his hand atop hers, he smiled at his daughter. He was no longer sad. How could he be since his little girl was so happy? As he escorted her out of the room to the back of the sanctuary, his thought was that God had blessed him, his wife, and his family over the past twenty years, and he welcomed all that the Lord still had in store for him in the future.

~ The End ~

ABOUT THE AUTHOR

Jadie Brooks has lived in the northwest for all but one year of her life, thirty-eight of them with her husband, Stan. She has two grown children and two exceptionally cute granddaughters. Because of the wonders of the internet, she has adopted many cyber kids as well. Travelling, reading, quilting, knitting, a bit of gardening, and, of course, writing are among her hobbies.

Jadie would love to hear from you at author.jadiebrooks@gmail.com

Made in the USA
Lexington, KY
09 November 2013